NIGHT SHIFTERS

Baen Books By
Sarah A. Hoyt

Draw One in the Dark
Gentleman Takes a Chance
Night Shifters (omnibus)
Noah's Boy

Darkship Thieves
Darkship Renegades
A Few Good Men

NIGHT SHIFTERS

Sarah A. Hoyt

NIGHT SHIFTERS

Draw One in the Dark copyright ©2006 by Sarah A. Hoyt.
Gentleman Takes a Chance copyright ©2009 by Sarah A. Hoyt

A Baen Books Original

Baen Publishing Enterprises
P.O. Box 1403
Riverdale, NY 10471
www.baen.com

ISBN: 978-1-4767-3651-8

Cover art by Tom Kidd

First Baen paperback printing, June 2014

Distributed by Simon & Schuster
1230 Avenue of the Americas
New York, NY 10020

Library of Congress Cataloging-in-Publication Data

Hoyt, Sarah A.
 Night shifters / Sarah A. Hoyt.
    pages cm
 ISBN 978-1-4767-3651-8 (omni trade pb)
 1. Dragons--Fiction. 2. Imaginary wars and battles--Fiction. I. Title.
 PS3608.O96N55 2014
 813'.6--dc23
                                    2014009917
Printed in the United States of America

10 9 8 7 6 5 4 3 2 1

CONTENTS

DRAW ONE IN THE DARK

Sarah A. Hoyt

⊰ DEDICATION ⊱

One of the amazing side benefits of becoming a professional writer is to be able to personally meet and become friends with people you've read and admired from afar.

I'd like to dedicate this book to David Drake, whose friendship, by itself, is enough to compensate for all the tribulations, sweat, and tears of a career in writing.

⊰ ACKNOWLEDGMENTS ⊱

I would like to thank Sofie Skapski, Kate Paulk, Pam Uphoff, and Lee McGregor for proofing and doing occasional continuity interventions. Without them, this story would be very difficult to follow. And I'd like to thank my husband, Dan Hoyt, who at a crucial point in the story came up and told me how much I was playing with his emotions and how he needed the rest of the story right then. It made finishing the book much more fun.

ACKNOWLEDGMENTS

The July night sprawled, warm and deep blue over Goldport, Colorado. In the distance the mountains were little more than suspicions of deeper darkness, a jagged outline where no stars appeared.

Most of Goldport was equally dark, from its slumbering suburbs to the blind silence of its downtown shops. Only the streetlights shone, at intervals, piercing the velvet blackness like so many stars.

At the edge of the western suburbs that climbed—square block after square block—into the lower slopes of the Rockies, the neon sign outside a Chinese restaurant flickered. *Three Luck Dragon* flared, faded, then flared again, and finally turned off completely.

A hand with nails that were, perhaps, just a little too long turned over a sign that hung on the window, so that the word "closed" faced the parking lot.

After a while, a sound broke the silence. A flapping, noise, as though of sheets unfurling in the silent night. Or perhaps of large wings beating.

Descending.

Had anyone been awake, he'd have seen a large, dark creature—serpentine and thin—with vast unfolding wings descend from the night sky till his huge taloned feet met the asphalt. He closed his wings about himself and waited.

He did not wait long. From alleys and darkened streets, people emerged: teenagers, in tight jeans and T-shirts, looking nervous, sidling out of the shadows, glancing over their shoulders as if afraid of being followed. From yet other alleys . . . *creatures* emerged: long, sinuous, in moist glistening colors between green and blue. They slid, monstrous heads low to the ground, curved fangs like daggers unsheathed in the moonlight. And sometimes dragons seemed to shift to naked teenagers and back again. In and out of the shadows, knit with walls and garbage bins, slithering along the hot cement of the pavements came young men who were dragons and dragons who were nervous young men.

They gathered in front of the Great Sky Dragon. And waited.

At length the dragon spoke, in a voice like pearls rolling upon old gold. "Where is it?" he asked. "Did you get it back?"

The amorphous crowd of humans and dragons moved. There was the impression of someone pushed forward. A rustle of cloth and wings. A murmur of speech.

The young man pushed forward was slender, though there was a suggestion of muscles beneath his leg-molding jeans and of a substantial chest straining the fabric of the white T-shirt. His bare arm displayed a tattoo of a large, green, glistening dragon and his eyes had an Asian fold, though it was clear from his light brown hair, his pale skin that he was not wholly Asian.

He was, however, completely scared. He stood trembling in front of the monster, who brought a vast golden eye to fix on him. "Yesss?" The dragon said. "You have something to report? You've found the Pearl of Heaven?"

The young man shook his head, his straight, lank hair swinging from side to side.

"No?" the dragon asked. Light glimmered on his fangs as he spoke, and his golden eye came very close to the boy, as if to examine him better.

"It wasn't there," the youth said, rapidly, his English not so much accented as retaining the lilt of someone who'd grown up in a community full of Chinese speakers. "We looked all over his apartment. It wasn't there."

The golden eye blinked, vein-laced green skin obstructing it for just a moment. Then the huge head pulled back a little and tilted. "We do not," it said, fangs glimmering, "tolerate failure."

It darted forward, so quickly the movement seemed to leave a green trail in the air like an afterimage. The fangs glistened. A delicate tongue came forth.

The boy's scream echoed a second too late, like bad special effects. It still hung in air as the youth, feet and hands flailing, was lifted high into the night by the great dragon head.

A crunching sound. A brief glimmer. Two halves of the boy tumbling, in a shower of blood, toward the parking lot.

A scurry of cloth and wings followed, as men and dragons scrambled away.

The great golden eyes turned to them. The green muzzle was stained red. "We do not tolerate failure," it said. "Find the Pearl of Heaven. Kill the thief."

It opened its wings and, still looking intently at the crowd, flapped their great green length, till it rose into the dark, dark sky.

In the parking lot below no one moved till the last vestiges of the sinuous green and gold body had disappeared from view.

✢ ✢ ✢

CHAPTER
1

Kyrie was worried about Tom. Which was strange, because Tom was not one of her friends. Nor would *she* have thought she could care less if he stopped showing up at work altogether.

But now he was late and she was worried. . . .

She tapped her foot impatiently, both at his lateness and her worry, as she stared out at the window of the Athens, the Greek diner on Fairfax Avenue where she'd worked for the last year. Her wavy hair, dyed in multicolored layers, gave the effect of a tapestry. It went well with her honey-dark skin, her exotic features, and the bright red feather earring dangling from her ear, but it looked oddly out of place with the much-washed full-length red apron with "Athens" blazoned in green across the chest.

Outside everything appeared normal—the winding serpentine road between tall brick buildings, the darkened facade of the used CD store across the street, the occasional lone passing car.

She looked away, disgusted, from the windows splashed with bright, hand-scrawled advertisements for specials—souvlaki and fries—$3.99, clam chowder—99¢, Fresh Rice Pudding—and at the large plastic clock high on the wall.

Midnight. And Tom should have come in at nine. Tom had never been late before. Oh, she'd had her doubts when Frank hired the young street tough with the unkempt dark curls, the leather jacket and boots, and the track marks up both of his arms, clear as day. But he had always come in on time, and he was polite to the customers, and he never seemed to be out of it. Not during work time.

"Kyrie," Frank said, from behind her. Kyrie turned to see him, behind the counter—a short, dark, middle-aged man, who looked Greek but seemed to be a mix of Italian and French and Greek and whatever else had fallen in the melting pot. He was testy today. The woman he'd been dating—or at least was sweet on, as she often walked with him to work, or after work—hadn't come in.

He gave Kyrie a dark look from beneath his bushy eyebrows. "Table seven," he said.

She looked at table seven, the broad table by the front window. And that was a problem, because the moon was full on the table, bathing it. It didn't seem to bother the gaggle of students seating at it, talking and laughing and eating a never-ending jumble of slices of pie, dolmades, rice pudding dishes, and olives, all of it washed down with coffee.

Of course, there was no reason it should bother them, Kyrie reminded herself. Probably not. Moonlight only bothered her. Only her . . .

No. She wouldn't let moonlight do anything. She wouldn't give in to it. She had it under control. It had been months. She was not going to lose control now.

The students needed warm-ups for their coffee. And heaven knew they might very well have decided they needed more olives. Or pie.

She lifted the walk-through portion of the counter and ducked behind for the carafe, then back again, walking briskly toward the table.

Her hand stretched, with the pot's plastic handle firmly grasped in manicured fingers, nails adorned with violet-blue fingernail polish. One cup refilled, two, and a young man probably two or three years younger than Kyrie stretched his cup for a warm-up. The cup glistened, glazed porcelain under the full moonlight of August.

Kyrie's hand entered the pool of moonlight, brighter than the fluorescent lights in the distant ceiling. She felt it like a sting upon the skin, like bathwater, just a little too hot for touch. For a disturbing second, she felt as if her fingernails lengthened.

She bit the inside of her cheek, and told herself no, but it didn't help, because part of her mind, some part way at the back and mostly submerged, gave her memories of a hot and wet jungle, of walking amid the lush foliage. Memories of soft mulch beneath her paws. Memories of creatures scurrying in the dark undergrowth. Creatures who were scared of her.

Moonlight felt like wine on her lips, like a touch of fever. She felt as if an unheard rhythm pounded through her veins and presently—

"Could we have another piece of pie, too?" a redheaded girl with a Southern drawl asked, snapping Kyrie out of her trance.

Fingernails—Kyrie checked—were the right length. Was it her imagination that the polish seemed a little cracked and crazed? Probably.

She could still feel the need for a jungle, for greenery—she who'd grown up in foster homes in several cement-and-metal jungles. The biggest woods she'd ever seen were city parks. Or the miles of greenery from the windows of the Greyhound that had brought her to Colorado.

These memories, these thoughts, were just illusions, nothing more. She remembered those times she had surrendered to the madness.

"One piece of pie," she said, taking the small notebook from her apron pocket and concentrating gratefully on its solidity. Paper that rustled, a pencil that was growing far too blunt and required lots of pressure on the page.

"And some olives," one of the young men said.

"Oh, and more rice pudding," one of the others said, setting off a lengthy order, paper being scratched by pencil and nails that, Kyrie told herself, were not growing any longer. Not at all.

Still she felt tension leave her as she turned her back on the table and walked out of the moonlit area. Passing into the shadow felt as if some inner pressure receded, as though something she'd been fighting with all her will and mind had now been withdrawn.

While she was drawing a breath of relief, she heard the sound—like wings unfolding, or like a very large blanket flapping. It came, she thought, from the back of the diner, from the parking lot that abutted warehouses and the blind wall at the back of a bed-and-breakfast.

Kyrie wanted to go look, but people were waiting for their food, so she set about getting the pie and the olives and the rice pudding—all of it pre-prepared—from the refrigerator behind the counter. Next to it, Frank was peeling and cutting potatoes for the Athens's famous "fresh made fries, never frozen," which were also advertised on the facade, somewhere.

While she worked, some of the regulars came in. A tall blond man who carried a journal in which he wrote obsessively every night between midnight and four in the morning. And a heavyset, dark-haired woman who came in for a pastry on her way to her job at one of the warehouses.

Kyrie looked again at the clock. Half an hour, and still no Tom. She took the newcomers' orders.

On one of her trips behind the counter, for the carafe of coffee, she told Frank, "Tom is late."

But Frank only shrugged and grunted, which was pretty odd behavior for the guy who had brought Tom in out of nowhere, hired him with no work history while Tom was, admittedly, living in the homeless shelter down the street.

As Kyrie returned the carafe to its rest, after the round of warm-ups, she heard the scream. It was a lone scream, at first, startled and cut short. It too came from the parking lot at the back.

She told herself it was nothing to do with her. There were all sorts of people out there at night. Goldport didn't exactly have a large population of homeless, but it had some, and some of them were crazy enough to scream for no reason.

Swallowing hard, she told herself it meant nothing, absolutely nothing. It was just a sound, one of the random sounds of night in the city. It wasn't anything to worry about. It—

The scream echoed again, intense, frightened, a wail of distress in the night. Looking around her, Kyrie could tell no one else had heard it. Or at least, if Frank's shoulders were a little tenser than normal, as he dropped fries into a huge vat of oil, it was the tenseness of expectation, as if he were listening for Tom.

It wasn't the look of someone who'd heard a death scream. In fact, the only person who might have heard it was the blond guy who had stopped writing on his journal and was staring up, into mid-air. But Kyrie was not about to ask a man who wrote half the night what exactly he had heard or hadn't. Besides the guy—nicknamed "The Poet" by the diner staff—always gave the impression of being on edge and ready to lose all self-control, from the tips of his long, nervous fingers to the ends of his tennis shoes.

And yet . . .

And yet she couldn't pretend nothing had happened. She knew she had heard the scream. With that type of scream, someone or something was in trouble bad. Back there. In the parking lot. At this time of night most of the clientele of the Athens came in on foot, from the nearby apartment complexes or from the college dorms just a couple of blocks away. It could be hours before anyone went out to the parking lot.

Kyrie didn't want to go out there, either. But she could not ignore it. She had the crazy feeling that whatever was happening out there involved Tom, and, what the heck, she might not like the man, but neither did she want him dead.

She gave a last round of warm-ups, looked toward the counter where Frank was still seemingly absorbed in his frying, and edged out toward the hallway that led to the back.

It curved past the bathrooms, so if Frank saw her, he would think she was going to the bathroom. She was not sure why she didn't want him to know she was going to the parking lot. Except that—as she got to the glass door at the back—when she saw the parking lot bathed in the moonlight, she thought that something might happen out there, something . . . Something she didn't want her employer to know about her.

Not that it could happen. There was nothing that could happen, she thought, as she turned the key. Nothing had happened in months. She wasn't sure what she thought had happened back then hadn't all been a dream.

The key hadn't been turned in some time and it stuck, but finally the resistance gave way, and she opened the door, and plunged into the burning moonlight.

Feeling of jungle, need for undergrowth and vegetation, her heart beating madly in her eardrums, and she was holding it together, barely holding it together, hoping . . .

She jumped out onto the parking lot and called out, "Tom—"

Something not quite a roar answered her. She stopped.

And then the smell hit her. Fresh blood. Spilled blood. She trembled and tried to stop. Tried to think.

But her nose scented blood and her mouth filled with saliva, and her hands curved and her nails grew. Somehow, with clumsy claws, she unbuttoned her uniform. She never knew how. As the last piece of clothing fell to the ground, she felt a spasm contort her whole body.

And a large, black jungle cat ran swiftly across the parking lot. Toward the smell of blood.

Soft pads on asphalt. Asphalt. The word appeared alien to Kyrie's mind, locked in the great loping body, feeling the movement, the agility, and not quite believing it.

Strange feeling on pads. Hard, scratchy.

Muscles coiling and uncoiling like darkness flowing in moonlit patches. Bright moonlight like a river of fire and joy. Running. Smelling with sense that no human ever possessed.

And the feline stopped, alert, head thrown back, sniffing. A soft growl made its way up a throat that Kyrie could only just believe was her own.

Smell—a rich, spicy, flowing smell, like cinnamon on a cold winter night in Kyrie's human memory, like rich molten chocolate, like freshly picked apples to that dwindling part of herself who thought with human memories.

She took a deep breath and felt her mouth fill and overflow with drool, while her paws moved, step on step, toward the smell, soft pads on asphalt, growl rising from throat.

What was it? What could it be? Her human mind could not

identify the smell that came at her with depth and meaning that humans did not seem capable of perceiving.

She felt drool drop through her half-open mouth, onto the concrete, as she looked around for the possible source of the wondrous scent.

There were . . . cars—she had to force herself to remember the word, to realize these were man-made and not some natural plant or animal in a jungle she'd never seen but that was all this body knew and wanted to remember.

Cars. She shook her great head. Her own small, battered Ford, and two big vans that belonged to Frank and which he used for the daily shopping.

Around the edge of the vehicles she followed the scent. It was coming from right there, behind the vans, from dark liquid flowing along the asphalt, between the wheels of the van. She padded around the vans. Liquid looked black and glistened under moonlight, and she was about to take an experimental lap when the shadow startled her.

At first it was just that. A shadow, formless, moving on the concrete. Something with wings. Something.

Her hackles rising, she jumped back, cowering, head lifted, growling. And saw it.

A . . . lizard. No. No lizard had ever been this size. A . . . creature, green and scaly and immense, with wings that stretched between the earth and the sky.

The feline Kyrie dropped to her belly, paws stretched our in front of her, a low growl rising, while her hair stood on end, trying to make the already large jungle cat look bigger.

The human Kyrie, torpid and half-dormant, a passenger in her own brain that had been taken over by this dream of moonlight and forest, looked at the beast and thought, *Dragon*.

Not the slender, convoluted form of the Chinese dragons with their huge, bewhiskered faces. No. Nordic. A sturdy Nordic dragon, stout of body, with the sort of wings that truly seemed like they could devour the icy blue sky of the Norsemen and not notice.

Huge, feral, it stood before Kyrie, fangs bared, both wings

extended, tip to tip probably a good twelve feet. Its muzzle was stained a dark red, and—as Kyrie knit her belly to the concrete—it hissed, a threatening hiss.

It will flame me next, Kyrie thought. But she couldn't get the big cat to move. Bewildered by something that the now dominant part of her couldn't comprehend, she lay on her belly and growled.

And the Kyrie part of her mind, the human part, looked bewildered at the dragon wings, which were a fantastic construction of bones and translucent glittering skin that faded from green to gold. And she thought that dragons weren't supposed to look that beautiful. Particularly not a dragon whose muzzle was stained with blood.

And on that, on the one word, she identified the enticing smell. Blood. Fresh blood. She remembered smelling it before the shape-shift. But it smelled nothing like blood through the big cat's senses.

With the feline's sharp eyes, she could see, beneath the paws of the dragon, a dark bundle that looked like a human body.

Human blood. And she'd almost lapped it.

Shock and revulsion did what her fear couldn't. They broke the human Kyrie out of the prison at the back of her own mind. Free, she pushed the animal back.

Push and push and push, she told herself she must be Kyrie. She must be human. Kyrie was smart enough to run away before the dragon let out with fire.

And never mind that the dragon might run her down, kill her. At least she would be able to think with a human mind.

All of a sudden, the animal gave, and she felt the spasms that contorted her body back to two human legs, two human arms, the solidity of a human body, lying on the concrete, hands on the ground, toes supporting her lower body.

She started to rise to run, but the dragon made a sudden, startled movement.

It was not a spring to attack nor a cowering in fear. Either of those she could have accepted as normal for the beast. It was a vague, startled jump. A familiar, startled jump.

Like coming on Tom around the corner of the hallway leading to the bathroom and meeting him coming out of it. Tom jumped that way, startled, not quite scared, and she always thought he'd been shooting up in there—must have been shooting up in there.

Now the same guilty jump from the dragon, and the massive head swung down to her prone body, to look at her with huge, startled blue eyes. Tom's eyes.

Kyrie. His human mind identified her a second before his reptilian self, startled, scared, surprised, would have opened his mouth and let out with a jet of flame.

His mouth opened, he just managed to control the flame. He tried to shape her name, but the reptilian throat didn't lend itself to it.

Tom felt his nictitating eyelids blink, sideways, before his normal eyelids, the eyelids he was used to, blinked up and down.

She stood up, slowly, shivering. She was honey-colored all over. Both sets of his eyelids blinked again. He'd always thought that she had a tan. No lines. And her breasts were much fuller than they looked beneath the uniform and apron—heavy, rounded forms miraculously, perfectly horizontal in defiance of gravity.

He realized he was staring and looked up to see her looking into his eyes, horrified. He tried to shape an apology but what came out was a semi-growling hiss.

"Tom," she said, her voice raspy and hoarse, her eyes frightened and . . . pitying? "Tom, you killed someone."

Killed? He was sure he hadn't. He stopped on a breath, then tasted in his mouth the metallic and—to his dragon senses—bright and delicious symphony of flavors that was blood.

Blood? Human blood?

The shock of it seemed to wake him. He looked down to see a corpse between his paws. His paws were smeared with blood. The corpse was a bundle, indistinct, neither male nor female, neither young nor old. It smelled dead. Freshly dead.

Had he run someone down? Killed him? Had he?

He tried to remember and he couldn't. The dragon . . .

He took his hand to his forehead, felt the clamminess of blood on his skin, and realized he was human again. Human, smeared with blood, standing by a corpse.

And Kyrie had seen him kill someone.

"No," he said, not sure to whom he spoke. "Oh, please, no."

Tom's voice was low at the best of times. Now it came out growly and raspy, like gravel dragging around on a river bottom. His transformation, much faster than hers, had been so fast that she'd hardly seen it.

He stood by the corpse, looking lost despite his broad shoulders, small waist, muscular legs, powerful arms. Except for his being all of five-six, and for the track marks on his arms, Tom could have graced the cover of bodybuilding magazines. Only his muscles weren't developed to the grotesque level the field demanded.

And above it all his face that managed to make him look like a frightened little boy.

His hair had come loose from the rubber band he used to confine it in a ponytail. Loose, it just touched his arms, in a rumple of irregular curls. His skin was pale, very pale all over. Not exactly vampire-white. More like aged ivory, even and smooth. And his eyes were a deep, dark, and yet somehow brilliant blue.

They now opened in total horror, as he stared at her and rasped, "I didn't. Kill."

Her first reaction was to snap out that of course he had. She'd seen him by the corpse, his muzzle stained by blood. Then she remembered she'd almost lapped the blood herself. Lapped it! And she'd known what it was before shifting too.

She shuddered, and remembered what the blood smelled like to the jungle cat. *The beast*, as she'd learned to call it years ago, when she'd first turned into it. Or hallucinated turning into it, as she'd convinced herself had happened over time. That theory might have to be discarded now, unless she was hallucinating Tom's shifting, too. She couldn't quite believe that.

"I don't remember chasing," he said. "Killing."

A look down at the corpse told her nothing, save that it had been mauled. But wouldn't Tom . . . the dragon have mauled it anyway? Whether he'd killed it or not?

Tom was looking down, horrified, trembling. Shock. He was in shock. If she left him here, he would stay like that. Till they were caught.

She reached for his arm. His skin felt skin cold, clammy to the touch. Was it being the dragon? Or being naked in the night? Or the shock? She had to do something about the shock. No. She had to do something, period.

"Come," she said. "Come."

He obeyed. Like a child, he allowed her to pull him all the way to the back door of the diner.

She stooped to pick up her clothes, trying not to get blood on them.

Tom stumbled after Kyrie, confused. The parking lot was cold. He felt it on his wet skin. Wet. He looked down and saw patches of blood on his body. Human blood.

"You're shaking like a leaf," Kyrie whispered. She opened the back door of the Athens and looked in, along the corridor that curved gently toward the bathroom. She said, "Go in. Quickly. Get into the women's bathroom. Don't lock it. I'll come."

He rushed forward, obeying. In his current state, he couldn't think of doing anything but obeying. But a part of his brain, moving fast beneath the sluggish surface of his shocked mind, wondered, *Why the women's bathroom?* Then he realized the women's bathroom was just one large room and locked, while in the men's restroom they'd managed to cram the stall and a row of urinals. And the outer door didn't lock.

Yeah, there would be more room in the women's bathroom to clean up, he thought, even as he skidded into the door to the bathroom, on damp, bare feet.

"Why didn't you turn the light on?" Kyrie said, coming in after him, turning the light on.

She went to the sink and started washing herself, making use of the paper towels and the water. Considering where she'd been, she had very little blood on her. Not like Tom. He tasted blood on his tongue.

And now he was shaking again.

"Stop that," Kyrie said. She was clean now, and putting her clothes back on. How had she managed to get out of her clothes before shifting?

He tried to remember his own clothes, and where he'd left them, but his memory was fogged and confused, intercut by the bright golden blur of the dragon's thoughts.

"Are you going to clean yourself or am I going to have to?" Kyrie asked. She'd somehow got fully dressed before he could notice. She stood there, looking proper, in her apron. She'd even put the earring back on her ear. She'd remembered to take that off. What was she? Some kind of machine?

Tom pulled his hair back from his face. "I'm naked," he said.

"I've noticed," she said, but she wasn't looking. And now she had the expression back on her face—the expression she'd shown Tom since the first day he'd arrived at the Athens and Frank had offered him a job. The expression that meant he was no good, he was possibly dangerous, and that Frank was crazy to trust him.

He knew she would glare at his track marks next and, damn it all, he hadn't shot up since he'd got—Well, since he'd got the job. He stopped the thoughts of whatever else he'd got forcefully. You really never knew what the other dragons could hear. He didn't think they were telepathic. He thought they were just watching him really closely. But he wasn't about to bet on it. No way. He wasn't about to let his guard down. He'd seen what they could do, way back when—

He shook his head and took deep breaths to drive away his memory—which could force him to become a dragon as fast as the shine of the moon or the smell of blood. He concentrated on the thought that it was nearby. It. The treasure he'd stolen. The magic that helped him stay himself.

A wet and cold paper towel touched his chest and he jumped. Kyrie's glance at him held a challenge. "I'll do it if I have to," she said.

He shook his head and pulled the towel from her hand, rubbing it briskly on his shoulders, his arms, his chest. He discarded it in the trash can, thinking about DNA evidence and trying not to. Telling himself he couldn't have done it, he couldn't have killed anyone. He couldn't. He just couldn't. That was something he couldn't live with—knowing for sure he'd killed anyone.

But the police would think— The police—

He started shaking again and took deep breaths to control it. He folded another mass of paper towels and wet it and ran it on his face, his hands. The face looking back at him from the mirror looked more red than white, smeared with blood.

Whose blood? Who had that person been, out in the parking lot? Tom didn't remember anything. Nothing, before opening his eyes, staring at the dead body, and seeing Kyrie. And that wasn't right. It had been like that at first, but it had given him more control and he was supposed to know what he'd done while in dragon form. He was supposed to remember.

Kyrie was looking at him, attentively, cautiously, like a bomb expert trying to decide which wire to cut in a peculiar homemade contraption.

Tom bit his tongue and managed a good imitation of his normal, gruff tone. "It's all right," he said. "I'm fine."

She cocked her head to one side, managing to convey wordlessly that there were about a million interpretations of *fine* and none of them applied to him. But aloud she said, "I'm going out for just a second. Lock up after me. When I come back I will knock once. Only once. Let me in when I do."

Tom locked the door behind her, obediently. He wondered where she was going, but it wasn't like he had any room left to argue about what she might want to do. He should count himself lucky she hadn't screamed bloody murder when she'd found him in the parking lot. Perhaps she should have screamed bloody murder. Wasn't that the name for what he'd done? No— He hadn't— He couldn't—

A muffled knock. He realized that not only had Kyrie been gone for a while, but also that he'd somehow managed to remove most of the red stains from his hands and face. His hair was a drying, sticky mass that he didn't want to investigate, much less clean.

"That will do," she said. "You can wear these." She extended to him, at the end of a stiff arm—like a person feeding a wild animal—what looked like a red jogging suit.

"It's mine," she said, as though mistaking his hesitation for a belief that she'd mugged a vagrant for the clothes. Or taken them from the corpse. "I usually jog in the morning before going home. Safer here. It's a main street."

He swallowed hard, trying not to think of what street would be less safe than Fairfax. But then if she lived nearby—as he did—in the interlacing warren of downtown streets, there would be many less safe. Well, not less safe in reality—the crime rate in Goldport was never that high and most deaths were crimes committed by and between gang members. But in the side streets, dotted with tiny houses, or with huge Victorian mansions long since turned into tiny apartments, a woman jogging alone in the wee hours of the morning would not be seen. And that, perhaps, meant she wouldn't be safe—because she could disappear and not be noticed for hours.

A thought that whoever tried to attack this woman would be far from safe himself crossed Tom's mind and he beat it down. Perhaps that was what she was afraid of. Of being mugged in the dark street and killing—

He grabbed the jogging suit. It felt too cold to his hands, and too distant—as if it weren't real fabric but some fabric-like illusion that his senses refused to acknowledge fully. As if he weren't really here. As if this were all a dream and he would, shortly, wake up back in the safety of his teenage room, in his father's house, with his stereo, his TV, his game system, all those things he'd needed when life itself wasn't exciting enough.

The clothes fit. Of course they would fit. Kyrie was his height, just about, and while his shoulders were much broader, and his chest far more muscular, she had other . . . endowments. A memory of her in the parking lot swept like a wave over him, and he felt a warm blush climb his cheeks and adjusted his—her—jogging pants and prayed that she wasn't focusing there just now.

But he might have been too late, because she frowned as if she were about to ask if blood turned him on. She didn't, though. Just said, "Wait for me. By the back door."

"The back?" he said. His voice came out too low and raspy. "But—"

"You can't walk through the diner like that. It's clear your hair is caked with blood. Someone might notice and say something. Later. When . . . someone asks."

The police. But neither of them mentioned it.

"I'm going to tell Frank I'm going out for a moment," she said.

He nodded. She was efficient. She was determined. And she was helping him. It was more than he could have hoped for. And certainly no fault at all of hers if it made him feel helpless and out of control.

As he hadn't been in six months.

CHAPTER
⊰ 2 ⊱

Kyrie wasn't sure what she was going to tell Frank. She had some idea he'd already be on simmer from what he would see as her sudden disappearance. In the ten steps between the bathroom and the diner proper, she ran her options through her mind—she could tell him she felt ill. She felt ill enough after the mess in the parking lot and the more specific mess in the bathroom. And the last thing any greasy-spoon owner wanted was to have a sick employee—visibly sick—tending to tables. On the other hand, if she did that, she was going to be some hours short this month. Because there was no way she could come back again tonight. And there was rent to pay.

She didn't know what she going to say at all until she emerged from the corridor into the yellowish light of the diner and said, "Frank, I need a few minutes, to go to Tom's." Which made perfect sense as she said it. A few minutes should suffice to go to Tom's house, because Tom walked here, and if Tom walked here, he couldn't live very far away. That meant a couple of minutes would also see him back to his home with no problem at all. And her back here, pretending she'd just dropped by his place.

Frank was attending to the students' table and had the sort of look on his face that meant he was trying very hard not to explode.

Kyrie had worked for him for a year and she'd been a reliable employee, never late, rarely sick, and trustworthy enough to be left alone with the register on occasion. None of which were easy to come by in a college town in Colorado for the late-night shift and considering what Frank was willing to pay.

He looked over his shoulder at Kyrie, and his brows beetled together, nonetheless, and he managed, "What? More minutes?"

"Tom is sick," she said. "He called me." Let Frank wonder why and how she'd given Tom her cell-phone number. "He wants me to buy him some stuff at the pharmacy and drop it by. Over-the-counter stuff," she added, thinking that most of what Tom probably took was not over-the-counter.

Frank looked like he was going to say something like that, for just a moment, but he gave it up. Probably he couldn't imagine Kyrie buying illegal drugs. And in that he would be right. She got enough lawlessness in her everyday life, enough to hide and disguise, that she did not need any more adrenaline.

So Frank shrugged, which might be taken for agreement, and Kyrie rushed back down the hallway, hoping to find Tom, hoping Tom hadn't shifted, hoping that for once things would go well. For just this once.

Tom was where she expected him—at the back of the diner, facing the door to the parking lot. He was pale and had started trembling again, and there wasn't much she could say or do for that. She wondered if he'd killed the man. She didn't want to think about it. It didn't matter. If he had, could she blame him? She knew the confusion of mind, the prevalence of the beast-self over every civilized learning, every instinct, even. How could she accuse someone else who'd given in perhaps further?

Of course she could, a deeper voice said, because she didn't give in. She'd fought her—as she'd thought—hallucinations tooth and nail and she'd held onto a normal life of sorts. No friends, no family, no one who might discover what she'd thought was her hideous madness, but she made her own money, she lived her own life.

She managed a weak smile at Tom by way of reassurance, as she turned the key and opened the door.

She took a deep breath to steel herself against the smell of blood, the light of the moon. She must stay in control. She must.

But she wasn't ready for the other smell—the hot, musky, and definitely male smell that invaded her nostrils as she stepped onto the parking lot.

Dizziness and her mouth went dry and her whole body started fluttering on the verge of shifting shape, and she told herself no. No. Regained control just in time to see it, at the edge of the parking lot, under one of the lights.

Not it. Him. The smell was clear as a hallelujah chorus in her head. He was at the edge of the parking lot, and he was tawny and huge and muscular.

A lion. He was a lion. Was he a lion like she was a panther and Tom was a dragon, or . . .

Or what? An invader from the vast Colorado savannah outside Goldport? Where lions and zebras chased each other under the hot tropical sun?

She shook her head at her own silliness.

Behind her, Tom drew breath, noisily. "Is it?" he asked.

"Yes," she said.

"But—" He drew breath again and something—something about the movement of his feet against the asphalt, something about his breathing, perhaps something about his smell (since when could she smell people this way?) made her think he was about to run.

She put out a hand to his arm. "Do not run," she said. "Walk steadily."

His arm felt cold and smooth under her hand. Light sprinkling of hair. Very little of it for a male. Perhaps being a dragon . . . She didn't want to think of that. She didn't want to think of Tom, muzzle deep in blood.

Which of course meant the lion could smell them. Smell the blood on them. "You mustn't run," she said. "We . . . Cats are triggered by motion. If you run he will give chase. Walk slowly and steadily toward my car. The small white one. Come."

They made their way slowly, steadily, across the parking lot, in the reek of blood. Perhaps the lion wouldn't be able to smell Tom in the overwhelming smell.

Perhaps they could make it to the car. Perhaps . . . perhaps the moon was made of green cheese and it would rain pea soup tomorrow.

He smelled powerful, musky. She could hear him draw breath, was aware of the touch of paw pads on the asphalt. She felt those movements as if they were her own, her heart accelerating and seeming to beat at her throat, suffocating her.

Paw touching asphalt, and paw touching asphalt, and paw touching asphalt. Measured steps. Not a run. Please don't let it be a run.

And her movements matched his—slow, measured, trying to appear unconcerned, escorting Tom to the car, guiding him.

Tom walked like a wooden puppet. Was he that terrified of the lion? Didn't he know in his dragon form he was as big? Bigger? Stronger? Why was he afraid?

But her rational self understood. He was afraid because he was in human form. And every human at the back of his mind feared the large felines who lurked in the shadows and who could eat him in two bites.

Kyrie herself was sweating and cold by degrees, and felt as if her legs were made of water, as she concentrated on following the beast's movements by sound.

They hit the moonlight, out of the shadow of the diner and into the fully illuminated parking lot. The heat of it felt like fire playing over Kyrie's skin and she kept her head lowered. She took deep breaths. Her heartbeat echoed some old jungle rhythm but she told herself she would not, she would not, she could not shift.

And the smell of him—of the lion—enveloped her, stronger than ever. Her senses, sharpened from wanting to transform, gave her data about him that a mere nose should not be able to gather. That he was young. That he was healthy. That he was virile.

She pulled Tom forward, and the lion followed them at a distance—step, step, step, unhurried, unafraid. She prayed he wouldn't start running. She prayed he wouldn't leap. And inside, deep inside, she felt as if he was toying with her. Playing. Like a cat with a mouse.

She was not a mouse.

Sweat formed on her scalp, dripped toward her eyes, made her blink. The car loomed in front of her, white and looking much bigger than it usually did. Looking like safety.

Kyrie pushed her key-fob button to unlock it, and felt as if her fingers slipped on the smooth plastic, as though she had claws and unwieldy paws.

No. She must not. She must remain human. She must.

Breathing deeply and only managing to inhale more unabashed male musk, she shoved Tom, slightly, and said, "Go around to the passenger side. Get in."

Go, give him a divided target. Go, but for the love of all that's holy, don't stop. Don't stop. Don't let him catch you. She didn't know which she feared most. The idea of being attacked or the idea of seeing Tom attacked, of seeing Tom torn to pieces. Of shifting. Of joining in.

She shuddered as her too-clumsy fingers struggled with the car handle. She saw Tom open the door on the other side. Get in. She struggled with the handle.

And the lion was twenty steps away, crouching in the full light of the moon, augmented by the light of a parking-lot lamp above her. He was crouching, front down low and hindquarters high.

Hindquarters trembling. Legs bunching.

Jump. He was going to—

He jumped, clearing the space between them, and she leaned hard against her car, her heart hammering in her chest, her body divided and dividing her mind. Her human body, her human mind, wanted to scream, to hide. Her human body knew that the huge body would hit her, claws would rend her. That she was about to die.

But her other mind . . . Her other mind practically died in the ecstatic smell of healthy young male. Her other mind thought the lion knew her, guessed her, smelled her for an equal. That the lion wanted— Not to eat her.

She realized she'd closed her eyes, when she felt him landing near her—landing with all four paws on the asphalt. Not on her, but so close to her she felt the breeze of his falling, and smelled him, smelled him hot and strong and oh, so impossibly male.

She felt her body spasm, wish to shift. She fought it. She struggled to stay herself.

Through half-open eyes, she saw a lion's face turned toward her, its golden eyes glowing, its whole expression betraying . . . smugness?

Then it opened its mouth, the fangs glowing in the light and a soft growl started at the back of its throat. She didn't know if it was threatening her or . . .

Something to the growl—something to the sound crept along her nerves like a tingle on the verge of aching. If she stayed— If she stayed . . .

The car door opened, shoving her. She leapt aside, to avoid being pushed into the lion. A hand reached out of the car, dragged her. She fell onto her seat. Blinked. Tom. Tom had pulled her into the car.

"Drive," Tom said. "Drive."

He reached across her, as he spoke and slammed the door. From outside, the lion made a rumbling sound that might have been amusement.

She didn't remember turning the ignition. She didn't remember stepping on the gas. But she realized she was driving down Fairfax. Tall, silent apartment houses succeeded each other on either side of the road, lighted by sporadic white pools of light from the street lamps.

"Where do you live?" she managed, glancing at Tom. Part of her wanted to tell him she hadn't been afraid, she hadn't been . . .

But she wasn't even sure she could explain what she'd been. She had been afraid. That was a huge beast. But also, at some level, she was afraid she would end up shifting, cavorting with him. Over a half-devoured human carcass.

"Two blocks down," Tom said, and swallowed, as if he'd had the same thought at the same time. "Audubon apartments. On the left."

She remembered the place. Not one of the graceful Victorian remnants, but half a dozen rectangular red-brick boxes sharing a parking lot. During the day there were any number of kids playing in the parking lot, and usually one or two men working on cars or drinking beer.

Now, in the dark of night, it was silent and ill lit. As she pulled into the parking lot, Tom asked, "It was one of us, wasn't it?"

"Pardon?" she said. She knew what he meant. She knew all too well. He was asking if the lion was like them. If the lion too had a human form and one not so human. But Kyrie had managed until very recently to convince herself she only had one form and that everything else was hallucination. Mental illness.

Now this whole thing felt like mental illness. She parked the car, turned the engine off.

"You know . . ." Tom said. His blue eyes were earnest, and he plucked at her sleeve like a little kid seeking reassurance. "You know, a shapeshifter. Like us."

She shrugged. "Seems unlikely it escaped from a zoo," she said. "Someone would have given the alarm, wouldn't they?"

Tom nodded, as if considering this. "What . . . what did it want?"

Kyrie shrugged. She wanted to say *he* wanted everything but all she had to go on was the smell. And she didn't wish to discuss her response to the smell with Tom.

"Do you think it killed the . . . person?"

Did you? Kyrie thought, but only shrugged. How did you ask someone who looked as bewildered and shocked as Tom if he'd committed murder? And was she really feeling sorry for Tom? *Must be going soft in the head.*

Tom got out of the car, patted down where the pockets would be in normal pants, and Kyrie realized he wouldn't have keys.

But he turned around and said, "Thank you for driving me," and pushed the door as if to close it.

"Wait, do you have keys?"

He shrugged. "The neighbor usually keeps them," he said. "For me. I keep his."

His? For some reason it had never occurred to Kyrie that someone like Tom could entrust his key—or anything else—to a male. If she'd thought of his social life outside work at all, she imagined a never-ending succession of sweet things across his mattress. But now she realized she was probably wrong. It was unlikely there was anyone on his mattress. He had come from a homeless shelter. And he was a dragon.

"Keith keeps my key and I keep his. . . . So if we lose it while we're out," Tom said, an edge of impatience in his voice. "He's a college student. They lose their keys." He hesitated a minute. "Gets stinking drunk too." He said it as if he, himself, never took any mind-altering substances.

And out of nowhere, an altruistic impulse, or perhaps the thought that he'd saved her—from what?—with the lion in the parking lot, made her get out. "I'll come with you," she said. "To make sure you get in okay."

She had a feeling, a strange feeling something was wrong. Wrong with this parking lot, with this entire area. There was a feeling of being watched and not in a friendly manner, but she wasn't sure by whom, or how. Any other day, any other time, she would have shrugged it off. But now . . . Well . . . perhaps she was picking up smell or something. Something was definitely wrong.

She got out of the car, unsteady on her legs, glad that the moonlight was hidden by the shadows of the buildings. The pressure of the full moonlight was all she needed now. At the same time, she felt as if the buildings themselves were looming shapes waiting to jump her.

It wasn't possible, was it? For the buildings to be shifters? With a human form? What was this? How many people did it afflict? And why was she afraid?

She wasn't sure of anything anymore. Sweat trickled down her back and her legs felt like water while she followed Tom to the steps outside the door of the nearest building.

"Keith might not be home," Tom said, pressing the button. Actually, it was damn bloody sure that Keith Vorpal would not be home. Keith was a film student at Goldport College and somewhat of a ladies' man. One or the other tended to keep him out of the house on warm summer nights. He always assumed Tom had the same sort of life and only seemed somewhat amused that Tom managed to come home naked so often. He took Tom's mutters of "some good beer" or a "glass too many" and asked no questions. Which in itself would be worrisome, except that Keith's own life was such a mess of perils and odd adventures that he probably took it for granted everyone else's life was that crazy. And no worse.

Their arrangement with the keys rested on a vague hope that one of them might be home when the other needed a key. So far it had worked out, more or less. But there was always the chance . . .

Tom rang again. A buzz he recognized as Keith's voice came through the loudspeaker. He couldn't actually understand what Keith said, but he could guess. "It's Tom, man," Tom said. "Lost my key, somehow . . ."

Another buzz that Tom—with long practice—understood to mean that he should ring Keith's door and Keith would give him the key. Then the front door clicked open.

"Sorry there's no elevator, but—" Tom started, and shut up. Most apartment buildings in Goldport, much less most apartment buildings in downtown Goldport, didn't have elevators. He must be having flashbacks to his childhood in an upscale NY condo.

As it was, the Audubon was more upscale than the places he'd lived in the last five years even when he'd been out of the shelter. There were no rats. The cement stairs covered in worn carpet were clean enough and didn't smell of piss. And if, now and then, like on the third floor, you could hear a baby cry through the thin door of an apartment, you could be sure the little tyke had just awakened and needed to nurse, and not that he was being beaten within an inch of his life.

These were solid working-class apartments, where people scrimped and saved to get by and might wear clothes from thrift-shop racks, but where most families had two parents and both parents worked, and where kids went to school and played, instead of doing drugs. Or selling them.

Yeah, it could be much, much worse. Tom rubbed his hand across his face as he climbed, as fast as his feet would carry him up to the third floor. He hated shifting shape—particularly shifting shape when he didn't mean to and staying shifted for . . . hours, he guessed, as his last memory was from when the moon first appeared in the sky, around maybe nine. He wondered what he'd been doing. It had been months since shifting had come with such total memory loss.

If he could find his clothes, he would know what had happened, but right now he only had a memory of fear—of fleeing. And then nothing at all until he'd come to himself in that parking lot, with Kyrie staring at him and the bloodied corpse at his feet.

They'd reached the landing on the third floor and he lurched to Keith's door on the left, and pushed the doorbell. Despite his having called, he didn't expect a fast response and didn't get it. From inside came Keith's voice and a higher, clearly female voice, and then the sound of footsteps, something falling, more footsteps.

Tom smiled despite himself, guessing that Keith had still been explaining to his visitor why the doorbell had rung from downstairs, when it rang again up here.

When the door opened, Keith looked disheveled and sleepy. He was a young kid—although to be honest he might be older than Tom. Tom just perceived him as much younger than himself—perhaps because Keith didn't shift. Keith was blond and generally good-looking. Right then, he was blinking, his blue eyes displaying the curiously naked look of the eyes of people who normally wore glasses and suddenly found themselves without.

His hair was a mess and he looked confused, but he was grinning as he handed Tom a set of keys. Though the student held the door almost closed, Tom glimpsed a redheaded girl behind Keith. He felt a little envious. It had been years since he'd even dreamed of sharing his bed with anyone. He could never guarantee he wouldn't shift and scare a date halfway to death. Or worse.

Then he realized Keith was looking enviously at him. Tom followed the direction of Keith's gaze, and saw Kyrie standing just behind him, hands on hips, as though daring Keith to make a comment. And Tom felt at the same time ridiculously pleased that Keith thought he could be involved with someone like Kyrie and a little jealous of Keith's admiration for her. Keith didn't even know her. He didn't even know who she was. He didn't know that she shifted as well.

"Thanks," Tom said, a little more dryly than he should. He

snatched the key from Keith's hand and started up the stairs at a faster clip than he should, considering how he felt.

Keith grinned. "No problem. But I have to go back. This girl is something else. She swears she saw a dragon flying over the building. A dragon." He shook his head.

A dragon. Tom managed a noncommittal sound of empathy. Probably Tom. But Tom didn't dare ask questions about what he'd been doing or what direction he'd been flying. Instead, he turned and started up the stairs. Up and up and up, to his fifth-floor landing, Kyrie's steady gait keeping pace with his.

His door was . . . locked. He let out a breath he hadn't been aware of holding in. After all, he did not know how or when he'd shifted and all he had was the memory of fear, of running away. It was possible *they* had found him in his apartment. It was possible . . . If they'd figured out his name, and they must have by now, it would have been easy.

But the door was locked, his doormat looked untouched. Everything was as it should be. No light came under his door. Everything was normal at least to human senses and he didn't want to use his dragon senses. He didn't want to reach for that other self, for fear it would bring them. And for fear of what he might do. He swallowed hard, thinking of the corpse.

There could be nothing odd in his apartment. The only reason his hand trembled was because of his being so tired. And the corpse and everything.

He slid the key in and turned it.

In the moment before Tom opened the door Kyrie had a wild surge of panic. She wanted to tell him to wait, but she couldn't speak. And she didn't know why he should wait. She just had a feeling— added up from rustling, from sounds she could not possibly have heard, from an odd smell, from a weird tingle up her spine—that something was wrong, very wrong.

Perhaps Tom was going to drag her into his apartment and— And what? Imagination failed her. She had seen him in that bathroom, so slow and confused he didn't even seem to know how to wipe away blood from himself. She had seen him standing there, helpless. She could hardly believe he would now turn around and rape her.

On the other hand, didn't they sacrifice virgins to dragons in the Middle Ages? She almost smiled at the thought of Tom as virgin-despoiler. The way he looked, he'd have trouble beating away the ones who threw themselves at him. Kyrie managed to calm herself completely, when Tom reached in and turned on the light.

The light revealed an unprepossessing living room, with the type of dark brown carpet that landlords slapped down when they didn't expect to rent to the upper echelons of society. But the rest . . .

The furniture, what there was of it—splinters of bookcase, remnants of couches with ugly brown polyester covering—seemed to have been piled up in the middle of the room as if someone had been getting ready to light a bonfire. And the window—the huge picture window opposite—was broken. A thousand splinters littered the carpet. Books and pieces of books fluttered all over.

Tom made a sound of distress and stepped into the room, and Kyrie stepped in behind him. He knelt by a pile of something on the carpet, and Kyrie focused on it, noticing shreds of denim, and what might or might once have been a white T-shirt. And over it all, a torn purple rag, with the Athens logo. The Athens sent the aprons home with the employees to get laundered at employee expense.

That meant that Tom had been ready to go to work when . . . The tingle in her spine grew stronger and the feeling that something was wrong, very wrong overwhelmed her. It was like a scream both soundless and so loud that it took over her whole thought, overcame her whole mind, reverberated from her whole being.

"Tom," she said, putting a hand on his shoulder. "Tom, we'd best—"

She never had time to finish. Someone or something, moving soundlessly behind them, had closed the door.

Kyrie heard the bolt slide home and turned, skin prickling, hair standing on end, to stare openmouthed at three men who stood between them and the door.

Men was dignifying them with a name they didn't quite deserve.

They were boys, maybe nineteen or twenty, just at the edge of manhood. Asian, dressed all in black, they clearly had watched one too many ninja movies. The middle one wore exquisitely groomed, slightly too long hair, the bangs arranged so they fell to perfection and didn't move. He must have spent a fortune on product.

The ones on either side were not so stylishly groomed, but one sported a tattoo of a Chinese letter in the middle of his forehead, while the other had a tattoo of a red dragon on the back of each hand—clearly visible as he was clenching his fists and holding them up in a gesture more reminiscent of boxing than karate.

The far one shouted something, and Kyrie grabbed hold of Tom's arm, and shoved him behind her. He was acting like a wooden puppet again.

The pretty boy in the middle laughed and said something—Kyrie presumed in Chinese—to his friend. Then added in English, "He only speaks English." But when he turned to Tom all traces of laughter had vanished from his expression, as he said, "You know what we want. You foiled the first fool who came looking, but, you see, we returned for you. Now give it to us, and we might not kill you or your pretty girlfriend."

Pretty girlfriend? Kyrie registered as if from a long way away that they were talking about her. Truth was, very few people ever had called her pretty. She was too . . . striking, and proud to be called that. Also at some level people must always have sensed what she was, because since she'd turned fifteen and the panther had made its first appearance, few men had made taunting comments in her presence. Hell, few men even addressed her in any way.

But if there was an instinct for self-protection, this trio was lacking it. The little one with the two dragons on the backs of his hands started laughing.

At least, he threw his head back and Kyrie thought he was laughing, a high-pitched, hysterical laughter. And then she realized what the laughter really was as his outlines blurred and he started to shift. Wings, and curving neck. All of it in lovely tones of red and gold, like all those Chinese paintings. But the features—which in paintings had always made Kyrie think of a naughty cat—looked malevolent. He hissed, between lips wholly unprepared for speech, "Give us the pearl."

Pearl? A pearl seemed like a very odd thing for Tom to steal. Was it some form of drug? Kyrie glanced behind her, to see Tom shaking his head violently. The fact that he was the approximate color of curdled milk, his normally pale skin looking downright unhealthy and grey, did not reassure her that by his shaking his head he meant he'd never heard of such a thing as a pearl.

"Tom?" she said.

He only shook his head again.

"Right," the middle one said. "You want to play rough, rough it is."

And suddenly a golden dragon took up most of the small brown room. And there were claws reaching for Kyrie. No. Talons. And someone's fangs were close to her face, a smell like a thousand long-forgotten sushi dinners invading her nostrils. A forked tongue licked her ear and through the lips not fashioned for speech, through the accent that he showed even in English, she nonetheless understood the young man's words as he said, "We're going to have so much fun."

She'd never shifted when she was scared. The few times she'd shifted it had been just the moon and usually summer calling to her, the feeling of jungle in her mind, at the back of her brain.

But as her fear closed upon her throat, making breathing almost impossible, as her heart pounded seemingly in her ears, as her blood seemed to race away from her leaving her cold as ice, she felt something . . .

She wasn't sure what was happening until she heard the growl erupt from her throat. A full growl, fashioned from melodies of the jungle.

Lizards. Uppity lizards, at that. They dared challenge her? Try to grab her?

Turning around, she swiped a giant paw across the tender underflesh of a clawed foot holding her. And then she leapt for the throat of the giant beast who was trying to claw her down.

It was—the part of her that remained human, deep in the mists of consciousness thought—like the armada and the English ships. The Spanish armada's huge, slow ships might be stronger and better armored. But they had no hope against the small English ships that could sail around them, landing shots where they wished till the giant ship was crippled.

Kyrie grabbed the beast by the throat, hanging on, till she tasted blood—and what blood. It was like drinking the finest champagne straight from the bottle.

The beast yelled and reached for her with its claws. It managed to scrape her flank, in a bright slash of pain. But she jumped out of the way before the creature could grab her, and she was on top of his head, as both his friends converged, trying to grab her. And she leapt at the soft underbelly of the red one—Red Dragon, the human Kyrie thought—in a mad dance of claws sinking into soft, unarmored flesh.

And then up again, and leaping at the eye of the next dragon.

That there were three of them was not an advantage. After all, three large, slower-moving beings only helped each other get hopelessly entangled while Kyrie danced upon them like a deadly firefly, in a frenzy of wounding, a joy of blood.

She was vaguely aware that she too was bleeding, that there were punctures on her hide and that, somehow, one of them had managed to sink his fangs into her front leg—her right arm. But she didn't care. Right then, allowed the madness she'd long denied, she jumped at the dragon's eyes, swiping her claws across them and relishing the dragon's shriek of pain, the bright blood jumping from the right eye. She jumped and leapt, possessed of fierce anger, of maddened, repressed rage.

But while the beast exulted in the carnage, while the feline gyrated in mayhem, a small trickling feeling formed at the back of Kyrie's mind. It was like the first melting tip of an icicle, dropping cold reason on her hot madness. The feeling, at first, was no more than that—just a trickling cold, protesting, demanding—she wasn't sure what. The beast, in its frenzy, ignored it.

Until slowly, slowly, the feeling became words and the words became panic in Kyrie's mind. She was fighting all three dragons. She was keeping all three dragons at bay—just. But there were three of them, there was one of her, and the beast's muscles were starting to hurt and . . . How could she get out of here?

There was no way of reaching the door. All the dragons were between her and the door and none of her sorties had brought her close to escaping.

Blood in her nostrils, mad fury in the beast's brain, what remained of the human Kyrie tried to think and came up with nothing but an insistent, white surge of panic. And she couldn't let it slow her down. She couldn't. If she did, all would be lost. But she couldn't fight forever.

In a twirl, claws sinking into the nearest dragon's hide, she thought of Tom. But the corner into which he'd shrunk when she'd shifted was vacant.

The coward had run out the door behind her back, hadn't he?

She felt a horrible sense of betrayal, a letdown at this, and her extended paw faltered, and the dragon above her reared.

It was the center dragon—who in human form had artificially smooth and immovable hair. In dragon form he had a tall crest, red and gold. Well, it had been red and gold, it was now much darker red in spots, thanks to Kyrie's claws. And blood ran down its cheek from one of its eyes. But the other eye was unblinking fixed hatred as it opened its jaws wide, wide, fangs glistening.

Kyrie needed to jump. She needed to. But her muscles felt powerless, spent. Stretched elastic that would not spring again.

So this is how it ends . . .

The big head descended to devour her, teeth ready to break her neck. And a taloned paw grabbed her roughly around the middle, swept her back.

She turned. She turned with her remnant of strength, her very last drop of fury, to snarl at the dragon behind her.

She snarled at him, Tom thought—amazed he could think clearly in dragon form. He'd willed himself into being a dragon. Willed himself into it.

He desired it and pushed. He knew she was going to have problems leaving. He knew she couldn't fly.

And he knew she was an idiot for even fighting. They had no chance. But then, neither could he leave her to die alone. She had taken care of him, when she'd found him in suspicious circumstances. She'd shown him more kindness than his own father had. And she was a shifter like him. They were family: bonded deeper than any shared genes, any joint upbringing.

He shifted suddenly, unexpectedly, leaping in the air, and out of his corner so quickly the other dragons didn't seem to register it. He had only the time to see that she was cowering, that the dragon above her would finish her. And then he was reaching for her, grabbing her, jumping out the open window, even as she turned to snarl at him.

But the snarl—lip pulled back from vicious fangs—faltered as she recognized him.

He held her as gently and firmly as he could. He mustn't drop her. But neither must he hurt her. He could smell blood from her. He could smell fear.

He unfurled his wings—huge parachutes. Above him, the other dragons hadn't appeared yet. Perhaps she'd done more damage than he'd thought. Perhaps they had a few minutes. A very few minutes.

Down in the parking lot, her car was a small abandoned toy. Her keys would be in his apartment, he thought, and shook his huge head, amazed at the clarity of the human thought in beast form. Normally he didn't even remember what he'd done as a dragon. Perhaps because he was responsible for another? He'd never been responsible for anyone but himself.

But they must run. They must get out of here very fast. And as beasts, he could not explain to her what danger they were in. He couldn't even think, clearly think, of where to run.

The dragon wished to crawl under a rock, preferably by a river, and hide.

But Goldport was not so big on rivers. There was Panner's Creek, which in the summer became a mere trickle winding amid sun-parched boulders.

He flew her down to the parking lot, slowly, landed by the car, and wished to shift. He didn't dare reach for the strength of the talisman to allow himself to shift. No. The dragons would sense that.

Instead, setting Kyrie down carefully, he *willed* himself to shift. He thought himself human, and shivered, as his body spasmed in painful change.

He was naked. Naked, sitting on the warm asphalt of the parking lot, next to Kyrie's car and a panther. No. Next to Kyrie. In the next minute, she also shifted, and appeared as a naked, bloodied young woman, lying on the pavement next to him.

"The car," he rasped at her, his voice hesitant, difficult, like a long-neglected instrument. "We must leave. Soon. They will pursue."

She looked at him with confused, tired eyes. Her chin was scratched, and there was too much blood on her everywhere. He wondered how much of it was hers. Did they need to go to the hospital? They healed very quickly. At least Tom did. But what if these wounds were too serious? How could they go to the hospital? How could they explain anything?

"I don't have keys," she said, and patted her hips as though looking for keys in pockets that were no longer there.

Tom nodded. He got up, feeling about a hundred years old after two shifts in such a short time. His legs hurt, as did his arms, and his whole body felt as though someone had belabored him with sticks.

But he was human now and he could think. He remembered.

One eye on the window of his apartment, wondering how long he had, he said, "I'm sorry. I'll pay." Then he grabbed one of the stones on the flower bed nearby—a stone-bed, to tell the truth, since he'd never seen flowers there. He smashed the window with the stone, reached in, unlocked the door.

Sweeping the crumbs of glass from the seat, he smashed the key holder, reached down to the floor, and grabbed a screwdriver he'd noticed there while Kyrie was driving him. "Remembered you had this here," he said, turning to see her bewildered expression as her car started. And then, "Get in. I'll pay for the damage. Just get in."

Was it his imagination, or had he seen the shadow of a wing in the window above?

He reached across to unlock the passenger door, as she jumped in.

She fumbled with the seat belt as he tore out of the parking lot in a screech of rubber. Sweat was dripping from his forehead into his eyes. He was sure he was sitting on a chunk of glass. It had been years since he'd driven and he found the turns odd and difficult. The car his father had given him as a sixteenth-birthday gift handled much better than this. Good thing there was almost no traffic on the roads at this time.

He tore around the corner of Fairfax, turning into a narrower street and hoping he was only imagining the noise of wings above. He tried to choose tree-lined streets, knowing well enough that it was harder to see into them from above. The vision of dragons seemed to focus naturally on moving things. In a street of trees, shaken by the wind, in which shadows shifted and shook, it would be harder to see them.

Some of these streets were narrow enough—and the trees above them well over a hundred years old—that it made it impossible to see the streets at all, except as a green canopy. He took one street, then another, then yet another, tearing down quiet residential streets like a madman and probably causing the families snug in their brick ranches to wonder what was happening out there.

They passed two people walking, male and female, he tall and she much shorter, leaning into him. Shorts, T-shirts, a swirling white skirt, a vision of normalcy and a relationship that he couldn't aspire too, and Tom bit his lip and thumped the side of the wheel with his hand, bringing a startled glance from Kyrie.

He'd gone a good ten minutes and was starting to think they'd lost their pursuers, when he thought of Kyrie. He turned to her, wanting to explain he really would pay and that she should not—

Her dark eyes gazed into his, unwavering. "How many cars have you stolen?" she asked.

The way he'd hot-wired the car, quickly—she swore it had taken him less than a few seconds—had chilled Kyrie to the bone.

She supposed she should have known someone with a drug problem, working minimum-wage jobs had to supplement with crime, but all of a sudden she realized he was more dangerous—more out of control than she'd thought.

More out of control than the other dragons?

And yet, after he'd driven like a madman for a while, he looked at her with a devastatingly scared expression in his pale face. Despite chiseled features and the now all-too-obvious dark shadow of unshaven beard, he managed to look about five and worried he'd be put in time-out.

"How many cars have you stolen?" she asked, before she knew she was going to say it.

His expression closed. She would not be able to describe it any other way. The eager, almost childish panic vanished, leaving in its place a dark, unreadable glare, his eyebrows low over his dark blue eyes. He turned away, looking forward, and shrugged, a calculated shrug from his broad shoulders. One quarter inch up, one quarter inch down.

"I used to go joy riding," he said. "When I was a kid. I got bored." And when she didn't answer that, he added. "Look, I've told you. I'll pay you for the damage." And again, at her continued silence. "I couldn't let us be caught. If they'd caught us, they'd have killed us."

At this, he stopped. He stopped long enough for her to gather her thoughts. She felt so tired that if she weren't in pain, she would have fallen asleep. But she hurt. Her shoulder felt as if it had been dislocated in the fight. There was a slash across her torso that she prayed wouldn't need stitches, and a broad swath of her buttock felt scraped, as though it had rubbed hard against a scaly hide. Which it probably had, though she didn't remember.

"Who are they?" she finally asked. "Why are they after you?"

"They're a Chinese triad," he said. "They're members of a . . . crime syndicate. Asian."

"Admirably described," she said, and heard the hint of sarcasm in her own voice, and was surprised she still had the strength for it. "But what do they want with you?"

He hesitated. For just a moment he glanced at her, and the scared little boy was back, with wide-open eyes, and slightly parted lips.

He looked back at the road in time to take them, tightly, around a corner, tires squealing, car tilting. "They think I stole something from them," he said, with the defensive tone of a child explaining it really, really, really wasn't him who put the clamp on the cat's tail.

Something. Kyrie was not so naive that she didn't know Chinese crime syndicates—like most crime syndicates—dealt mostly in various drugs. "A drug deal gone bad?" she asked.

He had the nerve to tighten his lips, and shake his head. "I don't deal drugs," he said.

Whee. There was one form of criminality he didn't stoop to. Who would have thunk it? "So . . ."

"I didn't steal it, okay?" he said. "I didn't steal anything. They think I did, and they're trying to get it back."

"Sounds ugly," she said. Somehow she felt he was lying but also not lying. There was an edge to his tone as if he weren't quite so sure how he'd got himself into this type of situation.

"It is," he said. "They've been after me for months." He shrugged. "Only they've just figured out my name, I think. Now they can follow me, wherever I live. They're shifters. Dragons."

"I gathered."

"They worship the Great Sky Dragon. . . ."

"Uh?" She had never heard of any shifter divinity. But then again, she'd never heard of any other shifters. All of a sudden, vertiginously, as though standing at the edge of a precipice and seeing a whole world open before her, she wondered if there was a whole culture, a whole society she didn't know about. Some place she belonged, whole families of shifters. Perhaps the only reason she'd never known about it was because she was adopted and she didn't know her own birth family. "Shifters have their own gods?"

Tom shrugged. "I think he was a Chinese divinity. Or one of their sacred animals, or something."

"Did you get involved with them because you . . . shift? Into a dragon? Is your family . . . does your family shift?"

Tom shook his head. "My father doesn't . . . No."

"Then how did you get involved with the triad?"

He looked confused, then shrugged—not a precise shrug. "I don't know," he said. He seemed on the verge of saying something, but shook his head, as if to his own thoughts. "My father—" He stopped dead, as though something in him had halted not just the words but the train of thought as well.

They were driving down a narrow, tree-bordered street. Ahead of them loomed the dark expanse of the Castle—officially known as Chateau D'Aubigerne, a castle imported from the Loire, stone by stone, by a man enriched in the gold rush. It now stood smack dab in the center of Goldport, abandoned and empty, surrounded by gardens gone to seed and an eight-foot-high iron fence like massed spears. Now and then there was talk of someone buying it, restoring it, and making it into a hotel, a mall, a resort, or just a monument for tourists to gawk at. But all those projects seemed nonstarters, perhaps because the Castle was well away from all the hotels and convention centers, in a street of tiny, workmen's brick ranches, with cars on blocks and broken plastic toys in the front yards.

Tom slowed down till he was going a normal speed and said, "Where can I take you?"

"Beg your pardon?"

He grinned at her, a fugitive grin that transformed his features and gave her a startling glimpse of what might lurk underneath the troubled young man's aggression—humor? Joy? "Where can I drop you off? Where do you live?" He smiled at her, a less naughty smile this time, more that of a patient adult facing a stupid child. "You can't go to work like that, can you?"

She shook her head, panicked. Gee. Frank was going to be mad. She might already have lost her job. A surge of anger at Tom came up, but then vanished again. Someone had once told Kyrie that if you lost a job making less than ten dollars an hour you could find another one within the day. In her experience this was true. And besides, it wasn't like Tom had asked her for help.

She'd just jumped in and helped him. Hell, she thought she'd learned not to do that years ago.

"My place," she said. "It's down the next street. Turn right. Third house on the left."

"House?"

"Rental. It's smaller than an apartment, really. I just . . . I don't like people around."

He nodded and maneuvered through the turn and up to her house, at a speed that could only be considered sedate after his early high jinks.

The house was tiny—eight hundred square feet and one bedroom, but it had a driveway—a narrow strip of concrete that led right up to the back door and from which a narrow walking path led to the front door. This late at night—or early in the morning—all of Kyrie's neighbors would be asleep and she was grateful for that.

As Tom pulled up to the back door, she had only two steps to go, stark naked. And she always left the key under a rock in the nearby flower bed. She hated to be locked out of her house and didn't know anyone in town she could trust with a key. It was one of the side effects of moving around so much.

As she started to open the door, she looked at Tom. He was sitting behind the wheel, the engine still going, looking forward. The car was hers, but she could hardly tell him to leave it and run off naked into the night. On the other hand—where was he going to go even with the car?

She had to invite him in. She didn't really want to, but she saw nothing else she could do. Nothing else a decent human being could do. She tapped him on the arm. "Turn that off. Come inside. Have a shower. I'll grab another jogging suit for you."

He looked surprised. Dumbfounded as if she'd offered him a fortune. "Are you sure?"

"Where would you go otherwise?"

He shrugged. "I'll figure . . . I'll figure something. I always do." For just a second a dangerous liquid quality crept into his voice, but he only shook his head and swallowed. "Look, it's not safe to be around me."

"I've noticed. But you have nowhere else to go. Come inside. I'll make coffee."

He took a few seconds, then grabbed the screwdriver and turned it. And nodded at her. "Can I come out through your side?" he said. "Less—"

"Exposure, yes," she said. "And don't break anything. I have a key." She dove out the door and retrieved her key from its hiding place.

✢ ✢ ✢

Later Tom would think he might never have agreed to go to Kyrie's house, except for the chunk of glass slowly working its way into his buttock.

It was clear she didn't really want him around, and he wasn't sure he could blame her. After all, he wasn't sure he wanted himself around most of the time. And she'd seen him at one of his most dangerous moments.

It would probably be a kindness for him to leave. But then he came up on the fact that he was naked, he was shaking with exhaustion, and there was a big glass chunk becoming a permanent part of his behind.

He turned off the car and waited till she was out and had opened the door before he dove out of the car after her. And stepped into a cozy kitchen—cozy and homey and like no place he'd ever been before.

His father's condo had been huge. This entire house would probably fit in the kitchen. And the kitchen of that house had been white and chrome, imported Italian marble and mosaic floors. But it was the domain of Mrs. Lopez, their cook. Never the family kitchen. Never a place where the family gathered for meals.

Of course no family could really gather in this kitchen either. Not unless they were all unusually close. It was barely big enough to contain both of them, a card table, two folding chairs, a refrigerator, stove, and a tiny counter with sink. Above the table, on the wall, hung a painting of an old-fashioned bicycle done in shades of red and pink on black, the front wheel dwarfing the rest.

Kyrie closed the door behind him. "This way," she said, as she led him out of the kitchen via the interior door, and into a hallway. She opened another door and turned the light on. "The bathroom. I'll go get you something to wear."

He stepped into the bathroom, where there was just enough space for himself between tub, sink, and toilet.

Kyrie returned almost immediately and knocked, and he hid himself behind the door as he opened it. It seemed silly when they'd been together, naked for most of the evening. But then Kyrie had put on a robe—a fluffy, pink robe that made her look young and feminine.

She handed him a bundle of clothes and said, "There's plenty of water. Outsized water heater, so don't worry too much. But I'd like to shower after you, so don't use more than you have to."

He nodded, took the clothes, set them on the toilet tank, and started the shower. Plunging under the water, he felt it like a warm caress. He tried not to notice that it ran red-stained down the drain. The corpse . . .

The corpse seemed wholly unreal in this white-tiled shower that smelled of lavender and a subtle hint of Kyrie's perfume. Tom had never noticed her perfume before, but it was definitely her smell. Something spicy and soft that he'd caught before as an undertone at work.

He removed the glass chunk from his backside, by touch, then soaped himself vigorously. He had no right to intrude on her life, nor to bring his own messes into her house. He had no right to endanger her. He should leave as soon as possible.

Guiltily, he used her shampoo, which was some designer brand and smelled of vanilla. His hair, too, yielded quantities of red bloodstained water.

What would the police think? Would the police track him? And Kyrie? He'd tell them she was innocent. He was the murderer.

Was he the murderer?

He couldn't think about it. Stepping out of the tub, he heard Kyrie knock at the door. She then opened it a sliver, and held out a towel. "Sorry. Forgot to give them earlier," she said.

And she was being kind to him. Far kinder than anyone had been in a long time. He thanked her, dried himself, combed his hair with his fingers, the thick black curls falling into their natural unruliness, and dressed in her jogging suit.

Coming out the door, he had his words ready. About how he would be going now, no time to chat, really, best thing would be to get out of her hair as soon as possible, and then—

And then she was waiting at the door and smiled at him. "I made coffee. It's in the kitchen. Do you drink coffee? I won't be a minute."

And she went past him into the steam-filled bathroom.

He couldn't exactly leave when she was being so friendly, so he went into the kitchen, where she'd run the coffeemaker, and set cups, sugar, and cream out. He didn't know whether to laugh or cry that one of the cups was embossed with a dragon, but he took it anyway.

Kyrie showered quickly, wondering what was wrong with her. Didn't she want him out of the house. Now? Yesterday?

But she'd never talked with another of her kind. And perhaps he knew what had happened. Perhaps he'd remember if he'd killed the person in the parking lot. And perhaps she'd be able to figure out how he'd got involved with the triad and if she'd now be in danger.

And perhaps tomorrow it would rain soup. And cream.

But there were more material considerations, too. Her arm, where Red Dragon—the one who in human form had two red dragon tattoos—had got in a glancing bite at the panther's paw. It looked like the tooth had pierced her arm. It wasn't exactly bleeding—just a trickle of blood that increased under the warm shower. She examined the puncture dispassionately. Her memory of the adrenaline-fueled fight had fuzzy edges and she could not remember if the bite had released, or if it had been fully completed before something she did caused the dragon to let go.

If the first, it was probably a narrow, not-too-deep cut. If the second . . . Well, she could easily be looking at a puncture all the way to the bone, and at an infection. She couldn't afford that, but neither could she afford to go to the hospital.

Oh, she could afford it monetarily. She probably could scrape up the money for a quick visit to the emergency room or one of the twenty-four-hour med centers. What she couldn't afford was for doctors to ask how she got her wound or for them to notice anything at all strange about the shape of the wound. For them to remember her wounds when someone brought the corpse in, certainly with similar wounds. No. Better to trust in Tom and ask him to help her clean her arm and perhaps bandage the wound. Better the devil you know.

There were other wounds too. One on her hip, which she could bandage herself, and then one across her shoulder, at the back, which she didn't think she could take care of without help.

She got out of the shower and dried a little more vigorously than she needed, to punish herself for her stupidity in getting involved in Tom's affairs. She bandaged her hip and her torso before putting on her robe again.

Frank was going to make her pay for the apron. But at least she still had a job. She'd called while Tom was showering. While Frank had been none too pleased to hear she wouldn't be back the rest of the night, neither had he fired her.

In the kitchen, Tom stood, holding the cup of coffee. The one with the dragon. Kyrie smiled. She hadn't even thought about his reaction. It had come, like most of her dishes, from the Salvation Army thrift store. She picked up the cup left on the counter and poured herself a cup of black coffee. He hadn't thrown a snit at the dragon. He hadn't imagined it was a dig directed at him.

Perhaps he was not quite so touchy and antisocial as she would have thought he was. Or perhaps . . .

Kyrie looked him over. He smelled of soap and her shampoo, and he looked far less dangerous than he had. His black curls were damp from the shower, dripping down his back. His expression was just bewildered enough to make him look younger the he normally did. Even the fact that he was frowning into his coffee cup didn't make him look threatening, just puzzled.

He looked at her, and the frown became less intense, but the eyebrows remained low over the blue eyes, which looked like they were trying to figure out something really difficult. Like the meaning of the universe. "Why?" he said. "I'm dangerous." He shrugged, as if he hadn't said exactly what he meant to say. "I mean, it's dangerous to hang out with me. You saw . . . my apartment." He took a sip of coffee, fast, desperately, as if trying to make up for words that didn't come out quite right. Then choked, coughed, and set the cup down to cover his mouth. "Why did you let me in here?" he asked.

Kyrie could have said many things. That his apartment was one of the reasons. Who would send him out there naked, in a car that looked, clearly, like it had been broken into? Who would send him out into the night with nowhere to stay, no safe place to crash?

But before she spoke, she realized that there would be many people—perhaps most people—who would do that. She'd met them often enough, growing up. The families who took foster children but didn't want them associating with their *real* children; the children at school who shunned you because you lived in a less than savory part of town; the teachers who assumed you were dumb and hopeless because you didn't live with your blood family.

Had she done the same with Tom, in shunning him because of his appearance? His drug habit? But no. She'd been justified in that. Those were things he could and should control. However, this trouble . . . Well, perhaps he'd brought it on himself. Perhaps at the root of it all was a drug deal gone bad, or the theft of something valuable.

She couldn't imagine anyone stealing anything valuable from a triad composed of dragon shapeshifters. She would have to assume Tom was brasher, and perhaps braver, than she. But she didn't know him well enough to rule it out, either.

And again, she had had plenty of experience with his type: the alcoholic foster parents, the doping foster brothers. You gave them chance and chance and chance, and they never improved, never got any better. They just told you more and more lies and got bolder and bolder.

She didn't know what to say and she couldn't guess in which category Tom would fall. So, instead, she stuck to the need at hand. That had always seen her through. When in trouble, stick to the need at hand.

"I need you to help me bandage my arm and disinfect my back," she said. And not sure why his eyes grew so wide at this request, added, "Please?"

He nodded and shrugged. "Of course," he said. His eyes remained wide, as if he were either very surprised or very skeptical. "Where do you keep the first-aid supplies?"

"They're in the bathroom," Kyrie told him. "Behind the mirror."

Tom headed that way. It was a relief to have something to do—to have something to think of. He'd been sitting there, feeling miserable, drinking his coffee, wondering what was the best way to leave.

The bathroom was still full of steam—but the smell was indefinably different there. Not just the soap and shampoo he'd used also, but something else . . . Something he could neither define nor explain. It smelled like Kyrie. That was all he could say. It was a familiar smell and he realized he'd smelled it around her even under the layers of odors at the Athens. A hint of cinnamon, an edge of burnt sugar. Only not really, but that was what the smells made him think of. Like . . . What the kitchen smelled like when Mrs. Lopez had been making pastries.

He opened the medicine cabinet and collected bandages, antibiotic cream, small scissors, bandages, hydrogen peroxide, and cotton wool. It was the best-stocked home cabinet he'd ever seen. Other than his own. shapeshifters. You came home cut, scraped, you weren't even sure how.

And Kyrie was one of them. Just like him.

That he was attracted to her didn't make it any easier. He'd been attracted to her from the first moment he'd seen her—giving him the jaundiced once-over when Frank introduced them. But his attraction to women had come to nothing these last five years, ever since he'd found out he was a shapeshifter.

There were too many things to be afraid of—shifting in front of her, for instance. Hurting her while he was shape-shifted. And then the whole thing with the drugs, with which he'd tried—unsuccessfully—to control his shifts. It made him associate with too many shady characters for him to want any girl he even liked involved with. And then, of course, the . . . He pulled his mind forcefully away from even thinking of the object. That. And the triad. This without even thinking of nightmare scenarios: pregnancy. A baby who was born shifted.

And now in one night he'd managed to visit all but the last of these scenarios. He'd shifted in front of Kyrie. He'd probably hurt someone else in front of her. And he'd landed her in the thick of his trouble with the triad. Damn. And all this when he'd just found out she was a shapeshifter too. She was one like him.

Oh, she was not the only one he'd met, in his five years of wandering around, homeless and rootless. But she was the first one he'd talked to, the first one he'd had anything to do with. The only female . . . Up to tonight, he would have sworn that only males shifted shape.

And what good did it do him that she too was a shapeshifter—that she would understand him?

Absolutely none. First, he had blown it so far with her that if his hopes were a substance they would be scraping them off the floor and ceiling for months. And second—and second there was the triad.

Tom had been attracted to Kyrie before tonight. Now he liked her. He liked her a lot. He might very well be on his way to falling in love with her. If he had the slightest idea what love was and how one fell in it, he would be able to say for sure. But here the thing was—he cared about her. He cared a lot. An awful lot. He didn't want her dead. As he was bound to be, soon enough, now that the triad had got really serious about finding him.

"It's right there on the shelf," Kyrie's voice said from the doorway. He turned to see her framed in the door, those big, dark eyes pensive and wondering.

"Oh, yes, right," he said. "It's actually in my hands." He turned around and lifted the hands filled with first-aid stuff. "I'm sorry. I spaced. I guess I'm tired."

She nodded solemnly. He didn't remember ever seeing her laugh. Smile, sure, a bunch of times, mostly the polite smile you gave customers late at night when they came in looking tired and out of it. But never laugh. Was laughter too far out of control for her? And why did he want to know? It wasn't as if he'd ever find out.

"Right," she said. "Shifting that many times in a row. Staying shifted that long. I've shifted, but not for long tonight, so I'm not—" She yawned and covered her mouth with her hand. "—that tired."

He smiled, despite himself, grateful that she couldn't see it because she had turned her back and was heading back toward the kitchen. Where she sat at the table, pulled the cord on the lamp overhead to turn it on, and rolled up the sleeve of her robe to show a narrow wound with bluish borders, like a bruise.

He sat on the other chair, laid the first-aid materials down on the table. "That looks awful," he said.

She nodded and turned her arm over. On the bottom there was another bruise, another puncture.

"It went all the way—" he started.

She shook her head. "No. The dra— He just bit me. I don't know how deeply. It feels different . . . in the other body." She'd lowered her head to look at her own arm, and her hair had fallen across her face. The temptation to reach over and pull that multicolored curtain back was almost more than he could endure.

"Have you had a tetanus shot?" he asked, going on routine. "Because if you hadn't, you should. I don't know how clean . . ." He realized he was about to say he didn't know how clean dragons' teeth were and caught himself in time. He smiled. There was no avoiding it. He was a dragon. She knew he was a dragon. And on that, at least, there was no reason for awkwardness. Hell, she shifted too. He had to keep telling himself that. He had to remember. "I, personally, brush and floss. Use mouthwash, even. But I can't answer to the cleanliness of another dragon's teeth."

That got him a smile. Little more than the polite smile that she gave customers, but a smile nonetheless, and even a teasing sort of reply. "No unified dental hygiene guidelines for dragons?"

"Afraid not," he said. He soaked one of the balls of cotton wool in hydrogen peroxide and gently started to cleanse the area. "Seriously, you really should go to a doctor. I know we shifters heal quickly, but these deep puncture wounds can be dangerous. Only a tiny area exposed to air, see. The space in there can develop an infection very easily. And you could get blood poisoning, something horrible." He looked up and saw her open her mouth. "I know what you're going to say, and I'm not going to tell you that you're wrong. The last thing we need. The very last thing is to call attention to ourselves—particularly with strange animal bites. And I understand how you feel about being in the hospital. I slept under a bridge many a night, rather than going to a shelter when the moon was full and the impulse to shift greater. But, Kyrie, I'm not joking." He pushed as much hydrogen peroxide as he could into the puncture, on both sides, by squeezing the cotton right atop of it. "If you get a fever, the first sign of swelling on your arm, you must—must—see a doctor. It could kill you."

"You know a lot about this stuff."

He nodded, pulling back the cotton wool, tossing it in the kitchen trash in the corner, and waiting while her arm dried. Then he got antibiotic cream and started slathering it on. There was no reason to tell her anything. Or maybe there was. He'd been so desperately alone all these years. "My mom is a doctor," he said.

"Is she . . ." Kyrie swallowed. "Is she . . ."

"She left Dad about ten years ago," he said. "When I was a kid. Went down to Florida with her new husband. I haven't seen her since. But up till I was ten I gave her many reasons to perform first aid on me, and I heard this speech a lot."

Kyrie frowned at him. Then shook her head. "I was going to ask if she was a dragon."

Tom shook his head, then shrugged. "I don't think so. I know Dad isn't. And I don't think Mom is. I've never . . ." He was about to say that he didn't know any older shifters, but then realized he did. He had seen a couple of derelicts shifting while he flew above in the middle of a summer night. It had been further out west, toward New Mexico, and they'd shifted into coyotes and headed for the hills. He remembered because back then, seeing the tattered men shift into ragtag coyotes he'd wondered if he'd end up like that. Old, still a transient, still homeless. It had been part of what led him to steal. . . . "I don't think it's hereditary, or at least not that way. Why? Are your parents shifters?"

She shook her head and shrugged, and her eyes got soft and distant. "I wouldn't know. They left me at the entrance of a church in Charlotte, North Carolina, when I was just a few hours old. I was found by parishioners coming out of the midnight services on Christmas night. There were headlines all over the papers, about it. But I never knew . . ." She shrugged again. "I was raised by foster families."

And perhaps that explained why she held herself under such tight control? Tom wouldn't know. He knew about as much about foster care as he knew about happy family life. A couple of his acquaintances of convenience, while he had been on the streets, had been foster children. They'd told him hair-raising stories about the system. But did it mean that every one was like that? Or only the ones who'd gone seriously to the bad?

He taped the bandages in place over the puncture. "Blood poisoning will make a visible circle, it will start just above the wound, and it will be a red circle that will slowly move upwards if it's not treated. If you see a circle on your arm, you must go to the doctor, immediately."

"Am I to assume personal experience speaks here?" Kyrie asked.

He managed a smile. "My best friend and I." He hadn't thought of Joe in years. Wondered where he was now. What he was doing. "We had these plastic swords, but you know, they were disappointing because they really couldn't cause enough damage. We could bang on each other all day long with them, they were too light and definitely not sharp. So we improved them by sticking nails in the tip. Rusty nails." He saw her wince. "Yeah. Lucky for us my mom caught the infection in time. Even then I was on antibiotics forever. Now that I think about it, lucky we were both lousy swordsmen, too. We never managed to kill each other, though we tried for a whole day."

He pulled her sleeve down, and started to gather the stuff.

"No," she said. "I want you to look at my back. It feels abraded." As she spoke, she loosened her robe, and edged it down at the back—to reveal a shoulder that had been stripped bare of skin.

"It's more than abraded," Tom said. And because the sight of the robe sliding over the raw flesh of her shoulder made him cringe, he added, "Let me," and pulled the robe down slowly, at the back. In the process, the front fell too, revealing one of her breasts almost to the nipple. Golden skin the color of honey, and it looked velvet soft. His fingers wanted to stray that way, wanted to feel . . .

He concentrated on her back, kneeling so that her back was all he saw. He found the end of the skinned portion where her shoulder blade ended. "This looks awful. How?"

"I think it was a paw swipe," she said. "The claws missed me, but the scales got me."

"Ah," Tom said. He had never thought he was that lethal in his dragon form, and to be honest, he wasn't sure he was. He didn't know how much he looked like the Chinese dragons. He was aware the tail was different, the paws more massive, but he'd never looked at himself in a mirror while shifted. Or if he had, he hadn't managed to remember it.

He got the antibiotic cream and started applying it in a thin layer to Kyrie's back, trying to touch so lightly that he wouldn't hurt her. She didn't seem to flinch from the touch, so he must be succeeding. There had been a time he wanted to be a doctor. Before . . . all of this.

"When did you shift for the first time?" Kyrie asked.

Tom's hand trembled immediately, as the memories flooded him. Flying over the city. Not the first time, but one of the first. Seeing everything. Then coming home. Breaking the bedroom window. It was devilishly hard to work the paws when you weren't even sure what was happening to you. And then his father. His father, with the gun, ordering him out.

Hell, he didn't even know his father had a gun until then. Until that moment, had anyone asked, he'd have said his father wouldn't have a gun in the house. Tom had heard his father go on and on about gun control quite often. And he was too young to understand hypocrisy.

He took a deep breath and managed to push the memory away. To this day he wasn't sure why his father had ordered him out of the house. He'd shifted back by then. He'd shifted back and grabbed hold of his robe. Which is why he'd ended on the street in his robe and barefoot.

But he controlled the memories, squeezed a dollop of cream from the tube. Kyrie hadn't asked again, so he probably hadn't taken that long to get himself under control. "I was sixteen," he said. "I never had any warning before. I just . . . Shifted. In the moonlight."

In the moonlight, in his room, with its comfortable bed, and all the posters, and the TV, the stereo, the game system. All the things he'd once thought needed to survive. "I was all excited too," he said. "That first time. I thought it was a cool, superhero thing."

She was silent, and he thought she was thinking about what a fool he'd been. He concentrated on what he was doing. Fingers on the wound on her shoulder, lightly, lightly, spreading a thin, shining layer of antibiotic cream.

"I was fourteen," she said, speaking as from a great distance. "I thought I was dreaming the first few times. And then I thought I was hallucinating. I thought I had . . . I don't know. Seizures or something. I used to imagine that my parents were two mental patients who'd had me and had smuggled me out of the madhouse so I could be raised on the outside."

He laughed despite himself and she turned to look at him, her expression grave. Not offended, just grave.

"I don't think there were any mental hospitals like that in the 1980s," he said. "Where they kept the children of the patients locked up along with the parents. Were there?"

Kyrie shook her head and smiled again, a smile fractionally warmer than the ones she gave the customers. "Not in this country, no, I don't think," she said. "But I was very young. Just a kid. I thought . . ." She shrugged. "Actually at first I thought someone was putting datura in my food or something."

"Datura?" he asked.

"A hallucinogenic. At least, Agatha Christie has a mystery in which someone is putting it in a man's shaving cream to make him dream that he's a werewolf, and I thought—"

"I read Christie too," he said. Often her books were the only thing available in safe houses for at-risk youth or whatnot, where he sought temporary refuge. That and the ever-yellowing pile of *National Geographic*. It was Tom's considered opinion that *National Geographic*s were alien artifacts routinely bombarded down onto the Earth. "But isn't datura something Indian, something . . ."

"I didn't tell you I was rational, did I?" Kyrie asked.

He shook his head and reached for the gauze, cutting it to fit the area on her shoulder, and laying it gently atop the wound.

"I thought someone was trying to make me think I was crazy.

Perhaps my foster parents. They get more for special-needs kids, you know? And then I read up on it, and I decided I was schizophrenic. I couldn't tell what I did while I was under this condition, so I started hiding. At first I was lucky that no one saw me, and then when I realized what caused it—the full moon, a feeling of anger. Anything. I was damn careful over the next four years. Always slept alone, even if arrangements called for other kids in the room. I'd take a blanket and go sleep in a tree, if needed. It . . . made for interesting times and made me change families even more often. And then I was on my own, and I've been careful. Very careful. But I still thought it was all in my mind. Till tonight."

Tom shook his head as he started taping the gauze in place. He couldn't imagine not knowing the shift was true. But perhaps it was different for dragons. He saw the city from above. He saw things happen. And, of course, within a month of his first shifting, his father had seen him shift and had shouted at him and . . . ordered him out. For shifting. Hard to tell yourself it was all in your mind after that.

"How many of us are there?" Kyrie asked. "I mean—there's you and the triad, but . . . You've known about this more and have been more places. How many shifters have you met?"

She had to talk to keep her mind off what he was doing. He wasn't hurting her. On the contrary. His fingers, touching her skin ever-so-lightly were a caress. Or the closest to a caress she could remember.

It had been too long since she'd even let anyone touch her. Certainly not since she'd started shifting. Before that there had been foster siblings who'd got close, some she'd hugged and who'd hugged her. But not since then.

Tom's touch was very delicate, as if he were afraid of breaking her. It felt odd. She didn't want to think of him, back there, being careful not to hurt her.

And she really wanted to know how many shifters he'd seen in the five years since he'd left his house. She hadn't been out much. Well, not out on the street and not out while aware of being in a shape-shifted body. She hadn't been looking for other shifters. But he might have been. Hell, considering his thing with the triad, he probably had been.

He paused at her question. He'd been taping the gauze down over her wound, and he stopped. For a moment she thought she'd offended him.

But he sighed. "I don't know for sure," he said. "I wasn't counting. Including the occasional enforcer for the triad or not?"

"The enforcers for the triad have been trailing you all this time?"

She was sure he'd smiled at that, but she wasn't sure how. His fingers resumed their gentle touch, taping the gauze in place.

"No," he said. "Only a . . . part of a year." He paused again. "Without counting them and . . . and the other triad dragons, of whom there are many, I'd say I've seen about twelve, maybe thirteen shifters. Not . . . not close enough to talk to. I've only talked to a couple. I never went out of my way to talk to them. And sometimes, it was ambiguous, you know. Like, you're walking downtown and you see someone walk in a certain direction and moments later a wolfhound . . . or a wolf . . . comes from the same direction. The only ones I knew for sure were the triad and the orangutan and the coyotes. There seem to be any number of them within the triad. Hundreds. And that might be hereditary. They seem to think they're descended of the Great Sky Dragon. They marry among themselves and they have rites and . . . and stuff."

"So—excluding the triad—a dozen in five years? That doesn't seem like many."

"No. And most of the time it was larger cities than Goldport. Large cities back east. New York and Boston and Atlanta."

"Odd," Kyrie said. "Because just last night—"

"Yes, you and me and that lion," Tom said, his voice grave, as he finished taping the gauze in place. At least she assumed he'd finished, because he lay the tape back on the table, with the scissors on top of it. And then, ever so gently, he tugged her robe back in place. "I've been thinking the same. Why that many in one night. With the triad here, too, we must be tipping the scales at . . . a lot of shifters. And I wondered why."

Kyrie wondered why too. She'd been living in Goldport for over a year. She remembered the Greyhound bus had stopped here and she'd thought to stay for a night before going on to Denver. But she'd never gone on. Something about Goldport just felt . . . right. Like it was the home she'd been looking for so long. Which was ridiculous, since it was what remained of a gold boom town that had become a University town. And she never had anything to do with either mining or college.

But Goldport had felt . . . Not exactly familiar, but more safe. Secure. Home. Like the home she'd never known. She had walked from the Greyhound station to the Athens and seen a sign on the window asking for a server. She'd applied and been hired that night.

But what attraction could the small, odd town have for other shifters. Well . . . Tom had come via the Greyhound too, she supposed. And Frank had offered him a job.

As for the lion . . . She wouldn't think about the lion. "It's probably just a coincidence," she told Tom. And it probably was. Three were not, after all, a great sample. Perhaps they were the only three shifters in town—other than the triad—and had just chanced to bump into each other. The blood had surely helped. She swallowed, remembering what the blood smelled like in the other shape.

Tom came around and started gathering the first-aid supplies.

"What kinds of shifters are there? What kinds did you see? Just big cats? And werewolves? And dragons? Or . . ."

Tom stopped what he was doing. He didn't drop the supplies, just held them where they were. He didn't look at her. "You're going to think I'm an idiot," he said.

"Um . . . no," Kyrie said. She couldn't understand why she would think he was an idiot now. She had a thousand reasons to think him careless, low on self-preservation instincts, and probably a little insane. But . . . an idiot? "Why?"

He sighed. "I swear one of those shifters was a centaur. I know what you're going to tell me, that centaurs don't exist, that I was just seeing a horseman, that—"

"No, I'm not," Kyrie said.

"You're not?"

"Tom, dragons are thought not to exist too."

"Oh." He looked shocked. As if he'd never thought of it that way. Then he grinned. "Well, then I can tell you. Another one of them was an orangutan. Little stooped man, sold roast chestnuts on the street near . . . near my father's house. And he shifted into an orangutan at night. He was a very nice man, once I got to talking to him. He told me that his wife and his daughters sometimes didn't notice when he shifted." He grinned at that, as he gathered all the first-aid supplies, and headed back to the bathroom.

Kyrie followed him, wondering what to do next. He'd helped her. And, whether his association with the triad was dangerous or not, he, personally, didn't feel dangerous. And they'd lost the triad for the night, hadn't they?

She was reluctant to send him out alone and barefoot into the night. What if he got killed? How would she feel when she heard about it? How would she live with herself?

And besides, having grown up without family, all alone, this was the first time she'd found someone who was genuinely like her. Not family—at least she didn't think so, though he could be a half brother or a cousin. One of the curses of the abandoned child was not to know—but someone who had more in common with her than anyone else she had found. And if he'd gone bad . . . She shook her head.

She didn't know why he'd gone bad. She remembered the smell of blood in that parking lot and the madness in the apartment. Clearly, she too had it in her to commit violence. She would have to control it. Perhaps he was just weaker than her? Perhaps he could not control himself as well.

He put the stuff back in the medicine cabinet, carefully organized, and turned around. "I'll get out of your hair now, okay. Just report your car stolen. You have insurance, right?"

"Yes, but . . ."

"Oh, I'll still pay you for the window," Tom said. "But it might take me a while to be able to get to an ATM. I have some money. Not much. I don't think I'll get my deposit back for the apartment. I thought I'd head out of town, lead the . . . the dragons away from you."

"And leave me stuck in the middle of a murder investigation?"

He opened his hands. "What else can I do? I can't undo what happened." He looked earnest and distraught. "Someone died. And, Kyrie, I wish to all that's holy that I could tell you it wasn't me who killed him. But I can't. He's dead, and I'm . . ."

He opened his hands, denoting his helplessness. "I wish I could tell you I never touched him and that I would never have done that, but my mind is all a blank. I don't even remember being attacked in my apartment, honest. If it weren't for the state it's in . . ."

His hair had fallen in front of his eyes, and he tossed his head back to throw it back. "Look . . . I might very well have done it, and they might find evidence linking me to it. I'm not sure how your DNA works when you're shifted. But if it was . . . If they think I killed him, all you have to say is that I asked you for a ride home, that you had no idea anyone was dead. You could have come out in the parking lot and never seen it, you know? It was behind the vans. I took advantage of your charity and stole your car. No one will hold that against you."

Kyrie bit her lip. There were other things he wasn't even thinking about, she thought. For instance, the paper towels. Properly looked over they'd probably find traces of her hair, dead skin cells, whatever.

But fine, the major evidence would point to him, and she could probably come up with a story that would let her off and get him out of her life forever. So, why didn't she want to? Was it because once he was gone she could go back to imagining that she was just hallucinating the shifts? And she wouldn't have a witness to her shape-shifting.

She put her hands inside the wide sleeves of her robe. "I think that's tiredness talking," she said. "I think if I can come up with an excuse, so can you. You're exhausted from who knows how many hours shifted. And you don't look well." This last was the absolute truth. Tom had started out looking shocked and ill, and he'd progressed to milk-pale, with dark, dark circles under his eyes, bruised enough to look like someone had punched him hard. "You could crash the car out there," she said, and seized upon that. "And I don't want it made inoperable. The insurance never pays you enough to junk it."

He frowned at her, the frown that she had learned to identify as his look of indecision.

"I have a love seat," she said. And to his surprised look added, "In the sunroom at the back. Sleeping porch, really, from when they treated tubercular patients in this region. They thought fresh air was essential, so they had these sun-porches. Someone glassed this one in, and there's a love seat in it. Nothing fancy, mind you, but you can have it and a blanket."

She could see him being tempted. He was so tired that, standing in the middle of her little bathroom, he was swaying slightly on his feet. She could see him looking in what he probably thought was the direction of the sun-porch, and she could practically hear the thoughts of the love seat and blanket run through his head. She could also see him opening his mouth to tell her thanks *but no thanks*.

Which was when the doorbell rang.

CHAPTER
⋖ 3 ⋗

The noise of the doorbell echoed, seeming to fill the small house.

Kyrie jumped and Tom turned his wrist toward himself, as though checking time on a watch he didn't wear.

She swept her gaze toward the narrow little window in the shower, instead, checking the scant light coming through, blue tinged, announcing the end of blind night, the beginning of barely lit morning.

"It can't be anyone about the . . . It's too early," she said.

And saw Tom pale, saw him start shaking. "Go to the kitchen," she told him, sure that in his mind as in hers was the memory of the bathroom at the Athens, full of bloodied towels, probably tainted with his hair and skin. And hers.

Why, oh, why hadn't she put the used towels in her car? Dumped them somewhere? But where? Outside Tom's apartment? They hadn't exactly had time to stop anywhere and get rid of things.

It was too late for all that, now. All her life, she had faced crises and looked after herself. What else could she do? There hadn't been anyone else to look after her. Now she had to look after Tom too. Not the first time she had this sort of responsibility. Younger kids at foster homes often clung to her, sure that her strength would carry them. And it did, even when she thought she had no strength left.

He was shaking, and she put a hand out to him, and touched his arm. It still felt too cold, even through the sweat suit. "Go to the kitchen. Sit down," she said. "Stay. I'll go see who it is. I'll deal with it."

She walked out through the kitchen and the hallway, to the front room with its curved Seventies vintage sofa that she'd covered in the pretty red sheet, and the table made of plastic cubes where she kept her books and her few prized possessions. It should give her a sense of security, but it didn't. Instead, she wondered what would happen to her books if she were arrested and what would happen to the house if she lost her job. Though it was just a rental, it was the first place she could call hers, the first place where she was not living on someone else's territory and on someone else's terms.

She shook her head. It wouldn't come to that. She wouldn't let it come to that.

The front door was one of the cheap hollow metal ones, but it did have a bull's eye. The neighborhood was quiet enough and the whole city was basically safe, so she supposed it had been put there to allow occupants to avoid Jehovah's Witnesses.

Now she leaned into the door and put her eye to the tiny opening. Out there was . . . a stranger.

He stood on her doorstep, and he was tall, blond. Broad shouldered, she supposed, but with the sort of relaxed posture and laid-back demeanor that made him look more like a surfer than a body builder. Increasing the impression was hair just on this side of long, the bangs overhanging his left eye. He wore a loose white linen suit that seemed to accentuate his relaxed expression. The sunglasses that covered his eyes despite the scant light made him look like one of those artists afraid of being recognized, or else like a man who'd just flown in from a vacation in Bermuda and had not yet fully realized that he was back home.

The sunglasses made his expression unreadable, but he seemed to be looking intently at the door. As Kyrie watched, he raised his hand and rang the doorbell again.

It was what? Four, five in the morning? Surely this was not a casual visit. Casual visitors didn't insist on being answered at this time of night. But then what? A rapist or a robber? What? Ringing the doorbell? Wasn't that sort of unusual? Besides, she could handle herself. Surely she could handle herself.

Kyrie unlocked the door and opened it the length of the chain. The chain was another puzzler. Either the neighborhood had been a lot worse when the security device was installed, or the Jehovah's Witnesses were unusually persistent.

"Ah," he said, when she opened the door, and smiled flashing teeth straight out of a toothpaste commercial. "Ms. Kyrie Smith?"

Before she could answer, there was a faint rustling sound behind her. She turned and saw Tom mouthing soundlessly, "Police?" He raised his eyebrows.

She shrugged. But it if was police, then she really needed to answer. Before he took too close a look at the car. The upholstery was doubtlessly smeared with blood. And, doubtlessly, some of it would be the murder victim's.

Tom nodded at her, as if to tell her to go ahead and open the door. And Kyrie did, about a palm's width further.

The man on the other side got closer. He wore some strong aftershave. No. Not strong, but insinuating. He looked down at her, his eyes unreadable behind the sunglasses. "Ms. Kyrie Grace Smith?"

She nodded. Smith was the name of a foster family she no longer remembered, but it had stuck to her throughout her growing up years.

He reached for a pocket of his linen suit, and brought out a leather wallet, which he opened with a flourish that must have taken years to learn. "Officer Rafiel Trall, Goldport Police Department. May I speak to you for a moment?"

Tom swallowed hard and was sure he'd turned pale at the announcement that the man on the other side of the door was an officer of the law. He'd had run-ins with the police before. He had a record. Oh, he'd never been arrested for more than a night or a couple of nights. And he'd been a minor. And every time his father had bailed him out.

But still, he didn't know what kind of record they kept or if it would have been erased when he turned eighteen. He was sure a couple of times they'd tried to charge him as an adult. Wasn't sure if it had stuck. He hadn't been paying much attention back then. He'd been cocky and full of himself and his family's power and position.

Since he'd left home, he'd done his best not to be caught. He tried to visualize being in jail, and needing to shift. Or shifting without meaning to. He imagined turning into a dragon in confines where privacy didn't exist. He couldn't be arrested. He wouldn't be. He would kill himself first.

Kyrie looked at the ID, then at the man.

"May I come in?" the man asked. "I have a few questions to ask you. Just a few minutes of your time."

Silently, Kyrie opened the door, and the man came in. He didn't look surprised at all at seeing Tom, whom he greeted with a nod. But then why should he look surprised? He couldn't know that Kyrie didn't have a boyfriend, could he?

Tom willed himself to relax, to show no fear. Fear would make the man suspicious and would make him look harder for something that had triggered that reaction.

"Look, this is just a quick visit," the policeman said. "A quick question. You work at the Athens on Fairfax, right?"

Kyrie nodded.

"Mr. Frank Skathari, your boss, said you had left about midnight?"

Had it been midnight? Tom wondered. It seemed like an eternity to his tired body, his dizzy mind. He saw Kyrie nod and wondered if she had any more idea of the time than he did.

"You didn't see any large animal in the parking lot?"

"An . . . animal?" she asked.

"There was a corpse . . . I'm sorry. You might not have noticed," he said. "It was behind some vans. But there was a corpse, and it looked like it died by accident. An attack by some creature with large teeth. We're thinking like a Komodo dragon or something."

Dragon. Tom felt as if the word were directed at him. The policeman looked at him as he spoke. Or at least, his face turned in Tom's direction. It was hard to see what the man was looking at, exactly, with those sunglasses on. "People bring these pets from abroad," he was saying, as Tom focused on him again. "And let them loose. It could be dangerous. I just wanted to know if you'd seen something."

"No," Kyrie said, and sounded amazingly convincing. "I saw nothing strange. I was just concerned with Tom . . ." She made a head gesture toward him. "With getting Tom his medicine."

"Medicine?" the policeman asked, as if this were the clue that would unravel the whole case.

"Migraine," Tom said. It was the first thing to cross his mind. His father, he remembered, had migraines. "Migraine medicine."

"Oh," the policeman said. "I see." He sounded alarmingly as if he did. He looked at one of them and then the other. "So, you won't be able to help me."

"I'm afraid not," Kyrie said.

"That," he said, "is too bad. I was hoping you'd have coffee with me tomorrow." He looked at his watch and nodded. "Well, later today—and discuss if you might have heard something suspicious or . . . found something. Perhaps in the bathroom of the diner. We haven't looked there, yet, you know?"

Tom heard the sound of a train, inside his ears, complete with whistles and growing thuds. He felt as if he would pass out. The bathroom. The damn man had looked in the bathroom and . . . seen the towels. And he going to use it to blackmail Kyrie? Blackmail Kyrie into what? What had Tom got Kyrie into?

He felt a spasm come over his whole body, and knew he was going to shift. And he didn't have the strength nor the will power to stop it.

Kyrie gasped. He managed to see her through a fog of pre-shift trembling, and realized she wasn't looking at him, but at the door she had just closed.

Then she turned around and something—something about him, about the way he looked, made her eyes grow huge and panicky. "No," she said. "No, you idiot. Don't shift."

Her hand grabbed firmly at his arm, and it felt warm and human and real.

+ + +

Kyrie turned from closing the door on the policeman's smiling face, and saw Tom . . . She couldn't describe it. He was Tom, undeniably Tom, human and bipedal, but there was something very wrong about his shape. His arms were too long, the wrist and quite a bit of green-shaded flesh protruding from the end of the sleeve. His hands were stretched out, too, his fingers elongated and the space between them strangely membranous. And his face, beneath the huge, puzzled blue eyes, looked like it was doing its best to grow a snout.

"No, no, you idiot," she said. "Don't shift. No. Calm down."

He stood on one foot, then the other, his features blank and stupid. His face already half-dragon and unable to show human emotions. His mouth opened, but what came out was half hiss, half growl.

She slapped him. She slapped him hard. "No," she said. "No."

And he shivered. He trembled on the edge of shifting. She realized she had smacked what could be a very large, very angry dragon in a minute. And then she smacked him again on the nose, as if he were a naughty puppy.

She judged how her shifts had left her, tired, witless. He'd shifted twice now. Oh, so had she, but the first time very briefly. How long had he been shifted? What had he done?

"You cannot shift now," she said. And slapped him again.

He blinked. His features blurred and changed. All of a sudden he was Tom, just Tom, standing there, looking like someone had hit him hard with a half brick and stopped just short of braining him. He seemed to be beyond tiredness, to some zombielike state where he could be ordered about.

"Oh, damn," he said, so softly that it was almost a sigh. He looked at her, and his eyes showed a kind of mad despair behind the tiredness. "Oh, damn. I can't be arrested, Kyrie, I can't. I was . . . when I was young and stupid. My father . . . got me out, but sometimes I spent a night in lockup. Kyrie, I couldn't survive it as a dragon. When my dad threw me out, I spent the night in a runaway shelter and . . . it was torture. The dragon . . . The beast wanted to come out. All those people. And being confined. If they take me in on suspicion of murder, if I have to stay . . . Kyrie, I couldn't. I'll kill myself before that."

Suddenly she understood why he'd started to shift, what the words of Officer Trall would sound like to him. She sighed, heavily. "No one is arresting you. At least not yet."

"But he *is* blackmailing us. He's blackmailing you. About the towels in the bathroom. He knows about the blood. And it's all my fault."

"Yes," Kyrie said, wondering if it was blackmail, or what it was, exactly. She remembered the expression in his eyes. Those eyes . . . If it was blackmail, what did he want, exactly? "He knows about the towels because he smelled them."

"Smelled?"

"He found them by the smell of blood, I'd bet. Before any other policemen got to them. He got to them and bagged them and . . . I presume hid them. You were starting to shift, so you probably missed it, but he lowered his glasses and I could see his eyes."

"And?" Tom asked.

"He had the same golden eyes as the lion in the parking lot," she said.

"He is . . . like us?" Tom asked, as his mind tried to adjust to the thought. "He is the lion? How can . . ."

"You know the lion was like us," Kyrie said.

He heard the annoyed note in her voice. She had slapped him. Hard. He'd almost gone to pieces in front of her. He felt like an idiot. "But, he's a policeman. He looks . . . he looks well-adjusted. And he traced us . . . And . . . he's in the police?" He swallowed, aware of sounding far less than rational and grown-up.

She nodded. "Yes. I'm very much afraid he's in the police."

"And he's like us . . ." Tom couldn't imagine it. How would he hide his shifts? How would he shift? How would he . . . Did his family know? Or didn't they care? He tried to imagine having parents—a family—who accepted your shifts, who loved you even when you, yourself, weren't sure you were human.

Kyrie shook her head. For just a moment there was empathy in her look. "I can't imagine it either," she said. "I suspect he normally works the night hours, though, just like us. Cops do, too, you know. It's a nocturnal occupation. So we will probably find some of our kind as cops. It's easier to control the shifting if you're awake."

Tom nodded. The whole thing was that even if you didn't shift, if you were a shapeshifter you felt more awake—more aware—at night. It was inescapable. So if you wanted to sleep and actually be able to rest, you did it during the day. And therefore, of necessity, you worked nights.

"Speaking of which," Kyrie said, "sun is coming up soon, and you're practically falling down on your feet."

"You've been yawning," he said accusingly.

She looked at him, puzzled, and he realized he'd said it as if he needed to salvage his manhood. While she'd just been . . . telling the truth.

"I'm sure I have," she said. "It's late. Come on. You can sleep in the back room."

Tom pulled his hair back and very much wished he had something to tie it back with. "I really should go," he said. "The triad dragons are after me and . . ."

"Oh, not that again," Kyrie said. "We've been over it." And she said it in such a tone of great tiredness that Tom couldn't answer.

Meekly he followed her back through the hallway, where she opened a linen closet and got out a thin blanket. And then she led him all the way back to the kitchen and opened a door he hadn't even been able to see, next to the fridge. It was a narrow door, as if designed for very thin people. At the very back of the house, a small room, enclosed all in glass, opened. There were blinds on the windows, which made it not quite like sleeping in a fishbowl. Besides, the backyard was the size of a normal flower bed. Maybe ten feet by ten feet, if that much, and surrounded by tall wooden fences. Not a fence belonging to it, but the fences of other houses that met there.

"Sorry there's not much of a view," Kyrie said. "I planted roses out there, to hide the fence, but most of them died in the drought. Only a couple survive and they're tiny."

He realized she thought he was looking at the fence in horror, and he managed a smile. "No, no. It's fine. I just need to sleep . . ."

"Well, this is the love seat. It doesn't open up, but it's fairly comfy. I've napped on it on occasion."

Tom felt the sofa reflexively, even as a voice at the back of his mind asked him what exactly he intended to do if he found it lumpy. Go and sleep in a better place? Like, for instance, all the hotels that accepted barefoot men without a dime on them?

He sat down on the sofa and clutched the thin blanket to himself. "Thank you, Kyrie. Thank you."

She looked surprised. Had he really come across as that much of a prick, that she'd be surprised because he thanked her?

Apparently so, because Kyrie stood there, looking at him, eyebrows raised, as though evaluating a new and strange artifact, before she said, "Goodnight," and left.

Tom lay down and pulled the blanket over himself. It couldn't have taken more than ten seconds before he fell asleep and into dreams populated by darkness, pierced by sharp claws and glimmering fangs—and a huge pearl, the size of a grapefruit and glowing like the moonlight at the full.

Kyrie frowned all the way to her room. She told herself that she must get her head examined, she really, really must.

In jerky movements, angrier at herself than she would like to admit, she undressed, throwing her robe over the foot of the bed.

Normally she slept naked. It was a habit she'd picked up since she'd started renting this house. All her life, up till then, she had been staying with someone else, under someone else's rules—when she was a foster child—or in a communal building, an apartment building where she didn't want someone to come in attracted by noise, while she was having what she thought of as one of her episodes, and find her naked. In retrospect, it was very foolish of her to think she didn't actually shift, since the *episodes* usually meant she woke up naked. At least, she told herself, she had learned to remove her clothes fast in the first throes of the shift.

Looking back, she thought it had all been an elaborate game with herself, to keep herself fooled about the nature of the shifting. After all, if she'd wakened with clothes nearby shredded to bits by large claws, she'd have had to think. She'd have had to admit something else was going on, right?

But in her own home she went to sleep naked, so that when she woke up naked she could pretend nothing at all untoward had happened in the night. Dreams, just dreams. She could tell herself that and believe it.

Only now, she stood naked in the middle of her bedroom and felt . . . well, nude. There was a man in the house. A young, attractive, and not particularly wholesome young man.

Okay, so he was in the back room and frankly, from the way he'd been swaying slightly on his feet, he probably wasn't in any state to be walking around. Not even stumbling around. And there was a locked—she paused and turned the key in the lock—door between them.

But still, she looked at herself in the mirror and she looked distressingly naked. Which meant . . . She blew out a breath, in annoyance at herself, as she scrambled to her dresser, got her loosest T-shirt and a pair of panties, and slipped them on.

What was she thinking? Up till this night she'd never found any reason to like Tom. And what had changed about this night? Well, he might have killed someone. And he was being chased by triads trying to recover something he'd been stupid enough to steal from . . . gangsters.

Yeah. There was a good reason to allow him to sleep in her house. There was a good reason to expose herself to the potential danger of a practically strange—no practically about it; in fact, she knew Tom was strange—man in the house.

She pulled back the covers on the narrow bed pushed up against her wall. The bedroom was barely large enough for the bed and the dresser—both purchased from thrift stores. It would be too small if she had a queensize bed.

She lay down on the mattress—or more accurately, threw herself down on it with the sort of angry fling of the body that a thin thrift-store mattress couldn't quite take.

She shifted position and flung the covers over herself, refusing to admit she'd bruised something.

There was a reason for Tom to be here. Sure there was. She didn't want to throw him out into the night, barefoot, tired, and confused.

Only, if she'd caught the drift of Tom's story right, he'd been surviving on his own, out there for a long time. He was a big man. Well, perhaps on the short side, but definitely well developed and muscular and . . .

No, this was worse than the lion. She turned facedown on the mattress and buried her face on her pillow.

The bedroom was in deep darkness, partly because it was the only room in the entire house that had only one tiny window—very small and high up on the upper corner of the back wall. Now she wondered if the full light of day was near.

What kind of an idiot was she?

Was she now suddenly attracted to hard-luck cases? She'd always laughed at women who came to the diner and, over breakfast with their equally clueless friends, complained about being disappointed by men that, surely, they knew were no good from the beginning. If you picked up with ex-cons, drug addicts, thieves—how could you expect anything good to come of it? Why would they respect you when they'd never respected another human being?

She knew this. So, why would she take this one in? Why? He wasn't even any good at being bad. He was a mess of trembling jelly between bouts of dangerous behavior.

She remembered him in the parking lot, under the moonlight. Pale skin and muscle-sculpted body, and those eyes . . .

Okay, so he was pretty. Since when was pretty worth all this trouble? The world was full of handsome men who weren't her problem. Men who would run the first time she turned into a panther.

And there was the problem, and there she came to and stopped. Because for all else that might be said for Tom, he wouldn't run.

Neither—probably—would Officer Trall. She remembered the disturbing moment when he'd lowered his glasses and fixed her with those recognizable golden eyes that, even in human form, with normal sclera, iris, and pupil, were unmistakable. And he looked just as good in human form.

She threw back the covers.

Again, pretty he might be, but that man was trouble. Pure trouble. He was a shifter, yes, but he was also a police officer. And what did the officer want with her? Why did he want to meet her? She was not so innocent that she didn't notice—of course she did—that he'd mentioned the bathroom, which meant the paper towels. Was it a threat? Was he blackmailing her? Blackmailing her into what?

She remembered the lion in the parking lot of the Athens—virile and energetic and very, very male.

She bit her lip. She wished she could convince herself that it would take a lot of blackmail to get her to what the Victorians called a fate worse than death. But she doubted it. If Tom hadn't been there, if he hadn't pulled her into the car, she very much suspected she would have shifted and . . .

And then there was Tom. His image flickered through her mind, as she tossed her thin blanket and turned first this way, then that. He'd been so gentle, so . . . respectful, when he helped dress her shoulder. Which, by the way, should hurt, shouldn't it?

She sat up in bed and prodded at her bandaged areas, but nothing hurt. Perhaps the antibiotic cream was also an analgesic. She had a bad habit of buying whatever was on sale without reading it too carefully. Well, just as well it didn't hurt. She lay down again, and closed her eyes.

But her thoughts went on behind her closed eyelids.

What was she going to do with Tom? Did she have to do anything with Tom? How far was she responsible for him?

She saw his features close at her comment, she saw his lost expression, all pale face and huge, shocked eyes. She saw him in the parking lot, dragon-form, muzzle bloodstained, and in the bathroom of the Athens, all over blood, his long, dark hair caked with it. She saw him in her living room, half-dragon and mostly man, clearly out of control.

What had he meant to do? Attack the officer? Why? For speaking out of turn?

All right. So, Rafiel Trall might have sounded like he was blackmailing her—blackmailing them. But she wasn't sure he was. There was something to his expression—a softness, a hopefulness . . . that made her doubt that he meant to threaten her. And even if he were. What did Tom mean to do? Eat him? Was he so devoid of any sense of right and wrong? Had no one ever told him you didn't eat people? Ever?

The bed felt too hard, the blanket too hot, the sheet too wrinkled beneath her tossing body.

She was never aware of the moment at which she fell into a dreamless sleep.

Kyrie woke up with the phone ringing.

The phone was on the dresser, across the room from the bed. The ring itself, seeming to run up and down her nerves like fire, carried her halfway there, still asleep, and she woke up fully with the receiver pressed to her ear, while she heard herself say "Hello" in a sleepy voice.

"Ms. Smith?" the voice on the other side was a masculine purr, dripping with sensuousness that caressed the syllables, making the "Ms." sound dangerously like "Miss" and "Smith" sound like a compliment, an indent proposition.

She knew it was Rafiel Trall without his announcing himself. She could see him at the other side of the phone, relaxed and seductive masculinity, poise and confidence and that something in his eyes, that something in his expression that said he was very bad for her. In the way that chocolate was bad for you. And all the more irresistible for being bad.

"How may I help you, officer?" she asked, making her voice crispy and official. All business. She had to keep this all business.

"In a lot of ways," he said. "But right now I just want to ask you a favor." She could hear him smile, and she couldn't quite tell how. One of her first jobs, out of high school, had been with a cold-calling telemarketing company. The job hadn't lasted long, though she'd been surprisingly good at it. Perhaps, she thought now, they could hear the harmonics of the panther in the human voice. And bought. And bought. And were very polite with it.

At that job they'd told her to always smile while she was talking because people on the other side could tell. She'd never believed it till now.

The silence lengthened between them, stretched like taffy, feeling sticky and endless, thinner and thinner, but never breaking. "All right," she said, at last. "Ask."

This time there was a very masculine chuckle at the other end.

"I can always say no," she said, tempted beyond endurance by the chuckle.

"You can," he said, gravely. "But I hope you don't. There's a restaurant about . . . oh, two miles from your house. It's the in-house restaurant at Spurs and Lace."

Spurs and Lace was the one good hotel in a Western town plagued with cheap motels and improbable cabin resorts, which catered to those families too poor, too numerous, or too shy to stay at the one Holiday Inn. The nineteenth-century hotel was in a completely different class. Once used by moneyed Easterners coming for the benefit of the mineral waters and the dry Western air, it had been renovated within an inch of its life, furnished with antiques and updated. It was now the haven of moneyed business travelers and honeymooning couples. An executive resort, Kyrie believed they called it.

"The restaurant is called Sheriff's Star, but despite the name it's good," Trall went on. "They serve brunch, which we're just about in time for."

Again, she said nothing. Oh, she could see where this was going, but she would let him come out and say it.

"I'd like to swing by your house to pick you up in about . . . oh . . . five minutes?"

"Why would you like to pick me up?" Kyrie asked, though her mind, and the recollections of his smell from the day before, gave her pretty good indications.

The chuckle again. "I'd like to feed you, Ms. Smith. Nothing worse than that. And if, during brunch, you should feel like talking to me about the diner, and what you think might have gone on in that parking lot in the dark, I will discuss the other cases we've had with you and—"

"Did you say other cases?" Kyrie asked.

"Indeed."

"Other cases of . . ." She remembered his story the day before. ". . . attacks by Komodo dragons?"

"Possibly. Mysterious attacks, shall we say."

"I see."

"Well, I think if we discuss it, we'll both see better," he said. "So . . . I'll pick you up in a few minutes, if that is acceptable."

"No," Kyrie said, before she even knew she was going to say it. But as soon as the word was out of her lips, she knew why. She knew she had to say it. Stranded at a restaurant with only this relative stranger and no way home on her own? No. She didn't think so. She might have gone stupid last night, but now it was the next day and she wouldn't be stupid anymore. "No. I'll bring my car. I'll meet you there. In twenty minutes."

She could see him hesitate on the other end of the phone. She wasn't sure how, or not exactly. Perhaps the letting out of breath, or perhaps some other sound, too light for ears to consciously discern. But it was there. And it was followed by a hesitant, "Your car . . ."

And now it was her turn to smile into the phone, "Why, officer. Would you be embarrassed to be seen with me, because of the condition of my car?"

"What? Of course not. It's just that I thought with the broken window, you have a security liability and—"

"Oh, I wouldn't worry, Officer Trall. After all, it's a good part of town, isn't it?"

After she put the phone down, she thought that it was a good part of town. And that her car might look ever so slightly embarrassing. But probably more so for Officer Trall, whom she doubted ever left the house without wearing pressed clothes.

She refused to be intimidated by him. Or scared by his obvious, open, clear sexuality. To begin with, whether he turned into a lion or not, he was—as she had reason to know, being a female counterpart—only human. Or possibly something less. How much the animal controlled them was something that Kyrie didn't wish to think about. And second, there was very little reason he would be romantically interested in her. She'd guess his suit had cost more than she made in a month.

Chances were he turned on that feline, devil-may-care charm with every female in sight. And meant nothing by it.

Still, she wouldn't look like a charity date. Not at the Sheriff's Star, she wouldn't. Too many times in childhood, she'd found herself dressed in foster sisters'—or brothers'—discards, cowering at the back of a family group, afraid someone would ask why a beggar was let in.

Now she might dress from thrift shops—her salary rarely extended to new clothes, except for underwear and socks—but at a size six that meant she got last year's designer clothes, donated by women so fashion conscious they spent half their time studying trends. That and a bit of flair, and her naturally exotic features, made most people think her beautiful. Or at least handsome.

Before getting in the shower, she checked her wounds under the bandages, and was shocked at finding them completely healed and only a little red. There would be scars, but no wound. Interesting. Very interesting. She must make sure to figure out what that antibiotic cream was. She needed to buy more of it. She always kept a well-stocked first-aid cabinet—part of her trying to be prepared to survive any emergency on her own—but this had been the first time she'd needed it.

She rushed through a shower, dried her hair properly into position and slipped on a white knit shirt with a mass of soft folds in the front that gave the appearance of a really deeply cut décolletage—but a décolletage so hidden by the swaying material in the front that it was a matter of guessing whether it was really there or not.

Then she put on the wraparound green suede miniskirt. No fishnets, which she occasionally wore to work. There was no reason to look like Officer Trall was having brunch with a hooker either and—with this outfit—fishnets would give that impression. Instead, she put on flesh-tone stockings and slipped her feet into relatively flat shoes.

Fully dressed, she thought of Tom. If she was going to leave him here alone, in the house, without a car, she should leave him a note.

Backtracking to her dresser, she grabbed the notepad and pen she kept in her underwear drawer, and wrote quickly, *I had to go out. There's eggs and bacon in the fridge.* Shape-shifting seemed to come with hunger and, from the way her own stomach was rumbling, Tom would be ravenous. *Don't go anywhere till I come back. We'll discuss what to do.*

She went to the kitchen and was about to put the note on the table when she heard a rustle of fabric from the doorway to the back porch.

Tom stood there, looking only half awake. But his blue eyes were wide open as they stared at her. "Whoa," he said, very softly.

It was, in many ways, the greatest compliment anyone had paid Kyrie in a long time. If nothing else, because it seemed to have been forced from his lips before his mouth could stop it.

Tom awakened with the sound of steps. For a moment, confused, he thought it was his upstairs neighbor walking around in high heels again. But then he realized the steps were nearby by. Very nearby.

He woke already sitting up, teeth clenched, hands grabbing . . . the side and seat of a rough, brownish sofa.

He blinked as the world caught up with him—the night before and the events all ran through his mind like a train, overpowering all other thought and leaving him stunned.

And then he realized he could still hear steps nearby. Kyrie. He was in Kyrie's house. She had put him up for the night, though he still couldn't quite understand why. He'd have thought he was the last person in the world whom she'd want around. But she had given him the sofa to sleep on, and the sweat suit, and . . .

Still half asleep, and with some vague idea of thanking her and getting out of her house and stopping endangering her as soon as possible, he lurched to his feet and stumbled toward the kitchen.

Kyrie stood by the table, her hair impeccably combed, as it usually was when she came to work. The first time Tom had seen her, he'd thought she was wearing a tapestry-pattern scarf. When he'd realized it was her real hair, he'd been so fascinated that he couldn't help staring at her. Until he'd realized she was looking at him with frowning disapproval bordering on hatred. And then he'd learned to look elsewhere.

But this morning, in her own kitchen, she looked far more stunning than she usually did when she came to work. There was this folded down front to her blouse that seemed—at any minute—to threaten to reveal her breasts. He remembered her breasts and his mouth went dry. Beyond that, she wore this tiny suede thing that looked like a scarf doing the turn of a skirt. Below it her legs stretched long and straight to her feet, which were encased in relatively low heeled but elegant shoes, seemingly made of strips of multicolored leather woven together.

The whole was . . . He heard himself exclaim under his breath and she turned around. He had a moment to think that she was going to disapprove of him again. But instead, she looked surprised, her eyebrows raised.

"I'm sorry," he said. "I'm not used to seeing you dressed up. You look . . . amazing." He just wished her little feather earring hadn't got lost. It would have looked lovely with that outfit.

"Thank you." She smiled, and her cheeks reddened, but for only a second, before the smile was replaced by a worried expression. As if she thought he wouldn't compliment her unless he had ulterior motives. "I was about to leave you a note," she said. "There's eggs and bacon in the fridge."

He realized he was starving. But still, it felt wrong to impose that far. She was being too generous. There was something wrong. "I should go," he said.

"Eat first. And then we'll talk," she said. She spoke as if she had some plan, or at least some intention of having a plan. She threw the note she had written to him into the trash, opened the cupboard above the coffeemaker. "There's cups and coffee beans here," she said. "The coffee grinder is behind the coffee beans. I'm going to go for brunch with . . ." She took a deep breath and faced him. "I'd rather you don't leave because I'm going to go for brunch with the policeman."

Tom felt a surge of panic. "You mean, he might want to arrest me?"

She looked puzzled. "No. I mean I might get some information out of him about what happened and what we can do, or even if there's any danger at all." She waved him into silence. "I know there's still danger from the triad, but I'm hoping there is no danger from the police. If there is, I'll call and let you know, okay?"

He nodded dumbly. Something in him was deeply aggrieved that she had dressed up to go to lunch with the policeman. But of course, there was nothing he could do about that. She wasn't his. He had no chance of her ever even looking at him like less than a dangerous nuisance.

And then for a moment, for just a moment, she looked at him and smiled a little. "Wish me luck," she said.

And she was out the door. And he silently wished her whatever luck meant to her. But he felt bereft as he hadn't in a long time. As he hadn't since that night he'd been thrown out of the only home he'd ever known.

Okay, and on top of everything else, the man is paranoid, Kyrie thought as she got out. *Why would he think I wanted to turn him in to the police?* In the cool light of day, her car looked truly awful, with its smashed driver's side window. She would have to get a square of plastic and tape it over the opening. Fortunately it rarely rained in Colorado, so it wasn't urgent. As for getting money to fix it . . . well . . .

She put the spare key in the broken ignition socket, thinking that would probably be more expensive to repair than the window. And she would make sure Tom paid. Yes, he'd done it to save their lives, but much too thoughtlessly. Clearly he'd either never owned a car, or never owned a car for whose repair he was responsible.

From the look of the sun up in the sky, it was noon and it was a beautiful day, the sidewalks filled with people in shorts and T-shirts, ambling among the small shops that grew increasingly smaller and pricier in the two miles between Kyrie's neighborhood and the hotel.

There were couples with kids and couples with dogs dressed like children, in bandanas and baseball caps. Lone joggers. A couple of businesswomen in suits, out shopping on their lunch hour.

Again Kyrie experienced the twin feelings of envy and confusion at these people. What would they do if they knew? What would they think if they were aware that humans who could take the shape of animals stalked the night? And what wouldn't Kyrie give to change places with one of them? Any one of them. Even the businesswoman with the pinched lips and the eyes narrowed by some emotional pain. At least she knew what she was. *Homo sapiens.*

She pulled into the parking lot of the hotel and, unwilling to brave the disdain of the valets, parked her own car. Wasn't difficult to find a parking space during the week.

Entering the hotel was like going into a different world from her modest house, her tiny car, or even the diner.

The door *whooshed* as it slid aside in front of her, and the cold air reached out to engulf her, drawing her into the tall, broad atrium of the hotel, whose ceiling was lost in the dim space overhead, supported by columns that looked like green marble. The air-conditioning cooled her suddenly, making her feel composed and sophisticated and quite a different person from the sweaty, rumpled woman outside in the Colorado summer.

The smoked glass doors closed behind her. Velvet sofas and potted palms dotted the immense space. Uniformed young men, on who knew what errands, circulated between. This hotel was designed to look like an Old West hotel, one of the more upscale ones.

She could all too easily imagine gunslingers swinging from the chandeliers, a bar fight breaking out, and the uniformed receptionists ducking behind their marble counter.

Kyrie hesitated but only for a moment, because she saw the signs to the restaurant and followed it, down into the bowels of the atrium and up in the elevator to the top floor that overlooked most of Goldport. Light flooded the restaurant through windows that lined every wall. Kyrie couldn't tell how big it was, just that the ceiling seemed as far up as the atrium's, but fully visible—a cool whiteness twenty feet up. Soft carpet deadened the sound of steps, and the arrangement of the tables, on different levels and separated by partitions and judiciously placed potted palms, made each table a private space.

A girl about Kyrie's age, blond and cool and wearing what looked like a business suit in pretty salmon pink, gave her the once-over. "May I help you?"

"Yes," Kyrie said. "I'm meeting a Mr. Trall. Rafiel Trall."

The girl's eyes widened slightly. And there was a gratifying look of envy.

What, thinking I can't possibly be in his league, sweetie? Kyrie thought, and reproached herself for her sudden anger and calmed herself forcefully, giving the woman a little smile.

"Mr. Trall is this way," the hostess said and, picking up a menu, led her down a winding corridor amid wood-and-glass partitions and palms. From the recesses around the walkway came the sounds of talk—but not the words, the acoustics of the restaurant being seemingly designed to give tables their privacy—and the smells of food—bacon and ham and sausage, eggs, roast beef. It made her mouth water so much that she was afraid of drooling.

Then the hostess led her around a wooden partition, and stepped back. And there, getting up hastily from his chair, was Rafiel Trall. He was perhaps better dressed than the night before, when his pale suit had betrayed a look of almost retro cool.

Now he was wearing tawny chinos and a khaki-colored shirt. His blond hair still shone, and still fell, unruly, over his golden eye. The mobile mouth turned upward in what seemed to be a smile of genuine pleasure at seeing her. "Miss Smith," he said, extending a hand. He tossed his head back to free his eyes of hair. There were circles of tiredness around his golden eyes, and creases on his face, as though he too had slept too little and not well.

He shook her hand hard, firmly. The hostess disappeared, silently, walking on the plush carpet as though gliding.

"Sit, sit," Rafiel Trall said. "Relax. I was horribly hungry, so I ordered an appetizer." He waved toward a platter on the table. "Seafood croquettes," he said. "High on protein, though perhaps not the kind . . ." He grinned. The golden eyes seemed to sparkle with mischief of their own.

Kyrie sat down, bonelessly. *What am I doing here?* she asked herself. *What does he want from me?*

And there, she knew the answer to the first one. She was here because he had blackmailed her into coming. Regardless of whether a threat had been uttered, regardless of what the threat he might actually mean, Rafiel Trall had mentioned those bloody towels in the bathroom.

Kyrie didn't own a television, but she had watched enough episodes of *CSI* on the diner's television, during slow times of the day, that she knew that on the show, at least, they could tell if someone had wiped someone else's blood off their skin with a paper towel. There would be skin and hair and sweat. . . .

But she remembered Tom and the way Tom had looked. What else could she have done then? Short of ignoring the whole thing and pretending it had nothing to do with her? And then what would have happened to Tom? She wasn't sure what she thought was worse—Tom eating the corpse, or Tom getting killed by ambush in his bedroom.

So she'd used the towels, and now Rafiel Trall held the towels over her head. And Tom's head. Which had brought her here.

But why did Officer Trall want her here? And what was the point of it all? Did he want to blackmail her for favors? No. If he wanted to do that, he would demand she meet him elsewhere, wouldn't he? However secluded the table might be . . . it wasn't *that* private.

Besides—she looked up at Rafiel Trall and refused to believe that he had that much trouble getting dates that he needed to force a girl into bed. Even if she admitted she didn't look like chopped liver.

She became aware that he'd said something and was now sitting, his napkin halfway to being unfolded on his lap, while he looked at her, expectantly.

There was no point lying. "I'm sorry," she said. "I have no idea what you said."

He smiled. "No. You were miles away. I said your outfit is very becoming."

Before she could stop it, she felt heat rise up her cheeks. "Thank you," she said. "But I would like to know why you asked me to come here."

He grinned at her. "I would like to have breakfast with you and to discuss . . . some cases the Goldport police force has encountered recently."

Her expression must have became frozen with worry, because he shook his head. "I do not in any way suspect you, do you understand? I just think you could—literally—help me with my enquiries. And I thought it was best done over a nice meal."

Kyrie nodded and picked up her menu, then put it down again, as the prices dismayed her.

"Ms. Smith—I'm hoping for your help with this. I'll pay for your meal." He smiled, showing very even teeth. "This is a business brunch."

She hesitated. She was aware that whatever he said, breaking bread with someone was an expression of friendship, an expression of familiarity. After all, throughout human history, enemies had refused to dine together.

"Look." He stared at her, across the table, and, for the first time since last night, didn't smile. "I'm sorry I mentioned the bathroom, which I meant to make you think of the paper towels. It was unworthy of me. And stupid. In fact, I . . . got rid of them, okay? I risked my position. But I'm sure . . . Just, I'm sorry I mentioned them. I didn't know any other way to make you help me, and we must talk. About . . . dragons and what's going on."

His voice was low, though Kyrie very much doubted anyone overhearing them would have any idea at all what they were talking about. But his expression was intense and serious.

She nodded, once. Not only was she starving, but she had left Tom in charge of the kitchen, with bacon and eggs at his disposal. Considering how many times he'd shifted the night before and how tired he'd looked, she was sure that he would have eaten all of it and possibly her lunch meat besides, before he could think straight.

Besides, what did Trall mean, *dragons*? He'd mentioned crimes. More than one? What had Tom done? Before she threw her luck in with his, she had to know, didn't she?

"Very well, Officer Trall," she said. "I'll have brunch with you."

He smiled effusively. At that moment, the server reappeared and he informed her they would be having the buffet. He also ordered black coffee, which Kyrie seconded.

The buffet spread was the most sumptuous that Kyrie had ever seen. It stretched over several counters and ranged from steamed crab legs, through prime rib, to desserts of various unlikely colors and shapes.

Kyrie was interested only in the meat. Preferably red and rare. She piled a plate with prime rib, conscious of the shocked glares of a couple of other guests. She didn't care. And at any rate, back at the table, she was glad to notice that Rafiel Trall's plate was even more full—though he'd gone for variety by adding ham and bacon.

They ate for a while in silence, and Rafiel got refills—how long had he been shifted the night before? Could a lion have killed the man?—before he leaned back and looked appraisingly at her. "How long have you known your friend? The . . . dragon?"

Kyrie, busy with a mouthful, swallowed hastily. "About six months," she said. "Frank hired him from the homeless shelter downtown for the night hours. He told me he was hiring him from the homeless shelter and that he thought Tom had a drug problem, so I'm guessing that Frank thought he was doing the world a favor, or was trying to garner a treasure in heaven, or whatever."

Rafiel was frowning. "Six months ago?"

Kyrie's turn to nod. "No, wait. A little more, because it was before Christmas when we were really crunched with all the late shoppers and people going to shows. And the other girl on the night hours had just left town with her boyfriend, so we were in the lurch. Frank got a couple of the day people to fill in, but they don't like it. Most of them are girls who think this part of town is unsavory and don't like being out in it at night. So he said he was doing something for community service, and he went and hired Tom."

Rafiel was still frowning. "And is he? On drugs?"

Kyrie shrugged. She thought of Tom, so defenseless last night, she thought of Tom, looking . . . admiring and confused this morning. And she felt like a weasel, betraying him to this stranger.

But she didn't seem quite able to help herself. Something was making her talk. His smell, masculine, feline, pervasive, seemed to make her want to please him. So she shrugged again. "Not on work time, that I've noticed," she said. She didn't find she needed to mention the track marks. To be honest, they might be scars. She hadn't looked up close. It seemed more indecent than staring at his privates. Which she hadn't done, either. Well, maybe she'd seen them by accident yesterday, but no more than to note he had nothing to be ashamed of.

"His name is Thomas Ormson?" Rafiel asked. "Thomas Edward Ormson?"

Kyrie shrugged again. "I've never known his middle name. I know he's Ormson because he introduced himself as Tom Ormson."

Rafiel made a sound at the back of his throat, as though this proved something. "If you excuse me," he said, standing up.

She ate the rest of her roast beef in silence, wondering if, by confirming Tom's name, she had given something essential away and if Tom would now be arrested. But Rafiel simply came back with yet another plate of meat. "How long have you known he was . . . a shifter?" Rafiel asked, cutting a bite of his ham.

"Not . . . not until last night. He was late. I heard a scream and I went to look. And he was . . . shifted." Why couldn't she stop herself talking? Why would she trust this stranger?

"And there was a dead person?" Rafiel asked.

Kyrie nodded.

Rafiel frowned. "Has he been late other nights?"

"No," Kyrie said.

"Are you sure? Not last Thursday? Does he work on Thursdays?"

Kyrie frowned. "He works on Thursdays, and he wasn't late."

"And he's been in town for more than six months?"

She nodded.

Rafiel Trall ate for a while in silence. Kyrie was dying to know what this was all about.

"Why do you ask?" she said. "You said there had been crimes, not one crime."

Rafiel nodded. "What I'm going to tell you is not known much outside the police department. There have been a couple of reported cases, but no one has put two and two together."

Alone in the house, Tom showered. He felt guilty about it, because it was Kyrie's shower. Her water. Her soap. Her shampoo.

But at this point he owed her a bunch of money, and he just added to it mentally.

Most of his time on his own, he'd found shelters for runaway kids and, then, when he was older, homeless shelters. He hadn't been homeless as such. He'd just moved from shelter to shelter in between bouts of getting in trouble and running away. He'd only slept outside when the moon was full. Shortly after leaving his father's house—even now his mind flitted away from the circumstances of that leaving—he'd thought it best to abandon New York City altogether. There were too many opportunities, there, for a rampaging dragon to do serious damage. And far too many people who might see him do it.

He'd drifted vaguely south and westward, moving when he thought someone had caught a glimpse of him in shifted form and, once, when a picture of him, as a dragon, in full flight, was published on the front page of the local rag. It had been syndicated to the *National Enquirer*, too. If his father caught a glimpse of it, on a supermarket line, would he have— But Tom shook his head. If he'd not actually given up on his father, he should have. Long ago.

But running or settled for a while in a town, he'd never had an apartment until these last five months. And all showers at these institutions had been rationed and far from private. All the soap had smelled of disinfectant, too.

The last five months, the showers had been heaven. And he'd bought the best soap he could find. His one luxury. But now he was homeless again, adrift. And, with the triad pressing down, he might have to leave.

He only hadn't left already because Kyrie had insisted he stay. And Kyrie was . . . the only one of his kind he'd ever got close to. Oh, he might also have quite a huge crush on her. But that didn't count. He'd had crushes before. He'd moved on. But Kyrie . . . He bit his lower lip, standing in her tiny bathroom and turning on the water.

Kyrie was something he didn't know what to do about. He didn't want to leave. He didn't want to lose the only kindred feeling and fellowship he'd ever known. But with the triad chasing him, what else could he do?

He showered, enjoying the water, then dried his hair and put the jogging suit Kyrie had lent him back on. He didn't own anything else. He didn't even own this. Nothing but his own skin.

A look outside, through the kitchen window, showed him a paper in the driveway. He wondered if Kyrie would mind if the neighbors saw him. But considering she hadn't told him anything about it, he'd assume she didn't.

He walked out to get the paper. It was noon, or close to it. The earliest he'd wakened in a long time. The air, though already suffocatingly hot, felt clear and clean, and he smelled Kyrie's roses, and the neighbor's profusion of flowers that spilled over the lawn and around the mailbox, in an array of pastel colors.

The neighbor, an elderly lady, sat on the porch with a tall glass of something, her white hair in curlers. She smiled pointedly at Tom and waved at him. Tom waved back and found himself grinning ridiculously. Bending to pick up the paper, he felt as if he were living something out of a movie. A domestic morning. And he wished madly that he could live that life and have that kind of morning. That kind of life. Just be a normal person with a normal life.

But, who was he kidding? Judging from all the trouble he'd got into before he'd started transforming into a dragon, his life wouldn't have been any different had he been perfectly normal. He'd probably still be running from town, a drifter. He probably still would have used. He probably . . .

He put the paper on the table, while he nuked himself a profusion of bacon and fried some eggs in a frying pan on the gas stove. He left half the eggs and bacon in the fridge. He could have eaten them all, easily enough, but he didn't want to do that to Kyrie. Yeah, she'd probably get lunch bought for her today, but what if she shifted again tonight and needed breakfast tomorrow?

Tom knew how much food cost. Over the last five months one of his delights had been learning to cook. He'd bought cookbooks at the same thrift stores at which he shopped for clothes and furniture. Since on a diner waiter's salary it was a challenge to cover everything and put money aside—as he felt he had to—he'd reveled in trying to create quasi-gourmet dishes from meats on special and discounted produce. And he'd eaten a lot of tofu.

Now he cooked quickly, peppering his eggs from a shaker by the stove. His stomach growled at the smell of the utilitarian fare. He knew, from other shifts, that the craving for protein was almost impossible to deny, the morning after a shift. Kyrie clearly knew it too.

Kyrie again. Sitting down to eat, he opened the paper. And choked.

Right there, on the front page, the headline above the fold screamed "Murder at Local Diner!" The picture of the Athens in black-and-white made the huge parking lot with the tiny diner beside it look like something out of a film noir.

The story was all too familiar to Tom. They'd found a body in the parking lot—of course anyone reading only the headline would think that they'd found it in the diner proper. Which meant that Frank was probably sizzling. If he was awake. Since he preferred to work nights, perhaps his day manager hadn't found it necessary to wake him and tell him about the paper. Then again, sometimes Tom thought Frank worked around the clock. He always seemed to be at the diner.

Frank's mood might matter or not. Tom hadn't decided yet what he was going to do about work. He needed the job. Wanted it. He'd enjoyed working at the diner more than he cared to think about. It had been his first long-term employment. A real, normal job.

Before this he'd just signed up with the day laborer places. But he'd enjoyed the routine, the regulars, and getting them served quickly, and getting their tips. Smiling just enough at the college girls to get a good tip without their thinking he was coming on to them. The minor feuds with the day staff, the camaraderie with Kyrie and . . . well, he wouldn't call it camaraderie with Frank, but Frank's gruff ways.

He had felt almost . . . human. And now it would all vanish. It all would go as if it meant nothing. Like, having a family. Like school. Like a normal adolescence.

He finished eating and cleaned his plate with bread from the red bread box over the fridge, before carefully washing the dishes and putting them away.

Normally he compensated after nights of shifting by grabbing some fried chicken on the way to work the next evening. Or by eating a couple of boiled eggs. Most of what he cooked at home was near vegetarian. So this might be the most protein he'd eaten at one sitting in years.

Oh, he could afford bacon and eggs, but he'd been saving money. He had some idea that he would go to a community college and get a degree. He'd dreamed of settling down.

Now, of course, as soon as he could swing by an ATM, he would have to empty the five hundred in his account to pay Kyrie for the car repairs and the groceries. And at that he'd probably still owe her money. But he would send her money from . . . somewhere.

And on this he stopped, because he hadn't told himself he was going to run. Not yet. But, after all, with the apartment in ruins, and the police investigating a crime around his place of employment, what else could he do? He had to run. Just as soon as he could retrieve . . . *it* from the Athens.

The doorbell rang. Tom thought it would be the police, come to arrest him. But how could they know he was here? Of course, Kyrie might have spoken, but . . .

He tiptoed to the door, trying to keep quiet, and looked through the peephole. Keith Vorpal stood on the doorstep, baseball cap rakishly turned backward and an expression of intense concern on his good-natured face. Since Vorpal didn't usually feel much concern for something not involving shapely females, Tom was surprised and curious. Also curious about how Vorpal had found him.

He opened the door on the chain and looked out.

"Man," Keith said as soon as he saw Tom. "Good to see you're alive. They think someone broke into your place and destroyed it, then tried to set fire to the pieces of furniture. It's all everyone talks about. Did you see anything weird when you were there?" He looked up at the space over the door, probably where the house number was. "I guess you spent the night here?"

Tom opened the door. "Come in," he said.

Keith came in, looking around the room with the curiosity of someone visiting a strange place.

"How did you find me?"

Keith shrugged. "Your boss, at that dive you work in. He said you were staying with the girl, Kyrie? And he gave me the address."

How did Frank know? Perhaps Kyrie had told him. She must have called in sometime after they got back to her place.

"Come on," Tom said. "I'll get you some coffee."

Moments later, they were in the kitchen and Tom had managed to get cups and coffee, and locate the sugar and milk.

"I guess you've been here a lot?" Keith asked.

Tom shrugged, neither willing to lie full-out, nor to destroy this impression of himself as a man in a relationship that Keith seemed to envy.

He wondered why Keith had come over. He seemed to be worried about Tom. But Tom wasn't used to anyone being worried about him. Did this mean the human race wanted him back?

CHAPTER
⤐ 4 ⤎

"There have been," Rafiel Trall said, leaning over the table and keeping his voice low, "a series of deaths in town. Well, at least they're classified as deaths, not murders. Bodies have been found . . . bitten in two."

"Bitten?" Kyrie asked, while her thoughts raced. Only one kind of thing could bite a person in two. Well, maybe many kinds of things, but in the middle of a city like Goldport, almost for sure all of those things would be shapeshifters. People like her. Tom had said that there weren't that many out there. But there were three of them and the triad. Were there more? And if so, what was calling them to Goldport?

"Bitten," Rafiel said, and his teeth clashed as he closed his mouth, as though the words had been distasteful for him to say. And he held his teeth clenched too, visible through his slightly parted lips. "Our forensics have found proteins in the bites that they say are reptilian but not . . . not of any known reptile."

He sat up straight and was silent a moment. "The theories range wildly," he said. "From pet Komodo dragons that escaped and grew to huge proportions, to an alligator, somewhere, to . . ." He shrugged. "An extinct reptile that survived somewhere in the wilderness of Colorado and has just now found its way into town. Though that

99

theory is on the fringes. It's not like we've called a paleontologist in to look at the bite marks yet. But . . ." He took a deep breath, and it trembled a little as he let it out. "But the teeth size and the marks are definitely . . . They're very large teeth, of a reptile type. I . . ." He shook his head. "You must realize in what position this puts me. Everyone at the police is talking escaped animals and Jurassic revivals. They've stopped just short of positing UFO aliens, but I'm very much afraid that's coming up next."

"And meanwhile none of them guesses the truth," Kyrie said, leaning back.

He nodded. "Or at least what might be the truth," he said. "You see in what kind of a position this puts me. . . ."

She looked at him across the table, and could well imagine that sort of divided loyalty, that confusion of identities. There were many things she wanted to ask. How many other shifters he'd met. Why he suspected Tom specifically. Instead, she heard herself say, "How did you become a police officer?"

He grinned. "Oh, that was easy. Granddad was one. Dad is one." Suddenly the grin expanded, becoming the easy smile of the night before. His hand toyed with his silverware on the side of his plate. "If I hadn't become a police officer, they would think there was something wrong with me. The shifting, they can forgive even if they can't understand. Not being a policeman? Never."

It was a large hand, with square fingers. No rings, except for a large, square class ring, and she scolded herself for looking for rings. Yeah. They could get together and raise a litter of kittens. What was she thinking?

Rafiel shrugged. "So, you see . . ."

"And your . . . shifting . . . when did you start?"

He took a deep breath. "It started when I was about twelve. My parents were aware of it first, as I did it in my sleep. They were a little scared, but I was normal otherwise, and how do you go and tell someone your kid . . . well . . ."

Kyrie nodded. "So . . . they aren't?"

"No. And Dad is retired now, but the first he heard about these corpses he asked if I knew . . ."

"And you think it's Tom?" Kyrie asked, her hands unaccountably clenched on the side of the table, as if this mattered to her personally.

He shrugged. "Just . . . the shape matches, and I've never met another one large enough to actually sever a body in two. But if he was in town that far back, and there were no murders something must have happened three months ago that triggered them. And then you say that he was at work on Wednesday. And on Wednesday we found a body right behind the Three Luck Dragon. Well, actually it was found on Thursday morning, but we think he died around midnight on Wednesday."

Kyrie thought back. As far as she could tell Tom had been at work and had been much as normal.

"Of course," Rafiel said. "The time is never exact. There could be a two-hour difference one way or another. And you see, I don't know any other shifters, any other shape that could just bite a man in half. And how common can a dragon be?"

Kyrie thought of the triad. "There are others . . . like Tom in town."

"Really?" Rafiel asked. He raised his eyebrows. "I've only met, truly met, another one besides you. He was a wolf and was passing through town. Transient. He was brought in for petty theft, and shifted while I was booking him. Fortunately Goldport has a tiny police force. Most officers are part-timers. And I was alone in the room with him at the time. I could . . . . . cover things up and talk sense to him. But that was only one I ever talked to. And he was a mess. Drugs, possible mental illness. I've . . . smelled others, but I don't know their shapes."

"Smelled?" Kyrie asked, aware of his smell so close, just across the table, that reek of masculinity and health and vigor—like the distilled scent of self-confidence.

He looked at her, with the look of a man who tries to evaluate whether someone is playing a joke on him. "Smelled—there is a definite scent to those . . . like us. A slightly metallic smell? An edge?"

Kyrie shook her head. She hadn't been aware of ever smelling people before. Perhaps because she hadn't been aware of really shifting shapes before. She thought of people as people, not smells.

And yet, as Rafiel mentioned it, she was aware that there was a slight edge in common in his smell and Tom's and perhaps her own. If their smell had been music, the metallic scent would have been a note, subdued but persistent, in the background. She blinked.

"These other . . . dragons," he said, lowering his voice on the last word. "Are they part of . . . the Asian community in town?"

"Why do you ask?" Kyrie said.

"Because all the victims were Asian or part Asian," he said. "That's why I was so surprised when I saw your . . . when I saw Thomas Ormson in his other form. Though thinking about it, he didn't look oriental even as . . . a dragon."

Kyrie shook her head. "Nordic," she said. "Like what they used to carve on the prow of Viking ships." She wondered if the Viking figureheads had been drawn from life. And if they'd really existed, all that time, in the past. "But yes, the other dragons are Asian. Tom said they are members of a triad." She hesitated.

"An organized Chinese crime syndicate?" Rafiel asked. Then added, "I see. Look, I know you feel like you're betraying him or something. But . . . put yourself in my place. The police will never be able to solve this series of deaths. And I know—or at least I think I know—something that could lead them to the truth. But if I speak, I won't be believed. And if I demonstrate it, I don't know . . . I suspect the first few of us who come out to society at large face the charming prospect of a life in the laboratory. I don't want that. I don't know anyone who wants that. I'm sure you don't. But at the same time I want to stop the murders. The people being killed . . ."

He shrugged. "They don't deserve to die, and we should put a stop to it. If the killers are like us—and there's a great chance they are—then it's our responsibility to stop it." He looked desperately up at her, his expression very intense and not at all like the relaxed image of the day before. "Do you understand what I'm saying at all?"

Kyrie understood. At least intellectually she understood. And suddenly, in a rush, she felt as if she, the orphan, had been adopted into a family, a family that came with obligations, with requirements. She looked at Rafiel's intense golden eyes, and hoped his smell was not influencing her as she said. "Yes, I see. But you must promise to do nothing against Tom on . . . anything else. Anything beyond the murders. It is not his fault if he is a shifter, and if he weren't a shifter, none of this would come out about him."

Rafiel nodded once and leaned forward. His plate was now empty and he pushed it forward and joined his hands on the place where it had been, his whole attitude one of intense attention to her.

She told him what had happened the night before. Her considerations and thoughts and final decision to take Tom home to his apartment. The condition of the apartment. The attack by the triad members.

She could no more stop herself talking than she could stop herself breathing. Her mind was powerless against his masculine scent.

Rafiel nodded. "That would make sense for the deaths we've been seeing." He pulled a notepad out of his pocket and noted down the description of the triad members. "Not that we can do anything about it officially," he said. "Because if they catch them then they'll . . . They might very well figure out about us as well, you know."

Kyrie nodded. The rules of this group to which she belonged despite herself were revealing themselves as complex. If they must be hidden—and they must, because revealing one of them would mean revealing all of them—then, surely, surely, they would have to police their own. Like other secretive communities of what had at the time been considered not quite humans all through history, they would have to take care of their own. Slaves, immigrants, serfs—all had policed themselves, to avoid notice from the outside, as far back as there had been humans in the world.

One way or another. She wondered what that meant. She could understand it to mean nicely or by force. And she wondered if Rafiel Trall understood it.

And looked up to find his intelligent golden eyes trained on her. "You know that means we might have to . . . take care of it on our own," he said. "I . . . never met any of *us* till a couple of years ago, and I never thought about it. The possibilities of someone going bad, doing something terrible and how the normals would never be able to take care of it and we'd have to step in. I never thought about it. I thought there might be a half a dozen of us in the world . . ."

Kyrie shook her head. "Tom has seen a dozen or so over five years. Not counting the dragon triad, where he thinks there could be hundreds. I think there's more than half a dozen. I wonder . . ."

"Yes?"

"I wonder how long this has been going on and why no one seems to know about it."

"I don't know," Rafiel said. "When my parents found out, they tried to research. They found legends and stories, poems and songs. And Mom, who reads a lot of scientific stuff, thinks there might be such a thing as . . . migratory genes. People attaching the genes from other species. Going partway there, as it were. But I'll be damned if that explains mythological species, too. Like dragons. Wonder if there are sphinxes and sea serpents, as well." He shook his head. "There seem to be a lot of legends about . . . people like us, until magic stopped being believed and science stepped in. I think we'll have to admit that we are not . . . things of the rational universe. I'm sure Thomas Ormson's shift violates the rules of conservation of matter and energy." He frowned, then suddenly grinned, a boyish grin. "Good thing that's not the sort of law I have to enforce."

Kyrie nodded. Men and their puns. "I've thought the same. But if we exist, if we exist anyway, how come no one has found out? How come one of us hasn't slipped spectacularly in a public place yet, and been found out?"

"Who says we haven't?" Rafiel said. "Have you ever heard of cryptozoology?"

"Bigfoot and the Loch Ness monster?" she asked, unearthing the word from a long-ago spree on the Internet looking up strange stuff.

Rafiel started to shake his head then shrugged and nodded. "For all I know, they're of ours too, yes," he said. "But more than that. Giant panthers in England, the lizard man of Denver, the thylacine in Australia that keeps being seen, years after it's supposedly extinct. And giant tigers and giant black dogs. All of those. And perhaps," he sighed, "Bigfoot and Nessie too." He looked at her. "They're all seen. They're all found. It's just that they're impossible, see. And the human mind is very good at erasing everything that is not possible. I . . . My mother says that the human mind is an engine designed to order reality." He paused and frowned. "You have to meet Mom to understand. But if she's right, then our minds are also designed to reject anything that introduces disorder, anything that goes against the grain."

"Our," she said, before she knew where her mind was headed. "You said the human mind and referred to it as 'our.' You think our minds are human."

"Do you think they aren't?" Rafiel asked. "Why?"

Kyrie shrugged. "Up until last night I thought I was perfectly human," she said. "I had no idea that I shifted shapes. I thought all that was an hallucination. Today I don't know what I think."

Something to the way that Rafiel's expression changed, and to his gaze shifting to a point behind her, made her turn. The server approached to drop off the bill. Rafiel glanced at it and handed it, with a card, back to the server.

"Look, when I went to bed yesterday—well, today at sunrise— we didn't have an ID on the victim yet. I'm scheduled to go and attend the autopsy today."

"Why?"

"Why the autopsy? Because we don't know exactly what killed the man. Our pathologist says the wounds look odd."

"No, why would they have you attend it? I've seen this in cop shows on TV, but I don't understand whey they need a policeman, who's not an expert in anatomy or anything of the sort to be there."

"Oh, that . . ." He shrugged. "Look, I'm the investigating officer. We don't have a murder department. Until these bodies started appearing three months ago, our murder rate was one or two a year and those usually domestic. And the investigating officer has to attend the autopsy. It's . . . That way we're there. They film the autopsy, you know, but a lot of it never makes it onto the film or even the official report. And we need to know everything. Even some casual comment, that the examiner might forget to put in the official report, or that the cameras might not catch. Sometimes, crimes are solved on little stuff." He grinned suddenly, disarmingly. "Of course, I'm going on my criminal-science class. As I said, most of the murders here don't involve much solving. The murderer is usually sobbing by the kitchen door, holding the knife. But the classes I took said I should be there. Also, if they find any evidence—dust or hair on the victim's clothing, I'll be there to take it into custody. Chain of custody is very important, should the case ever come to trial."

The victim's clothing. Kyrie remembered the sodden rag of a body the night before, soaked in blood. She hadn't been able to tell if he was wearing clothing, much less what it might be.

She emerged from the reverie in time to hear Rafiel say, "To the morgue?"

"Beg your pardon?"

"I was asking if you'd come with me to the morgue. To watch the autopsy."

"Why?" she asked.

He shrugged. "I don't know. Because though I'm not deputizing you, in a way I am? Because there might be something you see or notice. There might be a hair on the victim's body that is that of a diner regular—"

"I doubt they can find a hair, with all that blood," she said.

"You'd be amazed what's found in autopsy. And I think you can help us. Perhaps help me solve the whole thing." He paused a moment, significantly, playing with his napkin by folding it and unfolding it. "And then we can deal with it." From his expression, he looked about as eager to deal with it as she felt.

"Won't people mind?" Kyrie asked. "Isn't it irregular to have me with you at something like an official autopsy?" She imagined facing the dead body again. All that blood. It was safer during the day, but it would still trigger her desire to shift.

"I'll tell them you work at the diner," he said. "And that you're there because I think you might see or remember something. And if needed I'll tell them you're my girlfriend and you're thinking of studying law enforcement. But it should just be me, and Officer Bob—Bob McDonald. Good man, he usually helps me. He'll be there. But he was my dad's partner when Dad was in the force. Bob won't ask much of anything. He'll trust me. He thinks I'm . . . as he puts it: 'strange but sound.' And no, he doesn't know. At least we never told him. Of course, he's around the house a lot." He shrugged and set the napkin down, neatly folded, by his still half-full water glass. "So, will you come? With me?"

Kyrie sighed. She nodded. It seemed to be her duty to do this. Would it be her duty, also, to kill someone? To . . . execute someone? Until early morning today she'd never even examined her own ideas on the death penalty—she hadn't had any ideas on the death penalty, trusting brighter minds than hers to figure that out. But now she must figure it out. If Tom had killed the man yesterday, did they need to kill him? Was there another way to control him? How much consciousness did he have while killing? And would any considerations of justice or injustice to him have anything to do with it? Or would it all be overruled by the need to keep society safe?

The server dropped off the credit card slip, and Rafiel signed it.

"Your name," Kyrie said. "It's an odd spelling."

"Rafiel? I was named after an Agatha Christie character. Mom is a great fan."

"Jason Rafiel," Kyrie said. "*Nemesis* and *Caribbean Mystery*."

He smiled. "Mom will love you." Then he seemed to realize how that might sound, and he cleared his throat. "So, will you come with me?"

Kyrie sighed. "I really don't want to," she said. "But—"

"But?"

"But I think I might have to." She felt as if her shoulders were being crushed by the weight of this responsibility she didn't really want to take.

Tom had given Keith coffee and shuffled him to the back room where Tom had spent the night. He felt more at ease there, as if he were intruding less on Kyrie's privacy. She'd let him sleep here. It was a de facto guest room.

"I was just worried about you," Keith said, sitting down on the love seat as Tom motioned toward it. "The paper said a corpse was found behind that diner place where you work. And then with the apartment the way it looked, I thought—"

He had never clearly said what he thought, just frowned and looked worried. And Tom wasn't absolutely sure how to respond. It had been five years since he had actually needed to talk to someone or had a personal connection with anyone. And apparently socialization was reversible, because as far as making small talk—or any talk at all—he might as well have been raised by wolves.

He hadn't been a solitary child. He'd always had his buds, back when he was growing up, all the way from his playgroup in kindergarten to what—he now suspected—had been a rather unsavory group of young thugs in his adolescent years. In fact, it could be said that Tom, growing up, had spent far too little time alone with his own mind and his own thoughts.

But the last five years . . . Well, there had been interactions with other humans, of course, some of which still made him cringe. The man who'd tried to rob him outside his father's house. At least Tom hoped he'd been trying to rob him. Though why a barefoot kid in a robe would have anything worth taking, Tom couldn't understand. All he remembered was feeling suddenly very angry. He remembered shifting, and the dragon. And coming to with a spot of blood in front of him, and no one near him.

And there had been other . . . simpler interactions. But there had been practically no social interaction. Every time he'd talked to another human, or another human had talked to him, one of them had pretty clearly and immediately wanted something of the other.

Now, he couldn't see any signs that Keith wanted something of him. At any rate, there was nothing Tom had—what few possessions he'd owned had been destroyed at the apartment—his changes of clothes, his secondhand furniture, his . . . he realized with a start that his thrift-store black-leather jacket would be lost as well, and felt more grief over that than he'd felt over anything else. That jacket had been with him from almost the time he got kicked out of the house. He'd bought it almost new, with the proceeds of his first day as a laborer.

In many ways, that jacket defined him. It had a high enough collar for him to raise and hide his often-too-vulnerable face at moments when he wanted just his tough exterior to show. He'd learned early that looking tough and perhaps just a little crazy saved him from having to do real violence. Which, when anger could literally turn you into a beast, was half the battle.

Tom had lost his home and left without even the clothes on his body. For the second time in his life. And the thought that Keith might want Tom's body made Tom start to laugh—rapidly changed into a cough when Keith looked at him, puzzled. He knew Keith. That was not in the realm of possible.

Keith, for his part, just seemed to want to reassure himself Tom was okay. Having done that, he now sipped the coffee very slowly. "I guess your girlfriend is out?" he asked.

"Kyrie had an appointment," Tom said.

"She's cute," Keith said. "How long have you guys been together?"

Ah. "Well, we work together," Tom said, edging. "And one thing led to the other."

Keith nodded.

"You? Did the girl see any other dragons last night?"

Keith frowned. "Now that you mention it, yeah. She said she saw four dragons later on. One jumped down to the parking lot, and then three others flew away a while later." He shook his head. "I don't know. Maybe she has a dragon obsession. She's fun and all, but it might be more weirdness than I want to handle." He scratched his head and adjusted his hat. "I have weirdness enough at college."

Tom nodded, not sure what to say. And Keith launched in a detailed description of his college trouble, which involved pigheaded administrators and some complex requirements for graduation that Tom—who'd never been to college, only vaguely understood.

And then in the middle of it—he'd never quite understand it or be able to explain it—there were wings.

Only it wasn't quite like that. There was a powder. A green powder, like a shimmer in the air. Tom had sneezed and was about to say something about it, but it didn't seem to matter. It was as if he were floating a long way above his own body.

And Keith jumped up, dropping the cup that he'd been holding. Tom jumped for it, in the process dropping his own cup. Both cups shattered with a noise that seemed out of proportion to the event, and seemed to go on forever in Tom's mind.

And then he turned, but he seemed to turn in slow motion. For one, his body didn't understand that his legs actually belonged to him. And his legs felt like they were made of loose string, unable to support his weight. He tripped over his feet, and as he plunged toward the floor there were . . . wings over him. Green wings. Dragons. Green. Wings. Had to be dragons.

Suddenly the windows weren't there. Ripped? The screens were ripped from the frames. Glass lay at his feet. And the tip of a green paw came into the room, only it didn't look like a paw, more like a single toe with a claw at the end.

Tom grabbed for the low coffee table in front of the love seat. It was wicker and very unstable, but he struck out with it, hard, at the thing. There was a . . . tooth? fang? coming toward him, and he batted at it with the table. It made a hissing sound, not at all like a dragon sound. And it was dripping. At least Tom didn't think it was a dragon sound. He had no idea what he sounded like when he was shape-shifted.

Keith was kicking something large and green and shimmering.

"Stop," Tom yelled. "You can't kick a dragon. It will blaze you."

Keith looked at him, and Keith's eyes were huge, the pupils so dilated there was almost no iris left. It reminded Tom of something but he couldn't say what.

"Mother ship," Keith said. "The mother ship has landed. They're coming for us. I saw a movie."

"Really," Tom said, reaching out. "You shouldn't kick dragons."

Tom had managed to wrench the wooden leg away from the wicker table, and he had some idea he could stab the dragon with it. But one of the dragons was attacking Keith, while the other was . . . crouching against the glass door. If Tom could attack that one . . .

He started to go for the handle to the patio door, but all of a sudden it wavered and changed, in front of him, and it was the door to the Athens, with all the specials painted on. He pulled at it, but it wouldn't open. So he backed up, and kicked high at it.

The glass shattered with a sound like hail.

The big green body leaning against it shuddered and turned. Toward Tom.

Two toes-with-claws reached for him. A fang probed.

He had time to think, *Oh, shit.* And then he remembered what Keith's eyes looked like. They looked like his own, in the mirror, back when he was using.

The morgue of Goldport was in a low-slung, utilitarian-looking brick building. Someone with misconceived ideas of making it look like Southwestern architecture had put two obviously nonfunctional towers in asymmetrical positions atop the tile roof.

Rafiel Trall parked in front of the building, and Kyrie parked beside him. There were a couple of other cars and a couple of white panel vans parked in front. The street was the sort of little-traveled downtown street that connected quiet residential streets to the industrial areas with their warehouses and factories.

Rafiel put sunglasses on as he came out of the car, and Kyrie wondered for a moment if his golden eyes were unusually sensitive to light. It didn't seem like the most practical eye color to have.

He saw her staring and smiled at her, as if he thought she was admiring him. Kyrie looked away quickly. The man clearly had an ego as large as his shifted shape.

But he was quiet as they walked inside the building. Though it was air-conditioned, it didn't have the same feeling of clean cool as the inside of the hotel. Instead, the cold here felt clammy and clinging and there was a barely discernible smell. If Kyrie had been pressed to define it, she would have said that it smelled like her car a day after she'd lost a package of ground turkey in it, last May. It was the stink of spoiled meat, mixed with a faint tinge of urine and feces—what she'd once heard someone call the odor of mortality—but so faint that she couldn't quite be sure it was there.

"Have you ever been to this type of place?" Rafiel asked.

She shook her head.

"Sensitive stomach?" he asked.

She shrugged. She truly didn't know. She remembered the corpse last night and felt a recoiling—not because she'd been on the edge of losing her lunch over it, but because she remembered all too clearly how appetizing the blood had smelled. Appetizing was far worse than sickening. "I don't think so," she said.

And at that he gave her his bright smile, which seemed to beam rays of warmth through the chilly atmosphere. "Well, anyone of our kind has seen dead bodies, right?"

Kyrie blinked, bereft of an ability to answer. Had she seen dead bodies? Only the one yesterday. What was he telling her? She looked at the bright smile, the calm golden eyes, and wondered what hid behind it. Oh, she'd guessed—it wasn't that hard given his history— that Tom might have done things he was sorry for. There was that edging and shying away behind his silences. And a man like him who didn't seem totally devoid of interior life and yet ended up on drugs was clearly running away from something.

But until this moment, Kyrie had allowed herself to believe the something had been a few petty thefts, car joyriding, other things that could well fall under juvenile delinquency. Never . . . never murder. She'd never thought of murder, until Rafiel thought that. And now she wondered if the other shifters really had that much trouble controlling themselves in animal form that killing humans was common and accepted. And if it was, what was she doing here? What was the point of murderers investigating murders? If it was normal for shifters to kill humans, how much should the life of a human be worth it to them? How could Rafiel be a policeman? And how could Rafiel talk of it so calmly?

But she couldn't ask him. He'd continued ahead of her, down the cool tiled hallway, and she had followed him, without thinking, by instinct, like a child or a dog. And now he stood near a man who sat at a desk, and said, "Hi Joe. I'm here to see last night's pickup." He removed his sunglasses and pocketed them.

Joe, a middle-aged man, with a greying comb-over and a desk-job paunch, looked pointedly at Kyrie.

Rafiel smiled, that dazzling smile that seemed to hide no shadows and no fears. "Girlfriend," he said. "Kyrie is thinking of joining the force and I told her she should see an autopsy first. Kyrie Smith, this is Joe Martin. You know I've talked to you about him. He practically keeps this place running."

Kyrie, head spinning at being called someone's girlfriend, put her hand forward, to have it squeezed in a massive, square-tipped paw.

Joe gave her what he probably thought was a friendly smile, but which was at least three quarters leer, and told her in a tone he surely believed was avuncular, "You take good care of our boy, Ms. Smith. He's been lonely too long. Not that some ladies haven't tried."

And on that auspicious blessing, they walked past Joe and down the hallway, past a row of grey doors with little glass windows.

They all looked similar to Kyrie, and she had no idea what prompted Rafiel to stop in front one of them. But he stopped, and plunged a hand into his pants pocket, handing her a small notebook. She took it without comment, though considering the tightness of Rafiel's pants, she had to wonder what quantum principle allowed him to keep notebooks in there. When he handed her a pen too, from the same provenance, she was even more impressed, because sharp objects there had to hurt.

"Just take notes," Rafiel told her. "And no one in there will ask who you are. They'll assume you're a new officer I'm training. Goldport has one of the smallest full-time forces in the state. To compensate, we have a never-ending string of part timers, usually either people blowing through town for a few months, or people who took a couple of months of law-enforcement courses and decided it wasn't for them. If they ask, then I'll tell them you work at the diner and I want your opinion, okay?"

Kyrie nodded, feeling marginally better about being an apprentice policeman than about pretending to be Rafiel's girlfriend. A sense of unease about Rafiel built in her mind, even as she nodded and held the notebook and pencil as if she were official. Might as well make some notes, too. Hell. Who knew? She might need them. She was, after all, investigating this herself, wasn't she?

Rafiel opened the door and the smell of spoiled meat leaked out, overwhelmed—fortunately overwhelmed—by the smell of chemicals. She thought she detected rubbing alcohol and formaldehyde among them.

Inside was a small room, with tiled walls and floor, all leading down to a drain in the center of the floor, above which a metallic table was placed and into which something was gurgling. Kyrie knew very well what the something would be, but she refused to look, refused to investigate.

In the full light of day, without the pressure of the moon on her body and mind, it was unlikely that the smell of blood would be appetizing. But she refused to give it a chance, all the same.

The tiled room should have looked cold and sterile and it probably would have, had it been tiled in standard white. However, the walls looked like someone had either gone crazy with artistry or—more likely considering what Kyrie had seen of how the public departments of Goldport, from town hall to schools, operated—they'd received remnant tiles from various public projects.

Be it as it may, bright blue, fierce red, sunny yellow, and the curious terra cotta orange of Southwest buildings covered walls and floor.

It all went to make the man who stood in the middle of the room look greyer and more colorless. He would be, Kyrie judged, somewhat past middle age. Colorlessness came not only from his white hair, but from a skin that looked like he was never allowed out in the sunlight. He had an aquiline nose that looked broken but probably had just grown like that, and—on either side of it—brightly sparkling blue eyes, rife with amusement.

"Hello there, Rafiel," he said, and grinned. He wore a lab coat, and the sleeves—and his hands, in latex gloves—were stained as colorfully as the tiles that surrounded him. "We were just about to start, but Bob—" He nodded toward the other man in the room, who was somewhat past middle age, with a bald head surrounded in a fringe of grey hair. He wore a bright Hawaiian-style shirt, incongruously patterned with what seemed to be palm trees and camels on a virulently green background. "—Bob said it was proper if you were here, as there should be more than one of you watching."

"I'm sorry," Rafiel said. There was some change that Kyrie couldn't quite define to his tone. "We were having breakfast."

The man in the lab coat—a doctor?—grinned. "Breakfast, before this? Oh, no. You know so much better than that."

"To be honest, Mike," Bob said, "he hasn't tossed his cookies in about a year. Not since that vagrant found at the warehouse that had been there for over three months, last summer, remember?"

Rafiel said nothing, only shook his head and a light red tinge appeared on his cheeks. And Kyrie realized all of a sudden what his tone had been. The sound in his voice had been the sound of a little boy responding to his betters, of a young man convincing the elders of his worthiness.

"This is Kyrie Smith," Rafiel said, gruffly. "She'll be taking notes."

The two older men looked at her as if noticing her presence for the first time. The medical examiner smiled and Bob raised his eyebrows, his eyes twinkling with amusement. She rather suspected that, notebook or not, she'd just been relegated to the girlfriend realm again.

She ducked her head, while the examiner turned to a point in the wall, where a little light flashing and a glint of something seemed to indicate the presence of a camera, and said, "We have washed and set the body, ready for examination." He gestured toward the body on the table.

It looked much better than the night before. Or perhaps much worse. It was all a matter of perspective. The night before, it had looked like a piece of meat wrapped in blood-soaked rags. Now, laid out on the table, it looked definitely human.

"The victim," the medical examiner continued, in that officious voice that people get when talking into recording instruments, "is a Caucasian male, blue-eyed, five foot nine, two hundred and thirty pounds, probably between thirty and forty years old. As far as we can determine, he died of multiple stab wounds, by an instrument to be determined." He gestured toward a large Ziploc bag at the corner of the room, against the multicolored wall. It was filled with something that looked black and ragged. "I removed the victim's clothes—T-shirt and slacks—in the presence of Officer McDonald, and bagged them. They will be handed to the custody of Officer McDonald and Officer Trall for further analysis. As reported to me by Officer McDonald, the corpse was not found to have any identification and the police department is waiting for a missing-persons report that might give some clue as to his identity."

"Instrument to be determined, Mike?" Rafiel asked, leaning

forward to take a closer look at the very pale corpse crisscrossed by dark gashes.

The medical examiner looked up. "They don't look like knife stab wounds."

"What about . . . I mean, yesterday we thought it might be another of those animal attacks?"

"What animal . . . ? Oh, the victims cut in half?" Mike said. "Not that I can tell. I mean, yeah, the other ones have some marks consistent with perhaps animal teeth, though I would hate to see the animal with teeth that size. But this one . . ." He frowned. "More like he was stabbed multiple times by a weird implement. A nubby sword with a serrated edge, perhaps?"

Rafiel blinked. He looked toward Kyrie and frowned.

Kyrie felt relieved. Well, at least a little relieved. She took a deep breath. A nubby sword with a serrated edge didn't seem like anything that Tom could have been carrying on him. She had seen his teeth— glimmering in the moonlight—and they looked as polished and smooth as the best gourmet knives. So they couldn't be confused with these stabbing implements. And Tom hadn't had anything on him. She remembered him in the bathroom.

Her sense of relief surprised her. Did she care that much if Tom was guilty or not? But then she thought that considering she might be called on to administer justice, and considering she had already hidden him from the law, in a way, yes, she did care.

She made a quick note on the nature of the implements, and looked up to see that the doctor and Rafiel were removing something, with tweezers—from the man's grey hair.

"Looks like the same green powder found on the clothes and the body when we first examined it," Mike said. "We're sending it for analysis."

Rafiel was frowning at a little baggie into which he'd collected what looked like a sprinkle of bright green powder. "Looks like pollen," he said. "Anything flowering about now that's this bright green?" he looked at Bob.

"Not that I know," Bob said. "Label it. We'll hand it over to the lab. Who knows? They might actually figure it out."

He shrugged and Kyrie didn't know if he was being ironic. She also didn't have time to think about it, because Mike had sliced a Y shape on the man's chest and opened the body cavity.

The smell of death and corruption became all encompassing, and the sight of the organs . . . Kyrie swallowed. Even as she swallowed and struggled with nausea, she felt relieved that it wasn't hunger and that she wasn't finding this in any way appetizing. Perhaps panthers only ate fresh meat.

"Are you okay?" Rafiel asked.

She wasn't okay. The smell seemed to be short circuiting her brain and making her blood rush loudly in her ears. But she nodded and got hold of the considerable willpower she resorted to when she had to prevent herself from shifting. She nodded again. "I'm fine," she said, though her voice echoed tiny and distant.

"Look at that," the doctor said. "That's the stab that killed him. Right through the heart." He pointed at an organ that looked exactly like the others, to Kyrie, all of them an amalgam of red and green, yellow and the sort of greys that really shouldn't exist in nature. "There are several others that reached vital organs, but I'd say that's the one that stopped it. Pretty much ripped the heart to shreds, in fact."

Rafiel and Bob had moved closer, and were looking into the opened body.

"What are those white things?" Rafiel asked.

"Damned if I know," Mike said. "They look like some sort of adipose deposits."

"They look like huge ant eggs to me," Bob said. "You know, the kind you find when you break an anthill open in your garden? Just much bigger."

"They seem to be at all the stab wound sites," Rafiel said.

Kyrie wrote "white things" and "ant eggs" and "wound sites."

"So, some contamination on the blade," Rafiel said. "Can you put some—"

Then as the doctor handed him a bag and said, "You'd best keep it in a cooler, though, since it's not been exposed to the air."

Bob produced a normal picnic cooler from somewhere. It was

full of ice. He got the baggy and a couple other baggies of what the doctor thought might be contaminants in the wound, and put them in the cooler.

The autopsy progressed along lines that Kyrie had read about, but never been forced to watch before, and she had to call on all her self-control to continue watching, particularly when they sawed the cranium open to remove the brain. But there didn't seem to be any other surprises.

"I think," the doctor said. "There might be some drug in the blood, so I'd like to get that looked at also."

"Drug?"

"Some hallucinogenic. His pupils were like pie plates when they got him in. I'd say he was high as a kite."

She tried to imagine this man high. He didn't seem the type. Well fed, middling dressed, middle-aged. Oh, Kyrie and everyone in her generation had heard all the platitudes about drug use affecting every class and every type of person. And, as such, they might even be true. But there were two classes it primarily affected—depending on the drug—the very rich and the very poor. And within those, whatever drug was the current drug of choice tended to make people sickly or at least skinny.

This man looked robust and neither too rich or too poor. And yet, looking at him, something gnawed at the back of Kyrie's mind. She couldn't quite say what.

She took her leave, with Rafiel, and hurried out of the place. Outside, standing in the sun, holding a cooler with whatever samples they got off the body, Rafiel blinked. His enormous confidence seemed to have vanished and he looked confused and perhaps a little scared.

He looked over his shoulder, but Bob had stayed behind, talking to the examiner. "We have to find who did this, Kyrie. The sooner the better."

"Why?" Kyrie said. There were many things she wanted to ask Rafiel, like why he assumed that one of their kind was bound to have seen corpses before, and why, if that was the case, they should discipline this killer. And why he'd assumed that this too was a death by dragon—other than having seen Tom standing over the body. But she couldn't ask any of those, and anyway, the most important was this—why they particularly and not the police in general should find out what happened to this victim.

Rafiel blinked again. The gesture made him look slow of thought, though it was probably just a reaction to the strong sunshine. "What do you mean why?" he asked.

"Why should we care who did this, if it wasn't a shifter?" Kyrie asked.

Rafiel frowned. "No, but the victim was a shifter. Didn't you smell it?"

Rafiel insisted on following her home. There was nothing for it. "Can't you see?" he said. "I have to. If something is killing shifters . . ."

"How would they even know I'm a shifter?" she asked. "Wouldn't it take knowing the smell? And knowing what we are?"

Rafiel shrugged. "I can't answer that. Perhaps something like your triad friends. Didn't Ormson say that the triad had been shifters for centuries? That it ran in families? That they know what it means and even have a shifter god?"

She looked at him. A monstrous idea was forming. If someone was killing shifters, and if it was another shifter, wouldn't it make sense for it to be someone who . . . oh, worked for the police? Who could keep an eye on people without anyone getting suspicious? He could smell someone—once—and then realize . . .

She shook her head. "Why were you at the diner?" she asked. "Last night?"

Golden eyes widened. "I was coming for a cup of coffee," he said. "I was off work."

"You were coming for a cup of coffee in lion shape?"

He chuckled at that. Audibly chuckled. "No. Of course not. I only shifted when I smelled . . . I was in human form when I first saw you. When I saw you pull Ormson inside. Of course, I knew you were shifters."

"How?"

He looked at her as if she'd taken leave of her senses. "He was a dragon," he said.

"But then why did you shift?" Kyrie asked. "Why wouldn't you just call the crime in?"

"And catch you still shape-shifted?" he said. "I had to make sure you were out of there before I called it in."

"But why shift, then?"

He sighed. Something like a shadow crossed the serene golden eyes and he mumbled something.

"Beg your pardon?" Kyrie said.

"The smell of blood, all right? Combined with the moonlight it caused me to shift and it took effort to get back to my form. Because then . . ." He turned very red. ". . . then I smelled you."

Kyrie thought of the smell of him, rising in the night with all the blatant come-on of a feline-seeking-female ad.

She nodded once. She could believe that. But she still had a question, "Why come to the Athens for coffee? Pardon me, but I know even late at night there are better places open, and dressing as you do, surely you can afford better."

He shrugged. "I don't know, okay? Started going there about a year ago. I like . . . It's homey, okay? Feels homey. And there's you. You're . . . I could smell you were a shifter. And I like looking at you."

Kyrie frowned. "Fine," she said. But she wasn't convinced. For one, she couldn't remember having seen Rafiel at the diner, ever. Of course, considering how busy it got there at times, like the five a.m. rush just before she went off shift, he could have been dancing naked on a table and she would not have noticed.

She looked at him, and, involuntarily, pictured that. No. If he were dancing naked on the table, she would have noticed.

"Fine," she said again. "You can follow me home."

At the back of her mind, she thought that if all else failed, Tom would be there. And Tom could always help defend her against Rafiel. Okay, Tom might not be exactly a superhero. But it would be two against one.

✢ ✢ ✢

Tom had just kicked the door, and felt something—something giant and pincer-like reach for him when . . .

"What in hell?" came from the direction of the living room in a very male voice. A vaguely familiar male voice. And then there were strides—sounding echoey and strange through his distorting senses, advancing along, toward him.

Past the kitchen. He felt more than saw as two pairs of green wings took flight, from the backyard, into the dark night sky above.

And he turned in the direction of the steps to see Kyrie look at him, her mouth open in shock, her eyes wide, her face suddenly drained of color.

Keith was still doing fake kung-fu moves in the direction of the utterly broken windows. But Kyrie stood in the middle of the room, gulping air.

Behind her, stood the policeman lion, golden eyes and immaculate linen clothes, all in a vague tawny color. And he looked . . . disgusted.

Tom summoned all his thought, all his ability to speak, and came out with the best excuse he could craft. "It wasn't me," he said. "It was the dragons."

Kyrie stood in the middle of her demolished sunroom. The windows were all broken. As was the sliding door. And there was Tom—and he looked very odd. Tottery and . . . just strange. And there was another guy—his neighbor, she thought, from the apartment.

"I'm sorry," Tom said, again. "It was the dragons." He pointed at the backyard. "They were attacking."

His voice sounded odd. Normally it was raspy, but now it sounded like it was coming out through one of those distorters that kids used to do alien voices. And there had to be something wrong with him. He was walking barefoot on shards of glass. It had to hurt. In fact, she could see little pinpricks of blood on the indifferent beige carpet. But he didn't seem to be in pain.

"Tom, are you all right?" she asked. But by then she was close enough to look in his eyes. His pupils were huge, crowding the blue iris almost completely out of his eyes.

Kyrie took a deep breath. Damn, damn, damn, damn. She knew better, didn't she? Once a junkie always a junkie. And Tom was . . . Hell, she knew what he was. Shifter or not, someone with his upbringing wouldn't have fallen as low as he had without some major work on his part. He had to be totally out of control. He had to be.

But she'd almost believed. She'd almost trusted. She remembered how she'd felt bad about telling Rafiel on him. She remembered how she felt so relieved it wasn't a dragon's teeth on that man's body.

Hell, she still felt happy the man hadn't died by dragon. That meant she didn't have to keep Tom close until she figured out what to do about it. She just didn't have to. She was through with him.

"You're high," she said, and it sounded odd, because she hadn't meant to say it, hadn't meant to call attention to the fact, just in case Rafiel hadn't noticed it. But it didn't matter, did it? If Tom was this out of control, he was going to be arrested, sooner or later.

Tom shook his head, his dark eyebrows knit over his eyes in complete surprise. "Me?" he said. "No. Keith is high. He was talking about the mother ship. I mean, clear as day it was just two dragons."

Kyrie didn't know whether to laugh and cry. All these years she had kept away from dangerous men. She'd laughed at the sort of woman who let herself get head over heels with some bundle of muscles and no brain. And now she'd got involved with . . . this. Okay, so not involved, although if she told herself the truth, she had been interested in Tom. Or at least appreciative of his buff and sculpted body. She hadn't done anything even remotely sexual or physical to him, though.

Not that it mattered. She'd let him into her house. She'd let him stay here alone . . . And he'd got his buddy over, hadn't he? And they'd . . . what? Shot up? There didn't seem to be any smell of pot in the air, and besides she doubted that pot would cause this kind of trip. Of course, she knew drugs could also be swallowed or . . . And that wasn't the point. He'd gotten high and destroyed her property.

She looked around at the devastation in her sunroom, and wondered how she was going to pay for this mess. The landlord would demand payment. But she had no more than a couple of hundred in the bank, and that had to last for food and all till the end of the month. And she needed rent.

She took another deep breath. She was going to have to ask Frank for more hours. And even then, she might not make it.

Tom was looking at her, as though trying to interpret her expression, as if it were very hard to read—something he couldn't understand. "Uh," he said. "I'll leave now?"

Part of Kyrie wanted to tell him no. After all, well, he was still barefoot. And bleeding. And he was high. She should tell him to say. She should . . .

But no, she definitely should not. She'd kept him overnight, so he would be better off leaving in the morning. And now, what? He'd just caused more damage.

"Yes," she said. She heard her voice so cold it could have formed icicles on contact. "Yeah. I think it would be best if you left and took your friend."

Tom nodded, and tugged on the shoulder of the other guy's sweater, even as he started inching past Kyrie, in an oddly skittish movement. It reminded her of a cat, in a house where she'd stayed for a few months. A very skittish cat, who ran away if you so much as looked at her.

As far as Kyrie could tell, no one had ever hurt the cat. But she skidded past people, as though afraid of being kicked.

Now Tom edged past her the same way, while dragging his friend, who looked at Kyrie, blank and confused, and said, "It was aliens, you know. Just like . . . you know. Aliens."

She heard them cross the house, toward the front door. She didn't remember the guy's car on the driveway, but it wasn't her problem if they were on foot. In fact, it might be safer in the state they were. And she didn't care, she told herself, as she listened for the front door to close.

"Kyrie," Rafiel said. He stood by the windows, frowning, puzzled. "Something was here."

They'd been walking for a while, aimlessly, down the street, when Tom because aware of three things—first, that he was walking around in a neighborhood he didn't know; second, that he was barefoot; third, that his feet hurt like living hell.

He sat down on the nearest lawn, and looked at his feet, which were cut, all over, by a bunch of glass.

This realization seemed to have hit Keith at the same time, which was weird. As Tom was looking in dismay at the blood covering the soles of his feet, Keith said, "Shit. You're bleeding."

Tom looked up. He remembered seeing Keith's eyes, the pupil dilated and odd. But Keith looked perfectly normal now, even if a little puzzled. "What happened?" he said. And frowned, as if remembering some thing that didn't make any sense whatsoever. "What happened to us back there. What . . ."

Tom shook his head. He knew what Keith's eyes looked like. And Tom had some idea what mind-altering substances could do to your mind and your senses. Hell, for a while there he was shooting everything that came his way. Heroin by choice, but he'd have done drain opener if he had any reason to suspect that it would prevent him from shifting into a dragon. He suspected, in fact, that he had shot up baking soda in solution more than a few times. And who knew what else? It was miraculous enough he'd survived all those years. But nothing nothing, equaled the trip he'd just gone through, back there.

He put his face in his hands, and heard himself groan. He'd messed it up for good and all. Not that there had ever been any hope that Kyrie would see him as anything other than a mess. Not considering what he'd done the night before. The . . . corpse. And then his being so totally helpless. There was no way he had a chance with Kyrie. Not any way. But . . .

But now she thought him a drug addict. And the policeman had been with her.

"I'm going to get my car," Keith said. "Do you have any idea which way we came?"

"You have a car?"

"Yeah," Keith said. "I parked just a couple of blocks from . . . your girl's . . ." It seemed to hit him, belatedly, that perhaps Kyrie was no longer Tom's girl. Not after what they'd done to her sunroom. "Do you have any idea which way we came?"

There was something to the dragon. Perhaps seeing the city from above so many times, Tom had memorized it like one memorizes a map, or a favorite picture. Or perhaps being a dragon came with a sense of direction. Who knew?

But by concentrating, he could just figure out which way Kyrie's house was. He wondered if the policeman would arrest them for even coming near.

Standing up, unsteadily, he said, "Come on." He winced at the pain in his feet. "Come on. It's this way, up the road here two blocks, then up ten blocks, and then to the left another five, and you should see her house."

Keith took a step back. "Whoa, dude," he said. "You've gone all pale, just standing up. Sit down. I'll go get the car. You're sure of the way?"

Tom nodded. He wanted to say he would go with Keith, but he could tell he would only slow Keith down. He sat down on the grass, again, with some relief. "Sure," he said. "Sure. You should see it. If not . . . come back."

He put his face in his hands, again, sitting there. He didn't know how long he and Keith had been fighting the . . . dragons? He was sure they were dragons, but there was a feeling of strangeness, his memory kept giving him images of a big, horned toe. No. A tooth. No . . .

He sighed. He was never going to remember. And he had no idea what had got him so high. And Keith too. For all his attitude with the girls, the one thing Tom had never suspected Keith of doing was getting involved in drugs. In fact, he would bet his neighbor had never got high before.

So . . . How had they got high?

The sugar. It had to be the sugar. He'd drunk nothing but the coffee. No one, absolutely no one would put drugs in eggs or bacon. So, it had to be the sugar. He'd put three spoons in the coffee. Kyrie. Kyrie kept drugs in the house.

He blinked in amazement. Okay, so he'd stolen the—he'd stolen *it*—he forced his mind away from what *it* was—so he could give up drugs. There had been one too many times of waking up choking on his own vomit, struggling for every breath and not sure he was going to make it to the morning. There had also been the ever-present fear of being arrested, of shifting in a jail cell. Of eating a bunch of people.

So, he'd stolen *it* and tried to use it to control his shifts, so that he would stop waking up in the middle of the day dreaming he had eaten someone the night before and not being sure if it was true or not. The drugs weren't working so well for that, anyway. Or to make him stop hurting.

But, even with the . . . object in his possession he hadn't been able to give up on drugs, not entirely, until he'd started working at the diner, and he'd been . . . He'd seen Kyrie, and he'd seen the way she looked at him. And . . . he chuckled to himself. He'd tried to change. He'd really tried to change his ways to impress her. And all the time, all this time, she was doing drugs, too. Perhaps all shifters did them, to control the shift? Or perhaps she disapproved of him for other reasons. But, clearly, a straight arrow she was not.

"Are you okay?" Keith asked. He'd stopped the car—a beat-up golden Toyota of late Eighties vintage—in front of Tom and rolled down the window.

Tom realized he was laughing so hard that there were tears pouring down his face. He controlled with an effort. "Oh, I'm fine. I am perfectly fine."

He had, in fact, been an idiot. But not anymore.

When the office was empty like this, late at night, and Edward Ormson was the only one still at his desk, sometimes he wondered what it would be like to have someone to go home to.

He hadn't remarried because . . . Well, because his marriage had blown up so explosively, and Sylvia had taken herself such a long way away, that he thought there was no point trying again.

No. He was wrong. He was lying to himself again. What had made him give up on family and home wasn't Sylvia. It was Tom.

He looked up from the laptop open on his broad mahogany desk, and past the glass-door of his private office at the rest of the office— where normally his secretaries and his clerks worked. This late, it was all gloom, with here and there a faint light where someone's computer had turned on to run the automated processes, or where someone had forgotten a desk lamp on.

He probably should make a complaint about the waste of energy, but the truth was he liked those small lapses. It made the office feel more homey—and the office was practically the only home Ormson had.

The wind whistled behind him, around the corner of the office, where giant panel of window glass met giant panel of window glass. The wind always whistled out here. When you're on the thirtieth floor of an office building there's always a certain amount of wind.

Only it seemed to Ormson that there was an echo of wings unfolding in the wind. He shivered and glowered at the screen, at the message one of his clerks had sent him, with research details for one of his upcoming trials. Even with the screen turned on, he could still see a reflection of himself in it—salt-and-pepper hair that had once been dark, and blue eyes, shaped exactly like Tom's.

He wondered if Tom was still alive and where he was. Damn it. It shouldn't be this difficult. None of this should be so difficult. He'd made partner, he'd gotten married, he'd had a son. By now, Tom was supposed to be in Yale, or if he absolutely had to rebel, in Harvard, working on his law degree. Tom was supposed to be his son. Not the constant annoyance of a thorn on the side, a burr under the saddle.

But Tom had been trouble from the first step he'd taken—when he'd held onto the side table and toppled Sylvia's favorite Ming vase. And it hadn't got any better when it had progressed to petty car theft, to pot smoking, to the school complaining he was sexually harassing girls. It just kept getting harder and harder and harder.

He thought he heard a tinkle of glass far off and stopped breathing, listening. But no sound followed and, through the glass door, he saw no movement in the darkened office. There was nothing. He was imagining things, because he had thought of Tom.

Hell, even Sylvia hadn't wanted Tom. She'd started having an affair with another doctor at the hospital and taken off with her boyfriend to Florida and married him, and set about having a family, and she'd never, never again even bothered to send Tom a birthday card. Not after that first year. And then Tom . . .

This time the noise was more definite, closer by.

Edward rose from his desk, his fingertips touching the desktop, as if for support. He told himself there were no such thing as dragons. He told himself people didn't shift into dragons and back again.

Every time he told himself that. Every time. And it didn't make any difference. There were still . . . Tom had still . . .

No sound from the office, and he drew in a deep breath and started to sit down. He'd turn off the computer, pack up and go . . . well, not home. His condo wasn't a home. But he'd go back to the condo, and have a drink and call one of the suitably long list of arm candy who'd been vying to be Mrs. Ormson for the last few months, and see if she wanted to go to dinner somewhere nice. If he was lucky, he wouldn't have to sleep alone.

"Ormsssson."

His office door had opened, noiselessly, and through it whistled the sort of breeze that hit the thirtieth floor when one of the windows had been broken. It was more of a wind. He could hear paper rustling, tumbling about, a roaring of wind, and a tinkle as someone's lamp or monitor fell over.

And the head pushing through the door was huge, reptilian, armed with many teeth that glimmered even in the scant light. Edward had seen it only once. He'd seen . . . other dragons. Tom not the least of them. But he hadn't seen this dragon. Not more than once. That had been when Edward had been hired to defend a triad member accused—and guilty—of a particularly gruesome and pointless murder.

This creature had appeared, shortly after Edward had gotten his client paroled, and while Edward was trying to convince him to go away for a while and not to pursue a bloody course of revenge that would have torn the triad apart—and, incidentally, got him dead or back in jail.

This dragon—they called him the great something dragon?—had flapped down from the sky and— Edward remembered his client's body falling from a great height, the two pieces of it tumbling down to the asphalt. And the blood. The blood.

He swallowed bile, hastily, and stood fully again. Stood. Ready to run. Which was foolish, because the thing blocked his office door, and his huge, many-fanged head rested on its massive paws. There was nowhere Edward could run.

The dragon blinked huge, green eyes at him, and, as with a cat's secretly satisfied expression, he gave the impression of smiling. A long forked tongue licked at the lipless mouth. "Ormson," it said, still somehow managing to give the impression that the word was composed mostly of sibilants.

"Yes?" Edward asked, and found his voice wavering and uncertain. "How may I help you?"

"Your whelp has stolen something of mine," the dragon said. Its voice was only part noise. The other part was a feeling, like a scratch at the back of the brain. It made you want to flip up your cranium and scratch.

"My . . .?"

"Your son. Thomas. He's stolen the Pearl of Heaven."

Edward's mouth was dry. He opened it to say this was entirely Tom's business, but he found himself caught in an odd crux. If Tom had stolen something, then Tom was still alive. Still alive five years after being kicked out of the house. Had he learned something? Had he shaped up? He almost had to, hadn't he, or he would be dead by now? No one could continue going the way Tom had been going and still be alive after five years on their own, could they?

He swallowed hard. But Tom had stolen something. This seemed to imply he'd learned nothing. He'd not changed.

He clenched his hands so tightly that his nails bit into his palm. How could Tom still be a problem? How could he? Didn't he know how hard he made it on his father? Didn't he care?

"I don't know what my son has done," he said, and his voice came out creditably firm. "I haven't seen him in more than five years. You cannot hold me responsible for what he has done."

"He has stolen the Pearl of Heaven," the dragon rumbled, his eyes half closed and still giving that look of a secret smile.

"So, he's stolen some jewelry," Edward said. "Get it from him. I don't care."

Did he care? What if they killed Tom? Edward didn't know. He didn't even know if it would grieve him anymore. It wasn't supposed to be this hard. He'd been saying that since Tom was one. And it hadn't got any easier.

"It's not that easy," the dragon said. "The Pearl is . . . dragon magic. Ancient. It was given to us by the Emperor of Heaven. It will not do him any good, but it is the center of our strength. We need it, or we shall fall apart."

Great. Tom would manage to steal some cultic object. Hell, if he found an idol with an eye made of ruby, he'd dig the ruby out just to see what would happen. And Edward remembered all too well the incident in the Met Museum with Tom and the mummy when Tom was five. Other kids just never thought of this kind of trouble to get into.

"So get it. From him. I know nothing of it."

"Ah," the dragon said. And the sound, somehow, managed to convey an impression of disapproval, an impression of denial. "But the child is always the responsibility of the parents, isn't he? Your son has hidden the Pearl of Heaven. It is up to you to find it and give it back to us."

The *or else* remained unspoken, hanging mid-air, more solid, more certain than anything the dragon had said.

"I don't even know where he is," Edward said.

"Goldport, Colorado."

"Fine," Edward said, nodding and trying to look businesslike. He scooped up his laptop, picked up his case from the floor, started pushing the laptop into it. "Fine, fine. I'll call tomorrow. I'll make enquiries. I'll try to figure out where he—"

A many-clawed paw lifted. With unreal, careful precision, it rested atop the briefcase and the laptop and just touched the edge of Edward Ormson's hand. The claw shimmered, like real gold, and ended in an impossibly sharp talon.

"Not tomorrow," the dragon said. "Now."

"Now?" Edward blinked, in confusion, looking down at the talon on his hand, the tip of it pressing just enough to leave a mark, but leaving no doubt that it could press hard enough to skewer the hand through sinew and bone. "But it's what? Nine at night? You can't really book flights at this time of night. Well, not anymore. You can't just show up at the airport and book a flight on a whim. With the security measures that simply doesn't happen anymore."

"No airport," the dragon said, his paw immobile, the pressure of his talon palpable.

"Driving?" Edward asked, and would have sat down, if he weren't so afraid that some stirring, some careless gesture would make the creature stab his hand with that talon. He didn't know what would happen if he did that. He didn't know how Tom had become a dragon, but if the legends were right, then it was through a bite. Or a clawing. "Driving would take much longer. Why don't I book a flight tomorrow. I'll fly out before twenty-four hours. I promise."

"No driving. I'll take you. Now."

"You'll take me?"

The claw withdrew. "Pack your things. Whatever you need to take. I'll take you. Now."

There really wasn't much choice. Less than ten minutes later, Edward was straddling the huge beast's back, holding on tight, while they stood facing the place where the dragon had broken several panels of glass to get in.

There was a moment of fear as the dragon dove through the window, wings closed, and they plunged down toward the busy street.

A scream caught in Edward's throat. Not for the first time, he wondered why no one else saw these creatures. Was he having really vivid hallucinations while locked up in some madhouse?

No. No. He was sure other people saw them. But he was also sure they forgot it as soon as they could. He, himself, tried to forget them every time he saw them. Every time. And then they appeared again.

They plunged dizzily past blind dark offices and fully lit ones, toward the cars on the street below.

At maybe tenth-floor level, the dragon opened his wings, and turned gracefully, gaining height.

Edward was never sure how they flew. He'd always thought thermals . . . But these wings were flapping, vigorously, to gain altitude, and he could feel the back muscles ripple beneath his legs.

He'd put his briefcase's shoulder handle across his chest, bandolier style. And that was good because the dragon's scales were slicker and smoother than they seemed to be, and he had to hold on with both hands to the ridge that ran down the back of the dragon, as the dragon turned almost completely sideways, and gained altitude, flying above the high-rises, above Hudson Bay, circling. Heading out to Colorado. Where Edward was supposed to convince Tom to do something he didn't want to do.

Oh, hell.

"What?" Kyrie asked, looking at Rafiel who stood by the windows, frowning at them.

"This window was broken from the outside," he said. "Something ripped the screen aside, and hammered that window down. From the outside."

"How do you know?" she asked. She was looking at her patio door and wondering how she was going to be able to pay for all that glass. Safety glass, at that, she was sure. "How could you tell?"

"The glass fragments are all on the inside," he said. "And scattered pretty far in."

"The glass fragments for this patio door are pretty much inside, too, but there's a bunch of them outside," she said. "I think you're reading too much into it."

"No," Rafiel said. "I'm no expert, of course. I could bring the lab here, and they could tell you for sure. But—see, on the patio door, the glass is kicked all the way out there, almost halfway through your backyard."

"Which isn't very far," Kyrie said.

"Admittedly," Rafiel said. "But see, the door I'm sure was kicked from the inside. But the windows weren't. There's some glass that crumbled and just fell on that side, but most of it got pushed in here, all the way to the middle of the carpet."

Kyrie looked. There were glass pieces all the way through the room, to the foot of the sofa where Tom had slept. There were spots of blood, too, where Tom had walked on the glass, apparently without noticing.

Suddenly, it was too much for Kyrie, and she sat on the end of the sofa where there was no glass. "How could he?" she asked. "What was he high on, anyway? There was glass everywhere. Why couldn't he feel it? What's wrong with him?"

Rafiel looked puzzled and started to say "Who?—" Then he shook his head. "If you mean Ormson, I think there's a lot more wrong with him than even I could tell you. Though I think I'll do a background check on him tomorrow. His getting that other young punk here worries me. Perhaps he's a dealer? And that guy came by for a hit?"

Kyrie was about to say that she'd never seen any signs that Tom dealt—but what did she have to go on? She had suspected him of it. He'd said he didn't. And, of course, she would trust him because he was a model of virtue and probity. "What is wrong with me?" she asked.

And now Rafiel looked even more puzzled and she almost laughed. Which showed how shocked she was, because there really wasn't anything to laugh about.

The golden eyes gave her the once-over, head to toe. "I don't see anything wrong with you."

For a moment, for just a moment, she could almost smell him, musky and virile like the night before. She got up from the sofa. That was probably what was messing her up. It was all down to pheromones and unconscious reactions and stuff. It was all . . . insane.

She grabbed her right hand with her left, as if afraid what they might do. "Well, that's neither here nor there," she said. "Is it? These windows are going to cost me a fortune, and I will have to work a *bunch* of overtime to pay for it."

"I could talk to my dad. He knows— I could get someone to do the job and you could pay for them on credit."

Kyrie twisted her lips. One thing she had seen, through her growing up years, and that was that families usually went wrong when they started buying things on credit, no matter how necessary it seemed at the time. And since many of the foster families fostered for the money allowance a new kid brought, she had seen a lot of families who had gone financially to the wrong. "No, thank you," she said. "I can take care of myself."

"But this is wide open," he said. "And there's something killing shifters. What if they come for you? How are you going to defend yourself? I have to protect you. We're partners in solving this crime, remember?"

Kyrie remembered. But she also remembered that she wasn't sure what all this meant to Rafiel. And didn't want to know. She'd been a fool for trusting Tom. She'd be damned if she was going to repeat the mistake with Rafiel. What if he had the door fixed in a way that he could, somehow, come in and kill her in the night?

She couldn't figure out any reason why he would want to kill her. But then, she couldn't figure out any reason why anyone would want to go around killing other shapeshifters. It had to be a shifter. Only a shifter would smell them. So, what would he get out of killing his own kind? And who better to do it than a policeman?

"No, thank you," she said, again. "You don't have to take care of me. I can take care of myself. I've been doing it all my life. Pretty successfully, as you see."

"But—"

"No buts, Officer Trall." Without seeming to, she edged around him, and guided him through the doorway from the sun-porch into the kitchen. She locked the door to the outside, then grabbed the extra chair and wedged it under the doorknob, the way she'd secured her bedroom in countless foster homes, when she'd been lucky enough to have a room for herself. "You'd best leave now. I need to have something to eat, and then I'll go to the Athens early. The day shift is often a person late, and if I can pitch in at dinnertime, I can work some overtime, and that will help pay for this . . . mess."

As if taken off balance by her sudden forcefulness, he allowed himself to be shepherded all the way out the kitchen door.

"Thank you again," Kyrie said. And almost told him it had been lovely. Which could apply to the luncheon, but certainly was a gross overstatement when it came to the autopsy, and just plain silly when applied to what they found back here. Which, admittedly, wasn't his fault.

He was still staring at her, the golden eyes somehow managing to look sheepish, when she closed the door in his face. And locked it.

Alone in the house for the first time in almost twenty-four hours, she rushed to the bedroom. She needed to get out of her skirt and into jeans and a t-shirt. Then she'd eat something—at a guess bread, because she imagined that Tom would have eaten every ounce of protein in the house—and get out of here. The diner had to be safer. More people, more witnesses.

Although it hadn't helped the guy last night, had it?

She shuddered at the thought of that bloodied body on the slab. She would park up front, she decided. On Fairfax Avenue. Within plain sight of everyone.

"Damn," Keith said, after a while of driving in silence.

"What now?" Tom asked. He'd been sitting there, his head in his hands, trying to figure out what he was going to do next. He felt as if his life, over the last six months, was a carefully constructed castle of cards that someone had poked right in the middle and sent tumbling.

If Kyrie was no better than him, then maybe it was something wrong with the nature of shifters. Maybe that was why everyone he'd met was a drifter, or . . .

"I forgot to tell you why I came looking for you," Keith said.

"I thought it was to make sure I was all right," Tom said.

"Well." Keith nodded. "That was part of it, only . . . I went to pay the rent today and I got to talking to the building manager about what happened at your apartment and she said . . . The manager got a bunch of your things from the floor. Before she called the police to look at it."

"The police? To look at my things?" Tom asked. He was trying to imagine why the woman would do that. She was a little old lady who looked Italian or Greek and who had always seemed pretty nice to him.

"No, you fool. She got the things before the police came over, because she figured they were your things and you might need them, and the police would just tie them up."

"Oh, what did she get?"

"I don't know. It looked like was some of your clothes, and your boots, and a credit card."

Tom blinked. "I don't have a credit card." Had one of the triad dropped his credit card behind? Tom hadn't been impressed by the collective intelligence of the dragon enforcer trio, but that seemed too stupid even for them.

"Your ATM card, then."

"Oh."

"The manager said it was none of the police's business. She asked me to bring you by for your stuff." Keith looked at Tom. "But maybe I should take you to emergency first. For your feet?"

"No," Tom said. First, because he had enough experience in his own body to know that any wound would heal up seemingly overnight. And second because if he could get some clothes on, and his hand on his ATM card, he was going to find some stuff to buy. Heroin, by choice, but just about anything else would do, short of baking soda. This time he was going to get high and stay high. He would be feeling no pain.

CHAPTER

⇥ 5 ⇤

In jeans and a comfortable T-shirt, Kyrie went into the kitchen. She felt naked without the earring she normally wore. She'd found it in a street fair when she was fourteen and it had been her favorite piece of jewelry since. But there was no point crying over spilt milk or spoiled jewelry. She had lost it somewhere at Tom's house, while becoming a panther. She would have to look out for another one.

Meanwhile she needed to eat something, even if just bread and butter.

She put the kettle on for tea, and opened the fridge to see if perhaps a couple rounds of her lunch meat had survived. And was shocked to find eggs and bacon still sitting on the shelf, where she had left them. Looking at the containers, she determined he'd eaten about a third of her provisions. Which meant she would still have enough for the rest of the week, even if she shifted once or twice.

She'd long ago decided to make breakfast her main protein meal of the day. Even if she ate breakfast at the time other people ate dinner. Eggs and bacon, particularly bought on a sale, were far cheaper than meat for other meals.

She got the microwave bacon tray, and noticed Tom had washed it very carefully. She put the pan on for eggs, and again noticed it had been scrubbed with a soft, plastic scrubber, per manufacturer instructions for nonstick pans. Sitting at her little table, washing down the food with a cup of sweet tea—which she preferred to coffee unless she felt a need to wake up suddenly—she felt vaguely guilty about throwing Tom out.

Then she realized the source of her guilt was that he'd actually made an effort to wash the dishes and that, as ravenous as he must have been—she remembered what she'd felt like at the restaurant—he hadn't eaten all of her food. She smiled to herself. So, it was fine if the man were a one-person demolition engine, as long as he had good household habits?

She shook her head. Okay, she clearly was going soft in the head. Perhaps it was the shifter-bond. But if so, couldn't she feel more tenderly toward Rafiel? Was the way to her heart to give as much trouble and cause as much damage as humanly possible?

After washing her dishes, she grabbed her purse and hurried toward the Athens. She'd park up front. With the driver's window in the state it was, she didn't want to leave the car unwatched, anyway. She'd park up front, and keep an eye on it through her work shift.

Hopefully the diner would be short-staffed for the dinner shift, the last few hours of the day staff. Hopefully. They usually were, but then things never went the way one wanted them to, did they? And she'd have to buy another apron from Frank's stock, kept for when a staff member walked out of the job with the apron still on. Another expense.

She checked the chair under the lock between the kitchen and the back porch before leaving the house.

"We were all very worried something dreadful had happened to you," Mrs. Rizzo looked at him, her sparkling black eyes narrowed in what might indeed be worry. Or suspicion. Though that wasn't fair, because she'd never been suspicious of him.

A small woman, so short that she made Tom feel tall, she stood in front of her desk in the little, musty manager's office at the back of the apartment complex. Every possible inch of space on her wall was covered up in pictures—pictures of smiling brides, pictures of babies, and pictures of children looking sticky and sweet in equal measures and displaying mouths with a varying number of teeth in unguarded smiles. A set of pink booties, half knit, lay on her desk, with a gigantic ball of pink yarn and two green plastic knitting needles.

Tom had often wanted to ask her if the pictures were all her children, but he was a little afraid of the answer, and not quite sure if yes or no would be the scarier reply. Instead, he threw back his head to move the hair out from in front of his face—he really needed to find something to tie it soon. A rubber band would do—and smiled at Mrs. Rizzo. "Fortunately I was staying with a friend."

She cocked an eyebrow at him. "A girl?"

"Yes. She works with me."

Mrs. Rizzo grinned, suddenly. "Well, and isn't it about time you found someone to settle down. Is she a good girl?"

"Yes, a very good girl," Tom said. Or at least he'd thought that until today, and finding out about the sugar. But he wasn't about to discuss that with his apartment manager.

The lady nodded. "Good, maybe you can stay with her until we get your place fixed. It should only be a couple of weeks. Or we could move you to number 35, if you want. I talked to the owner, and he said it would be okay to give it to you. It's a little bigger, but he said you could have it for the same price."

A few hours ago, this would have been an offer for Tom to snatch with both hands. He could have got into the new apartment without paying a deposit, and with no real inconvenience. Oh, his furniture and utensils were gone, but he hadn't had all that much, and he could always replace them in a month or less from thrift shops and garage sales. A sofa first, until he could afford a bed, and a pan and a frying pan would do for cooking in, till he could get more complete utensils. And . . .

But he stopped his own thought, forcefully. He would have been very happy to do that a few hours ago. It would have made him non-homeless again. But a few hours ago, he now realized, he'd still been under the mistaken impression that Kyrie was some sort of ideal woman, something to aspire to. Someone whom, even if he could never have her, he could imitate and hope to be more like. Now . . .

"I don't know what I'm doing, yet, Mrs. Rizzo. I'll let you know in a couple of days, if that's all right." Of course he knew perfectly well what he was doing. He was getting heck out of Dodge before nightfall. He might come back later—if he could—for the . . . object in the water tank of the Athens's bathroom. But he wouldn't come back to live. He wouldn't go back to working there—with Kyrie. No way, no when, no how. And no one could make him.

Mrs. Rizzo sighed. "You're staying with her, right? Well, I hope it works. But if it doesn't, remember we have number thirty five. I'll hold it for you for another week." She smiled. "It's the one with the bay window." And sounded exactly like someone holding out a sweet to a kid.

Tom nodded. "I'll be in touch. But Keith said you had some of my stuff . . ."

She reached behind the desk and brought out a box that was larger than Tom expected. Protruding out of the top were his boots, and he gave a deep sigh of relief upon seeing them. Then, as he dug through, he found a couple of pairs of jeans, one black and one blue, three black T-shirts, and—carefully folded—his black leather jacket. He felt suddenly weak at the knees. It was like losing half of your identity and then retrieving it again.

At the very bottom of the box was his ATM card, and he found himself taking a deep, relieved breath. He wouldn't need to wait till the banks opened to get out his money before he got out of town. Next to the ATM card was a library book—*The Book of Sand* by Jorge Luis Borges. He could drop that off at the library depot on the way out of town. Good. The library was unlikely to make much of a search for him on the strength of a single hardcover book, but it was best to get out of town with as few things hanging over his head as possible.

Between the book and the ATM card was a red object, which at first he couldn't identify. And then he realized it was Kyrie's red plumed earring.

He should take it back. He should . . . His hand closed around it. Or not. Or not. He couldn't see facing her. He couldn't imagine her reproaching him for getting high and destroying her sunroom. He would have to tell her, then, that the least she could have done was tell him that the sugar wasn't exactly sugar. She must keep the real stuff somewhere. After all, they'd had coffee the night before to no ill effects. So, why didn't she tell him where it was? Tom would much rather have had it.

His hand closed on the plumed earring and he shoved it into the pocket of his jacket.

"You can change in the bathroom," Mrs. Rizzo said, pointing to a little door at the back. "If you want to."

The bathroom was a continuation of the office. Oh, there were no pictures on the walls, which was a very good thing. Tom would have hated to undress completely in front of a mass of staring babies and prim brides. But the hand soap was pink and shaped like a rose, and, on the toilet tank, a much-too-tall crochet angel with a plastic face, squatted contentedly over three spare toilet paper rolls, as though hoping they would soon hatch into chickens.

Tom had to watch that, and the mirror, and the vanity, because the bathroom was so small he could barely move in it. He removed Kyrie's jogging suit, folded it carefully, and put it beside the toilet paper angel. Then he put on his jeans and T-shirt with a sense of relief. He wished some of his underwear had been preserved, but if absolutely needed he could do without it a little longer.

Socks were something else—as was the need to put his boots back on. He hadn't felt any pain from his feet recently, but then he'd been . . . busy. He sat down on the closed toilet lid, to look at his feet. And was surprised to find he'd shed most of the glass shards. Only a couple large ones remained, embedded in his skin, but his skin seemed to be . . . He stared at it. Yep. His skin was pushing them out, forcing them out and growing behind them. The other cuts were already closed, though angry red and likely to leave a scar.

This was one of those changes that arrived when he started shifting into a dragon. All of a sudden, he could cut himself or scrape himself and it would heal in a day, or a few hours, depending on the depth of the injury. It was just about the only change that wasn't completely unwelcome.

He washed the bottom of his feet with damp toilet paper, and looked again. Nothing really. Just rapidly healing cuts. He slipped his boots on, wishing he had socks, but it couldn't be helped. With all his belongings still in a box, he went back to Mrs. Rizzo. "I'm sorry to bother you, but could I borrow a plastic bag? It's easier to carry than a box." Meaning, it would actually be possible to carry while he was in dragon form. Which was how he'd kept most of his belongings, while moving all over the country.

She nodded, and bent to get something from behind her desk. Tom wondered what exactly she kept back there, just as she emerged with a backpack, not a plastic bag. The backpack was pale blue and made in the sort of plastic that glistens. "The Michelsons left it behind, when they vacated number 22," Mrs. Rizzo said. "It used to have wheels, but they're broken. They left a bunch of the kids' old clothes, too. Ripped and dirty." She made a face. "When people do that, I wash them and fix them and give them to charities in town. Such a waste. People throw everything away these days. But the backpack I kept, if someone moved in with a school-age kid and needed it."

"It's all right," Tom said. "I only need a plastic bag."

"No, no. It's okay. You can have it. There will be two or three others by September, when school opens. People throw them away."

Well, the backpack was more practical because it closed. Though, in dragon form, he would still have to carry it the same way—by wrapping the straps around his huge ankle—the backpack zipped shut. And there was less chance of losing stuff. "Well, thank you then," he said, reaching for it.

Up close, as he stuffed his remaining belongings—and Kyrie's jogging suit—into it, he realized the full extent of his problem. The backpack had a little orange dragon with stubby wings on the back, and it said underneath, in fiery orange-red letters, "Scorchio." He scowled at it.

"Kids these days like the weirdest things, don't they?" Mrs. Rizzo said.

"Yes," Tom said. And then, with everything in the backpack, he had to say good-bye somehow. Only he'd never said good-bye to anyone or anything, and certainly not to anyone who liked him and whom he liked. "I'll be back," he lied. "In a few days."

"You do that, dear," she said. "I'll hold number 35 for you, okay?"

As he headed out, he caught a glimpse of his reflection in the window of the next door apartment. Against the dark drapes, he looked like something out of a horror movie—unruly hair, tight black jeans, black leather jacket. Even with the stupid pale blue backpack on, he didn't look like anyone that someone would want to bother.

He stalked off, down Fairfax Avenue, away from the Athens and toward the nearest ATM that way. He had a vague idea that he should go back and pay Kyrie for the mess. He would have done it the day before. But now he told himself there was simply no way. Not any way in hell. She should have told him about the sugar. It was all her fault. Yeah, he probably still owed her for the car—but because of the sugar he was now headed out of town, with nothing but a handful of possessions. He was going to need all his money.

He realized he was holding her responsible for the fact that she wasn't perfect. And that was fine, as far as he was concerned. Wasn't there someone—one person—in the world he could look up to?

"When is your break?" Rafiel asked. He'd been sitting at one of the small tables in the extension room that used to be the sun porch of the Athens and had been enclosed, sometime decades away, to make more space for tables.

Like a sun porch, it was informally furnished. Just plastic tables and chairs, of the type people used outside. On a Friday like this, and when the dinner hour was in full swing, it filled up fast.

A family group or a gaggle of laughing and screaming students surrounded every other table. Only Rafiel sat alone.

She'd smiled at him when first serving him, and the rest of the time she'd avoided looking too closely at him, as she served the noisy groups around him. But now she was pouring a warm-up of coffee into his cup, and he said, "Come on, please? I need to talk to you."

She would believe him a lot more and talk to him with a far clearer conscience if she couldn't detect, as an undertone to his soap and aftershave smell, the lion's spicy-hot scent. She didn't trust herself around that smell. She behaved very stupidly around it. Instead, she made a big show of looking around, as if mentally counting people.

"No way for the next hour or so," she said. "I have to keep refills and desserts and all coming. They allowed me to work because they were two people short. There's no way I can take a break."

To her surprise, he smiled. "Okay, then. I'll have the bowl of rice pudding. A la mode." He lowered his voice, "And then I want to talk to you. There's some very odd autopsy results."

Stealing the car wasn't hard. Tom walked along the darkened working class neighborhoods first, looking at all the old models of cars parked on the street.

It had to be an old model, because his way of starting a car without a key wouldn't work on the newer models. And in those streets, around Fairfax, with their tiny, decrepit brick houses, the cars spotted with primer on the front, there was a prospect on every corner. He could steal a dozen cars, if he wanted to.

Half a dozen times, he walked up to a sickly looking two-door sedan, a rusted and disreputable pickup and put his hand on the door handle, while he felt in his pocket for the stone he'd picked up from a flower bed near his apartment. The only other piece of equipment necessary to this operation was a screwdriver, which he'd bought from a corner convenience store.

He had everything. So, why didn't he just smash the window, break the ignition housing, start the car, and drive away? Most of these houses looked empty and people were probably still at work or already asleep.

But he'd put his hand on the handle, and reach for the rock, and remember how hard it was to make ends meet from his job at the Athens. How he had never been able to buy a car, but used to read the Sunday paper vehicles for sale ads with the relish of a kid looking through a candy-store window.

From those ads, he knew many of these cars would be a few hundred dollars, no more. But a few hundred dollars was all he had in his pocket, and it had emptied his account. And accumulating it had required endless small sacrifices, in what food he ate, in what clothes he wore. Hell, he didn't even shop the thrift stores at full price. It was always at half-price or dollar-day sales.

Oh, he wasn't complaining. He was lucky to have a job, given his past work history and his lack of training. Correction. He'd been lucky to have a job. Now it was over and he'd be lucky to ever have another. What were the owners of these cars employed at? What did they do?

Fuming, he turned away. Damn. This going-straight thing was like some sort of disease. You caught it, and then you had the hardest trouble getting rid of it. They probably didn't sell honesty-be-gone tablets at the local drugstore.

He walked down one of the cracked sidewalks that ran along the front of the pocket-sized lawns, kicking a stray piece of concrete here and there, to vent his anger. Damn. He couldn't walk out of the city on foot. And he wasn't at all sure he could start flying from inside the city. What if someone saw him? What if . . . *they* saw him?

He walked along as a thin rain started trickling down on him from the sky above. The rain felt . . . odd. He'd been living in Colorado for six months and this was the first time he'd seen rain. There was a feeling of strangeness, at first, and then, despite the warmth of the night, discomfort at water seeping everywhere and dripping from his hair onto the back of his neck, running down the back of his jacket.

He walked a long time on his still-tender feet and passed a roped-in car dealership. But it was the sort of car dealership you got in this kind of area—selling fifth-or sixth-hand cars. Of course, he thought, as he walked past, his hand idly touching the rope that marked off the lot, he could probably break into those cars far more easily than into any others. But . . . he stared at the wrecks and semi-wrecks under the moonlight. What were the chances that the owner of this lot was living so close to the bone that the theft of a car would really hurt him?

Tom looked at the facade of the dealership proper, and it was a well-known car dealer. Chances were they'd never feel it. His hand weighed the stone in his pocket.

On the other hand . . . On the other hand, the theft of a car—or one more car, as Tom doubted this would be the first—might be what caused the dealership to close doors at this location, to give up on this neighborhood, perhaps to give up on this level of car, at all. And then people in this neighborhood would find it harder to get a car. Perhaps harder to find jobs.

Tom dropped the stone out of his jacket pocket and kicked it violently aside. Then he dropped the screwdriver after it. He walked down the road, his hands shoved deep in his pockets.

He would have to walk, as far as he could out of Goldport. He'd go south, toward New Mexico. Lots of empty space that way, less chance of someone seeing or noticing a dragon flying against the sky. But damn, he could get much, much farther if he could ride. As it was, he'd almost surely get caught by the three dragons. And this time he would have to face them alone.

He realized he was chewing on his lower lip, as he walked down the street where the dilapidated houses gave way to houses in even worse state but divided into apartments, and then to warehouses tagged with the occasional gang graffiti.

He pulled the collar up on his leather jacket. Even with the ridiculous backpack on his back, he didn't think anyone would challenge him. Not for a moment.

Knowing this trip was likely to end in his death, he wished he could buy something to make it easier. Not a lot. Probably nothing to inject. Just some pot to smoke, to ease his nerves. He was going to die, he might as well go easy. Besides, he'd seen there was no point trying to escape the grip of drugs, if even Kyrie did them.

In his six months in the city, he'd seen plenty of drug dealers standing around in shady corners, waiting. This was the type of neighborhood to attract them. But perhaps the rain, unaccustomed in Colorado, had driven them indoors. Tom couldn't see anyone, and certainly not anyone with that pose of alert shiftiness that identified a dealer. He had money. He was willing. But no one was selling.

"Damn dealers," he muttered to himself under his breath. "Just like cops. Never around when you need one."

Wide awake and hopeless, he headed south and west while the sun set and the breeze grew cooler, ruffling at his damp hair, his soaking jeans.

✢ ✢ ✢

"Frank, do we have rice pudding?" Kyrie asked, coming near the counter.

Frank looked up with a frown, from a talk he'd been having with three customers seated at the part of the counter where you could get food served. His girlfriend wasn't around again, tonight, so he was in a mood. "I just came in and I haven't made any. If there's any, it's leftover from yesterday."

Well, it was all gone, then. But before Kyrie could turn to go give Rafiel the bad news, Frank added, "Is Tom coming in later?"

"Tom?" Kyrie didn't know what to say. She honestly had no idea. And for just a moment was startled that Frank would ask her about Tom. Except that of course, last night she'd taken time off to take medicine to Tom. Or at least that was what she had told Frank. And then she'd told Frank that Tom was in really bad shape and she had to take him home with her and watch him.

"I don't know," she said. "He left my place a few hours ago."

"Do you know where he was going?"

She shook her head. "He was with his friend. The guy who lives downstairs from him," Kyrie said, as she pulled a stray strand of hair behind her ear. And as she did, the customers at the counter looked up. And she froze.

They were the three from the night before. The three dragons. None of them permanently injured, as far as she could tell, though she was sure she'd got the eye of at least one of them in the battle.

But they sat there, at the counter, uninjured, and the middle one even had his hair arranged, as artificially perfect and smooth as before. They all wore tight jeans and satin-like shimmering jackets, with dragons in the back. They looked like something out of a bad karate movie, and Kyrie was so shocked at seeing them here, in . . . well, the glare of the fluorescent lights, that she didn't know what to do.

Red Dragon was the one sitting next to where Kyrie stood. He backed away from her, his eyes wide, and said something in Chinese that sounded like a panic attack.

The middle one said something in return, something she couldn't understand, and put his hand into his pocket, pulling out a sheaf of bills, which he laid on the counter. And then, the three geniuses, in massed disarray, started toward the door. A process only slightly hampered by the fact that not one of them was willing to turn his back on Kyrie. So they moved backward as a group, bumping into tables and booths, snagging on girls' purses and men's coats, and muttering stuff in Chinese that might be apologies or threats.

Clearly, they were rattled enough to forget their English. Clearly, they thought that Kyrie's panther form was too dangerous to anger. Although why they thought she would shift into a panther right then and take them to pieces in front of the diner patrons was beyond her.

Pulling and shoving at each other, they got to the door, then in a tinkling of the bells suspended from it, out of it, tumbling onto the sidewalk where the lights were starting to show, faintly, against the persistent glow of the sunset.

"What was that all about?" Frank asked. "Did those guys know you?"

"I have no clue," Kyrie said, choosing to answer the first question. And this was the absolute truth. She couldn't figure out why they would be scared of her. After all, even if she had been so stupid as to shift here, in the middle of the diner, they could have shifted too, and then they would have had the upper hand. There were three of them, after all.

Unless . . . She smiled faintly at the thought. *Unless the total idiots thought this was a shifter diner and that everyone here would be shifters.* If Tom was right the shifting was ancient, well established in their culture, and perhaps passed on in families. They had a lore and a culture. For people like that it must be utterly bewildering when strangers shifted. *Perhaps they think we too band together.*

Frank was glowering at her, and she realized she was still smiling. He reached for the plates and cups the guys had left on the counter and pulled them down, near the cleaning area, by the dishwasher, glowering all the while and banging the utensils around so much that, if they weren't break-resistant, they would probably have shattered.

"What's wrong?" Kyrie asked.

But he just glowered at her some more, grabbed a dish towel from the counter, and wiped at the serving surface with it. "Oh, nothing.

Everything is fine and dandy. You and Tom and . . ." He lifted his hands, upward, as though signifying his inability to understand any of them.

Kyrie skidded back to the sun-porch, to give Rafiel the distressing news about the rice pudding.

"There's no rice pudding," she said. "And the three dragons who were at Tom's apartment were just here."

"The dragons?" he said and started to rise. "Here?"

"In human form," she said. "They left." She frowned. "They seemed afraid of me."

He looked at her a long moment, then shook his head. "I don't know what to do. I wonder why they were here."

"Looking for Tom," she said.

"Oh." He looked out the window. "We could follow them, but there's only two of us—"

"And neither of us can fly," Kyrie said. "Besides, there's only one of us. I'm working. But since there's no rice pudding, you're free to follow them."

He just grinned up at her. "Oh, bring me pie à la mode, then. I don't care. I'm in it for the vanilla ice cream." And he winked at her.

"What kind of pie?"

"I told you I don't care," he said. "Just bring me a wedge."

"Green bean pie it is, then," she said, and walked away. To bump into Anthony, the last of the day shift to leave. He was in his street clothes, which, in his case were usually elaborate and today consisted of a ruffled button-down white shirt, red vest and immaculate black pants. "Hey," he said. "What's up with Frank? He's acting like a bear with two heads."

Kyrie shrugged and Anthony sighed. "What that man needs," he said, as if this summed up the wisdom of the ages, "is to get laid. He seriously needs to get laid. His girlfriend hasn't been in for too long." And with that, he twirled on his heels and made for the door. Kyrie had often wondered if in his free time he was a member of some dance troupe. At least that would explain the bizarre clothes.

Kyrie went back to scout out the pie, though the only choices were apple and lemon. She chose lemon, figuring he would like it less, and put two scoops of ice cream on the plate with it. It wasn't so much that she wanted to thwart Rafiel—but a man who ordered with that kind of complacency did deserve green bean pie. Or at least Brussels sprouts. Too bad they didn't have any on the menu.

She took the plate of pie in one hand, the carafe in the other, set the pie in front of Rafiel and went off, from table to table, warming up people's coffees.

Despite her best efforts to banish it, the image of Frank getting laid was stuck in her mind. She looked across the diner at Frank, behind the counter, his Neanderthal-like features still knit in a glower. She shuddered. There were things the human mind was not supposed to contemplate.

Edward Ormson's first thought was that they couldn't be in Colorado. Not so fast. Even by airplane it took over three hours. And they couldn't be flying at airplane speeds. Well, they could, but it would have left him frozen as a popsicle sitting astride that dragon.

And he hadn't been frozen, nor gasping for air. The temperature around him had remained even, and he'd felt perfectly comfortable. Only twice, for just a moment, light seemed to vanish from around them. But it was such a brief moment that Edward hadn't had time to think about it. Now he wondered if some magic transfer had taken place at that moment.

Oh, Edward didn't believe in magic. But then he also didn't believe in dragons, he thought and smiled with more irony than joy while the dragon circled down to a parking lot in a street of low-to-the-ground buildings.

They landed softly on the asphalt and the huge wings that had been spread on either side of him, coruscating and sparkling in the light like living fire, closed slowly.

"Down," the dragon said. Or perhaps not said it, because Edward didn't remember sounds. Just the feeling that he should get down. He should get down immediately.

He scrambled off, sliding along scales that felt softer on the skin than they should have.

But once he stood, in the parking lot, holding his briefcase, he realized that the front of his suit had tiny cuts, as though someone had worked it over with very small blades.

He frowned at it, then looked up at the dragon who glowed with some sort of inner fire, in front of him. The beast opened its huge mouth, and all thought of complaining about damages to his clothes fled Ormson's mind.

"Find your son," the dragon said, in that voice that wasn't exactly a voice. "Make him give back what belongs to me."

And, just as suddenly as he'd appeared at Edward Ormson's office, the dragon now stretched its wings, flexed its legs, and was airborne, gaining height.

Alone in the parking lot, Edward became aware that it was raining, a boring, slow rain. Behind him, a little Chinese restaurant called Three Luck Dragon had its open sign out, but there were no cars parked. So either it catered to a local clientele, or it had none.

Did the Great Sky Dragon mean anything by dropping Edward off here? Or was it simply the first convenient place they'd come to?

Edward saw the curtain twitch on the little window, and a face peer out. The lighting and the distance didn't allow him to see features, but he thought it would be the proprietors looking to see if he intended to come in.

Well, today was their lucky day. He'd go in and order something, and get out his cell phone. He would bet now he knew where Tom had last been seen, he would be able to find the boy with half a dozen phone calls.

One way or another, he always ended up cleaning up after his son.

Western towns don't taper off. Or at least that was what Tom had seen, ever since his drifting had brought him west and south to Colorado, New Mexico, and Arizona. You walked down a street, surrounded nice Victorian homes and suddenly you're amid five-floor brick warehouses, with the noises of loading and unloading, of packing and making of things resounding within.

And then, a couple of blocks away, you were in the middle of a high prairie, with tumbleweed blowing around. Looking back, you could still see the warehouses, but they were so incongruous that they seemed to be part of another world.

Tom turned to look at the dark edge of the warehouses. He stood on what had abruptly become a country road, its asphalt cracked underfoot. Looking just beyond where he was standing, he saw nothing but an underpass, just ahead. Why there was an underpass was a question he couldn't answer, as it was just two country roads meeting. Perhaps this was what people complained about, with public projects that made no sense.

But right then Tom was grateful of the underpass. In this landscape of brown grass and blowing tumbleweeds, there wasn't much cover, otherwise. He made for the underpass and stripped quickly, shoving all his clothes and boots into the little backpack with the happy dragon on the back. The boots were a tight fit into the small space, but he got them in, and zipped the thing. Then he loosened the back straps to their outmost, and put them around his wrist.

Willing yourself to shift was like willing yourself to die. Because the process of shifting, no matter how easy, always hurt. It took desire to do it, but it needed something else. He got out from under the overpass, and stood—naked in the moonlight, willing his body to shift, willing.

A cough shook him, another, heralding the preliminary spasms that often preceded the shape-shifting. Pain twisted in his limbs, wracked his back, as his body tried to extrude wings from itself. He opened his mouth and let the scream come—something he never did within a city—the scream of pain of his human self, the scream of triumph from the ancient beast once more let forth.

A car drove by, toward the outside of town. One of the tiny SUVs in white. A Kia or a Hyundai or one of those. Tom's confused senses were aware of its turning around and then zooming past again. But no one came out. *Worse comes to worst*, his still rational mind thought, as his body shifted. *They'll just call 911. And good luck with convincing a dispatcher they just saw a dragon.*

In the next moment it no longer mattered. The dragon was him. He was the dragon. His body fully shifted, Tom spread his wings fully, feeling the caress of wind and rain on them. He opened his mouth and roared, this time in triumph. His vision sharpened. He was in a vast non-cave. And the dragon knew they should go to ground, they should find a cave.

No, the human part of Tom said. *No. Not to a cave. We're flying west. Deep west, until we come to a town. We'll follow the highway that will take us to Las Vegas, New Mexico, by early morning. Then . . . cave.*

The dragon blinked, confused, because the image in its mind, for a cave, had mattresses and pillows and other things that made sense only to the human. But it had learned, over the years, to trust the ape cowering away at the back of its mind.

It trusted it now, even when it found something wrapped tightly around its front paw. The human mind said they were clothes, and that they shouldn't be discarded.

The dragon harrumphed, loudly. Then spread its wings again, sensing the air currents. Half of flying was coasting. If you needed to beat your wings the whole time, you were going to die of tiredness soon.

He felt the currents. He flapped a little. He gained altitude. He headed out of town.

"Break?" Rafiel asked.

Kyrie was about to shake her head, but stopped. The dinnertime crowd had thinned. Students had left for concerts or movies or whatever it was that college students did with their evenings. And the families, too, had vanished, probably home to their comfy chairs and their TVs.

The only two people in the diner were a man at the back, who seemed to be signing the credit card slip that Kyrie had dropped on his table. And Rafiel.

Kyrie looked at the wall clock. Ten-thirty p.m. That meant there would be a lull till eleven or thereabouts, when the late-night people would start coming in. And she only needed ten minutes.

She backtracked to the counter and put away the carafe she'd just used to give Rafiel a warm up. "Frank, is it okay if I take ten minutes?" she asked.

Frank turned around. He was still glowering. "Fine. It's fine," he said, as if he were saying that it was all completely wrong.

"Is there a problem?" Kyrie asked taken aback.

"No. I just wish your boyfriend had given us some warning before he decided to disappear."

"He's not due for an hour or so. I came in early," Kyrie said. "And he's not my boyfriend."

But it was hardly worth arguing. And Frank looked to be in a worse mood than she'd ever seen him. "I'll take a break now," she said. "If Tom doesn't come in, it's going to be a hellish shift, and that way I'll be able to stay till five a.m., okay?"

Frank shrugged, which looked like consent. He was grilling a bunch of burgers, though Kyrie had no idea why, given the deserted look of the diner. Perhaps he was precooking them a bit to allow him to cook them faster later on. It wasn't any of her business, in any case.

She backtracked to the enclosed-porch addition. Rafiel must have heard, or watched her conversation. He was standing as she approached. "Ready?"

She nodded. And gestured with her head toward the door at the back of the extension that led to the parking lot. She didn't want to go to the parking lot again. Truly, she didn't. On the other hand, neither did she want to talk to Rafiel in front of Frank. Frank was likely to decide that Rafiel was also her boyfriend and hold her responsible for whatever the policeman did in the future.

She had no idea what had gotten into her boss. He was usually grumpy, but not like this. And then there was Anthony's idea, which made her make a face, as she led Rafiel out the back door and onto the parking lot.

This time the parking lot was deserted, there was no smell of blood, and she took care to stay in the shadow of the building, out of the light of the moon.

Rafiel made a sound that seemed suspiciously close to a purr as he got outside, and he stretched his arms. "Do you feel it?" he asked, giving Kyrie a sidelong glance. "Do you feel the call?"

"No," Kyrie said, as curtly as she could. It was a lie, but only in a way. Yeah, she could feel the call, but she could feel the call every night. And it seemed to her Rafiel was speaking of another call. And there, as if on cue, she noticed his smell again. No, not his smell. His smell was soap and a little aftershave, nothing out of the ordinary. But the smell exuding from him right now was a thick, feline musk that made her think of running through the jungles, of hunting, of . . . "You said you had news that pertained to the corpse?" she said, turning her head away.

"Yeah," he said, and looked away from her, as though her turning her head to get fresh air, slightly less tainted by his musk, were an insult. "Yeah. We got a chemical analysis for the green stuff we found."

She looked at him. He nodded as if she'd asked a question. "The . . . Well, the lab thinks it's of insect origin, although not quite like anything they know from any insects."

"And?" Kyrie asked.

"And those things . . . the white stuff on the lungs?"

"Yeah."

"They think it's eggs."

Kyrie frowned at him and he shook his head, looking impatient and annoyed, as if resenting that she couldn't read his mind. "Not chicken eggs," he said. "They're insect eggs. They don't know what type yet, but they're getting in an entomologist from the Natural History Museum in Denver tomorrow. He's someone's brother-in-law or brother of a brother-in-law, and he's driving down day after tomorrow. He's supposedly one of those guys who can tell on sight what kind of insect laid eggs where. He's used for investigating crimes by all the local police departments."

"Okay," Kyrie said. "And why did I need to know this right now? Why was this so urgent that I had to take a break to hear it?" His smell was growing stronger. It seemed to fill her nose and her mouth and to populate her mind with odd images and thoughts. She found herself wondering what his hair would feel like to the touch.

"Because I think there was the same powder on your porch last night," he said. "Where those windows were broken."

"My porch? Insects?" she asked. "But Tom said something about dragons and his friend was going on about aliens."

"Well, yeah," Rafiel said, and shrugged. "But I don't think those two were exactly in the state necessary to testify in a court of law. Or for that matter anywhere else."

Kyrie conceded. And yet, she wondered what had happened in the porch while they were gone. Had bugs broken the window? In her mind was an image of masses of bugs crawling out of the loam, pushing on the window, till the sheer weight of their mass broke it. Yuck. Like something out of a bad horror movie. "Any dead bugs, or other pieces of bug in that powder?"

"No," he said. He looked directly at her, as if her face were a puzzle he was hoping to decipher. His eyes were huge and golden, and his lips looked soft. The musky smell of him was everywhere, penetrating her nostrils, her mind.

He leaned in, very close to her, and asked in a voice that should be reserved for indecent proposals, "So, can I come by? After your shift?"

The tone and the closeness startled her enough to wake her from the trance induced by his scent. She stepped back. "No. Why would you? No."

He took a deep breath as though he, too, had been affected by something, and stepped back. "So I can see if you have that powder in your porch or not. And to have it analyzed if you do." He shook his head. "What did you think I meant?"

"All right," she said, reluctantly. "If you want to come. But not when I get off work. Come later, around one or so." She wanted to get some sleep tomorrow. And besides, she was not absolutely sure about Rafiel Trall yet. She'd rather face him in the full light of noon, without the effects of whatever this smell was. "I'd better go back in. Frank is in a mood and I have repairs on a porch to pay off."

Edward Ormson got out of the taxi in front of the diner where he'd been told Tom worked. Finding this information had been a fast job.

He, himself, had found Tom's address on the Web, and his secretary had then called—from New York, that much more impressive—the boy's landlady and asked questions.

Closing the taxi door and waiting till the driver pulled away, Ormson frowned. In fact, in the whole story there was only one thing he didn't understand. And that was that his secretary had told him the landlady seemed fond of Tom.

Oh, it wasn't at all strange that a woman should have some interest in Tom. Even at sixteen, when the boy had left home, there had been to him that roguish charm that attracts a certain class of females. What was odd, though, was that he had reportedly been living within the apartment complex this woman managed for about six months, and she said he'd never been late with the rent, didn't have loud parties, hadn't given the neighbors any cause to complain. He didn't, in fact, seem to have any life beyond going to work and—according to the woman—reading out on the steps of the building when the weather was warm. Reading? Tom? Perhaps it was the wrong Thomas E. Ormson?

But no. It wasn't that common a name. And besides, there had been the dragon. Edward swallowed, as he headed toward the gaudy facade painted all over with the prices of specials in what appeared to be a full pack of primary color markers. It wasn't just that "Fresh Rice Pudding" was scrawled in vivid red that offended Ormson's sense of aesthetics. It was that above it "Fries Always Fresh, Never Frozen" was done in at least five different and mutually clashing colors.

And above the door, something that looked very much like a pink pig wearing a cook's hat and apron was tossing a succession of pancakes up in the air. The whole was so horrendous that it might very well be considered kitschy chic if it were in the right place. But around the diner, head shops, used record stores, and closed warehouses clustered. This was the type of area that would never be fashionable.

It stood as a bulwark against the fern bars and lofts proliferating just a few blocks away. Here dingy and strange would hold the line against quaint and overpriced.

Wondering about the hygiene of the place, and if it was quite safe to go in, he opened the door. A clash of bells greeted him, and a rough-looking, dark-haired, bearded man glared at him from behind the counter.

Ormson had intended on approaching the first person he saw and asking for Tom. But this man didn't look like the greatest of prospects. His eyebrows were beetled low over his dark, sunken eyes, and he looked positively murderous, an impression not improved by the fact that he held a very large knife in his right hand.

Hoping that his hesitation hadn't been noticeable, Edward made for the most distant of the many booths upholstered in dark green vinyl. He was about to slide into it, when the man behind the counter barked, "Hey, you." Edward looked up, not even daring to ask what he'd done wrong.

"That booth is for groups, Mister," the dark man said. "Take one of the smaller ones."

Edward obeyed, though wondering why the booth was being held for groups when, clearly, there was no one else in the place. But he really didn't want to argue with the man.

Instead, he slid into the smaller booth and made a big show of picking up the menu and studying it. Normal diner fare, all of it, as far as he could see, with a few Greek dishes thrown in. And though he wasn't sure he wanted to eat here, or even that the food here would be safe to eat, the place didn't smell bad. Greasy, sure. There was an underlying smell of hot oil, as if the place were used, day and night, to fry stuff. Which it probably was. But there were appetizing smells of freshly grilled burgers and fries riding on the sheer greasiness that put a sticky film on every vinyl booth and table. And those were making his stomach clench, and his mouth start to water.

It had been too long since he'd eaten anything. Since lunch the day before. The clock on the wall here showed eleven o'clock, which meant it was one in the morning back home. No wonder he was starving. And he'd eaten in diners when he was in college. To no ill effects. Of course, he'd been younger.

He looked around the still empty diner, hoping that the very angry man behind the counter was not the only person here, hoping that a waitress—or, for a choice, his son—would materialize somewhere, out of the blue.

Not that he had any wish to see Tom. Not really. He had no idea what he would tell the boy, or what the boy's reaction to him would be. Their last parting had been far less than amicable. But if he saw Tom and convinced the stupid boy to give back whatever it was to the dragons—and what kind of an idiot did you need to be to steal from organized criminals?—then he could go back home in the early morning flight. And wash his hands of the boy. And resume his lonely life. Lonely, yes, but at least untroubled by the stream of acts of self-destruction that was Tom's way of living.

He looked around enough, and no one came, and rather than order from the guy behind the counter, Edward thought he would leave. Leave now. The man would probably curse him, as he left, but it was obvious Tom wasn't here. And if Tom was the reason the man behind the counter was so furious, then what would happen if Edward mentioned Tom?

He'd started rising when a couple came in through a side door that seemed to lead to another part of the diner—the covered porch he'd seen from the outside. He first thought of them as a couple—tall, blond man and slightly smaller girl, with multicolored hair. But then he realized the girl was wearing an apron with the logo of the diner, and that the blond man was just following her. In fact, he headed for the door as the girl rushed toward Edward.

"Hi," she said, and smiled. "My name is Kyrie. What can I get for you?"

He thought of asking her for Tom right away, but . . . no. He was hungry, anyway. "I'll have coffee," he said. "And your souvlaki platter, and one of the large Greek salads."

"What dressing on your salad?" she asked.

"Ranch is fine," he said.

She nodded, and went over to the counter. He watched her, from behind as she went. She was quite an attractive girl, probably in her early twenties, with a trim body, hair dyed in an elaborate pattern, and the sort of face that reminded him that America was supposed to be a melting pot. Seen in a certain light, he supposed she could be Greek, or perhaps Italian, or maybe even Native American. . . . Or, he admitted, some other, far more exotic combination. He wondered what the truth was. He also wondered if anything was going on with her and Tom and if that was what had the cook's nose out of joint.

The girl came back in a moment, set a cup in front of him, and put down a container of sugar and another with creamers. She filled the cup and he—ignoring the sugar and the creamers—took a sip.

His surprise at the quality of the coffee must have shown, in raised eyebrows or some change in expression, because the girl smiled at him. And, oh, she had dimples. He grinned back. She wasn't that much younger than him, really, and besides, he went out with girls her age every other week. But was she involved with Tom? Or how did she feel about Tom? He had to ask about Tom, but was it going to ruin everything?

"Excuse me?" he said, before she could turn away. "I don't suppose I could ask you a question?"

She tensed. He saw her tense, as she turned around, even if her face didn't show anything as she said, "Yes?"

"I'm sorry to bother you," he said. "But does Thomas Ormson work here?"

For a moment her face stayed absolutely frozen, and he thought she was going to tell him to go to hell or something. Instead, she put a hand on the table, and it trembled. Oh, no. What was going on here? Was she Tom's girlfriend.

"I thought you looked like him," she said. "But I thought . . ." She swallowed and didn't say what she thought.

"I'm his father," Edward said, low enough that the gorilla behind at the grill wouldn't hear him. "My name is Edward Ormson. Do you know where he is?"

She opened her mouth.

"Kyrie," the gorilla said. And she looked around, as if wakening. People had come in while they were talking, and there were five tables occupied. And she was alone. Also, his dinner was now sitting on the counter, ready. She went to get it.

"I get out at five," she told him. "It might be easier to talk then."

It was night from hell. Or at least night from next door to hell. Nothing bad happened. Kyrie even managed—despite her mounting exhaustion—to not drop any trays full of plates, and not to mix up any orders.

But Tom hadn't shown up. She was of two minds about this. Part of her wanted him to show up. She wanted to . . . Well, for one his father had been at the Athens, and his father was asking about him. That certainly didn't seem like the kind of father who had thrown his son out of the house at sixteen. Then again, she thought—who knew what Tom had done, and how much he could goad people beyond their natural limits?

His father had left after half an hour, and she hadn't given it much thought, until, as she was getting ready to leave, she saw him waiting by the door, looking very proper in his expensive-looking, if somewhat rumpled, business suit.

She nodded to him, and went toward the counter, to tell Frank she was leaving. He glared at her, which was not really a surprise, since he'd been glaring at her—and to be honest at everyone else—all night. Then he motioned with his head toward Tom's father. "Another one?"

She sighed. "I have no idea what you're talking about. He's just . . ." She stopped short of telling Frank this was Tom's father. She wasn't even sure why. Just she didn't want the jokes following on Tom being her boyfriend and his father supposedly visiting her. "He just wants to ask me something," she said.

And anyway, she thought, as she walked toward Mr. Ormson, if Frank couldn't see the resemblance between Tom and his father— same pale skin, same dark hair, same blue eyes—then he didn't want to see it.

They stepped outside the diner, and the morning was lovely, just warm enough to promise heat later at midday, but not warm enough to actually be uncomfortable. Kyrie took a deep breath of the air that seemed much cleaner than it would be later on in the day when Fairfax became clogged with bumper-to-bumper traffic. "I don't know where Tom is," she told his father, quickly. "I saw him last about twelve hours ago. He left with a friend. I don't know where he is. I can give you his address if you want."

"I have his address," his father said. "His landlady said that he worked at the Athens and that she thought his girlfriend worked there too. You wouldn't—"

Kyrie felt herself blush. "No. He doesn't have a girlfriend, that I know." There was no point explaining, and yet she could tell he was looking attentively at her, as though trying to read her expression. Or most probably wondering why she was blushing. Damn her blush, really. For a woman who could and did tan easily enough, she had the most inconvenient blushes. And it really didn't mean anything, except annoyance at Frank thinking she was Tom's girlfriend.

"Can we go somewhere and talk?" Mr. Ormson asked, leaning slightly forward, as if eager to have her answer.

Kyrie shook her head. Her feet hurt, and she felt sticky all over, as she usually did when she'd been working long hours at the Athens. And this time she'd worked ten hours. "I really don't think I have anything else to tell you," she said. "I only know Tom from work." And why was her mind, unbidden, giving her images of his coming out of the shower, his hair still dripping. He'd been perfectly dressed too. Well, almost perfectly. One thing her house didn't have any of was male underwear. "And I really don't know where he could have gone. If you go where he lives, talk to his downstairs neighbor. I think his name is Keith. He might know where Tom went from there."

"Oh, but I think you might know more without realizing it," he said, and in response to what she was sure was very annoyed frown, he said, "I'm not underestimating your intelligence, it is just that I know people absorb things about other people, without meaning to. And you might know something about Tom, something that will give me a clue." He hesitated a long time, as if he were not sure a clue to exactly what. "A clue to where to find him."

Kyrie was sure, too, that this was not what he had meant to say. She looked up—Tom's father was considerably taller than him—at Mr. Ormson's chiseled profile, and she wondered what he was trying to find a clue to exactly, and why he'd come looking for his son these many years later. Or had he looked for Tom before? Had Tom refused to see him? Perhaps that was what he wanted a clue for? A clue as to why his son would reject him? Kyrie shouldn't be getting involved with this. She really shouldn't.

"Just a cup of coffee," he said, and looked wildly around, lighting at last at a coffee shop sign a couple of blocks away, the edge of the advance of gentrification of downtown Goldport. "I won't keep you long, I promise. I imagine you must be very tired."

"Yes, but—"

"Please," the man said. "Tom is my only son. If there's any chance I can . . . find him."

Again she had a feeling that what he had been about to say was not "find" but something else—persuade? Reach?

"All right," she said, setting off toward the coffee shop. "But just one cup of coffee." She had to admit to herself at least half the reason for allowing him that one cup of coffee was that she wanted to know what was happening—exactly what was wrong—between those two. Had Tom told her the truth about being thrown out of the house? Or had he run away? What had his father thought of the whole thing? Did his father even know that Tom was a shifter? And did he love him despite that?

Kyrie didn't have any personal interest in the matter, of course. Well, Tom's father seemed nice enough. Possibly too nice to be saddled with Tom as a child. But, really, ultimately, what drove her to walk those blocks to the coffee shop, what convinced her to sit across from him at the little, tottering table, amid the decor that tried to hard to be urban and sophisticated, was curiosity.

She had grown up with many families, but none of them hers. And none of her families had ever shown her much of the tangled feelings between close blood relatives. All she had of it was the understanding drawn from books and movies. She saw family and familial love through a mirror darkly.

So she went with Edward Ormson, and sat at the little table across from him, holding a cappuccino that she knew would have way too much milk, and watching the man sip his espresso grande, or very tall or whatever they were calling the huge cups these days.

"How long has Tom been working at the Athens?" Mr. Ormson asked.

"Six months," Kyrie said. Was everyone going to ask her this question? If Mr. Ormson's next question was about the murders three months ago, she was going to scream.

But he nodded. "And he's . . . he's a good worker?"

"He's responsible," Kyrie said, surprising herself with saying it. "And competent. He always shows up or calls if he's ill. This is the first night he missed work completely." And having said the words, she wondered where he was, what he was doing. She frowned at her cup of foam with very little coffee. She had as good as thrown him out. Of course, he deserved it. Or did he?

Rafiel's talk of an insect-origin powder, his talk of eggs in the wounds of the victim . . . Something was not right, and it seemed certain that high or not, Tom had been fighting something—some creature, possibly the same that had committed murder in the parking lot, just a day ago. But he had been high. And he should not have been high. He should have been more careful in her house.

Somehow this moral high ground was not as satisfying as it should be. She realized that Mr. Ormson was looking attentively at her, and she managed a smile at him, her professional smile that meant very little but seemed to make people feel at ease. "He was better than most servers we get at the Athens."

"Was?" Mr. Ormson said. His blue eyes, so much like Tom's, were filled with a coolly evaluating look that was nothing like Tom's at all.

She shook her head. "He didn't show up today. I'm assuming he gave up the job. I don't know . . ."

But Mr. Ormson continued looking at her, coolly appraising. "Do you . . . I don't quite know how to ask this question, but I need to— do you have any idea if my son might be involved in illegal activities?"

Oh, Lord, the drugs. Yes, she was fairly sure that Tom was involved in illegal activities. But talking about it to this stranger felt like a violation of trust. Stupid to feel that way, she told herself. Stupid. And ridiculous.

He'd broken confidence with her. He'd been a guest in her house and behaved with utter disregard, with utter—

But she thought of the food left on her shelf. She had expected him to eat it all. She wouldn't have held it against him if he had eaten it all. It must have taken a lot of willpower to control himself and not eat all the protein he could. She, herself, and Rafiel too, had binged shamelessly. But Tom hadn't. And if he'd given in to the drugs later, perhaps he hadn't realized what he was doing? Or perhaps he had but had no other choice?

She looked at Mr. Ormson staring at her. No. Tom was, if nothing else, another shifter, a member of this makeshift family in which she'd ended up plunged suddenly. She owed him that much loyalty, if nothing else. Even if he were really guilty of murder; even if she ended up having to fight him or take him out—he was one of hers. And Mr. Ormson, even if his looks were testimony of a genetic relationship to Tom, was not one of them.

She raised her eyebrows at Mr. Ormson, and he laughed, as if she'd said something very funny. Only the laughter echoed bitter and hollow at the edge of it. "Ah. I see," he said, though she clearly did not. "Let me tell you what I know of my son. Let me explain."

"You don't need—"

"No, please let me, then perhaps you'll understand better what I mean, and that I'm not merely fishing for something that will allow me to put my son away or something equally . . . drastic.

"Tom was never an easy child. No, perhaps I lie there. He was a happy baby, chubby and contented. At least, we had a nanny, but when I was home and the nanny brought him to me, he was usually asleep and sometimes he . . . woke up and looked at me, and smiled." He made a face, worried, as if trying to figure out, now, what those smiles might have meant, and suspecting them of some deeper and possibly bad meaning. "But then he started walking. And he started speaking. The first word he learned was no. And he said no very often over the next fourteen or fifteen years. His teachers told us there was nothing wrong with his mind, but his grades were dismal."

He frowned again and took a quick sip of his espresso, as if it could control the flow of words. "I was going to say the first call from the police station, saying he'd been arrested was a shock, but that isn't true. From nursery school onward, we got calls, from Tom's teachers and supervisors. He'd stolen something. Or he'd broken something. His language violated all the rules of every school that ever took children. He had . . . I think they call it appositional deviational disorder. He couldn't obey and he wouldn't submit to any authority."

Ormson's lips compressed into a bitter line. "By the time he became officially a teenager, I'd run out of options. Counselors and boot camps, and whatever I thought might straighten him out, just made him more violent, more unruly. His mother had left by then. She— I think she couldn't understand him. I couldn't understand him, either, but I had my work. She . . . she found someone else and moved to Florida, as far as she could from us and still remain on the East Coast. And Tom and I settled into a routine. As long as he kept his . . . infractions beneath a certain threshold, I could get him out of jail the same day, and no harm done. I thought . . . I thought he would grow out of it."

Kyrie finished her coffee. For some reason, the story was making her feel sorry for Tom. Oh, it was foolish. It was borderline suicidal to feel sorry for someone like Tom. But in his father's descriptions— it seemed to her, from kids she had known in foster care—she read a desperate desire of Tom's to be seen, to be noticed, to be acknowledged. Oh, she didn't think it could all have been solved with a nice talk by the fire. Life tended not to behave like a Disney special, so much more the pity. She suspected that by the time that Tom had learned to walk, learned to say that all-vital *no*, the problem was already intractable. But nonetheless it was possible to feel sorry for the man he might have been.

"There was joyriding," Ormson said. "And drugs. And one or two cases of lewd acts in semipublic places."

Was he watching her face to see if she was shocked? The only thing Tom hadn't told her about was the lewd acts, and she wondered how much of those was showing up naked in public places—something neither he, nor she, could control.

"So." He leaned back. "You can't possibly fear to let me know something he's done. You see, I know."

She inclined her head, in a gesture that might have been a yes, or just curiosity.

He smiled, a tight-lipped smile. "I see," he said. "Well, then I'll ask it outright. Do you have any reason to think my son did something . . . stole something from a . . . an organized crime group?"

She must have trembled, without meaning to. The triad, the three exceedingly dumb dragons at the diner today, all came to her mind, and she must have trembled as she thought about it. She immediately calmed herself down, and forced herself to relax, but there was that look of understanding on Ormson's face.

"You don't have to answer that, but you do have to answer me this. It's very important. Do you know where he's hidden it? The Pearl?"

The Pearl. Ormson wanted the same pearl the Chinese dragons had spoken of. How could he know about it? Clearly Tom hadn't told him about it. He hadn't even seen Tom and wasn't sure where Tom might be. So . . .

She looked at him, and in his intense expression read the same eagerness of the three dragons looking at Tom the night before. The Pearl, they had said. And they'd asked where he hid it.

On her feet, she pushed the chair forward. She remembered to take the cup with her, which was a little strange, in retrospect, and put it on the tray near the other dirty cups.

She headed toward the door at a good clip and got there before Mr. Ormson seemed to realize it, before he got up, before he came after her, with a haste that made everyone in the coffee shop turn to stare at them.

Kyrie was aware of their scrutiny as she ran out, into the still deserted early morning street. She heard him come after her, almost immediately, heard him call, "Ms. Smith. Kyrie. Please, I must explain."

But all she could think was that he—was he really Tom's father?—was working for the dragons. He had no more concern or care for Tom than he did for her. They were shifters, they were alone. They must look after each other.

She ran full tilt back to the Athens, and heard him run behind her, also at full clip. But she was much younger than him, and she ran faster, and was well ahead of him by the time she reached the Athens and headed for the parking lot.

It was only in the parking lot that she realized she hadn't parked there that day. And that was the least of her worries.

Tom was tired. At just that moment, he wasn't absolutely sure how the dragon felt. Though he was still the dragon.

He could feel the dragon's wings, suspended between the earth and the sky, the dragon's front legs tucked upward in flight position, the dragon's tail, serving as a rudder to direct the pattern of flight. But a part of him, a core, looking out through the dragon's eyes, and trying—desperately trying to find a populated place to land—was wholly human, wholly Tom. And tired.

He had to stop soon, he thought as the dragon flew above the spectacular painted desert, the brightly layered mesas of New Mexico. But New Mexico was empty. That was what had made it so attractive. It was a place he could hide, far from human contact. But he needed some humans. He was going to need food and sleep, soon. And he did not want to hunt for wild rabbits, eat them raw and fall asleep on the hard-packed desert dirt.

The dragon's eyes, more far-seeing than any humans, followed a highway and following the highway, a conglomerate of buildings. It wasn't very big. Nothing to compare to the Colorado cities Tom had left behind. It wasn't even as big as Goldport.

Memories from drifting west, through parts of New Mexico, months ago, brought up the name Las Vegas, New Mexico. One of those towns forever being confused with a better known town of the same name in a different state. It was the *only* city large enough to have a hotel in the area within reach of his flying.

He aimed for it and flew in its direction, determinedly, feeling the weight of the backpack reassuring on the dragon's ankle. He had money in there. And clothes. He'd land somewhere outside town, make himself decent for human contact, then slip into town and stop at some truck stop—he seemed to remember an awful lot of them in Las Vegas—for breakfast. And then find a cheap motel room to crash in. Anything, really, so long as it didn't rent by the hour. He wanted to sleep in peace and quiet.

And then he could start looking for something more permanent, and thinking of a way to survive. Some place to hide out for a few months, till the triad either found the Pearl on their own or forgot about him.

And then . . . He had a fleeting thought he could go back to Kyrie then, and maybe . . . But no. That avenue was closed and he knew it.

The human brain in control of the dragon body guided himself down and down and down, to land between two mesas, on rocky ground, where no one would see him.

He shifted, an effort even greater than shifting into dragon had been the evening before. When it was done, he was weak and pale and trembling, standing naked in between the two rock spires, holding onto the handle of the backpack.

How he managed to get dressed, he didn't know. It involved a lot of starts and stops. Even the times he'd run away from other cities, from other states, he'd never made himself fly eight hours straight, through the night.

Las Vegas could not be more than a mile away. He'd gauged it well when he'd landed. He didn't want to land so close to the populated area that someone would see him shifting. And he was right by the only road into town coming from the direction of Goldport.

He put his backpack on and summoned strength from determination. He must make it to town. It was the only way he was going to get eggs and bacon and a cup of coffee. He could almost taste the cup of coffee. Not to mention the orange juice. Hell, anything wet would do.

With the dry desert air stinging his nostrils and his parched throat, he headed toward Las Vegas.

CHAPTER
6

That she'd gone to the parking lot instead of up front where she'd parked her car was the least of Kyrie's worries because in the parking lot there was . . . She swallowed hard, trying to comprehend it and unable to. They were . . .

They were green and huge and glittering like jewels in the full light of day. And they were some sort of Amazonian beetle. At least, Kyrie remembered, vaguely, having seen much smaller versions of these creatures at the Natural History Museum in Denver, pinned solidly through their middle, against a background of black velvet. In a glass case.

But those were small. And dead. The legend had said something about them being used for jewelry, and she could kind of see that, from the way the green carapaces glowed with blue highlights, in the light of the morning.

It would be five-fifteen, she thought, or possibly five-thirty, and soon there would be people coming to breakfast at the Athens, and yet in the parking lot of the building, there were two giant . . . insects dragging something.

She couldn't even look at the something. She didn't need to look at the something. She could smell the symphony of blood sharp and clear as day from where she was standing.

Somewhere in the back of her mind, a steady and very worried voice was intoning, *oh crap, oh crap, oh crap,* almost in the tone of someone praying.

The little voice was prescient. Or more in tune than Kyrie's body and the rest of Kyrie's mind, which stood, amazed and immobilized, staring at the insects.

She didn't know when they first saw her—where were the eyes in those things?—but she noticed a little start and their leaning into each other, communicating—with what? Antennae?—somehow, and then they turned. They advanced on her.

At this moment the little voice that had been intoning *oh crap,* grabbed the rest of Kyrie. It turned her around. It sent her running, in broad strides, around the Athens and to her car. She had a vague impression of people inside the diner turning to look at her as she ran by at full speed. Would the beetles follow? Out here, up front? In front of everyone?

They wouldn't if they were shifters, but what if they weren't?

What, she thought, as she put her hand in through the broken window to release the latch, pulled the door open, and, without pause, dove headlong into her car. *They're the result of some nuclear accident? Or some exterminator's bad dream?*

She stuck the key in the ignition, started the car, and headed down the street. It wasn't until she was headed toward home, speeding as much as she dared in this zone, that she realized her moment of frozen panic couldn't have taken much more than a few seconds. It seemed much longer, subjectively, but as she pulled away from the curb, in her car, she saw Edward Ormson on the sidewalk, hands on sides, slightly bent over, in the position of someone who's run too fast, too far.

He had just—almost caught up with her. As for the beetles, they were nowhere in sight. Had she imagined them? She wasn't about to drive around the back of the Athens to find out.

Edward Ormson stared at the girl, his mouth hanging open in wonder.

She'd run away from him. She'd looked at him as if he were

something profoundly disgusting, and then she'd left without warning. This was not something that happened to him normally, when he was trying to ask someone questions.

Why had she run? What had he said that was so terrible?

Confused, he walked back up in the direction of the coffee shop, where the area was much better. His head ached and he felt very tired. Dragon-lagged, he thought. Whatever magic the dragon had used to get here had left Edward feeling as if he'd been beaten.

So . . . this avenue to find Tom hadn't worked. And he needed to get back to New York as soon as possible. He'd best find a place where he could call his secretary again and get her to call around and ask more questions, find someone who might know where Tom was.

It was eight a.m. in New York and the woman would probably be in the office.

He considered going into the coffee shop, but they'd seen the girl run away from him. At the very least he'd get pitying stares. At worst, they would think he was some sort of pervert and had said something to her that was over the line.

Shaking his head—he still couldn't understand why she had run—he walked past the coffee shop. And came to a sort of little park in the middle of the sidewalk. He sat down on the park bench set in the four feet of lawn amid three dispirited trees.

Tom walked in the shadow as much as he could. Partly because he was thirsty and partly because he realized a guy like him, in black leather, carrying a kid's backpack had to look incongruous. He was holding it by the strap, dangling it from his hand, instead of carrying it on his back.

He hoped anyone seeing him would think he was carrying it for a son or little brother and give it no thought. But you never knew. And he didn't want people to remember his coming through here. He didn't want the triad to be able to find him.

Just before he got to town—he couldn't see it, but he could smell it, a tinge of food and car exhaust in his nostrils—he saw a couple of cars abandoned. Something about the cars tickled his memory, but he couldn't quite say what. Well, at least one of them looked awfully familiar. But it was just a Kia something or other, one of those economy cars that tried to look like SUVs and rarely managed more than looking like a toy patterned on an SUV.

It wasn't Kyrie's car. That was white too, but much smaller. Besides, this one had a driver's side window, Tom thought, and felt very guilty he hadn't sent her the money to have that repaired.

He'd been so furious last night, so furious because she'd failed to live up to his high standards. *His* high standards at that. It took some nerve. Now, he felt mostly tired and vaguely upset at himself, as if he had let himself down.

Fine. He'd eat something, he thought, as he saw, in the distance, the outskirts of town—represented by what looked like an abandoned gas station. He'd eat something, he'd sleep, and then he'd think this whole thing over. If by then he still thought he had done Kyrie an injustice or somehow failed to live up to what should—*yes, indeed, by damn*—be his high standards, he would take as much of the money as he dared and mail it back to Kyrie before he vanished from her life.

He couldn't even tell why he wanted to deal straight with her. It wasn't because she was a shifter. He wasn't feeling particularly charitable toward Mr. Golden Eye Lion police officer. And it wasn't because they'd worked together all this time—because though he'd enjoyed work at the Athens, Kyrie had always looked at him as if he were slightly below subhuman. And it wasn't his attraction for her, because he'd already decided that he had not a snowball's chance in hell.

And then he realized it was how she'd treated him, when she had found him standing over that body. He'd been deranged. He'd been in dragon form. But she hadn't even hesitated. And she didn't even like him. He knew that. But she'd grabbed him, and helped him hide the evidence of his involvement in anything back there.

She'd been there when he needed her the most. Whether she'd disappointed him by keeping funny sugar around or not, she didn't deserve for him to leave her with a huge bill in car repairs. Okay—so that was that. He'd send her some money this evening, send her more when he settled some place and found a job.

The decision put a spring in his step, and he almost walking normally when he reached the gas station. Which was too bad. Had he been dragging along the road and looking all around in despondency and depression, he might have noticed something about the shadows, something about movement.

As it was, he walked by the squat brick building without a second glance. And didn't know anything was wrong until he felt the impact of something hard on the back of his head. And then he had no time to think about it, as darkness closed around him.

Kyrie was rattled. She didn't know if she had dreamed the beetles, out of being so tired, out of Rafiel's report on there being insect matter in and around the corpse last night.

Normally, Kyrie was very sure of her perceptions. She'd had to trust in them and them alone, as often those who were supposed to look after her or be in charge of her hadn't been very trustworthy at all.

But now? Now she wasn't sure of anything. The last two days had been a carnival of weirdness, a whirling of the very strange. Driving her car along familiar streets and around the castle just before her neighborhood, she thought she wouldn't be at all surprised to wake up in her bed, suddenly, and find that all this, from the moment she'd seen Tom as a dragon, had been a crazy dream. Although if that were true, then her subconscious harbored some very weird thoughts about Tom.

She pulled up at her house, and opened the front door, half expecting to find her house as ransacked as Tom's apartment. But everything inside looked normal and was in its usual place. She locked the door, picked up the mail that the carrier had pushed through the mail slot on the door. Junk, junk, and bills. Which seemed to be the modern corollary of death and taxes.

She went all the way to the kitchen, and saw her chair still under the door to the back porch. Had it really all happened? Had the little porch, which had been her main reason for renting this house, truly been destroyed?

She pulled the chair away, unlocked the door and looked at the broken windows, the glass on the carpet, the . . . mess. Then she turned on the light and walked into the room.

Rafiel had said that there was green powder on this carpet, like there was green powder on yesterday's corpse. She hadn't noticed. But now, by the light of dawn and the overhead light, she could see it—glistening on the carpet. It was even more visible because it must have rained sometime during the night when she wasn't paying attention to the outside—and the rain had puddled it into little rings and patterns on the beige carpet.

She wondered what it all meant, but couldn't even think straight. And she wasn't about to call Rafiel and ask him. Not right now, she wasn't.

Instead, she retreated to the kitchen, locked the door, and slipped the chair underneath. She wished the door were somewhat stronger than the hollow-core, Seventies vintage door it appeared to be. But it couldn't be helped. She was certainly not going to fashion a new door before going to bed. And she needed to go to bed.

She took a hurried shower, with torrents of hot water, and felt as if the heat and the massage on her sore muscles were reviving her. Coming out and drying her hair, she noted that Tom had hung up his towel very neatly on the hook at the back of the door. For some reason she'd expected it tossed on the floor.

As soon as she went into the bedroom, the phone rang. It was a cheap, corded affair and it was plugged in there because it was the only phone plug in the entire house. Possibly because the entire house was not hard to cross in twenty hurried steps.

Normally the only calls she got—at least since she'd got on the telemarketers do-not-call-list—were from Frank, asking if she wanted to come in and work extra hours. And if this were Frank right now, he could go to hell. There was no way Kyrie was about to turn around and go work another shift. Not with those beetles in the parking lot, and she didn't even care whether they were real or a product of her imagination.

But the voice on the other end of the phone wasn't Frank's. It was a voice that purred with masculine self-assurance.

"Kyrie?" it said, though she didn't remember giving Rafiel permission to call her by her given name.

"Yes."

"I have information on the victim."

So, he was going to call her every time he had information? But she bit her tongue and said, "Yes?" because she knew that anything else could start a debate or an argument and that would mean talking on the phone longer and staying awake longer.

"He was Bill Johnson. A roofer by trade. And apparently a coyote in his shifter form."

"A . . .?" How had Rafiel found that out? It wasn't exactly the sort of thing you could ask people about? Or . . .

"His wife had pictures."

"Pardon me?" Kyrie asked finding this, in some way, stranger than giant beetles in the parking lot of the Athens.

"His wife had pictures of him as a coyote. Lovely lady, I would judge about ten years older than him but looking and acting much older. A grandma type. She pulled out pictures, to show us, of what her husband looked like in his coyote form. She said he got the shape-shifting ability from his Native American ancestors and that he was, like their coyote of legend, a bit of a trickster. And then she said—"

"Showed *you* pictures?" Kyrie asked, as her mouth caught up with her brain in horrified wonder.

"Oh yes. She called him in to missing persons and Officer Bob and I and our one female officer, Cindy, all went along to take her statement and see if she had any pictures of the deceased. Because if it wasn't him, we didn't want to put her through identifying the body. Cindy came along on the principle that the lady might need a female shoulder to cry on."

"And?"

"And she took out the pictures and showed them to us. And the other two looked at each other and then at me as though they thought the poor lady was totally out of her mind with shock and all that. Which she probably was, of course. But still . . ."

"But still, he was a coyote. And she knew. And didn't mind."

"Mind? She was positively gleeful. Very sorry none of their six children inherited the characteristic."

"Children." Kyrie was beyond astonishment. That a shifter could secure all these things that she thought were out of her reach because she was a shifter felt absolutely baffling.

"They live in Arizona," Rafiel said. "Where Bill and his wife lived till about a year ago, when they drove through town and stopped at the Athens for breakfast and all of a sudden realized they'd never felt so at home anywhere. So they decided to sell the place in Arizona and buy a house here. Ever since then, Bill went into the Athens for his morning breakfast after roaming the neighborhood as a coyote."

"Well, at least no one would notice a coyote. Not in Colorado."

"Right. Lions and panthers are something else."

"And dragons."

"Yes."

She could hear him take a deep breath.

"So, we know that the victim was definitely a shifter."

Shifter. Victim. The back of the Athens. The beetles. Kyrie desperately wanted to go to bed, but she felt she should tell Rafiel. After all, he was a police officer. He would know what to do about it, right?

"There is more," she said.

"More about the victim?"

"More . . . another victim."

"What?"

"I was . . . I forgot I parked my car up front," she said. "Because of the broken window. So I went into the parking lot and there were . . . They were beetles. That type of shiny rain-forest type beetle that they make jewelry out of?"

"Someone made jewelry out of beetles?"

"No. It would take a very big person to wear those as jewelry. They were six or seven feet long and at least five feet across, and shiny . . ."

"Are you sure you didn't dream this?"

"No, I absolutely am not sure. But I think they were there. They were huge and green blue and they were dragging something. A corpse. I think it was a corpse because I could smell the blood."

"A corpse? In the parking lot of the Athens? Another corpse?"

"I didn't see it. It was just something—a bundle—they were carrying. And it smelled like blood."

"Are you sure this is not a dream you were having when I woke you up with my phone call?"

"Quite." Kyrie looked toward her still made bed. "Very much so. I haven't gone to bed yet."

"Fine," he sounded, for some reason exasperated. "Fine. This is just fine. I'll go to the Athens and check."

"Take . . . something. They might be dangerous."

"Oh, I wouldn't worry," he said, his voice dripping with sarcasm. "I have my regulation bug spray can."

She had a feeling he didn't believe her, and she couldn't really blame him because she wasn't a hundred percent sure she believed herself. "Right," she said. "And, oh, remember you wanted to know about the dust on the floor of my porch. There is dust. It's bright green."

"Lovely," he said. "I'll be there. Right after I check the parking lot of the Athens."

Tom hurt. That was his first realization, his first awareness that he was alive. The back of his head hurt like someone had tried to saw it open, and the pain radiated around the side of his head and it seemed to him as though it made his teeth vibrate. An effect not improved by a twisted rag, which was inserted between his teeth and tied viciously tight behind his head. His legs and arms were tied too, he realized, as he squirmed around, trying to get into a better position. It felt like there was a band of something around his knees, and one around his ankles. Very tightly tied.

With his eyes closed, trying to remember where he was and why, he smelled old car oil and dust and the mildew of long-unoccupied places. His face rested on concrete, but part of it felt slick.

The gas station. He must be in the gas station he was passing when . . . When someone had hit him on the back of the head. So. Fine. Shaking, he opened his eyes a sliver. And confirmed that he was lying in a vast space, on a concrete floor irregularly stained with oil or other car fluids. This must have been a service station at some point. Light was dim, coming through glass squares atop huge, closed doors that took up the front of the building.

He looked around, but his eyes felt as if they couldn't quite focus. And he wondered if he'd been attacked by some random local hooligans, who had felt an irresistible craving for his leather jacket and the kid's dragon backpack, which no longer appeared to be anywhere near. Or if it was the triad again.

Through the fogs of his mind, he remembered that the white car parked by the road side had been the same make and model as the one that had turned around while he was shifting before. Had they seen him? Had they followed him? Along the highway? If they'd seen him follow the highway, it wouldn't be hard to calculate that he would stop in Las Vegas, New Mexico. It wouldn't have been hard to figure out, either, that he'd land and shift some distance from town.

It couldn't have been hard to find a place to lie in ambush for him.

In the next minute, there was a sound of high censure, in some form of Chinese. Oh, bloody hell. And then, out of a darker corner of the warehouse they came, all three of them. Tom had run into them a couple of times, before the time they'd ambushed him in his apartment.

He'd privately nicknamed them Crest Dragon, Red Dragon, and The Other One. And his opinion that their intelligence and their viciousness were inversely proportional did nothing to make him feel better right now. The only good thing, he thought, as they advanced, speaking fast Chinese at him as though he should understand it, was that they were in human form and not dragons.

As usual Crest Dragon—in his human form a young man with hair so well groomed Tom had wondered if it was a wig—took the lead, walking in front of the other two, who flanked him, left and right. Crest Dragon was waving the backpack around, and shouting something in Chinese.

Truth was, even without having any idea what the complaints in Chinese were, Tom understood the gist of the matter completely. And the gist of the matter was that the Pearl of Heaven hadn't been in the backpack.

Exactly what kind of an idiot did they think he was? He glared at them. And how stupid were they, really? Did they think they would not feel . . . it, if it were in that backpack. Tom remembered holding it, remembered the feeling of power and strength and calm and sanity flowing from it. He could feel across miles, and he was sure so would they be able to, if he hadn't taken extraordinary precautions in hiding it. And they'd thought he'd carry it in a back pack?

He glared at them, which was harder to do than it should be, because his eyes seemed to want to focus in different directions. How hard had they hit him on the head? And did they realize how hungry he was?

Crest Dragon came closer, waving his arms in theatrical exasperation. Then he flung the backpack—with force—across the building, grabbed Tom by the front of the T-shirt and, lifting him off the ground, punched him hard on the face.

Tom screamed. The pain radiated from his nose to match the pain on the back of his head, but sharper and sudden, edged around with blood and a feeling that his nose had broken. His vision blurred. If not for the rag in his mouth, he'd have bit his tongue.

Another punch came, immediately after. And he screamed again. He tasted blood and didn't know if it was running from the back of his nose, or from his mouth. And it didn't matter. Pain after pain came. He was vaguely aware of being kicked, punched, and hit with something—he wasn't sure what.

On the floor, curling into a tight ball, he endured each sharp pain as it came, and screamed as loud as he could. In the back of his mind, words ran, words so completely calm and composed that he couldn't think they were his. But the thoughts couldn't have belonged to anyone else. And they made sense.

One was: *Scream. Stoicism is for fools.* Another, just as sudden, as complete, was: *Only idiots inflict pain for pain's sake.* And the third, very clear, very sharp, was: *I could shift. I could eat them.*

It was the third thought that caused him to scream louder than the pain. And the word he would scream, if his mouth hadn't been so firmly gagged, would have been, "No."

Oh, he could shift. He could undoubtedly shift. And the binds on his limbs would break away with the force of the shifting, the greater strength and size of the dragon. Of that he had no doubt.

It was even possible that he could defeat all three of them, even if they too shifted. They were not swift of mind and they always had trouble coordinating attacks. But—and this was a huge but—he wasn't absolutely sure he could prevail. Not as tired and weak as he felt.

And then, worst of all, the dragon was very hungry. Starving. Ravenous. The dragon wanted food. Protein. And Tom didn't think he could live with himself if he succeeded in eating another human being. Or even one of these three fools.

A foot—he thought—crashed against his face. It felt like his forehead exploded. Blood flowed down, making him close his eyes.

He screamed "No," as much at the dragon within as at the pain.

Kyrie had just fallen asleep when she heard something. At first it was a little sound. Like . . . something scraping.

The sound, in itself almost imperceptible, intruded into her dreams, where she dreamed of mice, nibbling on cardboard. In her dream, she was in the back hallway of the Athens, and she opened the back door to the parking lot to find thousands of mice nibbling on large piles of cardboard boxes.

As she stood there, paralyzed, the nibbling grew louder, and louder, and then the mice swarmed all over her, thousands of little paws all over her, insinuating themselves under her nightshirt, crawling up her belly, tangling in her hair.

She woke up and sat up in bed. No mice. But she'd been sleeping uncovered, on top of the bed, and there was a breeze coming in around the door to the bedroom, blowing with enough force to ruffle her nightshirt and give her silly dreams.

Kyrie looked at the clock on her dresser. Seven a.m. She should be asleep. She still had time to sleep. Turning her pillow over, she lay back down. And realized she could still hear the sound of mice nibbling on cardboard. She blinked. She was awake. She was sure of that. So why were mice . . .?

And why did it feel like her head swam? She felt dizzy, as if she were . . . anaesthetized? Drugged? Slow?

She looked at the shaft of light coming from the little window above her bed. Was that green powder dancing in the light? Was she dreaming it? And she still felt dizzy, as if her head wasn't quite attached to her body.

Getting out of bed, as silently as she could manage, she opened her bedroom door. The living room was empty and everything looked undisturbed. Definitely no mice. But she could still hear the crunching, shredding sounds from . . . the kitchen.

Even more cautiously, feeling pretty stupid for moving around her own house as if it were some sort of secret dungeon, she crept down the hallway toward the kitchen. But before she got there, the green glimmer in the air became obvious. It was no more than a glimmer, she thought, a soft shine, like . . . a cloud of green dust. Green dust in the air. Green dust on the corpses. Green dust covering her back porch the day that Tom claimed he had been attacked by dragons.

And she was light-headed and growing dizzy. As if she were being doped.

Had they been dragons? Rafiel had said the powder was of insect origin, but was it? They didn't even know what dragons were—exactly. Other than mythical beasts, of course. And she remembered the beetles in the parking lot of the Athens. It could be those.

She stood there, for a moment, in the hallway of her own house, feeling her head swim. She stared at the green dust, listening to what sounded like an attempt to break through the door—if the thing trying to break through were armed with claws and pincers.

Only, the attempt couldn't be very serious, could it? It was a hollow-core door. How hard could it be to break it down? No, the purpose was to put the green powder into the house first, wasn't it. And why would you do that?

She thought of the victim in the parking lot of the Athens, covered in the green powder. And then she thought of Tom and Keith, clearly high as kites.

Yes, Tom had seemed to do most of the damage she'd found in the sunroom. Yes, their response to the attack hadn't been the most effective. But they had been high as kites. What if they had been high as kites because of the green dust?

What if it that was what was causing her head to swim?

In a moment, she was sure of it. She remembered Tom's casual greeting of Keith when he'd stopped for the key. Friends? Perhaps, of a sort, the friendly acquaintance sort where you trust each other with a key in case you're locked out. Or where you might exchange greetings in the hall. Perhaps the kind where you go in search of your acquaintance when you hear a murder has taken place at their job site. Not the type of friendship, though, where you go to someone's house in order to share a drug with your friend.

Kyrie retraced her steps down the hallway, quickly. Why, oh, why hadn't she allowed herself to be so afraid of bird flu that she bought a couple of surgical masks? In the event, right now, all she could do was improvise.

She opened the door to the linen cupboard and got a washcloth, which she tied over her mouth and nose, careful to cover them as much as possible. Then she retreated further, into the living room where she grabbed the umbrella she had bought for what she thought was a fabulous price when she first moved to Colorado. As her year's worth of letting the umbrella sit by the front door had proven, the price hadn't been quite so fabulous as she then thought. Never mind. It would be of use now.

She grabbed the umbrella by the solid wooden handle that had so impressed her when she bought the thing and wielded it like a samurai sword.

Just in time. From the kitchen came the sound of the door breaking down and then a dry shuffle, shuffle, shuffle, as of chitinous legs moving over the linoleum of the kitchen. She heard her chair being dragged, the table overturned. And she heard the thing shuffle closer, toward the hallway. At the entrance to the hallway it stopped, and, in a series of dry scrapings, it sent forth another cloud of glowing green powder. From the other side of the house came the sound of the door falling down. The front door. Wouldn't the neighbors see it? And who would believe it? They could see it all day long. They'd think they were going crazy and not tell anyone about it.

Kyrie put her back against the hallway wall, as a cloud of green powder came from the living room side, too.

She prepared to sell her life dearly.

Tom woke up choking. A taste of blood in his mouth, and his nose felt wholly obstructed. He coughed, and it seemed to help, clearing both mouth and nose. But he was thirsty and he was still lying, twisted, on the floor of the old service station. And his mouth was still gagged.

"Are you going to talk or not?" Crest Dragon asked. He stood directly in front of Tom, hands on hips. "Are you going to tell us where you hid it, or will we have to hurt you again?"

Tom blinked. He opened his mouth, and screamed, because that was all he could do. With a gag in his mouth, it was very hard to tell the idiots he had a gag in his mouth.

Other Dragon, the one with the Chinese character tattooed on his forehead, screamed something menacing in Chinese in response to his scream, and struck a pseudo-karate position he had probably learned from movies. He came running toward Tom and Tom closed his eyes, fairly sure they were going to hit his nose again.

But before Other Dragon got to him, someone yelled. Red Dragon? Tom opened one eye. It was indeed Red Dragon. He spoke rapidly, pointing at Tom. And he had one arm in front of Other Dragon, who looked confused. Crest Dragon looked vexed. He turned toward Other Dragon. "You didn't remove the gag? I told you to remove the gag," he said, in rapid English, and threw a punch at Other Dragon who avoided it by ducking under it.

He didn't tell Crest Dragon, obviously the head of this outfit, that he too could easily have seen that Tom was gagged. Instead, he untied the gag at the back of Tom's head, his fingers scraping at Tom's scalp and tangling in Tom's hair as he did it.

As the gag fell away, Tom opened and closed his mouth, hoping his jaw wasn't dislocated. It hurt as if it were, but that was probably only the result of having his mouth open like that for hours.

"Now," Crest Dragon said, and smiled, graciously, looking much like some sort of society hostess. "Now, will you tell us where you hid it?"

Tom judged his chances. What he needed most—what he wanted

more than anything—beyond the inner dragon's wish to tear these goons apart and use them as a protein source, was water. Liquid.

He looked at Crest Dragon and, in a voice he didn't need to make any raspier, he managed, "Thirsty. Very. Thirsty."

Crest Dragon looked disgusted, and for just a moment Tom thought they were going to resume beating him. He turned around to the other two.

"You know they said we shouldn't hurt him to where he couldn't talk," Red Dragon said. "You know he has to be thirsty."

How long had it been since he'd been thrown here? It seemed like forever. And he hadn't drunk anything before. Tom closed his eyes, as his captors' argument progressed into whatever form of Chinese they talked, Mandarin or Cantonese or whatever. Red Dragon had said they shouldn't hurt him to the point where he couldn't talk. Tom had realized, sometime in the last few days, that stealing the Pearl of Heaven had been a grievous mistake. Oh, he remembered it from when he was a kid, in his father's house. He remembered some old Chinese guy showing it to Edward Ormson at his home office.

Hidden around the corner, the then very young Tom had seen the Pearl and felt it. He'd felt the radiance of it penetrating to the core of his being. Since he'd later come to realize that it was a . . . cultic object of dragon shifters, he supposed that the fact that it resonated with him, even then, must mean he'd already been a dragon. It wasn't a late-caught affliction, but something he'd had all his life and only became active in adolescence.

Years later, he'd felt the call of the Pearl and he'd slithered, among those other dragons, so different from himself, to a meeting, where he'd seen the Great Sky Dragon. And the Pearl. He hadn't understood almost anything of the meeting. But he'd seen the guy who had the Pearl shift back into his normal form. And he'd followed him to an unassuming little restaurant. Where he'd stolen the Pearl.

Oh, the reasons he'd stolen it seemed valid at the time. He'd thought since this was used by shifters, since it gave forth a feeling of safety and calm, it must be something that helped control shifts. And perhaps it was. At least, since he'd had it, Tom had been able to stop his drug-taking. Gradually, but he'd stopped it. And the withdrawal effects he'd expected from heroin—all the horrible vomiting and cramps he'd heard about—had never materialized. Or not to any degree worth talking about. It hadn't been much more than a stomach flu. So perhaps the Pearl had helped.

Only then the triad had picked up the scent, and Tom had found that unless the Pearl were kept submerged in water, every dragon within miles of it could follow it.

He didn't even know how many dragons there were around. But he knew that there were enough that they'd tracked him. They'd tracked him all the way to Colorado, tracked him to Goldport . . . And he had to leave the Pearl immersed in water, which meant he, himself, couldn't use it.

So, if he couldn't use it, he might as well give it back. Only he couldn't give it back, because he'd seen enough of the dragon triad, enough of the ruthless way in which they disposed of those who crossed them.

They were so mad at him that these—admittedly low-level—thugs had pretended to forget to remove his gag and had proceeded to beat hell out of him. And no, he wasn't so stupid he would believe that they'd actually forgotten to remove it. No. They hated him. They had it in for him. So . . . The minute he told them where the Pearl was, the moment one of them verified it, got his hands on it, and phoned the others back to tell them where it was, he was a dead man.

And Tom didn't want to die. Not yet. So many times over the last few years, he'd thought he would be better off dead.

He didn't know what was different now, to be honest. He still didn't have a chance with Kyrie. Kyrie was probably, even now, snuggling with her lion-policeman.

But, damn it all, Tom felt a sting to his pride, a sting to what he retained as his sense of self, to think that if he died now, Kyrie would only think of him as a fuckup, as a junkie so far out of control that he couldn't keep from getting high in her house—even if he used her drugs for it.

He took a deep breath. He wanted to live. He wanted to know why she kept drugs. He wanted . . . he wanted Kyrie, and a house, roses, and everyday paper delivery.

He wanted the normalcy that had never been his.

A hand lifted him roughly, and he opened his eyes, bracing for a hit. But instead, he found Red Dragon pressing the neck of a water bottle against his lips.

Tom drunk gratefully, as if the water had been the breath of life.

As his mouth and nose became hydrated, the smell of the other three became more obvious. There was some sort of cologne, cheap and probably bought in gallon bottles, and the smell of the masses of product that Crest Dragon had slathered on his hair.

But above it, stronger than all of that, was the smell of living flesh. "No," Tom said. It was all he could tell the inner dragon, who was slavering at the thought of eating these fools.

Edward Ormson walked along the street, too stunned to even hail a cab from the two or three that drove by. This was all very bewildering. Social workers down at the homeless center remembered Tom as one of their successes, the landlady liked him, the librarians at the public library down the street gushed over him.

Were they really talking about Tom?

And he still couldn't understand what had made the girl run. In fact, he had no idea at all.

He frowned. It didn't make any sense. What did she know? And who was she, really? She said she barely knew Tom. She said that they'd just worked side by side for about six months.

But there was something else, there. Something to the way she talked about him, to the silences, to what she didn't say.

Oh, Edward had always known that Tom could be very charming to women. In fact, it seemed to him that women tended to like rogues and fools and Tom had a strong component of both, so it shouldn't surprise Edward that women liked his errant son. Even when Tom was little, just toddling around the place, the cook, Mrs. Lopez had been quite smitten with him. It was all they could do to keep her from feeding him on cookies and cake constantly. And Tom took advantage of it, of course. He'd been all smiles to the woman, even when he threw tantrums at his parents.

And yet, Kyrie Smith didn't seem to Ormson as the sort of woman who would be attracted to men who were trouble. No. Despite her exotic features and odd hairdo, she'd come across as capable, self-contained, controlled.

So, why did she seem so protective of Tom? Was it possible that for once in his life, just once, Tom had managed to attract someone in more than a superficial way? Was it possible that for once in his life Tom had a real relationship going? Or did she know something about the Pearl of Heaven itself?

For Tom to steal from the triad seemed like the stupidest form of madness, the last loss of grip on reality that the boy could have come to. But what if this were a cunning plan, hatched by someone with better organizational skills than Tom's? What if Kyrie was behind it? What if she had something in mind for the Pearl?

Edward needed to know more. That's all there was to it. He needed to know more about this whole thing before they could expect him to find Tom and force the boy to give the Pearl back.

He hailed a cab. He'd go back to the restaurant in whose parking lot he'd been let out, and he'd go find out exactly what this was all about. He'd worked for triad members now and then. He was, after all, a criminal defense lawyer.

It had started with pro bono cases, when he'd been asked to represent indigent clients. One of them was associated with the triads somehow, and that had brought him the triad business.

He remembered how shocked he'd been when he'd first realized that some members of the triad of the dragon—the ones he dealt with—were shapeshifters, capable of shifting into dragons. But he had never expected that this would somehow make Tom into a dragon. And he was still not sure how that could have happened. Nor was he sure how Tom could have got involved with the group again after he left his father's house.

But he knew he had to stop it. Somehow. And soon. He had to get back home to New York.

✢ ✢ ✢

Beetles. Definitely beetles. There was no other name for it. Shiny green carapaces and pincers. Advancing toward Kyrie, one from either end of the hallway. And they hissed. Or at least, it wasn't a proper hiss. Not like a cat's hiss, or anything. More like . . .

More like a kettle left too long on the fire. Or more like the release of hydraulic pressure from a train as it stops. That type of hiss.

One hissed, then the other hissed. They were communicating. They were communicating as they hunted her, as one approached from each side and they contrived to capture her in the middle, Kyrie thought.

This wouldn't do. This couldn't do. If she let them continue to advance, she'd find herself impaled by those two pincer-ended arms that kept advancing toward her, advancing inexorably in front of the shiny blue carapace, even while the creatures behind the pincers hissed at each other.

She imagined the hiss saying, "There she is, we've got her cornered."

Fear and an odd sort of anger mixed in her. This was her house. This was the only house that had ever been truly hers. All those years, growing up, she'd gone from house to house, from foster home to foster home, never having a place of her own, never having a say in even something as little as the color of her bedspread or the positioning of an armchair.

This house, tiny as it was, was the first place that had belonged to her alone. Well, that she'd been sole renter of, at any rate. Where, if she so wished, she could put the armchair on the roof, and it would stay there, because this was her space.

And these things, these . . . creatures . . . had violated it. Worse. They'd come into her house before, and they'd made Tom . . . high. They'd made Tom destroy part of her house. They'd given her an entirely wrong impression about Tom.

Not that they could be the ones who gave her the impression that Tom was an addict—or an ex drug addict. But they, as they were, had given her the impression that Tom didn't care about being a guest in her house, that he'd violated her hospitality. And because of them, she'd let Tom go—no—encouraged Tom to go, out there, somewhere, with no protection.

For all she knew, he was already dead. His own father was looking for him for the dragon triad. And she had kicked him out. Because of these things.

Anger boiled through her, together with a not unreasonable fear that there was no way out of this predicament and that she was going to end up as dead as that corpse they had rolled about in the parking lot of the Athens a few hours ago.

She heard a scream tear through her throat, and it seemed to her that the more advanced beetle—the one coming from the kitchen—stopped.

It seemed to Kyrie too that—though there was nothing on the beetle, anywhere, that could properly be called an expression—the beetle looked like it had just realized it was in deep trouble. Perhaps it was the thing's vague, confused attempt at skittering backward.

And then Kyrie jumped forward. There was no use at all attacking the pincers, so she vaulted over them. She used to be quite good at gymnastics in middle school. In fact, for a brief period of time, she'd thought that she was going to be a gymnast. But the foster family she was with didn't have the time to drive her to the extra practices.

Yet, just enough skill remained to allow her to vault over the pincers, and toward the monstrous head.

Blindly, more by instinct than anything else, Kyrie stabbed at the thing where the head carapace met the body carapace. She stabbed the umbrella down hard and was rewarded with a satisfyingly squishy sound, a spray of liquid upward, and a shriek that was part steam release and part the sound of a car's valves going seriously wrong.

From the other beetle came a sound of high distress, and it advanced. But its companion's body—dead?—blocked its way, and Kyrie jumped down from the carapace, on the other side, ran through her kitchen and out through her ruined back porch.

In her tiny backyard garden, she realized in her human form, she could never get enough of a running standard to jump over the six-foot fence.

But, as a panther . . .

She had never cavalierly shifted. Certainly never during the day. And yet, she was so full of fear and anger, of adrenaline and the need to fight or fly, that it seemed the easiest thing in the world. She willed herself into cat form and, suddenly, a black panther was rearing and taking a jumping leap at the fence. She cleared it with some space, just before she heard a sound behind her. It was an odd hissing, and a sound like . . . wings?

She had an odd feeling that these beetles could fly.

"Will you talk?" Crest Dragon asked.

Tom shook his head. There had been more . . . beatings. At least he supposed they would call it beatings. More accurate would be brutalizing to within an inch of his life.

Tom knew he would heal. The problem was that he suspected so did his captors. And that they were being more unrestrained with him than they would be with practically anyone else.

His defense right now was to look more confused than he felt, to look more tired than he felt. He shook his head and mumbled something that he hoped passed for a creditable wish to speak.

Red Dragon said something in their language that, for all it was unintelligible, was still clearly scathing. Crest Dragon answered curtly and sharply. They both turned to glare at Other Dragon, who shook his head, said something, then shrugged. He disappeared into a corner, where they seemed to have piled up some bags and other effects.

He returned, moments later, with . . . Tom blinked, unable to believe his eyes. But Other Dragon was definitely holding a syringe. A huge syringe. Tom frowned at it. It looked just a little smaller than those sold as basters at stores. He'd once been tempted to buy one for about two minutes until he realized the amount of meat he could actually afford didn't ever require external basting, much less internal.

Now he blinked at the syringe, and looked up at Other Dragon in some puzzlement. What the hell was that? What did they think they were doing? What did they want to put into him? Truth serum? Or marinade? Did they think he would be all the better for a touch of garlic and a bit of vinegar?

Other Dragon seemed rather puzzled as to what he should be

doing, too. Twice he turned around to ask something in Chinese. Twice he was told off sharply—or so it seemed—also in Chinese.

At last he sighed, and walked up to Tom, and held the hypodermic in front of Tom's face and shouted something that sounded like a samurai challenge. While Tom blinked, puzzled, Crest Dragon said something from the back. Other Dragon turned. Then looked again at Tom and smiled. A very odd smile, Tom thought. A smile of enticement, of offer that would have made much more sense—as starving as Tom felt—if he'd been holding a rare steak. He leaned in close to Tom and said, "You want this, right?"

The syringe was filled with a colorless liquid. It could be . . . anything. And Tom realized, suddenly, with something like a shock, that he very much did *not* want it, whatever it was. Perhaps it was the Pearl of Heaven that had eased his way up from the pit he'd dug himself into, but he could remember the days he was using. It had seemed so simple then. It had seemed to him that he was sparing himself pain and thought, both.

A life that was too bizarre, too complex—his feelings for the home he'd lost, his wandering existence, and the dragon he could become suddenly, unexpectedly—had been suddenly simplified. He'd sometimes, before the drugs, forgotten what he'd done as a dragon, but when he'd started using, it had made it that much easier. He could either forget or pretend it was all part of a bad trip.

He didn't have to believe—in the unblinking light of day, he didn't have to believe that he had no control over the beast. And he didn't have to see that the beast existed. He didn't even have to be believe himself alone—expelled from the only home he had ever known.

No—the drugs had blurred his mind just enough to make him be able to pretend it was all a dream—just a dream. That he was still sixteen and still at home. That he was not a shapeshifter, a dangerous, uncertain creature.

He'd thought he was fine. He'd . . . He frowned at the syringe, thinking. He'd thought he was doing great. He'd anaesthetized himself into being able to bear his life.

Until he'd woken up choking on his own vomit once too many

times. Until he'd woken up, in the morning, naked, under some underpass or beside some shelter, wondering what the dragon had done in the night and why.

And then there were the dreams. Lying asleep in daytime and dreaming of . . . eating someone. Of chasing people down. Of . . . Oh, he was almost sure none of it had ever happened. There would have been talk. News reports. Someone would have noticed. But the dreams were there, and the dreams made him fear one day all control would slip from the dragon and the dreams would become true.

And then there had been the Pearl of Heaven. And the job. And . . . and Kyrie. Who was he to judge her if she too chose to anesthetize herself, sometimes? She had helped him when he needed it most. He wanted to remember that. And he wanted to control the dragon. He wanted to know what he did, to know it was true. He didn't want the slippery dream, again.

"I want to own my own mind," he said, his raspy, low voice startling him. It seemed to come from so far away. And the words were odd, too, formal, stilted, not like himself at all. "I don't want drugs," he said in a still lower voice.

Crest Dragon said something that had the sound of profanity to it. And Other Dragon looked back confused. It was left to Red Dragon, the brash, perhaps younger of them, to step forward and say, "Well, then, if you don't talk, we'll have to give you some."

Which, of course, made perfect sense. But Tom couldn't talk. Because if he talked they would kill him. But if he didn't talk, they would give him this stuff. Which, of course, would make him talk.

He—who just the night before had been looking desperately for a drug dealer—realized if he were going to die, he would rather die sober. He'd rather know whatever there was to know, experience what there was to experience, with a clean perception. But then . . .

But then, and there it was. If he told them they would kill him for sure. Possibly in a painful way. If they gave him the drug . . . perhaps they would leave him alone while they went to verify he'd told them the truth. Okay, it was unlikely they would leave him alone. But with these three geniuses it was possible. At any rate, it would take them longer . . . They would have to get the words from him—

and Tom had no idea what this drug was, or if it would make him talk quickly. Or at all. And then they would have to verify.

That would take longer than if he told them the truth up front and they rushed off right away to verify it. Or called someone in Goldport. And that meant there would be more time for something to happen. Something . . .

Red Dragon was waiting. He had his hands on either side of his skinny waist—a dragon tattoo shone on the back of each hand. "Well," he said, with a kind of petulant sneer. "Are you going to tell us where the Pearl of Heaven is?"

Tom grinned. It made his lips hurt, as cracked as they were and with dried blood caked on them, but he grinned anyway. He wished he could gather enough saliva to spit at them, but of course, he couldn't. "Your grandfather's wonton," he said.

And, as they held him down; as the needle went into his arm, he relished the look of surprise—and confusion—on Two Dragon's face.

Paws on concrete. The sidewalk—an alien word from her human mind, forced, unwilling, on the panther, intruded. Sidewalk. People. People walking.

There were screams. Mothers and terrified babies, hurling to the side of the street. A man standing in front of her, gun cocked.

Kyrie's human mind pulled the panther sideways. The bullet whistled by. The panther crouched to leap. Kyrie tugged at the panther.

Trapped. The panther's brain rushed to every nook and cranny, to every possible hiding place, but she was trapped. There was nowhere she could go. No safety. No jungle.

Smell of trees, of green. Smell of moss and undergrowth.

Like a passenger in a lurching car, Kyrie blinked, becoming aware that she was veering off the street and toward the triangular block of land where the castle sat, with its own little forest around it, surrounded by high black metal fence, full of Victorian scrolls and rusting in spots.

Leaf mold on paws. Trees rustling overhead. The pleasing sound of things scurrying along the ground, in the soft vegetation. Screams behind her. People pointing through the fence, screaming, yelling.

The panther ran and Kyrie guided it as she could. Through the undergrowth, to the thick clumps of vegetation. She told the panther they were being hunted. That something bigger and meaner was after them. The panther crouched on its belly and crept, belly to the grass, close to the ground, forward, forward, forward, till it found itself all but hidden under the trees.

Kyrie had lost sense of time. She didn't know how long she had been in the panther's mind—a small focus of humanity, of sanity, within the beast. But she knew it had been long, because she could feel pain along the panther's muscles, from holding the position too long.

The panther wanted to climb a tree, to watch from above. It did not like this cowering, this submissive posture. And Kyrie couldn't hear any noise nearby. What remained rational and sane of herself within the panther thought that the people had stayed at the fence, talking, whispering.

They would call the police. Or the zoo. Or animal control. They wouldn't risk their lives on this. No. The panther wanted to climb the nearest tree and Kyrie let it, jumping so quickly up the trunk that Kyrie didn't detect any raised voices, any excitement at seeing her.

The tree was thick, and heavily covered in leaves. And it was around a corner from the front of the house. This way she would see the animal control officers approaching with their darts. Perhaps she could escape.

She wasn't so stupid that she couldn't see the possibility for discovery, for being caught. But she wouldn't think of it. She wouldn't think past trying to escape. She thought, as fast as she could, as hard as she could. And she saw no way out of this. Unless animal control officers missed her. She didn't imagine this happening. She could picture them beating the garden, tree by tree, bush by bush, looking for her.

The other option, of course, was for her to shift. She blinked. It hadn't occurred to her before. Of course, it would be humiliating. But being found naked in a public garden had to be better than to be tranquilized as a panther, and become a woman under sedation. She didn't know if that would happen—but it could.

But . . . But if she were found naked in a public garden, and if her house were examined, wouldn't she be committed? Or in some other way confined? Who would believe she was okay when she'd left her house torn to bits behind and was now here in this garden? At the very least they'd think she was on drugs. It wouldn't do at all.

Edward Ormson waited for only one moment, in the shabby entrance of the Chinese restaurant. He'd expected the oriental decor, and it was there, in a round, white paper lantern concealing the light fixture on the ceiling, on the huge fan pinned to the wall behind the cash register, in the dragon statue carved of some improbable green stone or molded from glow-in-the-dark plastic, that stood glowering on the counter by the register.

But the man behind the register, though unmistakably Chinese, wore a grubby flannel shirt and jeans and managed to look as much like the Western rednecks around him as he could. And the TV hanging from the wall was on and blaring, showing the scene of a tractor pull.

He was drinking a beer, straight from the can. To the other side of the elaborate oriental fan hung a calendar with a pinup standing in front of a huge truck. Something about this—the irreverence, the Western intrusions, stopped Edward from his course, which was to ask about the Great Sky Dragon.

Perhaps the creature had only left him in the parking lot because it was convenient. But the name . . . Three Luck Dragon, while not unusual, seemed to speak of dragons, and dragons . . .

He realized he'd been standing there for a while in silence, and probably looking very worried, as the man behind the counter swiveled around to look at him.

"How may I help you?" he asked.

Edward took a deep breath. Come on, if worse came to worst, what would happen? He could always tell the man that Great Sky Dragon was just the name of another restaurant, couldn't he? That he'd got confused?

And besides, if he didn't ask, what would happen? It wasn't as if Edward was going to figure out where Tom was, much less manage to convince Tom on his own. And he had a sneaky suspicion that if he tried to just forget the whole thing and go back to New York, the creature would just come and pluck him out of his office again. Or his house. There was only so much plate glass he was willing to replace.

All this was thought quickly, while the man's dark eyes stared at him betraying just a slight edge of discomfort, as if he were waiting, madly, to go back to his tractor pull on TV.

"I was looking for the Great Sky Dragon," Edward said.

"What?" the man asked, eyes widening.

"I was looking . . . I wondered if you could tell me where to find the Great Sky Dragon," Edward said.

There was a silence, as the man looked at him from head to toe, as if something about Edward's appearance could have reassured him that this was something to do. Slowly, the cashier's hand reached for a remote near the cash register, turned the TV off.

Then he came out from behind the counter and said, "You come with me."

Edward took a deep breath. What had he got into? And what would it mean? Had he just managed to startle a member of the dragon triad who had no idea who he was or what he was doing? And if he had, would he presently be killed by people who didn't even ask him why he wanted the Great Sky Dragon, or what he wanted of him.

He was led all the way through, past a bustling kitchen and past a set of swinging doors, into a grubby corridor stacked high with boxes.

At the very back of the corridor, a door opened, and the cashier reached in, turned on the light by tugging on a pull chain on the ceiling.

Light flooded a room scarcely larger than a cubicle. There was a folding table, open. An immaculate white cloth covered it. And on the cloth was a mound of peas—some shelled, some still in their pods. On the floor was a bucket, filled with empty pods. Behind the table was a plastic orange chair.

"Wait here," the cashier said. "Just wait."

Hesitantly, afraid of what this might mean, Edward went in. The cashier closed the door after him. Edward could hear the lock clicking home.

"I'll go in and look for it," a voice Kyrie knew said.

"But I wouldn't be too alarmed. It was probably just a large cat. I very much doubt it was a panther. I haven't heard of any panthers having been lost by the zoo. And panthers are not common here, you know," Rafiel Trall's voice went on, as usual radiating self-confidence.

A babble of voices answered him and, from the panther's perch atop the branch, Kyrie gathered that the crowd out there were insulted that Rafiel thought they could confuse a large house cat with a panther.

And yet, the way Rafiel talked, that certainty that exuded from his words, was so convincing that she could also hear the resistance running away. She could almost hear people starting to doubt themselves.

"I'll go in," Rafiel said. "With Officer Bob. Just to be on the safe side, please no one follow us. We'll do a thorough search. If we find it warranted, we will then call animal control. Right now all this commotion is premature."

The panther heard them come into the garden. Wondered how long it would take them to find it. Them. Officer Bob. Kyrie wondered what Officer Bob would think if he found her.

But Officer Bob was looking one way, and Rafiel was looking the other. She could hear them separate. She could hear officer Bob walking away. She could hear . . . She could hear Rafiel following her trail here.

He followed it so exactly that she started wondering if he was following the trail of broken branches and footprints she'd doubtless left, or following her scent. She remembered he seemed to be able to smell other shifters. To smell them out better than she did, at any rate.

He came all the way to the bottom of the tree, looked up at her, blinked, then smiled. "Kyrie," he said.

His voice was perfectly normal and human, and yet there seemed to be something to it, some kind of harmonics that made the hair stand up at the back of her neck. Not fright. She wasn't scared of him. It was something else.

For just a moment, there was the feeling that the panther might jump down from the tree and roll on him and . . . No.

Kyrie tried to control the panther and had a feeling that the world flickered. And realized she was a naked human, sitting on a branch of a tree in a most unusual position. A position that gave a very interesting view to the man below.

She scrambled to sit on the branch in the human way, and fought a desire to cover herself. She could either hold on to the branch or she could cover herself. Between modesty and a fall, modesty could not win.

"Yes," she said. Heat climbed up to her cheeks and she had a feeling she was blushing from her belly button to her hair roots.

Yes, she was sure she was blushing from the way Rafiel smiled— a broad smile that exuded confidence and amusement.

But when he spoke, it was still in a whisper. "I have this for you," he said, taking it from his pants pocket and handing it up. "I stopped for just a moment when I heard the report on the radio. I told Bob I needed to use the restroom and let him radio we were taking care of it, while I went to a shop and bought this. I'm sorry if it looks horrible, my concern was that it fit in my pocket."

He handed up what looked like a little wrinkled square of fabric. When Kyrie caught it, she realized it was very light silk, the type that is designed to look wrinkled, and that there was a lot more material than seemed to be.

Shaken out, the fabric revealed a sheath dress. Kyrie decided it was safer to climb down from the tree, first, and then put it on. With the dress draped over her shoulders, she climbed down carefully, until, on the ground, she slipped the dress on. Of course, she was still barefoot, but on a warm day, in Colorado, in one of the old residential neighborhoods of Goldport, that was not exactly unheard of.

"Go out at the back," Rafiel said. "From what I could see when we approached, the part where the garden borders on the alley doesn't have any bystanders. If anyone sees you, tell them some thing about having come in to look for the panther, but the police ordering you out. And now, go." As she started for the path, he pushed her toward another path, the other way. "No, no," he said. "That way. If you go this way you will run into Bob and Bob is likely to have his gun out and be on edge. I don't want you shot. Go. I'll meet you at your house as soon as I can."

Her house. With the bugs. Kyrie shivered. But there was nothing for it. She had to go somewhere. At the very least, she had to go somewhere to get shoes.

Edward didn't wait long. He didn't sit down. He didn't dare sit down. There was only one chair, and it seemed to be in front of the table, with the peas on it.

Instead, he stood, uncertainly, till the door opened, and a man came in. He looked . . . Well, he looked like an average middle-aged man, of Asian origin, in Colorado. He wore T-shirt and jeans, had a sprinkling of silver in his black hair, and, in fact, looked so mundane, that Edward was sure there must be a mistake.

He opened his mouth to say so. And stopped. There was something in the man's eyes—the man's serious, dark eyes. They looked like he was doing something very difficult. Something that might be life or death.

"Mr. Ormson?" he said.

Edward Ormson nodded, and his eyes widened. Was this the human form of the dragon he had seen yesterday? He seemed so small, so . . . normal.

But in Edward's mind was the image of that last night before he'd . . . asked Tom to leave. He remembered looking out of the window of his bedroom, next to Tom's room and seeing a green and gold dragon against the sky—majestic against the sky. He remembered seeing the dragon go into Tom's bedroom. And he remembered . . . He remembered running to see it, and finding only Tom, putting on his bathrobe. He remembered the shock.

These creatures could look like normal people. Perhaps . . .

"My name is Lung," the man said, and then, as though catching something in Edward's expression, he smiled. "And no, I am not him.

But you could say I . . . ah . . . know him." Lung stepped fully in the room, and seemed to about to sit down in the plastic chair, when he realized that Edward didn't have anywhere to sit.

"They left you standing?" he asked. "I'm so sorry." He opened the door and spoke sharply to someone back there, then stepped fully in. Moments later, a young man, with long lanky hair almost covering his eyes, came in and set down a chair. Another one, swiftly, ducked in the wake of the first, to remove the cloth and all the peas in it. As soon as he'd withdrawn the first one showed up again, to spread another, clean tablecloth on the table. And after that, yet another one set a tray with a teapot and two tea cups on the table.

Lung gestured toward the—blue, plastic—chair they'd brought in. "Please sit," he said. "Might as well be comfortable, as we speak."

Edward sat on the chair, and faced Lung across the table. "Tea?" Lung said, and without waiting for an answer, filled Edward's cup, then his own. "Now . . . may I ask why you were looking for . . . him? His name is not normally spoken so . . . casually."

Edward took a deep breath. "How do you know my name?" he asked.

Lung smiled, again. He picked up his cup, holding it with two hands, as if his palms were cold and had to be warmed on the hot porcelain. "He told us. He told us he brought you to town. That you were to . . . convince your son to speak."

"Ah," Edward said. "I don't know where to find my son," he said, picking up his cup and taking a hurried sip that scalded his tongue. "I haven't seen Tom in . . ."

Lung shook his head. "I don't question his judgments. It wouldn't do to do such," he said. He looked at Edward and raised his eyebrows just a little. "He says you have been . . . useful to us in the past, so you know a little of . . . his ways. And of us. Do you not?"

Edward inclined his head. More than simple acknowledgment, but less than a nod. "I have defended . . . people connected to him, before. I know about . . ." He thought about a way to put it that wouldn't seem too open or too odd. ". . . about the shape-shifting," he said at last.

Lung inclined his head in turn. "But do you know about the other . . . about his other powers?"

Edward raised his eyebrows, said nothing.

Lung smiled. "Ah, I won't bore you with ancient oriental legends."

"Given what I've seen, what I've felt; given that I was brought here by . . . the—"

"Him."

"Him, I don't think I would dismiss it all as just a legend."

"Perhaps not," Lung said. "And yet the legend is just a legend, and, I suspect, as filled with imagination and wild embellishments. What we know is somewhat different. But . . . he is not like us. That we know. Or rather, he is like us, but old, impossibly old."

"How old?"

Lung shrugged. "Thousands of years. Before . . . civilization. From the time of legends. Who knows?" He drank his tea and poured a new cup. "What we do know is this—he has powers. Perhaps because he is old, or perhaps, simply, because he was born with more powers than us. I couldn't tell you which. But whatever powers he has, it is said that he can feel things—sense them. Perhaps it's less premonition than simply having been around a lot and seeing how things tend to work out." He inclined his head and looked into his tea cup as though reading the future in its surface. "If he thought you should be here, then he has his reasons."

"But I can't find my son. I haven't seen my son in years. I didn't even know if he was alive. The— he said that I was responsible for my son, but surely you must see . . . I haven't seen him in years."

Lung looked up, gave Edward an analyzing glance, then nodded. "As is, I think we have it all in hand. We know where your son is. We have . . . Some of our employees have got him. In a nearby city. And they're confident he will eventually tell them what he did with the object he stole. We don't know why *he* thought it necessary to get you, nor why *he* thought you should be here. But he is not someone whose judgments I'd dream of disputing."

A silence, long and fraught, descended, while Edward tried to figure out what he had just been told, in that convoluted way.

"Are you telling me I have to stay here, but you're not sure why?" he asked.

The back alley wasn't empty, but it was nearly empty. At least compared to the crowd that surrounded the castle garden in the front. Here at the back, there were only half a dozen people looking in, staring at the lush, green garden, spying, presumably, for movement and fur.

There were two boys and a young girl of maybe fifteen, wearing jeans, a T-shirt and a ponytail and holding a skateboard under her arm. The other three people looked like transients. Street people. Men, and probably past fifty, though there was no way to tell for sure.

Kyrie, still under cover of thick greenery, wondered at the strange minds of these people who would come and surround a place where they'd seen what they thought was a jungle animal disappear. What kind of idiots, she asked herself, wanted to face a panther, while unarmed and empty-handed? She might be a shapeshifter but at least she wasn't so strange as this.

They were all roughly disposed on either side of a broad gate that seemed to have rusted partly open.

Kyrie could, of course, just walk out and tell them what Rafiel had suggested—that she had felt a sudden and overwhelming desire to look for the panther herself. But she would prefer to find some way past them without having to speak. Remembering a scene from a Western, long ago, she looked at the ground and found a large rock. Picking it up, she weighed it carefully in her hand. Then she pulled back, and flung the rock across greenery, till it fell with a thud at the corner of the property.

Noise like that was bound to make them look. They wouldn't be human if they didn't. In fact, they all turned and stared, and Kyrie took the opportunity to rush forward and out of the enclosure.

They turned back to look at her, when she was in the alley, but she thought none of them would be sure he had seen her in the garden, and started walking away toward the main road and home.

"Hey, miss," a voice said behind her.

Kyrie turned around.

"Are you the one who owns the castle?" one of the homeless men asked.

She shook her head and his friend who stood by him elbowed him on the side. "The woman who owns the castle is much older, Mike."

She didn't stay to hear their argument and instead hurried home as fast as she could. Once out of the immediate vicinity of the castle, everything was normal and no one seemed unduly alarmed by the idea of a panther on the loose. So Kyrie assumed that Rafiel wouldn't have too much of a problem convincing them that it had been a collective hallucination.

Her house looked . . . well, wrecked, the front door open, crooked on its hinges, the door handle and lock missing. Inside, the green powder was everywhere underfoot and, in the hallway, where she had confronted the creature, there was something that looked like sparkling greenish nut shells. Looking closer, she realized they were probably fragments of the beetle—struck off when she'd stabbed it with the umbrella?

The umbrella was still there, leaning against the wall. But the beetles had vanished.

CHAPTER
⊰ 7 ⊱

Lung nodded, then shrugged at Edward Ormson's question. "I don't pretend to know why *he* wants you here, though I'm sure he has his reasons. However, you don't need to stress too much in search of your son. As I said, he is . . . We have him. And he will talk."

A cold shiver ran up Edward's back at those words. They had Tom? "What do you mean by having him? Do you . . . are you keeping him prisoner?"

Lung seemed puzzled by Edward's question—or perhaps by the disapproval that Edward had tried to keep from his voice, but which was still obvious. "He stole from us," he said. "Some of our men have captured him. They will find out where he put the Pearl of Heaven one way or another."

One way or another. Edward found his hand trembling. And that was stupid. All these years, he'd gone through without knowing if Tom was dead or alive, or how he was doing. He hadn't worried at all about him. Why should the thought that he was being held prisoner by a dragon triad disturb him so much? Why should he care?

Oh, he could hear in the way Lung said that Tom would tell them the truth eventually that they probably weren't being pleasant with him. He doubted they were treating him very well. But in his mind, with no control from him, was the image of Tom on that last night. Barefoot, in a robe.

Edward had thought . . . well, truth be told, he couldn't even be very sure what he'd thought. He'd seen the triad dragons in action often enough. He knew what they could do. He'd seen them kill humans . . . devour humans. He'd seen the ruthlessness of the beasts. Seeing his son become a dragon, himself, he'd thought . . .

He'd thought it was an infection and that Tom had caught it. He'd thought his worthless, juvenile delinquent of a son had now become a mindless beast, who would devour . . .

His throat closed, remembering what he'd thought then. He didn't know if it was true or not. He assumed not, since Tom wasn't a member of the triad and lacked their protection. If he'd been making his way across the country devouring people, he'd have been discovered by now. He would have been killed by now. So Edward was forced to admit that his son must have some form of self-control. Well. Clearly he had to have some form of self-control if he'd not given in to whatever persuasion they were using to make him talk.

He looked up at Lung, who was staring at him, obviously baffled by his reactions. "What are you doing to him?" he asked. In his mind, he saw Tom, that last night he'd seen him. He saw Tom who looked far more tired and confused than he normally was. He hadn't even attempted to fight it. He'd opened his hands palm up to show he wasn't armed—as if he could be, having just shifted from a dragon. He'd tried to talk, but he didn't make any sense. Something about comic books.

These many years later, Edward frowned, trying to figure out what comic books had to do with the whole thing. Back then he'd found the whole nonsense talk even scarier, as though Tom had lost what little rationality he had with his transformation. And he'd got his gun from his home office desk and ordered Tom out of the house.

Tom had gone, too. And, somewhat to Edward's surprise, he hadn't made any effort to get back in.

"I thought you hadn't seen him for years?" Lung asked. "That you didn't care what happened to him?"

"I don't. Or at least . . ." But Edward had to admit that this last recollection he had of Tom as a sixteen-year-old youth in a white robe, and looking quite lost was an illusion. A sentimental illusion. It was no more real, no more a representation of their relationship than the picture of Tom in the hospital, two days old, with a funny hat on and his legs curled toward each.

It was a pretty picture and one that, as a father, he should have cherished forever. But Tom had been very far from living up to the picture of the ideal son. And in the same way, at least five years had passed since Tom had been that boy of sixteen, and even if Edward had done him an injustice then—had Edward done him an injustice then?—the man he was now would have only the vaguest resemblance to that boy.

Back then, Tom hadn't known anything but his relatively sheltered existence. And though he'd been popular and had the kind of friends who had got him in all kinds of trouble, his friends were like him, privileged. Well taken care of.

Suddenly Edward realized where his uneasiness was coming from about Tom and who Tom was, and what he had assumed about Tom for so many years. "It's his girlfriend, Kyrie," he said.

"Girlfriend?" Lung asked.

"Yes . . . or at least, I think she is. She said they were just coworkers, but there is something more there. She seems to care for him. She was furious at me for . . . I think she realized I was working for you, and she was furious at me."

"The panther girl?" Lung asked.

"I'm sorry?" Edward asked confused.

Lung smiled. "The girl who was with him two nights ago. The one who shifts into a panther."

"She . . ." Edward's mind was filled with the image of the attractive girl shifting, shifting into something dark and feline. He could imagine it all too well. There had been that kind of easy, gliding grace in her steps.

"Oh, you didn't know. Yes, she is a shifter. But I never knew she was his girlfriend."

"I just thought . . ." Perhaps what had bound them was their ability to shift shapes? But what would a dragon want with a panther?

The images in Edward's mind were very disturbing and he found himself embarrassed and blushing. "There are other shifter shapes? Other than dragons?"

Lung smiled. "Come, Mr. Ormson, you're not stupid. Your own legends talk about other shifters . . . werewolves, isn't it? And were-tigers too? And the legends of other lands speak of many and different animals?"

Edward felt his mouth dry. "This has been going on all along? People shift, like that." He made a vague gesture supposed to show the ease of the shifting. "And they . . ." He waved his hand.

"We don't know for sure," Lung said, seriously. "He who brought you here says there have always been shifters, and as you know he's not the sort of . . . person, whose word one should doubt. He is also, not, unfortunately, someone one can question or badger for details. He says that there have always been shifters. But that shifters are increasing."

"Increasing?"

"There are more of them."

"How? Is it . . . a bite?" He'd thought that back then. He remembered being afraid that Tom would bite him. He remembered having gone through the entire house, trying to think whether he'd touched anything Tom had touched. Tom's clothes, his toothbrush had all been consigned to the trash at his order.

The man laughed. "No, Mr. Ormson. It is . . . genetic," he pronounced the word as if to display his knowledge of such modern concepts.

Edward felt shocked, not because the man knew the word—he spoke without an accent—but at the idea that such a thing could be genetic. "But there is no one in our family . . ."

Lung shrugged. "In our families, which intermarry with each other quite often, even then only one child in four, if that many, will have the characteristic. In other families, in the world at large, who knows? It could be not one in twenty generations." He frowned. "I have often wondered if it is perhaps that people travel more now, and meet people from other lands, carrying the same rare gene. And if that's the only reason there's been an increase. Although . . ." He frowned. "I don't know that this is entirely natural—or explainable by simple laws of science. We seem to heal quicker than normal people and unless we are killed in certain, particular ways—traditional ways like beheading, or burning, or destroying the heart, or with silver— we're nearly impossible to kill. And we seem to live . . . longer than other people. I don't know how long. Himself is the oldest among our kind. I've never enquired as to those of other kinds and other lands."

Edward swallowed. That gun, that night, wouldn't have killed Tom anyway. Good thing he hadn't fired it. It would be horrible to have to live with Tom after firing on him.

But beyond that, something else was troubling him. The thought that Tom had received that curse from him—and presumably from his mother—and yet, he'd thrown him out. And now . . . "What will you do to Tom, if he tells you where the Pearl is?" he asked.

"He will no longer be . . . a problem," Lung said.

Edward nodded feeling relief. So, they'd let Tom go. "Pardon me if I'm asking too much. You don't need to tell me. I know something of the working of the triads in this country and I know the Dragon Triad is not that very much different, but I must ask . . . Why the Pearl? You're the only ones who have it, right? It was shown to me, years ago, in my apartment, and I remember thinking it was very pretty. But I thought it was a symbol."

Lung smiled, a smile that seemed to have too many teeth and to slide, unpleasantly, over his lips. "It is not a symbol," he said. "Our legend has it that the Pearl was sent down with the Great—with him. The Emperor of Heaven, himself, is supposed to have given it to him."

"Why?" Edward said, asking why the man believed his legend when he had dismissed all others.

But Lung clearly misunderstood him. He shrugged. "Because dragons are by nature bestial, competitive, and brutal. The beast in us overrides the man. We could never band together, much less work together without the Pearl of Heaven. We must find it soon," he said. "Or we will destroy ourselves and each other."

It wasn't until Edward had left and stood outside the restaurant that it occurred to him that saying Tom would no longer be a problem was not a reassurance. On the contrary. Unless it were a reassurance that Tom would soon be dead.

Stopped, in the parking lot, he felt as if ice water were running through his veins. He took a deep, sudden breath and almost went back inside. Almost.

But then he thought it would only get him killed. How could he go up against almost immortal shapeshifters? How could he? He would only get killed. And for Tom?

He needed help. He needed help now.

Kyrie locked her front door as best she could, which in this case involved sliding the sofa in front of it, because the beetle had pulled the handle and the lock out of it.

If Kyrie survived all this mess, she would be so far in debt for house repairs that she would be arrested. Or die of trying to pay for it. Or something.

The back door was impossible to close, having splintered in a million pieces. She should have got a solid wood door, after all. And on that thought she got out the phone book, called her bank for her balance, which ran to the middle hundreds. Then she went back to the phone and started calling handymen, finding it somewhat difficult to reconcile her urgency in getting the doors fixed with the price any craftsman would accept for this.

She had just discovered an elderly handyman, who only worked two days a week, who could do both glazing and carpentry, and who thought her situation desperate enough to warrant immediate response when Rafiel came in through the ruined back door.

"Dragons?" he asked her, as she was hanging up the phone.

"No," she said. "As it turned out, beetles. Huge, green and blue and iridescent. If you go to the Natural History Museum in Denver, you'll find that the much tinier versions of the creatures are used as jewelry by some rain forest tribe or other."

He grabbed blindly for one of the overturned chairs, pulled it upright, and collapsed on it, looking at her. She'd put the kitchen table and the other chair up, and that was where she'd been making her calls. "I've just got hold of a handyman, who will be coming by to fix my porch and my two doors. I gave him the dimensions and he says he has some surplus, older doors he removed from a house and I can have them for nothing. Which only means I'll be broke, not in the red. At this rate I do not dare miss work for six months, but I will probably survive the experience."

But Rafiel only looked at her, the golden eyes dull and uncomprehending. "Beetles?" he said.

She nodded. "Very much so."

"So it wasn't a hallucination in the back of the Athens?" he said.

"Did you find a corpse?" Kyrie asked.

He shook his head slowly. "No. But I found . . . I could smell blood. I didn't want to shift to verify it, but I could smell blood. And death. Fresher than . . . two nights ago. So I'm sure you were telling the truth. Only till this moment I had hoped that you had seen it wrong and that it was actually dragons. Do you mean to tell me we have dragons *and* beetles?"

"It's worse than that. The green powder? I think it has hallucinogenic properties, that it's supposed to make the victim unable to fight. I think that's why I managed to fight them back. I tied a towel over my mouth."

"Ingenious," he said. "I could go back to the Athens tonight in . . . lion form and try to follow the trail of the blood. It's probably fresh enough and because there was no body, I wasn't forced to call out the rest of the force, so the scent won't be diluted." He paused for a moment. "I would have done it then, but I was afraid it would bring too much attention."

He nodded, as if satisfying himself of something. "Then as we were heading for the station, there was the report of a panther. Fortunately it turned out to be a sort of mass hallucination." He cleared his throat. "As you know, these are quite common. Seeing black panthers, I mean. There's whole counties in England afflicted by it."

He looked at her, and reached for her hand, where it rested on the table. "How did you escape them?"

For a moment, for just a moment, Kyrie had a feeling of misgiving. Was it that Rafiel wanted to know how she'd escaped so that he could warn the beetles? But no. The beetles already knew how she had escaped. He wanted to know. It made sense.

"I stabbed one with my umbrella." She nodded toward the umbrella resting a few feet away against the wall in the hallway. "Between the head and back carapaces. And it was immobilized. Which allowed me to jump over it and escape."

"So, the shift to panther was . . ."

"I thought its mate would chase me."

"It probably would have, except for its being daylight and a busy area." He sighed. "I don't like to think creatures like that have such control. They are shifters, they must be. But what kind of insane nature or magic or evolution could have caused such a thing as shifter beetles?"

Kyrie shrugged. "Whatever it was, it created dragons. Which brings me to Tom."

"Ormson? Must you?" Rafiel looked pained and vaguely put out, as if she were insisting on speaking about a distasteful subject.

"Tom Ormson," she said. "I have reason to believe I did him an injustice. If that powder from the beetles causes hallucinations, I think that might have been all he was high on. On top of that, there is his father."

"Ormson has a father?" Rafiel asked.

"Till this moment you assumed he reproduced by fission?"

"No, I mean he has a father around here, a father who is in some way involved in his life?"

Kyrie shrugged. "I don't think he is. Involved in Tom's life, I mean. I think he came from New York on purpose to find Tom. I think at the request of the triad."

Rafiel's eyebrows rose.

"I think he's a lawyer of some sort," she said. "I . . . vaguely remember Tom telling me that. And I think he is involved with the triads in some way. Well, with the shifter dragon triad, most of all."

"This family just keeps getting better and better," Rafiel said. "I suppose I'll look up the elder Mr. Ormson's background. And his name is?"

"His given name? Edward."

Rafiel nodded. "I'll check him out."

"Wait," Kyrie said. She didn't know she was going to say it, till it came flying out of her mouth. "Wait. I need to ask you a favor. Please. Would you . . . Would you check on Tom?"

"Check on . . .?"

"I think he's staying with his friend, Keith, who lives in the same building, third floor. Because he left with Keith. Keith would at least know where he was going."

"But why do you want me to check on him? Isn't he a grown-up and able to look after himself?"

Kyrie frowned. She had a sense of deep uneasiness and was quite well aware that a lot of it might be due to her guilt in having misjudged him over the drug stuff. "I . . ." She waved at her house and the destruction. "Until today I would have said I was able to look after myself, too, but it is not that easy, as you see. And then he had the triad looking for him too. And apparently his father, working for them." She took a deep breath. "Last night he missed work completely. I'd like to know he's okay."

She stood up. She had some vague idea that the gesture would encourage Rafiel to go. She didn't want to be so rude as to ask him to leave, not when she was asking him for a favor. But the handyman should be here any minute. And as soon as she had locking doors—with a few extra locks—she was going to have to shower and go work. On virtually no sleep.

Rafiel got up too and she was optimistic that he would leave now. But he was still holding the hand he covered with his own when they sat at the table. And now he leaned forward and said, "You don't need to go it alone."

And before she knew what he was doing, he'd covered her lips with his and was pulling her to him.

She'd never been kissed, not even in high school. Any boy smart enough to be interested in her was, presumably, smart enough to realize this was not exactly a safe course of action. Having her lips covered by his, his hands moving to her shoulders was novel enough to stop her from reacting immediately.

His hands were warm on her shoulders, and his body felt warm and firm next to hers. And his tongue was trying to push between her lips.

· She put her hands on his shoulders and pushed him back. "I'm sorry," she said. "I'm not . . . I'm not prepared. I don't think . . . Let us get through this first, and figure out what it's all about?"

He started to open his mouth, as if to answer, but at that moment a white-haired man, in impeccable work pants and T-shirt showed at the kitchen door. "Miss Smith? I'm Harold Keener. Ready to start work."

"Well," Rafiel said, looking perfectly composed as if just seconds before he hadn't been attempting to shove his tongue into her mouth. "I'll be going then, and check on Ormson."

Was it Kyrie's imagination, or had he pronounced Tom's family name with particular venom?

And what had Rafiel thought he was doing, she wondered, as she walked the handyman back to the porch to discuss the double-glazed versus single-glazed options and costs. Was he so used to any girl he came onto melting with pleasure that he didn't even bother to check for some signs of interest before jumping the gun? Or had she been giving signs of interest? She doubted that very much, as she wasn't even sure what the signs were.

On the other hand perhaps he just thought with both of them shifting to feline forms, they were perfect for each other? Was this all about creating a litter of kittens? Or was he trying to distract her from something in the conversation? Had he said anything he didn't want her to remember?

Edward Ormson had left the Three Luck Dragon feeling less assured of himself than he was used to feeling. Something in the conversation—perhaps the way these strangers spoke casually of holding Tom prisoner, of interrogating Tom, made Edward feel inadequate and ashamed of himself.

These were not feelings he normally entertained about himself, and he didn't feel right about entertaining them now.

He told himself that Tom had been a difficult child, a delinquent adolescent. But the words of Lung echoed in his mind, telling him that people who shifted into dragons had problems of that sort. That the beast often overruled the human. And if Tom had been born that way, if it was blind genetic accident, then it wouldn't be his fault, would it? He'd been difficult, but then he couldn't have been otherwise. Would parents who were more interested in him and less interested in—what? his career, himself, Tom's mother's devotion to medicine? all of those?—have done better for him? Could anything have prevented getting to this point where a criminal organization composed of shapeshifters was intending to eliminate Edward's son? And Edward could do nothing about it? Except perhaps help them?

The wrongness of it, the wrongness of his having worked for the group that was intending to kill his son, made bitter bile rise to his throat. But why should he care? Where did all this anguish come from? Hadn't he washed his hands of the boy five years ago?

Five years ago. Damn, the boy had only been sixteen. And Edward had ordered him out of the house. At gunpoint.

Edward had been walking along the road leading toward town. Not a pretty road—a place of warehouses and dilapidated motels— and it seemed to be making him think things he'd never thought before. This was all wrong, these unexpected feelings, the sudden guilt over Tom. It was all very wrong. He'd been fine with this for five years. Why should it torment him now?

He was tired. That was all. He was very tired. He hadn't slept at all the night before, and now it was afternoon. He'd hail the first cab that came by. He would ask to be taken to the best hotel in town. He would go to sleep. When he woke up, he would feel much better about this. He would realize that Tom had made his own bed and now should damn well lie in it.

His briefcase was heavy, pulling down on his arm. And no cab came by. Heck, no car came by. He walked on, into the Colorado night.

He should have rented a car, only he didn't think it would take him this long to . . . To what? Make Tom give back whatever he had stolen, like a naughty boy caught with another kid's lunch box?

What did he know of Tom now, really? He would be twenty-one. How he had lived the last five years was beyond his father's knowledge and probably beyond his father's understanding. Who was he, this creature he'd seen growing up till the age of sixteen, and then let go and not seen again?

Tom worked nights in a diner, he could shift shapes into a dragon. And he had the affection—or at least the interest—of that exotic beauty who did not look like the type to be easily rolled by some patter. And Ormson should know that, he thought, with a rueful grin. *I tried.*

He'd walked a few blocks and was near an intersection when, out of the corner of his eye, he caught the yellow glimmer of a taxi.

Waving frantically, he got the cabby's attention, and moments later was sitting on the backseat of an air-conditioned taxi heading downtown.

"Downtown?" he said. "Really."

"Oh, yes," the cabby said. "Spurs and Lace is the best hotel in town."

Edward leaned back against the cool upholstery and hoped they had room. He just needed to sleep. Just . . . sleep. And then all would be well.

"Kyrie," Tom called, and the sound of her name woke him from a nightmare of half-defined shapes and half-formed thoughts in which he'd been, seemingly stumbling without direction.

He didn't know what they had given him. He suspected it was supposed to be some form of truth serum. At least they had expected him to answer questions while under.

He suspected he hadn't. Part of it was because he had the feeling that he'd been touring random recesses of his mind, which, for some reason, featured not only an up-close and personal view of Kyrie's bared breast, but also repeated reruns of Keith's conversation about his problems at college.

And part of it was because, as he became aware of who he was, where he was, and what was happening around him, he heard the three . . . Oh, he must not call them the three stooges, not even mentally. The way he was feeling, it might come flying out of his mouth next thing, and, who knew, they might actually understand the reference. No. He heard the three geniuses arguing loudly in what he presumed was their native tongue. It didn't sound like an argument about which one would go for the Pearl and which one would wait until the order came to cut Tom's throat . . . or however they intended to dispatch him.

With a final scream, Red Dragon ran out the door. The other two shrugged, went to the corner, and came back with sandwiches and drinks.

The smell of food made Tom hungrier than ever. If it weren't for the fact that he was using all his concentration to keep himself from turning into a dragon, he might very well have broken down and told them where to find the Pearl.

The room was acceptable, though it was close to downtown and, from his fifth-floor window, Edward had a view of the area where Tom worked.

Standing there, looking out the window, he wondered if Tom had lived on one of those rectilinear streets that radiated from Fairfax Avenue and which were lined with tiny houses and apartment buildings. Probably, since Edward very much doubted that waiting at tables at night in a diner was a job that paid enough for a car. And then he realized he'd thought of Tom in the past tense.

Angry with himself, he took a shower, put his underwear back on, and got in bed. He was asleep before his head touched the pillow.

And he was fully awake, staring at the ceiling a few minutes later, while thoughts that shouldn't be in his head insisted on running through it. Thoughts such as—shouldn't Tom's father do something to save him? no matter how unworthy the boy was—and really, what had he ever done while living in his father's house that wasn't done by kids of his age and set? He'd gone joyriding. He'd been caught with pot, once. And he'd committed minor acts of vandalism. He'd been naked in public twice, both in his last week at home—after he'd started shifting. Nothing that other kids he ran with didn't do. Kids who were now, for the most part, at Yale and Harvard.

But Edward had kicked Tom out of the house. And never even

stirred himself to find out what exactly the boy was doing. Or even if he was alive.

"He was a shapeshifter," he said to the cool air of the room. "He was a dragon."

But the empty room seemed to sneer disdainfully at this excuse, and he sat up in bed, furious at himself. The truth was that since his marriage had broken apart, Tom had been more of a burden than anything else. A hindrance to just living the life of an unattached adult, with a job and a few casual dates and no significant obligations. Because, if Edward hadn't been around for a while, then Tom took it upon himself to get parental attention by getting himself arrested or by—and suddenly Edward smiled remembering exactly what that had looked like—shaving half of his head and dying the rest of his hair bright orange. Why was it that at a distance of eight years that memory seemed funny and endearing?

Fully awake, he dug into his briefcase and brought out his cell phone. He called information in Palmetto, Florida. And then he called Sylvia.

A kid answered the phone, speaking in the endearing lisp of a child whose front teeth are missing and when Edward asked for Sylvia, screamed at the top of his lungs, "Mom."

This was followed by the click of pumps on the floor, and finally Sylvia's voice on the phone. "Hello."

"Hi, Sylvia, this is Edward."

"Who?"

"Edward Ormson?"

There was a short silence, followed by "Oh." And, after a longish pause. "How may I help you?"

Exactly like the waitress at an impersonal restaurant, Edward thought, but then they hadn't seen each other in over ten years. She had another family. It was foolish of him to resent it. Well, it was foolish of him to call too, but he felt he had to. She had never even sent Tom a birthday card. Not that Edward had seen.

"I just wanted to know if you've heard from Tom?"

"Who?"

"Thomas. Your son?"

"Oh. Tom?"

Was she not sure who her oldest son was? Edward should have felt revolted, but instead he felt more guilty than ever. What a pair they had made. Poor boy. Poor screwed up boy who'd ended up with them.

She seemed to collect herself, from a long ways away. "Isn't he living with you?" she said.

Edward took a deep breath. "No." And he hung up.

He didn't know what he had expected. That Sylvia was secretly a great mom? After all, she'd turned Tom over to a nanny as soon as she could, and returned to her job before he was one month old.

He walked over to the window and looked out again. No. He knew what he had hoped for. He had hoped that Sylvia would behave like a responsible, caring parent and thereby redeem all his memories of Tom's childhood. Prove to him that the boy had had at least one attentive parent till the divorce. And that if he'd gone wrong it was entirely his fault and his parents couldn't be blamed.

If that could be proved to be true—well, then Edward would feel if not justified at least slightly less guilty in washing his hands of Tom.

But his ex-wife's behavior, his own memories of his behavior only proved to him that Tom had never had a chance. Not even the beginning of one. And yet, he was still alive, five years after being kicked out. And Kyrie Smith liked him. That had to count for something. He couldn't be completely lost to humanity if he'd engaged the interest of an attractive and clearly smart young woman.

Kyrie Smith. She was a panther in her other form, Lung had said. Perhaps she knew other shifters. With their help, perhaps Edward could go up against the triad. Perhaps he could rescue his son.

He wasn't sure he could have Tom move back in. He wasn't sure he could endure Tom for much longer than a few hours. He wasn't even sure that he should ever have had a son, since he seemed to have approached the enterprise with the idea that children were sort of animated dolls.

But he was sure the least he could do was save his son's life. Or not cooperate with his murderers.

CHAPTER
❧ 8 ❧

Kyrie was not in a good mood. Oh, she was sure most of the reason for her feeling as down as she did was the fact that she really hadn't slept much.

By her calculations, she had slept exactly two hours in the last forty-eight. And even with the best of payment plans—the handyman had allowed her to pay in installments for her new windows and doors—she would not have any spare cash for the next few months.

So she'd been going from table to table, forcing her professional smile and longing—just longing—for the end of the shift. It didn't help that the night was exceptionally hot and the single air-conditioning unit labored, helplessly, against the dry heat that plunged through the windows patrons opened and clung around Kyrie in a vapor of french-fry grease and hamburger smell.

"It doesn't help that Frank is acting like someone did him wrong," Anthony said, as he passed her on the narrow isle between the plastic tables in the addition and gave her a sympathetic scowl. "Couldn't you get your friend Tom to show up?" he said. "I mean, Frank said if I wanted to continue working here, I'd do this shift too."

"I don't know where Tom is," Kyrie said, her voice sounding even more depressed than she felt.

223

Anthony—tonight resplendent in a ruffled red shirt and his customary tight black pants and colorful vest—looked very aggrieved. "Only, I'm missing my bolero dance group practice." And, at the widening of her eyes that she couldn't control, "Oh, Lord. Why did you think I dressed this way?"

Kyrie just smiled and looked away. There was an answer she had no intention of giving. Instead, she took her tray laden with dirty dishes to behind the counter, scraped them, and loaded them into the dishwasher.

Needless to say the diner was crowded tonight. Probably because people couldn't sleep with the heat—since most houses in Colorado didn't have air-conditioning—and had decided to come here and eat the night away instead. Normally, Kyrie and Tom, after six months of working together, had things down to a routine. Whichever of them went to bus one of his tables did the other's tables too, if they needed doing. They'd worked it out, and it all evened out in the end. When the night was busy, it kept the tables clear so people could sit down as soon as other people left. And that was good. But Anthony, though he was a very nice man, wasn't used to Kyrie's routines.

Kyrie hesitated, alternating between being mad at Tom for not being here, and a sort of formless groping, not quite a prayer, toward some unnamed power to grant his safety. She had as good as kicked him out . . .

No. She wouldn't go there. Of all the useless emotions in the world, the most useless was guilt. She slammed the last dish in the dishwasher, and checked the cell phone she'd slipped into her apron pocket.

Rafiel had said he'd call as soon as he had checked on Tom. He'd call even if he couldn't find Tom. He hadn't called yet. Why hadn't he called?

Kyrie turned from the dishwasher, expecting to see Frank glaring at her for slamming the dish in. But Frank was leaning over the counter, seemingly elated by intimate conference with his girlfriend—or at least the woman he'd been seeing. Kyrie was afraid the staff had decided she was his girlfriend partly as a joke. Which was kind of funny, because the woman was not much to look at.

She had to be fifty if she was a day, with the kind of lined, weathered skin that people got when they'd lived too long outdoors. And she had the sort of features that were normally associated with British women of a horsey kind. Her hair was flyaway, mostly white, and if it could be said to have been styled, she'd been aiming to look like popular pictures of Einstein.

But Frank was leaning forward toward her, to the point where their foreheads almost touched. It revealed his neck, above the T-shirt, and showed a bandage there. Ew. Had his girlfriend given him a hickey?

They'd been seeing each other for a while, but today they seemed cozier than Kyrie had ever seen them.

On the way back to her tables, coffeepot in hand for warm-ups, Kyrie noticed that, despite the woman's weathered features, she wore a very expensive skirt suit. Maybe Frank was interested in her for her money?

"Or maybe he has no taste," she told Anthony, as they met one coming and one going into the addition. "But see, you wished him to get laid and there . . ."

"Don't say it," Anthony said. "Don't even say it. I don't have the money to buy as much mental floss as I'd need to get that image out of my mind." He made a face, as he moved the tray the other way, to clear the doorway. "But it's been going on for a while, now, hasn't it? I hear she's the new owner of the castle. And there's talk she's going to renovate it and use it as a bed-and-breakfast. So, perhaps it is just for money." He looked hopeful.

Kyrie gave her warm-ups and then started taking orders. Went back and gave the orders to Frank, whom, she was sure, was ignoring them. Or didn't even notice the new handful of orders spiked through the order wire.

Then she went back again, having caught movement by the corner of her eye, and the impression someone had sat in the enclosure. It wasn't until she was at the corner table, near the outer door, facing the guy who had just sat down, that she recognized Tom's father.

He looked like he'd been dragged through hell. Backward. By his heels. He looked like he hadn't slept in more hours than she'd been awake. His suit was rumpled, his hair looked like he'd washed it and not given it the benefit of a comb—or clergy, since it tossed in all directions, as if possessed of a discordant spirit.

His dark blue eyes stared at her from amid bruised circles. "Don't say it," he said. "I know what you think of me, but don't say anything. I think . . ." He swallowed. "I think that there's reason. Oh, hell. I think they're going to kill Tom. I need help."

That he needed help was a given. That he was so worried about their killing Tom was not. She glared at him. "You didn't seem to be worried about him at all before," she said.

"I . . ." He swallowed again. "I've been thinking and . . . I don't want them to kill him."

Well, and wasn't that big of him? After all, Tom was only his son. She narrowed eyes at him. The shock, when she'd realized he was working for the people who'd already tried to kill his son once, had turned her stomach. She still didn't feel any better about Mr. Edward Ormson. She'd be less disgusted by a giant beetle. "What will you be eating, sir?"

He looked as surprised as if she'd slapped him. "What . . . what . . . I need to talk. Seriously. They're—"

She took her notebook out of her apron pocket, and tapped the pencil on the page. "I'm at work, Mr. Ormson, and my job is to get people food. What can I get you?"

"I . . . whatever you want . . ."

"We're all out of rat poison," Kyrie said, the words shocking her as they came out of her mouth.

His eyes widened. "Coffee. Coffee and a . . ." He looked at the menu. "Piece of pie."

She wrote it down and walked away. She really, really, really needed to convince Frank to start making Brussels sprout pies. Or cod liver oil ones.

Tom woke up from a sort of formless dream. He didn't remember falling asleep. His last memory had been of Crest Dragon and Other Dragon having a picnic of sorts in front of him.

Now he opened his eyes to an empty building. He didn't know how long he'd slept, but his nose no longer hurt, and it seemed to him like the pain in his tied arms had eased a little too. Perhaps he'd gotten used to being tied up. Or perhaps his arms had been without circulation so long that he could no longer feel them.

The last should have been alarming, except it wasn't. Everything seemed very distant, as if a great sheet of glass made of indifference separated him from the world and his own predicament.

He lay there, and listened to his own breathing. He would assume he still hadn't talked, though it was—of course—possible he had said something while he was in a half awake state. And if he had . . .

Well, it was possible that the three dragons had gone off to get the Pearl and would presently come back and kill him. Tom could shift now, of course, but what if they were still here? Perhaps just outside? First, as tired as he was, he couldn't fight all three of them at once. Second, what if he ate them?

His mouth felt so dry—his tongue glued to his palate by thirst, that he was sure he would bite them just for the moisture. And yet, there was an off chance. Would he lie here and wait for death? No. He would shift. As difficult as it was, as tiring as it was, he would shift.

Before he could collect his mind enough to concentrate on the shift, though, he heard sounds outside. A couple of cars, a lot of voices. Speaking Chinese. He closed his eyes, and pretended to be asleep.

A group of people came in, babbling in Chinese. Several men, by the sound of it. Tom half opened his eyes, just enough to look through his eyelashes, without anyone realizing that he was actually awake. He forced himself to keep his breathing regular.

And then from the middle of the babble a voice emerged. "Hey. Hey, what's the idea?"

Keith. The voice was Keith's. What was Keith doing here, though?

"You're okay, you're okay," one of the other voices answered, in accented English. "As soon as your friend answers questions, we'll let you go."

And then two men came in, breathing hard, carrying a sack with something very heavy in it. "Where do we put her?" they asked.

"Here," another voice answered. The forest of legs in front of Tom parted enough for him to see, on the ground, a trussed-up human, and the big sack being laid down behind it.

"She's starting to wake up," one of the men said.

"That's fine," another one answered. "With the tranq she'll be weak as a kitten for a while."

A kitten. Tom blinked, trying to focus his gaze. A kitten. The sack—some kind of rough burlap—was large enough to contain a heavy feline. She. Kitten. Kyrie. Not Kyrie.

"Oh, look, he's awake," one of the men who'd come in—and who looked far smarter than the three reverse geniuses—said and grinned. "Yes, that is your girlfriend, but don't worry. So long as you tell us where you hid the Pearl of Heaven, she'll be just fine."

Kyrie. Tom didn't want to shift. If he shifted, he was going to eat someone. But he couldn't tell them where the Pearl of Heaven was, either. Because then they'd just kill him. And Keith. And Kyrie.

He felt his heart speed up and his body spasm. And there was no turning back.

There was blood. There was blood and screams and panic. Tom's vision—the dragon's vision, was filled with people. He flamed. There was the smell of fire, and of cloth burning. People with clothes on fire ran to either side of him.

The dragon wanted to feed. To the dragon's nostrils, all flesh was food. The smell of humans, the smell of fodder so close was more than he could endure. The dragon tried to nip left, right . . .

But Tom knew once the dragon started feeding, it wouldn't stop till all humans around it were eaten. He knew from some deep instinctive feeling that having reached the depths of hunger, the dragon would now eat past satiety. And he couldn't let it happen. He couldn't.

If he ate a human, he'd never be able to live with himself. And if he ate Kyrie . . . No.

Tom—what there was of Tom in the huge scaley body with the flapping wings and the tearing claws and the flaming mouth, controlled the body and the wings and the mouth. Forcefully, he walked forward slashing with his claws at all opposition. Taken by surprise, the others ran out of the way. Tom could hear, to his side, the cough-cough-cough like laughter of a dragon shifting. He would deal with that later.

Before the dragon shifted, before he had to battle others of his kind, he would free Keith. And Kyrie.

Disciplining the dragon, he bent over Keith, and, with a sharp claw, burst the ropes that bound his friend's legs and hands. Keith was looking at Tom with huge eyes and, for a moment, Tom thought he would run away. He remembered that Keith had no idea who the dragon was. But Keith was looking intently at him and said, "Tom?"

Tom nodded, rapidly, and managed to get out, through a mouth not well adapted to speech, "Run."

Then he bent and ripped the burlap bag open. He couldn't see the feline—definitely a feline shape—inside move, though. He felt more than saw movement from it, and then he heard a stumping step from the side, and knew that a dragon had shifted shape near him.

He turned, just in time to find Crest Dragon launching himself at Tom.

Tom jumped aside, enough to avoid Crest Dragon's slashing and then turned around. Then he bent low and slashed across Crest Dragon's belly with a claw.

Bright blood spurted, and there was something like a scream that sounded all too human. The blood made the dragon's thirst worse, but Tom wouldn't let it drink, and, instead, hopped back, to slash at Red Dragon who had shifted shape also, and was trying to sneak up on Tom with all the stealth of an elephant in a very small china shop.

Tom's dragon kicked out at Crest Dragon, who was coming at him again, his back claws leaving red stripes of blood on Crest Dragon's muzzle, even as his muzzle clamped tight on Red Dragon's arm and pulled, ripping it out of its socket.

"Look out, look out, look out," Keith screamed from beside Tom. And he'd grabbed something—Tom couldn't quite see what, but it looked like an ancient and rusted tire iron. Keith was looming with it behind Other Dragon, who had, in turn been sneaking out behind Tom.

Tom clashed jaws at Other Dragon, but Keith hit Other dragon a sideways blow with whatever the thing was. It must have been a hell of an implement, and heavy enough, because Other Dragon gave a high-pitch scream and fell forward.

But there were other dragons. Too many dragons. A lot of the people who had come in had been severely burned by Tom's original flaming, and lay fallen, some in various stages of shifting shape, but seemingly out of action. But then there were others. Many others.

As a dragon, Tom wasn't particularly good at counting. There was something in the reptilian brain that tended to simplify things down to the level of one, two many. But the human inside that brain could tell there were at least eight dragons. Maybe more. And Tom was tired. And weak.

He was surrounded by dragons, on all sides, snipping and biting at him. He could feel wounds, even if he couldn't stop. If he stopped, he would die. And though that seemed—eventually—inevitable, he wasn't ready to give up. Not yet.

He circled and nipped. Until his back was to a wall and he was surrounded by dragons. Truth was, he thought, they could already have killed him. They were holding back. They probably just wanted to hurt him enough that he wouldn't be able to resist—he wouldn't be able to stop them from making him answer . . .

But if they didn't want to kill him, that gave him the advantage. He kicked and bit with renewed vigor, and realized that he had allies. On the outer ring, at the edge, Keith was dancing, like a mad monkey—which was exactly how Tom's dragon brain thought of him—repeatedly bashing the dragons at the periphery with whatever heavy implement he'd grabbed.

Oh, they turned, and tried to flame him, but Keith was too quick for them, jumping and running into the darkness, only to appear again somewhere unexpected, and bash another dragon over the head.

And from the other side, another . . . person? Had joined the fray. Only it wasn't in person shape, but as a large feline.

In the semidarkness of the station—was it dark out now?—Tom couldn't see very clearly, but he could see that it was a feline shape. And it was roaring and clawing and biting.

Suddenly, Tom realized he had an open way out of there, to the front door. Awkwardly, his legs streaming blood, Tom ran for it, flaming everything that got in his way. The door had been left open. From carrying the hostages in? Outside in the parking lot there were a lot of cars, and two men who ran at the sight of Tom. Tom flamed the cars. They caught and some exploded. And then, as Tom slowed down, he felt a hand on his front leg. A human hand. Touching him.

He turned ready to flame, and saw Keith, who was physically pulling him forward, toward one of the cars. An undamaged one. "Dude," he said. "You have to change, or you'll have to go on the roof rack."

Tom was already shifting. It was the only way to stop from flaming Keith. He became human, and tired and in pain, in mid-stride, and it was only Keith's determination that pulled him forward, that shoved him into a car—huge car. Like a limo—from the driver's side, and pushed him over to the passenger side.

He threw something on the floor at Tom's feet. Tom was too tired to notice what and just leaned back, breathing hard. Keith waited, his hand on the ignition. Waited. Waited. And then something—Tom couldn't see very well, he was that tired and in that much pain—heavy hit the backseat.

Kyrie. Tom turned around, even as Keith reached back, grabbed the back door, pulled it shut, then started the car and took off, in a squeal of tires, weaving between the other parked cars on the way to the road, and then down it, at speeds that were probably forbidden in this neighborhood.

The feline looking at Tom from the backseat was not Kyrie. It was a lion. Tawny and definitely male.

As Tom watched, it morphed into police officer Rafiel Trall.

Edward Ormson didn't know what to say to this woman. Kyrie brought him back a cup of coffee and a slice of pie, and he actually reached forward and grabbed her wrist, before she could walk away.

"They have him prisoner," he said. "They have him prisoner and you must help him."

"I must help him?" Kyrie asked. She shook her hand, pulling it away from his grasp. "I must help him? How? Aren't you the one who has been trying to catch him, to get him to tell you everything for the benefit of the triad?"

Edward felt exasperated. The woman was beautiful. Her skin was just the tone, her features just exotic enough to make her look some ancient statue of a forgotten civilization—remote and admirable and inhuman. The tapestry-dyed hair only contributed to the impression. But she clearly didn't understand. "You're young," he said. "You haven't got any children. You wouldn't know what—"

"No," she said. And it sounded like an admission, but then she leaned forward on his table, her hands resting on it. "No, I don't have children. But if I did I am sure I wouldn't assume a . . . criminal group was in the right and he in the wrong."

"You don't understand," Edward said. "You don't understand at all. Why would he . . . Why would Tom mess with them? Doesn't he know better? Doesn't he understand? They're dangerous."

"Oh, I'm sure he knows that," she said. "And I'm sure I understand better than you do. I'm sure he had his reasons. They might have been wrong, but I'm sure he had his reasons. I've known Tom too long not to know that he had to have reasons for what he did. He's neither stupid nor crazy, though he is, perhaps, a little too reckless."

Edward snorted at this. "Look, I don't know how good my son is in bed, but—"

The moment the words were out of his mouth, he knew he'd said entirely the wrong thing. She drew herself up. Her face became too impassive, too distant. "Mr. Ormson," she said. "I think you've said enough."

"No, listen, I know he appeals to women, he always has, but he—"

She pushed her lips together and looked at him with an expression that made him feel as though he were something smelly she had just found under her shoe. She opened her mouth. "Mr. Ormson," she said. "I have no idea what you think my relationship with your son is, but—"

At that moment, a phone rang. Kyrie plunged her hand into the pocket of her apron. "Rafiel," she said.

✢ ✢ ✢

"Can I borrow your cell phone," Rafiel asked, all polite from the backseat.

"My . . .?" Tom asked. Couldn't the man see Tom was naked? Where did he think Tom kept a cell phone, exactly?

"The cell phone," Rafiel said.

"From your backpack, dude. All your stuff is in there," Keith said, looking aside from his driving, even as he took perilous turns at high speed on the country road. Behind them, in the rearview mirror, Tom could see a blaze going up.

"The other . . . aren't they chasing us?" he asked.

"Nah. You set fire to their cars and the station."

"I did?" Tom asked.

"Yep. As you came out. You were flaming all directions. I grabbed you to prevent you from flaming this car. Don't you remember?"

Tom shook his head. He didn't. But he'd been running on adrenaline.

"And Rafiel stayed behind to keep them in there, until the fire caught. Some must have escaped, but I don't think they're in a state to follow us." He looked at Tom, even as he took a sharp turn onto the highway toward Colorado. "That was awesome," he said, and grinned.

"Your cell phone?" Rafiel asked from the backseat. "If I may."

Tom forced himself to open his backpack. And almost wept at the sight of his black leather jacket, his boots, his meager possessions. He rifled through them, till his hand closed on the cell phone. He passed it to Rafiel, without even asking why or what was so urgent about a phone call.

"You could dress," Keith said. "You know . . ."

And Tom, obediently, without thinking, pulled out his spare T-shirt and pair of jeans and put them on. Then he slipped on his jacket and boots.

Rafiel was talking to someone on the cell phone. "No, damn it, he's fine. Well, he's bleeding, but you know we heal quickly. Don't worry. We'll be there in six hours or so."

"I have to drink something," Tom said. "I have to."

"Um . . . we might stop at a convenience store," he said. He leaned forward, toward Keith, and spoke urgently. "In this area, some of the convenience stores at the rest stops have everything. I could use a pair of shorts and a T-shirt."

Keith looked back, still driving, and grinned. "Yeah, you sure could."

"So," Rafiel said, into the phone. "Don't worry. We'll be there. Yes, I understand. We'll . . . discuss it later."

He turned the phone off and handed it to Tom, then leaned back in his seat.

Tom could only see him from the waist up, of course, but he seemed relatively unscathed by the ordeal. And he was . . . well, everything Tom was not. Much taller, much more self-assured. And a lion. Kyrie was a panther. Tom didn't have a chance.

"So," Keith said, oblivious to his friend's thoughts. "How long have you guys been able to change into animals, and how do I get in on this?"

Kyrie stood, holding the phone, not quite sure what to do or say. Edward Ormson was looking at her, attentively.

"Look," he said. "I know I have said the wrong thing." His expression changed as if he read a response she wasn't aware of expressing in her features. "Okay, many wrong things. But look, however misguided, however wrongheaded, your . . . your reaction to what I was trying to do, to my trying to obtain the Pearl from Tom woke me, made me realize how bizarre all of this was. I haven't seen Tom in five years, and I'll confess I was a horrible father. But I don't want him to die. Can you help me?"

Kyrie looked at him a long time. She'd taken his measure the first time they'd met. Or at least she'd thought so. He was cold and self-centered. A smart man and probably well-educated and definitely good-looking, he was used to having his own way and very little used to or interested in caring for anyone else.

He would have, Kyrie thought, viewed Tom as an accessory to his lifestyle. He'd have the beautiful wife, the lovely home and, oh, yes, the son. Tom—if Tom's personality had always been somewhat as it was now—must have been a hell of a disappointment. They must have clashed constantly—supposing Edward paid enough attention to his son to clash with him.

Weirdly, it was that resentment he felt toward Tom, the fact he talked about Tom as having been insufferable that gave her a feeling that, however hidden, however denied even to himself, the man must care for his son. Because if he didn't truly give a damn about Tom, Tom wouldn't get under his skin so much.

Then she realized she could very well be speaking about herself. She had spent an awful lot of the last six months reassuring herself of how impossibly annoying Tom was.

Of course, he was annoying. Tom was quite capable of sulking through an entire work shift, for reasons she never understood. And he had this way of looking at her, then flinching away as if he'd seen something that displeased him. Particularly on those silent, sulking days. He was also quite capable of doing exactly the opposite of what you asked him to do, if he thought you hadn't asked him nicely enough. But . . .

But Tom was also unexpectedly generous. He would cover for her if she needed it, not complaining about the extra work. He would cover her tables, too, if she was moving slow because she was tired or not feeling well. He would bus a disproportionate number of tables and not call her on it. He had a way of smiling and shrugging and walking away when she offered to give him part of her tips after he'd helped her with the tables. And once when she'd pressed him, he'd said, "Oh, it all evens out, Kyrie." She remembered that.

And he had a way of appreciating the funniest of their diners. Sometimes, while enjoying a particularly funny interaction between a college-age couple, Kyrie would look over and find Tom smiling at them, in silent amusement. And, of course, he was—she remembered him naked, in the parking lot—distractingly handsome. As disturbing as the circumstances had been . . . it couldn't be denied that he was attractive. Despite his height, she'd often seen college girls batting eyes and displaying chests and legs at him.

So, her constant annoyance at him might very well have been a defense.

She realized she was grinning, as well as blushing because Edward Ormson was looking at her as if she had just taken leave of her senses.

"I'm sorry," she said. "I just realized why your son annoys me so much," and was gratified to see him look puzzled at this. "But you don't need to worry about him right now. He is . . . fine now."

"He is?" Edward Ormson started to get up, then sat down. He looked as though someone had cut all his strings, or whatever had been holding him up. He visibly sagged in his chair.

He looked so relieved that she had to smile. She picked up his coffee cup. "Let me get you another coffee. Warmer."

But he got up and handed her a twenty-dollar bill. "No," he said. "No. I don't think I need the coffee. Or the . . . pie. I just need to go to bed. I'm . . ." He rubbed his hand across his forehead. "I find I'm very tired." He pulled something else from his wallet and wrote rapidly in the back of it. "This is my card. There's my cell phone on the front and I put my room number at Spurs and Lace." He handed it to Kyrie. "If Tom should . . ." He swallowed. "If you tell Tom . . ." He shrugged. "I don't want . . . Let him decide."

"I owe you about ten, twelve dollars change," Kyrie said. "Even with tip."

But he waved it away. "I don't want to waste time. I don't care. I'm very tired. I haven't slept in . . . much too long."

Kyrie almost argued, but then she saw him stumble to the door. She put the bill in her apron pocket. She would ring it up later.

She wondered where Tom was and how he really was. And what was happening.

When they stopped at the convenience store, Keith went in first.

"I forgot to ask if he had any money," Rafiel said from the back.

Tom had been dozing. He opened his eyes and looked back at Rafiel, then at the front of the brightly lit store and grinned. "I'd tell you that he probably does or he'd have said something, but since we're talking about a man who thinks driving while looking backwards to talk to you is a perfectly safe practice, I can't really be sure."

Rafiel nodded. He looked . . . less than composed and was hiding behind the backseat. Fortunately though even at this time of night the convenience store/rest stop was full of people, Keith had parked in a place with two empty spaces on either side. Of course, the store was brightly lit in front and even with the tinted windows, Rafiel had to feel awfully exposed.

"I don't think anyone can see in," Tom said, in what he hoped was a friendly voice. He was still starving and his mouth felt dry as sandpaper, but the brief doze had made him feel much more human, much more in command of his own faculties. He felt . . . almost like himself. Enough to feel sorry for the guy. Even if the guy had a lot more chances with Kyrie than Tom himself.

Rafiel raised his eyebrows at Tom's comment, and nodded. "I hope not, I would never live down being arrested for indecent exposure. Even if I explained it—somehow—and went free. It's not something police officers are supposed to do, walking around naked."

"Must be a bitch," Tom said, leaning back against the seat and closing his eyes. He wanted to go in and get water and food. All his money was still in the backpack. He'd checked. But he would prefer to go in with one—or preferably—two people who could grab him if he passed out. Or started shifting and tried to eat one of the tourists.

"Yeah," Rafiel said, quietly. "I have clothes hidden all over town." He was silent a minute. "I just never thought I needed them in the neighboring towns too."

Tom smiled in acknowledgment of the joke, and felt a hand on his shoulder.

"I don't think we've been formally introduced," Rafiel said. "My name is Rafiel Trall. I'm a police officer of Goldport."

Tom opened one eye to see a hand extended in his general direction. He shook it, hard. "Thomas Ormson," he said. "Troublemaker. Broadly speaking of Goldport, also."

Rafiel nodded. "I haven't thanked you for saving my life," he said.

"You don't need to," Tom said. "I thought you were someone else."

Rafiel smiled. "At least you had the excuse of darkness. Apparently other . . . dragons have trouble telling a female panther from a male lion. In full light."

"Ah . . . how did . . .?"

"Kyrie had sent me to check on Keith," Rafiel said, then frowned. "No. To tell you the truth, Kyrie sent me to look for you. She thought Keith might know where you were. So I was at his place when dragons came in. Through the window. So I . . . shifted before I knew what I was doing. And they tranquilized me. With a dart gun."

Tom nodded. "They really weren't very polite," he said, thinking how much preferable a dart gun would be than what they'd done to him. "I think they injected me with marinade."

Rafiel's face went very puzzled, but at that moment, Keith opened the door and threw a bundle at Rafiel. "Shorts, T-shirt, flip-flops. All in the best of taste and the cheapest stuff we could get and still make you decent. Enjoy."

Tom turned back to look at the clothes while Rafiel unfolded them. The T-shirt was white, with a mountain lion on the front and it said "Get Wild In New Mexico." The shorts were plaid and managed to look like a cross between bad golf clothes and a grandpa's underwear. And the flip-flops managed to combine green yellow and a headachy-violet in the minimal possible amount of rubber.

Looking at Rafiel staring aghast at the getup, Tom realized he really liked Keith an awful lot.

But Rafiel recovered quickly. "I'll pay you back, of course," he said.

Keith nodded. Tom, not sure Rafiel meant that as a threat or a promise, raised his eyebrows. Then he said, "Look, I'm dying of thirst. And hunger. I have some money and I want to go inside, but I want one of you to come with me. Or both, preferably."

"Why?" Keith asked.

"Well . . ." Tom shrugged. "I haven't eaten in very long. I also haven't slept much. When I eat I might pass out or . . . as soon as I'm a little stronger, I might try to shift and . . . eat tourists."

Keith's eyes went very wide.

Rafiel, moving frantically and, from the bits visible in the rear view mirror, dressing, in the back seat, said, "Even in Colorado that seems a bit drastic. And I don't even know if New Mexico's tourists are as annoying as ours." There was a sound of flip-flops thrown about, and then Rafiel opened the door. "Come on then. We'll escort you to the food and water."

Anthony had moved behind the counter and was turning burgers on the grill. That Frank didn't even seem to have realized he was cooking, was worrisome.

Anthony turned around, putting plates on the counter for Kyrie to pick up. "Those are your orders," he said. "And would you cover table fifteen for me? And table five?"

Kyrie nodded. She assumed that Frank hadn't responded to Anthony's requests that he cook. Considering that he normally wouldn't let them behind the counter for more than dishwasher-filling, coffee-pot-grabbing stints this was alarming indeed. But Frank was still bent over the counter, staring into the eyes of his dowdy girlfriend and whispering who knew what sweet nothings to her.

When had this become so serious? Kyrie had seen the woman around before, but never actually interfering with Frank's work.

They touched a lot, Kyrie noticed. More than they talked. Her hand was on his, her fingers beating a slow tattoo on the back of his hand. And his were on the side of her other arm, also beating some weird rhythm.

Ah, well. Dating for the speech impaired. And sight impaired, Kyrie thought, looking back at Frank's Neanderthal profile, and his girlfriend's faded lack of beauty.

But Anthony was moving the burgers and fries, mixing the salads, and generally cooking like a demon, and she didn't have much time to look at her employer as, over the next few minutes she carried trays back and forth, fulfilling long overdue orders for both her tables and Anthony's.

When she was caught up, she came back to get the carafe and the pitcher of iced tea for refills. Frank's girlfriend had got up and was heading out of the diner via the back hallway. Either that or going to the bathroom, of course.

And Frank had seemed to wake up. "No," he yelled at Anthony. "What are you doing?"

Uh-oh. Now the explosion came, Kyrie thought. But as she

approached, she realized Frank wasn't storming over the fact that Anthony had been manning the grill and the deep fryer. Instead, he was throwing a fit because there was a little insect on the counter, and Anthony had been about to squish it with a paper towel.

"What?" Anthony said, his hand poised above the little creature—which looked like a beetle of some sort, only too small to be any of the normal ones found in diners. "It's an IPS beetle, man. It lives in pines. It must have come in because the windows are open."

"There's no need to kill it," Frank said, pushing Anthony's hand away and taking the paper towel from it at the same time. With infinite patience, he coaxed the beetle onto the paper towel.

Anthony shrugged and turned the burgers. "It's not like it's endangered or anything, you know? They spray for them up in the mountains. They kill spruce."

But Frank didn't seem to care. He got the beetle all the way into the towel, then walked out back, along the hallway.

Half fascinated, wondering what could have turned Frank, purveyor of burgers to the masses, into a lover of the small and defenseless, Kyrie followed him part of the way. Enough to see him open the back door and put the beetle out, on the ground, close to the Dumpster.

Then he waved at his girlfriend, who was walking across the parking lot.

"Is she an animal lover?" Kyrie asked as Frank came back in.

"Debra? No. Why?"

Kyrie wasn't about to explain. Instead, she said, "Is it quite safe for her to walk home alone at night like that?"

He looked at her surprised. And behind the surprise something else. As if he were wondering why she was asking him the question. "Sure. She lives just at the castle. She'll be fine."

It didn't seem to admit further discussion.

"No more hot dogs," Keith told Tom. He handed him a thin pack of something cold. "Sliced ham."

Tom grabbed at it, trying to focus. He was vaguely aware that he'd eaten something like twenty-six hotdogs. And drunk something like four huge cups of something sickly sweet with a flavor vaguely reminiscent of cherries.

Somewhere at the back of his mind was the awareness that he was going to need to use the restroom soon. Even a shifter's bladder couldn't possibly hold that much.

But much closer at hand was a need for protein. Lots of it. He grabbed the pack Keith gave him and was about to bite it as Keith pulled it away.

"Whoa, you need to unwrap it."

Tom was aware of growling. Or rather he was aware of several faces of tourists roaming around turning to him in shock. He was aware of Keith jumping, then shoving the pack—now peeled halfway—back at him.

He shoved the ham into his mouth and ate it, becoming aware, halfway through, that his manners left much to be desired. And that the burning pit of hunger at the center of his being was . . . calmer, if not completely filled.

Rafiel, to whom Tom had handed a hundred dollars to deal with the damage, because he couldn't think and eat at the same time, approached them, carrying a bag of food. Tom could see a block of cheese and a couple of containers of what might be yogurt through the bag.

"Ready?" Rafiel asked. "You seem to have slowed down some."

Tom finished the last crumbs of meat, resisted an urge to lick the package. "I'll use the restroom," he said. "And I'll be right out."

"Good point," Rafiel said. "We grabbed you snacks but no drink. Keith, get us a six-pack of water." He passed Keith some money. "Tom, can I use your cell phone? In the car?"

Tom nodded.

When he got back to the car, Rafiel was behind the wheel and Keith next to him. "You get in the back," Keith said. "We figure you'd want to sleep some."

"There's cheese and cold cuts and stuff in the bag," Rafiel said. "If you're still hungry. And there's water. You can lie down. I drive better than he does."

"And there's a bag of baby wipes," Keith said. "Your face is caked with blood. I didn't even think how weird it looked till we went in there."

Tom climbed into the back. He was about to tell them he wasn't that tired, when he stretched out on the broad and comfy back eat. And then his eyes closed. And he didn't know anything more.

CHAPTER
❧ 9 ❧

He woke up with a running conversation up front.

"So, why was he so hungry again?" Keith said.

"The transformation takes . . . I don't know. Strength. Power. It costs us what seem to be parts of ourselves. The muscle needs to recover."

"Would he really have . . . Would he have eaten someone or was he . . . ?"

"I don't know," Rafiel said. "I don't know Mr. Ormson that well. I don't know how many shape-shifts he'd had without replenishing himself. I guess it's . . . I mean . . . I guess it depends. I've never eaten anyone." There was a short silence, and Tom saw Keith look at Rafiel.

"Well, at least not that I remember," Rafiel said. "When you're very hungry or very tired, or scared, or in any other way pressed, the memory of when you're . . . the beast . . . changes. And we smell dead bodies a long distance away. So . . . I found a lot of corpses. Still do. I don't think I've ever eaten anyone, though. And since in my job I deal with unknown deaths and disappearances, I probably would have heard of it. Or, when I was too young to be in the force, my father would have. So . . ." He shrugged.

Tom sat up and rested his face on the front seat, between the driver and passenger sides. "I might have eaten some of that corpse in the parking lot . . ." he said, and looked at Rafiel, in the rearview mirror. "I don't know if I killed him."

Rafiel shrugged. "As to that, I can reassure you, at least. You didn't. The corpse had no tooth marks, certainly no marks of being killed by a dragon."

"The guy who died?" Keith asked. "In the parking lot?"

Rafiel nodded, at the same time Tom asked, "But you said he was killed by a Komodo."

"Oh, that's right," Rafiel said. "We never told you . . . Kyrie and I when we came back you two were high because of the beetle powder. Well, insect powder, but Kyrie says it was beetles."

"Beetles?" Tom and Keith said, at the same time.

"There was green powder all over Kyrie's back porch," Rafiel said. "And it seemed to be of insect origin and . . . well, I have the lab checking for some form of hallucinogenic properties. But the lab seemed to think that corpse at least had some traces of hallucinogen in his blood. So, we think that the green powder caused both of you to get high and hallucinate."

"Oh," Tom said, and could say no more. Of course. It wasn't Kyrie's sugar. It was the things attacking them. He frowned as he tried to remember. He'd thought they were dragons, but looking back he wondered why. He could remember what seemed to be long, long limbs, with fangs at the end, and he remembered green wings, but they didn't in any way look like dragon wings.

"But you said something about Komodo dragons?"

"Well, yes. There have been a few deaths that seemed to be caused by Komodo dragons. Really large Komodo dragons. Because the victims were all Asian, I suspected it had to do with triad business, and now I'm almost sure of it. I suspect it's the dragon triad. Some way they punish their members. That seems to be totally unrelated to the thing going on with the beetles. You seem to be the only link, Mr. Ormson."

Tom groaned. "My father is Mr. Ormson. I'm Tom. Particularly . . ." He managed a tired smile but couldn't see if Rafiel responded because all he saw of Rafiel in the rearview mirror was his very intent eyes. "Particularly to people who've seen me wolf down two dozen over cooked convenience store hotdogs." He made a face. "They weren't even all that good."

"Oh," said Keith. "There were also two containers of cottage cheese while the man was cooking more hot dogs, and a couple of pepperoni."

"Pepperoni?" Tom asked, and felt a moan break through his lips. "I don't even like pepperoni."

"Well, if you're going to throw up," Rafiel said. "You'd best do it out the window. We're still in Raton and we have about two more hours before we get home."

"I'm not going to throw up," Tom said. "Now, if I had taken Keith's finger when he tried to pull the cold cuts away, then I might have."

"You growled," Keith said.

"Dangerous that," Rafiel said, and though Tom couldn't see his face, he was now quite sure there would be a smile twisting the policeman's lips. "Taking food from a starving dragon. Just so you know, it's not all that safe with a lion, either."

Keith made a sound that might have been a really fake whimper, then perked up and grinned at Rafiel. "Oh, well. Worth the price of admission just to have heard you explain to the cashier that Tom had an eating disorder. I don't know how they thought that related to the fact that his face was covered in blood. Why was your face covered in blood?" he asked, looking back.

"Well . . . I think I took Red Dragon's arm. Front paw. Whatever. But I think there was blood before." Tom touched a snaking pink scar that crossed his forehead. "They broke my skin there. And I think they might have broken my nose, though it looks the normal shape, so maybe they just hit it hard enough to make it bleed and tear the cartilage."

"But . . . How long ago?" Keith said.

"We heal freakishly fast," Rafiel said. "But you might want to use the wipes back there, anyway, Tom. I'd suspect you rubbed some of it off on the seat back there, but you still look like you were in an accident. And if you don't clean up and we stop for any reason . . ."

Tom noted that his first name had been used, as he grabbed the baby wipes and wiped at the mess, using the rearview mirror, for guidance.

"And are you undead?" Keith said. "I mean . . . can you be killed, unless it's a silver bullet, or whatever?"

Rafiel shrugged. "I don't know. Tom, have you ever been killed?"

"I thought I was going to be," he said. "Out there, alone with the triad guys. I thought if they didn't kick me to death, they were going to kill me some other way. And if not, I thought I would be killed if I gave them what they wanted."

"And what did they want?" Rafiel said, very softly.

"Well," Tom said. "I brought the conversation around because I thought you deserved to know, but I'm not sure how to explain. Let me start by saying my dad was a lawyer."

"Ah, well, all is clear," Keith said. "No wonder you turn into a dragon."

Tom grinned. "He's a lawyer with a big firm, in New York. Or at least he was, five years ago. His firm represented some Asian families that had . . . contracts with the triads. It wasn't so much, I think, that the firm set out to represent a criminal organization. More like they started representing people at the margins of it, and then eventually, they were defending members of the triad in criminal trials. And my dad is a criminal lawyer. So . . ."

Rafiel nodded. "Yeah. I suspect a lot of lawyers end up having contact with less than savory creatures."

"Well, at one point, some people came over to my father's house. There was something that had landed from China, and they wanted him to keep it safe for them till the next day. He was the only person they trusted in New York, one of the very few people they'd had contact with. They came to our condo, which I remember my father was very upset about because he hadn't given them permission.

"I was . . . oh, probably five? My mom was working. My nanny was watching soaps. I was very bored. So I snuck around to hear what my dad was saying. These people were not like the people who normally came to visit, you know—they wore actual Chinese outfits in silk. I was fascinated."

He was quiet a while. He remembered the Pearl unveiling. He remembered . . .

"And then?" Rafiel said.

"And then they explained to my father that this was the Pearl of Heaven. It had been given to the Great Sky Dragon by the Heavenly Emperor. They said that many of their members, though not all, had the ability to shift shapes to become dragons. I didn't believe them, of course. And I could tell my dad didn't. And then they put this felt bag on his desk, and they pulled it down. And the Pearl appeared. It was . . . Imagine something that radiates light, that makes you swim with happiness.

"They said that it was needed to keep peace amid shapeshifters who were dragons part of the time, because the characteristics of the dragons remained in the humans, and there was too much strife otherwise. As a kid—and you realize I never had what could be called a good family life, back then—all I could sense and feel was the warmth and approval of the Pearl. And that's all I remembered."

"And?" Keith asked.

Tom realized he'd been quiet for a long while. "And then at sixteen I started turning into a dragon. I had a little trouble believing it at first, and then I thought that it was very cool. Like a superpower."

"That's what I think," Keith said.

"And then . . . My father caught me coming in as a dragon and transforming. I actually had this down to a science. I could kind of perch on the balcony outside my bedroom, and shift back to human, and then drop into the room through the sliding doors. Anyway, my dad caught me. He must have seen the dragon fly in. And he came to look. I only had time to grab my bathrobe. He thought . . . I don't know what he thought, but he looked terrified. He ordered me out of the house. I thought he was joking. He got a gun."

Tom laughed without humor. "My father who was a member of I don't know how many antigun organizations. He had a gun somewhere in his desk. He ran to grab it. I thought he was joking. I thought he would calm down. He ordered me out of the house at gunpoint and I went."

"Barefoot and in a robe?" Rafiel said. "In New York City. Amazing you survived."

Tom shrugged. "There are organizations for runaways. I wasn't, but I was the right age, the right profile, and all I had to do was say no when they offered to mediate my return home with my father." He shrugged again. "In a year I was lying about my age and getting jobs. But I hated the shift. I hated that it came when I didn't expect it. And because I fought it till the last possible minute, I often couldn't remember what I'd done when I'd shifted. I . . ." He looked at Rafiel. "I tried street drugs."

"Anything in the last six months?" Rafiel asked. "Since you've been in Goldport?"

"Only whatever the triad boys injected into me," Tom said.

"Ah. We don't regulate marinade. The rest is really none of my business. It's all hearsay, anyway. I have no proof. You might just be nuts and think you used and sold drugs."

"I never sold it," Tom said.

"Good. That's harder to give up, sometimes," Rafiel said. "What with connections . . . So, you tried some funny stuff, to control it. Did it?" His interest sounded clinical.

"Not so you could notice. I was using mostly heroin because of its being a depressant. I thought it would stop the shift. Since the shift came with big emotions and such."

Rafiel nodded.

"So I wanted to give it up, but I was scared," Tom said. "The one thing the drugs did was make me forget. And make me calmer when I wasn't a dragon. They . . . simplified my life. I couldn't obsess about being a dragon shapeshifter or about the fact that my own father had kicked me out of the house, or any of that, because I was too worried about getting enough money for the next fix."

Rafiel nodded. "Weirdly, I've heard other addicts say that this was more important for them than the physical effects. The simplification of life and of choices."

"It was for me," Tom said. "And then one day, I was in a small city—I don't even remember where—and I felt . . . I felt the Pearl. And I got the bright idea that if I had the Pearl I wouldn't need the drugs. So I followed the feeling. And I came to this incredible meeting of dragon shapeshifters. It was dark and the little town was asleep. The parking lot was filled with men . . . And many dragons. And there was . . . The Great Sky Dragon. I don't know how to explain this.

"He's like a dragon god. Not like God, the God above, the one God, but like a god. Like . . . like the Roman gods would be to humans. That's how the Great Sky Dragon was to the rest of us. I could imagine people offering sacrifices and . . . virgins to him. Like in the legends. And he had the Pearl."

Tom heard himself sigh. "I wanted the Pearl. I'm not stupid. Not when I don't want to be. They were all basking in the glow of the Pearl and stuff. And they were all scared of the Great Sky Dragon. I'm not very good at being scared," he said, and watched Rafiel nod.

"I was impressed by the Great Sky Dragon," Tom said. "But not scared as such. So I paid attention to who took the Pearl, and it was another dragon in attendance. He put it in a wicker basket. And I loitered till the dragon shifted shape. He was the owner of a small Chinese restaurant in town. I followed him there. And then . . . I . . . well . . . I waited. And I watched. And I planned. And then I ran in, got the Pearl and got out of there fast."

Tom frowned. "I must have taken them completely by surprise, because they didn't even think to follow me for a while. And meanwhile I found out they couldn't sense or follow the Pearl by sense if it was submerged in water. I couldn't follow it if it was submerged in water. I brought it out West inside an aquarium packed in foam peanuts in a cardboard box, in the luggage hold of various busses."

"Did it help with the addiction?" Rafiel asked.

"It helped with controlling myself, not necessarily the addiction—though perhaps the two are related. When I got it out and looked at it, I felt . . . calm, peaceful, accepted. And then even if I shifted, I didn't feel like it was a terrible thing or that I should be shunned or killed for it. Does it make sense?"

Rafiel nodded. He was frowning. Keith was looking back, and his eyes were wide—and was that pity in them? Tom didn't want Keith's pity.

"Anyway," he said, looking out the window at the mostly

deserted landscape they were crossing, "anyway, I kicked the habit. It wasn't as difficult as I thought. Rough moments, but I think that the fact we heal so easily . . ." He shrugged.

Rafiel nodded. "It would help, wouldn't it? The tendency to reassert balance. And Keith, when you asked if we were, I guess, immortal? I don't know, not more than anyone else. It's hard to say. Until you die you don't know, and then it's academic. I try to stay away from people trying to shoot me with silver bullets."

"Or any bullets," Tom said, wryly. "And before you ask, I brought the Pearl with me to Goldport. And it's stashed in water. They want it back. To be honest, I wouldn't mind giving it back, but I can't. Because I think once I give it back to them, they kill me."

Rafiel made a face. "There has to be a way of giving it back." He was quiet a while. Then he said, "But I guess it doesn't have anything to do with the beetles, then?"

Tom shrugged. "I didn't know about the beetles till tonight."

"What would you estimate the percentage of shifters in the population is?" Rafiel said. "From your travels?"

"I don't know," Tom said. "Not very high. Considerably less than one percent. Even if we go on legends."

"Even if we go on legends . . ." Rafiel said, as an echo. "But you know, we know three at least, in our immediate sphere, and then there's the beetles, at least two. From their size, there's no way they can be non-shifters. And there's one of their victims who smelled like a shifter—though I only caught a bit of blood. And another that was definitely a shifter. The corpse in the parking lot." He nodded at Tom. "His wife said he was a coyote shifter."

"Lucky bastard," Tom said feelingly. "A coyote would be much easier."

Rafiel laughed and for a moment there was a bond. "Tell me about it," he said. "Here's the thing, though, Tom, why so many of us? And why is all this activity around the Athens?"

Tom shook his head. "I have no idea."

"Except," Keith said, "except maybe there's something like the Pearl of Heaven? Something that calls shifters there? That works on shifters?"

"Perhaps the Pearl?" Rafiel asked.

Tom didn't think Rafiel was working for the triad, but you never knew. "Not the Pearl," he said. "At any rate, where I have the Pearl, it's submerged. So it's not exerting influence on anyone. If the dragons who know what it feels like can't feel it, then neither can anyone else."

"Um . . ."

"Speaking of the triad," Tom said. "How come we're driving their car, and they're not hot on our trail?"

"Well . . . you flamed them pretty thoroughly," Keith said.

"Yeah, but . . . come on? No one has checked? And don't forget they have aerial transportation."

"Well," Rafiel said. "Two things. While you were in the bathroom at the station, I called some friends in New Mexico and told them the old station was a triad hangout and I'd heard from a friend that it had just gone up in flames. At a guess, any of them that got out is in too much trouble to talk, much less count the car wrecks in the parking lot. It's genuinely possible they think you burned."

Tom nodded. "And the other thing?"

Keith chuckled. "We bought three cans of spray paint. While you were in the restroom, we spray painted the top of the car. Just the top. So that aerial surveillance . . ."

"Painted? What color?"

"Mostly bright orange," Rafiel said. "It was what they had. The front is still black. We ran out of paint." He grinned at Keith who was still chuckling. "People did look at us like we were nuts."

"I bet."

"So what do we do now?" Keith asked.

"Well, first we get to Goldport," Rafiel said. "I'd like to change clothes . . ." He frowned down at himself. "And I probably should call in and figure out the news on the case. Also tell them I didn't drop from the face of the world, since I was supposed to be at work a few hours ago."

"And then?" Keith said.

"And then I think Tom and I, and Kyrie should get together and figure out what we're going to do. Both about the Pearl of Heaven and the triad and about the beetles." He looked back at Tom. "They attacked Kyrie's house, you know, after you left."

"Damn. Is she okay?"

"She's fine."

"My fault," Tom said. "I shouldn't have stayed there. They were probably after me."

"Don't be a fool. I think they were after her. She had seen them in the parking lot, dragging a corpse, and it was clear they knew she saw them."

"Hey," Keith said. "Why you and Tom and Kyrie? Why am I being left out of this? What have I done wrong?"

Rafiel frowned. "Well, you're not . . . one of us, are you? I mean . . . we have to police our own and help our own, because if one of us is discovered, the others will be too. But you don't have to help us. You're not . . ."

"Yeah, but I want to help," Keith said. "Can I like be an honorary shapeshifter or something?"

"Why?" Tom asked, puzzled.

"Oh, hell. You guys are cool. It's like SF or a comic book."

"Except you could get hurt. Quickly," Tom said.

"I could get hurt very quickly anyway. Look, they knew you were my friend, they came to my house to get me. Surely that means I'm already not safe. I might as well help."

"Tom, he has a point," Rafiel said. "Kyrie's house is clearly not safe. Your apartment is destroyed. I doubt that Keith's apartment is safe. And I . . ."

"You?"

"I live with my parents," Rafiel said. "They know I'm a shifter. They help me if needed. It's convenient."

"I didn't say anything," Tom said.

Rafiel shrugged. "But I can't bring you guys there. If we're tracked . . . I can't risk them. Dad isn't doing so well these days."

"So you're saying you don't know where we can get together?"

Rafiel nodded. "Drop me off at home first. Then call Kyrie and tell her to meet you somewhere. Then pick me up in her car. We should leave this one in a public park or something. I don't think they'll report it stolen, but you never know." He drummed his fingers on the side of the wheel. "And then we'll figure out where to go. Perhaps a hotel room? A hotel would be good, wouldn't it? It's so public that I don't think even the triad would risk it."

Tom nodded.

"And I'm in? I'm in, right?" Keith asked.

"You're in," Rafiel said.

"There's a distinct possibility you're too addled to be left on your own," Tom said.

"Hey," Keith said, but he was smiling.

Tom felt odd. There was a weird camaraderie. He hadn't had friends in a long time. He hadn't ever had friends, truly. Not real friends.

He only hoped he could keep them all alive by the end of this.

Kyrie was standing at the counter, adding up her hours, when her cell phone rang. She dipped into the apron pocket, and brought it out. "Yes?"

"Kyrie?"

It was Tom. Until she felt relief flooding through her, she didn't realize that she couldn't be absolutely sure he was still alive till she heard from him.

She almost called his name, but then realized that Anthony was behind the counter doing something and that she didn't know if Frank was hanging out somewhere. So, instead, she said, "Yes?"

"Thank God it's you," he said. There was a sound like coughing. "You didn't say anything and I wondered if I'd done something wrong and called the police department in New Mexico."

"What?"

"Later. Rafiel said he'd told you that you might need to pick us up."

"Yes."

"Well, can you come? We're in the parking garage for the zoo. We've parked on the third level, and we'll come down to meet you up front. In front of the zoo."

"We?"

"Keith and I. We'll swing by Rafiel's place on the way, okay?"

"Sure."

She hung up and found Anthony staring at her. "Was that Frank?"

"No."

"Damn," Anthony said. "I don't know where he's gone. I'm going to have to stay here and wait for the day-shift people. Will you wait with me?"

"I can't," Kyrie said. "I've got to meet a friend."

"The guy you were talking to?" Anthony asked, gesturing toward the enclosure. "He looks an awful lot like Tom."

"It's his father," Kyrie said, as she headed for the door. She'd parked up front again. She didn't think she could ever park in the parking lot again. Not for all the money in the world.

"Oh," Anthony said, just as she opened the door and went out.

Kyrie realized a little too late that Anthony might think that she was having an affair with Tom's dad. But she didn't think so. Anthony was a rather conventional person, other than the bolero thing, and was more likely to have her engaged to Tom in his mind—and to assume that his father's visit had something to do with finalizing the arrangements.

The drive to the zoo wasn't long. Just a few blocks down Fairfax and then a turn into a tangle of streets named after presidents.

It didn't really matter which you took, since they were all parallel. Either Madison or Jackson took you to a sharp turn at Taylor and then up Wilson where the street namers had run out of presidents and offered, instead, Chrysalis Street, which in turn, exhausted by all these flights of fancy ended in Main Parkway, where the zoo, the library, and the pioneer museum were all located.

Finding Tom and Keith at the entrance wasn't hard either. She simply took a long turn around the parking lot, and—circling by the door—saw the two only people standing there, since the zoo was still closed.

She very much doubted it would have been hard to find them even if there had been crowds streaming by the door, though. Tom looked like he'd been put through a shredder. There was blood on his face, his hair was a mess, and he looked like he was about to fall over of tiredness.

But he smiled when he saw her, and she couldn't help smiling back as she opened the door. For some reason, she expected him to be mad at her, for throwing him out—for thinking he'd gotten high. But he didn't look resentful at all. He sat in the passenger seat, while Keith took the backseat. And Tom strapped himself down with the seat belt, too, she noted.

"We have to call Rafiel and go get him," Tom said.

"We do?"

"Yes. He went home to change. His clothes were shredded sometime . . . around the time they captured him." He gave her a quick rundown of everything that had happened and Kyrie listened, eyebrows raised, trying not to show just how harrowing the account was. Particularly the torture.

When he was done she thought how strange he was that he should have endured all that torture and yet have roused himself to action when he thought Keith—and herself—were in trouble. She took a sidelong glance at Tom, who was dialing his cell phone. There was someone there, she thought. Someone salvageable despite whatever his upbringing and his unexpected shifter nature had done to him.

"Rafiel," Tom said into the phone. Followed by raised eyebrows and, "I see." Which was, in turn, followed by, "Sure."

"He wants to know where we're going to be. He says he'll meet us. He's looking up some data on missing people. He says there's a spike over the last two months. He wants to know what the chances are those people are shifters. Something in the family interviews might give it away, he said. And he definitely wants to figure out how many people were headed for the Athens or vicinity when they disappeared. So he says he'll meet us wherever we're going. And he asks which hotel."

Hotel. Kyrie had been thinking about this. There was an off chance the triad—or the beetles, whoever they were—would decide to call around to hotels for their names. But the hotels they would call around to—if they got around to that—would be in their price range. Not the Spurs and Lace.

"We thought it would be better to meet at a hotel," he said into the phone. "Particularly a large hotel. Lots of guests. No shapeshifter, even one not quite in his right mind, would want to have that kind of public revelation."

"Where are we going?" he said. "Rafiel says he'll meet us wherever."

"Tom . . . What do you think of your father?"

Tom's eyes widened. His face lost color—which she would have thought impossible before. "Why?" he asked.

"Because he's in town and he—"

"Hang on a second," Tom said into the phone. "I'll call you back in a couple of minutes." He hung up the phone and set it in his lap, then looked at Kyrie. "My father?" he said, not so much as though he were verifying her words, but as though he were in doubt that such a thing as a father existed.

"Your father came to town two days ago and he—"

"Oh, shit," Tom said. "You realize he's probably working for the triad?"

"He was," Kyrie said.

"And? What did he do? Where did he go?"

"He came to me."

Tom's hand clenched so hard on the phone that his knuckles shone white through the pale skin. His face remained impassive. "What did he ask you?"

"Many things. But most of all he seemed to be concerned with where you were, and I couldn't have helped him even if I wanted to."

Tom nodded. "And?"

"And I realized he was working for the triad and I was so shocked that I . . . I left."

"Good," Tom said, and picked up the phone again. "Now, where should we go to that Rafiel can meet us?"

"Tom," Kyrie said, speaking in a low voice because she felt as though Tom were something very unstable on the verge of an explosion. Should not be shaken, stirred, or even looked at cross-eyed, as far as she could tell. "Your father has a hotel room. At the Spurs and Lace."

She expected the silence, and it came, but then she expected a flip remark, and that didn't come. Instead, Tom's face seemed set in stone, his eyebrows slightly pulled together as if he were puzzled, his face expressionless, his eyes giving the impression of being so unreadable that they might as well have a blind pulled down in front of them.

"He said to call him if we needed anything."

"Kyrie," Tom said. It was a slow, even voice. "Are you out of your mind?"

"No." She was prepared to be firm. It was the best solution, and yes, she realized it would disturb Tom, but she was determined to keep them safe. By force if needed. "No. I'm not. He said to call him, and we can meet him at the Spurs and Lace. Our names won't be on the register and I don't think anyone will think that he and you will be under the same roof."

"And there are reasons for that," Tom said, his voice still even. "Kyrie, he's working for the triad."

"No, he's not. He realized that they wanted to . . . kill you. And he came to me. He wanted me to save you."

"No. That might have been what he said. But he was just trying to find me, to—"

"Tom, I am not an idiot," Kyrie said, and saw something flicker in his eyes and for just a moment thought that Tom was going to tell her she was. But he didn't say anything, and she went on. "I saw what he was doing first, but he changed. He said that he didn't want you dead. He came to the Athens in the middle of the night, looking like the walking dead. And he begged me to help him."

"Kyrie. He's a lawyer. Lawyers lie. It's right in the contract."

She shook her head. "He wasn't lying."

"No? How not? What sign did he give you of his amazing turnaround, Kyrie? Tell me. Maybe it will convince me. I know the bastard far better than you do." He left the phone resting on his knees and crossed his arms on his chest, in a clear body-language sign that like hell he'd listen.

"If he shifts into a dragon in the car, I'm jumping out," Keith said, quietly, from the back.

Kyrie ignored Keith. "I know he's changed in his view of it, because he tried to convince me how bad you are."

Tom's eyes widened. "All right, Kyrie. I was the one who was hit on the head, but you seem to be the one affected by it. He's always said how bad I was."

"No," Kyrie said, and shook her head. "Not like this. He stopped just short of saying you botched your spelling bee in third grade. Your father, Tom, realized suddenly that he messed up big with you. And he's trying to justify it to himself by telling someone in increasingly more ridiculous terms how nasty a person you are."

Tom didn't answer. He was biting the corner of his lower lip.

"Look—I—" She stopped short of telling him she had done the same. Just. "I tend to do what he was doing, so I understand the process. Besides, when I told him you were safe, when Rafiel called, he went all slack. I've never seen someone so relieved."

"Okay, so maybe he didn't want me to die. Maybe he was relieved at that. Doesn't mean he won't change his mind again when he actually sees me."

"I don't think so," Kyrie said. "I don't think he will. And Tom, we could use his room. I'm indentured for the next six months, you can't have that much money. We'd have to get Rafiel to pay for it. I'd . . . I'd rather not." The last thing she wanted to tell Tom was that Rafiel had kissed her. Oh, Tom had no reason at all for jealousy, nor did she know if she had any interest in Tom's kissing her—Okay. So, she had to stop lying to herself, she thought again, looking at his face— Yeah, she wanted to kiss him. She just wasn't sure where it would go and *that* she wasn't sure if she wanted. But Tom had no reason for jealousy and she doubted he would have any, but she would still prefer not to tell him about it.

"Kyrie, I don't believe in big turnarounds. I don't believe people change that much."

Oh, she was going to hate to have to say this. "I don't believe it either, Tom, but . . . You're no longer a hard-core drug user who would steal cars for joyrides without a second thought, are you? So there must be change."

Tom's mouth dropped open. For a moment she thought he was

going to ask her to stop the car so he could get out. His hand actually moved toward the door handle. And then he seemed to realize she wasn't insulting him. The meaning of her words seemed to actually penetrate through his thick head.

He took a deep breath and held the phone out to her. "You call Daddy Dearest."

It would have been easiest to tell him she was driving and couldn't, but Kyrie was aware of the victory this represented. So, instead, she pulled over into a vacant parking space on the side of Polk Street and grabbed the phone. Pulling Edward's number from her purse, she dialed.

The phone rang, and she asked for the room number from the bored-sounding receptionist. Then his bedroom phone rang. Once, twice, three, four times. She expected the message to come on, when the phone was picked up, and clearly dropped, and picked up again.

"Hello," a sleepy male voice said from the other side.

"Mr. Ormson?" Kyrie said.

"Kyrie." The name came out with force, as though it would be more effort to keep it in. "Tom. Is Tom all right? Anything wrong with—"

"No. Tom is right here. He's fine. We were wondering if we could camp in your hotel room for a few hours."

"Beg your pardon?"

"Tom and I, and a couple of friends. We're . . . in danger from . . . your friends and . . . other people. We wondered if we could hide there till we find a plan of action."

There was a silence from the other side. And then a voice that sounded as if he didn't quite know what he was saying. "Sure, of course. Sure." A small pause. "And Tom is with you?"

"Yes."

"Oh." A deep breath, the sound of it audible even through the phone. "Sure. Of course. Anything you need."

"Thank you," Kyrie said and hung up the phone. She handed the phone to Tom and said, "Call Rafiel."

"Daddy Dearest is even now calling the triad bosses," Tom said.

His mouth set in an expression of petulant disdain. "They'll be there when we get there."

"I doubt it," Kyrie said.

"And if they are, we fight them," Keith said, leaning forward.

Okay, so being "scared" didn't even begin to describe the state of Tom's emotions as they pulled into the parking lot of the Spurs and Lace.

The problem wasn't being scared. He was used to being scared at this point. In the last three days, he'd been scared so often that he thought he wouldn't actually know what to do if he weren't in fear of someone or something. But this time he didn't even know what he was scared of.

Okay—so, if the triad members were there, Keith was right. They fought. And if Tom had to sacrifice himself so Kyrie and Keith got out of this unscathed, he would do so. He'd been prepared to do it before, in the abandoned gas station. So, why not now?

So . . . that wasn't the big source of his fear. The big source of his fear was that his father would be there, without the triad, and that all would be seemingly nice between them. He couldn't imagine talking to his father as if nothing had happened, as if . . . Worse, he couldn't imagine his father talking to him like that. But he'd been worried about Tom. Tom couldn't understand that either.

He settled for thinking that his father had been exchanged by aliens. It didn't make much sense and it wasn't very likely, but heck, what around here was likely? He'd just think that this was pod-father, and with pod-father, he had no history.

He got out of the car, and followed Kyrie and Keith up to the elevator and up in the elevator to the room, only slightly gratified by the puzzled looks the staff gave him. Up at the fifth floor, they walked along the cool, carpeted hallway toward room 550.

Tom took in the trays with used dishes at the door to the rooms, and the general atmosphere of quiet. There were no detectable odors in the air. Down the hallway, an ice machine hummed and clunked.

The classiest place he'd been in before this was Motel Six. Oh, he supposed he'd been in hotels as a child. In fact, he had vague memories of a trip to Rome with mother and father and, of course, his nanny, when he was ten. But most of the stuff before he'd left home now seemed to him like scenes from someone else's life.

And perhaps that was the best way to think about it. The Tom who'd been ordered at gunpoint from his childhood home was dead and gone. This new Tom was a stranger to the man in the room.

But when Kyrie knocked, the door was open by a man who looked far too much like the father Tom remembered for Tom not to take a step back, shocked—even as his father's gaze scanned him indifferently once, before returning, and then his eyes opened wider, and he opened his mouth as if to say something, but closed it again in silence and, instead, stepped aside to let them in.

He was wearing the pants and a shirt for the type of suit that Tom remembered his father wearing—fabric good enough to look expensive without looking ostentatious. But this one looked like hell—or like he'd been sleeping in it. His hair too, was piled up in a way that suggested a total disregard for combs.

But the strangest thing was that, as he stepped aside, so they could enter the room, Tom's father stared intently at Tom.

Tom let his gaze wonder around the room, instead. It was . . . dark red. And opulent. There was a dark red bedspread on the bed and from its sheen it might have been real silk. Someone had pulled it up hastily and a bit crookedly, so Tom's father had probably been in bed when they called, and had tried to make the bed in a hurry. Tom felt a strange satisfaction about this. To his knowledge, it was the first time his father had engaged in housekeeping for Tom's benefit.

Besides the bed, there were a loveseat and three armchairs and two chairs, a huge desk, where his father had a laptop, resting. And a lot more empty space than there should be in a room with all that furniture.

Over the bed was an abstract collage that brought the art form completely out of the realm of nutty Seventies fads—a thing in deep textures and gold and bronze colors.

The bathroom, glimpsed as Tom was going past, was all marble and actually two rooms, the first of which contained just a sink with a hair dryer and various other essentials of toiletry. Tom ached for a shower with an almost physical pain, but he went in to the bedroom, quietly.

"Mr. Ormson," Kyrie said. "Thanks for letting us come in at such short notice."

He shook his head. "No problem. Make use of . . . whatever you want. Tom? Are you . . . There's blood on you."

Tom shook his head. "I'm fine." And then, as though betraying that he wasn't, he walked over to the most distant armchair and sat down, as far away from his father as he could get.

His father frowned at him a moment, but didn't say anything.

"I wonder if Rafiel is going to be much longer," Tom said, pretending not to feel the weight of that gaze on him.

Keith sat down on one of the straight-backed chairs, and Kyrie, after some hesitation, took the armchair next to Tom's.

She looked at him, too, but her gaze was not full of disapproving enquiry. Unlike his father's expression, Kyrie's was warm and full of sympathy.

He wanted to smile at her, to pat her hand. But just because the woman didn't want him dead; just because the woman didn't think he was dangerous or a criminal, it didn't mean that she had any interest whatsoever in him.

So instead, he fidgeted in the chair and looked out of the window into the parking lot. But he kept looking at her out of the corner of his eye. She looked good enough to eat—and not in the sense he'd threatened to eat tourists. That cinnamon skin, those heavy-lidded eyes. He looked away. If he allowed himself to contemplate the perfection of her lips, or the way her breasts—one of which he remembered with particular fondness—pushed out her T-shirt, he wouldn't be able to answer for his actions.

Instead, he looked again, at her tapestry-dyed hair, falling in lustrous layers. And he remembered he had something of hers.

Digging frantically in his jacket pocket, he brought it out. He saw her eyes widen, and her smile appear, as he offered her the earring on his palm.

"You found it," she said.

"My landlady did," he said. "And I took it. I was hoping . . . I was hoping I would see you again, to be able to give it to you."

He felt himself blush and felt like a total idiot. But Kyrie put the earring on and was smiling at him. He'd have been willing to go a long way for that. Coming to his father's hotel room seemed like a minor sacrifice.

Even if Daddy Dearest ended up selling them up the river.

CHAPTER
⇥ 10 ⇤

The boy looked tense, Edward thought. Only the thing was, he wasn't a boy, anymore, was he? The face looking back at Edward's with such studied lack of expression was covered in dark stubble. And the shoulders had filled out, the arms become knotted with muscle.

Tom was wearing a black leather jacket, ratty jeans, and heavy boots. His father could have passed him a hundred times in the street and never recognized him. Only the eyes were the same he remembered from childhood, the same that looked out of his own mirror at him, every morning. But Tom's eyes showed no expression. They allowed him to look at them, and then they slid away from contact, without revealing anything.

There was blood on him too, and a snaking scar on his forehead. Had the triad done that, or had Tom gone through worse scrapes in the last five years? There were many things Edward wanted to know. Unfortunately, they were the ones he would never dare ask.

He watched Tom for a while, watched him pull out the girl's earring and give it back to her. He wondered if the two young fools had any idea that they were giving each other sick-puppy-dog looks.

But not only wasn't it his place to interfere, he was sure if he tried to tell them, either of them would put him soundly in his place.

"Do you guys want some coffee?" he asked, "I'm making some for myself."

There were sounds that might be agreement from the bedroom, as he set up the coffee maker. Fortunately the Spurs and Lace went for normal-sized coffeemakers, not the one-cup deals that were normally the rule. And they provided enough coffee and enough cups. He set it to run and thought.

The boy needed a shower. And probably clean clothes. But Edward had a feeling that if he offered either Tom might very well fling out of the room in a fury. He got a feeling that Tom was holding something in, battling something. And that if he let it all blow, none of them would like it.

Of course, if Tom should shift to a dragon . . . Edward peered around the door at the young man and Kyrie, who were now talking to each other, while Tom had closed his eyes and appeared to be dozing.

Neither the young man nor Kyrie looked scared that Tom would shift into a dragon, so it couldn't be that frequent an occurrence.

The coffee was made, and Edward had a sudden flash of inspiration. Everything that he might offer Tom would be refused. But if he handed it to Tom as a matter of fact, there was at least the off chance that Tom wouldn't know how to refuse. He'd looked many things, none of them at ease.

So, testing his theory, Edward poured himself a cup of coffee, and then one for Tom, surprising himself with retrieving, from the mists of memory, how Tom liked his coffee. The boy had only started drinking it when he'd . . . left. But Edward remembered ribbing him about liking three spoons of sugar in it.

He now poured in three packets of sugar and then crossed the room, trying to look completely at ease. For all his appearances in uncertain cases, in courtrooms presided over by hostile judges, this was probably his greatest performance. "Coffee is ready," he told Kyrie and the other young man. "If you wish to help yourselves." Then he walked up to Tom.

The armchair the boy was sitting in was right next to a side table, and on the other side of that was the straight-backed chair normally used at the desk.

Edward put his own coffee cup down on the side table, and leaned over, touching Tom's shoulder, lightly. "Tom, coffee," he said.

Tom woke up immediately, and sat up, fully alert. Edward remembered that he used to sleep late and sometimes miss first period at school. When had he learned to wake up like this, quickly, without complaint. How had he been living that a moment's hesitation between being asleep and full alertness might make a difference?

He couldn't ask. "I put three packets of sugar in. The way you like it."

Tom looked surprised. He reached for the cup, took it to his lips without complaint. And Edward sat at the desk chair, and took a deep draught of his coffee, feeling ridiculously proud of himself. It had worked. If handed things straight off, Tom was too confused to refuse. It was the first time in years . . . No. It was the first time Tom's lifetime that Edward had set himself to learn how to get around his stubborn son without a confrontation. And it had paid off.

It was all he could do to keep himself from smiling in victory. Fortunately, at that moment, someone knocked at the door and Kyrie opened it.

"Mr. Edward Ormson, this is Rafiel Trall, a police officer of Goldport."

Officer Rafiel Trall was tall and golden haired, with the sort of demeanor one would expect from a duke or visiting royalty. He shook Edward's hand, but there was a slight hesitation, and Edward wondered what Tom had told him about his father.

But then, as the young people pulled chairs together to talk, Edward slipped out the door, quietly.

He didn't know if they were all shape changers, and he didn't know how they'd react to what he was about to do.

But he knew he had to do it.

Tom smiled at seeing Keith immediately assume the role of secretary of the organization. Sometimes people defied all categorization. He'd never expected his wild neighbor, of the late nights and the revolving girlfriends to be this . . . neat.

But Keith grabbed the pad and turned to them. "As far as I can see it," he said, "we're facing two problems. One is the beetles. Kyrie is the only one who's seen the beetles—right?"

"No," Tom said, amused. "We've seen them also. We just didn't remember. I think you thought they were aliens."

Keith looked wounded. "Whatever that powder was . . ."

"Yes," Tom agreed not particularly wanting to go there, not wanting to explain that he'd thought Kyrie's sugar was drugged. He looked at her out the corner of his eye, and realized that Rafiel was also looking at her with an intent expression. Well, if she had to go to someone else . . . But Tom very much hoped she wouldn't.

"They are blue and green and refractive," Kyrie said. "And they look somewhat like the beetles I've seen in the natural history museum in Denver. I vaguely remember they said they were made into jewelry, and I could believe it because they were so pretty. The little ones in the museum. Not the large ones."

"You don't know what their genus is, do you?" Keith asked, looking up. "Because we could look them up and figure out their habits."

Kyrie shook her head. "I never really thought knowing the name of a beetle would be essential to me," she said.

"Ah, but see, that's where you go wrong," Keith said. Scribbling furiously. "Beetles are always essential. You let them run around unnamed they start music groups and what not." He looked up. "Well, I'll call the museum later, or look it up on line. So . . . we have these huge beetles. Are we sure they're shifters?"

"They're the size of that bed," Kyrie said, pointing to the king-size bed behind them. "Or maybe the size of a double bed. Okay, maybe a single bed. But taller. Huge still. Where do you suppose their natural habitat would be? And why wouldn't it have been discovered long ago?"

Keith waved one hand. "Okay, point, point," he said. "But so, we have two shifters. How often is it that shifters get together? Same species shifters? Can you guys like . . . mate in your other form?"

Tom felt a burning heat climb to his cheeks. Without looking he could tell that Rafiel was now staring at Kyrie with a gaze set to smolder. And Kyrie was staring ahead, looking shocked, refusing to look at either of them.

It was funny. Because of course Keith had always assumed that Tom was a player like himself, that he was out there, every night, picking up girls. And of course, Tom's sexual experience, which could be written on the head of a pin, was all in very human form, and had all happened before the age of sixteen.

He threw his head back and laughed. "Keith, you've got the wrong guy, at least where I'm concerned," he said. "The dragons I've known were in the triad. So, I have no idea. Also, the legends are a little quiet on the mating habits of dragons."

"And I had never met another shifter till two days ago," Kyrie said, her voice small and embarrassed. "I suppose it's possible to mate in animal form."

Did she throw a quick look at Rafiel? Tom's heart sank.

"But I wouldn't like to do it," Kyrie said. She sat up straighter in her chair. "For the same reason I wouldn't really like to eat in the shifted form. Even if it's proper food, you know, not . . . people. I like being human. If I'm ever going to have sex, I'd like to be aware of who I'm doing it with and how."

"You've never—" Keith started, then shook his head.

Tom realized he was grinning, and forced his face to become impassive. He hoped Kyrie hadn't noticed.

Rafiel, meanwhile, was shaking his head. "Not in shifted form," he said. "Never. So, I too know nothing about sex between shifters. Though I suppose"—he gave Tom a sly look—"that the sex lives of lions are far better documented than the sex lives of dragons."

But he couldn't touch Tom's self-assurance at that point. Kyrie had just as good as confessed that her experience was not superior to his own. He wondered if she'd done it on purpose.

"You guys are a waste of shifting ability," Keith said, sounding vaguely disgusted. "So, you don't know if two shifters of the same kind, different gender met, if it would lead to . . ."

"Kittens in the basket?" Rafiel said.

"Eggs in the lair," Tom immediately interposed not to be outdone.

"Actually," Keith said. "I was thinking more than some species have truly bizarre mating habits. And if we're dealing with a mating pair, which . . . could we be?"

Kyrie leaned forward, holding her coffee cup in both hands, over her knees. "I think we could be, yes," she said. "I think . . . I got a feeling that was the case."

"So, if we're dealing with a mating couple, you know that insects can get really kinky, right? Like all the biting off of heads of males after mating, or while mating, and all that stuff. Is it possible that the killings are part of a mating ritual? Like where the male has to give the female a gift or something."

"Yes, that's quite possible," Tom said, feeling slightly dumb that this hadn't occurred to him. Possibly because in all he'd read of the mating rituals of beautiful jungle cats, there had never been anything about their requiring the gift of a corpse.

"It might be pertinent," Rafiel said. "That I suspect there have been about two dozen people killed, and that they were all or almost all shifters."

"How could you know that?" Kyrie asked.

"I don't know. I suspect. If you remember, I told you I wanted to wait a little before I came here, because I wanted to find out if there could have been more people who disappeared in that area and whose bodies haven't been found yet?" He took a sip of coffee. "Well, I figured it out. At least partway. There are at least fifteen other people who have been missing, all over the last month or so. And they all disappeared from around the Athens. They were all young and therefore we didn't pay too much attention. Otherwise the pattern would have become obvious. But most of them, the families didn't seem sure they hadn't run away, so we thought we'd give it a little longer . . ." He took another sip of coffee. "We're a small police department. Oh, and most people were either passing through or had just decided to move here. Some interesting things—they all seemed to really like the Athens and had been there more than once. And they all had, the sort of relationship with their families and people around them that . . ." He looked at Tom.

"Say no more," Tom said, and for the first time realized his father was nowhere around. Was he hiding in the bathroom to be out of their hair? Tom didn't think it likely, but then neither had he thought it likely that his father would still remember how Tom took his coffee.

"Well, here's the thing," Keith said. "If these are gifts perhaps they have to be shifters. Do you guys know when someone else is a shifter?"

"Sometimes," Kyrie said. "If you get close enough. There is a definite tang, but I'm not very good at smelling it."

"I can't smell it at all," Tom said.

"I smell it very well, but I have to be near the person and sort of away from everything else."

"And all shifters smell alike?" Keith asked. "Regardless of species?"

Rafiel nodded.

"So, perhaps the gift of the dead corpse has to smell like a shifter?"

"It's possible," Rafiel said. "We don't have enough to go on, but there are definite possibilities. Just the fact that it's a shifter couple is interesting. I'd imagine the odds against it are enormous, and I wonder how long they've been a couple."

"Probably about a month," Tom said. "Since that's when you started noticing the pattern."

"Good job, Mr. Ormson. You might have a future in law enforcement," Rafiel said.

The *Mr. Ormson* was clearly intended to be a teasing remark, and Tom was about to answer in kind, but he thought of his father. If he was in the bathroom, trying to stay out of their way, Tom didn't want to call the others' attention to his absence. Because if he did, and it was nothing, he was just going to sound totally paranoid. On the other hand . . . On the other hand . . . If he didn't call their attention, and his father had gone to the triad . . .

Tom got up, carrying his cup of coffee, as if he were going to get a refill.

"So I think on the matter of the beetles, the best thing really would be to look them up in the Natural History Museum," Keith said. "See if they have stuff about those beetles' habits, then see what helps. And then we have the matter of the Pearl of Heaven."

But Tom had reached the little alcove before the bathroom, the area with the sink and the coffeemaker and cups. Tom frowned at it, because it had no articles of personal hygiene, only one of those kits of horrible toothbrush with toothpaste already on that hotels gave guests who forgot their toiletries. And Tom couldn't believe that his father—of all people—would have forgotten his toiletries.

The door to the bathroom was closed, but not enough for the latch to catch. Tom reached over, and slid it open with his foot, slowly. No one.

There could be a perfectly natural explanation. There should be a perfectly natural explanation. Tom was sure of it. But his heart was beating up near his throat, his mouth felt dry, and his hands shook. He put the coffee cup on the counter, very carefully, and then walked out, feeling light-headed.

Had he really believed his father cared? Had the thing with remembering how Tom liked his coffee been enough to make Tom believe his father gave a damn? He must really be starved for affection, if he'd believe his father could be more than a cold and calculating bastard.

He walked outside to the bedroom, feeling as if his legs would give out under him. His father had gone to the triad. Was probably, even now, making some plan to deliver Tom to the triad. And Tom didn't want to be tortured again. Plus, they would probably be even more upset now, considering he'd just been the cause of death of a number of their affiliates.

"We should just leave it on some public place," Keith said. "Like we left the car. And get the hell out of dodge. Let the triad feel it and go get it."

Tom tried to shape his mouth to explain that his father had left, that he'd gone to denounce them—to denounce Tom—to the triad. But the betrayal was so monstrous that he couldn't find the words.

And then he heard the key slide into the lock, and he turned, barely staying human, poised at the verge of shifting . . .

And his father came in, alone, carrying two very large bags with the name and the logo of one of the stores in the lobby. And another smaller bag, with the name of another of the lobby stores. One that specialized in candy and snacks.

They faced each other, silently, and his father looked so startled, so shocked, that Tom wondered if he'd started to shift already.

"I'm sorry," his father said. "Was I needed? You guys seemed to be talking about things I didn't understand and I thought I'd get some clothes and a comb, since I left without any of that." He put the larger bags on the bed, then opened the small bag and fished out a red box tied with a gold ribbon. "I thought you might like these, Tom."

Nuts with chocolate and his favorite brand. Okay, this was becoming ridiculous. His father might have kicked him out of the house at sixteen, and he might know next to nothing about Tom's life since then, but, apparently, it was a point of pride that he remembered what Tom liked to eat and drink.

There was really no response for it, though, and Tom, no longer ravenously hungry, still felt peckish of sorts. Besides, this was a hideously expensive brand of chocolates and he hadn't been able to afford it in years.

While he was tearing the ribbon, he saw his father open a bigger assortment of different types and set it on the side table. "For you guys, since none of you look like you've slept enough."

Tom noticed that Kyrie's eyes widened and that her hand went out for a dark chocolate truffle. He would have to remember that. Forget dead bodies. Any female with even a bit of Homo sapiens in her was going to go for the chocolates.

To change subject, and disguise his attention to her every action—and also how scared he'd been at his father's absence—Tom looked at his father and managed to say in a voice almost devoid of hostility, "I wonder if you could talk to us about the triad," he said. "How you came to be here, I mean. And how they got you to come here."

"The Great Sky Dragon kidnaped me from my office," Tom's father said. He dipped into the common box, too, and got a nut chocolate also. It was one of the tastes they shared. "He picked me up and told me that my son was my responsibility and he was going to bring me here, and I could find you and the Pearl, after which he'd take me back to New York. He made it clear I wasn't to return until I'd found them their Pearl. Tom, why did you take it?"

Tom shrugged. He'd tried to explain this before, and was getting tired of explaining. Particularly because the idea seemed really stupid now, and also because he was starting to realize what he'd searched for in the Pearl was what he'd found with Kyrie and even with the guys—acceptance, caring for him, giving a damn if he lived or died.

Instead, he said, "Because hard drugs weren't working for me." And seeing his father look shocked, Tom smiled. "Because the Pearl made me feel loved and accepted and I hadn't felt that since . . . In a long time."

His father had gone slightly red, and was looking at Tom as though evaluating something. "So," he said, "do you still need it?"

Tom shook his head. "No. I told the . . . them." He gestured toward Keith and Rafiel. "I told them that I would give it back, if I could just figure out how to do it. I haven't really been able to do that. Not recently."

"What do you mean?" Edward asked.

"I mean that if I gave it back to them, they'd kill me. They made it very clear they didn't take kindly that I'd stolen it. It's their . . . cultic object or something. They don't like the idea that a stranger grabbed it. I think they'll feel the stranger must be killed. Considering what they did to me when they captured me . . ."

"Okay," Edward said, very calmly. "So, how about I take the Pearl back?"

Rafiel choked on his chocolate. "Not a good thing," he said. "Because if you do that, then I suspect they'll kill you. The whole thing they said about you being responsible for Tom?"

"Okay," Keith said. "I've already said it, but you guys were out of the room. I think the easiest thing is for us to take it somewhere public and leave it. Yeah, they might still come after Tom in search of revenge, but there is at least a chance that after the massive ass-whooping of last night, they would leave him alone as being way too much trouble to discipline."

"Well . . ." Tom said. "Yes, it's possible." It wasn't probable. And it wasn't the plan he would have picked, if he had any other semi-sane choice. But he didn't think he did, and leaving the Pearl somewhere public and running beat his plan to keep hiding it and running from the triad.

"You could leave it in front of the triad center here in town," Edward Ormson said. "You could put it at the door, in a bucket of water. Wait till the bucket dries. By the time the water dries and they feel it—if we hide it a little—we'll all be out of town."

Tom looked up. "Out of town?"

"You could come back home," his father said, suddenly animated. "Maybe go to college." He looked around at the rest of them. "And I'd arrange for the other two here to go wherever they want to go. College? Move and a business? Just say it. I assume Officer Trall would be safe, by virtue of his position?"

Tom could feel his jaw set. "The only home I've ever known . . ." he said. There was the thought that Kyrie might want to go to college, but he didn't think she wanted to go at his father's charity. *He* didn't want his father's charity. "The only home I've ever known burned a few days ago. I'll have to find some other place to live."

His father looked away and there was a silence from everyone else for a moment. "Anyway," Tom said, "leaving the Pearl somewhere and letting them know later is the best plan I've heard, Keith. Perhaps leave it in a bucket of water and call them though, instead of leaving it in the open and letting them sense it. We don't know if there are other dragons like me around and getting it stolen again would be a pain. They'd only come after me again."

"Yeah," Rafiel said. "So . . . where did you hide the Pearl and how much trouble do we need to go through to retrieve it?"

Tom did a fast calculation in his head. He wasn't sure of Rafiel or his father yet. Though, sadly, he was more sure of Rafiel than his father. Rafiel had at least fought against the triad dragons.

But he'd misjudged his father once. He looked sidelong at his father, and read discomfort and understanding in his eyes, as if he were completely sure Tom wouldn't trust him, and understood it too. As well he should. And yet . . . Tom was going to have to take the risk at some point. Might as well start.

"It's in the toilet tank at the Athens," Tom said. "The ladies' room. It has a huge toilet tank, the old-fashioned kind, so I just put it in there."

Kyrie's eyes grew huge. "What if the tank had stopped?" she asked. "What if . . ."

He shrugged. "It seemed fairly sturdy. Besides, I wrapped the Pearl in dark cloth, before I put it in. You know the light isn't very good there. If someone looked in there, as ancient as the tank is, they'd just think there was some type of old-fashioned flushing mechanism that they didn't understand."

"And it's been there?" Rafiel asked. "These six months?"

Tom nodded.

"Have you considered," Rafiel said, "that maybe it's the Pearl that's attracting people to the Athens and making them feel at home there?"

"I don't think so," Tom said. "If I can't feel it when it's submerged, if the triad dragons can't feel it while it's submerged, then how should strangers?"

"Besides," Kyrie said, "that feeling was there before. It was there a good six months before that. I felt . . . I know this is going to sound very strange, but I felt almost called to Goldport. Like I had to come here. And once I got here, I had to go to the Athens. Then I saw the wanted sign and I applied."

Rafiel fidgeted. "I developed the habit of going to the Athens for breakfast about a year ago too. And it's not near my house. I just felt . . . called to go there. And I felt okay once I was there."

Tom sighed. "I came to the Athens a few times for meals, before Frank noticed me. He asked if I wanted a job. I didn't want to take a job under false pretenses, so I told him the truth. That I was homeless, that I hadn't had a fixed address for a long time, that I'd never had a full-time job and that I had a drug habit I was working on kicking. He told me as long as I kept clean once he'd hired me, he didn't mind any of those. . . . What's weird is that I'd already stopped in Goldport, and I had no idea why. It was like something in my subconscious had called me here, and to the Athens."

"Aha," Keith said. "Beetles. Mr. Ormson, is your computer connected to the Internet, and can I use it?"

Tom's father nodded. "Sure. Why?"

"I want to search the Natural History Museum. They have a lot of their collections online now. And they have a bunch of links to other scientific institutions."

"What do you mean by *aha beetles*?" Tom asked.

"Well . . ." Keith blushed. "You see, I like reading weird things."

"You told us," Kyrie said. "Comics and SF."

"Eh. Those are actually the sanest things I read. I also read science books. For fun. As I said, biology is fascinating, particularly insects. I seem to remember that certain beetles can put down pheromones that attract other beetles and their particular type of prey to their environment." He shrugged, blushing to the eyes. "So I think we should find out if the beetle Kyrie says looks like the shifter beetles is one of those."

"Makes sense," Rafiel said.

"Let me help you navigate the computer," Tom's father said, "in just a moment. Meanwhile . . . Tom, I don't mean . . . Well, you have blood on your face and your hair, and I thought . . ." He'd walked to the bed and pulled up one of bags. "I don't think you've changed pants size, and I just got you XL shirts and that. I grabbed you some socks and underwear too. The store here only has designer clothing, but I didn't want to go outside and look for another store."

Clothes? His father had got him clothes? Tom's first impulse was to say no and scowl. But if he was trying to keep his purity from his father's gifts, he was a little late. While the others talked, he'd been happily munching away on his chocolate with nuts. And the box was empty. Besides, he hated wearing jeans without underwear; the leather boots, without socks, were rubbing his feet raw; and if he was to have to go out soon, then he would have to shower.

So instead of his planned heated denial, he said, "Fine. I'll only be a minute. If anyone needs my opinion on anything, call me."

He grabbed the bag from the bed and took it with him to the little alcove before the bedroom. It weighed far more than it should for a pair of jeans and a couple of T-shirts. Opening it, he found it had at least as many clothes as he had owned back in his apartment. Better quality though. And more variety. There were a few pairs of jeans, and chinos, T-shirts, and a couple of polos. And, yes, underwear and socks.

He wasn't sure if he was ready to forgive his father, yet, but he was sure that his feet would thank him.

He went into the bathroom and turned on the shower. Water poured out in torrents. Oh. He might have to take more than a few minutes.

Much to Kyrie's surprise, the museum did have information on its insect collection online. It wasn't complete. All they had was pictures of the insects and their names.

"Is it this one, Kyrie?" Keith asked. And because the three men remaining—while judging from the sounds from the bathroom Tom was doing his best to deplete Colorado's natural water reserves today rather than in the next fifty years—had all crowded together around the computer, behind Keith who was sitting at the desk, they had to part now, to allow her near enough to see.

The picture was very small, and clicking on it didn't make it bigger. But Kyrie was fairly sure it was the same creature. "Yes. I'm almost positive," she said.

"*Cryptosarcodermestus halucigens,*" Keith read. "Now a quick Google search."

The sounds from the bathroom had become positively strange. Kyrie had known Tom for six months. She would have sworn he was the last person to ever sing in the shower. And if he had ever sang in the shower, she was sure—absolutely sure—it wouldn't be "The Lion Sleeps Tonight." Although—and she grinned—there was always the possibility that he was trying to tweak Rafiel. And tweaking was definitely in Tom's personality.

She wasn't so stupid that she didn't realize that though the men seemed to get along with each other—fighting triad dragons must have done it—they seemed to have a rivalry going over her. Right now it was composed of mostly stupid things—like how she reacted to something each of them said.

Kyrie wasn't sure she could deal with any of it. She was sure she didn't wish Rafiel to kiss her again. Well, maybe a little. But not if it was going to hurt Tom.

"Aha," Keith said, from the computer. He'd brought up a colorful screen, surmounted by a picture of the beetle.

"Yes, it's that one," Kyrie said. "It definitely is."

"Well, it's our old friend *Sarcodermestus*," Keith said. "And listen to this, guys . . ." He stopped, as they heard the door to the bathroom open and close. "Might as well wait for Tom," he said, under his breath.

Tom, Kyrie thought, as he came toward them, barefoot, walking silently across the carpeted floor, was definitely worth waiting for. At least the man cleaned up well. He'd shaved and tied his hair back. The new clothes, jeans and a white T-shirt, seemed to have been spray painted on his body. They underlined his broad shoulders, defined his musculature, and made quite a fetching display of his just-rounded-enough-but-clearly-muscular behind. He looked far more indecently naked than he'd been when she'd found him with the corpse in the parking lot. And, as he pressed in close, he smelled of vanilla. Vanilla soap and vanilla shampoo, probably some designer brand used by the Spurs and Lace.

Kyrie swallowed. She wasn't drooling either. And besides, if she were, it would be because it was vanilla. She was almost positive.

He pushed in close, between her and Rafiel—he would—and said, "Listen to what? What have you found, Keith?"

"On the beetles," Keith said. "They rub their wings together to produce clouds of hallucinogenic powder to disable their victims. And the male puts down some sort of hormonal scent. It attracts the victim as well as the prey they need to reproduce."

"Prey?" Kyrie said. It was very hard to think next to a vanilla factory. Up till today, she'd always have said she was a chocolate type of girl. But apparently vanilla would to the trick. Provided it was good vanilla.

"They lay eggs in the bodies of freshly killed victims, which have to be of a certain species of beetle. By the time the victims have reached a certain point in the decomposition, the eggs are ready to emerge as larvae." Keith said. "They bury the corpses in shallow graves, so that the larvae can crawl out on their own."

"So, if I were a beetle, which I am not," Tom said, "where would I hide the corpses with the eggs in them?"

"Somewhere safe," Kyrie said.

"The parking lot of the Athens?" Tom said.

"Impossible," Kyrie said, aware of the fact that she might sound more antagonistic than she meant to. "Impossible. After all, it's asphalt. And besides . . ."

"It's public," Rafiel said from Tom's side.

"So, the male lays down a scent to attract the female, does he?" Tom said.

Definitely, Kyrie thought. *And it's vanilla.* Then stopped her thought forcefully.

"Why lay a scent at the Athens?" Tom asked.

"Easy," Rafiel said. "It's a diner. This means they get not only tourists passing through and the workers and students from around there, but also a large transient population. If it's true that shifters aren't all that usual, then it increases their odds of getting shifters—supposing, of course, shifters are the intended population."

"Well, since all the shifters here seem to have some form of the warm fuzzies toward the Athens, I must ask the non-shifters. Keith? Mr. Ormson?"

"It's a dive," Keith said.

"It . . . I only went there because Tom worked there," Edward said. "I wouldn't . . . I don't see any reason to go again."

"So," Rafiel said. "There is a good chance whatever the substance—if there is one—that the male slathered around the Athens attracts shifters only. Which would mean the eggs would need to be laid in shifters. Where around the Athens can one bury freshly killed bodies in shallow graves and not be immediately discovered? It's all parking lots and warehouses around there."

Kyrie had something—some thought making its way up from the back of her subconscious. At least she hoped it was thought, because otherwise it would mean that stories of corpses and weird shifters who lay eggs in corpses turned her on.

"This means that the male has to be a regular at the Athens," Rafiel said. "Or an employee."

"Don't look at me," Tom said. "I already turn into a dragon. Turning into a weird beetle too, that would require overtime. When would I sleep?"

"No," Rafiel said. "I don't think that we can turn into more than one thing. At least I can't and none of the legends mention it. No. But you know, it might be someone on day shift. In fact," he said, warming up to his theory, "someone on day shift or who only works nights very occasionally, would fit the bill. Because then when he's not serving, he could be tripping the light fantastic with his lady . . . er . . . beetle."

Whatever thought had been forming in Kyrie's mind disappeared, replaced with the image of Anthony turning into a beetle but retaining his frilly shirt, his vest. "Anthony," she said. "Perhaps he dresses that way to attract the beetle in human form."

Tom grinned at what he thought was a joke. "He's a member of a bolero group. They meet every night," he said. "He only works nights when Frank twists his arm, poor Anthony."

Okay, so maybe it was a joke, but still . . . "Are we sure he really does dance with this bolero group?" she asked.

Tom grinned wider. "Quite. He gave me tickets once. You wouldn't believe our Anthony was the star of the show, would you? But he was."

"So . . . what can we do?" Rafiel asked. "I can go in and make a note of all the regulars. Or you can point out to me the ones you thought started coming around about a year ago."

"Hard to say," Kyrie said. "I mean, I can easily eliminate those who haven't been there that long. But I can't really tell you if they've been coming for longer than a year, since I've only been there a year."

"It's a start," Rafiel said. "I'll come in tonight. You can point them out to me, and then I can run quick background checks on the computer. Mind you, we don't get the stuff the *CSI* shows get. I keep thinking that they're going to claim to know when the person was conceived. But we get where they live and such."

"There's the poet," Kyrie said.

Tom nodded, then explained to the other's blank looks. "Guy who comes and scribbles on a journal most of the night, every night.

Maybe he's writing down 'Plump and tasty. Looks soft enough for grubs.'"

"Or 'perfectly salvageable with some marinade,'" Rafiel said, looking over Kyrie's head at Tom.

Without looking, Kyrie was sure that the guys had exchanged grins that were part friendly and part simian warning of another male off his territory.

"So, I go into work as normal," Kyrie said.

"And me too," Tom put in. "Well, yeah, I know Frank should have fired me, but I don't think he will. I know how hard it is for him to find help at night."

"Yeah," Kyrie said. "Particularly since he's been weirdly absent-minded." She didn't want to explain about Frank's romance heating up in front of everyone. It was funny, yes, but it was a joke employees could share. Bringing it out in front of strangers just seemed like gratuitous meanness. "Poor Anthony ended up having to cook for most of the night yesterday."

"Which means you were alone at the tables?" Tom said. "I'm sorry."

And this was the type of moment that made Kyrie want to think of things she hated about Tom. Because when he looked at her like this, all soft and nice, it was very hard to resist, unless she could think of something bad he had done. Which, right now, was failing her, because the only bad thing she could think of was stealing the Pearl of Heaven. And he was ready to give it back, wasn't he? "Yeah, well," she said, lamely. "For some reason I'm sure you'd rather be attending to tables than being held prisoner by a triad of dragon shifters. So you're forgiven."

"Thank you," Tom said, and smiled. "So I'll come in tonight, with you, at the normal hour, and I'll . . . we'll watch and see if anyone looks suspicious." The smile became impish and the dimple appeared. "Besides, really, Anthony will thank me. His fiancé is in the bolero group too and by now she probably thinks he's found another one."

"So, that's what we do about the beetles," Keith said. "But what do we do about the triad dragons and the Pearl of Heaven?"

"I'm very glad we made Keith an honorary shifter," Rafiel said. "This guy has a talent for keeping us on target."

"Honorary shifter?" Kyrie asked.

"He wanted to help us. He's jealous of our abilities. So he said we could make him an honorary shifter," Tom said. "I don't think he told us what specifically he would shift into though. I say a bunny."

"A blood-sucking bunny with big sharp teeth," Keith said. "Seriously, how are you going to get the Pearl, Tom, and shouldn't we at least have a tentative plan in place for how to return it?"

"I need to find a container large enough for it," Tom said, showing the approximate size with his hands. It looked to Kyrie like about six inches circumference. "A plastic bucket, maybe. With a lid. Then I can put it in there, in water and carry it without its giving me away. A backpack to carry it in would be good. Not this backpack." He nodded to the thing he'd carried and which he'd let drop in a corner of the room. "Because if I go in with a kid's backpack, Frank will notice and ask questions."

"Right," Rafiel said. "I have a couple of backpacks from army surplus that I use when I'm hiking. I'll go grab one of them before you go in to work."

"Well, this just brings up one question," Keith said, turning his chair around to face them. "And that's how are we going to sleep. Because we all need to be fresh for tonight. Unlikely as it is, we might be able to pinpoint someone and follow them and find the bodies, but we don't want to be stumbling into walls."

"You can stay here," Tom's father said. "There's a few extra pillows and blankets in the closet and I'm sure the bed fits five."

But Tom's father should have known better, Kyrie thought a few minutes later. With Tom and Rafiel in full-blown competition for her attention, chivalry was thick enough in the air that one needed a knife to spread it.

So, despite her heated protests, it ended up with her on the bed, Tom—universally believed to have had the roughest few hours— stretched out on the love seat by the window, Keith curled up on the floor in a corner and Rafiel and Mr. Ormson staking out the floor on either side of the bed. Rafiel lay down between her and the love seat, of course—probably trying to prevent Tom from attempting a stealth move.

Kyrie would have liked to fall asleep immediately, and she thought she was tired enough for it. But she wasn't used to sharing a house—much less a room—with anyone.

She lay there, with her eyes closed, in the semi-dark caused by closing the curtains almost all the way—leaving only enough light so that they could each maneuver to the bathroom without tripping on other sleepers.

Tom's dad showered. She heard that and the rustle of the paper bag as he fished for clothes. She grinned at the way the older man had neatly outflanked Tom's stubbornness.

Tom was still suspicious of his father, and perhaps he had reason, but Kyrie heard the man lie down on the floor, next to the bed and seconds later, she heard his breath become regular and deep.

She was the only one still awake. She turned and opened her eyes a little. Tom was in the love seat, directly facing the bed. In the half-light, with his eyes closed and something very much resembling a smile on his lips, the sleeping Tom looked ten years younger and very innocent.

A tumble of dark hair had come loose from whatever he'd tied it with, and fell across his forehead. His leg was slightly bent at the knee, and he'd flung his arm above his head, looking like he was about to invoke some superpower and take off flying.

It was all Kyrie could do not to get up and pull the hair off from in front of his face. Forget special hormones laid down by male beetles to attract the females. The way some human males looked while sleeping was the most effective trap nature had ever devised.

CHAPTER
⇥ 11 ⇤

Kyrie woke up with a hand on her shoulder. This was rare enough that just that light touch, over her T-shirt, brought her fully bolt upright. She blinked, to see Tom smiling at her and holding a finger to his lips.

He appeared indecently well-rested and, unless it was an effect of the dim light, the scar on his forehead had almost disappeared. He pointed her toward the desk and asked in her ear, breath tickling her, "Do you like steak?"

She looked her confusion and he smiled. "I ordered dinner," he said. "From room service. My father said to do it, since we have to go in before the others."

"Your father?" Kyrie said.

"Don't go there," Tom said, giving her a hand to help her up. "Really, don't."

"No. He was awake?"

"I woke him to tell him I was going to wake you and we'd leave for work. They don't need to be there when we go to work."

Kyrie got up and stepped over the sleeping bodies in the room, to the bathroom. She washed herself, halfheartedly because she didn't have clean clothes to put on. By the sink there were now five little "if you forgot your toiletries" kits—she would love to hear how Edward had explained that to the hotel staff—and half a dozen black combs. Also, a brush.

"I thought you could use the brush," Tom said, putting his head around the doorway. "I got it from downstairs."

She thanked him, pulled the earring from her pocket, where she'd put it for sleeping, and slipped it back on.

The meal was a hurried and odd affair, eating in the dark. But more disturbing than any of it, was looking up from taking a bite and finding Tom watching her.

What did he want her to do? Swoon with the attention? Fall madly in love with him? What would they do together? Both worked entry-level jobs, which was no way to start a family. And if they did start a family, what would it be? Snaky cats?

She glared at him and to excuse the glare said, "Eat. Stop staring. We don't have that much time." And he shouldn't, he really shouldn't smile like that. There was nothing funny.

But she didn't say anything. They finished the trays, left them by the door, and hurried out. "Are you worried about what Frank will say?" Kyrie asked Tom as they got in the car.

Tom still had the goofy smile affixed on his lips, but he nodded. "A little," he said. "Just a little. Frank can be profoundly unpleasant."

"Yeah, and he's been in a mood," Kyrie said.

Tom didn't know whether to be relieved or worried that all Frank said was "I thought you'd disappeared."

"No," Tom said. "Wasn't feeling well for a while and my dad came to town to look after stuff, so I was with him. I'm sorry I forgot to call."

For some reason, this seemed to alarm Frank. "Your dad? You have— You're in touch with him?"

Tom shrugged. "He heard I wasn't okay and he came to check on me. It's not that rare, parents caring about their kids," he said. Of course, he had no previous experience of this, and he wasn't absolutely sure he trusted his father's newly conciliatory mood. But he'd enjoy it while it was there and not expect it to stay, so he wouldn't be wounded when it disappeared.

Frank looked upset with that. "Well, get on with it. You have tables to attend to."

To Tom it was like returning home. He realized, as he was tying on the apron—"And we'll dock the extra $10 from your paycheck. I can't figure out what you people do with your aprons. Eat them?"— that he'd missed all of this.

The air-conditioner was pumping away ineffectively, too far away from the tables to make any practical difference, which meant that the patrons had opened the windows again, allowing the hot dry air of Fairfax Avenue, perfumed with car exhaust and the slight scent of hot asphalt, to pour in and mingle with the hot muggy air inside the Athens, perfumed with clam chowder, burgers, and a touch of homemade fries.

It was almost shocking to realize, but he really loved the place. His mind went over the panorama of seasons and imagined the Athens in winter, when it was snowy out and cozy inside and customers would linger for hours at the corner tables—near the heat vents—drinking coffee after coffee. He'd enjoyed coming in from the freezing cold outside and encountering the Athens as though it were a haven of dryness and warmth. He felt happy here. He wondered if it was just whatever pheromones the beetles had laid down around this place talking.

And speaking of pheromones, he got to work, greeting now this customer, now the other, taking orders, refilling coffees. To his surprise people remembered and had missed him.

"Hello, Tom," one of the women who came by before going to work at the warehouses said. "Were you sick?"

"Yeah," Tom said, and smiled at her. She was spectacularly homely—with a square face and grey hair clipped short. But she seemed to treat him with almost maternal warmth, and she always tipped him indecently well. "Touch of something going around."

"You guys should be more careful," she said. "Just because it's warm, doesn't mean that you can't get sick. Working nights, and you probably don't sleep as much as you should. I abused my body like that when I was young too. Trust me, it does send you a bill, though it might come twenty years down the road."

"Well, I'm all right now. What will you have?" He leaned toward her, smiling. And felt a hand pat his bottom lightly.

He believed in being friendly to customers but this was ridiculous. He turned around ready to blast whoever it might be, and saw Kyrie, leaning against him to talk to the customer. "Is this big ape bothering you, ma'am? Should I remove him?"

The customer grinned. "My, you're in a good mood. I guess your boss's hot romance makes things easier, right? He's not on your case so much?"

"Hot romance?" Tom asked.

"Oh, you don't know?" the customer said. "He's been sitting there all the time holding hands with that woman who bought the castle. The one he's been seeing off and on. Now she's here all the time."

"I meant to tell you," Kyrie said. "But I didn't want to talk in front of people. They spent yesterday necking over the counter. It was . . . weird. Poor Anthony had cook all the meals. Slowed us down to a crawl."

"Well, Anthony is a nice boy," the woman said. "But not like Tom."

"Ah, so you wouldn't want our big ape removal services," Kyrie said, and smiled at the woman, then at Tom, and flitted away to go take the order of the next table.

She left Tom quite stunned. Had Kyrie smiled at him? And had Kyrie really patted his bottom? Forget pheromones. What were they pumping out of those air-conditioners?

"Well, have you asked her out?" the woman said.

"I'm sorry?"

"Oh, don't play stupid. Have you asked Kyrie out?" the woman asked, smiling at him with a definite maternal expression.

He felt his damn all-too-easy blush come on and heat his cheeks. "Oh, I wouldn't have a chance."

The woman pressed her lips together. "Don't be stupid. She might have talked to me, but that entire little display was for your benefit. You do have a chance."

Tom hesitated. He could feel his mouth opening and closing, as he failed to find something appropriate to say, and he was sure, absolutely sure, he looked like a landed guppy. "I don't know," he said. "I'm not anyone's prize catch."

"So?" the woman shrugged. "No one is. You don't make babies start screaming when they see you. You'll do."

He had to get hold of this conversation. And his own unruly emotions. He and Kyrie had things to do. Far more important things. The Pearl had to be returned. They had to stop whatever scary beetles were trying to kill them both. This was no time to go all googly-eyed at the girl. "Yeah, well . . . anyway, what will you be having?"

"The usual. See if you have apple pie. I don't know if Frank baked yesterday, he seemed so distracted with his girlfriend. Apple for preference, but cherry would do. And a coffee, with creamer and sugar on the side."

"Sure," Tom said and beat a hasty retreat around the edge of the booths and back to the counter. There was apple pie in the fridge. He knew the customer enough to put the pie in the microwave for a few seconds' zap to chase the chill away. He got the coffee and the little bowls with cream and sugar and put it all on a tray.

And turned around to see Frank and his girlfriend—and he almost dropped the tray.

There was something odd about Frank and his girlfriend, both, and Tom couldn't quite say what it was.

He'd seen them before together, but usually when she picked Frank up or dropped him off. Now, they were holding hands over the counter, quite lost in each other's eyes. They weren't talking. Only their hands, moving infinitesimally against each other seemed to be communicating interest or affection or something.

With such an intense gaze, you expected . . . talk. And you really didn't expect people their age to be that smitten.

He realized he was staring fixedly at them, but they didn't even seem to have noticed. They continued looking at each other's eyes.

There was other crazy stuff happening there, Tom thought. Because while the woman didn't look like a prize—she looked like she'd been run through the wringer a couple dozen times, and perhaps hit with a mallet for good measure—she dressed well, and she looked like she could do better.

And if she was really the new owner to the castle, she couldn't be all that poor. The property, dilapidated and in need of work as it was, was yet worth at least half a mil, just on location. Where would someone like her meet someone like Frank? And what would attract her to him?

He set the pie and the coffee in front of the customer, who said, "I see you've noticed the lovebirds."

"Yes," Tom said, distracted. "I wonder how they met."

"I don't know," the woman said. "It was at least a month ago. In fact, when I saw them first, a month ago, they were already holding hands like that, so it might have been longer."

A month ago. The cluster of missing people had started a month ago. How would those two facts correlate? Tom wondered. He smiled at the customer and said something, he wasn't sure what, then backtracked to get the carafe to give warm-ups to his tables.

Was he being churlish? After all, he also didn't compare to Kyrie. If he should—by a miracle, and possibly through sudden loss of her mind—manage to convince Kyrie to go out with him, wouldn't people look at them funny like that too, and say that they couldn't believe she would date someone like him?

But he looked at Frank, still holding the woman's hands. And Kyrie had said that the day before he'd been so out of it that he'd let Anthony work the grill. Frank, normally, would not let any of them touch the grill. He said that quality control was his responsibility.

Tom looked at Frank and the woman. He could swear they hadn't moved in half an hour. That just wasn't normal.

He tracked Kyrie through the diner, till he could arrange to meet her—as he went out, his tray laden with salad and soda, to attend to a table, and she was coming back, her tray loaded with dishes—in the middle of the aisle, in the extension where a whole wall of windows separated them from Frank and made it less likely Frank would overhear them.

"Kyrie, those two, that isn't normal."

To his surprise, Kyrie smiled. "Oh, it's cute in a gag-me sort of way."

"No, no. I mean it isn't normal, Kyrie. Normal people don't sit like that perfectly quiet, fluttering fingers at each other."

Kyrie flung around to watch him, eye to eye. "What are you saying?"

"That we're looking for a weird insect-like romance. And I think that's it. The pie-and-coffee lady says that they first met a month ago, at least. I didn't pay any attention when it started, just sort of realized it was going on. I guess the idea of Frank getting some and maybe leaving descendants was so scary I kind of shied away from it. But the pie lady thinks it was already going on a month ago. Though even she says it's getting more intense."

"I haven't given it much attention, either," Kyrie said. "A month at least, or a month?"

"At least a month, I don't know anymore."

Kyrie looked suitably worried. "Okay," she said. "Okay. I'll make enquiries."

Kyrie turned on her rounds, to stop by the poet, and give him a warm-up on his coffee. "We always wonder what you write," she said and smiled. All these months, she'd never actually attempted to talk to the poet, but she figured someone had to. And he was there every night the same hours.

He was the most regular of the regulars. If he had looked at all—and Kyrie had never been absolutely sure of the poet's being fully engaged with the world—he would know, better than anyone, how long Frank's romance had been going on.

The man reached nervous fingers for the ceramic cup with the fresh coffee in it, and fumbled with getting it to his mouth to drink. His pale-blue eyes rested on Kyrie's face for a moment, then away. "I . . . It's just a journal. My therapist said I would be better off for writing a journal."

"A journal," she said. She had a feeling the man wasn't used to much female attention, but if what he wrote was indeed a journal, then he would have all the data there, at his fingertips. "I would never be disciplined enough for a journal."

He grinned, showing her very crooked teeth. Then looked rapidly away and continued, speaking intently to the salt shaker. "Well, it's all a matter of doing it at the same time every day, isn't it? Just being regular and doing it at the same time. After a while it becomes a habit and you could no more go without it than you could go without eating or sleeping."

He looked back at her, just a little, out of the corner of the eye, reminding Kyrie of a squirrel, tempted by nuts on the sidewalk but hesitant about coming out in the open.

She smiled at him. "You must write all sorts of fascinating details about everything that happens in there. I mean, so much better than just memory. My coworker and I were just talking about how long our boss has been in love with that lady there." She gestured with her head. "And we couldn't remember when they started going out."

"Oh." The poet fumbled with his journal, flipping through the pages in a way that seemed to indicate he wasn't absolutely sure how to use fingers. The gesture of a terminally nervous neurotic. "I can tell you the exact day. I have it here, all written down, because it was so amazing. She came in, they looked at each other, and it was like . . . you know, the song, across a crowded room and all that. They looked at each other, their eyes met, and she hurried over there and they held hands." He found the right page and, for once, dared to look up at Kyrie, as he showed it to her. "There, there, you see. Almost exactly a month ago. And they've been like that ever since. Oh, not every night, not that . . . absorbed . . . but at least a few nights a week she walks him in or waits for him when he goes out."

The way he looked at Kyrie, shyly and sort of sideways, seemed to indicate he had his own personal dreams of getting to hold hands with her someday. Kyrie didn't feel that charitable, but smiled at him anyway, and glanced at the page—of which she could understand nothing, since it appeared to have been written by dipping a spider's legs in ink and letting it wander all over the page. "Very nice. Well, now I'll know what you're doing and I can tell the other people when they ask."

She wandered away to check on orders. So far, no one had asked for anything cooked, but it was bound to happen. "Tom, you might need to take over the grill," she said, as she passed him. "As people start coming in who want their early morning dinners."

He looked surprised. "Sure," he said. "I can probably load dishes while I'm up there too, if you want me to."

She didn't tell him anything about Frank and his girlfriend, but she was thinking. What she was thinking, mostly, was that this whole eyes meeting across a crowded room didn't happen to people. Not in real life. But it might very well happen to bugs who were acting on instinct and pheromones.

It turned out not to be as bad as Kyrie expected. The clinch of hands over the bar stopped before the crunch, and Frank took over flipping the burgers and cooking the eggs and what not.

From about ten to midnight they were so busy that Kyrie didn't even notice the other guys had come in—Keith and Rafiel and Tom's dad—until she saw that Tom was serving that table. And then she forgot about them again, as she was kept running off her feet, taking pie to one and a hamburger to another, and a plate of dolmades to a particularly raucous group in a corner.

As the crowd started thinning, past midnight, Kyrie went up to the counter to put the carafe back. And when she turned, Rafiel was standing by the counter. "Can you take a fifteen-minute break?" he said. "Tom says he can handle it till you come back."

"Frank," she said, and realized that Frank had heard them. He waved them away. "Go. If Tom can handle it, I don't care."

On the way to the front door, Kyrie told Tom, "Thank you."

He looked slightly puzzled and then frowned at Rafiel, which did not seem at all like a natural reaction. "Are you sure you asked him?" she asked Rafiel.

"Yes, yes, I asked him." He led her outside, toward his car, parked on the street. "I'm not saying he's incredibly excited about it, but I asked him."

"Rafiel, if he doesn't think he can handle it alone I shouldn't leave him." She started to walk back, but Rafiel came after her and grabbed her arm.

"Seriously," he said. "I don't think he minds the work. He minds you going out with me. Oh, don't look like that," he said, before she was aware of looking like anything at all. "He knows we have to talk. He says there's some stuff you found out."

"Yes," Kyrie said, and sat down on the passenger side of the car.

Rafiel had held the door open for her, and closed it as soon as she sat down. He then walked around the car to his side.

"I thought I'd take you for a cup of coffee, so we can talk? There's an all-night coffeehouse down the street."

Kyrie nodded. She had no need for coffee, but she wanted to tell Rafiel about the beetles, and what she thought of the beetles.

Edward watched Tom, after Kyrie left. He watched Keith too. Mostly because Keith puzzled him. He sat at the table, taking everything in, seemingly unaffected by the fact that there were not one but two types of shapeshifters that might want him dead.

Dragons and beetles and who knows what, oh my. "You're not scared at all?" he asked Keith, in an undertone.

Keith looked back at him, as though trying to decide exactly how many heads Edward might have. "Well," he said. "It's not so much that I'm not scared. Although . . . I don't think I am, you know?"

"Why not?" Edward asked. He thought of the Great Sky Dragon, flying through the sky and using what seemed to be magic to get from one place to the other without having to cross the space between. He thought of even Tom in his dragon form, of Tom's flying across the New York sky, seeming completely nonhuman.

"I don't know," Keith said. "I told them it was because I read so much science fiction and comic books—and that's probably true." He shrugged. "I mean, you see something very often, even if you know it's fiction, it makes an impression on you after a while and part of you hopes or believes it to be true, right? I mean, even if your mind knows it isn't."

"It's possible," Edward said. To be honest he didn't remember what it was like to be that young anymore. It had been at least twenty-five years since he'd read any fiction. No. More. In college, his fiction reading had just tapered away to nothing. "I suppose it's possible."

"Well, in a way it was like that," Keith said. "I mean, the idea would have probably struck me as much odder, much more impossible if I'd never seen it in stories. But the important thing is, I saw it happen in the worst possible circumstances." He lowered his voice. "They grabbed us and they took us in, and Rafiel was . . . um . . . shifted. And Tom was all tied up, and—"

"He was. Tied?" Edward knew what Lung had told him, and at some level, consciously, he knew that being captured by the triad could be no picnic. But somehow, seeing Tom walk into his hotel room had given him hope that it was all just a big fight. He knew Tom could handle himself in a fight. He wasn't so sure about Tom being helpless.

"Yeah. He was completely tied-up. And he . . . They'd . . . His clothes were caked with blood. They'd taken his jacket and boots off. I think they might have thought to keep them after they . . . you know, got rid of him. Or perhaps they thought that the leather would protect him. And then he . . . shifted. I knew it was still him because of his eyes. And he freed me. And I freed Rafiel, who recovered much faster than they expected. And then we were . . . fighting. And that's the thing you know." He looked at Edward and seemed to realize that Edward was trying very hard to imagine but didn't really know. "I realized they can be taken out with a good tire iron. You don't need to be one of them."

Edward was following his son with his gaze. Tom looked so . . . competent. He'd removed his leather jacket and was wearing a red apron with "Athens" on the chest, and doing a job his father had never, possibly, imagined a son of his doing. But he was doing the job competently.

There had been no complaints. On the contrary. People smiled at him and it was clear that several of the regulars were very fond of him. And he answered back and smiled, and seemed to be a part of this diner. A trusted employee. Which was more than—just five years ago—Edward could have imagined.

To be honest, he couldn't have imagined it two days ago. If he'd thought of Tom at all, he'd thought of Tom as being in jail, or perhaps dead. He would never have believed his son was sane and responsible enough to hold down any job.

"Really," Keith said. "I'd love to be able to shift, because it's cool, but I'm not afraid of them. I mean, the nice ones are nice. The other ones would probably be just as dangerous as normal people."

Edward frowned. That thought too would have been unbelievable five years ago. But he was looking at Tom, and thought Tom was not much different than he would have been if he'd never turned into a dragon. He was just Tom. And, on balance, a much better person than Edward had any right to expect.

Just then, Tom noticed him looking and arched his eyebrows. Edward looked away. He might have thrown Tom out from fear and confusion. Getting him back, however, was going to require a full and rational siege.

If only they managed not to get killed by any other shifters. Edward wished he had Keith's certainty that they could fight against shape changers on equal terms.

"We need to talk," Rafiel said. He pulled the chair out for Kyrie, and waited until Kyrie had sat down before going around to his side. He picked up both their orders too, her iced mocha latte and his tall cup of something profoundly foamy.

"Yes, I . . . Tom thinks—"

"Wait," Rafiel said. "We don't need to talk about the . . . creatures." He looked around again, as though afraid someone around them might understand the cryptic comments. "We need to talk about Tom."

"We—uh? What about Tom?"

"Well, he's not as bad as I expected," Rafiel said. "Not nearly. But he is . . . ah . . . Tom has issues."

Kyrie nodded. "Yes, but—" She didn't want to discuss Tom nor Tom's issues, nor could she imagine what Tom had to do with any of this. Tom's personality had nothing to do with the predicament they were in.

Sure, it would have been helpful if he could have managed to avoid tangling with the triad dragons. But that was, surely, just a fraction of his problems. The beetles loomed much larger in Kyrie's mind, perhaps because she had experienced them up close and personal. And Tom was not a were-beetle. Of that she was sure.

"No. I just . . ." Rafiel looked flustered, which was a new one for him. "I just am going to say this once and be done, okay? I can't help notice that he's attracted to you, and I think I've seen you . . . I mean, you give the impression of being attracted to him too, sometimes."

"I don't think I am," she said. "It's just that we've been working together for a while and I think I've misjudged him horribly, and I feel guilty about that. So I've been nice to him, but I don't think—"

"Good," Rafiel said. "I mean, really. Tom is not a bad person, but I think he's been through a lot in his life, and I think it makes him . . . well . . . I think he's sometimes not as well-adjusted as he would like to be. And I wouldn't want to wish that on you."

He put his hand across the table, on top of hers. Kyrie withdrew her hand, slowly, not wanting it to seem like a rejection. If she was reading this right, Rafiel had just tried to clear the field of his rival in a most underhanded way, something she thought only women did. Perhaps because she'd seen it between women and girls in her middle and high school years.

Fortunately, she wasn't sure she was interested in either of these men—or in any men. She'd seen too much of marriage and relationships through her time in foster care to think that she would ever take any relationship for granted or view it as a given. On top of that the kinks the shifters' natures would put into any relationship just about had her deciding to remain celibate the rest of her life. The knife-in-the-back approach to friendship and love certainly didn't incline her toward Rafiel.

"Tom thinks that Frank and his girlfriend might be the beetles," Kyrie said, rapidly, before Rafiel could resume his wholly inappropriate talk.

"Frank and his girlfriend?" Rafiel asked. "Why?"

Kyrie told him. She told him about the woman who ordered pie every night and who said that Frank and his girlfriend had held hands a month back, and about the poet and the whole eyes meeting across a crowded room thing.

Rafiel frowned. "Don't you think it's all a bit in the air?" he asked. "I mean, they're just a middle-aged couple, and perhaps they're not so good on the relationship and getting along with each other front. Perhaps they aren't very good at connecting with each other?"

"But . . ." Kyrie said, and seized on the one thing she was sure of.

"But his girlfriend first met him around a month ago." And then, with desperate recollection. "And, you know, he had a Band-aid on his neck the day after I speared the beetle."

Rafiel sighed. "He and how many guys in Goldport? Think. Perhaps he cut himself shaving."

"At the back of his neck?"

"Well, okay, so he scratched himself. Or had a pimple that blew up. It happens. Don't you think if he'd been stuck with an umbrella, even in another shape, it would require more than a Band-aid?"

"Not necessarily," Kyrie said. "We heal fast."

"I still say this is all in the air," Rafiel said. He sipped at his coffee as if he were angry at it. "You have no proof. There are probably dozen of couples—hundreds—with weird relationships, who started a month ago, and where one of them had some sort of injury on the neck that day."

"I doubt hundreds," Kyrie said. "And besides, you know, there is the fact that she has a very convenient burial ground."

"What?"

"The castle. She bought the castle. You've seen the grounds. She could bury a hundred people there in shallow graves and be fairly assured they wouldn't be found. That's pretty hard in urban Goldport."

"Not really," Rafiel said. "You know, people have backyard lawns."

Kyrie snorted with laughter before she could stop herself. "I suppose you could fit one corpse in my backyard lawn. Two if you put them very close together."

Rafiel was jiggling his leg rapidly up and down. "Yeah, but some people have bigger lawns." He frowned, bringing his brows together. "What do you want me to do about it, anyway? Do you want me to burst into the Athens and arrest them because they hold hands and don't talk?"

Kyrie wasn't used to getting upset at people. Normally, to get along, both as a foster child and as an adult, she'd learned to hide her anger from people. But she couldn't even hide from herself that she thought Rafiel was being unreasonable. That she suspected he was being unreasonable because he felt thwarted in his pursuit of her affections didn't actually make her feel any better.

"I want you to go in there and look around," she said.

His mouth turned down in a dissatisfied little-boy scowl. It was the type of expression she would expect from a five- or six-year-old who had just seen someone else get the bigger piece of candy. "I can't do that," he said.

"For heaven's sake, why not?"

"Because I don't have a warrant." Instead of getting louder, his voice had to lower and lower, until it was low and almost vicious, growling out its protest. "I'm a policeman. I can't go poking around people's property without a warrant. Citizens get all sorts of upset when policemen do that. They would—"

Kyrie didn't think this behavior was more endearing because of its sheer irrationality. She finished her frozen latte, and picked up the cup, which she'd got as a take-out cup, as she'd been afraid of having to finish it on the way back to work. "Officer Trall, if you can hide evidence, lie to other police officers, and suggest that we, as shifters, need to take our law into what passes for our hands, then, yeah, you could and should be able to have a look-see in someone's garden without a warrant. I mean, no one is asking you to go in with a police force. Just go there, shift, and have a good sniff. Death will out, you know?"

He narrowed his eyes at her. "I'm trying to stay on the right side of the law. I'm trying to enforce the law. I'm trying to be a good person, Kyrie, and somehow balance this with being a . . . shifter. I don't think you realize—"

"Oh, I think I realize it perfectly well. I just think you'd be far more energetic in pursuing this if I'd told you that the culprit in this case was Tom Ormson."

"That's underhanded. Tom is a friend. He risked himself to rescue me."

"Oh, and how well you thank him."

"I didn't mean it that way. If you took it that way it's because you chose to. Tom would be very bad for you, and just because—"

"As opposed to yourself? You would be great? What would your mother think of your dragging me home?"

He blinked, genuinely confused. "Mom would love you. I don't understand—"

"I mean, Officer Trall, that your parents might not be so happy that the son they've protected, the son they always thought would need their protection the rest of their lives has a life outside the family."

"That's ridiculous. Did you just call me a mama's boy? I don't think there's anything else I can say to you."

"Well," Kyrie said. She was leaning over the table, and he was leaning from the other side, and they'd been arguing in low vicious tones. Now she straightened. "That is very fortunate, because I don't think I want to discuss anything with you, either."

And with that, she flounced out the door, which—she thought, smiling to herself—the owners of this coffee shop must think was a normal thing for her.

She had gone a good half block before she heard him shout, "Kyrie," behind her, but she didn't slow down, just went on as fast as she could.

This time she didn't go into the parking lot. Didn't even think about it. Instead, she approached at a half run, toward the front door. While she was waiting to cross Pride, the cross street before the Athens, she was vaguely aware of a car squealing tires nearby, and then parking in front of the diner.

She didn't turn to look. Which was too bad, because if she had turned to look, Rafiel's hands on her shoulders spinning her around wouldn't have taken her so much by surprise. And his mouth descending on hers might have been entirely avoided. Or, if not, she might at least have avoided the few seconds of confusion in which her brain told her to get away from the man while parts far more southerly responded to his strength, his virility, and the rather obvious, feline musk assaulting her nostrils with a proclamation of both those qualities.

As it was, she lost self-control just enough to allow him to pull her toward him, to allow herself to relax against him. She lost track of who she was and what she meant to do through the feeling of firm male flesh, and the large hands on her shoulders, both compelling and sheltering her.

He slid his tongue between her lips, hot and searching and forceful.

And in her mind, an image of Tom appeared. Tom smiling at her, with that odd diffident expression when Keith had asked about sex as a shifter.

She pushed Rafiel away. And then she slapped him. Hard.

Tom would probably have missed the kiss, if he hadn't already been watching the door for Kyrie. But he was.

Okay, first of all, and stupid as it was, and as much as he was absolutely sure he didn't actually stand a snowball's—or a snowflake's—chance in hell—of getting near her, he'd been indulging himself in quite nasty thoughts about Rafiel.

So, okay, Rafiel needed to discuss the case with her. But couldn't he just have taken her on a quick walk down the block, then back again? Couldn't he have talked to her out there, against that lamppost in front of the Athens? Where Tom could have kept track of them through the big plate-glass window?

And then . . . and then there was everything else. If Frank and his girlfriend were the beetle couple, where did that leave Tom? Truth be told, Tom felt a little guilty for even suspecting Frank of that. Frank had given him a full-time job when no one else would.

Yes, but why had he? Tom wouldn't have hired himself, with his credentials at the time. And then there was his father. He'd told Kyrie not to go there, but it wasn't entirely avoidable. For one, his father was sitting at a corner table, in the extension, getting intermittent warm-ups of coffee and ordering the occasional pastry. He seemed to be discussing comic books with Keith, a scene that, before tonight, Tom thought could only come from his hallucinations.

And his father had already managed to ask Tom if Tom was warm enough—warm enough!—in the Colorado summer, where the temperatures reached the low hundreds in daytime and the buildings gave it back all night. Warm. Enough. It wasn't so much like this man's behavior bore absolutely no resemblance to the father Tom had known growing up. That was somewhat of a problem but, it could be said that any father at all would be an improvement over that man.

On the other hand, this particular father seemed to do parenting by instruments. Like a pilot, flying in a thick fog, might read his instruments to decide his location, how to turn, and where to stop—and if the instruments are faulty might end up somewhere completely different—Tom's father seemed to be trying to mend a relationship that had never existed in ways that didn't apply even to that hypothetical relationship.

Maybe it was that the only relationships Tom's father had ever taken seriously were courting relationships. At least that would explain his trying to win his way back to Tom's heart with chocolates. It didn't explain his thinking that Tom wore the same size pants he'd worn at sixteen though.

On the other hand, these pants were a great advantage, now he thought of it. He would no longer need to worry about siring an inconvenient shifter child—not if he wore them much longer. This, of course, brought his thoughts around to Kyrie again, and to the fact that she was five minutes over her break already.

Oh, he had no intention of telling Frank about it. Even if Frank were perfectly aboveboard and exactly what he claimed to be, there was absolutely no reason to let Frank know this stuff. He'd just get upset.

And so far Tom, moving rapidly from table to table, taking orders, distributing them, warming up coffee, was keeping on top of everything. In a little while, the crowds would drift back in again, and as long as Kyrie was in by then . . .

No. What he hated was the fact that he might be covering up for her necking time with Rafiel. Okay, he was willing to admit that Rafiel might not be exactly the scum of the earth. He could do worse. And she could do worse, too. In fact, any way he looked at it, Kyrie and Rafiel were just about a perfect match.

Despite her upbringing, Kyrie was fairly balanced. And Rafiel, after all, came from such a well-adjusted background that his parents knew about and abetted his shape-shifting. Surely, neither of them had anything in common with Tom, who had been thrown out of his house—at gunpoint no less—by the man who now thought he could heal it all with expensive chocolates and too-tight clothes.

They deserved each other. And neither of them deserved him in any sense. Which didn't mean he had to like it. It didn't even mean he had to accept it, did it?

He seethed, having to control himself to prevent slamming plates and breaking cups. He seethed partly at them, because he was sure they were taking advantage of his covering up for her to go and neck in some shady corner. And he seethed partly at himself, because, who was he to get angry at whatever they wanted to do?

And then, as he turned around, carafe in hand, he saw Kyrie come hurrying toward the door.

Alone. She was alone. He felt his heart give a little leap at this. Not hopeful. Oh, he couldn't have told himself he was hopeful. But . . .

And then he saw Rafiel come up behind her. He grabbed her by the shoulders. He spun her around. His mouth came down to meet hers. She relaxed against him.

The teapot escaped from Tom's grasp and fell, with a resounding crash and a spray of hot coffee onto the nearest bar stools and Tom's feet.

It took him a moment to realize the shattering sound had indeed come from outside his head.

Edward had never seen Tom tremble. He'd held a gun to the boy's head when Tom was only sixteen and he had never seen him shake. But now, he was shaking. Or rather, vibrating, lightly, as if he were a bell that someone had struck.

"I'm sorry I'm late with the warm-up," he said, and his face was pale, and his voice oh, so absolutely polite. "I dropped the carafe and had to brew another one."

"It's okay," Edward said. He'd been enjoying his conversation with Keith, partly because it distracted him from the fact that they might very well all be dead soon. And partly because in the middle of a lot of information about Keith—who apparently had parents and no less than four siblings somewhere in Pennsylvania—there was some comment and anecdote about Tom. Apparently Tom kept Keith's key and usually could be counted on to give it back when Keith came home drunk and confused, having left keys and jacket—and often other clothes—at the last wild party he'd attended.

Keith had engaged in some self-mocking on the subject of the number of times Tom had shown up without a stitch of clothing on, and how Keith had thought that Tom went to even wilder parties than he did. Now, of course, he understood. "He must go through an awful lot of clothes," Keith said. "They all must."

And Edward had nodded. He'd been relaxed. And Tom had looked happy and in his element. Why was he shaking now? Was it just the coffeepot? Was Tom so insecure he'd get that upset over a broken coffeepot?

"It's okay. I really don't need a warm-up," Edward said. "It's excellent coffee, but I've probably already drunk too much. Don't worry."

Tom nodded, and looked aside, as if getting ready to walk away. Then came back and sat down. He put the carafe down, with some care, on one of the coasters and leaned forward. "Father," he said.

It was the first time in five years he'd actually called Edward that. Edward took a deep breath. "Yes?"

"I need you do it for me, the delivery."

"What delivery?" Edward asked, puzzled. They were going to find the beetles, weren't they? What was there to deliver?

"The delivery of the Pearl," Tom said, lowering his voice. "In a few minutes, when I get a chance, I'm going to go into the bathroom and get it, I'll put it in the container before I take it out of the water, then put the container in the backpack. I assume you know where the center for the . . . Where their center is in Goldport, right?"

Edward nodded. "But . . . aren't we going to do that later? I thought we were going to—"

Tom pushed back the strands of his hair that had gotten loose in the course of the evening. "No. I . . . It's me. Look, it's just me. I know there's something wrong with me, but I just can't take it. I can't. I can't be around to watch it. So, you take the . . . delivery to the people looking for it, and I'll go, okay?"

Oh, no. This sounded far more serious than Edward had thought. And he didn't quite know how to handle it. The thing had always been, since Tom was two or so, that if he got something in his mind, no matter how misguided or strange, it was almost impossible to get it out. And if you pushed the wrong way, he only got mad at you and more determined to do whatever he'd set his mind on.

He didn't even want to ask about it in a way that would get Tom's back up. So he spoke as gently as he knew how. "Tom, I don't understand. What can't you take, and why are you going? And where?"

Tom shook his head, as if answering some unspoken question. "Kyrie. And . . . Rafiel. I can't take it. I know this is stupid, okay? I know it's puppy love, okay? But I've never been close to another woman. Well, not since I was sixteen. And I've never even thought about another woman as I think about Kyrie. I know it's stupid. You don't need to tell me—"

"I wasn't going to tell you that—" Edward started.

"But I know it's stupid. I know I never had a chance. Being as I am. Who I am. And I don't just mean the . . . shifting. I mean, just who I am. I know Kyrie deserves much better. I know that Rafiel is better. I've known that since I met him. But I'm too . . . I can't watch. I should be able to because they're both my friends, in a way, so I'm probably immature too, but there it is. I'm immature. I just can't . . . I'd end up getting in a big argument with her or him, or both of them. And I can't do that, because then . . . it would be worse than just leaving. So I'm leaving."

The words had poured in a torrent, drowning out any other attempts at speech, any other attempts at questioning. Now they stopped, and Tom reached for the coffeepot handle, as if to get up and resume his rounds.

"Tom," Edward said. "Where are you going?"

"It doesn't matter. Just . . . somewhere. Somewhere till things cool with the triad and until . . . No, I don't suppose I'll ever forget. I'm not . . . good."

"Perhaps you could consider coming home?" Edward said, and before Tom could correct it, "To my home. You can, you know. I don't mind."

He expected anger, or perhaps a huffing of pain. But instead Tom inclined his head once. "Maybe. After . . . when the triad isn't looking anymore. Perhaps they'll even give up on the idea of revenge, and calm down, and then, maybe."

Edward knew Tom was wrong. He knew Tom was wrong about Kyrie and Rafiel. He'd seen the three of them together and while Rafiel might look a lot at Kyrie, Kyrie looked at Tom. Now, most of the time she looked at Tom with annoyance or borderline irritation.

But that was part of it too, wasn't it? The ones who could annoy you most, the ones who could get under your skin most . . . He remembered what she had told him about how she knew that Edward still liked Tom, still had paternal feelings for him. How it was all about how he fought so hard to counter those feelings.

From what he'd seen, Edward guessed Kyrie had known from experience. She was, at the very least, seriously in lust with Tom. For a moment or two the day before, he'd thought she'd need a drool catcher to avoid staining the carpets of his hotel room. But he would bet there was more there, too. Because Kyrie was not the type to confuse lust with love.

He could let Tom go on believing this, being miserable. Tom would then probably end up in New York again and, knowing his intelligence and his new-found focus, be at Harvard or Yale within the year. And eventually he would find another woman.

But Edward looked at his son's pale face, his set mouth, which looked rigid enough not to tremble. Rigid enough not to betray the desolation within.

"Tom, I've watched her, and I think you're wrong. From her reactions, since I've met her, and from seeing her with him, I've . . . I don't think she's interested in him. And I think she likes *you* a lot."

Tom shook his head. "No, trust me. I had some hope. Not a lot. I mean, I know our different standings. But she was nice to me, and I thought maybe . . . But then I saw them kissing." He gestured with his head. "Up front. I know. I saw." He shook his head. "And I never expected it to affect me so much." He frowned, thunderous eyebrows low over his blue eyes. "I wanted to shift and flame something. Preferably his pants."

Edward almost laughed at this, because it was so much like Tom, to want to flame his rival's manhood right off. But he didn't want to laugh, not while Tom was in pain.

"I just thought you should know. I think you're wrong. But if you still think you must leave, then . . . I hope eventually you'll come back to my home. And before that, call me, okay? Tell me where you are. I'll wire you money. There's no reason for you to be deprived."

It was probably a measure of Tom's state of mind that he didn't protest the offer of money. Instead, he nodded and walked away.

"Man, he has it bad," Keith said. "I didn't realize it was that serious."

"I suspected it," Edward said. "I just didn't know he would take it in his head to run away from it all."

Was that what he'd taught Tom, when he'd thrown him out? To leave difficult situations behind?

Kyrie was shaking. Mostly with repressed rage. That Rafiel would dare grab her like that. That he would dare kiss her. And in front of half the diner too.

She put her apron on, and resumed serving her tables, but felt as if people were staring at her, and found herself blushing. *How could he?*

She suspected Rafiel was the center of attention to his parents, the center of their lives. His "handicap," the fact that he shifted, would make him far more precious to them, and they far more attentive to him. And he'd grown up to be the center of the universe.

Kyrie would bet too that with his body, his easy, self-assured personality, he would have girls falling from his hair and tumbling into his lap. She would just bet. So he probably was not too well aware of the meaning of the word no. Well, she would buy him a thesaurus at the first opportunity.

No, as in never. As in negation. As in I'm not interested. And even if the girl hasn't said it flat out, if she'd given him reason to think she was less than pleased with his interest, then Mr. Rafiel Trall would learn to keep his hands to himself. And his lips too.

She was so mad, that she banged a load of dishes into the dishwasher, after bussing the empty tables. This was the hour when people started leaving before the rush, and she'd bussed her tables, and Tom's too. She banged the plates and cups in, and she gave Frank a dirty look when he glared at her.

The dirty look must have worked, because Frank didn't say anything. Just turned away.

And Frank was, of course, a problem, as was Frank's girlfriend. Kyrie couldn't believe how obtuse and close-minded Rafiel had been. How could he not see that this series of coincidences, here, at the center of the Athens, was far more relevant than no matter how many couples who'd started dating a month ago, no matter how many men with bandaged necks elsewhere?

Damn the man. She couldn't believe someone like that, who was clearly smarter than dryer lint, would attempt to solve crimes using parts of his anatomy that lay below the equator.

She closed the dishwasher and started it, and turned to face Tom. He stood just behind her, his arms full with a tray of dishes.

"Oh, Tom, I'm sorry. That dishwasher is full. Let me open the other one. I'll put the dishes in for you if you want me to."

He shook his head. He was keeping his lips together, as if he were biting them to keep himself from saying something. How weird. It was an expression she'd never seen on his face. "Are you okay?"

"Fine," he said. "Just fine. I'll put the dishes in. You can go." His voice sounded lower and raspier than normal.

She went. She picked up tips, she tallied totals, she filled coffee cups.

On the way back from the addition to the main part of the diner, she saw Tom bussing a table, and thought that was as good a time as any to talk to him.

"I couldn't get Rafiel to listen," she said, in a whisper. "About Frank. He says it's all coincidences, and he refuses to help. What are we going to do?"

For a while, she thought that Tom hadn't heard her. He remained bent over the table, his hand holding a stack of plates to put on the tray, while the other hand held a moist cloth, with which he was poised to wipe where the plates had been. But he didn't move. He just stood there.

"Tom?" she said.

He put the plates on the tray, very slowly. Carefully, he wiped the table. Then he stood up and faced her. His face was stark white. Not the sickly pale it had been in the parking lot the night she'd found him over the corpse, but white—the white of paper, the white of the unblinking heart of a thunderbolt. "I don't know what you want me to do," he said, his voice calm, emotionless. "If you can't get Rafiel to listen to you, I fail to see where I can be of any use. I'm sorry."

"Oh, Tom, don't be an idiot," she said, in an urgent whisper, sure he had to have misunderstood it all. "I want to know what you and I are going to do about it."

Tom shook his head. "No. You don't understand. We're not going to do anything. After tonight, I won't even be here."

"Where are you going?"

He twisted his lips and shrugged. "Somewhere."

She watched him pick up his tray and his cloth and disappear toward the main diner, tray held at waist level.

What on earth was going on? First Rafiel had behaved like a lunatic, and now Tom. What had they been smoking? And why were they not sharing?

"What do you know about this?" she asked Keith and Edward, where they sat in their corner table. "Where's Tom going? What is wrong with him?"

Keith sat back on his chair, looking vaguely scared. "Whoa," he said. "That's one of the few rules of safety I've learned. I don't get in between this kind of stuff."

"What kind of stuff?" Kyrie asked, her temper rising. "What kind of stuff? What is wrong with every male here tonight?"

"I think," Edward said, his voice regretful, his tone slow, "that if I told you what Tom told me I would forfeit whatever trust I've been able to earn back from him. And you must see I can't do that. He might need me. I have to . . . stand by to help him if he needs it. I've got to tell you I hope he comes to his senses, but I don't think my explaining things to you would further this in any way."

"Oh," Kyrie said. "I see. He"—and she pointed at Keith— "Makes cryptic remarks, and you make longer cryptic remarks, with far better vocabulary. Whatever. Sure. What is this? Be Stupid Day for males?"

She glared at them a while, daring them to answer. When neither did, she huffed out of there.

They didn't answer because they had no answer. They knew damn well—had to know—that they were acting like idiots. All of them.

Well, she would show them. Rafiel might be more practiced at smelling shifters, but Kyrie would bet that even she, herself, in panther form, could smell a rotting body in a shallow grave. If she knew what she was looking for. Even at the morgue, with all the preserving fluids and embalming whatnots, she had smelled it. She was sure she could smell it undisguised and in the heat of day under a thin layer of earth. The only reason she hadn't smelled it before—if it was there—would have been that she was escaping beetles and cops with guns.

So, when her shift was over, she'd go up to the castle, and she'd shift. She'd sniff around. When she found the corpses, she would shift again, and she would call the police. Take that, Officer Trall. If someone called the corpses in, then Mr. Rafiel Trall would have to do something about it, would he not?

And as for Mr. Tom Ormson, she didn't know exactly what was biting him, but she was in no mood to find out, either. It occurred to her that he might have seen Rafiel kiss her. But if that was what had put his nose so severely out of joint, then Tom needed to take a chill pill, that was what he needed to do.

After all, what fault was hers if an idiot male decided to kiss her? She had slapped him for it, too. Half rocked his head off of his shoulders. And if Tom hadn't stuck around to see that, he was more of a fool than she'd ever thought, and she wouldn't mind if he left and never came back.

She avoided him the rest of the shift.

Edward received the backpack from Tom's hands, and pulled out his wallet to set the bill for the food he and Keith and Rafiel had eaten. He guessed Rafiel wasn't coming back, but he wasn't about to ask

Tom. There was absolutely no reason to get the boy even more upset than he already was.

Instead, Edward put the backpack on his back, sure it looked ridiculous with his nice clothes. He got up, and Tom was turning away, putting the bill with the money in his apron pocket. Edward grabbed at his son's shoulder. "Tom." It was as close as he dared come to a hug.

Tom looked back, eyebrows raised.

"I just want you to know," Edward said, "that if you need anything at all . . ." He gave Tom one of his cards. "You probably remember the home address," he said. "But this is the new office address and my cell phone and work phone. Call. Anytime. Day or night, okay?"

Tom nodded, but there was just that look of dubiousness in his eyes that made Edward wonder if he would really call. Or just get into trouble and not tell anyone.

He walked out of the diner, and out into the cooler, exhaust-filled night of Fairfax Avenue. Under the light pole, he noticed that Keith was behind him.

"Can I come with you?" Keith asked. "To deliver that?"

Edward took a deep breath. "I don't think so," he said. "I'm going to deliver it in person, you see, not put it down somewhere and wait for them to find it. I'm afraid they'll go after Tom again if I do that."

"So . . ."

"So the triads are dangerous. And the Great Sky Dragon is not someone—or something—one tangles with for sport. I think I'm fairly safe, because they depend on me for legal representation. But I don't think you'd be safe and I can't allow you to risk yourself."

"But . . ." Keith said. "I can take out dragons. With a tire iron."

Edward couldn't avoid smiling at that. "I know," he said. "And I'm proud to have met you. But I really think this is something I have to do alone."

Keith took a deep breath, and shrugged. Then frowned. "You're not going to allow me to, are you? No matter what I say?"

"I'm afraid not," Edward said. "I'm afraid it wouldn't be safe."

"Okay. Then . . . I'll stay and keep an eye on Kyrie and see in what direction Tom leaves, okay? I'll tell you. When I see you."

Edward nodded, and put out his hand, solemnly. Keith shook it just as solemnly.

Add to the things Tom had accomplished the fact that he seemed to make worthy friends. And that was something that Edward had never expected of Tom. But he was glad. He started walking up the street, to where Fairfax became a little better area. It would make it easier to hail a cab. Once he caught a cab, he would call Lung.

If he didn't give them much time to react, perhaps they wouldn't have time to summon the Great Sky Dragon. Edward wasn't sure he could face that presence.

In fact, he wasn't sure at all he would survive this experience. Despite everything he'd told Keith, he was sure that the triad could buy a replacement lawyer, once they got rid of him.

The funny thing was that he didn't much care if anything happened to him, provided nothing happened to Tom. He'd never got around to changing his will, and if he died, at least Tom would be taken care of. It wasn't like he'd ever been much of a father.

Kyrie hung up her apron and picked up her purse. It hit her, suddenly, and with a certainty she'd never felt before that whatever happened tonight was decisive.

Because, if she went to the castle and found nothing, she'd have to live in hiding. Perhaps move. Because she couldn't know what the beetles knew or where they were.

On the other hand, if she went up there tonight and found corpses . . . well, it might be the last time she hung her apron on this peg and headed out, at the end of the shift, into the Colorado morning with the sky just turning pink, Fairfax Avenue as deserted as a country lane, and everything clean and still.

She got in her car and drove home, but only opened her front door to throw her purse inside the living room. Then she put her key in her pocket and headed back out.

The way to the castle was quick enough and at this time of morning there wasn't really anyone out. Kyrie could walk unnoticed down the streets. Which was good, because whether Frank and his girlfriend were shifter beetles or not, Kyrie didn't want him to know that she suspected him or his girlfriend. She wanted him to think that she had gone home, normally, and stayed there.

In a way she wished she could. Or that she—at least—had Tom or Rafiel with her. She couldn't believe that both of them had turned on her at the same time, and she wondered if it was some argument they'd had, of which she was only catching the backlash. Who knew?

The castle looked forbidding and dark, looming in the morning light. Most of the windows were boarded up, except for some right at the front, next to the front door. She supposed that Frank's girlfriend, not needing all the rooms—at least until such a time as she opened a bed-and-breakfast, if those plans were true—had opened only those in which she was living.

Kyrie wondered what Frank's and whatever her name's plans were, if they really were the beetles and if they truly were in the middle of a reproductive frenzy.

Were they intending on having all their sons and daughters help in the bed-and-breakfast? Or simply to take over the castle with their family? Kyrie seemed to remember that beetles were capable of laying a thousand eggs in one reproductive season, so even the castle might prove very tight quarters. And how would they explain it? And would the babies be human most of the time? Or humans all the time till adolescence?

There was no way to tell and Kyrie wondered if other shifters worried about it. She did. But others were, seemingly, in a headlong rush to reproduce, regardless of what it might mean. She thought of Rafiel and scowled.

As she approached the front entrance to the garden, Kyrie saw a woman in a well-cut skirt suit and flyaway grey hair walking away from the alley where the back entrance opened. She was walking away from the castle, toward Fairfax. Maybe she was going to pick Frank up from work.

Which would mean, Kyrie supposed, that they weren't guilty and were just an older couple in dire need of social skills.

But it would also mean it was safe to go into the castle gardens. Kyrie ran in.

The gardens were thick and green in the early morning light.

There was dew on the plants, and some of it dripped from the overhead trees. Above, somewhere, two birds engaged in a singing competition. She started toward the thicker part of the vegetation, where she could undress and shift. She didn't think that the woman living here now had any domestic help, but if she did, Kyrie didn't want some maid or housekeeper to scream that there was a girl undressing in the garden. Embarrassing, that.

Avoiding a couple of spiders building elaborate webs in the early morning sunlight, Kyrie made it all the way to the center of the garden, somewhere between the path that circled the house, and the outside fence.

There were ferns almost as tall as she was and she felt as if she'd stepped back into another geologic age when the area was covered in rain forest. She removed her clothes quickly and with practiced gestures. Shirt, jeans, shoes, all of it neatly folded and set aside. And then she stood, in the greenery, and willed herself to change.

It came more easily than she expected. The panther liked green jungles and dark places. It craved running through the heavy vegetation and climbing trees.

Kyrie forced it, instead, to stand very still and smell. It didn't take long. The smell was quite unmistakable.

"Hello," Edward said into his cell phone in the back of the car. "May I speak with Mr. Lung?"

There was no answer, but a clunking sound as though the phone had been dropped onto a hard surface. From the background, Edward could hear the enthusiastic voice of a monster-truck rally narrator. Then, as if from very far off, the shutting of a door echoed.

Edward hoped this meant that someone was calling Mr. Lung. It was, of course, possible that once it had been determined that Edward hadn't called to order an order of moo goo gai pan with fried rice on the side, the cashier had simply left. Or gone to the kitchen to pinch an egg roll or his girlfriend's bottom.

It took a long time, but at long last, Edward thought he heard, very faintly, approaching footsteps. And then—finally—the sounds of a phone being moved around on a counter.

"Mr. Ormson?" Lung's voice asked.

"Yes. I have what you . . . I have the object you require. I'm heading to the restaurant to return it."

"You are? And your son?"

"We'll leave my son out of this," Edward said.

"I see. Will we?"

"Yes."

"Your son caused much damage and death to our . . . organization."

Edward said nothing. What was he supposed to say?

After a long while, Lung sighed. "I see. But you are returning the object in dispute."

"Yes."

"Well, then I shall wait anxiously. I will see you in how long?"

"About ten minutes," Edward said, and hung up the phone. He looked at the light growing brighter and brighter in the east, every minute. If he was very lucky, then they wouldn't summon the Great Sky Dragon this close to dawn. Or if they did, he wouldn't make it here.

If he was very lucky.

He felt he could stand just about everything short of facing that huge, enigmatic presence once again.

CHAPTER
⇥ 12 ⇤

The panther scented the corpses right away. Fortunately, they were a little past ripe, even for its tastes. Kyrie was grateful for this.

Locked at the back of the huge feline mind, she could feel the huge paws tread carefully through the undergrowth, and she could feel the big feline head swaying, while it tasted the air. Death. Death nearby.

The death smelled enough like what the animal recognized as its own mortality to slow down its steps, and it only continued forward because Kyrie forced it to.

But it continued. Around the lushest part of the vegetation and toward a little clearing of sorts, in the midst of it all.

The vegetation that had once grown here had been torn out, unceremoniously, by the roots, rose bush and fern, weed and bulb, all of it had been pulled up and tossed, unceremoniously, in a huge pile beside the clearing.

What there was of the earth there had then been turned. Graves. Kyrie could smell them, or rather the panther could.

Kyrie was sure the smell would be imperceptible to her human nose, but her feline nose could smell it, welting up through the imperfectly compacted earth—the smell of decay, of death, of that thing that inevitably all living things became.

Only this death had the peculiar metallic scent that Kyrie had learned to recognize as the smell of shifters. The people laid to rest here had been shifters. Her kind. She looked at the ground with the feline eyes, and forced the feline paw to make a scratching motion on the loose earth.

It didn't take long. The hand wasn't much more than fifteen inches down.

The panther wanted to run away and to forget this, to pretend it had never existed.

But Kyrie forced it to walk, slowly, ponderously, to where Kyrie had left her clothes. Kyrie would shift. And then she would call the police.

But before she got to where her clothes lay, she found herself enveloped by a cloud of green dust. It shimmered in the morning air, raining down on her.

Pollen. It had to be pollen. Just pollen. She wished it to be pollen. But she could feel the panther's head go light, and indistinct forms take shape before her shifted eyes. Game, predators, small fluffy creatures and large ones, all teeth and claws, formed in front of the panther's eyes, coming directly from her brain.

Kyrie could feel the huge feline body leap and recoil, as if the things it were seeing were normal.

And then . . . And then she saw the beetle. It was coming through the vegetation, blue-green carapace shining under the morning light.

Not quite sure what she was doing, Kyrie forced the panther throat to make a sound it had never been designed for. She screamed.

The Chinese restaurant looked dismal grey in the morning light, as Edward got out of the cab in front of it.

As he was paying the fare, the cabby gave him an odd look. "They're closed, you know," he said. "They only open for lunch and that's not for seven hours."

"I know," Edward said, giving the man a generous tip and handing the credit card slip back. When you're not sure you're going to live, you can be very generous. "I'm meeting someone."

The cabby frowned. An older man, with Anglo-Saxon features, he was one of those men whose expressions are slow and seemingly painful, as though their faces had been designed for absolute immobility. "Only," he said, "they've found corpses in this parking lot, all the time. I've read about it in the paper. Are you sure you want . . . ?"

Edward nodded. He wanted to explain he was doing it for his son, but that made it sound way too much like expected a medal for doing what any decent father would do. Brave death to keep his son safe. Only . . . he supposed he hadn't been a decent father. Or not long enough for it to be unremarkable.

"I'm sure," he said. "I'll call you for the trip back," he said. "Your name is on the receipt, right?"

"Right," the cabby said, but dubiously, as though he couldn't really believe there would be a trip back.

The truth was neither did Edward. As he walked away from the cab—already peeling rubber out of the parking lot—and toward the silent door of the Three Luck Dragon, with the closed sign on the window, he would have given anything to run away.

But instead he fumbled off the backpack as the door opened a crack and Lung's face appeared in the opening. "Ah, Mr. Ormson," he said. Then he stepped aside and opened the door further. "Come in."

"There is no need," Edward said. "I have what you want, here. Take it and I—"

But the door opened fully. And inside the room were a group of young men, all glaring at him. They all looked . . . dangerous. In the sort of danger that comes from having absolutely no preconceived notions about the sanctity of the human life.

"I said, come in," Lung said.

It wasn't the sort of invitation that Edward could refuse. For one, he was sure if he did those dark-haired young men glaring at him out of the shadows would chase him down and drag him back. The only question was whether they would shift into dragon form first.

Edward suspected they would.

Walking away from Goldport by the shortest route did not require going near Kyrie's house. However, walking away from

Goldport and not heading out of town via the route to New Mexico did lead Tom down Fairfax Avenue, in the general direction of the castle and Kyrie's neighborhood. Though those were a few blocks north from his path.

Kyrie. The name kept turning up in Tom's mind with the same regularity that a sufferer's tongue will seek out a hole in a decaying tooth. It hurt, but it was the sort of hurt that reassured him he was still alive.

Kyrie. The problem was that he'd actually had hope. He'd seen her look at him. She'd patted his behind. She'd smiled at him. He'd had hope, however foolish that hope might have been. If he'd never hoped for anything, he wouldn't have been so shocked and wounded at seeing her with Rafiel.

And, yes, he was aware that the fact he couldn't bear to see them together was a character failing of his, not of theirs. He was also aware she hadn't betrayed him. Looks and even pats on the bottom are not promises. They certainly are not a relationship. They are just . . . Lust.

Perhaps, he thought, as he walked in front of closed-up store doors and dismal-looking storefronts in the grey morning daylight, *perhaps she lusts after me—though who knows why—but when it comes to love, when it comes to a relationship, she's a smart girl. If she were interested in me, it would only be proof of either stupidity or insanity.*

But . . . but if it wasn't her fault, why was he punishing her?

He scowled at his own thought. He wasn't punishing her. If anything, he was keeping himself from being punished daily by the sight of her with Rafiel.

It hurt. No, it wasn't rational, but it hurt. Badly. And Tom didn't do well with hurt. He wasn't punishing Kyrie. He'd go out of town, through Colorado Springs. Probably buy a bus ticket there. Maybe go to Kansas for a while. It had been a long time since he'd been in Kansas.

But, the relentless accusing voice went on in his mind, if he wasn't trying to punish her, why was he leaving Kyrie to face the beetles alone? Why was he leaving her when she couldn't even sleep in her house?

Because it wasn't his problem. Because she wasn't his to worry about. She could always bunk up with Rafiel, couldn't she? And she was sure he'd keep her safe. She wasn't Tom's to keep safe.

If she had been, he would have given up his life for her, happily enough.

But what kind of love was that? He minded seeing her with Rafiel? He minded her being happy? But he didn't mind leaving town while she was in danger?

No wonder she'd picked Rafiel. Tom's love was starting to sound a lot like hate.

As the last few thoughts ran through his mind, Tom's steps had slowed down, and now he stopped completely in front of the closed door of a little quilting shop, just one crossroad past where he would have turned up to go to Kyrie's place.

Maybe he should go and check on her. See if she was home. See if she was well . . . Then, if she told him she was fine and that Rafiel would take care of her, he could leave town with a clear conscience and never worry.

He turned around, in front of the shop—the window screaming at him in pretty red cursive that summer was the ideal time to quilt—and headed back toward the crossroad. He'd just turned upward on it, when he saw, ahead of him, just scurrying out of sight on a bend of the road, a giant beetle, its blue carapace shining in the sun.

Kyrie, Tom thought. He knew there were other places they could be headed. But right then he thought of Kyrie. He thought only of Kyrie.

And then the scream came. It was all Kyrie and yet not human— a warbling mix of terror coming from a feline throat designed only for roaring and hissing.

Without even noticing what he was doing, he broke into a run. He made the turn ahead in the street in time to see the beetle creep into the greenery-choked garden of the castle.

And the scream came again.

Kyrie was hallucinating. Or rather, the panther was. In front of the feline eyes arose a hundred little animals that needed hunting, or rearing predators.

And yet, at the back of the panther's mind, Kyrie managed to remain lucid, or almost lucid. There was a beetle. She must not lose track of that. A beetle with a shimmering blue-green carapace. And it was trying to kill Kyrie. And lay eggs in her corpse.

This certainty firmly in mind, Kyrie aimed at anything green-blue that she caught amid the snatches of illusion clogging the panther's vision. The panther's claws danced over the extended limbs with what looked like a poison injector at the end but might merely have been a lethal claw of some sort. She careened over the bug's back, and scrambled halfway away before the beetle caught up.

They were right over the graves, and the funky smell of them disturbed the panther, even through the hallucinations.

And at the back of the panther's mind, Kyrie knew soon she would be dead and buried in this shallow grave.

Tom had run full tilt into the garden of the castle, before he realized what he was doing. He was only lucky the beetles were too busy to realize he was running after them.

Of course, what they were too busy with was Kyrie. And once they noticed Tom they would start pumping the green stuff, and make Tom high as a kite and his fighting totally ineffective.

Twenty yards from them, seeing the huge black feline leap and dance ahead, in mad attack, Tom stopped. He pulled his jacket off, and tossed it in the direction of a tree, making a note where it was. He would come back for it. Then he peeled off the white T-shirt and, wrapping it around his head, tied it in a knot at the back. Its double thickness of fabric made it hard to breathe, and he could wish for better clothes to fight in than the pants that were slowly castrating him.

But he didn't get his choice. And it didn't matter. He must fight for Kyrie.

He grabbed a tree branch and plunged forward into the battle swinging it at any beetle limbs within his reach.

Clouds of green stuff emanated, turning the air green and shimmering.

Tom realized the smaller beetle—the one he'd followed?—was immobile and rubbing its wings to emit cloud after cloud of green powder. Meanwhile the one fighting Kyrie—and so far not losing, though also not managing to get any hits in—was not emitting green powder.

Interesting. So, they could only make people hallucinate when they weren't actively fighting, was that it?

Well, he thought, jumping back and landing atop the beetle, with a huge tree branch in hand. *Well. He was about to take the fight to the enemy.*

And now Kyrie was sure that she, personally, was hallucinating. On top of the panther-conjured images of scared little furry things, there was . . . Tom. Oh, not just Tom, but Tom in gloriously tight jeans, with his shirt removed, and his muscular chest bare in the morning sunlight.

Of course, the shirt he'd taken off was tied around his face, which seemed a really odd hallucination for her to have. And she would think she would dream of his grabbing her and kissing her, rather than of his hitting some very hard blows on the beetle with a huge tree trunk—far too big to be a branch—he'd got from nowhere.

And yet, she thought as she tried to concentrate on hitting any green-blue bits of bug that she could see through the panther's addled eyes. *And yet* the sight of him fighting the bug was far more distracting than the sight of the small furry things could be for the panther.

She bit and snarled and clawed at bits of bug, but in her mind she was admiring the way Tom leapt, the way he could turn on a dime, the force he put into the swing of that tree branch in his hand. From his movements, he too must have taken gymnastics or dance, or something.

Absorbed between her fight and disturbing glimpses of half-naked Tom, she could barely think. She heard the squeal of brakes toward the back entrance of the garden, but she paid it no attention.

Which is why she was so shocked to see Rafiel running toward them, gun drawn, blond hair flying in the wind and his expression quite the most distraught Kyrie had ever seen. He was screaming something as he ran, and it seemed to Kyrie—through the panther's distorted senses—that one of the words was "die." The other words, though, were "gravy" and "pick." She wasn't sure what gravy had to do with it.

Rafiel let out shots as he ran, aimed at the beetles, and from the high-pitched whining of the one that Tom was beating, Kyrie would guess at least one of the bullets had found beetle flesh. Whether that meant it had also found any lethal points was something else again.

Behind Rafiel, Keith came, running up, with what looked like a hoe in his hand. Where had he found the hoe?

Tom heard a bullet whistle by and looked up to see Rafiel running into the garden firing wildly. Still beating on the beetle—smacking it repeatedly on the head seemed to make it too confused to either fight, flee, or put out green powder—Tom wondered if he was the intended victim of the beetle.

But the next bullet lodged itself solidly in the beetle's—Frank's?—flesh, and the creature emitted a high-pitch whine. And then it went berserk, limbs failing up toward Tom, trying to dislodge him, trying to stab at him.

Tom hit at the limbs, wildly. Keith was running up, behind Rafiel, and as Rafiel leapt toward Kyrie's beetle and shifted shapes mid-leap, his clothes falling in shreds away from the lion body, Keith grabbed the falling gun and aimed it at Tom's beetle.

Kyrie was grateful when Rafiel, now in lion form, joined the fight, but—though the panther was having trouble seeing clearly—she could see enough to see Keith grab the gun and point it in the general direction of Tom.

She didn't think that Keith would hurt Tom. Or not on purpose. But from the way Keith was holding the gun, she could tell there was no way in hell he could hit the broadside of a barn.

Unfortunately, he wasn't aiming at the broadside of a barn. He was aiming at a general area where Tom was a prominent feature. Without thinking she leapt, hitting the still-human Tom with her weight and bringing him rolling off the bug and onto the ground, with Kyrie just by his side.

Just in time, as the bullet whistled through the space where he'd been.

Kyrie was attacking him, Tom thought, as he hit hard on the ground, just barely managing to tuck in his head enough that he wouldn't end up unconscious. Why was she?

And then he realized that Keith had a gun and clearly had no idea what to do with it, as several erratically fired bullets flew over the beetle's carapace. Just where Tom would have been.

Still stunned by his fall on the ground, Tom put out an hesitant hand toward the huge mound of fur beside him. "Kyrie?" he said.

A tongue came out and touched his hand. Just touched, which was good, because it felt just like a cat tongue, all sharp bits and hooks.

A non-feline hissing sound, a scraping, and Tom saw the beetle was turning around and was aiming sharp claw-like things at Kyrie.

Before he could think, he knew he was going to shift. He had just the time to kick off his leather boots as his body twisted and bent. And he was standing, as a dragon, facing the bug. He did what a dragon does. He flamed.

First, Kyrie thought, flames weren't particularly effective in these circumstances. Tom's flame seemed to glance over the beetle's carapace, without harming it. And second, if Tom continued flaming, he would hit a tree and roast them all alive.

But before Kyrie could change shape and yell this at Tom, who was clearly addled by adrenaline and change, Keith came flying out from behind them, hoe in hand. He had dropped his gun. Which was good. But Kyrie wasn't sure that a hoe was the most effective of weapons.

Only she couldn't do anything, except shift, in a hurry and scream, "Don't flame, Tom," as Keith landed on top of the beetle and started digging into the joint between the neck and the back carapace. Digging, as if he were digging into soil, making big chunks of beetle fly all over.

The beetle went berserk.

Sometimes the only way to stop a flame that is doing its best to erupt from a dragon's throat is for the dragon to force himself to become human. This Tom did, forcing his mind to twist his body into human shape. Just in time to avoid burning Keith to a crisp atop the beetle. Which was good, because Keith seemed to have hit on something that worked. He was digging up large chunks of beetle flesh, throwing them all around in a shower of beetle and ichor.

And the beetle was stabbing at him, fortunately pretty erratically. The beetle's arms weren't meant to bend that way. Not upward and toward something on its back. Only, even an erratic blow was bound to hit, eventually. Unless . . .

Tom grabbed the tree branch he'd let drop, and started beating at beetle limbs. From the other side, Kyrie was doing the same.

Kyrie was back to her human form, and Tom couldn't look at her with more than the corner of his eye. Not if he wanted to continue fighting in any rational manner at all.

But, damn, that woman could swing the tree branch with the best of them.

As the beetle stopped moving, and its high-pitched scream grew, Tom became aware of another sound behind him. A feline protest of pain. He turned, in time to see the beetle get a claw into Rafiel between shoulder and front leg.

For a moment, for just a moment, Tom thought, *Good. He deserves it.*

But an immense feeling of shame swept over him. Why did Rafiel deserve to die? Because he'd bested Tom in winning the affections of a woman?

Hell, by that criteria there would hardly be any males left alive in the world.

Shame made Tom jump forward, toward Rafiel, tree branch in hand, beating at the beetle. Just in time, as Rafiel was crawling away, bleeding.

And now Keith scrambled up on the back of this beetle. He looked like nothing on Earth and certainly no longer like the hard-partying college student. His clothes were a mess, he seemed to have bathed in greenish-brown ichor, and he'd lost his cap somewhere.

But he had an insane grin on his face, as he started digging up chunks of this beetle. And Tom concentrated on keeping the beetle from stabbing his friend, by beating the beetle's limbs away. Kyrie joined in on the other side.

Soon the beetle had stopped moving.

But from behind them there was still a high-pitched sound, like the beetle's scream.

Tom turned around, expecting to face yet another beetle. Instead, he saw Rafiel desperately clutching his shoulder and struggling to get up while pale, white, giant worms swarmed over him.

Tom didn't understand where the worms came from, but they had big, sharp teeth and were biting at Rafiel.

Tom ran toward Rafiel and started grabbing at the worms trying to eat Rafiel, while Kyrie ran up to smash the ones that were merely around Rafiel.

A second later, Keith and his hoe joined in.

Grubs, Kyrie thought. The more advanced grubs on the corpses beneath the thin layer of soil had come alive at the smell of Rafiel's blood, and were swarming him.

She saw Tom jump ahead and start to pull the grubs off Rafiel. As mad as she was at Rafiel, she didn't want him eaten alive by would-be insects. And besides, Rafiel had got in this trouble by trying to help her in the first place.

She jumped into the fray, gleefully smashing at the grubs with her heavy branch.

And Tom had got the last grub off Rafiel—who seemed more stunned than hurt, and was swinging the huge piece of tree he carried, likewise beating down the bugs. Keith joined in with his hoe.

There were a lot of grubs, more and more—pale and white and writhing—pushing up out of the soil, as soon as they smashed a dozen or a hundred.

So absorbed in what she was doing, her arms hurting, while she kicked away to keep the grubs from climbing her legs, Kyrie didn't keep track of Rafiel.

Until she smelled gasoline and realized that Rafiel had got a huge container of gasoline from somewhere and was liberally dousing the clearing and the surrounding vegetation.

Tom had just realized what the worms were. They were grubs. Babies. It seemed odd to be killing babies who were acting only on instinct.

But . . . were the babies human? He couldn't tell. They looked like white grubs, featureless, except for large mouths with sharp teeth. With which they'd probably been feeding on decaying human flesh.

Would they ever be human? How could Tom know? Except that, of course, their parents had been human. At least part of the time.

He swung the tree branch and smashed little beetle grubs while wondering if with time they would learn to be human babies and human toddlers. But . . . would they? And even if they did, when adolescence came, when most people started shifting, would they be able to control their urges to shift? And their urges to kill people so they could lay eggs in the corpses?

He just decided that he'd hit all of them who attacked him, but he would not, could not, kill any that might still be asleep beneath the soil. They should take those, and see if they became human babies as they developed. If they did, chances were they wouldn't shift again till their teen years. And meanwhile, they could see that they got a good education, and didn't believe they could kill people for their sexual gratification.

If shifters would look after punishing their own criminals, then they had to look after educating their own young, didn't they?

He'd just thought this when he smelled gasoline, and, looking up, saw Rafiel spreading gasoline over the entire area and the surrounding vegetation.

Tom had to stop him. He had to. He was going to kill all the babies. And themselves with them, probably.

As tired as he was, he didn't realize he'd shifted and flamed until he saw fire spark on the gasoline-doused tree on the other side of the clearing.

Oh, shit.

CHAPTER
⊰ 13 ⊱

"Run," Kyrie screamed, managing to grab at Keith's arm, and making an ineffective grab at Tom's wing, as she scrambled ahead of them toward the back entrance of the garden—the nearest one.

If she thought for a minute she could go over the fence, she would have done it. She couldn't pull Tom, though, and he seemed dazed, staying behind, staring at the flames.

"Tom, run," she yelled, but there were sheets of flames where they'd been, and she couldn't stop, but ran. Ran all the way out the gate. Where she collapsed in a heap on the beaten-dirt of the alley, a few steps from Rafiel's car.

Rafiel was facedown in the alley, but he was clearly alive, taking deep breaths that shook his whole body.

Kyrie heard Keith ask, "Are you all right, man?"

And realized Rafiel was on all fours, throwing up.

Tom ran out of the gate, fell, then scrambled up, holding on to the eight-foot-tall metal fence of the castle to pull himself upright.

And Kyrie couldn't help smiling when she realized he was wearing a jacket and a pair of leather boots. And nothing else. So, that was why he had delayed? Tom and his jacket and boots.

He dropped something at her feet. "I tripped on these."

Her clothes. As she shook them out, even her earring dropped out.

But he had his back to her, and was still clutching the fence posts, while he stared at the roaring inferno growing inside the garden.

"We have to go," Kyrie said. "We have to get out of here. The fire department will be here in no time."

"But . . ." Tom said. "The babies."

"You mean the grubs? Tom, those weren't human. They tried to eat Rafiel."

Tom made a sound half growl. "We don't know if they were babies. Do we know what we were during gestation? Perhaps they would have shifted when they were fully grown, and only a few of them would ever shift again and not for years."

"Tom," Rafiel said. His voice sounded shaky. "I understand the feelings, but we had to kill them. We couldn't afford for the corpses to be found with those larvae. They would be taken to labs. Do you want them to figure out shape-shifting? They might very well come after us and kill us all, if faced with a dangerous example like that."

"So, you killed them to save your life? Is that right? Do you have the right to kill things just because there's a remote chance it would eventually lead to your death?"

"Hell, yes," Rafiel said.

"It's not moral," Tom protested.

"If I'm dead, morality doesn't matter to me anymore. Tom. Look, they bit me." He showed round bite marks, as if from a hundred little mouths equipped with sharp teeth. "They were dangerous. They would have bit other people. Killed other people. Besides," Rafiel shrugged. "Technically *we* killed them. You flamed them."

"Only because I was trying to prevent you from killing them," Tom said, and realized how stupid that sounded.

"Tom," Kyrie said. "It was self-defense. The heat of battle. And they were probably dangerous. Please calm down. We need to get out of here before those fire trucks get here. Hear them?"

Tom heard them, the wailing in the distance, getting near.

"We can go to my house," Kyrie said. "Take showers. I'll make something for us."

Just then, Tom's phone rang in his jacket pocket. "What now?" he said, grabbing the phone and taking it to his ear.

"Mr. Ormson," a cool voice on the other side said.

"Yes."

"We have your father," the voice said.

Oh, shit. The dragons. "But you have the Pearl of Heaven too," Tom said.

"Yes. But . . . There is someone who wishes for more than the return of the Pearl." The voice on the other side was slick and uncaring an inhuman. "He says there must be punishment."

"What punishment?" Tom said, feeling like he'd been punished enough this last hour.

"Severe punishment," the voice said. "One of you will be punished. Either you or your father. We're at Three Luck Dragon, on Ore Road on the other side of town. If you're not here in half an hour, we'll punish your father. The Great Sky Dragon is tired of waiting."

The phone line went dead and Tom thought, *So, let them punish my father. He deserves it. He's the one who got involved with the triad.*

But Tom was the one who had stolen the Pearl of Heaven. Worse, Tom was the one who had asked his father to return it. And his father had gone, without complaint. Even though, knowing even more about the triad than Tom did, he must have realized this was the kiss of death.

Tom didn't realize he had made a decision until he was running down the alley.

"Where is he going?" Rafiel asked Kyrie, as Tom started running.

Kyrie shrugged, but Keith said, "Something must have gone wrong with his father taking the Pearl out to the triad."

"What?" Rafiel said.

"Whatever happened to we'll leave the Pearl somewhere?" Kyrie said. "And let them find it?"

"I guess that wasn't practical," Keith said. "Since Tom was heading out of town."

"He was? Why?"

"I don't know," Keith said. "But he'd seen the two of you kissing and he said he couldn't stand to stay around."

"Oh no," Kyrie said.

"He's not going to get very far dressed like that, before someone arrests him for indecent exposure," Rafiel said, as Tom hit the end of the garden, and turned onto Fairfax Avenue. And then he jumped, and opened the door of his car. Getting into the driver's seat, he yelled, "Get in now."

Kyrie had barely the time to scramble in, beside Keith on the backseat, before Rafiel tore out of the parking lot in a squeal of tires and a smell of burning rubber.

He pulled onto the curb just ahead of the running Tom, leaned sideways and opened the passenger door. Then before Tom could swerve to avoid it, he yelled out the door, "Get in now, Tom. Get in."

"I don't want to get in," Tom said, stopping.

"That you might not, but you're naked. Someone will arrest you long before you get where you're supposed to go," Rafiel said, way too reasonably.

Tom looked down. Yeah. He supposed a leather jacket and a pair of leather boots didn't constitute decent clothing. And he had to get to the restaurant without being arrested.

He flung into the passenger seat of the car. "I need to go to Three Luck Dragon on Ore Road on the south side."

"I know where it is," Rafiel said, starting the car up. "Wonderful Peking duck." Then, as though realizing that Tom's driving motive wasn't a wish for food. "Your father?"

"Yes," Tom said, and covered his face with his hands. "I should never have sent him to them. Hell, I can't do anything right. Damn."

He felt a hand on his shoulder, from the back, and heard Kyrie's voice. "If you were planning to go out of town, you did the only thing you could do," she said. "And your father, did he protest?"

"No," Keith said. "He knew there was a danger. He wouldn't let me go with him. But he, himself, went willingly. Tom. Your father is an adult. He made his own decision."

"Doesn't mean we'll leave him to die," Tom said.

"Right," Rafiel said. "Which is why I'll get us there as soon as possible. Meanwhile, there are clothes under the front seat, Kyrie, if you could get them. There should be at least two changes of clothes. And there should be a pair of pants and a T-shirt Tom could use. They'll be large as hell, but they should make him decent."

Before Tom could protest, he found Kyrie handing him a T-shirt and a pair of sweatpants. Removing his jacket and boots and putting clothes on was difficult in the tight confines of the car. And Tom wasn't absolutely sure if the dragons cared if he had any clothes on.

But he understood there would be a psychological advantage to being fully dressed when he got there and tried to negotiate his father's release with the dragons. If he were naked, he'd be embarrassed, and that would put him at a strong disadvantage. No. He had to be dressed. And he had to get his dad out of this.

He should never have involved his dad in this.

Before they got to the restaurant Kyrie could smell the shifter scent in the air. She wondered how many of them were there.

Speeding down the—at this time—deserted Ore Road, lined by warehouses and dilapidated motels, then made one last turn . . . And then she saw it. At least she imagined that was it. She couldn't imagine any other reason why the parking lot in front of a low-slung building ornamented with an unlikely fluorescent green dragon on the roof would be crammed—literally crammed with men.

No, she thought, as she got closer. Men and dragons.

And at the head of it all, golden and brilliant in the morning light, was a huge dragon. Ten times bigger than Tom in his dragon form. And even bigger than that in presence. He *felt* a hundred times larger than his already immense size.

In his front paw, raised high above the assembly, he held Edward Ormson.

Kyrie wasn't close enough to see Edward's expression. But she could see his arms moving. He was alive.

Rafiel stopped the car in front of the parking lot. Impossible to turn into it. And besides, Tom was already struggling with the latch, trying to jump out.

Kyrie opened the door, too, as soon as the car stopped. And was hit by the silence of the hundreds of beings in the parking lot.

It was the silence of suspended breath.

Tom had *never* been so scared. Not even when he'd been sixteen and his father had thrown him out of the house at gunpoint. Not even in the wild days and terrifying nights afterward, while he tried to learn to live on the street while not dying of sheer stupidity.

It wasn't only his terror, he realized. It was the terror and awe of all those around him. He could hear it in their silence, see it in their absolute immobility. And he could feel it rolling in waves over him whenever he looked at the great golden dragon who stood in front of the multitude. Holding Tom's father.

Right.

There were moments, Tom had learned, when fear was the best thing. Fear of the street thug kept you from saying something that would have made him kill you. Fear of the poisonous snake kept you too far away from it to be bitten. And fear of some animals would make you stand absolutely still, so that their eyes, adapted to movement, couldn't see you.

And there were moments when fear had to be ignored. His fear was perfectly rational. He could sense the menace of the Great Sky Dragon and the fear that infected those around him, crowding the parking lot. He could feel it, and it made him struggle to draw breath. It made him have to fight his every instinct to be able to step forward into the crowd, which parted to allow him through.

His fear was the most natural thing in the world and it came from the fact that he did not wish to die. And it didn't take a genius to know that was the most likely outcome of this situation.

And yet . . . And yet, of course Tom didn't want to die. There had been enough ambiguity in the exchanges in the car that he thought he just might still have a chance with Kyrie. And who, thinking of Kyrie—particularly when she'd smiled at him—could want to die and not even try for something more with her?

But all of that was irrelevant, for the same reason that it was irrelevant whether or not Tom could or wanted to eat some human beings on occasion. It was irrelevant because if Tom did it and succeeded he wouldn't be able to live with himself afterward.

As he wouldn't be able to live with himself if he walked away now and let them kill his father. His father had walked into this at Tom's request. It was Tom's doing, and it was high time Tom dealt with his own mistakes.

He walked forward through the crowd, which parted for him, leaving him a wide aisle to walk through.

He could hear his friends walk behind him, but he didn't turn to look. That would only make what he needed to do harder to accomplish.

Edward wasn't really scared until Tom showed up. Before the Great Sky Dragon arrived, even, while Lung and his minions had kept him prisoner in the entrance area of the restaurant—where the TV blared endlessly about round-the-clock monster truck rallies—he'd realized what was going to happen and he was prepared to take it.

Funny how, just days ago, when the Great Sky Dragon had told him that he held him responsible for Tom's actions, Edward had bridled at the idea and tried to deny it. Now it seemed absolutely self-evident.

Tom was something that Edward had made. Not only by inadvertently passing on some long-forgotten gene that had caused the boy to turn into a dragon—no. Of that guilt he could have easily absolved himself, because . . . who can be sure of what he's passing on to his sons? And who can control what his children inherit?

But these days with the other shifters—getting acquainted with Kyrie and even the policeman—Edward had realized that he'd done something else, something drastically wrong with Tom. Because the other shifters weren't as troubled and hadn't gone through so much to get to a place of balance. And hadn't made mistakes nearly as bad as the ones Tom had achieved.

Which must mean that shifters weren't inherently unstable. Of course, Edward had tried to tell himself that Tom was inherently unstable; that there had been something wrong with the boy from the beginning. But he'd seen Tom at the diner—Tom holding down a job and establishing contact with other human beings all around him.

There was nothing wrong with Tom. If he'd gone around the bend, it had to be his father's doing.

And so, Edward was ready to pay for his crimes and for the fact that he had been a truly horrible father. So he'd been perfectly calm, in the Great Sky Dragon's grasp, while the dragon lifted him above the crowd. Even though he'd been held there, immobile, for half an hour, he didn't feel scared or upset.

He devoted his time to a vague dream that Tom would come back; would figure things out with Kyrie; that sometime in their future they would have children. Even if Edward would never get to see his grandchildren, he could imagine them vividly. And it was worth it to him to sacrifice himself for them.

And then the car stopped. And Tom showed up. The four of them—the four children, as Edward couldn't help thinking—walked through the massed triad crowd toward the Great Sky Dragon.

Tom was at the front, looking pale and drawn and absolutely determined.

"Tom, no," Edward shouted. "It's not worth it. Leave."

But Tom shook his head, black curls tossing in the light of the morning. He frowned. He walked all the way to the front of the Great Sky Dragon and stood, feet planted apart, arms crossed on his chest. "I've come," he said.

Edward had the impression the giant creature holding him laughed, though there was no sound. "It is good that you come," he said. "And now, what do you want to do?"

"I want you to let my father go," Tom said, casting his voice so that, normally low as it was, it could be heard all over the vast parking lot.

"Or?" the Great Sky Dragon asked.

"I don't think there's any or," Tom said. "You're much bigger than I am, and we're surrounded by all your minions. I'll fight you, if you want me to, but I don't think there would be any contest."

"No," the Great Sky Dragon said. "There wouldn't."

"So, I'm here. You do whatever you have to do, but you let my father go first."

"Tom, no," Edward said. "Don't do this. I don't want you to sacrifice yourself for me. I was a horrible father."

At that something like amusement flickered over Tom's face, which, from where Edward was looking at it, looked like a terrible, pale mask incapable of human movement. For just a moment, Tom blinked, and looked up at his father, and his eyelids fluttered, and his lips pinched upward in an almost smile, "No shit, Sherlock. Did you have to consult many experts to come to this conclusion?" He shook his head. "But it doesn't matter, because I've always been an even worse son, and—" As Edward opened his mouth, Tom held up a hand to silence him. "What's more, I brought this final situation on by my own actions. I'm not stupid. I wasn't a baby when I stole the Pearl of Heaven. Nor were my impulses uncontrollable. I knew what I was doing. I knew whom I was messing with. And I did it anyway. So, you see, it's my doing, and who but I should suffer for it?"

Tom looked away from his father. "Let my father go," he told the dragon. "And promise me that all my friends will be able to leave safely. And then do whatever you think you have to do to even the score."

Edward felt himself being lowered, slowly, until his feet touched the pavement. He put out a hand and grabbed at Tom's shoulder. "Tom, no. Please. I can't live knowing—"

But the dragon flicked a toe at Edward's back. Just, flicked it. And Edward went flying, backward, head over heels, to land bruised and stunned at Kyrie's and Keith's feet.

Tom watched the dragon flick his father out of the way and send him flying. A look back over his shoulder showed him that his father was alive and well. He turned back to the dragon.

Having no illusions about how long—or how little—remained for him to live seemed to make everything around him very bright and sharp. The dragon glittering in the light of the morning was a thing of beauty, golden and scintillating. And the sun coming up over the Three Luck Dragon painted the sky a delicate pink like the inside of certain roses when they're just opening to the light of morning.

As for the morning air, it smelled of flowers and it felt cool to the skin, with only a hint of warmth to indicate the scorcher the day would later become.

I'll never see another sunrise, Tom thought. *Yesterday was my last sunset. That meal eaten with Kyrie, hastily, in my father's hotel room, was my last meal. Worse, I'll never kiss a girl, beyond the half-hearted kisses and gropes I got back before I knew I was a dragon. I'll never kiss Kyrie.*

Weirdly, none of this seemed startling. It was as though all his life he'd been hastening toward this. Or rather, as if all his life he'd been worried about how he was going to die and what would put an end to his life. Now he need worry no more. He knew exactly where he would end and how.

A brief thought of whether there was anything after flickered through his mind. His parents were Catholic—or at least Catholic of the sort that didn't believe in God but believed that Mary was His mother. They went to mass sometimes. Certainly for big occasions and momentous parties, like weddings and baptisms and funerals. And Tom had attended catechism lessons in the faraway days of his childhood. Well, at least he'd been present while dreaming up ways to trip up the catechist, or look up her skirt.

He had no objections to the idea of an afterlife. But he also couldn't believe in it. Not really believe. If there was anything on the other side of this, he sensed it would be so different that who he was and what he thought on this side would make no difference at all. For all intents and purposes, Tom Ormson would stop existing.

He wanted—desperately wanted—to look over his shoulder at Kyrie. He heard her back there, her voice muffled, as though someone held a hand over her mouth. She was yelling, "Tom, no."

But he didn't dare look. If he saw her. If he actually saw her, he knew his courage would fail him. Instead, he stood, legs slightly apart for balance, letting his arms uncross from his chest and fall alongside his body. In a position that didn't look quite so threatening.

He looked up at the huge, inhuman eye of the Great Sky Dragon.

"Ready?" the creature said.

"Ready," Tom said.

The creature lowered its head to be level with Tom's and said—in a voice that was little more than a modulated hiss, "You have great courage, little one."

And for a moment, for a brief, intense moment, Tom had hope.

Then he saw the glimmering claw slice through the air. It caught him just above the pubic bone. Tom saw it penetrate, before the pain hit. It ripped upward, swiftly, disemboweling him from pubic bone to throat.

Looking down, Tom saw his own innards spill, saw blood fountain out.

I'm dead, he thought, and blinked with the sort of blank stupidity that comes from not believing your own eyes.

And then the pain hit, burning, unbearable. He screamed, or attempted to scream but nothing came out except a burble of blood that stopped up his throat, filled his mouth, poured out of his nose.

He dropped to the ground and for a second, for an agonizing second, struggled to breathe. His rapidly fading brain told him it was impossible. He was dead. But he tried to breathe, against pain and horrible cold and fear.

He inhaled blood and heard Kyrie call his name. He thought he felt her grab his hand, but his hand was as distant and cold as the other side of the moon.

And then there was nothing.

"Tom."

Kyrie had struggled against Rafiel and Keith, as they held her back, struggled and kicked and tried to yell at Tom not to do this. It wasn't worth his sacrifice. It just wasn't.

They could fight the dragons. They could.

"No, we can't," Rafiel told her. "He's giving himself up so that the rest of us can get away in peace. If he doesn't do that, all of us will die."

"There's hundreds of them and five of us, Kyrie," Keith said. "We'll all die."

"Then we'll all die," she yelled. "Can you live with the idea you calmly allowed him to sacrifice himself for us?"

"I can't," Edward said. But he was gathering himself up from the ground, and he looked bruised and tired and hurt. He didn't look like he would lead any charges against any dragons.

So Kyrie yelled, "Tom, don't do it," and tried to struggle free, to go grab him. If they ran. If they ran very fast . . .

But Keith and Rafiel both grabbed her and held onto her arms, and covered her mouth.

She was twisting against them, writhing . . .

And it all happened too fast. That claw rising and falling, in the morning sunlight, catching Tom and ripping . . .

Kyrie saw blood fountain at the same time that the men, startled, let go of her. She careened forward, under the power of her own repressed attempts at movement, and the burst got her to Tom just as he was falling, his face contorted in pain.

She didn't even—couldn't even—look down to where his body had been ripped open. His insides were hanging out, and he was twisting, and his face looked like he was suffering pain she couldn't imagine.

His wide-open eyes fixed on her, but she didn't know if he could see her. She fell to her knees, and grabbed his hand, which felt too cold and was flexing in what seemed to be a spasmodic movement.

"They can still save you," she said. "They can still save you. The wonders of modern medicine."

But blood was pouring out of his mouth, blood was bubbling out of his nose, and, as she watched, his eyes went totally blank, in the morning light. Blank and upward turned, and wide open.

She couldn't tell if his heart was still beating and, since it was probably in the mass of organs exposed in the front of his body, she couldn't check. And she didn't need to. She knew he was dead.

She stood up, shaking slightly. And then she lost it.

She never knew the exact moment when she lost it. When she realized she was doing something stupid, she had already flung herself forward, at the Great Sky Dragon, arms and legs flying, mouth poised to bite.

"You bastard," she said. "You bastard." Only it wasn't so much a word as a formless growl, and she kicked at the golden foot and tore with her nails at the golden scales.

She felt more than saw as several of the human spectators, the triad members, plunged forward to grab at her, and she didn't care because she could take them all. All of them.

Only the Great Sky Dragon grabbed her in his talons, one of them still stained red by Tom's blood, and brought her up to his face, to look at her intently with his impassive eyes. "Pure fire," the voice that wasn't a voice said. "I wonder if he knows what he holds."

And then she was tumbling down, and hitting the ground hard.

As she struggled to sit up again, she could see the Great Sky Dragon already high in the sky, flapping his wings—vanishing.

Around them, the other men—or mostly dragons—were disappearing. Some flying and some just . . . scurrying away.

Aching, Kyrie looked over at Tom's corpse. He was still staring blankly at the sky. What did she expect? That he would get up and say it was all a joke? Corpses rarely moved.

She swallowed hard. Grief felt like a huge, insoluble lump in her throat.

But the madness was gone. She knew she couldn't avenge herself on the dragons. Or on any of them. She knew as she knew she was alive and that Tom was dead that there was no remedy for this.

She scooted forward and took hold of Tom's hand. "I'm sorry," she said. She knew he couldn't hear her, and she'd never devoted any thought to the possibility of life after this one. But if there was anything, and if he could hear her . . . "I'm sorry. This is not how I meant for this to go. I didn't even realize . . . I didn't know myself until just now." She squeezed the cold hand, knowing it was beyond comfort.

"Kyrie, you have to get up," Rafiel said. "I'm going to call the police. You have to get up from there."

She shook her head. "No. I'll stay with him. I'll go with him. We can't leave him alone here." She saw a fly try to alight on Tom's wide-open eyes, and she waved it away with her free hand. Oh, she knew he was dead and he couldn't feel it, but it seemed . . . indecent.

"Kyrie, he's going to the morgue. You can't go with him. You don't want to. Let me help you up," Rafiel said.

She felt him tear her fingers away from Tom's hand. As if from somewhere, far away, she heard her own thoughts tell her that she was in shock. And she believed them. It just didn't change anything, did it?

There were sounds of someone throwing up behind her. She thought it was Keith, but she didn't turn to look. It had to be Keith, anyway, since there were only the five of them . . . the four of them here. And it couldn't be Edward because he was crying, somewhere to her right side. He was crying, loudly and immoderately. And she thought that was weird because she didn't know lawyers could cry.

Rafiel threw something warm—a jacket?—over her shoulders. "You're trembling, Kyrie. You need something warm," he said.

"Tom's jacket," she said.

"What about it?"

"It will be ruined," she said. "All the blood. He's going to be very upset." And then she realized what she'd said was nonsense, but she couldn't seem to think her way out of that puzzle.

She felt Rafiel lead her very gently. And then there were lights, and noise, and a siren, and someone was asking her something, and she heard Rafiel's voice say, "She really can't talk now. She's in shock. I'm sorry. Perhaps later. We were walking across the parking lot to see when the restaurant opened, and this giant Komodo dragon came running out of nowhere, and it attacked Tom. I'm not really am not sure of the details. It all happened so fast."

Kyrie felt Keith shove her into a car. She didn't care whose car, nor where she was going.

CHAPTER
❧ 14 ❧

And then life went on, somehow. It all seemed very odd to Kyrie that life could go on after something like that. She'd seen someone die—no. She'd seen Tom die. She'd seen Tom die so that the rest of them would be allowed to go free.

It all seemed very strange, and she thought about it very deeply. She thought about it so deeply that the rest of life seemed inconsequential.

It all seemed a great mystery. One minute Tom had been alive and well and afraid, and making wisecracks and being himself. And the next minute—no, the next second, he was so much flesh, on the ground. No life, no spirit, no breath.

It was very odd that such a great change could be effected so quickly and that it could never be reversed.

There should be, she thought, and realized she was in her kitchen, sitting at the table and staring down at the pattern of the table—whirls of fake marble engraved on the Formica—*there should be a rewind button on life. So that you could press the button and life would be again as it was before. And the horrible things wouldn't have happened.*

Someone was knocking at the door. At the kitchen door. Tom. But no. Tom would come no more.

But someone was knocking on her kitchen door. And she was sitting at her table in her robe and—she looked—yup, a long T-shirt. She was decent. And someone was knocking, so she guessed she'd better let whomever it was in.

She stood up, opened the door. Keith was there, on the doorstep, wearing his ridiculous backward hat. Only it had to be a new one, because the other one had burned with the castle, had it not? She seemed to remember . . .

He had her newspapers under one arm, and was staring at her, in utter dismay. "Kyrie," he said. "Have you slept? Eaten anything?"

"I don't . . ." She frowned. "I don't remember."

"You don't remember?" Keith asked. He looked scared. "Kyrie, it's been two days."

Two days? Since Tom had died?

"I just realized I'm . . . in my robe. In my home . . ."

"We brought you back. Mr. Ormson . . . Edward put you to bed."

He had? For some reason the idea of a strange male—of a strange older male—undressing her didn't embarrass her. Not even a little. It didn't matter.

She became aware that Keith had dumped the papers on the table, and was bustling around, setting a teapot on, opening the fridge, letting out with exclamations of dismay, if at her housekeeping or the lack of food in her fridge, she didn't know.

It seemed like all of a sudden, he was putting a cup of tea, a plate of toast with jam, and a peeled boiled egg in front of her.

"I'm not the best of cooks, Kyrie, I'm sorry," he said. "This is about all I can cook. But will you eat? A little. For me?"

He was looking pleadingly at her, and he looked far younger than she thought he was, and she thought if she didn't eat he might very well cry.

The toast and the egg tasted like straw to her, but she forced herself to eat them. The tea, at least, was sweet and warm, and she swallowed cup after cup, while Keith poured.

"Have you talked to Rafiel?" Keith asked.

Kyrie had to concentrate to remember Rafiel. It all seemed such a long way away and vague. After a while she shook her head.

"Well, they found journals. Apparently Frank kept journals. He'd managed to keep the beetle under control until just a few years ago and then . . . biological clock or what not and he went insane and started . . . laying down pheromones bait, to attract females and victims. He wrote all about it in his diary. He started laying the pheromones over a year ago. As if he were trying to reassure himself he wasn't crazy. Though most of the killings were the female's doing. He just helped drag the corpses to the castle, afterward."

She nodded, though what Keith was saying only made sense in a very distant and impersonal sort of way, as if he were talking about people who had been dead for centuries and whom nothing could affect.

"He was intending to make Tom the fall guy for it all, you know. That's why he hired someone from the homeless shelter with a history of drug abuse. The idea was to make all corpses disappear, except a couple, which would be found near Tom's apartment, and it would be thought that Tom had killed them all, that he had gone over the edge. The beetle's hallucinogenic powder would have helped. That's why they attacked us here. They wanted you to throw him out. They didn't want anyone to be around him, or to know him that well."

Well, and that had worked. And had led by degrees to everything else. But Kyrie felt too numb to even feel guilt. None of it mattered. She put her empty cup forward, and Keith filled it again.

"Kyrie, can you take a sleeping tablet? I bought some over-the-counter ones. I couldn't . . . I couldn't sleep without having nightmares. I have one. Can you take them? Or will they cause you any problems?"

"I can take them," she said, her voice sounding pasty and altogether like a stranger's.

He put the small yellow tablet in her hand. She swallowed it with a gulp of tea. Presently she felt as if the world around her were becoming blurry.

She was only vaguely aware of Keith's leading her to her bed, and tucking her in. For such a young kid—though he might be her age in chronological years—he had an oddly paternal touch as he tucked the blanket around her.

"Sleep," he said. "I'll take a key. I'll come check on you."

"This too shall pass," Kyrie said, and startled herself with saying it. Keith had come and checked on her and forced her to eat and sleep for the last two days.

This morning she'd woken up realizing that she couldn't go on like this.

Life would go on, even when there didn't seem to be any point to it. And it wasn't as though she could say, "Please just stop my subscription, I don't want to play anymore." Nor did it seem to matter. Not that way.

A wedge of sanity was forcing itself into her shock and grief. She'd liked Tom. She'd liked Tom a lot. Although at least part of the feeling was probably lust. She remembered his sprayed-on clothes, and she could smile, in distant appreciation.

She got up out of bed. It was eight a.m. Keith had been dropping by every morning at ten, after early classes. She didn't want him to catch her naked. And she really should stop being a burden to the poor young man. It was time she got herself together.

A glimpse in the mirror showed her how fully horrible she looked, with her unwashed hair matted and falling in tangles in front of her face. Witch of the Rainbow Hairdo, she thought and smiled, an odd smile, from pale, cracked lips.

She opened her dresser and got out jeans and a dark T-shirt, and underwear. She lugged everything to the bathroom, where she realized she still had her red feather earring on. She couldn't remember preserving it through the fight at the castle, but she must have, because she was wearing it.

She took it off and laid it, reverently, on the vanity. Tom had saved that for her.

Under the hot, full shower, she washed rapidly. Shampoo. Twice to get rid of all the grease she'd allowed her hair to accumulate in the last . . . three? four days? And then conditioner. And then soap her body, slowly, bit by bit, making sure every bit got properly scrubbed.

She doubted she had washed . . . since. There was green-red ichor on her legs. And her arms and hands were stained the dark—almost black—red of dried blood. Tom's blood. She watched it wash down the drain, in the water.

Damn. It wasn't only that she'd liked him. It wasn't only that she lusted after him and she'd never had a chance to do anything about it. It was that she'd only realized what he was made of as he was dying.

Oh, not just because he stepped up and offered himself in exchange for his father—and safety for all of them—but because he'd done it without complaint. And as a matter of course. Even the creature . . . the dragon, had told him he had courage.

Why you'd say that to someone who was about to die was beyond Kyrie. Maybe the dragon believed in an afterlife. Maybe he'd thought it would make things easier . . .

She finished showering and dried. Tom's towel was still there, hanging from the hook at the back of the door. She resisted a wild impulse to smell it, to bury her face in it and see if any of his scent remained on the fibers.

But no. That way lay madness. That way lay people who kept the rooms of dead people just the way they'd been when the person died. That way lay widows who slept with their husband's used clothes under their pillows. And it wasn't as if she had the right, even. He wasn't her husband. He wasn't even her boyfriend. Until a few days ago, she would have told people she didn't like him.

She dressed herself, combed her hair, carefully, put her earring in.

The face that looked at her from the mirror was still too pale, and she looked like she'd lost weight too. Her cheekbones poked out too far. But there was really nothing for it, was there? Life went on.

She'd got to the kitchen and put on the kettle, when someone knocked at the kitchen door. She thought it was Keith. He'd taken a key—what did he think she was going to do? try to kill herself? did he think he'd need the key to get in and save her?—but he still knocked before getting in.

"Come in," she said.

"I can't," a muffled voice said. "It's locked."

She reached over and unlocked the door. And . . . Edward Ormson came in.

He stood just inside the door, as if uncertain what he was going to do or say, or why he'd come here at all.

Kyrie turned from the small pan in which she'd just put an egg to boil. Keith must have brought eggs one of these days, because there were two cartons in the fridge. "Do you want an egg?" she asked.

"No, thank you," he said. His skin looked ashen. His eyes, so much like Tom's, were sunken in dark rings. "I've . . . eaten."

She got a feeling that what he was really saying was that he never wanted to eat again. Ever.

"I . . ." He hesitated. He was wearing cargo pants and a T-shirt and looked ruffled and uncertain and a long way from the smooth lawyer who'd landed in town however many days ago. "I would like to talk to you."

"Sit," Kyrie said. "As long as you don't mind if I eat while you talk."

As a matter of fact, though, she got two cups down from the cupboard, and grabbed the sugar bowl, which she put between them. She poured a cup for Edward and said, "Put sugar in it. Even if you normally don't. It seems to help. Keith has been making me drink it."

"Keith . . ." Edward said.

And Kyrie thought that he was going to accuse her of having an affair with Keith right after Tom had died, as if she'd made Tom any promises. And besides, she wasn't. Having an affair with Keith. She'd barely been aware of him here, to be honest, except for his making her eat and drink. And she thought he'd done the dishes once, because everything was out of place in the cupboard.

But Edward grimaced, and ran his hand back through his hair, just like Tom used to do. "Yeah, Keith has been coming to my hotel room every morning, too. And making me eat. He wrangled a key from the front desk somehow. I have no idea what the front desk people think is going on, and I'm afraid to ask." His grimace became an almost smile. "But he's kept me alive, I think. It didn't seem . . . to matter for a while."

"I'd have thought you'd be back in New York," Kyrie said. "With your family."

He shrugged. "There is no family. There was Tom. And I couldn't leave . . . yet. They're going to give me back the body tomorrow. I'll be flying it back with me for burial. Our family has a plot in Connecticut." He hesitated. "There will be a funeral. Probably closed-casket funeral. I wouldn't want . . ." He shook his head. "I thought you might want to come. I . . . you don't have to but if you want to I'll pay your fare. I've asked Keith, too. Other than that it will just be me and my business associates. I think . . . some of Tom's friends should be there."

Kyrie contemplated this. She wasn't sure. On the one hand it might offer . . . closure. On the other hand, she just wasn't sure. After all—she knew he was dead. Did she need to see him buried too?

And yet, it did seem right that he should have friends there with him, didn't it? He shouldn't go into the ground watched only by people who thought he'd gone bad. Poor Edward's son who'd gone to the wrong.

"I'll try," she said. "Yes. I think I would like to go."

"Good," he said. "And that brings me to what I wanted to talk to you about. You know the Athens is closed. From what I understand it is about to be foreclosed on. Not only had . . . the owner no living relatives that anyone can find, but he hadn't paid the mortgage in about three months. Apparently whatever frenzy . . . well . . . He wasn't taking care of business."

She nodded, not sure what he meant.

"I wanted to offer you . . . I wanted to . . . I know you're unemployed now."

Kyrie shook her head. "Waiting jobs aren't hard to come by," she said. "Particularly late-night ones. People offer them to you for being alive and breathing."

"I know," Edward said. "But I would like . . ." He took a deep breath, as if steeling himself to brave a dragon in full rampage. "Tom liked you an awful lot."

She nodded, then shrugged. It didn't seem to matter.

"I'd like to offer you college money," Edward said. "And however much money you need to live while you're in college. You can study whatever you want to." He swallowed, as if something in her expression intimidated him further. "I can't help you much in most professions, but if you take law, I can see to it that our firm hires you, and if you're half as smart as you seem to be, I can probably nudge you up to partner before you're thirty."

She heard herself laugh and then, in horror, she heard abuse pouring from her lips. She called him every dirty word she could think of. And some she wasn't sure existed.

His eyes widened. "Why . . . why?"

"You're trying to make reparations," she said, and the sane person at the back of the mind of the raving lunatic she seemed to have become noted that she sounded quite wild. "As if Tom were responsible for my being without a job. Tom isn't, you know. It was not his fault that the beetles ran wild. It was not his fault—"

And then the tears came, for the first time since all this had started. Tears chased each other down her cheeks, and there was a great sense of release. As though whatever she'd kept bottled up all this time had finally been allowed to flow.

She became aware of Edward's hand, gently, patting her hair. "You have it all wrong," he said. "I'm not trying to make up for anything Tom did. It's just that without Tom, I really have no family. And besides, I owe him a debt. Whoever started it—and it can be argued I did—right there in the end, he gave his life to end it, so that I could go free. That's a debt. I'm trying to look after the people he cared for. Don't deny me that. I've offered the same thing to Keith. Anything I can do to help, in his studies or his career . . . I'm a fairly useless person. Most of what I can offer is money. But that's yours, if you need it."

As suddenly as they'd started, the tears stopped. Kyrie wiped at her face, and swallowed and nodded. "I don't know, yet," she said. "I just don't know. I'll. I'll come to the funeral. And then we'll see."

"There are jobs with the police force, if you should want them," Rafiel said.

He stood by her kitchen door, looking, for the first time since she'd known him, stiff and ill at ease.

Kyrie sat at her kitchen table. She'd been going through all the newspapers, one by one. The one from after Tom's death talked about the two horrible tragedies in town—the group of people who seemed to have died in the garden at the castle. And Tom's death. The headline screamed "A Tragic Night In Goldport."

She looked up at Rafiel. "Surely the CSIs could tell that the bodies had been dead a while and buried," she said.

Rafiel seemed to take this as encouragement to come further into the house. "Yes and no," he said. "They could see . . . sort of, that things weren't exactly textbook. But the thing is that the fire got really hot there, at the center of the garden, and they couldn't say much for sure about each of the corpses, except identify them through dental records."

"The . . . beetles . . ."

"They must have reverted, in death or in burning, because they found skeletons." He sat down at the table, across from her. "They identified Frank and the woman who owned the castle. The castle itself survived, by the way. There's talk of someone buying it to make a school for deaf and blind kids."

Kyrie nodded, and flipped through the other papers. There were pictures of all the other dead. Even Frank, with his Neanderthal brow, graced the front pages of all newspapers. All of them smiled from posed photos or looked out from poses obviously clipped from candid snapshots. All except Tom.

"There are no pictures of Tom," she said.

Rafiel shook his head. "No," he said. "His father's picture of Tom, in his wallet, is from when Tom was six. We didn't think it was appropriate. And while his father thinks there are mug shots from his juvenile arrests, he didn't think those were appropriate either. And no one has tracked them down, possibly because the record is sealed."

Kyrie felt bereft. She couldn't explain it to herself, but she felt like she needed to see Tom's face, just once more. She was afraid of forgetting him. She was afraid his features would slip from her mind, irrecoverable.

While she'd come to accept that she'd live on past this, that she might very well live on to find someone and marry, maybe, sometime—her shifter handicap being accounted for—she couldn't bear the thought of forgetting Tom. "It's just . . . I would very much like to remember his face," she said.

Rafiel looked at her, intently. He was wiggling his leg again, this time side to side, very fast. "About what I said about Tom, the day . . . I was an ass, Kyrie. I could tell you were interested in him, and I was afraid. You . . . are very special to me, Kyrie."

She didn't know what to say to that, and just looked at him, with what she was sure was a vacant look.

He laughed, a short laugh, more like a bark. "And I'm being an ass again, aren't I? I can't give you a picture of him. Unless you want the one from when he was six and I don't suppose . . ." He sighed. "Would you like to come to the morgue? To see him? He's being given back to his father tonight, so if you want to see him, it has to be now."

Kyrie thought of Tom's face contorted in pain, as she'd last seen it. She wasn't sure that was the memory she wanted.

"He doesn't look like he did, you know. In death . . . His face has relaxed. They . . . the coroner closed him up. He doesn't look gross at all. More like he's sleeping."

"You were there?" Kyrie asked. "For the autopsy?" She thought of what she'd seen done to the corpse in the parking lot—the body opened, the brain sawed out of its cavity.

"There was no autopsy. It didn't seem needed. We supposedly saw death, you know, attack by wild animal. They found a couple of scales on his body. They're not exactly Komodo dragon scales." He frowned. "To be honest, they were in his boots and were probably . . . his . . . but they analyzed as reptile scales and the paper is printing something about the danger of exotic pets. They love to preach. And his father didn't want him autopsied, so he wasn't. He really looks . . . very natural."

Kyrie wasn't sure. The morgue had scared her. But perhaps seeing Tom without that expression of agony on his face was all she needed.

She nodded. In the bathroom, she caught herself putting on lip gloss and combing her hair. As if Tom could see her.

Feeling very silly, she headed out the door with Rafiel.

✢ ✢ ✢

The morgue was . . . as it had been before. The guy at the desk didn't even make much fuss over Kyrie coming back. Just tipped his hat at her, as if she were a known person here.

Rafiel led her down the cool, faintly smelly corridors, to a door at the end. He opened the door and turned on a very bright fluorescent light, which glared off tiled walls. In this room, the tiles were white, and it made the whole thing look like an antiseptic cell. Or the inside of an ice cube.

It wasn't an autopsy room. Just a small room, with a collapsible metal table set up against one wall. On the table was something—no, someone—covered with a sheet. The room was just this side of freezing.

"We don't have drawers," Rafiel said. "Just ten of these rooms. If needed we can cram three people per room, but I don't think we've ever needed to. The closest we came were the bones, from the castle, and those we just put all together in one room, while we sorted out who was who and identified victims by dental records and DNA."

She nodded. She didn't remember walking up to the table, but she was standing right next to it, now. She couldn't quite bring herself to reach out her hand and pull the sheet back.

Rafiel reached past her, and pulled the sheet back. Just enough to reveal Tom's face and neck.

He was right, Tom didn't look as he had at the time of his death. He also didn't look as other dead people that Kyrie had seen. She expected wax-dummy pallor. She expected the feeling she'd had when she'd seen other dead people—even when she'd seen Tom dead, in the parking lot. That feeling that all that mattered had fled the body and the only thing left there was . . . meat.

But there wasn't that sense. Instead, there was as much color as she'd seen on Tom when he was pale. Not the paper-white pallor of his anger, and not the sickly pale of the parking lot, when they'd discovered the corpse. Just, even, ivory white. His lips even had a faint color—pale pink. And his eyelids were closed, his quite indecently long eyelashes—how come she never had noticed?—resting against the white of his skin and giving the impression that at any minute his eyes would flutter open and he'd wake up.

She looked up to ask Rafiel if embalmers had worked on Tom, but Rafiel had left. Very decent of him. Giving her time alone with Tom.

She ran a hand down Tom's cheek. It felt . . . warm to the touch. She didn't know embalmers could do that. She caught at a bit of his hair. It felt silky soft in her hand. Clearly, they'd cleaned the body of blood.

Bending over him, she caught herself and thought this was insane. She couldn't, seriously, be meaning to kiss a dead man? But he didn't look dead. He didn't *feel* dead, and it wasn't as though she meant to French him. Just a quick peck on the lips. A good-bye.

She bent down all the way, and set her lips on him for a quick peck.

His lips were warm—warmer than she would expect, even from someone alive who was lying down in a refrigerated room—and she would swear they moved under hers.

And then she heard him draw a breath. She felt breath against her own lips. His eyes flew open. He looked very shocked. Then he smiled, under her lips. He wrapped his arms around her shoulders. He pulled her down onto him.

And he kissed her very thoroughly.

It should have been scary, but it was not. It was just . . . Tom. And his mouth tasted, a little, of blood, but it wasn't unpleasant. As soon as he allowed her to pull up, she said, "You're alive."

He frowned. "It would seem so. Shouldn't I be?"

She shook her head. "We're at the morgue."

He raised his eyebrows, but the mild curiosity didn't stop him from pulling her face down toward him, and kissing her again.

"Oh, hell," a voice said, startling them both; sending Kyrie flying back from Tom; and making Tom sit up and the sheet that covered him fall.

He pulled it back up, to make himself decent, but left his chest exposed, and Kyrie blinked, because where she was sure there had been a torso-long rip that exposed his insides, there was now only a very faint scar, as though he had only had a superficial cut.

They turned to the person who'd said, "Oh, hell."

It was Rafiel, and he was leaning against the wall, by the door, looking at them with wide-open eyes. "Shit," he said very softly. "It's nice to see you well, Tom, but how the hell do I explain to the coroner that his corpse with massive trauma is going to walk out of here?"

"Tell him reports of my death were greatly exaggerated?" Tom asked, raising an eyebrow and smiling.

"But we need to get him out of here soon," Kyrie said. "And get him some clothes. He's going to catch his death of cold."

"I doubt it," Rafiel said. "I very much doubt it. Unless cold is a silver bullet."

CHAPTER
❧ 15 ❧

And life went on even when the best that could possibly happen had happened. The day that Tom was let out of the morgue—though the coroner had insisted he go to the hospital for X-rays and a full checkup before admitting that Tom might, just possibly, be alive—they'd bought a daybed and a dresser for the back room.

They'd been quite prepared to use the rest of Tom's money and get it from the Salvation Army, but Edward had insisted, and so Tom had a matching daybed and dresser in Southwestern style, as well as a bookcase and a bunch of books his father had bought him to replace the ones that had been destroyed in his apartment.

The back room was now his, and for the use of it, the kitchen and the other common areas, he would pay half of Kyrie's rent, and half the utilities. Kyrie's bathroom had acquired a bottle of something called Mane and Tail, which she'd told Tom seemed more appropriate for Rafiel, and shouldn't Tom's shampoo be Wing and Scale?

But they weren't living together. Not exactly. They were roommates, not lovers. They hadn't slept together, didn't know if it would ever happen.

For now there were kisses, now and then, and the occasional

holding of hands. Tom had explained what he wanted with disarming frankness. "I'd like to date," he'd told her the night he'd got out of the morgue—was it only two weeks ago?—over dinner. "I've never dated, you know? Not even high school dating. I groped a few girls in school." He'd grinned. "They all complained. And I think I suck at relationships. Of any sort. I need practice. I'd like to date. Well . . . go together, as if we were kids. And then work up to the rest, if it works out."

The decision to share a house seemed odd in light of that, but it wasn't. Between two shifters, one of them should be able to watch out for the other. And also, they'd both realized that they'd been awfully lonely. And whether they were ever anything else again, they were friends.

They were also partners. Not in a romantic sense, but in a business sense.

Kyrie remembered a whole afternoon of shouting between Tom and his father. Both men assured her they'd never raised their voices, but she remembered sitting on the sofa in her living room while they glowered at each other and shouted, both of their expressions very much alike, and both far more intense than the argument warranted.

The gist of it was that Edward wanted to give Tom the moon, the stars, and happiness on a plate—or at least the only form of it Edward could give him. He wanted Tom to go back to school. He wanted to pay Tom's expenses while he did. He still wanted to pay Kyrie's too. Both studies and expenses.

Tom . . . wanted something completely different. He wanted the Athens. He would accept enough money to go to cooking school. Not chef's school. Far too fancy. Tom wanted to learn enough to be the cook for the Athens. And he wanted Kyrie to have part ownership of it.

Which brought them to this evening, two weeks later, standing outside what used to be the Athens. There was a new sign, up front, and Keith, perched up on a ladder, was finishing painting it. It said, in fancy old-English script "The George" and, in case someone missed the reference, there was a cartoonish drawing of Saint George, spearing a flaming dragon.

It was all very baffling to Kyrie, but Tom had insisted. And when Keith came down from his ladder, to much applause from the four of them—Kyrie, Tom, Rafiel, and Edward—and took a bow at his artistry, and Tom led them inside, the bafflement continued.

Tom had found somewhere, in the bowels of the Salvation Army—while he was trying to find replacements for some of his personal effects behind his father's back—an old, possibly antique, and definitely disgusting painting. It showed Saint George on a horse putting a lance through the chest of a dragon, who fountained quantities of blood. He now proceeded to hang it over the big booth at the back, the only one that could sit ten people.

"I hope you realize it's in extremely poor taste," Kyrie said.

"Yeah," Rafiel said. "That would kill you. That was the difference between you and the other corpses. The Great Sky Dragon didn't get your heart."

"I wonder if it was on purpose," Keith said.

"I'm sure it was," Tom said, finishing nailing his picture and jumping down from the vinyl seat, and backing up to admire the effect. "I suspect he considered it the equivalent of turning me over his knee."

"Has the coroner recovered yet?" Kyrie asked. "From having one of his corpses walk out?"

"Well—" Rafiel said. "He's now talking about how Tom was in comatose shock from the injury. In another five days he'll have convinced himself that he never pronounced Tom dead. I mean, if he told the truth, people would wonder if he'd been drinking his own formaldehyde. *He's* probably wondering if he's been drinking his own formaldehyde. People hate doubting their own sanity. He'll make . . . adjustments."

"But could the Great Sky Dragon know that?" Keith asked. "Wouldn't he have feared Tom's coming back would hit the papers and blow the whole shifter thing sky-high?"

"I doubt it," Tom said. He turned around, a frown making a vertical wrinkle between his eyebrows. "I very much doubt it. He's been around a lot. He knows people."

"What I want to know," Rafiel said softly, "is if the great triad presence in town was because of the Pearl of Heaven and if they'll now thin out, or if we're stuck with them for good. We don't have the police force to deal with an international criminal organization . . ."

"I wonder if they'll leave us alone," Kyrie said. "They strike me as people with notoriously little sense of humor—whatever the Great Sky Dragon has. And they're bound to be a little . . . miffed at us." She looked out the corner of her eye at Edward, who had already declared his intention to leave the firm that worked so much for the triads. He'd start again on his own. He'd made some noises about maybe moving to Denver. She wondered if any of these intentions would survive once he got back to New York.

But Edward didn't notice her look. He was still staring at the picture of Saint George, wide-eyed. "Good Lord, Tom," he said. "It will put customers off their food."

"I very much doubt it," Kyrie said. "Tom has been hiding talents. He can actually cook."

"And college students will eat anything," Keith said.

"There is that," Kyrie admitted. Then she looked at Tom, who was looking at her with a little smile. When he looked like that, it was very hard not to kiss him, and she'd been trying very hard not to kiss him in public. It only gave people ideas. Besides, they were at The George. They were supposed to behave as business partners. "So, what's the symbolism, Tom?"

"Can't you tell?" he asked softly. "I thought you'd get it." Smiling, he looked around at the still empty tables. The door was closed, the Closed sign firmly in place. In a minute, Keith—who wanted to work for them part-time, at night, even while going to college—was going to go out and hang the "Grand Opening" and "Under New Management" signs out there. But for now everything was quiet.

"The pheromones that Frank laid down will take years to wear out," Tom said. "Rafiel," he looked at the policeman, "has had them analyzed, and they are very potent. It's not unusual for little beetles to lay down chemical signs that attract mates and prey from miles away. These ones might very well act on the whole country. And they're specific for shifters. We'll have shifters coming out of our ears for years to come. Chances are," he said, looking at Rafiel, "that we'll have to keep order in our own little strange community. So many occasions for people to go over the edge. And we can't afford for the more out-of-control of us to expose us all to danger. So . . ." He waved expansively toward the picture on the wall. "We get to be both the beast, and the dragon slayer. It's perfect."

"If you say so," Kyrie said.

"There's people milling around out there," Keith said.

"Those aren't people, darling," Kyrie said, turning around, and surely surprising poor Keith with the playful appellation. "That's the poet and pie lady. They just want to come and loiter all night, eating too little food." She grinned at him. "Go open the door."

"And I suppose I'd better eat something," Edward said. "I'm taking the last flight to New York." He looked at the menu. New menus, freshly laminated. "Good Lord," he said. "What are these?"

"It's old diner lingo. Tom insisted. There's a translation in front of each item."

"You really have to learn to start saying no to that boy," Edward said, smiling. "He has entirely too many crazy ideas for his own good."

"Oh, trust me," Kyrie said. "I say no enough." And had Tom's father blushed?

He looked away from her and backed, to sit at a table facing the counter. Keith was opening the door. Behind the counter, Tom had put his—blue, emblazoned in gold—apron on. Yesterday he'd spent the whole day scrubbing the counter and kitchen area till it glimmered. And they'd interviewed and hired the staff. Anthony. And a couple of the day girls. And Keith, and half a dozen other new faces.

They, themselves, would have to work twelve hours or more a day, everyday. It didn't matter. That it was their place made all the difference.

Keith was writing stuff on the glass window. Most of it incomprehensible to the normal—or even abnormal—mind because it was taken from Tom's research of old diner lingo. There was for instance "Moo with Haystacks," which she thought was supposed to be burger and fries, for $5. She was going to have a talk with Keith and get him to write stuff everyone understood.

But for now, it was the first night, and she didn't mind if only the regulars came in.

Edward looked up from his menu. "I think I'll try the hash," he said.

"Really?" Kyrie asked.

"Really. I haven't had it in years, and since my own son is cooking, the chances are low he'll poison me. They're there, but low."

"All right," Kyrie said, and glanced in the menu to see the fancy name that Tom wanted hash called. Getting back to the counter, she looked over it at Tom.

He'd tied his hair back and tied a scarf over it, pirate style, to keep hair from the grill. Which just meant that he wasn't in the spirit of cooking in a diner yet. And he smiled at her, which made all thoughts flee her mind for a while.

It took her a few seconds to remember Edward's order, and to relay it in the new-menu-speak. "Gentleman will take a chance," she told Tom.

His features crinkled up in a smile. "Oh, yes. I am quite sure he will."

⊰ **AFTERWORD** ⊱

When you've written as many books as I have, you get used to their showing up in the strangest ways.

Yes, there are the books that someone else – agent or editor – suggested, there are the books that I proposed in cold, clear-eyed rationality because I thought they'd do well just then. There are books like *Darkship Thieves* which I wrote and no one seemed to want until, thirteen years later and almost by accident I decided to let an editor see it, and it sold and did well. And there are books that appear fully formed and run me to ground, no matter how busy I am, until I write them.

Of all the books I've written, *Draw One in the Dark* has perhaps the oddest origin story.

It was 2003 and my world had come to an end. Well, at least my writing world had, or so I thought. After sixteen years of struggling to break into the field and watching my very first series get scheduled for hard cover, I had the bad luck of having the first book come out in the month after 9/11/2001. Perhaps it would have not done well, anyway, but coming out just then, as an unknown, with no publicity, in hard cover, was disastrous. The series trickled through two more books, but by then it was obvious there was no breathing life into it.

So, there I was, thinking I'd never get published again. And I had a dream.

I'd like to point out this dream itself is not unusual. I had at various times in the past dreamed about seeing my published work. The dreams usually showed the title of some story I hadn't written or I hadn't written yet, and chances were by the time I woke up fully I'd forgotten all about the story, so I can't even tell you if they came true.

However, this time I went cunning. It was as though there was my dreaming self, and then my real self, in my head, watching my dreaming self. So I had some control.

The setting was an outdoor signing, of the sort they do at World Fantasy Convention when it's in a warm climate. Writers were sitting at little outdoor tables, each table with a candle on it, so there was this vast darkness, with only a tiny pool of light right in front of each writer.

I was sitting with the Baen writers – something I did even before I was a Baen writer – and as I sort of tuned in to the dream, I expected the normal thing, where I sat there while people on either side of me had lines, and got a fan now and then with one of my three published books (or my half a dozen published short stories) to sign.

Instead, I realized there was a line. This is where my real self, inside my dreamed self perked up. I thought, "Oooh. A line."

And then the first person in the line put a box on the table, and started taking out books. I'd seen them do this for other authors who had a vast oeuvre.

The first set in front of me was my three (then) published books, the Shakespeare Fantasy series. Then there were the musketeer mysteries at the time only in proposal. I said, "Oh, I see you're a real fan. You have everything."

And the young woman smiled and said, "Yes, I found you with your Shifter series, and then I bought everything you ever wrote."

And my dreaming self went "Shifter what? I've never written shifter anything!"

Meanwhile she's unloading books on the table, and she pulls out this one: *Draw One in the Dark*. And my dreamed self looked at it and recoiled. You see, it was a hard cover of the first edition. And I said, "Oh, you have one with the awful cover." And she said, "Yeah, you wouldn't believe what I paid for it, it's a collectible you know."

At this point I'd become alert to the fact that this series was special, somehow, so I got my dreamed self to do the smart thing. Under the pretense of admiring the preservation of the book, I turned it over and read the back blurb, then while talking to the fan, read the first three pages.

When I woke up I wrote half of it. And when Jim Baen, months later, asked if I had a book I wanted to sell to him, I suggested *Draw One in the Dark*.

Finishing it, I knew it was, up till then, the best thing I'd ever written. So I was somewhat dismayed (but no one can say I wasn't forewarned) when I saw the singularly inappropriate first cover. (Which, fortunately, was rendered somewhat better by cover design, then changed for the paperback edition. Yes, there were reasons for that first cover. Let's say it was a perfect storm of circumstances.)

Now, as I write this, I'm doing the final polish on the third book, *Noah's Boy*, and have contracted for the second edition of the first two books.

I see no sign of its being such a success that some fan will discover me through it. But then, if you'd asked me even two years ago, I'd have told you I didn't think there would ever be a re-edition.

This series seems to have a mind of its own – the third book takes it to a whole other level of complexity – and all I can say is . . .

If in some years, you come to a signing with a box of my books and see the scene I described above play itself, say hi. This book – this series — wouldn't exist except for you.

GENTLEMAN TAKES A CHANCE

Sarah A. Hoyt

From near and far the creatures gather—winged and hoofed, clawed and fanged, and armed with quick rending maws. Great hulking beasts appear that the world has not seen in uncounted ages: reptiles that crawled in great primeval swamps long before human foot trod the Earth; saber-toothed tigers and winged pterodactyls. And others: bears and apes; foxes and antelopes, all converge on a small hotel on the outskirts of Denver, as a snowstorm gathers over the Rocky Mountains.

Outside the hotel, some change shapes—a quick twist, a wrench of bone and flesh, and where the animals once were, there now stand men and women. Others fly into the room, through the open balcony door, before changing their shapes.

In there—in human form—they crowd together, massing, restive. Old and young, hirsute and elegant, they gather.

Outside the day dims as a roiling darkness of clouds obscure the sun. Inside the men and women who were—such a short time ago—beasts wait.

Then of a sudden *he* is there, though no one saw him shift shapes; no one saw him arrive.

He is not huge. At least not in his human form. A well formed man, of Mediterranean appearance, with well-cut if somewhat long lanky dark hair, sensuous lips and a body that would not have looked out of place in a Roman temple. He appears to be in his middle years and wears his nakedness with the confidence of someone who feels protected in or out of clothes.

But it is his eyes that hold the assembly in check—dark eyes, intense and intent—that look at each of them in turn as though he knew not only any of their possible sins and crimes, but also their nameless, most intimate thoughts.

"Here," he says. "It is here. It is nearby."

"Here," another voice says.

"Nearby."

"So many dead. Shapeshifters. Dead."

"We can't let this stand," someone says.

"It won't stand," the leader of the group says. "We'll find those who killed the young ones of our kind. And we will kill them. The blood of our children calls to me for revenge. I've executed the murderers of our kin before and I will do so again."

"The deaths happened in Goldport, Colorado," a voice says from the crowd and a finger points. "That way."

"I will be there tomorrow," the leader of the meeting says. A tenseness about him indicates certainty and something else—an eagerness to kill again.

Kyrie Smith looked up at the ceiling as a sort of scraping bump came from the roof of the tiny workingman Victorian that she shared with her boyfriend, Tom Ormson. The sound reminded her of ships at high sea—of the shifting and knocking of wood under stress. How much snow was up there by now? And how much could the roof withstand?

From the radio—high up on the shelf over the card table and two folding chairs that served as dining nook—came a high-pitched whistle, followed by a voice, "We interrupt this program to issue a severe winter storm alert. All city facilities are closed and everyone who is not emergency and essential personnel is requested to stay indoors. Goldport Police Department is on cold reporting. Should your home become unsafe or should you believe that it will become unsafe, these are the public shelters available."

There followed a long list of public buildings and churches. Kyrie thought briefly that with the weather the police couldn't be on anything but cold reporting—icy in fact—though she knew very well they meant that any accidents should be reported later. Cold seemed such an apt adjective for what was happening outside.

Not that she anticipated needing shelter. The little Victorian cottage had been here for over a hundred years and presumably had survived massive snowstorms. But though it was only three p.m., with the scant light outside, the swirling darkness looked more like stormy midnight than the middle of the afternoon.

It was her first blizzard in Goldport, Colorado. She'd lived here for just over a year, but the last winter had been mild, sparing her one of the legendary Rocky Mountain blizzards. Which she wouldn't have minded so much, except for the fact that those blizzards grew ever larger in the tall tales of all her neighbors, acquaintances, and the regular diners at The George.

For the last week—while the weathermen screamed *incoming*—the clientele at The George had been evenly divided between those who'd say not a flake would fall and those who insisted they would all be buried in snow and ice and future generations would find them like so many Siberian mammoths buried in permafrost, the remains of their last souvlaki meal still in their stomachs.

Kyrie suppressed a shudder, gave a forceful stir to the bowl of cookie dough she held against her jean-clad hip, and told herself she was being very silly. It wasn't like her to have this sort of fanciful, almost superstitious fear. She'd like to think she had imagination enough, but she'd never had time to let it run riot.

She had been abandoned as a newborn at the door of a church in Charlotte, North Carolina, on Christmas Eve, and had lived in a succession of foster homes, having to fend for herself more often than not. She'd grown up slim and graceful, with the muscular body of a runner.

At almost twenty-two, she'd been an adult and on her own for about four years. She rarely stayed at a job for very long. What she had thought for many years were dreams of turning into a panther—and now knew was true shape-shifting—usually scared her away from any given place, job or relationship and had kept her moving before anyone became too close. She'd been afraid of being made to see a psychiatrist. She'd been afraid of being given antipsychotic drugs. Sane or not, she wanted to know her thoughts came from her own mind, not from some chemical. And her madness—as she thought it—hurt no one. It was just dreams.

For years she told herself she didn't miss people, or relationships, or those other things that seemed to be a given right of all other humans. She kept her own house and her own mind. And, until three months ago, when Tom had become her boyfriend and started subletting the enclosed porch at the back of the house, she'd been lonely. Very lonely.

Then suddenly she'd had to believe she was a shifter. That the panther she dreamed of being was her other self. And that there were others like her. This had tossed her head first into a sea of new relationships, new ties.

This house and Tom were the closest thing she'd ever had to a family. Probably the closest thing he'd ever had to a family, too. Oh, he'd grown up with wealthy parents, she knew. He'd been raised in New York City by professional, well-to-do mom and dad. But that hadn't made them a family. It wasn't just that Tom's parents had divorced when he was very young. People might divorce and yet raise their children well and as a family. It was more that his mother had never cared again if Tom lived or died. And his father had left Tom to be raised by hired help, and only took notice of him when Tom got in some scrape and had to be bailed out—which he did regularly—possibly because it was the only time he got attention. And then, when Tom was sixteen, his father had walked in on him changing from a dragon to a human, and—horrified or scared—had thrown Tom out onto the streets of New York City in nothing but a robe.

After that Tom, too, had drifted aimlessly, living as he could, without anyone to rely on, without anywhere to call home. And now . . .

And now they lived together. And they were dating, presumably with a view to marriage, not that it had ever been mentioned. Of course, since Tom's father had bought the diner for them jointly, they were already part of a partnership.

And a touch of Tom's calloused hand could still set her heart aflutter, just like a sudden tender look from him, across the diner on a busy day, could make her feel as though she were melting from the inside out.

Still all their kisses and their caresses had an end. Tom always pulled back, before things went too far. Everyone in the diner—everyone who knew them—assumed that, since they dated and lived together, they were sleeping together as well. And Kyrie didn't know what to think. Tom said that he wanted to take it slow, to give them both time to establish a normal relationship before they became more intimate. And yet . . .

And yet sometimes, when he pulled back, she caught a hint of something in his eyes—distance and fear. Was he afraid he'd shift during lovemaking? It wasn't that unusual to shift under strong emotions, so that might be all it was. Or perhaps he'd realized he'd made a mistake and she was not whom he wanted?

A wave of protectiveness and of almost shocking possessiveness arose in her—the need to protect this, the one haven she'd found. Something—someone—must belong to her. And Tom was hers. Oh, not against his will. But hers to protect and hers to love.

Setting the bowl down, she pulled back her waistlong hair with a flour-covered hand, marring her carefully dyed-in Earth-tone pattern—that gave the impression of a tapestry whose lines shifted whenever she moved—with a broad streak of white. She frowned at the little door that led to the back porch where Tom was still asleep.

Would Tom be upset that she had turned off his alarm clock? They both worked the night shift at The George—a long night shift, often seven p.m. to seven a.m.—and he always set his alarm for two p.m. But she had turned it off because she thought there was no point going into the diner today and Tom might as well rest. The chances of their having enough customers to justify the money used in lighting and heating The George were very low. And even though it was only a few blocks away, Kyrie didn't want to drive in the storm howling outside. And she certainly didn't want to walk in it.

Whether Tom agreed with her was something else again. She looked down at the bowl of dough. A succession of never-ending foster homes had taught her that the easiest way of managing men was by setting something sweet down in front of them. It tended to distract them long enough that they didn't remember to be angry.

Still, as she knelt down to rummage under the cabinet for her two baking sheets, she tensed at a sort of half-gasped cry from Tom's sleeping porch. Rising, she held the trays as a shield, and looked at the door into the enclosed back porch. Tom didn't cry out in his sleep. The house was barely large enough to swing a cat. If he sleep-screamed, she'd know by now.

He didn't yell again, but there was a deep sigh, and then the slap of his feet—swung over the side of the daybed—hitting the wooden floor of the sleeping porch. The sound was followed by others she knew well, from normal days. A confused mutter that, had she been close enough, would reveal itself as "What time is it?" followed by a cartoonlike sound of surprise, which was followed, in short order, by the sound of the back blind being pulled aside to allow him to look outside, and then by words she couldn't hear well enough to understand but which—from the tone—were definitely swearing.

Then Tom's bare feet padded towards the door between sleeping porch and kitchen. Kyrie who, in her short time of sharing the house with a male, had learned that if you appeared to be totally in command and quite sure you'd done the right thing, men—or at least Tom—were likely to go along with it, so she set the tray down on the card table at which they normally ate and started studiously setting little balls of cookie dough down on the tray, two inches apart.

Tom cleared his throat, and she looked up, to see him in the doorway. Her first thought—as always—was that, despite being all of five-six, he looked amazing, with pale skin, the color of antique ivory; glossy, curly black hair just long enough to brush his shoulders contrasted with intensely blue eyes like the sky on a perfect summer day, and generously drawn lips that just begged to be kissed. Her second thought was that the most sculpted chest in creation deserved better than to be encased in a baggy green T-shirt that read *Meddle you not in the affairs of dragons, for thou art crunchy and good with ketchup*. Even if she'd bought him the T-shirt. And the best ass in the tri-state area should not be hidden by flannel checker-pattern pajama pants in such virulent green and yellow they could give seizures to used car salesmen.

"I take it The George is closed?" Tom said, and raised his hand to rub at his forehead between his eyebrows.

He squinted as if he had a headache and there were heavy dark circles under his eyes. Granted, skin as pale as Tom's bruised if you sneezed on it, but he didn't normally look like death warmed over. She wondered why he did now. "It's either closed now or it will be very soon. I called Anthony and he said it was pretty slow. He wanted to shut down the stoves and all, close and go home. So I told him fine. I know we could probably walk to The George but—"

"I looked out," he said. "We might very well not find The George in this. Blinding blizzard." He blinked as if realizing for the first time what she was doing. "Cookies?"

"Well . . . the radio said that there will be emergency shelters and I could only figure two reasons for it. Either the snow is going to be so heavy that the roof will collapse, or they're afraid we'll lose power. Can't do anything about roof collapsing. Not that tall. But I can preemptively bake cookies. Make the house warm."

He came closer, to stand on the other side of the little table. Though he was still squinting, as if the light hurt his eyes, his lips trembled on the edge of a smile. "And we get to eat the cookies too. Bonus."

"Make no assumptions, Mr. Ormson." She waggled an admonitory finger. "This is the first time I've baked cookies. They might very well taste like builder's cement."

His hand darted forward to the bowl and stole a lump of dough. Popping it in his mouth, he chewed appreciatively. "Not builder's cement. Raisin *and* chocolate chip?"

She shook her head and answered dolefully, "Rat droppings. The flour was so old, you see."

He nodded, equally serious. "Right. Well, I'll take a shower, and then we can see how rat droppings bake."

Down the hallway that led to the bathroom, she heard him open the door to the linen closet. Using a clean towel every day was one of those things she didn't seem able to break him of. But part of living together, she was learning, was picking your battles. This was one not worth fighting.

She heard him open the door to the bathroom as she put the cookie trays in the oven. She was setting the timer when she heard the shower start.

And then . . .

And then the sounds that came out of the bathroom became distinctly unfamiliar. They echoed of metal bending under high pressure and tile and masonry cracking, wrenching, subjected to forces the materials weren't designed for.

Her first thought was that the roof *had* caved in over the bathroom. But the sounds weren't quite right. There was this . . . scraping and shifting that seemed to be shoving against the walls. The cabinet over the fridge trembled, and the dishware inside it tinkled merrily.

Kyrie ran to the hallway and to the door of the bathroom.

"Tom?" she said and tried the handle. The handle rotated freely—well, not freely but loosely enough that the door clearly was not locked. And yet it wouldn't budge when she pushed at it. "Tom, are you in there?"

A growl and a hiss answered her.

The lion leapt across the entrance of the Goldport Undersea Adventure. He bounded across the next room, amid two rows of large tanks. The private company that had bought out the municipal aquarium had outfitted this room to look like a submarine's control room, with gauges and the sort of wheels that turn to activate pressure locks, and buttons and things. When the aquarium was open and functioning, the screens above the controls showed movies of underwater scenes in various bodies of water around the world.

Now dead and silent, with the aquarium closed due to inclement weather, they were just large, dark television screens. The whole building was empty except for a woman in the back office and the lion, who sniffed his way down the pretend mountain path that wound among tanks stocked with fish from the world over.

As he padded past the tank with piranhas, the lion growled softly, startling the exhibit of sea birds on an elevated area and causing them to fly up till they met with the net that kept them within their space.

The lion didn't care. He had picked up the scent he had been looking for. A sweetish, almost metallic scent. The smell of shapeshifters. He put nose to the ground and followed it, growling softly to himself, past the little suspension bridge with the artificial river underneath—momentarily disoriented where water had sprayed and diluted the scent. But the scent picked up on the other side of the bridge.

The lion couldn't think why the scent was important. There was a part of his mind—as if it were someone else, another mind, locked deep inside his brain—telling him the smell related to death and killing.

The lion didn't know why death or killing would be important, and he couldn't smell death in the air anyway. There was no decay, no blood. Just a smell of fish and water and chemicals, and the smell of people, many people, some of whom had probably passed by days ago but left behind the olfactory trail of their passage.

Then there was the clear bright scent of a shapeshifter. Not that the lion knew what a shapeshifter was, or not really. Just that this was the scent he was seeking, the scent he must follow, deep into the broad chamber decorated with a cement chest and a hoard of plaster coins that his other mind remembered as unconvincingly painted to resemble gold.

The chamber was vast, with a tall ceiling lost in darkness. The lion crouched close to the ground, and followed two trails of smell—or rather, one trail that wound itself around, in front of two vast tanks. Inside the tanks swam creatures the lion's inner mind told him were sharks. Large, with sharp, serrated teeth, they swam towards him, while he sniffed at the glass.

The lion paid them no more attention than he did the yellow tape that blocked one of the tanks and the service stairs, discreetly hidden behind some plastic fronds, leading back to the top of the tank. There was no smell there at all, and the lion didn't look at it. Instead, he turned to follow the interesting scent out of the chamber, towards the front of the aquarium.

And stopped when he heard a voice, coming from the opposite direction of where he had come. "Officer Trall?"

The words made the lion turn, giving something like a half-grunt under his breath, as he loped very fast back the way he had come. Very, very fast, his paws devouring the distance he had traversed so cautiously.

Steps followed him. Human steps. Steps in high heels—the inner voice told the lion. A woman.

The lion gave a soft, distracted roar as—the inner voice yelled to hide, to change, to do something—he leapt into a corner of the entrance chamber, around the side of the ticket booth, and into the narrow hallway that led to the bathrooms. He hit the door of the men's bathroom at a lope, and rolled into the room.

As he rolled he . . . shifted, his body twisting and writhing even as he tumbled, till a tall, muscular blond man landed, from a somersault, in the middle of the bathroom, by one of the closed stalls.

From outside the door, the voice called, "Officer Trall?"

"In here," the man who had been a lion answered, his voice shaking slightly. "Just a moment."

And it was just a moment, as he reached for his clothes—khaki pants and a loose-cut shirt that, with his mane of long, blond hair, gave him the look of a surfer about to hit the waves—and slipped into them and his shoes with the practice of someone who changed clothes several times a day.

In fact, Officer Rafiel Trall of the Serious Crimes Unit of the

Goldport Police Department, had clothes hidden all over town and in some of the neighboring towns as well. One thing shifting shape did—it ruined your wardrobe. Though he controlled himself—well enough during the day, with more difficulty at night—he still destroyed clothes so often that he'd developed a reputation as a ladies man throughout the department.

Every time he came back wearing yet another set of clothes, all his subordinates, from his secretary to the newest recruit, elbowed each other and giggled. Rafiel only wished his sex life were half as exciting as they thought it was. Not that he could complain, or not really. He dated his fair share of women. He just couldn't allow any of them to get close enough to see his . . . changes. So he had a lot of first and second dates and rarely a third.

He looked at himself in the mirror, frowning, as he combed his fingers through his hair. Receptionists, women officers, even the medical examiners and legal experts who had sporadic contact with the Goldport Police Department, all warned each other about him in whispers. He'd heard the words "fear of commitment" so often he felt like they were tattooed on his forehead. And it wasn't true. He'd commit in a minute. To any woman he knew would accept him and not freak out. In less than a minute to a woman like him, a shifter. Of his kind.

The thought of Kyrie came and went in his mind, a mix of longing and regret. No point thinking about it. That wasn't going to happen.

Instead, he opened the door—his relaxed smile in place as he met the aquarium employee who waited outside, a slightly worried look in her eyes. She was small and golden skinned, with straight black hair and the kind of curves that fit all in the right places. Her name was Lei Lani—which made him think of her as one of the Bond girls—and she was a marine biologist on some sort of inter-program loan from an aquarium in Hawaii.

Looking at her smile, it was easy to imagine her welcoming tourists in nothing but a grass skirt. Of course, thinking about that was as bad as thinking too much about her first name. Neither encouraged his good behavior.

"I'm sorry," Rafiel said. "One of those sudden stomach things."

"Ah. I was just checking, because I really should lock up and go home. I mean, everyone else has, and I only stayed because I live so close by here."

"Yeah. How bad is it out?"

"Blinding. As I said, if I didn't live within walking distance, I'd have left long ago. I mean, I'm not even sure you should drive in this. Perhaps you should stay at my place till the weather improves."

Was that a seductive sparkle in her eye? Did Rafiel read it correctly? It wasn't that he wasn't tempted, but right now he had other things on his mind.

He shouldn't have been so reckless as to shift shapes while there was someone else in the building, but the hint of shifter scent he'd been able to pick up even with his human nose had forced him to check it out. After all, a shapeshifter at a crime scene could mean many things. The last time he'd picked it up, it had, in fact, meant that the shifters were the victims. But there was always the chance it meant the shifter he smelled was the killer. And a murder committed by shapeshifters, properly investigated, would out them as non-mythological. Which meant—if Rafiel knew how such things worked—that at best they'd all be studied within an inch of their lives. At worst . . . well . . . Rafiel was a policeman from a long line of policemen. He understood people would be scared of shifters. Not that he blamed them. There were some shifters that he was scared of himself. But the thing was, when people were terrified, they only ran away half the time. The other half . . . they attacked and killed the cause of their fear.

"I'll be okay. I have a four-wheel drive, and I've lived here all my life. This is not the first blizzard I've driven in," he said. He was still trying to process the input of the lion's nose. There had been a clear shifter scent trail throughout the aquarium. It had circled the shark area.

The shark area where, yesterday, a human arm had been found— still clutching a cell phone—inside a shark. The aquarium had been shut down—though the weather provided a good excuse for that. And the relevant area was isolated behind the yellow crime-scene tape. The dead man had been identified as a business traveler from California, staying in town for less than a week.

The question was—had he fallen in the tank or been pushed? And if he'd been pushed, was it a shifter who'd done the pushing?

The sound of the roar-hiss from the bathroom made Kyrie stop cold. Tom didn't—normally—roar or hiss. But the dragon that Tom shape-shifted into did.

She frowned at the door, trying to figure out how Tom could have become a dragon in the bathroom. And why. While Tom was a short human, as a dragon he was . . . well, he had to be at least . . . She tried to visualize Tom in his dragon form and groaned.

With wings extended, Tom had to be at least twenty feet from wing tip to wing tip and she was probably underestimating it. And he was at least twelve feet long and his main body was more than five feet wide, with big, powerful paws and a long, fleshy tail.

Now, your average bathroom might—for all she knew—be able to contain a dragon. But the bathroom in this house was not what anyone could call a normal bathroom. In fact in most other houses it would be a closet and not even a walk-in closet. It was maybe all of five feet by four feet—the kind of bathroom where you had to close the door before you could stand in front of the sink and brush your teeth. There was no way, no way at all, a dragon could fit in there.

"Tom," she yelled again, pounding on the door. "Tom! Please tell me you didn't turn into a dragon in the bathroom."

The sound that answered her was not Tom's voice—in fact, it resembled nothing so much as a distressed foghorn—but it carried with it a definite tone of apology and confusion.

"Right," Kyrie said, as she tried to push the door open. The problem, of course, was that the door opened inward. That meant to get in—or get Tom out—she must swing the door into the bathroom which was, in fact, already filled to capacity with dragon. The resistance she felt was some part of Tom's flesh refusing to give way.

She stopped pushing. She had no idea what had caused Tom to shift. Normally he only shifted involuntarily with the light of the moon on him and some additional source of distress working against his self-control. But what could make him shift, in the middle of a blizzard, in the bathroom?

She needed to get him to shift back. Now. Knowing why he shifted would help, but if she couldn't find out—and he wouldn't be able to answer questions very intelligibly—then she must get him to shift back by persuasion.

The door dated from the same time as the house—somewhere around the nineteenth century, when Goldport had been built from the wealth flowing from the gold and silver mines around the area. The wealth hadn't reached into this neighborhood of tiny houses—originally filled with workers brought from out East to build the mansions for the gold rush millionaires. Oh, the house was still far more solid than houses built today. The walls were lath and plaster or brick, instead of drywall. It was framed in heavy beams. But the doors—as she'd discovered when repairing hinges or locks before—were the cheapest, knottiest pine to be found in any time or place. One grade up from kindling. Further, to make their construction cheaper, they were not a solid panel, but a thicker cross-frame filled out with four veneer-thin panels.

Kyrie silently apologized for any injury she might do Tom, but she had to bring him out of this somehow. She went to the linen closet and wrapped her hand in a towel. Then she aimed at the thin pine panel and punched with all her strength.

The panel splintered down the middle and cracked at the sides. It remained in place, but only because it was held together by countless layers of paint. The dragon inside the bathroom made a noise like a foghorn, again.

Kyrie ignored the noise and, instead, started tearing at the door panel, pulling it out piece by piece. When she had all the pieces out, she leaned in to look into the bathroom. Which was not as easy as she'd anticipated. First because it was dark in there. Whatever else the dragon had done in the shifting, he'd definitely broken the ceiling light fixture. Judging by a sound that evoked a romantic brook running through unspoiled mountains, he had also torn the plumbing apart.

Worse than that, what she was looking at resembled a nightmare by Escher, where nothing made any sense whatsoever. There were green scales, and she expected green scales, shading to blue in spots. But part of what she saw was the bluish-green underbelly of the dragon Tom shifted into. And right next to the missing panel, a claw protruded—huge and silvery, glinting like metal in the moonlight. Next to it was crammed what looked suspiciously like a bit of wing.

"Tom," she said, trying to sound reasonable, while speaking to a mass of scales that, she realized, was *pulsing* rapidly with the sort of panting rhythm a frightened person might breathe in. "Tom, shift back. You can't get out like this. Shift back."

The scales and wing and all slid around, scraping the door. The dragon moaned in distress. For a moment, the huge claw protruded through the opening, causing Kyrie to jump back, startled. When everything was done moving around, a dragon eye looked back at her through the opening. The tile balanced just above its brow ridge only made it look more pitiful.

The eye itself—huge and double-lidded and blue—except for size and the weird additional inner lids, was Tom's eye.

Kyrie spoke to Tom's eye. "Tom, please, you must shift. I understand there had to have been something to make you shift. But if you don't shift back now I can't get you out of there. And that bathroom is going to freeze."

She didn't need to be a building expert to know the tiny window into the bathroom had to be broken. The sudden moisture at her feet made her cringe. First, they were going to flood the house. And then they were going to freeze it. And it wasn't even her house. She rented it. Good thing she'd long ago resigned herself to the idea she'd never see the security deposit again. And good thing she didn't expect to ever be rich. After paying for these repairs, she'd be flat broke.

"Tom," she spoke as calmly as she could, though she felt her heart racing and was holding back on a strong impulse to shape-shift herself. She could feel it as her nails tried to lengthen into claws, as her muscles and bones attempted to change shape. She gritted her teeth and forced herself to remain human. To remain sane. Becoming a panther now would only add to the confusion. "Tom, you must shift back. I don't know why you shifted, but there is nothing that we can't face together. We've done it before, remember?"

The eye blinked at her, panic still shining at the back of it.

"Look, breathe with me—slow, slow, slow." She forced her own breathing to a slow, steady rhythm. "Slow. Everything is safe. And if it isn't, you can't fight it while crammed in that bathroom. You must be human and come out of there first. Then we'll talk."

She spoke on so long that she almost lost track of what she was saying. It was all variations on a theme. The theme of being calm. Very, very calm. And shifting back.

Water was running under the door, covering the pine floor of the hallway in a thin, shimmering film, but she didn't dare move or stop talking. Was she having any effect? Tom's eye continued to glare at her, unblinking. She only knew he was alive because she could hear the dragon's breathing huffing in and out of huge lungs.

And then there was a sound like a sigh. Or at least a short intake of breath followed by a long, deep exhalation. The dragon flesh filling the broken part of the door trembled and wobbled. The distressed foghorn sounded again.

Other sounds followed—sounds Kyrie knew well enough and which she felt a great relief at. Not that she'd show her relief. She didn't want to startle Tom and stop the process. That was the last thing she wanted. Instead, she took deep, deep breaths, feeling Tom breathe with her, while muscles slid around with moist noises, and bones made sounds like cracking of knuckles writ large.

Tom sat there, on the soaked floor of the bathroom, on what remained of his ripped pajama pants and T-shirt. Plaster dusted his hair. His naked, muscular body showed a landscape of scratches and bruises.

He looked at her, mouth half open. Then he keened. It was neither crying, nor screaming—just a sound of long-held, pent-up frustration. He raised his knees and wrapped his arms around them, lowering his head and taking deep deliberate breaths.

She'd seen this before. She knew what it meant. He was fighting the urge to shift back. But he had it under control now. And he would be mortally embarrassed as soon as he had the time to be.

Kyrie did what any girlfriend—what any friend—could do under the circumstances. "Right," she said. "Don't go anywhere. I'm going to go turn off the water valve to the house."

Tom was mortally embarrassed. Once past the panic of the dragon and the heightened senses of the beast and the pain of being forced into what seemed to the dragon like a very tiny box—once he was himself—he didn't need to examine his surroundings to know the damage he had done.

The toilet was broken, the pieces shattered everywhere. The plumbing was torn apart. Faucets bent beyond recognition. Walls with their inner layer scraped off, in a way that was probably not structurally sound. The window was smashed—leaving jagged pieces of glass glinting in the frame. The shower enclosure destroyed. What had, less than half an hour ago, been a bathroom was now a disaster zone.

And Tom was sitting in the middle of it, looking up at Kyrie, who stared back in shock. She was very pale. No doubt toting up the expenses he had caused her. The lease was in her name. They'd be lucky not to get kicked out, even after they repaired the damages. And all because he couldn't control his shifting and had gotten scared by—

In that moment, staring openmouthed at Kyrie—who looked, as she always did, like a Greek goddess who had consented to come down from her pedestal and wear jeans and a T-shirt and a single, red-feather earring—he remembered what had made him shift.

There had been a *voice* in his head. There had been a *voice*—echoing in his mind as clearly as though it were coming through his ears, which it wasn't. The voice had been of an entity known to Asian cultures as the Great Sky Dragon.

Whether he was really the father of all dragons as legend maintained, or not, Tom could not know. What he did know was that he was the leader of Asian triads in the west—that he ruthlessly murdered and stole and sold drugs and did what he had to do to keep his people safe and prosperous. And his people were only those who could shift into dragons. A specific kind of dragon. A kind Tom wasn't.

Their last meeting had brought Tom closer to his death than he ever cared to go. As close as he could go and still come back. And now he had pushed his way into Tom's head.

Tom shuddered as panic tried to establish itself and force him to shift again.

No, and no, and *no*! Nothing would be served by becoming a dragon. There were threats that the human brain was best suited to handling, no matter how much the puny human body might not be a match to claws and fangs and wings.

He heard himself make a sound—a half scream of frustration at the body he couldn't control—as he lowered his head and concentrated on breathing. Just breathing.

In this state he only half heard Kyrie say something about the water valve. He heard her walk away as he controlled himself. And then he smelled burning. The cookies.

It was, strangely, a welcome relief from other thoughts. He got up. Everything hurt. He felt as though every fiber of his body had been bruised and as if all his bones had cracked, crazed, like plates exposed to high pressure. Groaning, holding on to walls and furniture, telling himself he didn't have time to be in pain, he didn't have time to heal; he padded through the soaked hallway to the kitchen where just the barest bit of water was making it over the little metal lip dividing the kitchen linoleum from the hallway wood flooring. His feet slipped as he hit the linoleum, but he balanced, and rushed to the oven—as much as he could rush without screaming. He remembered one of his nannies reading him the original story of

"The Little Mermaid" and how, after the mermaid had traded her tail for legs, every step she took would be like walking on knives. This felt like that, except the knives were also throughout his torso and down his arms, and small daggers seemed to stab through each of his fingers as he flexed them.

Oven mitts on, he pulled the tray of cookies out and set it atop the stove, then carefully turned the oven off. The cookies were less burnt than he'd expected—just looked like they'd gotten a suntan.

Right. He'd best make himself decent quickly. They had bigger trouble than the cookies, and there was absolutely no way he could take a shower now. But if he remembered correctly, when you turned off the water valve to a house, whatever water was in the pipes or in the heater remained. That might just be enough to, at the very least, get the grit of masonry off his skin and hair.

He limped to the hallway closet, full of purpose—because any purpose, and any thought was better than to think again of what had made him change or to acknowledge his pain—and grabbed a handful of washcloths and a towel. And he tried not to think of the pain. It would pass. He would be fine. Shifters healed very quickly. Particularly well-fed shifters.

He wet the washcloths at the faucet in the kitchen, and put soap in about half of them—then retreated with them and the towel back to his room.

Fortunately he was familiar with this sort of ad hoc washing. He'd had to do it often enough when he was living on the streets and only working occasional day jobs, between the ages of sixteen and twenty or so. Contrary to public perception, given a supply of paper towels and soap, it was possible to wash up—at least enough to not stink—at a stall in a public bathroom. It didn't, by any means, beat a long soak in a tub, or even a hurried shower, but it would do if it must. And clearly it must.

He was going through the motions of wiping down with soap, then wiping the soap off, noting that the soap stung in a high number of abraded places, and that just touching his skin brought on a pain on the edge of unbearable, when he heard the back door close and Kyrie call tentatively, "Tom?"

"In here," he said. "I'll be out in a moment."

She didn't come in. Their rules for when they were allowed to see each other naked wouldn't make sense to anyone else. They didn't even make any *rational* sense to Tom himself. But they made *emotional* sense.

Because of the shifting, they had seen each other naked long before they had a relationship, and often saw each other naked in all sorts of situations. But while human and not coming off from a shift, they respected each other's privacy as much as possible. Kyrie would no more walk into his room while she knew he was naked than he would walk in on her in the shower. Oh, yes, they were dating. They were in love, or at least—Tom smiled to himself, as he extracted as much masonry as possible from his long dark hair—he thought so. His opinion might be insufficient, since he'd never had any experience with the emotion before. Still, he would give his left hand, or wing, or claw for Kyrie and she'd proven often enough she'd do the equivalent for him.

But they were both intensely private people. And neither of them had experience of relationships before. So they were taking it slow and trying to establish the feelings and the boundaries before becoming more physical. Not the least because neither of them was sure how the beasts they shifted into would react to *more physical*. The prospect of becoming dragon and panther during sex could be regarded as either hilarious or terrifying, depending on how macabre one's sense of humor.

Having finished his Spartan wash, he dried with the towel, tied his hair back—after rummaging for the elastic in the bedclothes—and slipped on a pair of jeans and a loose white T-shirt. Remembering the water in the hallway, he put on socks and his leather boots and came out of his room to find Kyrie coming in too, from the other side, duct tape in hand.

"I wiped the water from the floor in the hallway and sealed the bathroom," she said, matter of fact. "So the cold doesn't come into the rest of the house." Then looking at him, she smiled. "You cleaned up."

He felt himself blush that she was surprised he'd take the trouble to clean up. "I didn't think masonry was the in look this winter."

She nodded solemnly, stowing the duct tape in the drawer under the coffee maker. "There's coffee," she said, while pouring herself a cup. "I'd started it when—" She stopped. "Thank you for saving the cookies."

He bit back the obvious answer: "You don't need to put on the politeness. No need to thank me, since I was the one who made you forget them." Most of his life, long before he'd found out he was a shifter, at sixteen, he'd been giving the answer guaranteed to infuriate people and rejoicing in getting a reaction. Any reaction. He didn't know why. That was just the way he was.

It was tempting to say that he'd become a hostile bundle of aggression because both his parents were busy professionals, too busy in fact to notice their son existed. Tempting and, no doubt, some psychologist would say it in all seriousness.

But Tom didn't believe in psychology any more than he believed in any other organized religion. And at some point a grown-up had to stop blaming his parents for his quirks. Perhaps that was what had set him off . . . perhaps not. Perhaps some accidental genetic combination had caused him to be born hostile and contrary. But three months ago, when he'd moved in with Kyrie, he'd decided that habit stopped and quickly too. So now he bit his tongue and sighed. "They are a little too tanned."

She smiled back, as if she knew of the averted response and appreciated his effort. "No matter. Still edible." Picking up a cookie, she sat down.

He got himself coffee. Her whole attitude said *we have to talk,* and he supposed they did. He used the time of filling the cup and sugaring his coffee to think of what he could say that would mitigate what he had just done.

I'll pay for it was obvious, though he had exactly zero clue how. All the money he had—just like all the money Kyrie had—was part shares in The George. And, unlike what he would have imagined before getting into it, profits and debts weren't as clear-cut as they seemed. His father—in an impulse for atonement that could not be gainsaid—had bought them the building and equipment for The George. That much they had. But it wasn't money. You couldn't walk into the mall with five bricks and buy a T-shirt. And there was no way he could swap one of the industrial freezers for the repair bill on the bathroom. For one, because they needed the freezers.

Which was the issue with the money. The George was doing well. Money came in every night and day. The few upgrades he and Kyrie had been able to afford here and there—a coat of paint, new Formica on the tables, re-covering the vinyl booths, a new stove—were drawing in a better clientele, too. In addition to the manual laborers and students who had always drifted to The George, they now got young professionals from the gentrified area a few blocks away, amused at the dragon theme of the restaurant and intrigued by Tom's culinary experimentation.

They were—from what Tom understood of the raised eyebrows of his accountant, who was a man of few words—doing very well indeed, having unwittingly become the spearheads of the push for gentrification in *that* area of Fairfax. But the money that came in went out again very quickly, and the improvements fueled other improvements. There were waiters to pay and Anthony's salary had been raised since he'd become manager. To keep the better clientele, Tom had bought new silverware and dishes and improved the quality of everything from the paper goods to the coffee mugs. His own self-respect as a cook had forced him to buy better quality meat.

His father—when they talked—assured him all this would eventually pay off and while the cycle seemed fruitless and inane right now, eventually the money coming in would outstrip the need for improvements and Tom and Kyrie would find themselves wealthy or close to it. Today was not the eve of that day, though. Their separate bank accounts, if pooled, would net them maybe two thousand dollars. On which they had to live for the month. Not enough for this type of repair.

He could, of course, ask his father for help, but just the idea of it was enough to give him heartburn. He'd solved—he thought—his life-long struggle with his father. While his father was not the best of parents, neither was Tom the best of sons. But still . . . Edward Ormson had forced his sixteen-year-old son out of the house at gunpoint onto the streets of New York City on the day he found that Tom shifted shape into a dragon.

Tom could forgive, but he could not forget. He'd accepted the diner, but even that had smarted, and he'd only accepted it because he could tell how much Kyrie wanted it. And he'd talk to his father and be civil when he called because the man was trying his best to establish a relationship. And Tom was not so flush with friends that he could turn down anyone willing to befriend him. Even if it was his own father.

But he'd be damned if he was going to go cadging his father for money. He'd be damned if he'd go back to his father every time he found himself in a scrape. He'd be damned if he gave his father reason to think of him—ever again—as his fucked-up son.

He'd rather live on the streets, he thought decisively, as he made his way back to the table and sat down, cup in hand. He'd done it before.

He looked up, frowning slightly, to meet Kyrie's attentive gaze on him. She was examining his face—probably for signs of the madness that had caused him to shift in the bathroom.

When she saw him looking, she smiled. "Have a cookie."

What Kyrie wanted to know was why he'd shifted. But she was terrified that if she asked him, he'd feel the need the shift again. After all, whatever it was had to be powerful enough to cause a visceral panic reaction. Thinking about it might bring on another shift.

His eyebrows lowered a little and as he took a bite of the cookie, he did it as if it required a large amount of concentration. When he looked back at her, his gaze remained worried and more than a little bit confused.

"I figured," he said, his tone slow and calculating. "I might be able to get a loan. But I don't know how because I don't want to mortgage The George because that's yours too and, you know—"

"What?" She hadn't meant to interrupt, but the last thing she'd expected was for him to start talking money.

"The bathroom," he said, gesturing airily.

"Oh, that. I looked at the walls and they seem to be fine. You just peeled the tile off and destroyed the plumbing and appliances. Cosmetic stuff. We'll find a handyman. Place is solidly built." She shrugged. "Yeah, we'll borrow if we have to. We could do it all ourselves, you know, with a good how-to manual, but we don't have that much free time and a functioning bathroom is kind of a necessity." Seeing him open his mouth, she went on, redirecting the conversation, "Which is why I think we should go to The George."

He blinked at her. "What?" he said, his tone exactly matching her earlier one as, clearly, the gears of his mind had been grinding at a different place.

"I think we should go to The George until the blizzard is past and we get the bathroom repaired. While I don't like the idea of driving in this, we'll have a bathroom at The George. I mean—no place to take showers, though we can probably get a room at the bed-and-breakfast next door for that—but we'll at least have a place to go to the bathroom. The weather—not to mention the neighbors—kind of precludes just peeing in the yard."

Her absurd words managed to bring a smile to his lips, but it vanished very fast. "Yeah. We'll have to go."

"Yes. I know we could just stay at the bed-and-breakfast, but if we're going to be that close to The George, we might as well open too. I'm sure you don't want to spend however long in just a tiny rented room. And we might get a few diners, and it might just pay for that opening. And the bed-and-breakfast. I mean, we could go to one of the emergency shelters, but you and me and an enclosed space with a lot of people . . ." She shrugged. Given what had just happened to him, in the bathroom, she didn't need to draw pictures of a dragon and a panther rampaging amid distressed refugees.

He nodded and took a sip of the coffee. "Okay," he said. "I'll take a sleeping bag. In case we rent a room with only one bed." He got up and headed for his sleeping porch, clearly intent on packing. "And my laptop. Perhaps I can do some of the paperwork that's been accumulating."

"Tom . . ." She didn't want to ask, but she'd have to. "Why the shift? Was it the storm? You don't normally shift during the day, much less—" She stopped.

He'd turned around, a hand going up to his head, as if to pull back hair that didn't need it—a habit of his when he was nervous. His Adam's apple bobbed up and down as he swallowed. He sighed. For just a moment, it seemed to her, he was concentrating very hard on not shifting. "It was the Great Sky Dragon," he said. "I . . . I don't know how to put this without sounding like a science fiction story, but I heard him in my mind. Without sound." He took a deep breath like a drowning man who has succeeded in getting his head above water for a moment. "I know I sound crazy, but . . . He was there."

She shrugged at him. They were people who could—and did—change into animal shapes with or without wishing to. And still, he was afraid she'd think having experienced telepathy made him sound crazy.

"So you heard him in your mind," she said. "Did he threaten you?"

Tom shook his head. "No, that was the odd part. He warned me. But it wasn't a threat. He said someone he called the Ancient Ones wanted to kill us. That we should beware."

"Right. We'll stay out of retirement homes," Kyrie said, and immediately after, "I'm sorry. It isn't funny. But why should he warn us now, when he went out of his way to almost kill you before?"

Tom shook his head and looked startlingly naked and vulnerable—as if it cost him something to admit this. "I don't know."

The phone rang.

For an intense panic-filled moment, Tom thought it would be the

Great Sky Dragon calling him to repeat the vague warnings he'd spoken within Tom's mind. It took a deep breath and remembering the damages to the bathroom to keep him from shifting again right then and there. His back brain equated *dragon* with *safe*. He told himself the phone wouldn't eat him, as he stretched his hand to the phone on the wall and picked it up.

The caller ID window read "Trall, Rafiel" which made him draw a sigh of relief. For all his faults—and there were many—and despite the fact that he still carried a torch for Kyrie, Rafiel was the closest thing Tom had to a friend. He was, with Kyrie, almost the only other shifter Tom was friends with. Almost because an addled alligator shifter who went by "Old Joe" didn't exactly qualify as a *friend*. Not so long as friendship involved more than Tom covering up for Old Joe's shifts and giving him bowls of clam chowder on the side. Kyrie, Rafiel, Old Joe, an orangutan shifter, two now-dead beetle shifters and the dragon triad were the only adult shifters Tom had ever met, period. He guessed there weren't many of his kind in the world. The few, the proud, the totally messed up.

"Yeah?" he said, into the phone.

"Uh," Rafiel's voice said from the other end, as though the phone's being answered were the last thing he could possibly expect. Then, "I'd like to . . . I need to talk to you and Kyrie, when you have a minute."

There was that tone in Rafiel's voice—tight and short—that meant he was on the job. Tom wondered if Rafiel was alone or if he was picking his words carefully to avoid scaring a subordinate. Aloud he said only, "'Ssup?"

"Murder. There's . . . been . . . well, almost for sure murder. Human bones and stuff at the bottom of the shark tank at the aquarium."

"And?" After all, solving murders was Rafiel's job and he usually managed it without a little help from his friends.

"And I smell shifter," Rafiel said. "All over it."

"Oh," Tom said. "We'll be at The George." And suddenly he felt exactly like a man in the path of an oncoming train.

His dreams had been full of a nightmare about some ancient

menace; the Great Sky Dragon had spoken in his mind; and now there was murder, with shifter involvement.

Was the shifter a murderer or the victim? Either way, it could make Tom's life more of a mess than it already was.

"Don't shift! Don't shift! Don't shift!" Kyrie told herself. But she wasn't at all sure she was listening, and she kept looking anxiously at her hands, clenched tight on the wheel. Her violet nail polish was cracked and peeled from her run-in with the bathroom door, so it was hard to tell whether the nails were lengthening into claws or not. Part of the reason she kept her nails varnished was to make sure that she saw the first signs of her nails lengthening into claws. Today that wouldn't work.

Outside the window, in the palm of visibility beyond the windshield, white snowflakes swirled. Past that, the flakes became a wall of white, seemingly streaming sideways, shimmering. Somewhere out there, in the nebulous distance, there were twin glimmers of dazzling whiteness, which were the only indications Kyrie had that the headlights of her tiny car were on.

"Maybe we should have walked," Tom said. He shuffled in his seat and leaned close to the snow-covered windshield, as though he could lend her extra vision.

Kyrie gritted her teeth. Maybe they should have, except that the three steps they'd taken on the driveway, their feet had gone out from under them, and they'd only remained upright by holding onto the car. From which point getting in the car had seemed a given. She slowed down—which mostly meant defaulting to the fractional amount of sliding the car seemed to do all on its own—and twisted up her windshield wipers' knob, not that it did much good.

"How can you see?" Tom asked.

"I can't," she said, just as a sudden gust of wind cleared the space ahead enough for her to see they were at the intersection of their street and the next perpendicular one. And that a massive, red SUV was headed for them at speed.

Don't shift, don't shift, don't shift, Kyrie thought, as a mantra, even as she felt her whole body clench and her muscles attempt to change shapes beneath her skin, to take the form of a panther. *Don't shift, don't shift, don't shift,* as she struggled to keep her breathing even, and bit into her lower lip with teeth that weren't getting any longer, not at all, not even a little bit. She maneuvered quickly with a tire up on the sidewalk, tilting crazily around the corner, even as the SUV went by them and buried them in a shower of slush. Bits of ice rattled against roof and windows.

A moan from Tom reminded her she wasn't the only one worried about panic setting off a shape-shift reaction. "Perhaps," he said, in the voice of a man working very hard to control himself. "I should get out and . . . fly?"

"What? Shift twice without eating? First thing in the morning? And the second time after getting hurt?" she said, and on that, as he moaned again, she realized she'd said the wrong thing. Shifting shapes demanded a lot of energy and, for some reason, it set off a desperate craving for protein. So did the lightning-fast healing of shifters. All Tom had eaten since shifting was half a dozen cookies. And there was no protein at all around. Except, of course, her. She wasn't about to volunteer. And she knew Tom would rather die than eat a person, much less her.

She pushed the gas, taking advantage of a momentary break in the storm that allowed her to see a major crossroads ahead. Too late, she saw the light was red, but she was sliding through the intersection on the power of her momentum and slamming on the brakes only caused her to fishtail wildly and finally pivot halfway through to the left. Fortunately this turned the car right onto Fairfax, where she was supposed to be. Sliding, she pressed the gas cautiously. Their shifting position caused the snow to seem to shift directions, so that she could now see—more or less—out her front window, but nothing on the side.

I'll never find The George, she thought to herself, and glared at her nails telling them they weren't becoming claws, no they weren't, *not even a little bit.*

A sudden dazzling purple light to the left made her breathe in relief and confusion. The George's sign was still lit. Thank heavens. Anthony mustn't have closed yet, which meant, of course, that lights and heat would still be on, and less trouble than turning them on again. It also made the diner easier to find.

She brought the car to a minimally-sliding, almost-complete stop and took a deep breath. Normally, turning left into the parking lot of The George from Fairfax involved taking your life in your own hands. Fairfax was a four-lane road, the main east-west artery of Goldport, and it was heavily traveled all the time. In addition, mistimed traffic lights ensured there was no break in the two lanes of traffic across which you must cut to make it into the parking lot.

Today, it involved another kind of risk. She couldn't see at all through the storm, to find out if any traffic was oncoming. Just white blankness. True, there were very few vehicles out, but she'd managed to almost run into two of those few on the way here. Kyrie took a deep breath. There was nothing for it but to turn. And she wasn't going to shift. *Not at all.*

She turned the wheel, fully expecting to go into a spin, but the tires grabbed onto some bit of yet unfrozen pavement and propelled them in a queasy slide-lurch across the other lanes of the road and up a gentle ramp into the parking lot.

The snow didn't allow her to see any other cars in the parking lot, and Kyrie didn't care. Bordered by the blind, windowless wall of a bed-and-breakfast and a warehouse, the parking lot gave on to the back door of The George and, through two outlets, to Pride and Fairfax Streets both. Right now, she waited until the car stopped sliding, then put it in park and pulled the parking brake, and leaned over the wheel, breathing deeply. *You're safe, you're safe. Don't shift.* There was no point even trying to find parking spots in this mess.

When her racing heart had calmed down, she lifted her head and saw the parking lot—as much as *could* be seen. Drifting snow spider-webbed by the light of two street lamps and the purple glare from the diner's back sign obscured everything save for the two large supply vans parked in the middle of the lot. She looked to the passenger side of the car, where Tom was blinking and, she suspected, had just opened his eyes after calming himself.

"We should really—" Kyrie started and stopped. Through the snow she'd glimpsed something, half seen. She thought it was . . . but it couldn't be. Surely . . .

"Was that," Tom said, his voice small, "a dragon's wing?"

"Go inside," Tom said, as he glimpsed the wing again, through the multiplying flakes. "It's a red wing. It's . . ." He didn't say it. He couldn't quite assemble words.

His brain, still fogged from his quick shift into dragon and back, still laboring under the guilt of what he'd done to the bathroom—let alone the terror of the precipitous drive here, which had felt less like driving than tumbling down a chute—could not manage to describe the wing. But he was sure, from his two brief glimpses, that it was a Chinese dragon. An Asian dragon like the Great Sky Dragon and his cohorts.

Feeling for the door handle with half-frozen, still aching fingers, Tom managed to grasp it and throw the door open against resistance of what he hoped was stiff wind, and not a dragon tail or claw, as he yelled over the howling storm at Kyrie. "Go inside. I'll deal with it."

He plunged out of the car, his hair and his unzipped black leather jacket whipping about in the howling storm, just in time for his feet to go out from under him, and to reach, blindly, for the car door for support, and bring himself upright, and stare into . . .

He was big and red. No. As he blinked to keep his eyes from freezing, he thought he wasn't that big. Smaller than Tom himself in dragon form. But he was also horribly familiar—more familiar as

Tom focused on the details and noted that the dragon's front left paw was much smaller than the other. He was . . . Red Dragon. Not only was he was one of the Great Sky Dragon's cohorts, but when Tom had last seen him there had been a big battle, and Red Dragon had ended with his arm ripped out at the roots. Or rather, Tom had ripped Red Dragon's arm off, then used it to beat Red Dragon with.

Tom knew—from experience—that his kind was hard to kill. But this was a particular foe he'd never thought to see again; one he was sure had more reasons for vendetta against him than anyone else alive.

He felt his throat close and the panic he'd—barely—managed to control in the car surged through his body like electric current, seeking grounding. Not finding it, it twisted in a sparkle through his flesh. He felt his bruised, battered limbs wrench, and his body bend, and a hollow cough echoed through his throat mingled with a scream of pain that he could no longer keep back. His mouth opened, and he swallowed an aspiration of snow, cold and suffocating. He knew, absolutely knew, that if he shifted he would attack Red Dragon and probably try to eat him. He was *that* protein-starved. A protein-starved Tom ate uncooked meat and whatever else he could get his hands on. A protein-starved dragon would hunt live prey.

"Run," he told Kyrie with what was left of his human mind and his human voice, already sounding slurpy and hissy as his teeth shifted position. "Run inside, Kyrie."

He could just tell in the periphery of his beclouded vision that she was not obeying. Not even considering it, and he wondered if his voice had already changed too much. If perhaps she couldn't understand him. His body twisted again, the pain of shifting unbearable on his bruised flesh and caked bones, and he kept his eyes on the other dragon, in case he should have any ideas of flaming or striking. Dragons were hard to kill but not impossible. This Tom knew. If you severed the head from the rest of the body, if you divided the body in two. If you incinerated the body. Possibly if you destroyed the brain. Those deaths even a dragon could not overcome.

Tom had to think of how to inflict them on his foe, and he had to protect himself from them. He felt his fingers lengthen into claws and—

"No," it was Kyrie's voice, decisive sounding. And Kyrie—slim, unshifted, very human Kyrie—stood between the two dragons, her dark blue ski jacket making her just slightly bulkier than normal as she yelled at both of them. "No. You're not going to change, Tom. Deep breaths. I'm not having you pass out or worse when you shift. Don't you dare."

There had been a time when Tom had sought out cures for his condition. He'd tried to prevent his shifting with illegal drugs and with will power, with perfect diet and with lack of sleep. He'd visited places where people said native tribes had once worshiped. He'd taken yoga and tried to meditate. None of it had worked.

In times of stress, or when the moon was just right, causing some change in the tides of his being; when panic or excitement overcame him, he would change. And he couldn't control it, any more than a human being can stop sneezing by wishing to stop. But Kyrie standing in front of him and saying "no" tore to the very center of his being and stopped the already started process.

He groaned as he felt his muscles return to their normal position, his bones resume proper human shape. In this state, it was like being filleted, his body sliced by a thousand sharp knives, but it was needed and he willed it to happen.

She'd made him think even if what he was thinking was that they were both in great trouble. The red dragon had come back to seek vengeance. And, being a triad member and therefore an outlaw, he would stop at nothing. Tom's life, Kyrie's life, their friends, the diner—all of it would be in danger. And behind Red Dragon stood the powerful, mysterious figure of the Great Sky Dragon, who had taken Tom's life only to give it back again, and whom Tom didn't even pretend to understand. But Tom stopped and thought long enough to realize that if he were to shift now he would, probably, as Kyrie had said, lose consciousness. And that would not solve anything. Even if Red Dragon didn't take advantage of his weakness to behead him, an unconscious dragon in the parking lot becoming hypothermic would only add to Kyrie's troubles.

Through clenched teeth he asked Red Dragon, "What do you want?" But Red Dragon only glared and bobbed his neck up and down, waving his head like some deranged bobble-toy, his mismatched limbs rearing, his wings flaring.

"Go inside," Kyrie answered, looking at Red Dragon, but speaking to Tom, impatiently. "Go inside, Tom. We can't have you here. Not weakened. I'll find out what this . . . what he wants."

"But—" Tom said, and stopped as he realized he was about to say "I'm the man. I'm supposed to protect you." He could not say that. Man or not, he was in no state to protect anyone.

Feeling his cheeks heat in shame, he retreated. He retreated step by step, while staring at Kyrie. He walked backwards, through the blowing snow, till Kyrie and the red dragon were no more than outlines of themselves, patterns of shadow drawn on the surrounding whiteness. He felt his heart beat, hard in his chest. He was sure it was beating hard enough that if he looked down he'd see it pound even through the shirt and his black leather jacket. His mouth was dry and tasted vaguely of blood as though the hoarse cough that normally heralded his transformation had stripped it of its lining. He cleared his throat, more because he wanted to remind Red Dragon and Kyrie that he was still there—more because he felt like a coward and a fool, backing away from confrontation and leaving his girlfriend to face evil alone. But he didn't know if the sound carried that far, and besides, what good was it to remind them he was there, when he could do nothing to defend the woman he loved?

Oh, sure, Kyrie was a were panther. Oh, surely, she could defend herself. She had fought these creatures before but . . .

But if he'd not helped Kyrie then, she would have died. And now he was going to leave her alone with one of these—a creature that was bigger than her feline form, a creature that could burn her to cinders. Everything that was Tom—normal and human and responsible— wanted to stay and protect Kyrie. But he knew better, he knew how sensible Kyrie was. And he knew his body would not stand another shift.

He wished there was someone he could call to, but all the shifters he knew for a fact were shifters were a homeless man and Rafiel— who might or might not be inside. Was Rafiel inside? He'd called Tom. Had he had time to get here, yet?

Tom must check. He stepped back faster and faster. He couldn't see so clearly through the snow anymore, but Kyrie seemed to be circling the dragon, or the dragon seemed to be circling Kyrie. It couldn't be good, but at least he saw no flame. That at least was better than it could be.

He stepped back. As he walked into the purple glow of the sign at the back door he felt the warmth of the diner behind him. Even through the glass door at the back, enough heat escaped that, without looking, he could tell where the door was.

Stepping back towards the warmth, he heard the key in the lock, and then the door opened, right behind him.

He turned. "Anthony!" he said, or rather gasped in surprise, turning back to look and see if Anthony—who had no idea shapeshifters or dragons existed—would see the dragon through the snow before the door closed. But there was nothing out there, just the briefest of shadows, and did he hear Kyrie's car trunk open? What was she doing? Stashing the defeated body of her opponent? Well, it could be worse. If she was opening a car, then she had to be alive. Probably.

"Tom?" Anthony asked. He was slim and Italian or perhaps Greek or maybe some flavor of South American. Or maybe he had all those in his ancestry somewhere. Olive skinned, with curly dark hair, and a Roman nose, Anthony was a local boy, grown up in this neighborhood. He was Kyrie's and Tom's guide to local stores and events. And every small business owner seemed to know Anthony, whose approval counted for more with them than their better-business-bureau rating. He was also the leader of a bolero dancing troupe and newly married. And the one person they trusted enough to let him manage the daytime shift unsupervised.

"Yeah."

"You guys came in."

"You're open."

"I was going to close, but then people started trickling in and kept coming in. Cold, you know. Or just wanting to see people." He shrugged. "And there's freaky stuff around here, and . . ."

But Tom was listening, wildly, for the sound of the car door, for the sound of Kyrie, for what might be happening out there, in the howling snow.

Kyrie knew this was crazy, but it would be crazier to do nothing. She circled around the red dragon, looking up at the creature, as it circled in turn, to keep her in sight. She could feel her other form itching to take over, but she didn't think that would be the best of ideas. Because the dragon wasn't attacking her. Why wasn't the dragon attacking her?

Truth be told, from what she remembered, Red Dragon had been the least effectual of the triad members. Why would he be the one sent? Unless—she took a look at his shrunken arm—he was trying to avenge himself all on his own.

He opened his mouth and she tensed, ready to hit the snow and roll away from his breath. Instead he made a pitiful sound, low and mournful in his throat.

"What?" she said, as if she expected the creature to speak. Instead, it made the sound again, and then it coughed. The cough was just like Tom's when he was about to change. Or when he was about to flame, of course. She tensed and circled, watching. It moaned and circled in turn. Suddenly, it spasmed. Contorted.

It was changing. Kyrie, who'd thrown herself to the snow-covered ground, looked up to see the creature bend and fold in unnatural ways, seeming to collapse in on itself.

It was shifting. It was becoming human.

But why is he shifting? Wouldn't his dragon form give him the advantage? What could he gain by becoming human?

What he couldn't gain, clearly, was warmth, because in the next moment he stood there, looking like an instant popsicle in the shape of a young Asian male, skinny and very, very naked in the howling storm. He covered his privates with one hand—the other arm being rather too short to allow him to reach that far, and he looked at her with pitiful eyes, even as his skin turned a shade of dusky violet.

"What do you want?" she asked, using all her will power to keep her teeth from chattering. "What do you want? What do you wish from me?"

He shook his head slowly, his eyes very wide. She wondered if he looked like that out of fear of her, and realized it was more likely that it was the cold. "I . . . Must speak. I was sent to speak. To you. I must protect . . . Him."

"Protect the Great Sky Dragon?" Kyrie asked.

Red Dragon shook his head. He had a crest of hair in the front—rumpled—probably a natural cowlick, and in human form, his eyes looked small and dark and confused. "No, not him. He sent me."

He did not speak with an accent so much as with the shadow of an accent—as if he felt obligated to sound Asian, even though he didn't. It made his words seem stilted. He talked while shivering and the words emerged through short panting breaths. "He sent me to redeem myself. The Great Sky Dragon. Sent me."

"To redeem yourself?" Kyrie yelled as the snow blew into her mouth. She looked at the snow-covered ground for a stone or something with which to hit the enemy. Nothing was visible under the snow, but she must find something. Because she now knew he had come to kill Tom.

And then Red Dragon wrapped his arms around himself, a curiously defenseless gesture. "He send me to protect the young dragon. He says I must prove I'm worthy before I'm trusted, and this is where he wants me to prove myself. I am to defend the young dragon from the Ancient Ones."

"Defend?" Kyrie asked, her voice a mere, surprised whisper as her mind arrested on the word she could not have anticipated. "Defend? Defend Tom?"

"Tom," Anthony's voice said from behind Tom, as Tom tried to see beyond the light of the diner's back window, beyond where it seemed a dazzle upon a confusion of snow. Beyond all that, he was sure now, there were two human figures. And that must mean . . . Both of them were alive, which he supposed was good.

"Tom," Anthony's voice again. "Look, I don't suppose you and Kyrie are going to stay?"

"We have to," Tom said, still intent on the two people out there in the snow. Why weren't they walking any nearer? He had no doubts that Kyrie could more than hold her own in a fight with Red Dragon, provided they were both in human shape, but all the same, he wished that they would come closer—that he could hear what they must be saying. "We need a bathroom."

It was only as the silence lengthened that Tom thought his remark might be cryptic and he was trying to figure out how to describe what had happened in their bathroom, without giving away that he shifted shapes. A daunting task. "The pipes burst," he said at last, which, of course, was true. He stared into the snow. Were they now, finally, walking towards the diner?

"Oh," Anthony said. "So you two are staying? Because, you know, my wife is alone, and we don't have groceries and if we end up not being able to . . . I mean . . . If we're snowed in for a week or . . . I know I'm supposed to work, but, you see, my wife is not used to Colorado weather, and she's nervous at all the emergency announcements on the radio and—"

Tom looked over his shoulder at Anthony's anxious face, and understood what Anthony hadn't quite said. "You want to go home," he said. "Sure. Go."

"I hate to leave you guys in the lurch, but all the prep stuff is done, and there's a pot of clam chowder and I left a large bowl of rice pudding in the freezer and—"

"Go," Tom said. He was now sure that Kyrie and Red Dragon— in human form—were coming towards him, but they were walking very slowly, and he could not figure out why. Unless Red Dragon was still naked, but Tom knew Kyrie kept a bunch of spare clothes in her car. Had she been caught short for once?

"There's . . . look, Tom, you're going to think I'm crazy, but . . ."

He had to turn around, no matter how much he wanted to keep an eye on Kyrie. And then he realized all of a sudden perhaps Kyrie was delaying coming inside because she could see Anthony there behind Tom and there was something she didn't want Anthony to notice. Like the fact that she was naked. Or the fact that she could change shapes. It was a strange part of their secretive life to know a person they trusted absolutely with their business and their local connections could not be trusted to know what they truly were. But neither Tom nor Kyrie were willing to risk the reaction.

So Tom turned, away from the door, away from the parking lot, and towards Anthony, who, looking relieved to have Tom's attention at last, held the door open, stepped aside and gestured Tom towards the inside of the diner as he said, "Tom, look. It's . . . oh, this is going to sound stupid, but . . . You see, you might have to call animal control."

"Animal control?" Tom asked, as they walked the long, slightly curving hallway that led from the back door to the diner proper. They passed the door to the two bathrooms on the left, the doors to the freezer room and the two storage rooms on the right, and then found themselves at the back of the diner, looking at the newly re-covered brown vinyl booths, the five remaining green vinyl booths that Tom planned to upgrade as soon as possible, and tables newly covered in fake-marble formica. Out of habit Tom counted: five tables occupied here and, from the noise, another five or six occupied in the annex— a sort of large enclosed patio attached to the diner, which had larger tables and which was preferred by college students who arrived in huge, noisy bands.

Tom took off his leather jacket, folded it and stuffed it in the shelf under the counter, then reached to the shelf under that for an apron with The George on the chest. Then felt around again for the bandana with which he confined his hair while cooking—usually to prevent hair falling on the food, though today it would also keep the grill masonry-free, as he was sure his hair was still full of drywall, grout and tile fragments.

"Look, I don't know who deals with situations like this," Anthony said. He frowned. "For all I know it escaped from the zoo or something."

"What?"

Anthony looked embarrassed. "It's an alligator. I know you're going to think I'm completely insane, but I went out there, to throw some stuff away just a few minutes ago. Because, you know, Beth didn't come in, and we don't have anyone to bus, and the kitchen trash . . ."

"Yes." Beth was the new server, and not the most reliable of employees.

"Yeah, anyway, so, I went out there to throw the stuff away, and you . . . Oh. You're going to think I've gone nuts."

"I doubt it," Tom said flatly. He'd just noticed—sitting in his favorite table, by the front window, under a vivid scrawl advertising meatloaf dinner for $3.99—the blond and incongruously surferlike Rafiel Trall. He managed to look like a refugee beach bum, even while wrapped in a grey parka and miles from the nearest ocean. Rafiel looked up at his gaze, and raised eyebrows at Tom.

"Well . . . whatever. If you think I'm nuts, fine, but I swear there was an alligator by the dumpster, eating old fries and bits of burger."

"An alligator?"

"I know, I know, it sounds insane."

And Tom, to whom it did not sound insane at all—Tom, who, in fact, was suppressing an urge to blurt out that it was nothing but a homeless gentleman known as Old Joe, who happened to be an alligator shifter—instead shrugged and said, "No, it doesn't sound insane. You know, people buy them little as pets, then abandon them."

"In restaurant dumpsters?" Anthony asked, dubiously.

"I don't see why not," he said. "People abandon cats here all the time. Why shouldn't they abandon alligators?"

Anthony took a deep breath. "Well . . . sewers in New York, and I've heard of alligators in reservoirs here, but . . ."

"People are weird," Tom said, squirming, uncomfortable about lying to his employee and friend.

"I guess," Anthony said, frowning slightly, as though contemplating alligator-infested restaurant dumpsters were too much for him. He rallied, "Well, be careful when you go back there, all right? I beaned him with a half-rotten cantaloupe and he hid behind the dumpster but I don't think he's gone away."

"Yeah." He hoped Old Joe hadn't gone away. He was totally harmless, and mostly in need of a minder. And that minder, for the time being at least, was Tom.

"And I may go? Home?"

"Yeah." Tom saw Rafiel had stood up and approached the counter and now leaned behind Anthony, trying to catch Tom's eye. He remembered Rafiel's call had been about murder. "Yeah, go home, Anthony. I've got it covered."

He turned blindly—more on instinct than on thought—to the far end of the counter, where no customers sat, and where the two huge polished chrome coffee machines stood, probably a good twenty years out of date. They shimmered because Tom had taken steel wool to them last month, during a long, slow week, and now they managed to look retro, rather than obsolete.

On the way he grabbed still-frozen hamburger patties from a box Anthony had left beside the grill. He didn't think before he grabbed them, and he didn't think before biting into the first one. It was hard, and the cold made his teeth hurt, but he couldn't stop himself. He needed protein. He desperately needed protein, with an irrational bone-deep craving. If he ignored the craving, then there was a good chance the customers would start looking like special protein packs on two legs. Particularly since his body would be trying to heal the damage he'd caused by shifting in the cramped bathroom.

The third patty in his hand, holding it like a child holding a cookie, and hoping no one was looking too closely, he peered at the coffee machines. The caffeinated side was low, and he thought he should also bring the small backup coffee maker from the back room and use it to run hot chocolate, because on a day like this they should offer a special on hot chocolate. And doing this work at the end of the counter would allow Rafiel to approach him and talk to him without either calling attention or risk being overheard. Which was essential if that murder truly involved shapeshifters. And it probably did, because Rafiel wasn't a fool. Impetuous sometimes and a bit too cocky, but not a fool.

Tom got the spare coffee maker from the back room, and then the good spicy hot-chocolate mix from the supplies room. He darted to the front and wrote on the window with a red dry-erase marker, hot chocolate, 99¢ a cup and was setting up the coffee maker—scrupulously cleaned—to run hot chocolate, when he heard Rafiel lean over the counter. At the same time, he heard steps down the hallway. Kyrie's steps—he'd know them anywhere—and someone else's.

Behind him, Rafiel's voice hissed, suspicious, "What is *he* doing here."

Kyrie should have known that Rafiel would be at The George. As she came in with Red Dragon—in the grey sweatsuit that Tom kept in the back of the car, in case of unexpected shifts—she saw Rafiel ahead and bit her tongue before she echoed his question.

Instead, she shoved Red Dragon ahead of her, hissing as she passed, "Tom, the tables."

He looked around at her, unfocused, and she realized he was holding a hamburger patty in his hand. His eyes still had that odd, semi-focused look they got when he hadn't fully recovered from a shift. She doubted he fully understood what she told him and, anyway, it didn't seem to her as if he'd know what to do with the tables, right now. Hungry dragon. Tasty customers. Perhaps this was not the best of ideas.

"Never mind," she said, and she shoved Red Dragon into a tiny booth covered in tattered green vinyl. Customers never picked it unless the rest of the place was full. It barely fit two people and those people had best be very close indeed. Also, now that Tom had started having some of the booths re-covered in new brown vinyl, the older ones, with their cigarette burn marks and the scuffs on the fifties-vintage green vinyl were ignored. That Red Dragon let her just push him, and fell to sitting, like a little kid, reaching out with his shrunken arm to hold onto the table, filled Kyrie with something very close to irritation. "Sit. Stay," she told him.

She ducked behind the counter and picked up her apron—green and embroidered with The George on the chest, atop a little figure of a cartoon dragon.

The pocket still held her notebook and pen. She picked up a coffee carafe and started towards the tables, dispensing warm-ups and taking down orders for this and that, all the while thinking of what might be going on. What on Earth could the Great Sky Dragon mean by sending Red Dragon to *protect* Tom? What could Tom need protection against? What was all that talk of *redeeming* himself? And what could Red Dragon, who could barely challenge Kyrie herself, *do* to *protect* Tom?

She came back to Tom and passed along orders for half a dozen burgers and fries, a platter of souvlaki and a bowl of clam chowder, before ducking behind the counter and assembling two salads. Tom seemed to have finished bingeing on raw beef, and his eyes looked more focused. He also looked vaguely nauseated, as he usually did when he'd just realized he'd eaten something odd.

"What does Rafiel want?" she asked Tom as she worked. Rafiel had gone back to his booth. "I know he called, and said something about a murder, but then we got . . . sidetracked."

"There was a murder," Tom said, in an undertone. She noted that there was now an assembled burger near the grill, and that he was taking bites of it between flipping the burgers on the grill. This was good, because it meant Tom had become himself enough that he wanted his meat cooked, and with mustard and whole wheat buns and lettuce and pickles.

"And he thinks it involves shifters," he said, taking a bite of his burger.

"Oh," Kyrie said. "When it rains . . ."

"Yeah, apparently it pours when it snows too," he said, with a significant look at the windows, fogged with the inside heat and humidity and still being dusted with an ever-thicker snowfall.

He set the food on the counter, neatly grouped by table for her to deliver and said, still in that undertone, "I take it he poses no threat?" He gave a head gesture towards Red Dragon who sat in his booth looking forlorn and as confused as a little kid among strangers.

Kyrie frowned. "Ask me again in half an hour," she said, and delivered all the orders before making her way to Rafiel. She had left him sitting at his table, without so much as taking his order, because he was a friend and, as such, not likely to take offense if she didn't attend to him.

"I'm sorry," she said, as she approached him. "We're very shorthanded today."

He nodded, though his glance went, inevitably, to Red Dragon with his foreshortened arm, as if he suspected her of making a bad joke. "It's okay," he said. "I just came to ask you and Tom to come with me. I need your help. Well . . . I need the help of . . . people I can trust, and I don't want to . . ." He shook his head, and looked at Tom behind the counter. "I don't suppose you could get someone else in, to look after the place? While you come with me? Or could Tom manage alone?"

Kyrie looked up as the bell behind the front door tinkled, and yet another couple came in, muffled to the eyes and sliding on the coating of snow and ice that covered the soles of their shoes. They dropped into seats at a nearby table, and Kyrie said, "I don't know how Anthony managed alone, Rafiel. I don't think we can go anywhere now. Besides, how do you propose to drive in that?"

Rafiel shrugged. "Four-wheel drive and I'm used to this. I learned to drive in this."

Kyrie nodded. Rafiel, like Anthony, was local. "Well, I still don't know how I can come with you. Not with . . ." She waved around at the diner, and nodded towards the new customers, assuring them silently that she could see them and would be with them shortly. "Maybe if one of our employees shows up," she said, doubtfully.

"Yes. Get me a coffee and a piece of pie, please. I'll wait."

She frowned at him, because his willingness to wait meant he was convinced this did indeed involve shifters, and that meant there was no one else he could trust.

Looking towards the booth, she assured herself that Red Dragon was still there, now looking fixedly at Rafiel with a scared expression. Perhaps it was Rafiel that he thought he had to protect Tom from.

She took the order of the new couple—two coffees, which meant they had braved the walk just to be near other people—and went back to grab the pie for Rafiel.

"Chick-pea pie," she announced, as she set it down in front of him—a joke that had developed from the fact that Rafiel never specified what kind of pie he wanted, which led to her inventing more and more outrageous pretended contents to his food. "And your coffee."

"What does he want?" Rafiel asked, looking at Red Dragon and not even acknowledging her joke.

"He says he's come to redeem himself by protecting Tom," she said, and was gratified to watch Rafiel's eyebrows shoot up. She wasn't the only one who found this absurd.

"Kyrie says that you can't manage the diner alone," Tom heard Rafiel say, in barely more than a rumbling whisper. Tom had just moved the furthest away from customers possible, while remaining behind the counter. The sheer pileup of dishes from the tables Kyrie was cleaning demanded that he put them in the dishwasher, which was around the corner from the coffee maker, and almost to the hallway.

He looked up from slamming the dishes down. Rafiel had a slice of apple pie in one hand and his coffee in the other and was standing by the portion of the counter where Tom normally put the dishes for Kyrie to carry away. Past him, Kyrie was cleaning one last table. There remained four fully occupied ones, but everyone had been served, and had gotten their bill, and seemed to be just sitting around, talking, reluctant to face the storm again. "Maybe if it slows down now." "It might, you know?" "It's nasty out."

"I'm surprised there's anyone here," Rafiel said. "At least anyone who doesn't need to be here. What possessed you to come in?"

"I shifted," Tom said, slamming the last few plates into the dishwasher, shutting it and turning it on. "In our bathroom. There's . . . uh . . . no bathroom left."

He looked up, to see Rafiel staring at him, as he half expected, openmouthed. "In your bathroom? Why?"

Tom shrugged. "It will sound very strange."

"Not as strange as deciding to shift in the bathroom. How could you possibly think you'd fit. Or that there would be—"

"Fine," he said. "There was a voice in my head. The Great Sky Dragon's voice."

"The . . . ?"

"Yeah."

Rafiel looked at Red Dragon. "Threatening?"

Tom shrugged. "I thought so at the time. Now I'm not so sure. He was talking about some Ancient Ones or others who were, supposedly, after me."

"I see," Rafiel said, in that way he had that made it clear he did not see at all. He ate his apple pie in quick bites.

"At the time," Tom said, "I didn't even realize the voice was in my head. It sounded like he was talking to me through the bathroom window. Considering the last time I met with him . . ."

"He almost killed you?"

"Yes. Panic had carried me halfway through the shift before I realized he was in fact in my mind, and for some reason this failed to be reassuring."

"Ancient Ones," Rafiel said. "Shifters?"

"I don't know. He didn't say. I just . . . I'd had a weird dream about . . . very old shifters. Some with shapes that . . . well . . ." He felt stupid, but had to say it. "A saber-toothed tiger and all that."

"Stands to reason," Rafiel said. "We're not easy to kill . . . so some of us would be very old."

"Well . . . we don't know if our longevity is any greater. Legends aren't exactly clear on that, are they? Vampires, sure, but shifters . . ." He shrugged. "If we lived that much longer than normal people, wouldn't the world be overrun by us? And wouldn't it be far more obvious that we exist?"

"How do we know there aren't a lot more of us than we thought? I mean, we know shifters are attracted to this place. Do you know how many of your customers are shifters?"

"Yes. You and Old Joe out back, though I'm not sure I'd call him a customer." He added at Rafiel's blank look, "The alligator." He took a quick look around the diner. "Speaking of which. I should check on him. If Kyrie asks, tell her I just went out back and will be right back."

He ducked out into the back hallway, hoping that Old Joe would still be there. The man seemed to be old and confused enough that he shifted shapes at all sorts of times for any reason or no reason at all. And Tom dreaded the thought of his being naked and lost in the snow, scared away by the cantaloupe that Anthony had thrown at his head.

Rafiel heard Kyrie behind him. No. He smelled her before he heard her—that sharp tang that indicated a shifter, followed by the symphony of scent that was Kyrie herself. She didn't wear perfume—that would probably have covered up all other scents to him—but her smell reminded him of cinnamon and fresh cut apples and the smell of fresh mown grass. All of those were very subtle undertones overlaid on a smell of soap, but they twisted together in a scent that meant Kyrie.

"Tom went outside. Something about an alligator," Rafiel said without turning back.

Kyrie gave what was not even a suppressed sigh, just a slightly longer breath. He could almost hear her shrug. He couldn't tell if it was impatience or exasperation. "Yeah," she said. "He's one of Tom's strays."

There would have been a time when Rafiel would have pursued that hint of impatience with his rival. No matter how much Rafiel might deny it or what he might say, Kyrie remained his dream girl, whom he thought the perfect woman for him. The one he loved and could never have.

For a moment, a nonphysical ache seemed to make his heart clench, and then he shook his head. "Look, it's just . . ." He shook his head again when he realized he was about to tell her that he couldn't discuss Tom without appearing partial because he still wanted her and wanted her badly. Then he realized he couldn't tell her that.

The problem with it, he thought, repressing an impulse to kick something, was that he liked Tom. They'd saved each other's lives, more or less, a couple of times. They'd fought side by side. There was something in that for men—something older than time, older than human thought. It made them blood brothers; comrades at arms. But beyond all that, he *liked* Tom. Tom was odd and he did things Rafiel couldn't fully understand but then, in a way everyone appeared like that to everyone else.

Tom came in the back door then. Because of the slight curve of the hallway, Rafiel couldn't see him, but he could hear him, talking to someone who answered back in a raspy voice. This presumably meant, Rafiel thought, that Tom was bringing back the former alligator now in human form. Not that he put it past Tom to drag an alligator into the diner. And the fact that he could easily convince everyone in there that this was perfectly normal and nothing unexpected was part of what was unique about the man. Part of the reason Rafiel knew it was no use to try to seduce Kyrie. Not anymore. He had seen his competition and he knew he didn't measure up.

Instead, he turned around, to look at Kyrie, who was staring down the hallway, towards the sound of an opening door. "He keeps old clothes in one of the storage rooms," she said. "For Old Joe. Because he shifts for no reason, and it means he ends up naked a lot."

Rafiel shrugged. "The reason I came," he said, "is that we found an arm. At the aquarium."

"An *arm*?" She looked at him blankly, with a horrified expression. "An *arm*?"

"There was a cell phone ring that came from inside one of the sharks," Rafiel said. "The cleaning divers heard it. They thought, you know . . . the shark had swallowed a cell phone. People lean over—there's an observation area—and they drop things in the water. But then they found the bones at the bottom of the tank. Human bones. That's when we were called in, to determine if they were, in fact, human. They were. A couple of vertebrae. Some toe bones." He waved his hand. For some reason the finding of those fragments of humanity at the bottom of a shark tank affected him more than finding a whole decomposing body, as he often had. They were more pathetic and more anonymous, demanding more of his pity, his outrage—and his justice.

He shook his head, to dismiss the image of the bones—a handful of them, no more. Kyrie looked at Tom, leading Old Joe—a man so old he was almost bent over, and whose skin and hair were not so much white as the curious colorlessness of the very aged—to one of the corner tables, and now Tom was ducking behind the counter and getting a bowl of clam chowder and taking it back to Old Joe.

"So they opened the shark," Rafiel said, hearing his own voice sound toneless. "And they found a human arm, still clutching a cell phone."

"Someone fell in the aquarium?" Kyrie asked, and now Rafiel had her full attention, and Tom had come up and was nearby, his eyebrows raised.

"Was it a shifter?" he asked. "Who fell?"

Rafiel shook his head. "No. It wasn't . . . it's just . . . we went over today, with a team, and did the full work-up, and while we were there, I kept smelling this shifter smell, around the shark tank and up to the little observation area. And then around the offices, too. So I made sure to forget one of my notebooks behind, and I went back to pick it up. There was only one employee there, closing up for the day, really, and she didn't mind having me look around the crime scene." He cringed inwardly, knowing exactly how many violations of procedure he had incurred, but knowing that procedure, somehow, failed to account for shifter criminals and the shifter policemen whose life might be destroyed by them. "If it's even a crime scene, of course."

"And?" Kyrie said.

"And there was a definite trail of shifter-smell winding around the observation area from which the vic could have fallen into the tank."

"But surely," Tom said, "it could also mean that of the many visitors to the aquarium, one was . . . you know, like us."

Rafiel nodded. "Oh, it could mean that. Definitely. And that's the problem. I couldn't smell all around and . . ." He shrugged. "I wanted your noses on the case, as it were. I . . . stole a set of keys while the employee was busy." That she had been busy on a wild goose chase for the wallet he claimed to have dropped somewhere only made him feel slightly guilty. He noted that neither Kyrie nor Tom looked shocked by his behavior, either. Tom chewed his lip and looked like he was thinking. "I truly can't go," he said. "Kyrie is not that good on managing the grill area. It's new. The whole stove is. She's not used to it yet."

Kyrie looked as if she would protest, but was sweeping automatically back and forth across the tables with her gaze, even as she frowned. "Perhaps," she said, "I can come with you if we do it briefly?"

Rafiel looked towards Tom. He knew very well that Kyrie didn't need anyone's permission and, in fact, he was perfectly well aware that Kyrie would resent his openly asking if Tom minded her going with him. Because it would imply Kyrie needed a minder and that she was less than a fully conscious participant in the relationship. Both of which were lies.

So Rafiel didn't say anything, but he looked at Tom.

There had been times, only a few months ago, when Tom would have been very upset at thinking of Rafiel and Kyrie going anywhere together without him. But now he just looked towards the booth where Red Dragon sat and asked, "Can you take him with you?"

Rafiel raised his eyebrow, in mute question, wondering if Tom meant to use Red Dragon as a chaperone. But the look back was guileless and open. "It's just I'd rather not have him around when I already shifted once today. And not in the diner. I don't want to shift again, and I don't want to do it here. And there are two of you . . ."

Kyrie nodded. She had that jutting-lower-lip look she got when she'd determined on a course of action. "Let me talk to him, first," she said, and walked towards the booth, carrying the coffee carafe and a cup, in what might be a gesture of hospitality or, simply, the most discreet weapons she could carry in this space.

Red Dragon was still huddled in the booth where Kyrie had left him, and looked around with huge eyes, as if he expected everyone in the diner to shift shapes and devour him.

And he says he wants to protect Tom, Kyrie thought, and shook her head slightly at the absurdity of it. *It has to be a joke. Perhaps not his joke, but the Great Sky Dragon's.*

She pushed a cup in front of him, and poured coffee into it from the carafe and just as she was thinking that no matter how many packets of sugar Red Dragon put in it, he needed protein and she ought to have thought of it, Tom set a plate in front of Red Dragon, containing two whole wheat buns and what appeared to be a triple hamburger and a whole lot of cheese.

Considering that she knew very well how Tom felt about Red Dragon, Kyrie felt her heart melt. Tom was like that. He would give up his own shirt to clothe someone else, even if it was his mortal enemy. This both scared her and made her think her boyfriend was the best person in the world.

Red Dragon looked sheepishly at Tom who said, "Protein. After shifting."

The young man nodded at Tom and picked up the burger with shaking hands, while Kyrie looked up at Tom and gave him her warmest smile. He looked worried enough, but he winked at her, before returning behind the counter to fool with the grill or start preparations for the next dish, or whatever it was he did back there half the time. Kyrie was quite contented to leave the cooking to Tom, and most of their clientele seemed to approve of the decision.

She turned back to Red Dragon, who was wolfing down the burger.

"I can't call you Red Dragon," she told the creature who faced her, clutching the burger tightly as if he were afraid she'd take it away. "Do you have a name?"

Red Dragon blushed and paused, caught just after taking a bite, his mouth full, the burger awkwardly in his hand. "I'm . . . My name . . ." He blushed darker and looked down at the burger, setting it slowly down on the plate, as he hastily chewed what was in his mouth. "My name is Conan Lung."

"Conan?" Kyrie asked. She didn't know whether she believed it, and she almost laughed at the idea of this man, who was shorter even than Tom, much slimmer, and—definitely—no barbarian hero, being called Conan.

"I . . ." He sighed. "My parents used comic books to improve their English, and they liked Conan."

That he was descended from the sort of people who thought that their son was likely to grow up to be a barbarian hero, might explain his delusional thoughts of protecting Tom. *Might*. She doubted anything *could* fully explain that.

"Right, then, Mr. Lung," she said. "What I want to know—"

"Call me Conan," Conan Lung said, quickly, and in the sort of undertone that implied he expected a rebuff.

"Right then," Kyrie said, thinking to herself she hoped the creature wouldn't think they were the best of friends, now. In his last foray into their lives, he'd chased them all over town and he'd helped catch and torture Tom. She knew that like all cowards, he could be exceptionally cruel in a fight. And she didn't want to have him at her back in a dangerous situation. In fact, she didn't want to have him anywhere that she couldn't keep a sharp eye on him. "You said you came to protect Tom?"

Red Dragon cast a fearful look at Tom, then another back at Kyrie. "The Great One said that I must come and protect the young dragon," he said, and bobbed a small bow, as though just speaking of the Great Sky Dragon must entail a need to kowtow. "He said I should answer for his life with mine."

Kyrie frowned. Conan sounded terribly earnest and she didn't think just now, scared as he looked, that the man was capable of lying so convincingly. However, having met the vast golden dragon that was master of all other Asian dragons in the West, she couldn't imagine his sending Conan to Tom as a protector.

"You're . . . He told you you're to protect Tom? You're a bodyguard of sorts, then?"

Conan bobbed his head again, then shook it desultorily. "Not . . . a bodyguard. My . . . my fighting is not all that could be desired. But I am one of the Great One's . . . you know? One of his vassals. I'm supposed to . . . to report to him what's happening around . . . the young dragon. To . . . to call him if needed."

"Do you mean," Kyrie started, narrowing her eyes, "that you are spying for the Great Sky Dragon? That if there is any trouble . . ."

"He can be here in no time at all," Conan said. "He tried telling the young dragon to beware, but the young one didn't seem to understand him, so I am here to protect him." A bite of the burger and a fleeting look under his—annoyingly thick and long—lashes at her. "And . . . and you. By making sure the Great One can chase away any enemies before they can harm any of you."

"But protect us from what?" Kyrie asked. She didn't at all like the idea that the Great Sky Dragon had effectively planted a spy among them. She wasn't sure she trusted his intentions or his ideas of what was proper. And she was very sure she didn't trust the Great Sky Dragon, himself. A creature more than a thousand years old—and from what Kyrie understood, the Great Sky Dragon was several thousands of years old—would have seen generations come and go. What would others' lives be worth to him?

Oh, he could have killed Tom, three months ago—killed him in such a way that even the amazing healing power of dragons would not have reversed. And he'd chosen not to. But how did Kyrie know that it was ever a choice? How could she know that under what must surely be an alien honor code, the Great Sky Dragon hadn't been forbidden from killing Tom then? And how did she know that he didn't mean to make up for it now, by setting a trap in which Tom would be caught and killed?

She looked towards her boyfriend, who was leaning on the counter, chatting animatedly with Rafiel, and again felt a sick lurch in her stomach. In place of the family she'd never known, she had a man who loved her and who was—she believed—one of the best people in the world—dragon shifter or no. And she had friends: Rafiel and Anthony, and a young man named Keith who was, now and again, a part-time waiter at The George.

Kyrie was not willing to give up any member of her chosen family, nor any corner of her domain to shadowy creatures whose life span might be many times as long as hers, but whose moral compass left much to be desired.

"Stay here," she told Conan, as she got up, collecting the carafe. She must talk to Tom and Rafiel and try to figure out what they should do with Conan and what the Great Sky Dragon could be *trying* to do.

Whatever it was, they would be in as much danger as she would be—perhaps Tom would be in more danger, in fact—and she couldn't make a decision for either of them.

"Seriously," Rafiel said, speaking in an undertone to Tom's back, as Tom industriously scraped at the grill. "How many of your clients are shifters?"

Tom gave Rafiel a look over his shoulder, half startled. "I told you. You and Old Joe."

"You know better. You know because of the pheromones the . . . former owners . . . sprayed this place with, it attracts shifters. They attracted you and Kyrie, didn't they? Right off the bus. Unless you have a better explanation as to why you and Kyrie found little

Goldport, Colorado so irresistible. They attracted me, which is perhaps more easily explainable, since I'm a policeman and I work the night shift. So, failing a really good twenty-four-hour doughnut shop in town . . ." He smiled a self-conscious smile, glad Tom was turning around—spatula still in hand—and answered his joke with a chuckle. "You could say an all-night greasy spoon is the closest thing to my natural habitat. But how can you truly believe we're the only ones?"

Tom shrugged. "I don't know, Rafiel. I don't think there are that many of our kind of people, period. There was an orangutan shifter, back in New York. And of course, the Great Sky Dragon and his brood. And there is, of course, Old Joe and you and Kyrie. But that's out of thousands of people, Rafiel. I don't think there are that many of us to gather here. Or anywhere."

"What you mean is that you don't think there are that many of them in the vicinity. But how far does the call of the pheromones extend? How far will it bring shifters, do you know? How many casual travelers, how many students, will stop here and stay? How many of those do you have as regulars, Tom?"

Tom shrugged. He set the spatula down and leaned over the counter, so that they could talk to each other in a whisper and with a modicum of privacy. "I don't know," he said. "You figured out how to smell shifters before either Kyrie or I did. Can't you smell out shifters in the diner, and tell *me* how many shifters there are here?"

Rafiel shrugged. "Not always. When people wear perfume, or even cologne, sometimes it's hard to tell. When I was in high school—" He stopped abruptly.

"Yes?" Tom asked.

Rafiel shrugged. He'd never told Tom this. He had never told anyone, not even his parents. The incident, secret though it was, had crystalized for him exactly what risk shifters were in, and how their very natures placed them outside the purview of normal legality. Of what other people would see as reality.

Tom was watching him intently and Rafiel sighed and gave in. "When I was in high school, I had a girlfriend. This was around the time I started shifting, but I shifted mostly late at night, and provided I took care not to have dates on full-moon nights, we were okay. She was . . . she seemed very easygoing and was willing to postpone dates and take my less than convincing excuses. Still, when I graduated I went away to Denver to study law enforcement, and it was either break up or get married and, you know, I couldn't get married. Not and risk her figuring out what I really was. So we broke up. Alice stayed behind and worked . . . actually at The George. The Athens as it then was. And then when I came back for Christmas . . ." He shrugged. "Well, you know, being a shifter and all, and the first year at college I had to be in dorms . . ."

"I always wondered how that worked," Tom said.

"Not well. So I was convinced I wanted to quit school, and I came back home for Christmas, and I was going to tell Dad I couldn't be an officer, after all, which would break his heart. Anyway, when I got here I found out Alice was missing. Had been missing for some days. I shifted. I trailed her . . . well . . . her scent. I found her dead. She had been killed because she was a shifter. She was . . ." He looked up at Tom and saw, reflected in the other man's face, the strange, hollow grief he himself felt. "She was a lion shifter. And her new boyfriend caught her shifting and . . . you know . . . killed her. He was scared. I . . ." He shook his head, trying to free himself of memories of the past and Alice's soft brown eyes. "I never knew it. Even though I was with her, every day, I never smelled the shifter in her. She wore a perfume that had the same sort of undertone, and it got lost in the perfume."

He was quiet a while, unable to find words to continue.

"I'm sorry," Tom said, in a low voice.

Rafiel managed a chuckle. "Well, it was a long time ago. Ten years. But you see, if I could smell shifters that well, I'd have *known*. I did not."

"And you became a policeman," Tom said, softly.

Rafiel shrugged. "Someone official needs to be looking out for our kind, which is what this is all about. I didn't count on the diner becoming the center of shifters for miles around." He gave Tom a smile he was sure looked sickly.

"And why are you so interested in how many of our regulars might be shifters?" Tom asked.

"Well, I figure the aquarium isn't that far away, and if there was a shifter . . . well . . . it might have been one of your regulars who was there, and we might be able to tag him on his specific scent. And then I could question him, you know, without seeming to, and if it turned out to just be someone who went to the aquarium for fun or something . . ." He drew to a halt slowly. The truth was he didn't want this murder to involve any shifters. He didn't want to have to lie and skulk and go behind his superiors' backs.

Oh, Goldport was a small enough town, and the police department was somewhat informal and friendly. Rafiel was a third generation cop in the same department. He could get away with a lot. But he didn't like to. He was a policeman because he prized the idea of a justice system based on laws. He didn't approve of anyone defiling it. Not even himself.

"Rafiel," Tom said, laughter at the back of his throat, trying to cut through the words. "Are you truly suggesting we go up to all our regulars and smell them? Half of them are college students or warehouse workers who come here after work. You know what they smell like."

"No. I mean . . . no, I don't think that would work. Perfume and all. But . . . just keep your nose open, okay?"

Tom nodded and opened his mouth as though he were about to add something, but at that moment Kyrie came up to them. "He says he was sent to protect you, Tom. That the Great Sky Dragon said he tried to warn you and you didn't seem to get it."

"Why would anyone—particularly anyone ancient and presumably intelligent—send *Red Dragon* to protect . . . me?" Tom said.

"He says his name is Conan," Kyrie said, looking at Tom, but with an unfocused expression that indicated her attention was on her thoughts and not on their conversation.

"Conan?" Rafiel asked, before Tom could.

Kyrie turned to him. "His parents liked comic books, he says."

"So it stands to reason he should be the hero to protect me? And protect me from what?" Tom said.

"Are you sure you don't remember what the Great Sky Dragon told you?" Kyrie asked. "Perhaps . . ."

Tom shook his head. "It was all very confused." Just thinking back on that precise, booming voice in his head made his muscles clench and made him fear he would shift without warning. "I know he said I had violated old and sacred customs. The laws of our kind . . ." He shook his head, unable to remember.

"Our kind has laws?" Rafiel asked, at the same time that Kyrie said, "That doesn't sound like he wanted to protect you."

"No," Tom said. "It didn't sound that way to me, either, which is why I thought . . ." He clenched his hands on the counter, digging his nails against the hard formica top and making not an impression. If he'd been in dragon form . . . he would have dug his nails right through it. But he would not allow himself to change. Not now. Not today. Not again.

He took deep breaths, trying to forget the voice and the sense of urgency, trying to remember only the words and not the fear they'd induced. "I remember his saying something about Ancient Ones, but I wasn't sure what he meant—the laws or some people who were very old."

Kyrie nodded. "Well, we're stuck with Conan the Wonder Dragon over there, unless you can get rid of him in some way."

Tom looked at her. In some way. It occurred to him it would be very simple to get rid of him the dragon way—flames at twenty feet. When they'd fought as dragons before, Tom had ripped off Red Dragon's arm and beaten him over the head with it. But somehow he didn't think that was what Kyrie meant for him to do. And as for himself . . . well, until proven otherwise, he couldn't really say killing Red Dragon would be in self-defense. The rather pitiful creature, cowering in their smallest booth, warming his hands on a cup of coffee, could be said to be many things, but life-threatening wasn't one of them. Whatever he'd been or done in the past, right now the adjectives that came more readily to mind echoed more of *wet* or perhaps *spineless.*

Tom knew better than to discount the creature just because he cringed and hid around the corners. Tom had lived on the streets and seen many a beggar who seemed meek and mild turn suddenly and go on a rampage. But still, the truth remained he was not openly threatening Tom. If Tom killed Conan now, even in what could be considered a fair duel—as fair as it could be when only one of the duelists was in possession of a backbone—then he would forever feel he had murdered a defenseless being. And murdering defenseless beings would mean that Tom was not just a shifter, but an animal. It would make it very hard to look at himself in the mirror. Which would make shaving a challenge.

He shrugged. Aloud, he said, "Well, the Great Sky Dragon sent him to us for a reason."

"As a spy," Kyrie said. "It seems he has orders to report all we do . . . or at least anything we do that might be dangerous to the Great Sky Dragon. He put it as he can call the Great Sky Dragon and the Great Sky Dragon will come—or at least send help—when needed."

Tom looked at her for a moment, then shook his head slowly. Hadn't she understood the significance of the Great Sky Dragon in Tom's head? "Kyrie, he can reach into my mind with his voice at will."

"No," Kyrie said. "Conan says that you shut your mind to the Great Sky Dragon, and that's why he sent Conan to us as a spy. To keep an eye on us."

"Perhaps," Tom said. "But then again, if there's going to be a spy among us, is it not better that it be a spy we know? We can keep an eye on him, keeping an eye on us."

"That sounds strangely unhealthy," Rafiel said. "Like one of those situations where you end up being your own grandpa."

"Perhaps it does," Tom said. "But the truth is, you know . . . better the devil we know. And we do know this devil."

"We'll let him stay then?" Kyrie said, doubtfully.

"Better yet," Tom said. "We'll give him a job. That way we can keep an eye on him to make sure he's doing his job and to make sure he's not trying to kill me. All in one."

Kyrie didn't look convinced. "And what if he attacks?"

"Then," Tom said, and graced her with his best, bare-teeth smile, "I attack back. And I'm bigger and faster."

Kyrie sighed, as if conceding a point. "I don't like it," she said.

"I don't either," Tom said, and reached under the counter for an apron to give to Conan at the same time the front doorbell tinkled to let in the tall, thin blond man who usually spent the night in the diner, writing in a succession of cloth-bound journals. They called him the Poet though it was more likely—from the nervous look of him—that he was writing about conspiracy theories. He took his normal table, with his back against the wall. "But we must make the best of a bad situation, and look at it this way, if I get him to serve at tables, you can probably go with Rafiel and be fine. I'll get him a couple of flip-flops from the storage room."

"You're going to make him a waiter?"

"Why not? While protecting me, he might as well hand out some souvlaki," Tom said. Smiling with a reassurance he was far from feeling, he advanced on the small booth. Red Dragon jumped a little when he saw Tom approach, and looked up at Tom with an expression of such abject terror that Tom thought, *Oh yes, if the time comes, I can take him.* But he hoped it wouldn't be needed. He gave Conan a pair of red flip-flops, explaining, "Health regulations." Then he watched the man put on the apron, while he gave him the speech on waiting tables that had been given to Tom himself, when he'd taken a job as a waiter almost a year ago. "Don't be rude to the customers, no matter what they say; write down the orders, no one's memory is perfect." He took a notebook and pencil from the pocket of the apron and waved it at Conan. "And when you go out to take an order always take the carafe with you and give refills to the people who are having coffee." He glanced at Conan's shrunken arm. "You can put the carafe on the tables without damaging them, at least the new ones. And the old ones, who cares? They're all stained and burned, anyway."

Conan nodded, looking as self-conscious as a kid in new clothes, in strange company, and Tom pointed at the table the Poet had just occupied. "There you go. Take his order. It's probably just coffee, but you never know."

Then he turned to look at Rafiel and Kyrie who were both staring at him with a bemused expression. "What?" he asked in an undertone. "We don't have enough hands on deck today, and if he's going to stick around, he might as well make himself useful." He shrugged. "Besides," he dropped his voice further, "I might as well keep him too busy to think of something creative to do in the way of getting rid of me."

Rafiel shook his head but didn't say anything, and Tom covered up his apprehension with a smile. "Go on. Now Kyrie can go with you for half an hour or so. We won't be leaving the tables unattended."

Kyrie sat down in Rafiel's car, narrowing her eyes at him. "You won't shift while driving?"

Rafiel gave her a blank, puzzled look. "Why would I do such a stupid thing?" He frowned. "It would end up in an accident."

Kyrie shrugged. She'd rather cut her own tongue out with a blunt knife, than tell him how close she'd come to shifting, herself. "I just thought, you know . . . since one shifts when stressed . . ."

He looked away from the windshield past which Kyrie could see no more than a dazzling whiteness of snow, seeming to radiate from the center of the two light cones cast by the headlights. "Why would I be stressed?" he asked. He held the wheel lightly enough to make her want to growl at him—and she was fairly sure that this had nothing to do with an urge to shift.

He put the car in gear and started out of the parking lot, seemingly perfectly sure of where he was going. How he could be sure, Kyrie didn't know. Perhaps he was flying by instruments. She glared at him.

He looked out the windshield again and drove at what seemed to her a disgustingly high speed towards Fairfax. As the silence lengthened between them, he turned. "What?" he said.

Kyrie was so surprised he seemed to be aware of her disapproval that she felt her cheeks flush and started to open her mouth to justify herself. Before she could, he reached over and patted her arm awkwardly. "I grew up here," he said, in a tone that made it almost an apology. "I learned to drive in winter." He shrugged, as he stopped for a light that was no more than a diffuse red glow ahead. "I'm sure you'll get more comfortable with it in time."

The tone was sympathetic and attempting to be friendly but it felt patronizing and she had to bite back a wish to swat his ears and put him in his place. The image that came to her mind was of a paw swatting at his feline ears. She felt her lips twist upwards, and looked out the passenger window—though she could not see anything more than blinding white snow. "So, how do you think shifters are involved in this?" she asked, in as serious a voice as she could muster.

Without looking, she could sense he'd shrugged. Probably some slight rustle of cloth as his shoulders rose and fell. "I don't know. Not as victims."

"So you think they are . . . ?"

She looked back in time to see him shake his head. "I don't know," he said. "We've already found that some shifters feel the urge to kill in their . . . well . . . their other form. Perhaps that was it."

"Or perhaps just . . . you know, shifters that kill, like other people kill."

He gave a startled bark of laughter. "Oh, yes, very sensible. I should have thought of that, of course. I mean, we're shifters, we're not saints. The animal urge is not necessary to explain killing, is it? As I know only too well from police work."

"Well . . ." Kyrie said.

"No, trust me, it makes sense. Sometimes, with all this, we run the risk of thinking we're completely apart from humanity and different from them, and of course, we're not. We're humans, like all others. Or almost."

"Given a certain tendency to change shapes, yes, exactly," Kyrie said. "Just like all others."

Rafiel slowed down and leaned all the way forward. "I hope this is Ocean Street," he said. "Because I surely can't read that sign."

"So glad to know the superpowers of Colorado natives don't cover everything."

"You should be, otherwise imagine the envy you'd be forced to feel. Everyone would want to be born in Colorado. It would get crowded in the hospitals," Rafiel said. "But what I was saying . . . perhaps I'm foolish to feel guilty for all shifters, or at least to feel I must protect them from . . . you know, the majority of people—like I must . . ." He turned neatly into the parking lot beside a tall cylindrical building with broad rounded windows. "Like I must be the law for our people—those of us who hide amid other people." He looked at her, and for the first time in a long, long time, she detected a look of insecurity about him, as if he were young and not completely confident about what he thought or should be doing. "I guess you think I'm an idiot. I mean, we don't even know how many of us there are, and here I am, trying to keep them safe, as if I knew them personally."

"Not an idiot," she said, immediately, in reaction to his expression more than anything. "You feel a duty to . . . people like us, I guess." A little gurgle of laughter tore through her throat, surprising her. "Frankly, at first, that was why I helped Tom last year, when he found the body in the parking lot. I wasn't sure if he'd killed anyone or not, but I'd never met anyone else like me—you know, never having had a family. So I figured, he was my responsibility to look after. I'd guess you feel something like that."

"Yeah, but I'd feel better, if I didn't have reason to suspect a lot of our people . . . I mean, a lot of people like us have . . . issues controlling themselves."

"Other people do too," she said. And shrugged. "Now, let's go see if I can confirm your supposed shifter-smell. It's unlikely I can help you, since you have a better sense of smell than any of us."

"I just want . . . second opinion," he said. And got out of the car. On the road, behind them, tires squealed.

"Hey, can I help you with the waiting on tables?" a voice asked behind Tom, as Tom prepared a stack of burgers on the grill.

It was a well known voice—that of his friend Keith Vorpal, the only one of the non-shifters who knew shifters existed. Keith was a film student with an unshakeable joi de vivre and an absolute certainty that being a shifter was the coolest thing since being a superhero. He'd gotten embroiled in their affairs and taken part in some life-and-death struggles. Though he'd acquitted himself well enough, he was sure shifters got to have more fun than he did. Sometimes he claimed to be a human shifter. He shifted between a human form and a stunningly similar human form.

However that was, Tom felt strangely grateful that Keith, not a shifter, didn't feel either horrified by them, or forced to turn them in as abominations. And the fact that Keith knew the routines of The George, where he worked part-time, seemed like a godsend right now, when Tom had been doing his job and continuously prodding the hapless Conan to do his.

"Keith," he said, turning around. "Keith."

Keith smiled at him. His tumbled blond hair was in disarray, and his glasses fogged, from having come from cold to warmth. He unwound a bright red scarf from around his neck, as he spoke. "So, you need my help?"

"Yeah, all we have is Conan, and it's his first day." Tom said, and hoped against hope that Keith would have no memory of Red Dragon.

"Conan?" Keith said, as he ducked behind the counter, removed scarf and jacket. Tom heard the sound of Keith sliding the time sheet from under the counter and smiled.

"The new employee. Over there."

"Over . . ." Keith took in breath sharply. "But Tom, he's . . . that is . . ."

Tom was afraid Keith would blurt out loud that Red Dragon was just that, and the enemy besides. And since Kyrie had left, a sudden inrush of customers had come in, ten or twenty in all, all sitting at nearby tables, ordering hot chocolate and burgers and whatnot. He reached over and put a hand on the young man's shoulder, to arrest the flow of words. "It's all right, Keith, truly. I'm keeping an eye on him."

"If you're sure . . ." Keith said, looking confused.

"Yeah, sure about everything but his ability to wait tables. Why don't you go and—" But before he could suggest that Keith should relieve Conan of some tables and give him breathing room, Tom looked up at the booth where he'd left Old Joe. The clothes he'd loaned the old vagrant were still there, but Old Joe was gone. "Shit," Tom said, which made Keith look at him sharply, because Tom rarely swore out loud. "Man the grill, Keith. Just a couple of minutes."

With a suspicion that he knew very well where Old Joe had gone, Tom ducked out from behind the counter and ran down the hallway, just in time to hear the back door creak open, and to see, as he turned the corner, an alligator tail disappearing through the door.

He knew he should have locked it.

The aquarium looked like a cylindrical grain silo—at least if a silo could be massive, made of glass and concrete and rise ten stories into the air. Once you got inside, there were very few staircases where the public was supposed to walk—from the entrance room, outfitted to look like something from *Ten Thousand Leagues Under the Sea*, with rusty-looking ship wheels and riveted panels on the walls, to the restaurant on the other end. Instead, it was all gently sloping floors.

"Surveillance system?" Kyrie asked, looking at the blank screens in the entrance room and wondering exactly what to do if there was one. After all, she was here with a policeman. But policemen—she was fairly sure of this—weren't supposed to break into the scenes of crimes, alone or with civilian friends, after everyone else had departed. She wondered how this would play in court, if it ever came to court. And that was supposing, of course, that the killer wasn't a shifter. Because, if he was . . .

She shivered. She didn't know what to do if the killer was a shifter, and she would bet Rafiel didn't either. You couldn't let a shifter be arrested and end up in a jail, where his secret would inevitably come out. Particularly not if he was the sort of wild, barely contained shifter who would kill without a thought. If you allowed him to be arrested, you might as well confess that you were one too, and let them come for you. Because once the existence of shifters was discovered, then the sort of accommodation, the sort of looking out for each other, covering for each other, that she and Rafiel and Tom all did, would become impossible. People largely failed to see them because they didn't expect them. If one of them were revealed, then all would be.

But what could they do, if a shifter were guilty? How could they prevent him from being arrested? Cover for him, and allow him to go on murdering? Or take justice in their own hands and kill him? Who knew? The last time, they'd killed the murderer, but that had been self-defense, because he'd been trying to murder them. This time, they might have to make a dispassionate decision.

"Nah," Rafiel said. He'd barely looked at the screens. "First thing we asked was if they had a surveillance system. But they didn't. They said that they've never had issues with break-ins or vandalism. Normally the restaurant is open half the night, you know. So there's people around."

He led her past various incredibly unconvincing concrete caves. "You can shift in the bathroom," Rafiel said. "The ladies' room is there," and he pointed at a little artificial stone grotto amid which a small door opened with the universal symbol of the stick figure in a dress and the words shad roe. It was, Kyrie thought, very good that there was a picture, since she failed to know what either Shad or Roe meant. The only thing she could think was that Shad Roe was the Russian relative of Jane Doe.

She ducked into the bathroom—a utilitarian thing, with metal sinks and beat-up beige-painted stalls. Perhaps it was supposed to evoke a ship, she thought, and resisted an impulse to duck into a stall before shifting. There was no point at all. They were alone here, and besides, her panther self would be utterly confused, dealing with claws and a door lock.

"Right," she told herself. She removed her clothes swiftly. She concentrated. Shifting was hard, but she'd learned to do it volitionally in the last few months. As she felt her body spasm and shudder, she caught a glimpse of herself in the mirror, her eyes going slitted yellow, her features growing into a muzzle, her teeth into fangs.

She looked away from the mirror, as the image it reflected became a big, black-furred cat. It caught at the edge of her sense, the sweet-tangy scent that the human part of Kyrie knew meant a shapeshifter had been here, and recently too.

Tom ran down the hallway, full speed. He doubted that Old Joe could have run faster than Tom could walk. But the alligator that Old Joe shifted into could. He moved at a frighteningly fast clip, tail swaying. The door slammed shut behind Joe.

Tom hit it a couple of seconds later, the full impact of his body on the cold glass making it swing open. Snow flew into his mouth and stung his eyes, and as he looked around, frantically, all he could see of Old Joe was a trail in the snow, fast becoming covered by the more recent fall.

"Joe?" he said, stumbling along the trail, to where the dumpster stood, surrounded by a brick wall on three sides—presumably to hide from the customers' minds the ultimate fate of their leftovers.

A happy sort of clack-clack sound, not unlike castanets, made him veer sharp left, into the enclosure and almost step on Joe's tail. "There you are," he said, relieved that Old Joe had gone no further. "You really shouldn't wander off like that. You can have warm burgers inside, why are you—"

He froze as he heard a high-pitched animal battle scream and hiss—and almost ran forward, past Old Joe's front paws, to where he could see a little kitten, just inches from Old Joe's happily clacking snout.

It was orange and fluffy and tiny—maybe eight weeks old. Old enough to have open eyes and stand more or less firmly on spindly legs. Tom felt mingled dread and relief. Relief because he'd had other images in his mind, including a helpless baby shifter dragon. Dread, because instead of running, or jumping on the dumpster—if he could jump—the silly little creature stood facing Old Joe, hair fluffed out all on end, blue eyes blazing. As if it thought it could scare away a huge, armored gator. As Tom watched, it emitted another high-pitched battle scream.

Old Joe lunged. Before his teeth could grab the little creature, Tom stooped and picked it up. "No," he told Old Joe. "This is not dinner." He felt the kitten sink all claws into him, even as Old Joe looked up with a look of intense disappointment in his eyes.

Tom absently held the kitten close to him, hoping that the warmth would mollify him. He didn't dare put him down. Even if he had owners—and it was possible he might, and had only wandered in called by the smell of the diner refuse—what kind of owners let a baby this size walk around outside in a snowstorm? Making his voice stern, he yelled at Old Joe, "Shift. Now. Into human form."

The alligator looked up at him with such a sad look that Tom expected it to start crying. A different type of crocodile tears, Tom guessed. He cleared his throat, to avoid showing weakness, and said, "Now. You have no business being out here shifted. You know what kind of trouble Kyrie and I could get into if they found you. Do you want us to get in trouble?"

The alligator shook his head, earnestly.

"Right. Then shift," he said, and averted his eyes from the vagrant's form, as it writhed and twisted, from crocodile to human.

"Better," Tom said. "Now stay. Don't you dare shift again or wander off." Aware that the poor creature was naked, he darted inside, grabbed the discarded sweats, and brought them out.

Old Joe put them on, with the expression of a school child obeying an unreasonable taskmaster. He looked resentfully at Tom from under lank clumps of steel-grey hair. "It's tasty. It's been too long since I've eaten an animal."

Tom shuddered. "You're not going to eat this one, either," he said, firmly, holding and sheltering the orange fluffball in his hands. The kitten had started cleaning himself, in affronted dignity, as though to let Tom know he could take care of himself fine, thank you so much.

Old Joe didn't say anything else about it. He gave Tom a half-amused, half-sad look. Though his eyes could be called brown, they had faded as much as the rest of him, so that they looked even more pitiful and washed out. The grey sweat suit—picked up at the thrift store down the street and faded and washed out as it was—looked like a scream of color on the small, short body. As Old Joe stood up, he never straightened to his full five feet or so of height. Instead he stooped forward, bent, and shuffled along.

Tom shifted his hold on the kitten, and held Old Joe's arm, as he led him inside.

"Walk better as a gator," the man said in a raspy voice, tainted with an undefinable accent.

"Undoubtedly," Tom said, maneuvering to open the door, without dropping either of his charges. "But alligators are not native to the Rockies, and if anyone sees you, they'll call animal control. And then what are we supposed to do?"

Old Joe nodded, but Tom wondered how much he understood of his speech. Most of the time Old Joe's hold on reality was thread-thin, no more than a dime's edge worth of awareness. Sometimes, though, when he spoke, Tom glimpsed . . . he wasn't sure what. Perhaps the man that Old Joe had once been—sharp and incisive, bordering on the acerbic. And sometimes, sometimes, he seemed old and wise and world weary, but very much intelligent and capable of logical thought.

The thing was, you just never knew which Old Joe you had. It could be the wise old man or the crazy old codger. His shifting between an alligator and a human wasn't nearly as confusing as that. At least that you could tell. What went on inside his mind wasn't nearly as obvious.

Tom led him inside and to the booth, and said "Stay," then ducked behind the counter, to ask Keith to get a burger started. He cursed himself, inwardly. He'd given the old man clam chowder, because he'd been thinking he'd be cold, of course. But the thing was, he'd just shifted, so of course he'd gone outside, in search of protein. "Make that a triple," he said.

Keith looked at him, as he threw three patties on the grill. "Hungry?"

"Not for me. Old Joe. Bring it to the table when you're done."

"Sure," Keith said.

Tom went back to the booth, where he'd left Old Joe. He didn't want to leave the old man alone too long, for fear he'd shift and escape outside again. At a guess, Tom imagined the only reason he'd managed to get away unnoticed is that there hadn't been anyone seated close enough to him to see him. But three more tables had gotten filled up since then, and while they were too far away to hear him, they had full view of the table. And Tom had no idea how to convince spectators that all twelve people at those tables had hallucinated a man changing shapes into an alligator.

So instead, he slid into the pockmarked green vinyl seat across from Old Joe, who looked up at him, suddenly, with startlingly focused eyes. "They're here, you know?" he said. "They're in town."

"Who is in town?" Tom asked. Through his mind, like a scrolling list, went the names of everyone that Old Joe might be referring to: the Great Sky Dragon's people; whoever had killed the people at the aquarium; some unspecified group that hated shifters.

"Them," he said, and shrugged. "You know, the Ancient Ones."

And all of a sudden, either dredged from memory or created by his mind on the spot, Tom had a comic book cover in his mind, showing the Greek gods in full array and under them the words "The Ancient Ones."

He sighed. "Right." In the morass of Old Joe's mind, who knew what was true and what wasn't. And now the kitten was asleep on Tom's palm, as Tom shielded him with his other hand, so that Old Joe wouldn't see him and get hungry. "Right."

At that moment, Keith dropped the burger in front of Old Joe, who grabbed it as if he'd been lost in a burgerless desert for centuries. "Sorry," Tom said, in an undertone. "I should have remembered you'd need protein. It was stupid of me. No wonder you changed."

Old Joe shook his head, as emphatically as the alligator had, near the dumpster. "That's not why I changed," he said. "It was the Ancient Ones. I can't take them like this. They might kill me, you know?" His eyes gave Tom an appraising look from under the long grey hair. "You know what they're like."

"Actually," Tom said, "I don't." He wondered if Old Joe was talking about something real or something out of his nightmares.

Old Joe devoured the burger, with its bun and pickles, in fast, ravenous bites, all the more surprising because his teeth appeared to be broken and stained, and possibly moss-covered. How old was he? Tom had heard—and had observed in his own years on the street—how hard a life like that could be on people. When you threw in the alcoholism and drug use that plagued people on the streets, how likely was it that Old Joe was no more than middle-aged? Forty. Maybe fifty.

On the other hand, Old Joe was a shifter. So was Tom. And through five years of sleeping outside and roughing it through horrible winters, and working at the roughest manual labor, and shooting up and smoking and eating any amount of drugs . . . Tom had never managed to look his age, let alone unnaturally aged. At twenty-one, he looked closer to eighteen, except for the dark shadow of beard on his face. Even with his five o'clock shadow, he still got carded every time he tried to buy a beer. So Old Joe could not have aged all that fast, could he? Not unless he'd come up with some pinnacle of self-destructiveness that Tom had left untouched. And that, Tom found very hard indeed to believe.

But then again, perhaps alligators aged differently from dragons.

How was Tom to know? The problem, he thought, as Old Joe demolished the burger, is that he knew so few shifters. Not enough to give him a statistical universe, truly.

He adjusted his hands, trying to remove one, to rub at his forehead, and stopped short when the kitten emitted a vaguely threatening purr and put out a paw to hold Tom's hand in place. He was so much like Kyrie, asleep, on the sofa, putting out a hand to hold Tom back when he tried to walk off, that Tom smiled. A smile that died quickly, when he heard Old Joe say, in an almost singsong voice, "They want to kill you, you know?"

It was all Tom could do, not to look over his shoulder at where Conan was talking to a customer. "Who?" he asked, instead. "The Ancient—"

Old Joe nodded. "You see, they formed"—he wrinkled his forehead—"many years ago." He waved a hand with short, broken, dirty nails. "To punish those who hurt shifters. And to create a law for shifters. And they know about the deaths. At the castle." His voice was raspy, and he looked one way and another as if to make sure he couldn't be overheard.

"Many years ago?"

"Before cars. Or airplanes or . . . gaslight." His eyes seemed to be looking far away into the past. "Or horses."

"I see."

"I was young, you know? And they said that shifters needed rules and laws to protect them, and to rule themselves, that they needed to defend themselves against the others . . . the ones who would hunt them. And then they formed a . . . a group."

"I see. And why do you think this group is after us? Just because so many young shifters died?"

Old Joe shook his head, then shrugged. "He came to me, when I was outside. Dante Dire did. He came to me. He's the . . . killer for the Ancient Ones, the . . . how do you call it, when someone kills the condemned for a king? The executioner!" He looked very proud of himself for having come up with the word. "That's what he is. He punishes those who hurt shifters. And he came to me and said that many young and blameless shifters had died, and that it was all your fault, and . . . yours and . . . your girl and the policeman. And he wanted to know your names."

"How could he know we did it, and not know our names?"

"He can feel it. Many people can. Well, ancient shifters can."

"And he wanted to know who we were?"

"Yeah. He tried to get me to change," Old Joe squinted. "But I wouldn't. And then, you know, your manager came out, and he went away, but I was hit with a cantaloupe."

Tom tried to think through the confusion of articles, then shook his head. It didn't matter if it was all a dream of Old Joe's. Or rather, of course it did, since dreams couldn't possibly kill them, and real, pissed-off shifters on a rampage could. But . . . but for now, not knowing to which aspect of Old Joe he was addressing himself, he had to treat the thing as if it were deadly serious. "Is there some way they could figure out who we are? Since you didn't tell him? And why did he come to you?"

"He didn't come to me," Old Joe said, somewhat defensively. "He came to the diner because of the smell that attracts shifters, you know. And then he figured this is where all shifters came. And he recognized me. So he asked. I didn't tell him." He folded his gnarled hands in front of him, on the formica table, looking for all the world like a schoolboy who expects a reward, then looked up and smiled a little. "I wouldn't worry. You're safe. I saw Dante Dire again, just a little later. When your girl and that policeman . . . what's his name? When they went out, he got in a car and followed them." He patted Tom's hand, reassuringly. "So, you see, you are safe."

Tom didn't feel at all reassured.

"So . . . what have we learned, children?" Kyrie said, in a singsong voice, as she dressed herself in the chilly bathroom. "We've learned that shifters piss."

She and Rafiel had gone all over the aquarium. Much to her chagrin, she had confirmed Rafiel's smelling of a shifter around the aquarium and up the stairs to the little observation area over the shark tank, where the smell became far more intense, as though the shifter had lingered there.

But that was all she'd learned. The only thing she could contribute—as she walked out of the ladies' room, to meet the again-human Rafiel, outside his bathroom—marked salmon, according to some bizarre logic where all salmons were male, she guessed—was, "I could smell it strongest in the ladies' room."

"Really?"

"Really. So I'm guessing that shifters piss," she said, with an attempt at a smile.

But Rafiel frowned at her, as though lost in intense thought. "And that it's a female."

Kyrie immediately felt like slapping her forehead. That hadn't even occurred to her. "Or that. Or of course, it comes in after hours and isn't sure whether it's shad roe or salmon. Not that I can blame him . . . er . . . her . . . it there."

This got her a very brief smile. "I'm more worried that it lives here."

"What do you mean . . . Oh. You mean one of the sharks?"

He nodded. "I tried smelling the covering to the tank at the top, where they open to feed them and to go in and clean, but couldn't smell anything. Hell, the smell through half of this place is faint. But I think I detect a trace of whatever it is they use to clean the aquariums with, and I wonder . . ."

"But wouldn't they go nuts, staying shifted and in the aquarium the whole time?" Kyrie asked.

Rafiel shrugged. "I have no idea. Truly. You see . . . sometimes I think that if I lived somewhere in Africa, I'd just walk out one day into the savannah, and become a lion, and never, ever, ever change back."

Kyrie stared at him, shocked. She'd always thought of the three of them, Rafiel was the best adjusted. He had a family who knew what he was and collaborated in hiding him. He had the job he wanted to have, the job he'd dreamed about as a little boy. If anything he'd seemed in danger of being conceited and full of himself, not lost and full of doubt. But as he said those words, she felt as if he'd undressed. His expression had for a moment become innocent and vulnerable, making him look like a confused young man faced with something he couldn't understand nor deny.

"Never mind," he said, and managed a little smile. "It's just sometimes it's so hard being both, you know, living between worlds. I've tried to be human, and I can't—not all the time. And it just occurred to me, if I could *just* be a lion—be a lion all the time and stop . . . stop thinking like a human, stop caring about what humans think . . . it would be easier."

There were many things Kyrie wanted to say. That she understood—though she wasn't sure she did. She relished her rationality too much to let it go in exchange for a promise of simpler thinking. That she felt for him. That she could think of what it all must mean to him. But instead, what came out of her lips, was, "There's always the zoo."

As soon as she heard it, she was afraid he would be offended. And that was a heck of a thing to do to him, anyway. He'd just revealed an inner part of himself—at least she didn't think he was playacting, though with Rafiel, it was sometimes pretty hard to tell—and she'd answered with a joke.

To her surprise, he gurgled with sudden laughter. "Oh, yes . . . But if I couldn't control the changing even then, it could get a little embarrassing, no? Not to mean dangerous, right there in the feline enclosure."

"Yes," she said. Then changed the subject quickly. "But you think one of the sharks might have done it?"

Rafiel shrugged. "It still doesn't make any sense, does it? I mean, they get fed, as sharks. Why would she . . . or whatever . . . feel a need to come out and push humans into the tank?"

"Perhaps she has a taste for human flesh," Kyrie said. "Or perhaps there was someone who saw her shift, and had to be eliminated."

The refrain in Tom's mind had changed to *oh shit, oh shit, oh shit*, and he jumped up from the seat. Kyrie and Rafiel were being stalked by someone called the executioner for whatever the Ancient Ones were.

He ducked into the storage room and dialed Kyrie on his cell phone. There was no answer. It rolled over much too fast, in fact. He bit his tongue, thinking. Kyrie never charged her cell phone. Which meant, he had to get to her—somehow.

Oh, maybe Old Joe was dreaming it all up, but this seemed a bit complex, and the man's hesitations about time and place were much too realistic, and unless Old Joe's dreams came in technicolor and surround sound, Tom didn't think it was a dream at all. No. Tom thought that Old Joe was somehow trying to reassure him and claim loyalty points for not having turned him in.

Had he not turned them in? Who knew. Maybe he had. Or maybe he had turned Kyrie and Rafiel in. His primary loyalty seemed to be to Tom, who fed him and looked after him. Everyone else was a distant concern. He might care for Kyrie because Tom did. On the other hand, Kyrie thought that Tom encouraged Old Joe to hang around, and endangered them, and she made no secret of her feelings.

Tom came out of the storage room and dove behind the counter, kitten in hand. "Here," he told Keith, handing over the small, orange fluffball, and ripping off his apron over his head.

"What am I supposed to do with him?" Keith asked, holding the puzzled creature, who was meowing and hissing at having his sleep disturbed. "No matter how much Old Joe wants him, I'm not grilling him."

"No," Tom said. "He's not dinner. Just put him somewhere. I have to go out . . . uh . . . for a few minutes. I'll be right back, I swear."

Keith looked closely at the kitten who was wearing the universal kitten expression that means *let them come, all together or single file. I have my claws.* "How am I supposed to keep him from wandering around? Let me tell you how many health violations—"

"Oh, I'm sure. But if we let him go, Old Joe is likely to eat him. Just tie him up or something. Some sort of a leash."

"A leash? A cat?" Keith asked, in the vaguely horrified voice of someone who's just been instructed to confront a savage creature.

"Well, something," Tom said. "Please? And mind the place. I need to go out. Truly." He looked doubtfully at the kitten trying to claw at Keith. "Give him some food or something. Cats stay where they're fed, right?" And to Keith's look of incredulity, "Look, just try."

Tom had wanted a pet. The closest he'd come to having a pet was having fish. But those were more like animated swimming plants, as far as he was concerned. From the ages of five to ten, he had spent hours dreaming of various pets, from cats to horses. But his parents' lifestyle did not include time for animals. Truth be told, it barely included time for Tom. So he didn't have much idea what one did with pets, beyond a vague idea you told them what to do and they did it. At least, that seemed to be the interaction of owner and dog that he observed at various parks and in various streets. Except perhaps in the matter of bodily functions, dogs pretty much obeyed. It was all go here, come here, and stay. And by and large, the various mutts did. Surely cats couldn't be that much different. He had a lurch of doubt when he realized that save for a very old lady with a hairless cat on a leash, he'd never seen a cat be walked. "Er . . . just don't let him poop anywhere, okay?"

"Right . . ." Keith said in that tone of voice that indicated that as soon as Tom left the diner, he was calling the men in white coats to go after him. And Tom thought he very well might, but it didn't matter. He ran down the hallway to the back door, and out in the blinding storm where, more by instinct than by sight, he found the car where Kyrie had parked it. Fishing in his pocket, he found the car keys. He undressed, shivering under the snow and shoved his clothes and shoes into the car trunk, and shut it with a resounding thud, even as he felt his skin bunch and prickle with cold. He hooked the keys to a link in a bracelet that Kyrie had made for him. It was silver, but made of the sort of elastic weave—somewhat like chain mail but not really—that adjusted to his changes in size as he shifted from man to dragon and back again.

A brief thought of Conan came to him, with a sharp stab of annoyance. Don't let Conan see him. Don't let Conan realize he was gone. The last thing he needed, right now, was Conan's intervention, or to have to drag Conan with him on this dangerous expedition. Conan was a complication he didn't need. He wished with all his strength, with everything he could, that the Red Dragon shifter wouldn't realize he was gone until Tom was well away.

And then he forced his body—unwilling and fighting and screaming with pain and begging for more time to recover—into the series of spasmodic coughs and twists that changed the shape of bones and muscles, and made wings grow from the middle of the shoulders.

Wings that spread and flapped, once—twice—powerfully, lifting the dragon aloft in the blinding snow.

"Nasty way of getting rid of your exes," Rafiel said. And shook his head. "Or of course, perhaps we are completely wrong. The smell wasn't continuous. At least for me, it wasn't. You?"

"No, I couldn't follow it from the bathroom to the shark tank. Also, I thought there was a faint trail in the jellyfish and crab area, and all the way to the seafood restaurant." Which she privately thought was the height of bad taste to have attached to an aquarium, though right now, after shifting, those fishies in the tanks were starting to look startlingly like protein packs with incidental fins. "But it wasn't truly contiguous, and it . . . well, it didn't feel quite the same to me. I'd say there were two trails. Maybe three."

It was only as she saw the sudden look of alarm cross Rafiel's face, that Kyrie realized this was probably not the right thing to say.

"Three?" he said. "Are you sure?"

She shrugged. "Rafiel," she said, unable to fully keep her impatience out of her voice. "You know very well that you are the best sniffer of us all, when it comes to shifter-scent. I can only tell you what I smell . . . and it's probably less than you can sniff out."

But he shook his head, and swallowed hard. "No, the problem is that when you said it, it made sense, it clicked. Not one interrupted trail, but three trails. What the hell does that mean? A cabal of shifters, ready to kill people at the aquarium? What are we looking at here? A mob of shifters who have turned on all non-shifters? A shifter religion sacrificing the non-shifters?"

Kyrie shrugged. "Or just, perhaps, three people who happen to be shifters and who walked through the aquarium."

Rafiel grimaced, but nodded. "Oh, perhaps you are right. Perhaps I'm paranoid, but . . ."

"But our situation encourages paranoia?" she said. "Hiding from the world, unable to reveal what we are. Even in this multi-culti time, when every minority gets a pass simply for being a minority, we will never, ever, get such a pass. Because we are . . . dangerous?"

Another grimace that might have been an attempt at a smile. "I was going to say that sometimes paranoia is right, however little we like to admit it."

"Uh." Kyrie shrugged. "I would say we have insufficient data to say."

She started walking away from the bathroom area, and out of the monitors and clearly fake, Victorian-looking submarine hardware area, towards the stairs. The stairs were broad and spiral and surrounded by glass—giving them rather the look of an aquarium designed to contain people.

"Come on, Rafiel," she said, staring out at the blizzard's magnificent raging whiteness. She would guess during one of Colorado's many unclouded days, one would have a magnificent view from here of the city of Goldport, such as it was, sprawling at the base of the Rockies. Now you couldn't even see the office tower across the street. It was just white and more white, blowing and swirling as far as the eye could see.

And just as she thought this, she realized she was wrong—because in the middle of the storm, a flash of green and gold showed, at her eye level, three stories up from the ground.

"What the—" Rafiel blurted out from behind her. "Is that—"

And in the next second, Kyrie was sure that that was indeed her errant boyfriend in dragon form, because Tom, all of him, emerged from the storm, as close to the glass as he could fly and not crash into it. His expression looked alarmed as he stared in at them. If alarmed at his proximity to the glass, or with flying in a storm, or something else, it was hard to tell.

There was just a flash of terrified blue eyes, the dragon's mouth open in silent protest. And then . . . Tom flying away.

"Tell me he didn't just fly here through the storm to check on us?" Rafiel said.

And part of Kyrie wanted to tell him exactly that, except it depended on what Rafiel meant by checking on them. Kyrie was willing to bet that Tom wasn't jealous of their being out, alone, together. She was willing to bet that, because Tom had all but encouraged them to go out, even Tom wasn't that . . . paranoid as to change his mind so quickly. Besides . . . besides, if he didn't know he'd won that contest and won it for good, then Kyrie would give up on the whole relationship right now.

But it had looked to Kyrie exactly as though Tom had been checking up on them. Not in jealousy or fear that they were about to betray him, but in confused fear for them . . . Fear of something happening to them.

Where had he got that idea? And was he right?

Flying in the snow was far easier to talk about than to do. The part of

Tom that remained Tom at the back of the dragon's brain was fairly sure that the dragons—if they'd ever existed except as shifters—could never have been creatures of cold climates.

A string of complaints came from the dragon's body, penetrating Tom's mind. Cold might make him ache less, but cold hurt by itself. And he couldn't see. And the wings got no traction against this air laden with snow, which kept accumulating on their broad and outspread surface, thereby multiplying the cold and the lack of movement.

It felt as though the dragon's wings and his toes would presently freeze so absolutely that they would fall off, like so many enigmatic pieces of flesh raining on urban Goldport. Rain of dragon parts. That would be a new one at least. Forget rains of fish.

And yet, Tom's mind, deep within, like an implacable rider on a restive horse, insisted with all his will power that they must—*must*—go to Kyrie. They must protect her. And Rafiel too. The big lump might have been Tom's rival at some point. He was still, doubtlessly, a big lump. Also, generally speaking, a pain in the behind, always appearing so relaxed and laid back and comfortable with himself, while Tom most of the time felt that his personality and mind were sort of like one of those statues kindergartners sculpt: made of itty bits and pieces too mishandled to ever cling together properly, and forming no more than a suggestion of a shape, rather than the shape itself. But still, Rafiel was a friend. Pain or not, he would stand—had stood by Tom—when it was down to kill or be killed. And also, Tom suspected, deep within, Rafiel was a more honorable man and a more noble one than he liked to admit even to himself.

Be it how it may, Kyrie was Tom's girlfriend and Rafiel was one of his very few friends. They would not be allowed to stand alone as they faced whatever and whoever that executioner creature might be.

His purpose impelling him, he flew as fast as he could through downtown, sometimes descending to the top level of the high buildings, where the houses and offices formed a sort of sheltered canyon. He wondered if someone would see him, out of a window or a door—or rather if they'd see the suggestion of a dragon flying in the storm. He wondered what cryptozoology rumors would rise from it—like the Lizard Man in Denver, or all those black panthers and black dogs that appeared everywhere.

By the time he reached the aquarium, minutes later, he'd almost convinced himself that Old Joe had dreamed the whole thing. It was all a nightmare conjured from the old shifter's brain and whatever memories remained in that confused amalgam of personality. There would be no one there with Rafiel and Kyrie, and he would be in trouble with Kyrie for having left the diner for no reason at all. He almost looked forward to that monumental scolding, because if Kyrie was scolding him, that would mean that she was all right. And that all his fears were unfounded.

And yet, dipping towards the parking lot of the aquarium, as he approached, to check how many people might be within and if he might have to shift form and hide, before he exposed them all, Tom saw that Rafiel's big, black SUV was not alone there. Parked just across from it—in what might have been, had the lines under the snow been visible, the immediately opposing space—was a low-slung Italian sports car.

Tom-the-dragon blinked at the red car, in confusion. It looked like a dormant beast that would, at any minute, fling up and fly or attack. Definitely attack, judging by the look of the vehicle.

Perhaps it is the car of an aquarium employee, said Tom's more reasonable human mind.

Right. Right, Tom's unreasonable human mind answered. *I'm absolutely sure it is. Scientists and fish-feeders often own cars that look like that.*

Well, the place has a restaurant, too. Perhaps it's the car of the owner.

To this, even the doubting Thomas within could not have interposed any serious rebuttal. Instead, it settled into a non-verbal response—a prickling at the back of Tom's long dragon neck . . . a feeling of uneasiness in the pit of his stomach. And it was no use at all his telling himself that he was being silly. He flew around the building and thought he caught a glimpse of Rafiel and Kyrie on the third-floor stairway, but it was not something he could swear to. The glass was thick and curved, and probably designed to ensure the privacy of those within at the expense of the curiosity of those without.

He flew around again, hoping they would come out, because then he could change and warn them. But there was nothing, except a suggestion of movement in a room where the aquariums seemed filled with the spindly forms of crabs. Tom had visited the aquarium with Keith once, a month ago—because one of Keith's would-be girlfriends worked there—and seemed to remember just such a room, right next to the restaurant. He and Keith had joked that the crabs were all probably terminally neurotic and tormented by dreams of drawn butter. But the movement—what seemed like a woman or a small man flitting around a corner was too brief to make sense of.

And yet, he worried. What if the executioner, whoever he was, was already inside, getting ready to ambush Kyrie and Rafiel around the corner of some tank, or push them into the shark tank? What could Tom do from out here?

He decided to land somewhere and shift, then see if he could break into the aquarium. In his misspent years as a transient, he'd often broken into places. Mostly into cars, when he absolutely needed transportation for a short period of time. Sometimes, into garden sheds, carriage houses or garages, in the coldest nights, to get some protection from the weather.

He'd never stolen anything in those break-ins and he'd felt positively virtuous about that, until Kyrie had made him understand the damage he caused, however minimal, still disturbed the lives of innocents.

Still, he had experience breaking into places. Granted, a garden shed was bound to have a flimsier lock than . . . well, a municipal aquarium, even—or perhaps particularly—a municipal aquarium run by a seafood restaurant chain. But all the same, he should be able to break in. And he should be able to find Kyrie and Rafiel. And warn them. Before they got pushed into the shark tank.

He took a half-circle flight away from the windows, looking for a place to land and shift, where he would be less likely to be seen from nearby buildings. This objective was made only slightly more difficult because he could not see into any of the buildings around, and therefore could not tell if anyone might be looking out of a window, and have enough visibility to survey the parking lot of the aquarium. He kind of doubted it, though.

His memories of the location of the aquarium, gathered during his visit, in sunnier—if briskly cold—weather, was that it sat on a corner, bordering two fairly well-traveled streets—Ocean Street, where the aquarium's postal address was—and Congregation Avenue, which led straight to the convention center in less than a mile. On the other side of those roads were office buildings. The chances of anyone being in one of those buildings, on a snowy evening, were very low. In fact, possibly, nonexistent. He'd just land somewhere.

Down below him, in the parking lot, a car door banged. Somehow, in his mind, a voice echoed—not the Great Sky Dragon's voice, but a voice just as immense, just as overpowering—*Hey, Dragon Boy!* it said. *Come and be killed.*

Tom looked down. By the Italian sports car stood a slim, dark-haired man, his head thrown back in defiance. He was naked, but he didn't seem to either realize it or care. He wore his nudity like others wore expensive suits. His head tilted up, he favored Tom with a wide and feral smile. *What is it, little one? Afraid of me? I'll take you in fair combat. As fair as it can be when pitting an adult against an infant.*

Tom wasn't afraid—at least the dragon Tom had become wasn't afraid. The human, locked within the dragon's mind was not afraid either, or not exactly. He was not afraid of that creature down there, even if he was the vaunted executioner. For all he knew, the man would also change into a dragon, and come after him. And then he might be afraid. And then he might find a reason to kill this creature. But not yet.

And he didn't react to the voice in his head, as he had first reacted to a similar intrusion by the Great Sky Dragon. Finding someone in your mind once—like any other type of event that is supposed to be impossible but isn't—could hurtle anyone into a panic. The human mind was an amazing instrument, though. The second time of someone *speaking* in his mind didn't make Tom feel as violated, or as scared. It was just a voice. Just a voice in his mind. Nothing more.

He took a slow pass over the parking lot, looking down at the person standing by the car. All too human and weak-looking. If Tom was worried about anything, it was not the possibility this person might kill him. No, it was the fear that he might kill this person.

For years, while Tom was a transient, without friends or a fixed place, one fear had pursued Tom relentlessly: the fear that he would shift and lose self-control, and kill someone. It had been his first fear when he'd shifted into a dragon.

And he'd managed to control it—most of the time. The only people he'd ever killed were shifters who were trying to kill him. And even then, if there had been another way, he'd have used another way to stop them. He didn't think he'd ever eaten anyone—not even in the drug-haze days of his past.

He didn't want to kill anyone now. Not even this creature—whether or not he was the executioner that Old Joe had gone on about. Tom swooped again, around the man, slightly lower, trying to think of what to do.

His instincts told him he should leave now, but if he did he would leave Kyrie and Rafiel unprotected. *That* he couldn't do. That would negate his coming here to protect them. He had to, at least, warn them.

He swooped down again, closer. There had to be something he could do, without killing the man. Grab him by an arm and throw him away from the aquarium, perhaps. Then, while he took time to return—or while he shifted into a dragon and came after Tom, Tom would have a chance to warn Kyrie and Rafiel.

But as Tom got close, he saw the man was smoking a cigarette, completely impassive, disregarding the huge dragon closing in on him.

Tom could have bit off his head with a single motion. He could have rent it from his body with his claws. But he couldn't do either, not to a defenseless-seeming human.

Instead, he flew by so close the tip of his wing almost touched the man, but he sheared off, sharply, and executed a circle, coming back, still aware that he couldn't kill the man—that his own self-control wouldn't allow it—but hoping, hoping against hope that the man would be scared.

Oh, are we playing a game? a laughing voice asked in his mind. And suddenly Tom had no control over his body. None. He fell from the sky, like a pebble, unable to stop himself.

Hurtling towards the parking lot, Tom saw the man shift. Not into a dragon. The creature who stood in the parking lot hadn't been seen on Earth for millennia uncountable. Tom recognized it, immediately, from its display in Denver's Natural History Museum, though. It was a dire wolf: tall of shoulder, massive of bone, its teeth huge, unwieldy daggers flashing in the light.

And in that moment he regained control of his body, enough control at least, to tumble to an ungraceful semi-stop, skidding on his tail on the frozen ground.

The creature sprang, with a lightness that belied his size. A sharp pain stabbed into Tom's awareness, and his wing was seized and ripped. He turned, claw raised, ready to strike, but the dire wolf had moved, quickly, more quickly than should be possible, and bit hard on Tom's wrist. Only Tom's last-second recoil prevented him from ripping out Tom's throat. The yellow eyes of the monster shone with unholy glee amid grey fur, and Tom would have flown away— maimed wing and blood-dripping paw. But he couldn't. Kyrie and Rafiel were in there. They could be coming out any moment. What would this monster do to them?

"What the—!" Kyrie said, as she came through the door, and saw Tom being attacked by a creature out of a museum's diorama. For a moment that was all she could think, her mind seemingly frozen on that point—wondering if she was dreaming, if all those visits to the museum had finally affected her sanity, as she told Tom they were bound to. The museum was his favorite haunt, when they took a day off to go to Denver, and sometimes she felt as though she could have drawn every display from memory—including the broken places in the bassilosaurus skeleton.

She heard a soft growl at her side. Rafiel. A look at the policeman showed him, by touch, without even seeming to notice, stripping off his clothes.

And Kyrie, feeling the shift shudder through her, as she stared at the unlikely creature striking at her boyfriend, thought that this creature moved like nothing she'd ever seen. His movement was like a special effect, where the movie editors cut and pasted frames without regard, so that they displaced someone from one place to the other, without moving them the intervening distance. She was sure this was not what was happening, but the effect was rather as though the creature teleported from one place to the next instantly. And it was biting, rounding on Tom, and slashing, rending, always attacking.

Rafiel, already in lion form—tawny and sleek and large, though not half the size of the creature battling Tom—rushed into the battle, his mane snow-flecked. And Kyrie charged, right behind.

It was folly, her human mind said, sheer folly, to rush like this into battle with a creature that seemed supernatural in its movements. But what else could she do?

The creature teleported towards Rafiel—materializing right in front of him, Tom's blood dripping from the huge dagger teeth, a look of unholy amusement in the slitlike yellow eyes. It lunged at Rafiel and it was clear from the movement that it meant to take Rafiel by the throat, or perhaps to bite his neck in two, killing him in one of the few ways a shifter could be killed.

But as the massive-fanged mouth opened, Tom leapt, and bit the creature sharply on the hind quarters, causing it to close its jaws just above Rafiel's neck, barely touching him with its fangs.

And now Tom was raking what seemed to be a badly bleeding paw across the creature's flanks and making a high, insane hiss of challenge.

And Kyrie, who could see that the creature's eyes were—startlingly—more amused than scared, jumped in, her fur ruffled, growling low in the back of her throat.

The creature rounded on her, ignoring Tom's attack on its exposed flank and pinning Rafiel, casually, beneath a massive paw. It sniffed at Kyrie and the slitted yellow eyes looked more unholy and more amused than ever. *Hello, pretty kitten girl. It would be a shame to kill you, wouldn't it?*

The voice, in her mind, made her jump. She knew it was this creature in front of her, and not the Great Sky Dragon, but she suddenly understood why Tom had reacted as he did to the dragon in his mind. She heard a keen of not quite pain escape the panther's throat and she felt what seemed like a dirty finger rifling quickly through her mind. *Interesting mind, Kitten. Better defended than Lion Boy's.* The feel of unholy laughter. *But not by much.*

And then, suddenly, there was a streak of red from above, and a thing that looked much like a falling boulder through the snow resolved itself into Red Dragon, flying in.

It roared something that sounded much like "No," or as close to the word "no" as a dragon's mouth could form. And in the next moment it landed in front of the dire wolf. Kyrie expected the wolf to port away or to attack, but he didn't do either. Instead, he stood in place, looking confused.

Red Dragon let out a stream of flame at the dire wolf, just as Kyrie wondered why Tom hadn't done so. And the dire wolf wasn't there.

What sounded much like "spoilsport," echoed in her mind, and the dire wolf seemed to be quite gone, though they couldn't tell where. Moments later, a sound that seemed disturbingly like human laughter floated from the place where it had retreated.

For Tom it all went too fast. First, he was fighting a creature that seemed to be everywhere at once. His only hope was to take to the sky, but before he could—his bleeding wing, hurting every time he moved, threw off his balance—the creature struck him again. And again. At both front paws, and back paw.

And slowly it dawned on Tom that if the dire wolf could strike him like this, at will, and wherever it chose, then it could have killed him. That it wasn't killing him should have been a relief, but it wasn't. Because he had a feeling that the creature was playing with him the way cats play with mice.

And then there was Rafiel, who seemed to appear out of nowhere, and Tom wanted to yell at him and Kyrie to run, but the dragon throat didn't work properly and he couldn't give them the warning in a way that they could understand. And the only thing for it was for him to intervene and save Rafiel from the dire wolf, even though it probably would mean Tom would die for it. But he'd come to save Kyrie and Rafiel, and he was going to do it, if it was his last action on Earth.

He launched himself at the dire wolf, biting and scratching where he could reach. And then . . .

And then the creature sniffed Kyrie—at least it seemed like that to Tom, through the red mist his vision had become—and then . . . and then there was Conan. Conan had flamed towards the dire wolf, making Tom wonder why he, himself, hadn't. What was wrong with him? He'd sat here and let the creature maul him, with hardly any attempt at defense. Certainly without using his main weapon. Why?

And then the creature fled and there had been a suggestion of mocking laughter in Tom's mind. He stood, under the snow, bleeding, shivering, wondering if the creature was gone for good, or it was waiting for Tom to shift, if it was waiting for Tom to become more vulnerable, if—

"Shift, Tom," Kyrie said. "Now. You can't get in the car as a dragon."

"You left without me—" Conan was saying, clearly already shifted. "You left without me. Do you know what Himself would have done to me if you had died?"

"Shut up, Conan," Kyrie's voice, curt. "Tom, shift *now*."

And Tom realized Conan and Rafiel and Kyrie were in the car, and that they had clothes, and Kyrie was dressing in the backseat, and he blinked, once, twice, once the human way, up-down, then the dragon way, his nictating eyelids flickering side to side, then the human way again, and he groaned out loud as his body twisted and bent and . . . shifted.

His muscles were still writhing to proper shape beneath his skin, his scalp tingling as the bones of his skull adjusted, his vision double as his eyes changed, when he flopped into the back seat of the SUV, falling across the scratchy fabric.

Kyrie, mostly dressed, reached across him to shut the car door. As it slapped shut, Rafiel stomped on the gas. The wheels spun a moment, and then they were hurtling out of the parking lot in a guided slide that careened gracefully around a curve and past a—he was sure of it—red light.

"What if he had come back?" Tom asked. "As . . . as a dire wolf? And killed us while we were human and vulnerable?"

"Was that what that was?" Rafiel asked. Incredibly, he seemed to Tom to be dressing and driving at once, through the blinding white snowstorm. Tom blinked, but the impression remained, as Rafiel put on a sleeve of his shirt, while he held the wheel with the other hand and then presumably steered by the force of his imagination while he used both hands to quickly button his shirt. "A dire wolf?"

"Yes," Tom said, throwing himself back against the seat, and straightening as he felt the pain of open wounds at his back. "Oh, damn, I'm bleeding all over your upholstery."

"Never mind that," Rafiel said. "My uncle has a car detail place. Kyrie, would you look under the seat? There's a first aid kit there, and there should be another pair of pants and a shirt, too, besides the ones Conan got. They'll be long on you, Tom, but it's all I have."

"I left clothes, in the trunk of Kyrie's car."

"Of course. You can change into them there, if you prefer . . . I just thought . . ." Rafiel took another corner in a way that appeared to be skating on two tires. "Kyrie? How badly wounded is he?"

Kyrie had turned Tom halfway towards the window. "Gash across the back," she said. "I suppose that's the tissue your wings extrude out of. Looks vicious but it's mostly skin, and the antibiotic cream is stopping the bleeding, I think."

"Should we go to the hospital?" Rafiel asked.

"Not for this, but his hands . . ."

And Tom, who was aware both his hands stung like mad, but also that he could still use them—he'd checked—growled low in his throat. "No hospital. What are we going to tell them? Animal bite? Leave it alone. You know it will heal fast."

"Dragons heal very fast," Conan said quickly, in the sort of singsong voice that denoted he'd learned this somewhere, by rote.

By touch, almost by instinct, Tom reached into the first aid kit, grabbing cotton wool and hydrogen peroxide and a roll of self-clinging bandages, cleaned away the worst of the wounds and started bandaging his left hand with his right. Kyrie started helping him halfway through, and by the time she'd got his left hand neatly bandaged, and snipped the excess bandage, she said, "He'll do, Rafiel. And it should be all right by tomorrow. Will hurt a bit to use his hands, but . . ."

"You'll go to the bed-and-breakfast next to the diner," Rafiel said. "What is it called?"

"Spurs and Lace," Kyrie said. "It's not as kinky as it sounds. I think they thought it was an allusion to the Old West."

"Whatever. Tom, I want you to go to Spurs and Lace and go to bed. I'll man the diner for the rest of your shift."

"Like hell you will," Tom said. "Don't be stupid. You can't handle the new stove and grill. And you don't know anything about cooking or serving, either. And that is if Keith hasn't set the place on fire in the last half hour, because he doesn't know much more than you do." He set his jaw, and caught sight of himself in the rear view mirror and realized with a shock that he looked much like his father in a mood. "I'll do the rest of my shift, thank you very much. We'll see if Anthony can come in tomorrow morning, and if not we'll call our backups till someone makes it in. There was that woman—Laura Miller?—who applied last week. We could always give her a chance."

Rafiel seemed confused. He cleared his throat. "But you'll be in pain," he said. "And I . . ." He cleared his throat again. "I owe you my life."

Tom shrugged. "So, shut up and drive."

"I think," Kyrie said, "you should at least go to Spurs and Lace for a few minutes and shower. At least if they have a room and they should. They usually have rooms during the week. On the weekend they get all booked up with romantic couples or whatever."

Tom sniffed at himself. "All right," he said, realizing he needed to concede on something, and also that fighting a dire wolf had not improved his rather dubious hygiene from this morning.

"Just don't shift in their bathroom," Kyrie said, as she slapped bandages on his back, then handed him a bundle of clothing. "You might as well wear this and take the other clothes to change." And then, quickly, "Tom, why didn't you just call? I mean, you had my cell number, and Rafiel's. I understand you came over to protect us from this—that you knew this . . . creature was after us, somehow, but . . . Why not just call?"

Tom shook his head. "Your phone battery was out, Kyrie. You never remember to charge it."

"Oh," Kyrie said.

"All right," Tom said again as he slipped the rather loose, long pants on. "Rafiel, I want you to come with me."

"What? To shower?" Rafiel asked. "I said thank you already—"

"Feeble," Tom said, rating the joke. "No. So I can talk to you about what sent me out there, and what I think that creature is. Without anyone in the diner listening in."

"I should come," Conan said. "I should listen in. I'm supposed to protect you."

All three of them yelled "No" at the same time, leaving it to Tom to explain, "No offense, Conan, but you're not exactly a friend."

"You hired me! And I was sent by Himself, I—"

"Himself is not exactly a friend, either," Tom said. "At least he hasn't proven himself one."

Conan frowned, wrinkles forming on his forehead, as though he were trying to understand a very difficult concept. "You're a dragon," he said. "You belong to him!"

"Beg your pardon? I don't belong to anyone but myself," Tom said, his voice echoing his father's iciest tones. "In case you haven't heard there was this guy called Lincoln who freed the slaves."

"No," Conan shook his head, looking forlorn. "You don't understand. You're a dragon. You belong to Himself. Like . . . like family."

"Oh, and if you think that's a recommendation or reassuring, I should tell you a bit more about my family," Tom said, grinning impishly. Kyrie smiled at him. "I have never gone out of my way to obey them or to belong to them, either."

Conan opened his mouth, as though to reply, but seemed to realize it would be useless, and frowned slightly, as if he were facing a situation for which no one had prepared him.

"Won't it look weird?" Rafiel asked. "My going in with you, when you're going to get a room and shower?"

"I'm going to get a room for myself and Kyrie, for tonight and tomorrow," Tom said. "Probably three nights, actually. I can't imagine us going home before that. Heck, if we go home before a week, it will be a small miracle. I'll explain in detail what happened to our bathroom. But as for why you're going with me to the room, that's obvious." He raised his bandaged hands. "I was in an accident. We'll let them think it was a car accident. And you want to make sure I'm not going to pass out or anything."

"Oh," Rafiel said.

"And then I can tell you about the dire wolf. If I'm not mistaken, he's the person that Old Joe described as the executioner for the Ancient Ones."

"What did you mean 'executioner'?" Rafiel asked. He leaned against a heavy carved rosewood table in Tom's rented room at Spurs and Lace.

Kyrie must have been right about the crazy idea behind the name. The suite felt like a mashup of Old West and Old Whorehouse. It was bigger than a room, consisting of a bedroom with a queen-size bed, a sofa dripping in velvet and fringe, a dresser that would take five men and a winch to transport, and a hat rack with three cowboy hats on it, and a small sitting area in a projection that was part of a tower, surrounded by windows. The sitting area was outfitted with two too-precious-for-words carved wood armchairs, whose cushions were tormented by a print featuring cowboy boots and roses in random profusion.

Then there was the bathroom, which had a heavy rosewood table facing it. Above the table hung a gold-leaf-framed mirror and above that, on the flowered-wallpaper wall, a pair of spurs.

Rafiel shut his eyes, because you could go nuts trying to make sense of this stuff, and said, "What could he mean by executioner? And why would anyone want to execute us?"

"I think it was the larvae, you know, the ones who died in the fire. Old Joe says the Ancient Ones can feel . . . death on that scale. And that they're looking for the culprits."

"The culprits!" Rafiel heard the sound that came out of his throat, derisive like a cat spitting. "What about the shifters who were being murdered before that?"

"I don't know," Tom sounded exhausted. Rafiel heard the water go off, then the shower curtain close. "Perhaps they think that we did those too."

"And who are they?" Rafiel asked, feeling the anger in his voice and knowing he was projecting his fear into anger and throwing it at Tom. "These Ancient Ones," Rafiel said with less force. "It's pretty absurd to be judged by people you don't know and whose rules you can't understand. Who are they? What do they want?"

Tom came out of the bathroom, fully dressed, though it didn't seem like he'd have had time. He was limping, and his foot showed red slashes across it. Rafiel remembered the dire wolf biting at Tom's back paw.

Tom limped to the bed, sat down, and started putting socks on. "They're a group. I think they're a group of shifters who have lived very long lives."

"Oh?" Rafiel said. "What's very long? And should we be looking for a group then, or just one man?" Something tickled at the back of his mind, but he couldn't quite pinpoint it.

Tom shrugged. "I honestly don't know," he said. "Because, you see ... Old Joe ..." He shrugged again, wincing as he stood tentatively on his wounded foot and looked about for his boot. "Old Joe, you know, is vague. He drifts in and out of reality, and it's hard to tell. He told me that the Ancient Ones were around before horses."

"Before horses evolved? Or before they were domesticated?" Rafiel asked. "Because either way ..."

"It's unlikely? Yeah. I know. That's why I said he's unreliable. And he said that this creature, the dire wolf, had come to town, that he was their executioner, but he didn't say that the rest of them hadn't come too. Or how many there were. For all I know, and presuming that this story is true—and the executioner thing seems to be—then, you know, it could be that we're looking for anything between a busload of shifters as old as time, and two or three sixty-year-old shifters." He shrugged. "I couldn't tell you."

But his words had tickled something in Rafiel's mind. Two or three shifters. "At the aquarium," he said, "Kyrie and I caught at least two different scent trails. Maybe three."

"Oh?" Tom tensed, looking up. "Any of them our friend the wolf?"

Rafiel shook his head. "I don't think so," he said. "At least the smell wasn't right. Though all the scents were so faded ..." He shrugged.

"You know," Tom said, "that's the other choice. No Ancient Ones, no conspiracy of shifters. Just Old Joe going senile, and one homicidal dire wolf shifter." He'd found his boots, and was putting them on. "Who knows how many of us are homicidal? It was always my fear that I'd go that way." Tom's boots were work boots, probably picked up second- or thirdhand at some time when Tom was doing manual labor. But even looking vaguely like weapons of mayhem, they were part of Tom.

Rafiel had seen Tom turn back into high danger to recover them. Lacing them as tightly as that had to hurt his injured foot, but who was Rafiel to interfere with his friend's masochism?

"Unfortunately," Tom said, "I don't think that's it. I don't think it's just Old Joe and our dire acquaintance. When has our life been that easy?"

Kyrie shaved broad swathes off the gyro beef roast rotating on its vertical metal spike, and turned her back to the counter and the customers, to eat with the voracious appetite a recent shift brought on.

The diner had become packed, while she was gone—every table filled, even the table at which she'd first seated Conan. A couple was squeezed together into the too-small booth, cooing and billing and holding warm cups. Keith was working the grill like a pro, though Kyrie noted that he sometimes let things go a little too long, and the edges of omelets were often brown as Tom didn't allow them to be, and the bacon seemed full of burnt crunchy bits. And he was clearly late with the orders.

However, to do Keith justice, that last might not be so much his fault as Conan's. The new waiter, newly returned amid the tables of the packed diner looked much like a fly that had hit the window pane once too many times. He was trying to serve everyone clamoring for his attention and seemed completely lost. That he only had one good arm to hold the serving tray didn't help, as his other arm, at best, helped stabilize things, but could not help with the weight, which meant he carried far less per trip out to the tables than she normally did. The orders were piled on the counter. As Keith turned and put another one down and called out, "Table 23," he seemed to realize the futility of it, saying, "Oh, never mind," and putting five or six orders on a tray, he rushed out to distribute the platters, far faster than Conan seemed able to.

"That little rat you guys hired left me alone while you were gone," Keith said. "I don't know where he went but . . ."

"Don't worry about it," Kyrie said. "He went to help us. We know where he was."

Keith raised his shoulder sulkily, but didn't say anything for a while, till he said sheepishly, "I've kept people quiet," as he returned in what seemed like seconds, to tend to the grill, "by giving them free hot chocolate. I hope that's okay."

"It's fine," Kyrie said.

"Also, of course, there's nothing else open today which helped keep them here."

Kyrie took the point, and having finished a plate of gyro meat, she put the plate with the others collected from tables, and reached under the counter for her apron, intending to go out to clear the backlog as fast as possible. Only her hands, thrust under the counter, met with something like sharp little needles. On her pulling the hands back, the needles withdrew, only to stick her again when she reached out once more, only much less further in than before. "What the—?" she said, reaching out.

"Oh, that's Not Dinner," Keith said, flipping a burger.

"What?" she asked, as she knelt to look in the dark shelf where they kept folded aprons to the left and the time sheets to the right. Golden eyes sparkled back at her, and she looked closer, to make out a little orange ball of fluff making his way very fast to lie possessively atop the time sheets. "It's a kitten."

"Yeah," Keith said. "Not Dinner."

"I don't have the slightest intention of eating him," Kyrie said, upset, as she reached in and managed to retrieve the apron before the avenging claws got her. "You know you can't have your pet here. We're not allowed to have animals, except service animals, on the premises."

"He's not my pet."

Kyrie took a deep breath, deciding everyone had gone mad, and Keith right now was representative of everyone. What on earth could he mean? That the diner was suffering an infestation of cats, like some places had sudden infestations of rats? It didn't bear probing, not now. Grabbing a tray and filling it with orders, and picking up the coffee pot for warmups, she started among the tables, clearing up the backlog.

Many regulars looked happy to see her, and other people just looked happy to get their orders at last. In a few minutes, she had the main of it taken care of and, having directed Conan to start bussing newly emptied tables, returned to fill the dishwasher, restart the coffee, and pursue the interesting matter of a sudden plague of kittens.

Before she could, though, and while she was bent over the dishwasher, filling it with dirty plates, Tom and Rafiel came in, and Tom made an exclamation of distress and touched Kyrie's arm. "Kyrie, where's Old Joe?"

She looked up. "I don't know. Where was he?"

"I left him in booth number five."

"Well, he wasn't here when I came in," she said.

Tom swore under his breath and, at her startled look, said, "Not your fault. He must have gone alligator again. I hope he's not going to go after one of the customers in the parking lot. And I hope we find him, because we need to talk to him."

As he spoke, Tom reached over the grill, as Keith pulled a stack of cooked burgers aside and said, "I made these for you. I figured you'd need them."

"Great thought. Thanks," Tom said, grabbing the burgers and eating one after the other, like a kid with candy. "I'll take over the grill in a moment."

"I gave Not Dinner some milk and a few pieces of hamburger," Keith added.

"Not . . . oh. The kitten," Tom said. "Good."

Kyrie noted that Tom seemed to know about the kitten. In fact, she would bet the kitten was Tom's. Tom and his *strays*! Meanwhile, Rafiel had gone out the back door. He returned in a moment, snow glinting in his hair. "He's not out back, Tom. I can't find him. There's no trail I can see."

Tom took over the grill. "Go attend to the tables," he told Keith. "I'll take care of cooking."

Keith hesitated, and Tom was sure that he was hoping to hear what was going on, but he wanted to talk to Kyrie and he didn't want to leave the tables unattended. "We'll let you in on it," he said. "I promise."

"That's not it," Keith said. "I want to talk to you." He spoke in an undertone, and looked worried. "There's someone . . ."

"Right," Kyrie said from Tom's side. "I'll go do those two tables that just came in."

"So?" Tom said.

"It's this girl . . ."

Tom choked on gurgled laughter at the idea that anyone at all would come to him for romantic advice, but he managed to stop and make his features attentive. "Yes?"

"She's . . . she goes to school with me, and she looks really . . . I don't know how to put this, but I think she's a shifter. That was why I came by today. If I bring her, can you . . . sniff her out?"

Tom looked at him, and felt his brow wrinkle into a frown. "Probably," he said. "Rafiel can for sure. Why do you think she's a shifter?"

Keith shrugged. "I can't quite put my finger on it, but she looks tired in the morning, and . . . you know . . . she talks a lot about strange animals. She had a book on cryptozoology. It just seems . . ."

"Does she change clothes a lot?"

"Not that I've noticed, but . . ." Keith shrugged. "Just a feeling, okay? I've been around you guys enough for that."

"Yeah," Tom said. "Fine." He returned to cooking and, remembering that Rafiel, too, would be having shift-hunger, he grabbed one of the frozen t-bones from the freezer by the grill, and threw it on. His mind was working on the problem he and Rafiel had discussed. The idea of a group or groups of shifters skulking around making decisions about their lives, that they could not possibly anticipate. Did this group have anything to do with the bones in the aquarium? And how could Tom and Kyrie defend themselves from the dire wolf, who seemed capable of teleporting?

They spent the rest of the night watching the door and looking out back around the dumpster, but as far as Tom could tell, both any possible hostiles and the alligator shifter were miles away.

On a normal night there were several lulls, but as the wind howled, fiercer and fiercer outside the diner, rattling gusts of snow against the broad windows and leaving them spattered as if with the spray-snow people used for decorations, customers drifted regularly in and out.

It seemed to Tom, though he didn't look closely at anyone at the tables—kept busy with constant cook orders instead—that some people came in several times during the night. They were probably being kept awake by the wind and the snow, or perhaps the Victorians converted into apartment houses around here weren't exactly airtight and had inadequate heat. Tom remembered staying in many rental rooms and apartments where the temperature, on full-blown heat, never reached above tepid.

The constant stream of orders changed overnight, from burgers to pies and coffee and finally to omelets, eggs and bacon, sausages and hash browns. He felt as if he would never want to smell a cooking egg again in his life, and the pain in his wounded hands—continuously rehurt by his ceaseless work—had gone from a dull throbbing to a barely-keeping-from-screaming burn. He'd sent Kyrie away to rest a couple of hours ago, afraid that if no one else came in to relieve him at the grill he'd have to let Kyrie relieve him, and give her a quick crash course on breakfast dishes on the new stove.

He could have cried with joy when he saw Anthony come in. "It was getting cabin feverish at home," he said, sheepishly. "It's only a one-bedroom apartment. And the wind seems to have died down some, so Cecily fell asleep. You guys can go rest some."

Tom nodded and removed his apron, shoving it under the counter. He was surprised by a sudden feel of pinpricks piercing through his bandages. Looking under the counter, he got a sudden hiss and battle scream from the orange kitten.

He took a quick look over his shoulder at Anthony. He couldn't imagine leaving the kitten behind for Anthony to deal with, so as he grabbed his jacket from under the counter and slipped it on, Tom reached under and grabbed the protesting bundle of kitten and, ignoring the yowls of defiance, slipped it into his pocket.

Kyrie woke up to someone snoring on top of her. In a moment of unique confusion, she thought Tom must have decided to sleep on the bed after all, and he must be snoring, only the snore was so distant and tiny, that it couldn't be Tom. She wondered, momentarily, as she struggled with what seemed to be several tons of gravel on her eyelids, whether Tom could have shrunk, because she felt a very warm and vibrating body—if a very tiny one—laid across the space between her breasts.

Her mind finally added up that these impressions made no sense, and brought her awake with a sudden jar. Her beginning to rise was met with sharp little needles to the chin and, opening her sleepy eyes, she saw a small orange blur. "Uh?" she said, which seemed the height of eloquence just then. She blinked and saw the sun shining fully across the room and onto the bed, and Tom blissfully asleep mostly on and partly off the sofa next to the bed. He had dark shadows under his eyes, and looked paler than usual. He'd taken his boots and socks off in his sleep, allowing her to see the bandage on his foot, and he was sleeping on his side, probably to avoid hurting his injured back.

Kyrie blinked at the kitten on her breasts. "Hello, Not Dinner," she said in a singsong voice. "Are you one of Tom's strays?"

The kitten purred and licked first one paw, then the other. Kyrie had to admit he was handsome, "In a conceited male feline sort of way." She put her hand out to his tiny head and petted it, feeling the curve of the cranium beneath her fingers. "Mind you, you're much cuter than Rafiel and you can tell him I said that." She cast another look at Tom. She was sure she knew how this story went. Her boyfriend had found the kitten out, somewhere, under the snow. And since he couldn't resist strays, be they human or not, he'd brought it in out of the cold.

She wondered if Tom had thought that cats pooped or that he needed to provide himself with a litter box for the critter. "What are we going to do with him?" she asked. "He adopts the most impractical creatures." But, as Not Dinner purred happily and started a kneading motion at her throat, she couldn't blame Tom. And she hoped Tom liked hapless felines. She happened to know that the bed-and-breakfast allowed pets. There was a big sign in the foyer proclaiming four-pawed guests welcome and Kyrie didn't think it meant shifters. And she was sure the lady, a great cat lover, would find her a litter box for the newest member of the family.

Then she must find someone to fix the bathroom so they could return home. She wondered if one of Rafiel's ubiquitous and very useful relatives happened to be a plumber. If Rafiel found them help within his odd family, it would save explaining what sort of cataclysm had happened in that bathroom. Rafiel could make up whatever he wanted or nothing. His family had to know that there was something very strange about their relative, but none of them seemed to mind covering up for him.

"Right," she said, picking up the kitten, as she slipped out of bed, and dropping him atop the sleeping Tom. "You keep the dragon company while I get decent and go about finding you a litter box."

She fumbled in her suitcase for her robe and slipped it on, before opening the door. And then she saw the headline on the local paper laid outside the door. And shrieked.

Tom woke up with Kyrie shrieking, and saw Not Dinner rush towards her and the open door. "Kyrie," he said. "Not Dinner."

Kyrie bent down just in time to stop the tiny animated projectile attempting to run out the door, and grab him in her hand, even as she scooped up the paper with her other hand. She closed the door with her foot and returned to Tom. "Look at this," she said, and turned the paper towards him so that he could read the above-the-fold headline.

The *Weekly Inquirer*—which was a daily paper, a dissonance of nomenclature that bothered no one in Goldport—normally printed city news first page, relegating the national and international news to the middle sections where—it was felt in town—the rest of the world belonged, being far less important than their concerns.

Local news normally consisted of some business moving to town, some business moving out; an event of importance in the life of the mayor; some trial for fraud or embezzlement; a parade; or what Tom referred to as "pretty puppy" news. Today Tom would have expected the big headline to be about the snowstorm. And it was. At least the headline just beneath the title of the paper, in dark blue letters, was "Goldport Slammed by Storm." But above the fold, and in screaming red letters just beneath the newspaper's name was "Strange Animals Seen Around Town." And beneath that "Dragons and Saber-Toothed Tigers and Smoking Squirrels."

"Smoking squirrels?" he said, looking up at Kyrie, whose hand was shaking so much that the newspaper was oscillating before his eyes.

"Whatever. But dragons? Saber-tooth?"

"It wasn't a saber-tooth," Tom said, reasonably. "It was a dire wolf."

"Oh, yes, and I'm sure that the international spotters of extinct animals would care," she said, as she set the kitten on top of him and started reading from the paper. "Last night, amid the howling gusts of the storm—who writes this paper? The Bronte sisters?—a man passing by a building near the aquarium swears he saw in the parking lot a dragon or some other large creature battling it out with what he swears was a saber-toothed tiger. With great presence of mind he snapped a photo with his cell phone." Kyrie stretched the paper towards Tom so he could see an indistinct picture of dark shapes amid white snow. "He took a picture of us." Kyrie said.

If Tom squinted and sort of looked at it sideways, the dark blobs in the snow did look like Kyrie, the dire wolf and himself. In shifted forms. Or perhaps like three sacks of potatoes. "Kyrie, it's completely fuzzy. No one could recognize a dragon in that."

"No, but . . . if it hadn't been snowing, someone could have gotten a real picture of you and me and the dire wolf."

"All right. I will do my best not to get in fights with homicidal maniacs," he said, and sat up. "At least not when people might get a clear picture of me. Do you have any idea how I should sell this truce to the homicidal maniacs?"

But Kyrie only looked at him with a blank and panicked look. "But they know. Someone knows."

"Kyrie!" Tom said. "How many times do people read this sort of thing, or think they see it, or report it? It doesn't make any difference. Black panthers up in Ohio, I remember reports of that—"

"Yeah, a lot of them when I lived there."

"Oh, really?" he smiled briefly. "Well, I was on the cover of the *Inquirer* once. I mean, the real one, the tabloid. Someone got me, flying over town, with a telephoto lens. No one believed it of course. Not after half the tabloids spent the nineties reporting on the president's alien baby." He put his hand out to her, and held her wrist. "No one will believe it, Kyrie. That picture doesn't look any better than the countless pictures of the abominable snowman. And if it did, people would say it was Photoshopped. Calm down will you? Everything is fine. And look, about the cat, if you don't want it—"

"No, I always wanted a cat and he seems very nice . . . in an insufferable male feline way."

"I don't know if he's a male, I just—"

"Oh, he's a male, trust me. I just know." She grinned, and tossed the newspaper down. "Right, I must go and find him a litter box."

By the time she came back, carrying a small plastic box filled with grey granules, Tom was reading the paper, frowning, very puzzled over reports that a giant squirrel—the size of a German shepherd— had been seen in various locations downtown "wearing a beret and smoking cigarettes," he told Kyrie. "I mean, and you're afraid people will believe the thing about the dragon when they finish with this."

Kyrie looked confused. "Are you sure it's not someone like us? I mean . . . a shifter squirrel?"

"'The size of a German shepherd and wearing a beret? What are the chances?"

"Not high," Kyrie said. "But if it's true . . ."

"If it's true," Tom said, feeling as though he had a bit of ice wedged in his stomach, "then he's gone completely around the bend. Which I suppose would make him an ideal suspect for the aquarium murder."

"And perhaps for whoever unleashed the executioner on us," Kyrie said.

At that moment, the phone rang. And Kyrie sprang towards it. "It's Rafiel," she said.

Tom raised his eyebrows at Kyrie, as she pushed the button on the speaker and Rafiel's voice filled the room. He sounded nervous . . . or perhaps hassled was a better term. "Kyrie?"

"And Tom," Kyrie said. "We're on the speaker."

"Oh? Oh. Good. That saves me telling you stuff twice."

"What stuff?" Tom asked.

"Well . . . this morning, we got a call. At the station. They found . . ."

"Another arm?" Kyrie asked.

"Yes, but in this case, there was a body attached to it. Badly mauled. Aquarium. We're . . . processing it."

"Do you need our help?" Tom asked.

"Processing a body?" Rafiel asked, incredulous.

"No. With . . . anything."

There was a hesitation. Rafiel cleared his throat. "Yeah, but I can't . . ." His car horn sounded. "Did you see the paper, this morning?"

"The squirrel?"

"And the . . . you and the dire wolf."

"And?" Tom asked impatiently, waiting—fearing—what would come next but needing to hear it because until he heard, it was always worse than he thought. Until he heard it, he would think he'd been found, he'd been recognized, he'd been . . .

"And this morning, when we were called in, there were already reporters in the parking lot. From the *Weekly Inquirer*. They were looking for fur or scales, or who knows what. But they got hold of the murder, right at the beginning. And considering, they seem really interested . . . you know, the thing is the *Weekly Inquirer* was bought recently?" He seemed to wait for them to comment and when all that Kyrie and Tom did was exchange a look, he clicked his tongue. "The *Weekly Inquirer* was bought by Covert Corp."

"Covert what?"

"The corp. thing is sort of misleading. I mean, they are a corporation. But they are a family company. They own several magazines. Crosswords, mystery. But the most important property, the one they started with, is called *Unknown*. It's a magazine of cryptozoology."

"Crypto what?"

"Animals that aren't supposed to exist, or animals that aren't supposed to be there. Dragons and . . . that."

"Oh. But if they own many companies . . . What could it mean for the *WI* in particular?"

"The patriarch of the clan, Lawrence Stoneman . . . He's very hands-on, you could say. He seems to keep one of his kids in charge of each place the corp buys. His daughter, Miranda, is in charge of the *Weekly Inquirer*. And she grew up on cryptozoology. I think their interest in the murder is secondary, frankly, as opposed to what interesting animals they might find lurking around. In other words . . ." Rafiel hesitated.

"We can none of us afford to be obvious?" Kyrie said.

"With a maniac stalking us, and a second murder at the aquarium—where there are two, maybe three shifters running around?" Tom said.

"Exactly. So, yes, I do want your help, but I do need to be more careful about getting that help than I've been. I'll come in if I can, tonight. Meanwhile, if you must shift, be careful where you do it, and who might see you. More careful than normal, that is."

"Right," Tom said. And sensing Rafiel was about to hang up, he added, "Oh, do you have any relatives who could fix our bathroom?" And in response to a scowl from Kyrie, he added, "Not for free. We'll pay. I'd just like to get someone who can start right away, so we can move back home soon, and who won't ask . . . awkward questions." This brought up his deep-seated envy of Rafiel, who not only hadn't lost his family over his shifting nature, but whose family stood ranked behind him, solid, bolstering and protecting him.

Tom had been told that Rafiel's parents knew he was a shifter. This explained—or at least Rafiel thought it did—why Rafiel still lived at home. Tom didn't know how many other members of the extended family knew about it, and he was afraid to ask. In a world where the lack of safety of a shifter meant revealing the existence of them all, he didn't want to learn of the possible issues with Rafiel's security. Rafiel's family seemed to have done well enough with the secret so far, and Tom, who had no personal knowledge of how real families behaved, would not judge.

"Oh," Rafiel said. "I see. Yes, we have plumbers in the family, and one of my uncles can probably do the drywalling stuff or tile or whatever." There was a silence that gave the impression he was trying to think things out. "Yeah, it will do very well. It will give me an excuse to come by the diner later this evening. We'll just have to be careful there."

Rafiel disconnected, and Tom limped towards the shower to wash. He and Kyrie needed to eat something, and one of them should probably go in early to relieve Anthony. Normally, they should have had three shifts. They hadn't, mostly because Tom hadn't had time to even think of hiring a third manager, much less one who was practiced in using the complex new stoves. But they couldn't ask Anthony to do a twelve-hour shift, not when he was newly wed, anyway, so Tom would go in early. He grabbed a change of clothes and headed towards the bathroom, Not Dinner happily winding in and out between his ankles. "I wonder if that Laura person who was supposed to come for an interview yesterday will show up today. Do you think they've cleared the roads enough for traffic?"

Kyrie giggled, and as Tom stared, she said, "I'm sorry, but with everything going on, it's so much like you to be worried about the diner, and getting another manager/cook for the diner."

Tom grinned, seeing her point, but shrugged. "Well, Kyrie, look at it this way—if we survive this, then we'll need the diner in good shape, particularly considering the repairs to the bathroom. And if we don't survive, the fact that I was worried about running the diner won't make a bit of difference."

But Tom found, as he crossed the slush-filled parking lot of The George, that things were not that clear-cut in his mind. It was sort of like telling someone to stop worrying because nothing could be done about a problem. It wasn't in the human mind to stop worrying—to stop looking for the door out of the sealed room; to stop searching for the one true route through the labyrinth. He was sure that if the world were doomed to destruction by asteroid within a day or two, and everyone on Earth were informed of it, at least half of them would go to their graves still frantically looking for an escape from the approaching cosmic collision. In the same way, the sane thing to do, surrounded by problems he couldn't solve, might be to concentrate on the problems he could solve—on the diner, his bathroom, and the fact that his hands—though well enough to go without bandages—still hurt and would probably be sensitive to the heat from the stoves.

That would be the sensible thing to do, and the sane one. Which meant, of course, that his mind insisted on going through everything he couldn't do anything about—the murders at the aquarium; the executioner come to town; whatever the organization might be of old shifters, and beyond that where Old Joe might have gone and whether he was alive.

The weather had done one of those sudden reversals that Tom's almost year of living in Colorado had got him used to—it had gone from several degrees below freezing the day before, and blowing snow and howling wind, to fifty degrees with a very slight breeze which stirred the branches of the icicle-hung trees. All the icicles were dripping, too—from the branches of the trees and the edges of the buildings, a drip drip drip that seemed to be waiting only for a conductor and some rhythm to turn into an animated movie's symphony of thawing and spring.

Only it wasn't spring at all. And tomorrow could very well be freezing again. Or alternately it could be eighties, with everyone wandering around in sandals and T-shirts.

As Tom took a long detour around a melting pool in the middle of the parking lot, he fancied that even the birds on the trees that lined the streets were piping in tones of surprise, as if asking themselves if this was the last of snow or the beginning. He was smiling to himself at the idea of birds driven to Prozac by Colorado weather, but his detour brought him full-face with a poster on the wall of the diner—where it wouldn't have been visible from the back door. That wall was in fact where the storage rooms protruded a little from the otherwise square plan of the building.

The poster was glued at an angle on the whitewashed wall, and it was the sort of poster—printed on cheap paper, in two colors—that normally advertised a dance or a new more or less non-registered nightclub or, alternately, some new band come to town. At first Tom thought it was a new band. It might still be a new band. Only what the words across the top read, in huge bright red type—rodent liberation front. Beneath it was a rant in pseudo-Marxist terms, urging "The downtrodden, the despised who live at the edges of society" to "rise up and take what you want. No more foraging for fallen nuts, no more eating discards. Rise up and take your freedom in your hands. There are more of us than them. Rodents of the world, unite. You have nothing to lose but your mousetraps."

Tom blinked at the page. It was possible it was all allegorical and meaningful and too symbolic for words. They were, after all, not that far away from CUG—Colorado University at Goldport—and since fully half the students seemed to eat at The George any given day—

or more typically night—Tom was aware how the minds worked who might be behind this poster. They were the sort of minds that were convinced coming up with a particularly clever image or metaphor excused not having anything new to say.

Without his knowing he was going to do it, his hand reached out and plucked the paper from the wall. It could be a metaphor, a clever image, a college thing to delude themselves that they were doing something to save the world. But in his gut—in a big, insoluble cold lump at the pit of his stomach—he knew it wasn't. He knew it was . . . shifter business. Squirrels the size of German shepherds smoking cigarettes. Crazy. But how crazy did the dragon thing sound to other people as well?

He folded the poster and put it in his pocket, and started walking towards the diner. And heard the splish-splosh behind him of someone stepping on ice, then on water, then falling butt-first into the water. And turned to see Red Dragon—no, Conan. He had to get used to calling him Conan—sitting in a puddle of water, looking very surprised.

Surprised was the least of his problems, though, to tell the truth. He didn't look good. Not good at all. His skin was pale enough to look almost the color of Tom's and he had big circles under his eyes, and to make things worse, he was attempting to get up, but not managing to balance himself enough to do so, because of his shortened arm.

"I shouldn't go to him," Tom told himself. "I truly shouldn't go to him. How stupid can I be? One day I'm going to help someone who is going to kill me."

But in his mind was his sixteen-year-old self, alone, on the streets of New York City in a bathrobe and as lost and confused as any kid could ever have been anywhere. And he'd survived only because the gentleman down the street—an orangutan shifter, though his family didn't seem to notice he was one—who sold roasted chestnuts on the street corner, had seen him and taken him in, and given him a jogging suit, and let him stay there a couple of days, till Tom had caught hold of the idea of day labor and had got a fake ID that said he was eighteen and could, therefore, be hired.

And he was closing the distance to Red Dragon and holding him on the side of his weak arm and hauling him up, even as he looked down at what he was wearing—the jogging suit that Kyrie had given him and a pair of those shoes that you slip your feet into, which have an almost completely smooth bottom. No socks. "You need boots," he said. "For this weather. We'll take you to the thrift store tomorrow or something, okay?"

"I have money," Conan Lung said, in the tone of someone protesting charity. "I brought money with me. In a pouch. I could buy new boots."

"Oh? Good for you," Tom said, not sure whether to be amused or saddened and being, after all, wholly skeptical. If he had money, why grab the elastic shoes? They weren't that much better than the flip-flops Tom had given him. "And you have family in Goldport, too, don't you?" he added, remembering that their past adventures seemed to involve Goldport's minuscule Asian minority.

He shook his head. "Tennessee," he said, and wiped his dripping nose to his sleeve, and looked back, at a bottom that was entirely soaked in runoff from melted snow.

"Oh, now, you're just putting me on," Tom said. "And don't worry about the sweatsuit. I have a couple others in the storage room. For . . . this sort of situation." He decided he didn't want to talk about Old Joe to the Great Sky Dragon people. "I'll get you one. Socks too."

"I'm not putting you on," Conan said. He sounded aggrieved and tired, and just the slightest bit exasperated—though Tom couldn't tell at whom. "Mom and Dad have a restaurant in Knoxville. People don't all come in to New York City anymore when they immigrate. Planes go everywhere."

"I'm sorry," Tom said, holding onto himself with all his will power to prevent himself from giggling at the fact that Conan had completely forgotten to have an accent. Or completely forgotten to have an Asian accent. Now that Tom thought about it, there was just an edge of a southern twang to his voice. It sounded, Tom thought, like something he'd tried very hard to rid himself of. Something that he hadn't quite managed to leave behind him. And quite out of place in a triad member.

"And I do have money. In a pouch. I wear it on a flexible anklet when I shift," Conan added, sullenly, clearly having caught Tom's disbelief.

"All right. You have money. Couldn't you have got yourself decent shoes, then?"

Conan shook his head. "No," he said. "I got them at the Short Drugs down the block, and this was the best they had. It was this or flip-flops."

"You know . . ." Tom said, leading him towards the back door of the diner and opening it for him. In the hallway, Conan wiped his feet on the mat at the entrance, and duck-walked into the hallway, his cheap shoes squeaking on the concrete. "It might surprise you, but in a list of shoe stores, Short Drugs wouldn't be in the first hundred, being a drugstore and all."

Conan sighed, a sigh half of exasperation, as if Tom were being particularly daft. "I couldn't let you go, could I? I went to Short Drugs because it was just down the block."

And Tom, having closed the door, froze. "Couldn't let me go? As in, you're keeping me prisoner?"

Conan looked back, and now his voice was definitely furious. "No, you fool. I couldn't leave you unprotected." He blushed, hard, whether with embarrassment at proclaiming himself Tom's protector, or with anger, Tom couldn't tell. "What if I left you, and they killed you?"

"Shhhh," Tom said, forcefully, leaning against the wall, finger against lips, concerned most of all with the fact that Conan had yelled, and people might have heard him. "Shhh."

As if on cue, Anthony's worried face peeked around the corner in the hallway. "Tom? Everything all right?"

"Everything is fine," Tom said, talking over Conan's shoulder. "Conan fell in the parking lot. I'm going to grab him some dry clothes, and then I'll come in and you can go home."

"Oh, good," Anthony said. "Because you know Cecily will get worried." He smiled, but still looked somewhat worried, as he looked at Conan. However, he seemed reassured enough that Conan and Tom weren't about to come to fisticuffs.

Tom opened the door to the storage room, and pulled out a sweat suit. "Okay," he said. "You're here to protect me. You've told me this before. But I must ask you—because you never told me—what are you supposed to protect me from . . . ?"

Conan looked back at him. There was naked fear in his eyes, followed by something very much like defeat or humiliation. He took the sweat suit—grey, much washed—that Tom was holding out to him. "I don't know," he said, miserably. "He didn't tell me. Just that they were bad and . . . very powerful. And very large. And knowledgeable and . . . shifters."

"And he sent you? To protect me?" Tom asked. And realizing what he'd just said, and that Conan's hand was clenching hard at the end of his atrophied arm, he added, "I'm sorry, but . . . you're smaller than I in both forms, and with that arm . . ."

Conan shook his head. "You don't understand. You don't understand, okay?" His voice started rising again in a note of hysteria, and Tom pulled him into the storage room and closed the door after them, because the only other choice was pulling him into the bathroom and *that* would look funny. The room was piled high with boxes of paper napkins, potato chips and crackers. All the edibles were sealed in plastic or foil and it shouldn't have smelled, but they still did, so that it was a lot like being locked inside a giant box full of stale crackers.

"What don't I understand?"

Conan clutched the sweat suit in his good hand, clenched his other fist, and spoke through his clenched teeth. "Any of it. I was in high school. I was in the drama club and the choir and . . . and I was in the Latin club, too. And then . . ." He shook his head. "I shifted. And the next thing I know my parents were calling on . . . on Him. And he took me away. Because I was a dragon. I belonged to him. I was his to . . . protect and order. Like . . . like feudal, you know?" His shoulders sagged, despondently. "I was going to be a Country and Western singer. I was . . ." He shook his head.

And before Tom could think of what to say—lost in his own forgotten dreams, though he didn't remember ever wanting to be anything so definite and wholesome as a singer—Conan said, "It doesn't matter." He spoke in a flat tone. "You see, my parents didn't know what else to do with me, and . . . I don't have anywhere else to go. It's all . . . Well, honor and that. I disgraced the Great . . . Himself. I . . . didn't get the Pearl of Heaven for him. So . . ."

Tom remembered the long torture session that Conan and the others had subjected him to. He'd have felt angry, but he didn't know what had been at the back of it. He was just starting to glimpse what drove those he had assumed were crazed gang members. "So you have to redeem yourself."

He almost added that he didn't feel very reassured by the Great Sky Dragon sending Conan, anyway. But he didn't. He was learning that what came flying out of his mouth might hurt other people, even, possibly, people who didn't deserve to be hurt. And besides, he had a feeling—not quite a rational feeling, not even a thought, more of a prickling at the back of his neck that told him that the Great Sky Dragon's plans weren't as simple as they seemed. Instead, they were folded over themselves, more intricately than a highway map. And what he saw might not be all of it. He just wished he could be sure the rest of it was not against him.

"Well," he said, "I'll leave you to change." And escaped out the door of the storage room, to find Anthony in the hallway, looking at him with a very strange expression.

Tom wasn't sure how much Anthony had overheard, or what had caused him to come and look. But all Anthony said was, "I thought you'd have him change in the bathroom. He's going to get mud on the packs of napkins."

Kyrie was dozing on the bed. She would have liked to fall fully asleep again, but this seemed to be beyond her ability while a small creature lay down purring, squarely between her breasts, and punished any attempt at moving with sharp little claws at the base of her throat and a sort of soft "mur" that sounded like an admonition.

So she lay there, on the bed, on her back—which was far from her favored sleeping position—with a patch of sun squarely in her eyes. She tried to move her head just a little sideways. The needlelike claws got her at the hollow of her throat. "Mur."

"Yes, yes, I get it. I'm not allowed to move. I get it."

"Mur!"

She opened a cautious eye, in time to see Not Dinner curl up into a ball. But he remained facing her, and one of his eyes opened just a little.

Kyrie would have giggled, but she was fairly sure that this would have brought the claws out again, so she closed her eyes and tried to get back to dozing. Which was not exactly as easy as it might sound, while her mind kept giving her images of Tom fighting the dire wolf. There was something wrong about that creature. Besides the fact that it should have been extinct long before humans walked the Earth. The way it had moved . . . She shivered, and instinctively lifted a hand to ward off the claws, and the phone rang.

She jumped up and grabbed the bedside phone, but the ringing continued, and she realized what was ringing was her cell phone, and jumped for her purse, which was propped up against the sofa.

The phone showed Rafiel's number. She opened it. "Yeah?"

She remembered, belatedly, that she'd dumped the kitten on the bed and hoped he wasn't hurt. A look at him revealed him angrily licking himself and pointedly ignoring her.

"Kyrie?" Rafiel said. He sounded weird. Detached and breathy as if he had lost his voice and were speaking on echoes alone, unable to put any emotion in his words.

"Yes? What is wrong?"

"Nothing. Everything is fine."

"You sound very odd."

"Oh, got . . . something in my throat. Look, I don't suppose you can meet me at your house?"

"At my house? Why?" she said. And when he didn't answer immediately she said, "Is it about the bathroom?"

"Exactly," he said. "The bathroom. I've got someone to fix it. If you'll just meet me there . . ."

"When?"

"Now?"

"No can do. Must de-stink and put clothes on."

"Oh, why bother? We're only going to take them off."

"What?" She actually removed the phone from her ear and looked at the caller ID, to make sure that it was really Rafiel.

"I'm sorry. Bad joke."

"Very bad joke." Rafiel hadn't said something like this since she and Tom had got together. She wondered if he was trying to revive that rivalry, then realized it was probably just his idea of a joke to break the tension. He'd been with her in the SUV, and he hadn't even looked at her in a suggestive manner. "Okay. Give me half an hour," she said, matter-of-factly. And hung up.

Tom had taken over the grill, and was keeping an eye on Conan as he cooked. He'd found out Conan had camped out on the steps of the bed-and-breakfast all night, which he supposed explained the fumbling way he was moving and how bleary eyed he looked.

The problem, as Tom saw it, was that he could easily get Conan to crash in their house—if their house were operational. But their house was nowhere near operational. And in the bed-and-breakfast, they couldn't exactly offer him the living room floor and Tom didn't feel quite sanguine enough about letting him sleep on the floor of the suite. Inoffensive, he might be, but Tom could hear just the right note of sarcasm in Kyrie's voice if he told her that Conan would be sleeping on their floor. He could tell Conan he could sleep in the storage room, but beyond the fact that this would freak out Anthony, he wondered if Conan would do it.

He'd just settled on offering him the back of one of the diner's vans—in which he and Kyrie did supply runs to the local farmers' markets twice a week in season—and telling him he could park the van in front of the bed-and-breakfast—and look out the window for all Tom cared, when Anthony reappeared from, apparently, making sure Conan hadn't willfully destroyed supplies.

"Everything seems to be fine in the supply room," he said, removing his apron.

"Mmm," Tom said, noncommittal, as he turned to shave an order of gyro meat off the hunk slow-roasting.

"Well, you know . . . he's still a newbie," Anthony said. "So, you never know." He folded his apron and put it under the counter. "Keith left today at around ten, said something about bringing a girl to meet you."

"Yeah. Someone from college." Tom shrugged. "Maybe he wants me to give her a job."

"We do need people," Anthony said. "That Laura woman, whom we were supposed to interview, said she would come by as soon as the snow has melted. Something about not having a four-wheel drive." He shrugged. "So, if you're sure you don't need me anymore . . ."

"No, I don't. That's cool, you can go."

"Right. I'll come back late in the afternoon, if you need a break. Just call me. And speaking of calling?"

"Yes?"

"Your dad called."

Tom felt every muscle in his body tense. He might be closer to Tom than he had been in Tom's entire life—close enough that he was closing his New York City law practice and uprooting it to Denver. Of course, Denver—three hours away—was the smallest city that he considered "livable." And Tom wouldn't mind it at all, if it weren't for Edward's seeming conviction that, as the largest city—and capital—of Colorado, Denver must be well known to everyone who had lived in the state for any amount of time. Not only that, but it must be within easy reach of anyone wishing to, oh, look up an apartment for their erratic father.

The other thing was, his dad had his home number and his cell phone number. Why was he calling The George during the daytime?

He knew very well his son tended to be awake nights and sleep during the day.

"He said that the cable guy is coming to his loft this week, but he can't fly to Denver till next week, and . . ." Anthony hesitated. "He seemed to want you to go to Denver and wait for the cable guy at his place."

And, though he might try to become closer to his son, Edward remained as self-centered as a gyroscope. "Right," Tom said, ticking up *call Dad* in his long list of things to do and worry about. "I'll deal. I have to explain to him that even if I could normally have gone to Denver over the week—which I doubt, as shorthanded as we are—there's snow all over and the highways are closed."

Anthony seemed to be unsure whether he should say something, but finally it came hurtling out, "Well, I told him the highways were closed," he said defiantly.

"And?" Tom asked, surprised by the tone.

"He said you should fly," Anthony said. "Does he have any idea how small our airport is or how hard it would be to operate in inclement weather?"

"None," Tom said. "Don't worry about it. He's my dad. I'll deal with it. He's not a bad guy he's just . . . you know how it is. Lived his whole life in the Northeast." He set the platter of gyro meat, fries and pita bread on the counter and rang the bell to call Conan's attention. And managed, very nearly, not to grit his teeth. There was no way to tell Anthony that no, Tom's father didn't expect his son to take an airplane. He expected his son to fly as a dragon.

Which was how Edward's mind worked. Once having convinced himself that Tom's ability to shift was not dangerous, he'd become determined to use it as much as he could, and to derive usefulness from it as much as possible. Tom had to remind himself it was, in a way, an endearing quirk, a lot like Keith's absolute certainty that being a shifter dragon would be just like being a superhero. And that his father could have absolutely no idea of the troubles besetting Tom at every side.

He pulled over a huge bowl of peeled potatoes—essential ingredient of The George's famous fresh fries, never frozen proudly advertised in marker on the huge plate glass window up front—and started slicing them into sticks on a broad expanse of cutting board, while he watched Conan give warm-ups and draw up bills for a couple of customers. He'd be just fine.

"Anthony," he said, before the young man turned away. "You didn't . . . see the alligator out back again?"

Anthony blushed. "Oh, geez, about that . . ." He sighed. "I've been thinking about it, and look, it was pretty late last night, and I think I just imagined things. It must have been the shadows, and the snow blowing, you know? I just got a bit goofy."

Tom shrugged. "Okay, just making sure." He hesitated a second. "And you haven't seen Old Joe, either?"

"What? Oh, the old man . . . He's probably downtown at the shelter, you know? The city shelter lets people in when it's this cold, even when they wouldn't let them in regular times. You know, no sobriety check or what have you."

"Yeah. He probably is." And maybe he was, though Tom doubted it. He knew—none better—how shifters felt about crowded rooms, where your roommates could start looking like potential snacks, if you got stressed enough. "Don't worry about it. I just thought, since it's this cold . . ."

"Yeah," Anthony said. "Okay, call me if you need me." He got his jacket from under the counter and put it on, pulling the hood on over his head, till he peered from under a welter of fake fur, like an Eskimo prepared for the arctic.

"Right," Tom said.

And when Conan swung by to drop off orders, Tom grabbed his good arm. "Listen. I was thinking—I know you won't want to sleep in the storage room or whatever because we might go out behind your back. But how about sleeping in the diner van parked in front of the bed-and-breakfast?"

Conan looked startled. "Why?"

"Well, you can't go on sleeping on the steps. You don't look any too awake, just now."

"Oh." Conan sighed. "Look, I have money."

"So you keep telling me."

"If you promise that you won't go anywhere without waking me first . . . I can rent a room at the bed-and-breakfast."

Tom thought about it. It seemed a little odd to have to notify his jailer that he intended to leave. On the other hand, perhaps Conan was a bodyguard not a jailer. Tom wasn't sure he understood anything anymore. He certainly was sure he didn't understand the Great Sky Dragon. "Well . . ." he said, after a wait. "Yeah. I suppose I can do that."

"Only you have to make sure you do," Conan said. He shot Tom a resentful look. "When you disappeared yesterday and I had to go find you . . . If you'd died, you know . . ." He shook his head. "I was so busy at the tables I didn't see you leave, and let me tell you, Himself wasn't happy."

"How did the Great Sky—"

"Shhh," Conan said.

"How did Himself know?" Tom asked and resisted an impulse to roll his eyes and refer to *he who must not be named*. "Did you tell him?" It seemed to him the height of stupidity for Conan to confess to have lost track of Tom for any time at all, much less to call the Great Sky Dragon and confess his misdeed.

Conan sighed. "What do you think would have happened if I hadn't told him?" he asked. "They're everywhere. Someone would have told him, sooner or later. And then he'd have killed me for not telling him."

"Killed you?" Tom thought how ridiculous it was to kill someone for such a small offense. Particularly in a creature that claimed to want to protect Tom. He wanted to rebel. He very badly wanted to rebel. But not when Conan would be the one to pay for it. He nodded. "I'll tell you before we go out."

And turned in time to see Rafiel come into the diner.

Sometime between sixteen and twenty, Kyrie had simplified her getting-ready routine. The makeup that had seemed essential at sixteen had now gone by the wayside. The one fussy bit about her appearance was her hair dyeing and that she did once every three months and touched up once a month, and that was about it.

In the bed-and-breakfast, she didn't even have her shampoo or the shower gel she liked to use. Since the bathroom had been obliterated, and all her products with it, all she had was what Spurs and Lace provided, in an artistic little basket lined with lacy fabric. There were three bottles of shampoo, all seeming to belong to some brand that invested a lot in aroma therapy. Vanilla, mint and— bizarrely—coffee. Preferring her coffee on the inside, Kyrie grabbed the vanilla. There were three bars of soap for her perusal, but a look in the tub revealed that Tom had already started a bar that smelled minty fresh. He had also used up a bottle of shampoo labeled chamomile. She was sure he was missing his Mane and Tail, the worst-named shampoo for a dragon to use since the dawn of time.

The shower proved to have a torrential flow of water, and she washed quickly under it, only slightly hampered by the fact that, two minutes into her shower, Not Dinner screeched from outside the shower "Mur?" and patted tentatively at the shower curtain.

"Er," she said. "I'm fine."

"Yow?"

"No, really. We humans don't mind water. Heck, we like it."

A disbelieving "Nahooo?" answered her and she grinned. "I'm only a kitty part of the time, and I refuse to lick myself for hygiene."

"Mur!"

"Yes, I know, quite terrible of me, isn't it?" She finished rinsing and came out of the shower, drying herself briskly, and rubbing her hair almost completely dry with a towel, before combing it. Judging by the drip-drip-drip sounds from outside the bedroom window and the brilliant sunshine which had disturbed her sleep, the weather had turned some sort of corner. Which was very good, because she didn't think she could go outside with damp hair, otherwise. She had vague visions of doing that and having her hair freeze to her head as a large, unwieldy mass.

While she was home, she should grab a couple of hats for herself and Tom, she thought, as she slid into jeans, a red sweatshirt that was probably originally Tom's, but which she'd claimed by rights of laundress, and had been wearing for the last two months. The man never wore long sleeve shirts, anyway. Just his T-shirts under his black leather jacket.

She put her shoes on and told Not Dinner, "Now, Notty, try to be good. I'll ask the lady to bring you some food, until we can buy you some kitten cans."

"Mur?" he followed her to the door with the dancing step of young, overconfident kittens and seemed terribly disappointed that she wasn't willing to let him follow her outside. An ill-fated last minute rush at the door made her grab him in her hand—where he fit, fairly comfortably, then toss him into the room, as she quickly shut the door.

She asked the proprietress—a large, maternal woman named Louise—to feed the delinquent and informed her that he was a flight risk. It wasn't till she got to the car that she thought she should have asked Louise for a recommendation to a vet. She would need to get Notty his shots, and she should probably have him microchipped, at least if he had wandering paws.

Perhaps she would ask Rafiel, she thought, and smiled absently. He should know everything there was to know about the care of male felines in this town. But her smile died down, as, maneuvering through the mostly-melted streets, she wondered what Rafiel could possibly want. Oh, he'd said that he wanted to meet her at her house. And he'd said it was because of the bathroom . . .

Or *had* he said that it was because of the bathroom? Kyrie couldn't remember exactly. She frowned. Was there another reason? He'd sounded so odd over the phone—as if he'd been not so much talking as making modulated breathing sounds. But no . . . that wasn't right either. It was just as if there were no force of vocalization behind his words. No real sound. He'd said he had something in his throat. Like what? An elephant?

A brief image of Rafiel prowling the zoo and taking a big bite off an elephant amused her. And she smiled at herself, but as she entered her neighborhood, she went back to frowning. Rafiel's car wasn't parked on the street. This was like an itch at the back of her mind, an itch to which her brain responded by coming up with lots of reasons for the absence—his car had broken down, and he was borrowing someone else's; he had parked in the driveway; he was late.

But if Rafiel's car had broken down, he was likely as not to let her know in advance, so she would know the car to look for. It wasn't the sort of thing Rafiel forgot. Rafiel was a policeman. Details were his life. And he never parked in the driveway, which was a minuscule comma beside the tiny dot of the house and had barely enough space for Kyrie's subcompact. When Tom worked later and had to drive the diner's van home, he had to park on the street. And not just because he didn't want to block Kyrie in, but because there was no way to park two cars in the driveway without one of them having half of its back wheels on the street.

And besides, as Kyrie got to the driveway, it was empty and wet from melting ice. She started to pull in, while the back of her scalp bunched up. *Something is wrong,* an inner voice said. *Something is very wrong.*

But that inner voice was wrong nine times out of ten. Fact was, Kyrie's inner voice was a paranoid patient, and had to be kept carefully locked up in its rubber room, or else she would never hear a sound that wasn't suspicious, she'd never approach a place that didn't feel eerie, and she would spend her entire life running from shadows. Deliberately, she stopped within sight of her kitchen door, and put the car in park, the wheels slightly turned so that—should the car roll down the driveway—it would rest across the bottom of it, instead of slipping out into the street and potentially running into other cars.

Her foot remained on the brake, her hand resting on the keys, her car idling.

Run.

No. No, she wouldn't run. She had run too many times, after she was out of foster care—after she was on her own. Without family or any close friends, with nothing to anchor her down, she had drifted. Convinced she was hideously insane—with her dreams of turning into a panther, her secret fears of eating people—she had kept everyone at arm's length and ran every time someone got too close, every time anyone seemed hostile. Every time a shadow waved in the wind. But now she had a place, she had a job, she had Tom. She had something that was hers, and she wasn't running.

She pushed the parking brake in, relishing the feel of it under her foot, the slight grind of its going in. Then she reached for her purse, from the floor of the passenger side of the car. Where was Rafiel? This was so much like him, telling her to come to the house, and then not being here when she got here. And immediately, she scolded herself, because no, it wasn't like Rafiel at all. He was arrogant, not careless. If he said he would be somewhere, he would be there. He might act put out because she hadn't rushed to meet him, unwashed and in robe and slippers, but he would be there.

She bit her lip. Okay. All right. So something had happened. Could be anything. He was on a murder investigation. Perhaps someone had called and told him he had to be at the morgue now. This minute. Or perhaps . . . or perhaps something else had happened. Perhaps he'd had a fender bender. Or something.

A brief image of Rafiel laid out on a hospital bed made her wince. He wouldn't like that. They all tried to stay out of hospitals as much as possible. Besides being a crowded place, with lots of other humans—it would be a mess to shift in—their healing rate would call too much attention.

She reached for her purse, pulled out her phone. She would call him, figure out if anything had happened to him. Help him, if she needed to.

But the phone was dead. Out of batteries. Kyrie caught herself growling under her breath. She could swear she had recharged it last night. Clearly she hadn't.

She resisted an impulse to throw the phone—with force—across the driveway, and instead put it back in her purse and zipped her purse shut forcefully.

Okay, so Rafiel wasn't here, and she couldn't call him. What then?

She could go back. She could go to The George. It was only five minutes away. She could call Rafiel from there.

But what if he showed up as soon as she drove away? What if it was only a small delay, some administrative thing that kept him back? Then he would be there any second, wouldn't he? And when he got there, he wouldn't find her.

But she could call him.

In five minutes. What if by then he had driven away, furious? Oh, he had no right to be furious. He'd called Kyrie out of the blue. He'd told her to be here. There was no reason at all she should have obeyed him. And he'd said—or at least, he'd agreed—this was about her bathroom. Which meant he wouldn't be coming by alone. He would be with his uncle or cousin, or whoever in his vast tree of relatives was a plumber or a tile layer, or a good enough handyman. And that meant he wouldn't leave in five minutes.

But none of these rational arguments amounted to a hill of beans. After all, Rafiel was all male cat in this one thing, that he could act as capricious as he pleased, and make everyone else seem like they were the irrational ones, the ones who were failing him in some horrible way.

Besides, she realized, she had a phone in the house. Oh, they rarely used it, and in fact Tom had suggested they give it up and go all digital. But his father had protested that it was a number where he always knew he could reach them, even when their cell phones were out of a charge or they were out of range. In fact, it seemed that the phone, on the wall of the kitchen, and possessed of a built-in answering machine, mostly existed to take Edward Ormson's messages.

Which didn't mean it couldn't call Rafiel's cell.

Full of new decision, Kyrie got out of the car and slammed the door behind her. The driveway wasn't anywhere near as icy as it had been the night before, which was good. She should probably shovel the walk while she was here. Although most people in Colorado left their snow and ice on the sidewalk and let it merrily accumulate through the cold days, the law, technically, said that they were supposed to shovel within twenty-four hours of a major snowfall. The snow was melting on the sidewalks across the street, but not here, and Kyrie shuddered at the thought of what might happen if the postal carrier slipped and broke a leg on the way to their front door.

She paused at the door to the kitchen, frowning. The door itself was old, much painted, and starting to peel, a layer of red showing beneath the current decaying layer of white paint. It didn't matter, because it was normally covered by a screen door, which had a glass screen, conveniently slid down for winter. Kyrie was sure—as sure as she was of having charged her phone—that Tom had closed that screen door. She remembered him half-skating back through the ice that then covered the driveway to do it. He'd mumbled that otherwise it would probably fold back in the wind and maybe be wrenched off. So, why was the screen door half open now?

Run.

No, nonsense. Probably some weather-defiant Jehovah's Witness had come and opened the screen door to knock. Or perhaps one of their neighbors, worried about the lack of lights in the house had come to check on them. Most of the people in this neighborhood were elderly and retired and took an inordinate interest in Kyrie and Tom because they weren't and perhaps because they reminded them of their grandchildren.

She got her keys from the pocket of her winter coat, and unlocked her door into the kitchen. The house felt empty. It had that cold/empty feel of a house where no one is.

It should feel empty. They'd never given Rafiel a key. They were friends, but normally they met at the diner.

Right. I'll just call the arrogant lion boy, she thought, as she walked the four steps across the kitchen to the phone. But as she picked it up and before she could dial, a smell rose around her.

It was thick, miasmalike, overpowering. Her throat and nose closed. She gagged. It was like . . . like walking into a closed shed at the zoo, where someone had been housing several hundred wild animals.

And then there was the voice, a voice without vocalization behind it, a voice that seemed to come from the phone and yet not, a voice that seemed curiously devoid of sound, "Welcome, Pretty Kitten."

Gasping and gulping, through the horrible smell, Kyrie turned.

Run.

␡ ␠ 🐻 ␡ ␠

"Hey, Rafiel," Tom said, as Rafiel walked up to the counter, "I thought you said you'd come by this evening?"

Rafiel shrugged. "I was going to, but I talked to my cousin Mike, and he said that he could go by this afternoon, and I happened to be in the neighborhood, because I have to . . . do some interviews." He looked around. "In relation to the case in the aquarium." Shrug. "So I thought I'd drop by and get the house keys from you."

"All right. If you want to come behind the counter, they're in my jacket pocket under there," he said, as he flipped a couple of burgers. And broke two eggs onto the griddle surface of the new stove. He looked over his shoulder and was amused to see Rafiel gingerly lift the pass-through portion of the counter, as though he was afraid it might be spring-loaded or something. He didn't remember if Rafiel had ever been behind the counter, for all he'd offered to man the diner, just yesterday.

"Yeah," he told Rafiel. "Down there. Just under the edge of the counter. You're going to have to look, because there's Conan's stuff under there too, and there's the time sheet boards. At least there isn't a cat today."

"A cat?"

"Uh . . . Kyrie and I have a cat. I mean, a kitten. He's barely larger than one of the burger buns. Full of himself, though." He heard his own voice become embarrassingly doting, sounding much like the voices of old childless people who dressed their pets in costumes for Halloween and took them out trick or treating. He changed the subject, abruptly, "Hey, why didn't you just go to Kyrie? She's probably awake by now."

"I'm sure she's awake," Rafiel said. "I went by there. The owner— Louise?—said that Kyrie had left to go check on something back home. Yeah, I could have gone by your place, but that was out of my way and this isn't. What?"

The "what" made Tom aware that he was standing there and staring at Rafiel with an idiotic expression on his face. He felt oddly betrayed, and he couldn't have explained to himself why. But the idea of Kyrie going back to their place without telling him made him feel like she had shut him out or something.

Of course, this was very stupid. It wasn't like he and Kyrie lived in each other's pockets, or anything. Sometimes he woke up in the afternoon, and she was gone—gone to the store, or to do laundry or something. Of course, she always left him a note on the table. Of course, that might also be because when she went she took the only vehicle they normally kept at home, and if she wasn't going to be back in time, it meant Tom had to walk to The George.

"Nothing. I just . . ." Tom said, struggling with the feeling of betrayal, and not knowing what to say. "She didn't tell me she was going to go home, that's all."

"No?" Rafiel said, and frowned slightly, his blond eyebrows meeting up above his oddly golden eyes. "Weird."

"Well, not really," Tom said, almost defensively. "I mean, it's not like I own her, or she needs to tell me where she's going to be, or . . ."

"No, but you'd think she'd tell you anyway."

Tom thought perhaps Rafiel thought this meant he and Kyrie had had a falling out, and he wasn't really ready to be a rival with Rafiel for Kyrie's affections, again. He said, "Look, I don't think she means to dump me or anything, it's just . . . I'm guessing she went home because she realized she missed something. We left kind of in a hurry and didn't bring a lot of stuff." Of course, most of that stuff, like their toothbrushes, hairbrushes and most of their toiletries had, presumably, been ground to dust by his shifting in the bathroom.

"Yeah, but you'd think she'd tell you so you could tell her if you needed anything from home, too."

Tom shrugged. "I can walk there, if I do. It's no big deal. I was just surprised, that's all. It doesn't mean there's anything wrong."

"No," Rafiel said. He was still squatting by the space under the counter where they put their jackets and where they stored aprons. He had Tom's jacket in his hands, but he hadn't pulled it out yet. "It's just . . . very weird? I mean, I have this feeling it's weird. I know that I don't know Kyrie as well as you do, that I don't know the . . . patterns of your relationship, like you do. But it seems to me she always tells you when she's not going to be where you expect her. How many times have I been here, talking to you—or at home talking to you, for that matter—and you get a phone call from Kyrie saying she's going to the supermarket or the thrift shop, or the bookstore, and do you want anything. Or she tells you if she's going to have the oil changed, and it's going to take a while."

"So maybe she thought it would be very quick and wasn't worth mentioning," Tom said. But he felt it too, the wrongness of it. He just didn't want Rafiel to start thinking along the *Kyrie might be available again and I might have a chance* lines. "Anyway, my keys should be in there, righthand pocket. Yeah, that's it. My house key is the simplest one. Yeah. The keys for this place are way more complicated." He watched Rafiel remove the house key from the ring, fold the leather jacket carefully and push it back under the counter.

Meanwhile, Tom assembled two Voracious Student specials, with the double cheeseburgers and the egg and enough fries to sink a small ocean liner, and set them on the counter ringing the bell and announcing "Eighteen and ten."

Conan scurried towards the counter. He was getting better, Tom thought. He was also learning to carry the coffee carafe in his weaker hand. Tom had no idea how much longer it would take for the full arm to grow in, and it just now occurred to him that they would need to make some explanation to Anthony. He was thinking experimental treatment. It covered a multitude of sins, and most people didn't enquire any further.

Rafiel straightened up, slipping Tom's key in his pocket, and at that moment Keith came in, more or less towing a young woman. Keith was wearing his normal attire when the temperature went above freezing but not over 80—a CUG T-shirt, this one reading "I'm just a CUG in the college wheel," and jeans, topped by an unzipped hooded jacket in sweatshirt material. The girl with him, on the other hand, was dressed as if she thought she was going on a hunting expedition in the arctic wastelands. She was wearing a sweatshirt, a huge, puffy ski jacket in bright shocking pink, and the sort of fuzzy pink muffler that Tom associated—for reasons known only to his psychiatrist, should he ever acquire one—with Minnie Mouse. The rest of the girl's appearance certainly said mousie, if not necessarily Minnie. She was too skinny, the type of too skinny that the nineteenth century would have associated with consumption and a romantically early death, pale and had colorless white-blond hair that seemed insufficient for her head size and age. It was cut in a page boy just at her ears, but it gave the impression of having trailed off of its own accord and stopped growing due to either lack of energy or effort.

And yet, the way Keith looked at her, Tom saw that he seemed to be attracted to her. Who knew why? It made absolutely no sense to Tom, but then very few pairings did. He supposed his was as much of a surprise to everyone as theirs was to him. After all, what on Earth was a cat doing with a dragon? Or vice versa? And what was a nice girl like Kyrie doing with Tom?

"Hey Keith," he said. "Is this the friend you told me you'd bring by to meet me?"

The girl blushed furiously and Keith smiled. "Yeah, this is Summer Avenir, Tom. I've told her this is the best place in the world to get a burger, besides being my own, personal hangout, which, of course, immediately makes it better."

"Of course," Tom said. "Nice meeting you, Summer. And this is Rafiel. He's a friend."

Keith did a double take at Rafiel. "Taking a real job in your spare time, Officer Trall?"

"Nah. Just came by to talk to Tom," Rafiel said, looking embarrassed at being caught behind the counter as though he were an employee. "I'll be going now. Nice to meet you, Summer. Watch out for Keith. He's a troublemaker."

Tom caught Keith's questioning look at him, and frowned. Perhaps it was that he was behind this counter and cooking, with the scent of fresh fries, hamburgers, melting cheese and toasting bread in his nose. Perhaps through all this, it was too much to expect that Tom could smell another shifter. But though he could smell Rafiel faintly—the metallic scent associated with shifters coming through a mask of Axe cologne—there was no other hint of a shifter-scent. At least not close enough for him to track.

As Conan ducked behind the counter, to grab the coffee pot, Tom could smell him too, his scent a little sharper than Rafiel's and not overlaid with anything but soap and water. But, as far as he could tell, there was no other shifter-scent at all.

He would have to ask Keith why he thought this girl might be a shifter.

Kyrie couldn't breathe. Her chest ached and her throat stung and she couldn't breathe. It was all she managed to do not to claw at her own neck in frantic attempts to somehow force herself to get air in, through the miasma that surrounded her. It made no sense, because she knew she was breathing—somehow, she was still breathing, otherwise she would have passed out long since. But at the same time, the stink around her was so prevalent that she felt sure she couldn't be breathing. She just couldn't.

The smell surrounded her, intrusive, offensive. It seemed to her that she was not only inhaling it, but that it was coming through her ears and her pores as well. Pinning her down.

Where are you trying to go, Kitten Girl? Do you think I'd hurt a pretty thing like you?

Kyrie turned around. She wasn't sure why, but she felt as if the thoughts were coming from behind her, as she tried to get to the kitchen door—and somehow couldn't because the stink held her back, held her in place.

As she turned, she saw she was right. He stood in the shadows of the door from the hallway, just off the kitchen, and he seemed to be wearing a shimmery silver turtleneck and tailored black pants. He held a cigarette in his hand.

"We don't . . ." Kyrie said, slowly, because speaking hurt, thinking hurt, assembling thoughts into words seemed a labor worthy of Hercules. "We don't smoke. In the house. We don't approve of smoking. In the house."

She realized how ridiculous she sounded, as she was barely able to breathe and wondering what this . . . creature was and what powers he had over her. They'd determined in the parking lot that it could somehow reach into their minds and touch them. It could change what they were thinking. It was clear even to Kyrie's befuddled mind that it could also cause her to smell what she was smelling. There was no other way anything—human or animal—could smell that strongly, and the creature was or appeared to be in human form, standing in the demi-shadows of her hallway, smoking.

Kyrie hadn't been able to really look at him before—not in the parking lot at night, and under snow. But now she observed him. Was she seeing who he was, or who he appeared to be? And in either case, what could she deduce about him?

He was short for a male. Maybe an inch taller than Tom—she would guess him at five eight or thereabouts, and well built—that much was obvious from his huge shoulders, his muscular arms, his whole posture. The silvery turtleneck shimmered over muscle definition that would have made a gym bunny cry. This was not surprising. In Kyrie's experience most male shifters were built. Something about the animal form and the posture they assumed in their animal form made them exercise as humans normally didn't. In fact, what was strange was people like Conan who seemed to have not one functional muscle in their wiry, stringy shapes.

Beyond that, he was gold-skinned—a tone that Kyrie thought of as vaguely Mediterranean. Anthony's color. Could be anything from the southern regions, from Europe to the Americas. His hair was black, lank, and just a little long in front, falling in smooth bangs over his forehead, though the back seemed perfectly molded to the contours of a well-shaped head.

Other than that there was not much unusual about him—his nose was sharply aquiline, but not remarkably so. His forehead was high, but didn't give the impression of a receding hairline. His lips were broad and seemed sensuous, particularly now when they distended in a come-hither smile. But none of it would have made the man stand out on a crowded street.

None of it but the eyes. His eyes were gold. More gold than Rafiel's, which fell in the outer limits of brown. This creature's eyes were gold to the point of having an almost metallic shimmer to them. And like metal they were cold, unfeeling, blank. A blankness somehow lit from behind, like the screen of an old-fashioned computer.

The result was a look of perfect madness, the look of someone who had gone beyond normal human thoughts, normal human processes. Perhaps beyond thoughts at all.

He grinned at her as though he were a famished wolf and she a particularly tasty morsel of steak. Which might be an analogy much too close for Kyrie's comfort. She backed up, slowly, fighting against the smell, which seemed to hold her in place, to prevent her from moving, to drain her of all energy. It wasn't real, she told herself.

But she still couldn't reason her way to turning around and unlocking the door and running out onto the driveway. And perhaps that was not as irrational as it seemed to be. She didn't want to turn her back on the thing smiling seductively at her. The idea of turning her back on him, made her think of his being on her suddenly, biting into her, savaging her.

She backed against the door, without taking her eyes off him. If she was going to die, she would die with her eyes open. She would face her death without flinching.

Back against the door, she took a deep breath and told herself she was not smelling anything. Nothing at all. It was a smell of the mind, as she fancied Shakespeare might have said. Something that didn't exist. The air in her kitchen would be as untainted as it was when she came in. Cold and clammy, with a hint of disused space, and perhaps the ghost of cookies past, but nothing else.

"What do you want?" she asked the man smiling at her from the shadows. "What do you want from me?"

And the moment she asked, she recoiled, because it seemed to her like inviting the vampire into your home. This gave the creature a chance to say that he wanted her to die. And then, somehow to make it so.

But he laughed, a full-throated and very masculine laughter that she might have found pleasant under different circumstances. He emerged from the hallway and grinned at her. The light from the kitchen window behind her fell fully on his face. It should have made him look less unpleasant or more human. But all it did was gild the planes and features so that he looked like the antique funeral mask of an ancient and cruel emperor. The kind that would have ordered hundreds of thousands of people killed at his funeral rites.

"I just want to know you better," he spoke. It was, she realized with a shock, the first time she heard his voice. Before, he hadn't deigned to speak in audible words, but had tried to reach into her mind. She wondered if this meant that she'd scored a point. She very much doubted it.

Fighting against the smell that surrounded her, fighting against the suggestion that she was a small, frail, young thing at the mercy of this ruthless primeval evil—something she was sure he would like her to believe—she made her voice cutting and as sarcastic as if she were talking to Tom and Rafiel. "The normal way to get to know a woman is to go somewhere she is and introduce yourself. Some of the more polite people might ask her for coffee."

His laughter jangled, pleasant and cultured, but with something just slightly off-key behind it. It was, Kyrie thought, like when you heard thunder overhead, and the glassware in your cupboards tinkled in tune with it. A false note, a strange intrusion in what she was sure he wanted to be a perfectly polished image. She tried to keep this knowledge from her eyes, though, and must have succeeded, because he bent upon her an expression of great amusement—as though she were a particularly clever pet or a favored pupil.

Bending at the waist, hands on his thighs, the red glow of his cigarette end turned outward, he said, "Dante Dire at your service."

"Cute," she said, keeping her voice sarcastic.

"Nothing comes of denying what you are, Kitten. It is better to embrace it."

"I am not 'Kitten.' And I don't care to embrace anything." Said primly and with her back to the door and her lips taut.

"Really?" His insane eyes danced with merriment. "Don't you now? Oh, don't worry about it, I'm not going to eat you." He took a pull of his cigarette. "And if I did, you'd enjoy it." Again the mad dance of his insane eyes, followed by, "What do you think I am? Why do you think I'd want to hurt you?"

Because you broke into my house. Kyrie thought. *Because you are using a smell that can only be supernatural to keep me cowed. Because you talked in my mind. Because you attacked and wounded my boyfriend. Because you speak to me as if I were not an adult.*

She kept these thoughts up front, while behind them she ran others. She thought that if he was using his mind power on her, if he'd used some trick of pretending to be Rafiel—she was sure of it now—to lure her, it must mean he didn't want to or couldn't face all of them together. She didn't know why, since he had seemed to do pretty well with it in the parking lot of the aquarium. But it was clear he didn't like it, and didn't care to repeat it. And that was fine. Absolutely fine. But there was more. The fact that he was keeping the smell on her, and feeling that the smell was suffocating her, must mean he was afraid of her thinking clearly, of her thinking what she must do.

The thought sneaked behind her mind, afraid to be seen by whatever mind-scan capacities he had, that she should turn around and open the door. But . . . no. She couldn't do it, even if she tried. Simply couldn't.

"You have nothing to fear from me," Dire said. "I don't know what you were told about me, but you can think of me as a private investigator. I'm here to find out what is killing our people."

Kyrie made a sound at the back of her throat. "Our people?" she asked. "I am not a dire wolf."

He made a dismissive gesture with his cigarette. "Shifters."

Behind it all her thoughts went on. So she couldn't turn her back on him. It would be just too creepy. Which left her with no other choice . . . or perhaps . . . Like a glimmer, at the back of her mind, came the idea that she could move *towards* Dire, instead of away from him. Move towards Dire, but maneuver so the little folding table and chairs that she and Tom used for their meals would always be between them, and her back too close to the kitchen counter and stove to allow him to teleport behind her. She was sure that there were some rules to this teleportation thing, if teleportation it was and not just an ability to make people forget they'd seen him move through the intervening space. She was sure even if he could instantly magic himself across the room, he couldn't do it when there was a good chance he would end up with a table, a chair, or a fridge embedded in his toned-and-tanned body.

She took a step towards him, and saw his eyes widen in shock, and the stench vacillated for a moment, allowing her to take a breath of the cold, untainted air of the kitchen. The stench returned, of course, but she knew now more than ever that it was fake. Another step, and it seemed to her that a flicker of something moved behind his eyes, as if he, himself, had been on the verge of taking a hasty step back. She sidestepped, then sidled rapidly around the table.

"Why are you afraid of me?" he asked, his voice trembling slightly. "If you're not a traitor to our people, you have no reason to fear me."

Ah! "What is a traitor to our people?" she asked, her voice cutting and slow, though she felt it coming from a shaking brittle place inside her. "I've never had any people. The only one I've ever belonged to is Tom."

"The dragon boy?" the creature asked, and there was real anger behind the words. "He's less than nothing. A larva. Not even a young one. Ignorant. Weak."

Kyrie read something in that, an echoing, resounding jealousy. Jealousy of Tom? Or jealousy, simply, that they had a relationship? What in this creature's past made him so angry at her?

"Tom is the only other shifter who ever took my side. Who ever cared for me."

"All of us care for you," the creature said. "It is the duty of shifter to look after shifter. You should always be loyal to your kin. Your people."

"I have no kin," Kyrie said. "I was adopted."

And before the creature could answer the flip response, she'd managed to reach her objective—the phone hanging on the wall of the kitchen. They should have a mobile phone, she thought. It had never seemed important before, and this phone had been practically free at the thrift shop, but if they had a mobile one . . .

The phone cold in her hand, she pushed the automatic dialing button to get the diner. She saw the creature lunge towards the phone, finger extended, to disconnect her. But if he was afraid to stop her calling for help, that meant help was possible.

With her free hand, she grabbed one of the chairs, and threw it, as hard as she could, at the creature, then, grabbing the other chair, used it to keep him away from the phone, in a move reminiscent of lion tamers at the zoo.

"Put the phone down," the creature said, his voice sounding like sweet reason. "Put the phone down. I only want to talk to you. If you're not a murderer, I won't hurt you."

Oh, sure you won't. And what's a murderer to you, buddy? she thought; at the same time her mind flooded with sheer relief at hearing Tom's voice answer the phone, brightly, "The George, your downtown dining option twenty-four hours a day, seven days a week, how may I help you?"

"Tom," she yelled. "Tom. I'm home. And there's a creature. The dire wolf. Help."

She let the phone dangle before she heard Tom's response. From the other side of the table came growls and fury, as the creature, seemingly giving in to an uncontrollable impulse, shifted into his animal form.

Kyrie grabbed the chair and huddled in a corner holding it—legs out—like a defensive shield. Shifting would earn her nothing but the loss of her clear mind. She might not be able to defend herself this way, but she had to try. And she had to hope she would still be alive when Tom arrived.

Rafiel saw Tom reach for the phone and because Tom had just blocked his obvious path out from behind the counter—not on purpose, Rafiel was sure, but simply by reaching for the phone—Rafiel started going around his friend, to edge behind him and reach over to open the portion of the counter that allowed egress.

He heard Tom give his cheery signature-line response to the phone and rolled his eyes. As if anyone actually would consider a greasy spoon their choice for dining downtown, no matter how many times Tom repeated it. He found Kyrie's "The George" answer far more palatable.

Touching Tom's shoulder with his fingertips, Rafiel expected to cause the other man to step away, however briefly. But instead, Tom stood, frozen. Rafiel became aware that the voice coming teensy and distant through the old-fashioned phone was Kyrie's and that Kyrie sounded hysterical. He didn't remember Kyrie ever sounding hysterical, not even when she thought she was seeing Tom die before her eyes.

The fingers he had prodded Tom's shoulder with, in a very masculine keeping of distance in a friendship type of gesture, now became a full hand laid on Tom's shoulder. "What's wrong?" he asked, as he realized that Tom had gone frighteningly pale, and that his throat was working, his Adam's apple moving up and down, as if he were trying to speak through a great lump in the way.

But when Tom spoke, it wasn't to answer Rafiel. Instead, it was a raw scream, that seemed to have been torn out. "Kyrie!"

People at the nearby tables turned to look, and Conan looked up from a bill he was totaling up. Keith and his girlfriend, too, looked towards Tom, alarmed.

"What—?" Keith said.

But Tom spoke to Rafiel, apparently having totally forgotten that shifter business was secret, or that they might be in as much danger from being overheard as they would be from no matter which arcane shifter might be threatening them or, for that matter, murdering people at the aquarium.

"It's Kyrie," he said, and swallowed. "It's the . . . creature from the aquarium. He . . . I must go. I must go to her."

And as he spoke, he tore from around his head the red bandana which he usually wore, pirate-style, while cooking, and he pulled his apron off.

"Tom," Rafiel said, in warning tones, afraid that his friend would decide to shift, right there in the diner. But Tom, clearly, wasn't that completely lost to reason. He ducked under the pass-through in the counter, and ran towards the hallway.

"Keith, take the grill, please," Tom called over his shoulder, thereby proving that he wasn't completely lost to reason at all, or perhaps that his devotion to the diner outweighed everything else, even his love for Kyrie.

Rafiel didn't stand around to see if Keith took over the grill and stoves. Instead, he ducked under the pass-through on his own, and ran down the hallway after Tom. "Let me go," he said, as Tom, in what seemed to be a blind rush, struggled with the back door. "Let me go. I can go. I can defend her."

"No," Tom said, with a sound like a hiccup. "No."

"You don't think I would fight for her?"

Tom had managed to unlock the door and now pulled it open and walked out into the parking lot, and, after looking around— Rafiel hoped he was making sure that no one was coming or going close enough to see him—ducked behind the dumpster, where he would be invisible from nearby Pride Street.

He started undressing, rapidly, rolling his clothes in a bundle. "Stay," he told Rafiel. "Give Keith a hand. I'm sorry if I was too loud in there. She's in trouble. It's not that I don't think you'd fight for her. But flying is faster."

And like that, Tom kicked his boots aside, dropped his pants and underwear in a bundle, pulled off his shirt and writhed and twisted, coughing, once, twice, three times, as his body changed shapes and textures, the smooth skin becoming green scales, the head elongating . . .

Before Rafiel could blink twice, Tom was lifting off, flying across the clear skies of Goldport towards his own neighborhood.

A curse sounded from the door of the diner. "He swore he'd tell me." There was a sound of ripping clothes. And then a red dragon rose, also, following Tom across the skies.

This was folly, Rafiel thought, particularly while journalists obsessed with cryptozoology were already suspicious of the existence of dragons in town. But it didn't seem to matter, not just now. Nothing mattered, except Kyrie.

Rafiel wanted more than anything to go and save her. He understood Tom's impulse completely. His body strained to be in the sky, speeding towards her, ready to help in any way he could. But Rafiel couldn't fly and Tom had asked him to stay here and, Rafiel realized, with Conan gone, following Tom, and Keith at the grill, there would be no one to wait tables.

There weren't many people inside, but Rafiel was willing to bet there were more people than Keith could handle on his own, while cooking. *Right.* He ran his hand backward through his mane of unruly blond hair, aware, as he did it, that he would be making his hair stand on end and look more lionlike than ever. Right. Sometimes your duty requires you to be a hero, and sometimes it requires you to wait tables.

He turned to do just that and opened the door to The George. As he stepped into the cool shadows of the hallway, he saw a woman's figure retreating rapidly, ahead of him.

"May I help you?" he asked.

She turned around. It was Keith's blond friend, with her much-too-thick jacket and that look she had of having been dropped headfirst into a fish tank and still not being able to tell the piranhas from the goldfish. "I was . . . looking for the bathroom," she said.

It might very well be. Well—it could be, at least. If she was as confused as she looked, she might have walked all the way to the end of the hallway somehow managing to go by two bathrooms marked with the international icons for stick-figure man and stick-figure woman wearing triangle skirt without noticing them. He would even be willing to understand this confusion if the bathrooms had been marked salmon and shad roe, but since they seemed to be marked restroom it made the confusion less likely.

On the other hand, perhaps she was a shifter. If that was the truth, she might have understood more of the conversation than she'd seemed to, and she might have been in search of further confirmation.

And yet, she still didn't smell like a shifter to Rafiel. He'd keep a very close eye on her, even as he helped Keith sling the hash or at least the burgers, and prayed with as much faith as he could possibly muster that Kyrie would be all right.

She might not be his—she would never be his—but he was not willing to face a world from which she was gone.

To shift or not to shift. Tom—as a dragon—landed on the driveway, just behind the car. He'd been thinking—as far as he'd been thinking at all—that he wouldn't shift. The dragon was a far more impressive foe than Tom, with all of his 5'6", no matter how strong, no matter how muscular.

But he couldn't even get close to the door as a dragon, let alone enter through the back or front door and go to Kyrie's rescue. A quick look to the house next door, where an elderly couple lived, reminded him too that the longer he stayed here in dragon form, the more likely someone would see him and report him. A vision of journalists with snapping cameras had taken hold of his brain and he was struggling to shift back to human form, as—behind him—he heard a dragon land.

Already in human form, Tom looked back, startled, to see a red dragon on the driveway. Conan. And Tom hadn't called him. But Tom didn't have time to discuss it with Conan, or even to worry about what the Asian dragon might do. Instead, he must go to Kyrie, if Kyrie was still alive, if Kyrie could still be saved. And he didn't even want to consider the possibility of anything else. He plunged through the kitchen door, into a scene of chaos and a gagging animal smell.

"Tom," Kyrie said. She was on the floor, with a chair held as a shield. Across from her, biting and growling and lunging at the chair was the dire wolf, his fur on end, his eyes mad, saliva dripping from his daggerlike teeth.

He can take me in one bite, Tom thought. *He can behead me with a single bite. I'm going to die. But I can't become a dragon here. I can't. It would destroy the room and kill Kyrie, and he'd just port elsewhere.*

Blindly, he reached for the rack of utensils that Kyrie had put on the wall, next to the stove. He rarely cooked at home—both he and Kyrie normally ate at the diner, or else brought home food from the diner. However, Tom was taking cooking courses and on the rare occasions when he did cook at home, he felt the need for semi-decent implements. So Kyrie had tacked up to the wall one of those things with leather pockets normally used in workshops to keep hammers and whatnot. And over the last couple of months, they'd been buying good implements: chopping knives, spatulas, a meat-tenderizing hammer.

Tom saw the dire wolf turn towards him, and he knew he had only seconds, and he knew that he couldn't turn his back on the creature. So he reached with his right hand and grabbed the first handle he could. What he got was a polished, sealed-wood handle, and, from the heft, the meat-tenderizing hammer, with a weighted hammer on one side and a hatchet on the other. Too short to keep the wolf's jaws from closing on his head. He reached again, and brought out . . . an immense skewer. It was Kyrie's latest acquisition, and Tom wasn't absolutely sure what she meant him to use it for. It wasn't a classical skewer as such, but it had a skewer in the center and then four, smaller, metal prongs, on the bottom. Kyrie had said something about a TV commercial for it that mentioned roasting a chicken in a standing position. Since Tom couldn't imagine why anyone would want to do what sounded like a convoluted form of medieval torture—at least if the chicken were still alive—he'd thanked her effusively and set the skewer in the wall pocket, determined to forget it.

Now he realized it was a formidable weapon. He turned to the dire wolf, holding the hammer-ax in one hand, and the skewer in the other, and opened his mouth to say something pithy and challenging on the lines of *make my day*. And the smell enveloped him. It was like the smell of a hundred cats in heat; the smell of a thousand unwashed, wet dogs. It filled his mouth, his nostrils, his every pore. It made it impossible for him to think, impossible for him to move.

"Look out," Kyrie yelled and, rising from her defensive position, hit the dire wolf hard across the back of the head with what remained of her portable chair.

Tom felt the teeth clamp on his leg, and screamed, inhaling more of the smell. He knew what he should be doing. He should be attacking the creature, making him back up, allowing Kyrie to go behind him, allowing them both to escape, with Tom guarding the retreat, towards the car and away.

But no matter how much he thought of it, as the feral mad eyes faced Tom's, as the creature growled and snarled and salivated, all Tom could think was that he couldn't move. That the stench enveloping him was somehow preventing his movement.

"Tom, damn it," Kyrie said, her voice high and hysterical. "Do something. We're going to die."

And at that moment . . . there was a voice. It was the voice that Tom had heard in the shower before, the voice of the Great Sky Dragon. It echoed in his mind, filling up all of his senses, so that it was visible sound and scented words, and seemed to touch him all over, as if in an enveloping blanket.

Mine, the voice said. *Mine. Under my protection.*

Like that—with those words—the horrible gagging smell was gone from Tom's nostrils, from Tom's mind. The feel of the Great Sky Dragon's words still echoing in him—seeming to make his very teeth vibrate—Tom stepped forward, and brought the skewer in hard on the creature's eye, thinking only that if he destroyed the brain it might be the same as beheading. But the dire wolf had jumped backward just in time. The tip of the skewer cut a deep gash down the side of his face, while the ax, which Tom had managed to swing as a follow through, cut across his left ear.

The creature screamed. Blood spurted. And through it all, his voice, less powerful than the Great Sky Dragon's but also echoing inside Tom's head and not outside, as voices were supposed to, sounded, *He must pay. He must pay. And he's not yours. He's not Asian. You can't claim him.*

The stench came back, less overpowering, but back, nonetheless. But only for a second. The Great Sky Dragon's voice sounded again, and clearly he was a creature with a very simple philosophy. *Mine,* he yelled. *Mine. I've claimed him.*

The stench vanished. The dire wolf growled. Tom swung forward, skewer and ax swinging. Making a space behind him. "Go, Kyrie, go," he said. "The car, now."

She got up and lurched, behind him, towards the door, while he moved to block the dire wolf from getting to her. The creature wasn't teleporting or giving the impression of teleporting. Whatever it was that the Great Sky Dragon's voice caused, it seemed to cause the dire wolf to become unable to create what, for lack of better words, one must call supernatural effects.

"Come," Kyrie yelled, as she opened the door, and ran full tilt outside. "Come."

"I will," Tom said, kicking the door fully open with his foot, and backing into the open door, still holding the skewer and the ax.

The dire wolf made a jump—a clumsy jump—towards him. There was no Great Sky Dragon voice, but Tom swung at him, hard with the ax, and cut him across the nose.

Kyrie honked the horn, and now Tom turned, thinking it was the most stupid thing he could do, but also that he ran much faster that way. The passenger door of the car was open, and he more threw himself at the opening than ran into it.

His head on Kyrie's shoulder, he reached to close the door, even as she started the car and backed out of the driveway. The dire wolf came running out of the kitchen and chased them. Kyrie turned abruptly, hitting the wolf with the back left wheel and saying, under her breath, "Sorry, it wasn't intentional."

Tom took a deep breath, two. He straightened, and buckled his seat belt. "To whom are you apologizing?"

"You. Him. I don't know. I didn't mean to run him over. Did I run him over?"

Tom looked back at what looked very much like a bleeding dire wolf still chasing them. "I don't think so. Can you go faster?"

She pressed the gas down, taking these little residential back streets at speeds normally reserved for the highway, and breathing deeply, deeply, as if recovering from shock.

It took Tom a moment to realize that it wasn't breathing, it was sobs. "Kyrie," he said, aghast. He'd never seen her cry. He'd never heard her cry before. Not like this.

"I can't help it," she said. "Reaction." She turned again, seemingly blindly. "I thought I was going to die. And then I thought you were going to die and I . . ."

"I thought you were going to die," a voice said from the back. Conan's voice. He popped from the back seat like a deranged jack-in-the-box, and Kyrie slammed on the brakes hard, stopping them suddenly in the middle of a tree-lined street. "I thought you were going to die. You screamed. So I called Himself. I told him I couldn't go in, but I thought the enemy was in there. And then . . . he aimed for your mind and the enemy's mind."

"What the hell?" Kyrie said. And it was all that Tom could do not to turn around and plant his fist in the middle of Conan's smug-looking face.

Instead, he turned around and said, "What are you doing? What do you think you were doing, hiding back there?"

Conan's expression shifted, from smug to sullen. "I wasn't hiding from you," he said, in the tone that a kid might use to say it wasn't him who drew on the wall. "I was hiding from the dire wolf."

"Oh, that makes it ever so much better," Kyrie said. "Not."

"Just go," Conan said. "He's going to come for us."

"I don't think so," Tom said, looking behind them. "He's not back there, and besides, he knows where we're going to go, doesn't he?"

"Does he?" Conan asked.

"The diner," Kyrie said. And then, softly, "Hopefully, he's not so brazen as to come and attack us in the diner, in the parking lot, in front of everyone."

"Hopefully," Tom said. "Or we'll be dead. I mean, it's not like we can, realistically, stop showing up at the diner."

"No," Kyrie said. She started the car again, going more slowly. "But perhaps once he calms down, he won't be as dangerous? I mean, I get a feeling we pushed him over the edge, and he didn't very well know what he was doing."

"*We* pushed him over the edge?" Tom said. "*We?* What were you doing at the house, anyway? And without telling me. If Rafiel hadn't told me—"

"You should have asked Rafiel what I was doing at the house," Kyrie said. She drove with jagged movements that caused the car to lurch one way then the other. "He called me and told me to meet him there. Something about one of his relatives repairing the house. And then he wasn't there."

"He called you?" Tom asked. He remembered Rafiel coming into the diner, his confusion at not finding Kyrie in the bed-and-breakfast. He didn't even want to think that Rafiel might be working with the dire wolf. If Rafiel was . . . If Rafiel had betrayed them . . .

"He called me on my cell phone. Told me to meet him at the house ASAP. I thought it was a little weird, but he said he had everything ready to go right then, so I showered and went."

Tom groaned. Either Rafiel was mind-manipulated, or Rafiel had defected to—for lack of better words—the dark side. Either way, it could not be good. "But . . ." he said. "But . . ." And swallowed hard.

"The only weird thing," Kyrie said, "is that his words seemed to have . . . oh, I don't know how to put it . . . no sound. No vocalization."

Tom found his forehead wrinkling in worry before he could think that he was worried. That didn't feel right. Kyrie's purse was at his feet, as it normally was when she was driving. He bent down and picked it up. "May I get your cell phone?" he asked. He didn't like to reach into her purse without an invitation.

"Sure," she said, as she turned onto Pride Street. Five minutes from The George.

He reached into the little pocket on the front lining where she normally kept her phone. He picked it up. "He called you on this cell phone?" he said. It wouldn't turn on, there was no battery. So, he grabbed his cell phone from his pocket, and swapped the batteries. Then he turned the phone on and looked through calls received.

"Yeah."

"When?"

"This morning, almost right after you left, I think. I was lying in a patch of sun and unable to sleep, and then the phone rang."

Tom looked up and down through the list of numbers. The latest call the phone showed was three days before. He took a deep breath, and waited till she pulled in the parking lot of The George to speak. He wasn't sure what telling her while she was driving would do.

"Kyrie," he said. "There's no record of any such call."

"What?" Kyrie asked. She pushed the parking brake down with her foot, as she reached blindly for her cell phone. "Let me see that."

She pulled the cell phone from Tom's nerveless hands, and went to the menu and calls received, and paged, frantically, up and down the list.

She realized she was shaking violently, and she put the phone down on the seat, very slowly, then very slowly lowered her head towards the wheel, until she rested her forehead on it.

"You mean the whole call . . ." she said, at last. "You mean, he just reached into my mind." For some reason the thought made her physically ill. Reaching into her head to trick her seemed like the worst violation possible. "How could he? How?"

"I don't know. I think he has some sort of mind power," Tom

said, hesitantly. He laid his palm gently on her shoulder, as if he were afraid of touching her. But when she didn't protest, he enveloped her in his arms and pulled her to him. "I'm sorry, Kyrie. I think this is worse than anything we faced before."

For a moment, it comforted her, that he held her like that, tightly, against his body. He was still naked—she was quite sure he had forgotten that—and his skin smelled of the hotel's soap overlaid with sweat from fear and fight. It was not unpleasant. His hair was loose— as it always was after he shifted back and forth. He kept a package of hair ties in the glove compartment of the car, in a kitchen drawer at home, and in one of the supply rooms in the diner. His hair brushed her face, softly, like silk.

And for a moment—for just a moment, as her breath calmed down—this felt good and protective and healing. She had a sense that she belonged to him—that she was his, that Tom was somehow entitled to hold her like this and that he—as scattered and lost as he'd been most of his life—he was somehow protecting her. As he'd protected her, or tried to, in that kitchen.

But slowly the thought intruded that he was just looking after her because he looked after everyone—Old Joe, Conan, Not Dinner, and even Keith and Anthony to an extent. Tom seemed to think it was his duty, his necessary place in life, to go through it helping everyone and everything. And this made his arms around her, his soothing voice, the hand now gently stroking her hair and cheek, utterly meaningless.

She shrank back, laughing a little, disguising her embarrassment at having been, momentarily, emotionally naked. "You must put clothes on," she said. "What if someone looks in the car and sees me sitting here with two naked guys?"

"I don't have clothes," Conan said from the back seat, his voice dull and seemingly trying to be distant, as if he were apologizing for being present during their embrace. He hardly needed to.

Tom pulled back. He took a deep breath, as if he needed to control himself, and she didn't look down to see if he needed to control himself in that sense. It wouldn't help to know he'd been embracing her out of automatic pity but that lust had mixed in. She wanted to know he had held her for other reasons—she wasn't even sure what reasons she wanted it to be. Perhaps because he felt so incomplete without her, that he had to hold her and protect her to be able to hold and protect himself. She wanted him to think of them as a unit, she thought. As belonging. And perhaps that was, ultimately, her greatest foolishness, that she so desperately wanted to belong with someone. Not to. She had no fancy to be owned or restricted in that way. For much too long, growing up, she had belonged to the state of North Carolina—had been in effect the child of the state—that she did not want to belong to anyone. But she wanted to belong with someone, to be part of a group. Not at the mercy of passing bureaucrats and their whims, but able to contribute and be taken into account by a group.

She'd thought she was part of that. Even days ago, if you had asked her, she'd have said that she and Tom and Rafiel were just that sort of group. A *you and me against the world* group.

But now the dire wolf could get in her mind and force her own friendship for Rafiel to betray her. And Tom was determined to protect the world and its surroundings. "There's clothes under the seat," she told Conan. "Get some for Tom too. We stuff them there, when we go shopping. We buy extra stuff, I wash it and stuff it down there. From the thrift shop, so they're clean but worn."

"Worn is fine," Conan said, as he passed, over Kyrie's shoulder, a grey pair of sweat pants and a red sweat shirt to Tom.

"I think you should go shower," Kyrie said. "Both of you. I'll go inside"—she made a head gesture towards the diner—"and hold the fort, while you guys make yourselves decent."

Tom frowned a little but then nodded. "If he comes in the diner—" he said.

"I'll call, okay? I don't think he's going to do much in front of every customer at the tables, truly."

"You don't know that," Tom said. "He could reach in and touch your mind. Like he did before. We don't know how many minds he can touch. He could make everyone in the diner ignore him, as he kills you or dismembers you."

"I'll call you. I'll call you as soon as he comes," she said, almost frantically, wanting to go back to the diner, which right now represented routine and normalcy, and to be allowed to go on with life, to forget that someone out there—someone who didn't wish them well—had the power to reach into her mind and make her hear and think things that had never happened.

"I don't know what the owner is going to think, of my keeping going to the bedroom with different guys and coming out in new clothes," Tom said, under his breath, but Conan only gave him this unfocused, uncomprehending look, as if he were talking about some different planet, or something so strange that Conan's mind couldn't begin to understand it.

Tom was fairly sure this was not true. After all, the man had grown up in Tennessee, no matter how strange his parents' culture might have been. He'd watched the same shows, read the same newspapers—generally speaking—and listened to the same music— well, perhaps more country and western—that Tom listened to.

And yet, he genuinely seemed to have no idea why Tom going to his rented room to shower with different guys accompanying him might make the owner of the bed-and-breakfast a little uncomfortable.

"She's going to think I'm running a business," Tom added, under his breath. But it was all pointless: his worrying and Conan's—had to be deliberate—lack of comprehension. They met no one as they walked along the oak-floored hallways of the bed-and-breakfast. The room, when Tom opened it, was as Kyrie must have left it—with the bed coverings thrown half back, and her hair brush thrown on top of the clothes.

Almost by instinct—he certainly had not had time to get used to this—before Tom opened the door fully, he opened it a crack and put his hand in the opening, as if to catch a baseball. Seconds later a furry warm ball hit it, and clung to his wrist with sharp little needle claws. Tom laughed, as he brought the creature up and held him against his chest. "Hello, Not Dinner. Foiled again." Then he opened the door fully, allowing Conan into the room, and closing it and locking it afterwards. "You can shower first," he said. And realized that Conan was barefoot. "Did you leave your shoes . . . ?"

"Somewhere in the parking lot," Conan said, sullenly.

"I left mine in the diner, near the entrance," Tom said, looking down at his toes. "Well . . . I didn't even realize I was barefoot till now. We get used to this stuff."

"Yeah," Conan said, and went into the shower, to emerge, just seconds after, wearing the same clothes but looking far cleaner, his odd crest of hair standing up. Tom realized in losing his left arm, Conan had lost the red dragon tattoo he'd once had upon his left hand. He wondered if the new one would grow in with the same tattoo. No, it couldn't. That would require something uncomfortably like magic. Then would Conan have to go and tattoo the same image on the back of his hand?

Putting Not Dinner down on the bed, where he proceeded to attack some dust mites floating on a ray of light, Tom got up, wondering what part of Conan's belonging to the dragon triad was volitional, and what part was enforced. He remembered his saying that his parents had more or less turned him over to the Great Sky Dragon because he was a dragon and therefore belonged to him. Belonged. What a very strange word to use.

And Tom knew he should be furious with Conan for allowing the Great Sky Dragon to aim for Tom's mind once more. But he'd aimed for the dire wolf's mind. And Tom had no delusions. He knew that if the Great Sky Dragon hadn't spoken in his mind, the chance was good that he'd now be dead. Dire wanted to kill him. And he couldn't defend himself against Dire. That much was clear.

Tom turned the water on high and hot, and opened a new soap from the little basket of toiletries. Stupid as it was, he, who had for so long washed himself with soap from dispensers and with a combination of wet and dry paper towels at an endless succession of public restrooms throughout the land, felt an almost physical repulsion at the thought of using the same soap Conan had used. The soap Kyrie used, sure. No problem there. She was his, he was hers, in all but the legal marriage sense. He couldn't imagine life without Kyrie and he very much hoped she could not imagine life without him.

But the idea that Conan had used that soap and that there were sloughed-off, Conan skin cells in it made his flesh crawl. Which was stupid, he thought, as he washed himself almost vengefully, under water so hot that it made his skin sting. Conan looked clean enough, and he seemed to be a nice guy.

And then Tom realized it was the thought of the intimacy of belonging. Families used the same bathroom, the same soap. He wasn't ready to admit Conan into his family—if he would ever be. Conan belonged to the Great Sky Dragon—that creature that had now made free of Tom's mind, twice, without a welcome mat.

While the thought that the Great Sky Dragon could make free of his mind didn't fill him with the same horror that having her mind manipulated by the dire wolf seemed to fill Kyrie—understandably, because all the Great Sky Dragon had done was talk in his mind, not manipulate him into believing things that weren't true. Also, arguably, because the Great Sky Dragon, at least at this very moment, didn't seem to feel like killing Tom—it made him feel uncomfortable and used.

He'd brought his underwear, jeans, a T-shirt and socks into the bathroom with him. He'd packed—as he always did—a half-dozen rubber flip-flops, bought at the end of summer. He'd wear those till he could get back to his boots. He could lend a pair to Conan, as well. They wouldn't be much worse than his stupid elastic shoes. He dressed in the bathroom and emerged into the bedroom, with words on his lips which summed up the whole issue he had with this situation: "I don't belong to the Great Sky Dragon," he said, defiantly, saying the words aloud—even though he knew it would bother Conan.

Conan had been playing with Not Dinner—or at least submitting mutely to having his sleeve climbed, and his hair and ear played with.

He looked up, startled, and frowned at Tom, "You have to," he said. "You're a dragon."

"I'm not a dragon like you," Tom said forcefully, almost viciously. "In case you haven't realized, we don't look at all alike. As dragons. My body type is completely different. *I* am like one of those dragons that Vikings used to carve in the front of their ships. Perhaps there was once some organization I belonged to, like you belong to the Great Sky Dragon. But I don't belong to him. Or to you."

He felt vaguely guilty saying this, as if he were proclaiming the superiority of Nordic dragons over Asian dragons. In truth, he didn't feel like that at all. He was sure the Asian dragons were far more adept at surviving, for one. Look at how they had an organization that looked after them. And look at how their legends had managed to convince people that they were good and righteous—while all the European dragons had managed to do was simultaneously convince people that they were dangerous and that they slept on massive hoards of gold. Thereby creating perfect conditions for people to hate them and to steal from them—to take their valuables and proclaim themselves heros in doing this.

He wondered if the hoard and treasures were true, and then thought that if shifters really lived as long as Old Joe claimed—as long as the Great Sky Dragon appeared to have been alive—then it could very well be true. If you looked at the panorama of your life as covering hundreds or thousands of years, then everyone got to live in interesting times. Every long-lived shifter's life could cover wars and revolutions and endless upheavals. And gold often saw you through all of those. So why not hoard?

"It doesn't matter," Conan said. "It doesn't matter if you are an Asian dragon or not. You are a dragon. You're a child of the . . . of the G . . . of Himself."

Tom frowned at him. That was what he had wanted to fend off, he realized. Not the fact that the triad dragons were Asian—he really couldn't care less about that. What he wanted to fend off, more than anything, was Conan's—and seemingly the Great Sky Dragon's—belief that Tom belonged to him from birth. That Tom had no choice in this matter.

Tom had never been good at obeying. His inability to obey his parents, his teachers, his counselors or his advisors had made his—and probably his parents'—lives living hell long before he had turned into a dragon and been kicked out of the house. He always felt like, should someone tell him to go one way, he must immediately go the other. It was something deep within himself, something he was aware of but didn't feel he could change without becoming someone else—without dying, in a way.

And now this organization he didn't like or trust, this organization that was involved in criminal activities, and whose code of honor was as quirky as that of any mafia throughout history, wanted to claim him. He shrugged, as if to throw back their imagined weight from his shoulders, and picked up a hair tie from the packet he'd left on top of the dresser. Confining his still-damp hair into a ponytail, he said, jerkily, "I am not his child. And even if I were, that wouldn't mean I was *his*. That I *belonged* to him."

Yet Conan had allowed himself to be mutely handed over to this organization by his dutiful parents. Tom thought it was better—and more humane—to force your kid out on the street at gunpoint, as his father had done, than to hand him over to the designs and whims of a supernatural creature who probably would care nothing for him.

He saw Conan's small despondent shrug, which seemed to signify he couldn't do anything about either Tom's belonging to the Great Sky Dragon or Tom's stubbornness, and Tom said, "I am my own."

And in the next moment wondered how that could be true, when the Great Sky Dragon had the ability to enter his mind and make him hear his thoughts.

Rafiel kept his eye on Keith's friend as he moved around the tables taking orders. He'd never really had a job as a waiter, but he had

helped Alice sometimes when she worked at this same diner, back when it was The Athens. It was amazing how it came back to him and, except for the fact that Tom's menu was far more elaborate than that of the old Athens, and that he wasn't really desperate to get tips to supplement his income, it was just like being back in time.

His gestures came back, too—the broad wipe at the table before taking orders—the scribbling of orders on his pad, the carrying of the trays, one-handed and perfectly balanced.

As he approached the table where a new customer had just sat, he did a double take. The customer had pulled her—fake-fur fringed—hood back from her face, and was unbuttoning her black, knee-length knit outer coat. Underneath it, it was Lei, from the aquarium, with her long, sleek black hair, her exotic features, and her very shapely body, highlighted by a miniskirt and tight sweater. At least, Rafiel thought, as he ran his gaze over her legs—purely out of concern, of course—she was wearing thigh-high leather boots. He still didn't understand how anyone could, voluntarily, wear a miniskirt in this weather, but then again he couldn't really understand how anyone could voluntarily wear any skirt in cold weather. He'd consider it a peculiarity of the female brain—like inability to feel your legs from the thigh down—were it not for all those proud Scots and their kilts.

"Hello," he told Lei, smiling at her, and giving the table a quick wipe. "How may I help you?"

She was staring at him, openmouthed, just like he had grown a second head, or possibly stood on his head, and it took him a moment to realize in what capacity she had met him, and what she must think of him. A brief, lunatic impulse commanded him to tell her that he was his own underachieving twin, but this he conquered, forcefully. Instead he told her, "I'm just giving some friends a hand for an hour or so. I haven't changed jobs."

Lei turned very red, as though she'd been thinking exactly that, then grinned. "Oh well," she said. "I had been thinking that the police in Goldport must pay very poorly if their officers moonlight in diners."

"Nah. I'm friends with the owners and they had to go out for a little bit." *Please let it be only a little bit.* He gave her his best dimpled smile, which had made weaker women melt. "So, what will you have?"

"Just . . . a hot chocolate," she said, looking at the menu then folding it and returning it to its holder on the edge of the table. "I was just walking by and I felt like coming in." She shrugged. "I guess the aquarium being closed, and my not having to go to work left me with this great need for human company or something."

Rafiel's curiosity peaked at the mention of her having had an impulse to enter the diner. But a deep breath brought him no whiff of shifter-scent. Only the smell of washed female flesh and some perfume that was deep and spicy and hot, and probably cost upward of his salary per ounce and likely sold under some name like Dagger or Treason or something of the sort. And then, after all, people did sometimes feel an impulse to just go in somewhere without being shifters or smelling the specialized pheromones that infused the diner. He shrugged. "Right. I'll bring it to you, right away."

He went back, and drew the hot chocolate, and got a baleful look from Keith. "Do you have any idea how long Tom is going to be? People are ordering souvlaki, and I'm sure he keeps some pre-made, somewhere, but I can't seem to find it."

"No clue," Rafiel said, as he added a dollop of whipped cream atop the cup of rich, dark hot chocolate. "Sorry. But they should be back soon. They said it was only for a few minutes."

"Right," Keith said, but in a tone that implied he didn't believe it. He lowered a basket of fries into the oil, causing a whoosh that seemed deliberate and, somehow, irritated. "You know, I wasn't intending on having to work. I just came in to introduce Summer to you guys, and now here I am, working."

"I know," Rafiel said, trying to be patient. Sometimes it was hard to remember that Keith was younger than all of them. And sometimes it was much too easy. "I know. I'm sure they didn't mean to go out either. Quite sure."

Keith made a sound under his breath. It could probably be translated as "harumph." Rafiel couldn't answer that in any way, so he turned his back, and took Lei her hot chocolate, which she received with a wide smile, as if he had just fetched her fire from the mountain.

"I don't suppose you can sit and talk?" she said.

He looked around, and at the moment there wasn't any customer clamoring for his attention, so he shrugged. "Not sit," he said. "But I suppose I could talk a little. It isn't as though I'm going to get fired. It's just if I stand, at least anyone who needs something knows whose attention to get."

"Oh," she said. And "Yes."

He smiled. "So, what do you need to talk about?" He wondered about her brittle frailty and once more it seemed to him as though she were trying to make a play for his attention—whether his romantic attention or his friendship, he couldn't tell.

All other things being equal, he would have discouraged her. It was often easier to get rid of prospective romantic interest before the first date than after. It saved the girl some hurt feelings and him some of that fury to which hell could not compare.

However, Lei was involved—by working in the aquarium, if nothing else—in the case with the sharks. And Rafiel was never sure when a romantic come-on was just that, or an attempt by an otherwise awkward bystander to tell him something about a case in progress.

"It's not so much that I need to talk," she said, and looked down at her hands, one on either side of the hot chocolate cup. They were nice hands, the nails clean of any polish or shine, but carefully clipped and filed into neat ovals. "I just . . . I was wondering how long till the aquarium is allowed to open again, because, you know, the thing is that . . . Well, I know I'm only an intern of sorts, and I'm there to study as much as to work, but you know, they pay me, and I count on that payment to help make my tuition at CUG."

She looked up at him, intently, pleadingly almost. Her eyes were black, which was something Rafiel had never seen. You always heard talk of black eyes, but you never saw them. Instead, you saw eyes that were deep, dark brown, or something like that, but never that pure black, unreflective.

"We are working as fast as we can," Rafiel said. Except, of course, when he wasn't, like right now, when he was waiting tables, while he should have been visiting people who'd been around the aquarium a week or so before the first human remains were found—around when they'd calculated the first victim had fallen or been thrown into the shark tank. And selling his superiors on the need to do that would be interesting enough—though no one was likely to ask him for a very close accounting of his time for a week or so—because after all it would seem more logical to investigate who had keys to the aquarium, and who might have gone there since it had been closed to the public and in the middle of a snowstorm.

The second corpse—or the bits of it the sharks hadn't eaten—had shown up in an aquarium closed to the public. The suspects should, obviously, be the employees or—if his superiors ever found out that Rafiel had abstracted a key—Rafiel himself.

Only, having found out how easy it was to steal a key, Rafiel could argue—was arguing, with himself, just as he would with his superiors should they call him on it—that other people might have done so. And given his privileged knowledge that there were shifters and that two, maybe three of them, had been to the aquarium around the time of the first crime, he thought it made perfect sense to find out if one of those might have stolen the keys, as he had, and had copies made, and if the crimes were, somehow, being committed as part of a shifter imperative, driven by the animal half of some poor slob with less self-control than Rafiel himself had.

"The police are pursuing enquiries?" Lei said, ironically.

"Well, as a matter of fact the police are," Rafiel said and sighed. "You know"—he wiped at the table in what was more a nervous gesture than anything else—"it's amazing how often those words are true and how often they define most of what I do in my work. We pursue enquiries. We go from place to place and ask questions." He smiled. "All those TV series with heroic detectives who can flourish a gun and threaten a suspect just in the nick of time, or who have the ability to magically assemble pieces of evidence given by some amazing new scientific machine for analyzing skin cells, or whatever, do my job a great disservice. Most of what we do is just . . . patient, slow work. I'm sorry it's affecting your job. I'm sure it affected the job of the poor slob who got killed, also."

"Yes, of course," she said, looking guilty as people had a tendency to when they complained about a murder disrupting their lives and somehow managed to ignore that it had ended someone else's life. "It's just . . ." she shrugged. "Of course I'm very sorry for the man. The TV says he was an out-of-town salesman, or something, but you know, I still need to work and I need a paycheck."

"We will solve the murders as fast as we can," Rafiel said. "Trust me, I don't want some lunatic at large, pushing people into shark tanks."

She looked up at him and her curiously opaque black eyes managed to project an impression of innocence and confusion. "Are you sure that is what happened? I mean, couldn't people just have fallen in? Or . . . or jumped in, even?"

"Oh, sure," he heard himself say. "The first one, maybe. But this one? With the aquarium closed? Are you honestly suggesting that someone took it into his head to steal keys to the aquarium and go in to commit suicide by shark? What kind of person does that? Given how cold it was, it would have made more sense for him to stay outside and let himself die from hypothermia. Alternately, to jump from a very high building. But jump into a tank full of creatures with sharp teeth? Who views that as an easy way out?"

"Well, not easy, perhaps, but quick," she said, hesitantly. "Or perhaps they just were drunk, and dropped into the tank? Who knows?"

"Who knows indeed?" he said, thinking that it was very clear that Ms. Lei Lani knew less than nothing. "Do you often have drunken visitors who take the trouble of copying keys and come in after hours?"

She opened her mouth, then closed it, then opened it again. A blush suffused her cheeks. "I don't know why you keep talking about people stealing keys," she said. "It's not needed, you know. When the restaurant company took over the aquarium, they never bothered to change the locks. They're the same we had when the aquarium belonged to the city and was so poor we had fewer fish than your average pet store—or at least that's what I've heard. I wasn't here, back then. But they never changed the locks and some of the . . ." She blushed darker, a very interesting effect on her tanned cheeks. The more he talked to her, the less he was confident identifying her as a native Hawaiian, and the more it seemed to him she was probably Mediterranean or generic white, who just happened to have dark hair and a generally broad face. "You know, some of the guys who work there, like, some of the ones who clean the aquariums, talk about how easy it is to pick the lock, and about breaking into the aquarium and bringing dates there. I don't know if it's true or if they just talk about it to . . . to tweak me. But I know when we clean that observation area just over the shark tank, we often find . . ." She looked away from him, past him, at the front window and the sparse traffic out there on Fairfax. "We often find used condoms in the planters."

Rafiel raised his eyebrows. "Interesting," he said, while trying to sound, in fact, perfectly disinterested. Not that he was. She might simply be repeating salacious tales her male co-workers told each other. Most of the people who worked at the aquarium were high school or college age, and Rafiel knew better than to put any stock in the stories told by males in that age group. On the other hand, they might very well be true. And if true, they would open a whole other front of investigation into these crimes.

At that moment, he heard Keith say, "Oh, thank God, Kyrie, you're here," and looked up to see Kyrie duck behind the counter, looking like she had been crying but noticeably in one piece.

"Excuse me a moment," he said. "I'll go see if they still need me or if I can go back to my real job."

Kyrie saw Tom's clothes and boots at the back entrance to the diner, just under the overhang that prevented them from getting dripped on by the gutters filled with melted runoff. She picked them up, carrying them in with her. In her mind, she could see Tom shuffling out of them, hurrying to her rescue. She'd seen him do this before, and knew that he always kicked off his boots before he shifted.

He was lucky, she thought, that no one had stolen his boots yet, as likely as he was to leave them in all possible—and some distinctly impossible—locations around town. But the thought that he had been in a hurry to come to her rescue remained, as she stepped into the warm atmosphere of the diner, perfumed with the homey scent of fries and redolent of basil, fennel and mint.

Before they'd taken over, there had been an underlying bad smell to the diner, as though the old grease was never completely cleaned from the various surfaces. As they'd found in their grand cleanup and repainting before reopening under their management, this was by and large true. But now all that you could smell in the diner was the clean aroma of well prepared food. Tom was as fanatic about hygiene as he was about helping people who just didn't seem able to make it on their own. People and animals, she thought, as she remembered Not Dinner. Not that she resented Not Dinner. As someone who had long ago accepted it would be neither safe nor sane for her to have children, a pet might be as close as she came to motherhood.

She put Tom's boots on the lower shelf of the space behind the counter, the shelf into which all of them shoved either uncomfortable or too-heavy shoes on occasion—as well as purses, or bags of purchases. She smiled at Keith's enthusiastic and somewhat shaky salutation, and wondered if Keith had been worried about her, or even knew why Tom had left.

Grabbing an apron from beneath the counter, she said, "Tom will be in in just a second, and then you can go."

"Good," Keith said, sounding even more relieved. "You know, I was supposed to bring Summer here, and introduce her to you guys, and then take her out for a movie, or something. I was not supposed to bring her here, duck behind the counter, and leave her all alone. I don't even know where she's gone now." He cast a panicked glance around the tables—of which only five were occupied, and none of them except the one table with the dark-haired woman who was talking to Rafiel, showing anyone even remotely in Keith's age range.

"What does she look like?" Kyrie asked.

"Blond. Wearing a pink coat."

"Maybe she got bored and went for a walk," she said. Privately, she was thinking that if the girl got bored that quickly and went for a walk instead of, say, sitting at the counter and talking to Keith while he worked, she might not in fact be very interested. But she didn't say anything aloud.

She didn't remember being Keith's emotional age. Chronologically, they weren't that far apart. They were both, roughly college age—but Kyrie couldn't remember a time when she had felt so incapable of standing on her own two feet that she needed the props of a group, or of a friendship, or even of a boyfriend. In fact, until very recently, she had none of those. However, Keith clearly needed friends or a girlfriend or something and even in the months she'd known him, she had seen him assume that people liked him or even loved him on very scant evidence. It would be cruel to disabuse him of it.

Instead, she said as tentatively as she dared, "So this was a date?"

He shrugged. "Something like it. I mean, I told her I wanted her to meet some of my friends, but the idea was that I was going to take her to the morning showing of *Monsters of the Deep* at the Imax at the museum, and then we were . . . you know, going for coffee or something."

Ah, yes, Keith, take the girl to the Nature Museum Imax, why don't you? Dazzle and seduce her. She'll never know what hit her, Kyrie thought. After all, who was she to judge the mating rituals of others. It wasn't like she had a great deal of experience with mating or dating. And Keith, being a confirmed geek, was probably following the right tactic in looking for a girl who could share his obsessions. "Sorry to leave you stuck here," she said. "Maybe she's just outside looking at shop windows or something."

"Maybe," he said, sullenly. "But it's not even that. If Rafiel hadn't offered to help, I don't know how I would have managed both the tables and the cooking."

"Well," Kyrie said. She looked up to see that Rafiel was indeed wearing the red apron of The George, and smiled despite herself. What would the police force think of its officer moonlighting in this way? "I'm glad he stayed, then."

At that moment, Rafiel excused himself and sailed towards her across the diner, notebook in hand, a smile on his all-too-handsome face. "So glad you're here and okay," he said, in an undertone that couldn't be heard by anyone but Keith. "Are the two guys okay, too?"

"Yeah. They're showering," Kyrie said. "They'll be here any moment, or at least Tom will." And then, rapidly, "Rafiel, Tom says you didn't call me and ask me to meet you at my place?"

"Huh?" Rafiel said. "No, I didn't. I went by the bed-and-breakfast to get the key and when you weren't there, I came here to get Tom's. That's it."

She had known it before, but hearing it now made her heart sink. Hearing that Rafiel had never called, confirming absolutely that it must have been the dire wolf playing mind games brought on a slight shake, and caused her to reach for the counter for support. She must also have gone pale, because Rafiel said, "What's wrong?"

She told him, rapidly, in just slightly above a whisper. When she finished, she realized that Keith too was staring at her. "You're saying this thing was in your mind? That it made you think things had happened?"

Kyrie nodded.

"Wow," Keith said. "That's like some supervillain. Much worse than the last time." He sounded vaguely fascinated and excited about it.

"You know, Keith," Rafiel started. "This is not—"

"I know, I know, it's not a game or a play. It's the true thing, and it's true for all of you. But the idea . . . It's just cool. So, how are you guys going to defeat him?"

"I don't know," Kyrie said, as she looked over Rafiel's shoulder towards the door, where the bell tinkled indicating someone had come in. Her heart skipped a beat, and it seemed to her that her breath caught in her throat.

The man who had come in was not wearing a silvery turtleneck or black pants. He was rather more elaborately dressed, in an impeccably cut pair of grey trousers and a button-down silver shirt mostly covered by a blazer that must be made of the finest fabric available and fashioned by master tailors. But he was undeniably the same creature who had just fought it out with her and Tom in their kitchen.

"But he has just come in."

Kyrie stared at the dire wolf—Mr. Dire—in his neat attire, as he made his way between the tables, straight at her. Tom's fears came back to haunt her.

What if Dire reached into her thoughts and made her follow him somewhere he could kill her? What if he reached into the minds of the ten or so people in the diner and made them not see or not remember anything as he dragged her off, or even savaged her right here?

She remembered Tom hitting him repeatedly with the meat-tenderizing ax and the skewer, but Dire showed no sign at all of having been cut, or hurt in any way. His skin looked smooth, flawless, with only the shadow of beard marring its otherwise golden complexion. Had he been cut? Had that been an illusion? Or was this the illusion?

The counter had a series of bar stools on the far end, away from the grill and stove. These were rarely used during the day, though they were often occupied at night by single males who came in for their dinner, or by people who couldn't find room at the tables and booths. At this time, just before the dinner rush, they were all empty—a line of chrome and vinyl stools, fixed in a silent row.

Dante Dire flowed into one of these, straddling it. He smiled at Kyrie, revealing perfectly shaped and perfectly human teeth. She shook herself, realizing that she had been expecting him to reveal the saberlike teeth of his other form. "Could I have a coffee, miss?" he asked, just loud enough for his voice to carry to where she and Keith and Rafiel huddled.

"Don't do it," Rafiel whispered. "I'll take care of it."

But Dire smiled mockingly, and looked straight at Kyrie as he said, "Come on. It's not like I'm going to eat you."

It wasn't as though he was going to eat her, Kyrie thought. He kept telling her that, and perhaps he meant it, or perhaps it was one of those things where people keep denying their deepest thoughts. In either case, what did it matter?

Either he had no intention of killing her—and it seemed to her now, on cold reflection, that given the time it had taken Tom to come and rescue her, he could easily have finished her before the cavalry arrived—and therefore was merely toying with them, or perhaps giving her some warning of what his true powers were, or he in fact intended to kill her, and had just fallen in the rather bad habit of playing with his food. This last speculation went well with the insanity behind his eyes, and with the resemblance that he seemed to show to some of the crazier Roman emperors, those who thought they were gods and treated all life around them with the suitable disdain of immortals for mere mortal, ephemeral creatures.

So, he either could spirit her away from here, or kill her right here, without suffering any consequences, or he couldn't. In either case, it seemed to her it didn't make any difference to let Rafiel serve him. No difference, that is, except to make him despise her by thinking her a coward. And whether he intended to kill her or not, having him think worse of her would probably make it easier for him to treat her badly.

"No, I'll take care of it," she told Rafiel, as she poured a coffee, grabbed a bowl of creamers and a handful of sugars from beside the coffee maker, and set it on the counter beside Dire.

This—or the fact that despite herself her hand trembled as she set the coffee before him—seemed to amuse him. "Thank you," he told her. "I take my coffee black."

She nodded to him and started to walk away, but he said, "Stay!"

The voice was authoritative enough that she stopped walking and turned around.

"Stay," he repeated. "I think it's time I talked to you and explained what is going on."

"You don't need to," she said, her voice hollow. "You don't have to." She wasn't sure she wanted to know what Dante Dire thought was going on—at any rate she had a feeling his narrative would be highly colored and personal, and not factual or dispassionate.

"I want to," he said. "Look, it's like this . . ." He paused and took a sip of his coffee and his eyes focused to the side and behind her. Kyrie knew, without turning to look, that he was looking at Rafiel and Keith who had, doubtless, abandoned the lit stove and all other duties to come and stand beside her, as if their mere presence could protect her against this ancient and powerful creature. She had to repress an impulse to giggle, as well as an impulse to turn around and shake her head at them for being ridiculous. Instead, she looked at Dire, her eyebrows raised.

Dire looked from one to the other of the men, then back again at her. "Tell the ephemeral one to leave," he said. "This is shifter business. Not his. I want to talk but only to those who might understand it."

Kyrie froze. She heard Keith draw breath, and she knew he was getting ready to make some protest. She was almost relieved when it was Rafiel who spoke: "He's our friend. He has saved our lives in the past. There is no reason for us to banish him from any conversation. We trust him. He's one of us."

Dante Dire looked up. The gaze which he bent upon Rafiel was so coldly calculating that Kyrie felt as if she were frozen by proximity. "He is not one of us," Dire said, letting his eyes drift just enough to indicate he was surveying Keith disdainfully. "He can never be one of us. Nor can he ever truly understand us. Those of his kind who pretend to understand or like our kind, are only waiting to slip the dagger in."

Kyrie opened her mouth, in turn, to speak, but Dire looked at her. "You are young," he said. "The young make mistakes. I am not young and I am not going to suffer for your mistakes."

"But—" Rafiel said.

"We don't really want to hear what you have to say," Kyrie said, finding her voice. "We don't know that you'd tell us the truth. So far you've attacked us, nothing more. We don't see why we should trust you now."

He looked at her, eyes half closed. Slowly, slowly, his lip twitched upwards on the right side, as though she was a particularly clever child saying some interesting nonsense. "I have not attacked you," he said, didactically. "I have tested you. And having tested you, I've decided you are worthy of being told the truth. There are many of our kind," he said. "A great many more born than ever survive to their twentieth birthday let alone their hundredth. Some are killed by their own stupidity and others . . . find ways to die. Few find comrades worthy of them, or fight, as they should, for other shifters and themselves. Those that do are interesting. Interesting enough to deserve to be told . . . some things they should know."

"I don't really care if you find us interesting," Kyrie said, thinking that, on the contrary, she cared a great deal. She could feel his interest in them being exactly the same as the interest of a kid in the bugs he burns with a magnifying glass. And she didn't like it. But she would be damned if she was going to let him see the cold pit of fear in her stomach. "And I don't know what you have to say that we might want to hear."

He toyed with one of the bright pink packages of sweetener that she had left by his side on the counter. He had incongruously large hands, which looked calloused, as if he normally engaged in repetitive manual labor. Agile fingers with slightly enlarged knuckles. Did shifters get arthritis in their old age? And what had he meant about fewer shifters living to be a hundred? How old was Dire, after all? Oh, he changed into a prehistoric, long-extinct animal, but that might not give any indication of how old he himself might be. After all, Tom changed into a mythological being. And it wasn't as though Tom was mythological. Though he often could seem highly improbable.

"You want to hear what I have to say," Dire said. "Because otherwise you'll die from not knowing it. Already, you've broken the rules of our species. You can plead ignorance, and given enough good will, we might listen to you. But you have to show good will. You have to show a willingness to listen."

"So our special circumstances can be taken into consideration?" Rafiel said, ironically. "By a benevolent judge?"

This time Dire's look at him was amused. "Something like that," he said. "You should understand my point. I'm a policeman of sorts myself. And he"—he pointed a long, square-tipped finger at Keith—"is outside my jurisdiction."

"Well, if what you have to tell us is essential to our survival, then shouldn't we wait for Tom to hear it?" Rafiel said, challengingly. And, bringing up Tom before she could, made Kyrie feel guilty that she hadn't done it first.

But Dire shook his head, and shrugged, dismissively. "The dragons look after themselves," he said. "He's a shifter, but not my problem. The old daddy dragon has made it clear that your friend is one of his fair-haired boys and that I can't touch him no way no how, so why bother? He's protected or not, and if anyone does spank him, it will be his own kind. This is what I meant when I said there are things you must learn, before you get in worse trouble. There is nothing—nothing I can do to him, without precipitating a war between dragons and other shifters, the likes of which hasn't been seen on this Earth for thousands of years. I have no wish to see another one of those. The record of the last one still echoes through the legends of the ephemerals. Another one might very well destroy their puny civilization." He grinned suddenly, disarmingly. "And their civilization makes our lives much too comfortable to be allowed to vanish without a trace."

"Uh," Rafiel said, as though trying to figure out what to say.

"Fine, I'll go," Keith flung. "Being ephemeral and all, I'd better make sure that the stove doesn't catch fire. All I have to say is that Tom had better come in and look after it, as I'll still be close enough that I might, accidentally, catch wind of this highly forbidden knowledge, and we can't have that, can we?"

Kyrie wanted to turn around and apologize to Keith, but she also wanted to know what Dire had to say. She was starting to suspect that, biased or not, it would be informative. There did seem to be way too much that they didn't, in fact, know. Like how long their kind lived. Or the story of their relations with the rest of the human race. And it was becoming clear to her, more so than it had been when they'd last tangled with the dragon triad, that there was more to shifters than little groups of them struggling to survive, or loners like Old Joe.

She heard Keith retreat towards the stove, as Dire said, "Now, I'm one of the oldest shifters currently alive—"

Tom came in, followed by Conan, and surveyed the diner with a dispassionate look. Only a dozen people, in all, and all of them eating. "I think table six and eight could use coffee warm-ups," he told Conan, and instinctively looked around for Kyrie, because Kyrie was usually very good with refilling people's coffee and it wasn't like her to ignore the need for warm-ups. He found her and Rafiel behind the counter, at the point they were furthest from the customers at the table. Facing them was . . . He felt his mouth fall open, and the dragon struggle within, attempting to make him shift into his bigger, more aggressive form.

He'd come here, as they'd feared he'd come. He'd come here and tried to . . . He didn't even know what Dire was trying to do, but he was talking to Rafiel and Kyrie, and it seemed to Tom that if this creature was talking to Rafiel and Kyrie, then it must have them under some kind of mind control, because it was impossible that his friends had taken such complete leave of their senses as to listen to him like that. Wasn't it? Shouldn't it be?

He ducked rapidly under the counter, to the other side, and started towards them, but Keith grabbed his arm. "No use, old friend," he said. "That's a conference for non-dragon shifters only. I'm excluded because the bastard says I'm ephemeral, whatever that means. And you're excluded because you're the Great Sky Dragon's pet and the old bastard doesn't want to start a war. Is this the creature who fought you, outside the aquarium? He didn't seem so afraid of causing a war then."

"No," Tom said. "He didn't."

Conan, who had ducked behind the counter also, and was putting his apron on, said, "But then he didn't know Himself was protecting you personally."

Tom bit his tongue, so as not to tell Conan what Himself could do with his personal protection. He suspected if he were to name the exact unlikely anatomical feat he would like to see the Great Sky Dragon perform, it would only cause poor Conan to become speechless. Possibly forever. He couldn't even say the creature's name. How could he possibly hope to resist him? So, instead, he said, "And?" to Keith, instead of to Conan.

Keith shrugged. "He's apparently issuing some sort of warning to them about my kind and your kind, or whatever. He says he's a policeman, so perhaps he thinks he's Rafiel's colleague."

It was clear to Tom that Keith was offended at being kept out of the conference and he wanted to tell him that this was a fraternity he should count himself greatly lucky to be excluded from—that it was better to be excluded than to be claimed by old, amoral creatures. And he was sure if he said it, it would have no more effect than to have told his young, bereft self that it was better to be kicked out of the house with exactly a bathrobe to his name than to be handed over to a criminal, or at best an extra-legal organization, by doting and dutiful parents.

So instead he turned, to rummage under the counter. He found his boots there, and wondered whether Rafiel or Kyrie had taken care of that. He put them on, laced them, then put his apron on. Conan was already among the tables, giving warm-ups and taking other orders, or drawing tickets. But he kept looking over his shoulder at Tom, as if afraid Tom was about to do something stupid.

And Tom, who felt a great roil of anger boiling at the pit of his stomach, looked at the three people talking. Talking, as if this were a perfectly normal social occasion, talking as though the dire wolf hadn't tried to kill them just moments before. In the shower, he'd washed and disinfected a wound, halfway up his calf, caused by the monster's teeth. He was sane enough to realize that the creature could have hurt him much worse. It could have bitten his head off. It could have dismembered them all. It could have closed its teeth on his calf, and now Tom would presumably be growing a new foot, just like

Conan was growing a new arm, just like . . . But this wasn't rational. This wasn't even sane. He looked at that creature—who showed no sign of their pitched battle—talking to Kyrie, and he wanted to grab another meat-tenderizing hammer and a fresh skewer and renew the wounds he was sure he had made on that impassive, inhuman face.

"I was born a long time ago," Dire said. He looked at Kyrie first, but then up at Rafiel, as though making sure that he, too, was following the story. "It's hard to say exactly when, because, you know, in those days the calendar was different and more"—he flashed a humorless grin—"regional. Limited. The birthday of the god, or the such and such year of the city." Something like a shadow passed across his eyes, as if the visible reflection of all the passing years. "I can tell you it was before Rome. Probably before Rome was founded, certainly before it was heard of in our neck of woods, which was somewhere in the North of Africa—I think. Geography was arbitrary too, and your city, your people, your land, were the only people, the only lands, in the middle of the ocean, where true humans lived."

Rafiel tried to imagine that type of society. He could not. Or rather, he could all too well, but it came from his reading, from movies, someone else's imagination grafted on his own, and he was sure nothing like the real thing. He very much doubted that these people had ever been noble savages, or that such a thing as noble savages existed. On the other hand, he also doubted it was quite as hellish as other movies and books had shown it. In his experience, people were mostly people.

Dire's gaze changed, as though he'd read Rafiel's mind, and so perhaps he had. "I don't know how many shifters there were in the world at that time, but it's been my experience a lot more of us are born than ever survive to reach even human maturity. As I said before, most succumb to the animal desires, when they first change. And then others are the victims of other people's fear, then as now. Now perhaps less, because we are told that shifters don't exist. Back then, they believed we were evil spirits, or the revenge of prey upon their hunters, or other curses, but no one doubted that we existed.

"I was lucky enough to be born in a small village, where my shifting was viewed not as evil, but as a sign of favor from the gods. I was made their priest, and asked to intercede for my people with the wolf gods." He shrugged and again there was that feeling of a dark shadow crossing his eyes, implying to Rafiel that something more had happened.

It would be much like Rafiel saying, "I knew this girl named Alice, and then she died." In the spaces between the words lay all the heartbreak. He found himself feeling an odd tug of empathy towards this man, this creature, who had just declared himself older than time, and he wondered how much of it was true, and how much projected by the mind powers of their foe.

He steeled himself, crossing his arms on his chest, trying to present less of a sympathetic facade, and therefore invite less interference in his thought processes. Kyrie looked impassive, as if she were listening to a story that had nothing to do with any of them.

"It was fine while it lasted, but my people didn't last that long. We were conquered. I think, in retrospect, our first conquerors were Egyptian." He shrugged. "Hard to tell, and I certainly couldn't place it by dynasties. Then there were . . . others." Again the shadow. "And what is a power greatly appreciated in a shaman of the people, is not a quality appreciated in a slave. I shifted. I killed. I ran. I shifted again.

"Through most of history, shifters were neither appreciated nor protected." He showed his teeth in something between menace and grin. "But the truth of it, in the end, is that we scare ephemerals. Our greater powers terrify them. But until we group together there is not much we can do, and we certainly can't exert revenge. Over time . . . we formed such a group. Many of us, most over a thousand years old by the time we met, got together. We formed . . . something like a council of peoples. The council of the Ancient Ones. And we made rules and laws, to defend ourselves. There are many more of them than there are of us, and no matter how long we live, we lack the sheer numbers. So . . . we made rules. One of them is that it is illegal for anyone—even shifters—to kill great numbers of other shifters. Particularly young ones, who cannot have learned to defend or control themselves yet.

"And it is, of course, illegal for ephemerals to go after shifters in any way. These laws are ours." He tapped on his chest. "Our people's. We do not recognize anyone else's right to supersede them or to impose their rules on us."

Rafiel asked. He had to. The memory of those fragments at the bottom of the tank was with him—the idea that his people were causing deaths, causing people to be killed. Shifters like him were killing normal humans. None of Dire's carefully codified laws had anything to do with that. "Can shifters kill . . . other humans?"

Dire laughed, a short, barking sound. "What should we care, then? If our kind kills the ephemerals? Their lives are so short anyway, what should we care if they are shortened a little further. No one will notice and there are too many of them to feel the loss of a few, anyway."

Rafiel saw Kyrie wrap her arms around herself as she heard this, as if a sudden breeze had made her cold, and he said, "And what if the crimes lead the ephemerals, as you call them, to find us, and to go after us? What if the crimes lead to the discovery of the rest of us in their midst? And they turn on us? In these circumstances, you must agree, the security of one of us is the security of all."

"Is it?" Dire asked. "I thought that was why you were a policeman, Lion Boy. Yes, I have investigated all of you—and I thought you were a policeman so that you could keep yourself and your friends safe."

"It's not exactly like that," Rafiel said, and then hesitated, feeling it might not be safe for him to tell the dire wolf that he felt obligated to defend the lives of normal humans as well—that he'd become a policeman because he believed in protecting every innocent from senseless killing.

But before he could say any more, Kyrie spoke up, "You said there was a feud with the dragons? Or a war?"

Kyrie knew Rafiel too well. She knew this dire wolf, this creature talking to them with every appearance of urbane civility, would lose his civility, his compassion, his clearness of mind and word, the minute he thought that one of them wasn't in full agreement with him. She also knew Rafiel's deep-down pride in being a policeman and in his duties and responsibilities to those he served.

He was the third in a family of cops. His grandfather had been a beat cop. His father had been a detective in the Serious Crimes Unit. So was Rafiel. That was the type of tradition that left its mark on the soul and mind. Rafiel hadn't chosen to be a policeman. Rather, he was a policeman, who had simply felt he had to join the force.

And his loyalty to his family—whom Kyrie realized Dante Dire would call *mere* ephemerals—wouldn't allow Rafiel to stay quiet while their lives were deemed expendable by this ancient being who had never met them—and who clearly had no understanding for nor appreciation of normal humans.

She'd heard Rafiel hesitate, and she expected the barrage that would follow. And after that, she knew, it would take axes and skewers again, or worse. She interrupted, blindly, with a question about dragons, which pulled Dante's observant gaze from Rafiel's face, to look at her.

All of a sudden he looked older than he was, and tired. "It was a long time ago," he said. "At first . . . when we formed, dragons were part of our numbers. There were a good number of dragon shifters— in the Norse lands, and in Wales, in Ireland, and all over. And some of them formed part of our council, became Ancient Ones with us.

"I thought your boy dragon was descended from one of these lines—from these great tribes of dragons that lived all over the globe.

I thought . . ." He shrugged. "That he was a young one like any other. That he didn't matter."

"And he matters?" Rafiel blurted behind her, still half-bellicose, but at least not openly antagonizing Dante Dire.

Dante shrugged. "Their daddy dragon seems to think he does, even though he doesn't look a thing like his spawn. If he has decided to claim dragon boy, who am I to dispute it? We had a war with them, once, before human history was recorded. Our emissaries ran into his, into his kingdom as he called it. Yes, I see by your eyes that you doubt it, but yes, it was the same being, the same creature. And under him, organized, were the same people—well, some, of course. Some have died, and been replaced. I gather, like the Ancient Ones, he doesn't put much value on anyone until they've proven themselves, only in his case they can't prove themselves until they are over a hundred years old or so. Till then, he counts them as meaning little and being worthless, and he plays his games with them like a child with toys."

"So, is this a game?" Kyrie asked. "That he's playing? With Tom?"

"I don't know," Dire said. He hesitated. "That could be all it is. Your friend could interest him, purely, as a toy, something amusing to play with and to see what he does. Or he could interest him for . . . other reasons. It is not mine to judge. Except that it is clear he's keeping an eye on him through that younger dragon." He pointed towards Conan.

Tom had been on slow boil, anyway, looking at Kyrie sitting there, as if it were normal to talk like a civilized human being with that ancient horror who had been in her mind, who had manipulated her, who had, in fact, violated her thoughts in a far worse way than a violation of her body would have been. He wanted to do something. Like hurl cooking implements at the dire wolf shifter's head. Or perhaps beat him repeatedly with something solid—like, say, the counter top. Or perhaps simply request that he leave the diner.

He crossed and uncrossed his arms, looking towards him—without appearing to—listening to the things he was saying and studiously ignoring Keith's attempts at making Tom take over the stove so that Keith could beg off.

And then he heard the dire wolf say that Conan—hapless, helpless Conan—was not only, as he'd told Tom, an inadequate bodyguard, sent to protect Tom from the Ancient Ones, but he was, also, somehow, a spy. Or perhaps a listening device. He couldn't stay quiet. He took two steps forward. He put his hand on Kyrie's shoulder, to warn her that he was going to speak, and then he said, "What do you mean he's keeping watch over me? Conan? Yeah, we know Conan is a spy. What of it?"

"Oh, he's more than a spy," Dire said, amused. "He can do things."

Tom frowned. "What can Conan do?"

He saw that Conan, having approached the counter to drop off an order, was standing there, with the order slip in his hand, staring dumbly at Tom and then at the dire wolf, and then back at Tom again.

The dire wolf shifted his attention to Tom and inclined his head slightly, in what might be an attempt at a courteous greeting. Then he looked at Conan and something very much like a contemptuous smile played upon his lips. "Him? I imagine he can't do much. In and of himself. I gather he was recently wounded and those limbs take their sweet time to grow in, when you're that young." His eyes twinkled with malicious amusement. "Who wounded him? You?"

Tom nodded.

"Yes, that would suit the daddy dragon's sense of humor, to send him to guard you, after that. And no, I don't expect he would be any good at it. Certainly no good at all, against someone like me. But unless I'm very wrong, the daddy dragon already has more able forces stationed nearby. He would have sent this creature because he looks helpless and inoffensive, and you, if the thing with the alligator shifter is any indication, have a tendency to take in birds with wounded wings, do you not? So he figured you'd take him in."

"And?" Tom asked, his voice tense as a bowstring, as he shot a look at Conan, who looked ready to drop the order slip on the counter and run screaming into the night. He felt nausea again, the old sense of revulsion at the idea that the Great Sky Dragon knew him; understood him; was playing him.

The dire wolf shrugged and seemed altogether too pleased with what he was about to say. "You see, as you age, you acquire other powers. What a lot of people would call psychic powers, I guess. The ability to enter minds, and to make them think things, or to activate their thoughts . . ."

"Yes, yes, we've gathered that," Kyrie said, mouth suddenly dry.

"I suppose you have," the dire wolf said, and smirked. "But the thing is, you see, that we can also use other, younger shifters, particularly those with whom we have a connection of some sort, as long-distance hearing devices. My guess is that this young one has sworn fealty to the Father of All Dragons, and the Father of All Dragons has, therefore, reached into his mind and made him into his very own listening device. He is listening to us now," the dire wolf bowed courteously in Conan's direction. "I don't know what his game is with you, but I am telling him now that I am staying out of it, and that no harm will come to you through me. None at all. You are his."

Good, the word in the voice Tom had heard before echoed through his head, and suddenly he wondered if that had been what that first touch of the voice, while he was in the shower, had been. An attempt at getting him to admit fealty or subservience to the Great Sky Dragon. Doubtless, that would allow the old dragon to put a spy device directly in Tom's head itself, and not have to bother with Conan. Tom had a strange, sudden feeling that if he had accepted that, Conan wouldn't be alive. He had only crawled back, just in time, to have his boss find himself in need of a pitiful, inoffensive-looking creature. That was the only reason that Conan had been spared.

"Not good," Tom said, making his voice just loud enough to sound forceful, without speaking to the whole diner. "I don't know why the Great Sky Dragon thinks he speaks for me, but he does not. I am not his to either condemn or protect or play games with. You came here to judge me and my friends, and my friends are the only group I owe any loyalty to. If you are going to condemn any of them, Kyrie, Rafiel or Keith, then I demand you condemn me as well," he said. "We are all one. What we did, we did as a group."

He expected . . . oh, he didn't know. Outrage from the Great Sky Dragon. And possibly something more from the dire wolf—rage maybe. Tom could deal with rage right about now, even if he didn't want to have a shifter fight in the diner.

This was not a game. He was not a pawn. And neither was anyone else, here. The sheer denuding of the humanity of everyone, shifter and not, that these old shifters seemed to do, so casually, made Tom want to hit someone. "We are not toys," he said.

There was nothing from the Great Sky Dragon. Not a single word echoed through Tom's mind, and Tom had a moment of strange relief, when he thought he'd set himself free and that the Great Sky Dragon had, somehow, set him adrift. But then the dire wolf threw his head back and laughed so loudly, that a few people turned to look at him.

He brought himself under control with what looked like an effort, reached for a napkin and wiped tears of laughter down his face. "Very funny. Very brave and gallant. No wonder the lady appreciates you, Dragon Boy. You say those things as if you really believed in them. But you know better and I know better. Your elder has claimed you, and in light of your elder's claim, I know you're his, and therefore I am keeping my hands off you. It is not part of my mandate to get people into a war, or to cause trouble for any other ancient shifters. So, I regret to inform you, but you're his, and his you'll remain."

"And what do you intend to do about the rest of us?" Rafiel said. "While there were deaths, as you and the others have felt, they were in self-defense. And as for the young ones who died, it was an accident."

There was a baring of teeth. "I am investigating," he said, slowly. "You know what they say about police work. Most of it is boring and painstakingly slow. I'm going over reports of the case in the local

paper. I am looking at the site. I'm making my own determinations."
He stood up. From his pocket, he removed the amount of money for
the coffee, and carefully laid it on the counter. "I will try to keep
shifters from being hurt," he said.

And then he was gone, gliding towards the door, or perhaps
teleporting towards it, with a grace so quick and irrevocable that they
couldn't have stopped him had they tried.

Tom, on the tip of whose tongue it had been to ask exactly what
had happened to the alligator shifter, exactly what this monster might
have done to the old friend—the old dependent—that Tom was in
the habit of feeding and looking after, was forced to be quiet.

Forced to be quiet, standing there at the counter, looking at his
hands slowly clenching into fists. He wanted to scream, or pound the
counter. He wanted to shift. And what, with one thing and another,
he hadn't taken the time to eat any protein. He hadn't done anything
to recover from his last shift. And it didn't seem to matter. He could
feel his hands trying to elongate into claws. He could see his
fingernails growing.

He stumbled, like one drunk or blind, towards the back door, and
outside, stepped into the cold air of the parking lot, suddenly startled
that darkness had fallen and that it was snowing again—a steady
snowfall, with large flakes. The surprising coldness of the air stopped
his fury—or at least acted like a slap in the face, making him take long
breaths, and pace a little, stomping his feet, trying to calm down.

He wasn't going to shift. He wasn't going to. As he passed the
stove, Keith had called out to him that he needed to go. Tom couldn't
leave Keith stuck with this. And while he could, possibly, call
Anthony in, if it was snowing again Anthony might be reluctant to
come.

He stomped his feet again. There were no windows looking over
the parking lot, and the only light came from the two street lamps,
which shone, in a spiral of light as though the light were a fracture in
the glass of the night, a crack through which something human
shone.

There was nothing, Tom thought, blankly. *Only the beast and the
night. They resent humans for their light, for their bringing light into*

the night hours. For their science, for their thought. They resent us. I am human. I might be something else as well, but I'm not one of those. I'm not like them. I am not owned. I don't care if I was born of them. I don't care what unnameable offenses they think they suffered at the hands of those they call ephemerals.

He stomped his feet again, and walked out to the parking lot, then back again, the snow falling on his head and, he hoped, cooling it. *Shifters are dangerous. Any humans who tried to defend themselves against my kind probably had good reason to. We are dangerous. It's not like we are a harmless and persecuted minority. Oh, there are plenty of those in the world, and the crimes imagined against them are numberless. But no one has to imagine crimes against shifters. No one needs to create grand conspiracy theories to think we control the world or the markets, or even the arts. No. Our crimes are obvious and brutal.*

He put his arms around himself, as he realized he was out without a jacket and that the bitter snow-laden wind was cutting through his sweat shirt to freeze the beaded sweat of anger on his body. *I have met less than twenty adult shifters in my life and half of those were murderers. I cannot, I will not, believe it is wrong for people like Keith to suspect us of intending ill to the rest of them. Clearly this Dire creature intends plenty of ill to normal humans. Clearly. And the others . . .* He shook his head.

"Tom?" Kyrie's voice said, hesitant, from the doorway of the diner. "Tom?"

Rafiel knew a thundercloud when he saw one. He knew that Tom was leaving to deal with anger. He'd been around Tom enough to recognize the signs—as well as the signs that the man was fighting hard not to shift in front of all his customers.

Rafiel could also understand, from the tightening of Kyrie's jaw and the way she looked as if she'd like to bite something in two, as she watched Tom head out the back door, that there might be a storm brewing there.

Had he been an uninterested observer, he might very well have stayed around and convinced both of his friends to act like civilized, mature human beings. He might point out to Kyrie that killing Tom might seem like a really good idea, except that if she should succeed she would spend days not eating and moping about wishing she had him back—and that miracles rarely happened twice. He might point out to Tom that if he wanted a woman with an actual spine he had to allow her to think with her own mind, even if at times her actions seemed strange or ill-advised to him.

But Rafiel wasn't an uninterested observer, and inserting himself into his friends' possible argument seemed to him the worst possible way to bring about a reconciliation. They were all too aware—as he was—that he'd wanted Kyrie for himself. So he would leave them alone and hope they cooled off.

As for Rafiel, he must go interview the people who had signed the guest book at the aquarium the week before the first bones were found. It was probably a quixotic endeavor and a foolish one, to try to find the shifters by following up on the people who had been at the aquarium at one time or another. Surely, it was stupid. He wouldn't have signed that visitors' book, so why should anyone else? Particularly anyone else who was a shifter, who had something to hide and who didn't want to be confronted with the evidence of where he'd been and what he'd been up to.

He wasn't supposed to conduct interviews this late, but then, it was just on five o'clock, the early darkness an artifact of the season, the proximity to the mountains and the impending snowstorm. And these interviews were not, strictly speaking, procedure. In fact, he still wasn't absolutely sure how to justify them to his superiors.

While in his car, heading for the first address listed in the guest book, he dialed his partner at the station. "McKnight?" he said.

"Yeah? Where have you been? We have—"

"Later. I'm following an idea of my own. I was just wondering if you'd do me a favor, and check on the aquarium again. Did anyone do a thorough sweep of that platform above the shark tank?"

"We looked at dirt and prints on the railing and that, yeah," McKnight said. "Well, except the railing seemed to have been cleaned up, but we looked at the floor and all, for all the good it did us. The thing is, you know, it couldn't be just accidental falling in. There's normally a cover there, and it's quite sturdy enough to withstand the weight of an adult falling in. It's only removed to allow the cleaners to get in the tank. At this point, frankly, we're wondering if it's not so much murders as a body disposal system. The coroner hasn't looked at the body yet, so I can't tell you if our boy drowned or was otherwise killed. We might not be able to find out, anyway. Among the things not present seem to be his lungs."

"Yeah," Rafiel said, mostly to stem the flow of words. McKnight was new, and Rafiel was supposed to train him. An endeavor only slightly impaired by the fact that McKnight had just come out of college, with a degree in law enforcement. He was, therefore, to his own personal satisfaction, the highest authority possible on how to solve murders. Rafiel's own training and years of experience were dwarfed by McKnight's learning of the *latest techniques,* the *latest research,* the *latest ways to go about it.*

Which in the end boiled down to McKnight's opinions, nothing else. "This is something different," Rafiel said. "I talked to one of the aquarium employees." Let McKnight think that he had in fact spent the entire day in pursuit of that all-important interview. And let McKnight not guess that he'd been doing double duty as waiter at The George. Though given that he'd interviewed Lei while there, Rafiel thought he could convincingly—if falsely—make a case for having spent his day hiding, in disguise, while he waited for Lei to come in. "And she said not only were the door locks easy to open, but that male aquarium employees were in the habit of bringing dates there. She said that often there were used prophylactics in the planters around that small platform. I don't suppose those have been swept for clues."

McKnight was silent for a moment, which had to count as a miracle in several religions, Rafiel thought. When he came back, it was with less than his normal, self-assured verve. "I don't know about that," he said sullenly. "That platform is actually fairly broad, and the planters are pretty far away from the place where the vic fell or was pushed into the aquarium. So, there's no telling what people might or might not have looked at, that far away."

Rafiel, who had become skilled in the doublespeak employed by McKnight and other young hires, knew what that meant. What it meant, simply put, was that McKnight had been the one in charge of looking all around the area for clues and had decided—from his naturally superior knowledge—that there was no point in looking through the planters. That they were too far away from the area of the crime and that he was, therefore, safe in ignoring them. "I would appreciate it if you'd go over with someone and do a thorough looking over at that area. I don't need to tell you the possibilities it opens, including that of a romantic spat."

"Uh . . . both the vics were male."

"Yes, indeed," Rafiel said, tartly. "And of course, we only know of the male employees using the area as a love nest. However, my information was given to me by a female, and she might not have wished to implicate female employees, don't you think?" He didn't even wish to go into other possibilities with McKnight. "Just go and see what there is to find and how easy the area might be to get into after the place is locked down." And when one hasn't taken the trouble to procure copies of the keys, of course. "I will talk to you again in the morning."

Before he could hang up, McKnight's voice came through, high, upset, "Now? You want me to go now?"

"No time like the present, and you know how it is in these investigations. It might all be hanging on some little fact."

"But . . . but the weather channel says it's going to snow," McKnight said. "They say it's going to snow a lot. Another big blizzard headed our way in fact. I don't want to go out there in a blizzard."

"Well, then," Rafiel said, reasonably. "I would go out there now, before the snow becomes a blizzard."

From the other end of the phone there was something very much like an inarticulate exclamation of protest that, should it be more closely listened to, might translate into a profanity.

Rafiel chose not to listen to it any closer. Instead, deliberately, he pressed the off button of his phone, and turned his attention to navigating the maze of small neighborhoods, the opposite side of Fairfax from the one Tom and Kyrie lived on.

The neighborhoods weren't very different, though. In the early twentieth century, they might have been colonized by Irishmen or Poles, instead of the Greeks that had colonized the area north of them. Yet the houses all looked very much alike. Less brick here, and more the sort of elaborate, architecturally detailed Victorian houses that looked like mansions shrunk down to pint size. These houses often had three floors, but the floors would each contain no more than one room and a landing for the stair leading to the next floor.

They had, at one time, housed the laborers—many of them highly skilled—imported from Europe to build the elaborate mansions of the gold rush millionaires. The men and women enticed over to work for the newly rich had stayed and built their own dollhouse version of the boss's manor. And when the gold had evaporated and the silver lost its value they had stayed behind and added far more solid wealth to Colorado than mere metal could ever bring it.

Now in the beginning of the twenty-first century, the houses were mostly occupied by another kind of skilled laborer. While the neighborhood where Tom and Kyrie rented had never decayed appreciably, it had also never been exactly rehabilitated. Instead, the original Greek settlers had stayed, and the power of family and community supervision had kept the area, as the saying went, poor but honest. And now, when the younger generations were more likely to go to Denver to study, and then out of the state to work, it was mostly the realm of retirees, with no life and immaculate lawns.

The neighborhoods on the other side of Fairfax had been more ethnically diverse, and when the wealth of gold had rushed away from Goldport, there had been nothing there to keep people behind—no family, no weight of tradition. So instead they had moved on, restless, probably to Denver, where there were still mansions to build and money to be made.

In their absence, and with Colorado University right there, a few blocks away, another type of person had moved in. In the sixties, that type of person had often lived fifteen to a two-bedroom Victorian, and grown weed in the basement and generally destroyed the neighborhoods.

And then, recently, the sort of people who liked to buy destroyed properties and improve on them had moved in. Intellectuals, artists, a good number of childless couples with nothing but time on their hands to work on the houses. The houses looked pretty and almost newly built, though after coming across two of them painted in purple and accented with pink, Rafiel wished that these people had never heard the term *painted lady* or that they might have procured a translation of the term *good taste* before engaging in wanton remodeling.

He consulted his planner, and found that all three of the people he meant to see lived in this crisscrossing of pathways, shaded by century-old trees. The first one was on Meadoway, and he turned sharply onto it, admiring the faux-Victorian street light fixtures, and wondering if they were paid for by the neighborhood association or if anyone in the area had friends in city hall.

The first house he was looking for turned out to be one of the smaller ones—a two-floor Victorian with steeply descending eaves and a sort of look of being a Swiss chalet treasonously transported to the middle of Goldport, painted a weak aqua accented with green, and still feeling a little shell-shocked about the whole thing.

When Rafiel rang the doorbell, he was answered by a man who looked as if he could be cast, with no effort at makeup, as a hobbit in *Lord of the Rings*. Well, a rather tall hobbit, since he was about Rafiel's own height. But he had the hair perfectly right, and he was smoking a pipe. He was not wearing shoes, and Rafiel had to keep himself from looking down to see whether his toes were covered in curly hair, as Tolkien had insisted Bilbo Baggins' toes were. Instead, he focused on the amiable face, whose wrinkles showed it to be somewhat past middle age.

The man didn't smell like a shifter, and he'd seen nothing at the aquarium, and was shocked, shocked—as it turned out by the reports of cryptozoological discoveries in the parking lot of the aquarium and not by the deaths within. Before Rafiel could escape him, he had to be told that the man was a retired used- and rare-book seller, and to be given—he never understoodd why or how—a lecture on American horror writers of the nineteenth century and the value of their various first editions.

He escaped, gritting his teeth, to follow the winding Meadoway to Mine Street, where the next person lived who'd left both name and address at the aquarium at the time when it was probable the first man had gone for a totally unprotected swim with the sharks. This one was a bigger house, or at least taller, and instead of looking like a Swiss chalet, it looked exactly like a Southern antebellum mansion as it might have looked if Sherman had found himself in convenient possession of a shrinking ray.

The people who lived in it were obviously aware of the resemblance, as they'd painted the house aristocratic white, and had two rocking chairs on the diminutive porch.

Rafiel rang the doorbell twice, but no one answered, even though he could see the blue glow of a television through the windows of the darkened front room. He had visions of people dead in front of a TV screen, but he knew how unlikely that was. Far more likely that they had the sound turned way up and were far too interested in their program to listen to his ringing, or, after a while, knocking on their door. Or it was entirely possible they'd gone out for a burger or something they thought they needed to weather the coming snowstorm, and had left the TV on. People did that.

Before giving up, he sniffed around the door. It was unlikely he would be able to smell a subtle and old shifter smell without shifting, himself. But then again, this was not the aquarium, where shifters might or might not have passed. And even there, he'd picked up the original scent while in his human form and had only needed to shift to pinpoint its location.

In this case, if shifters lived here, it should be much easier. But his sniffing around the house, and around the driveway failed to raise even a vague suspicion of shifter-scent.

So, chances are that it's not here, he thought, and headed for the number three on his list, which was only a couple of blocks down at Skippingstone Way.

The house was yellow and narrow, set on a handkerchief-sized lawn bordered by what, to judge from the pathetic, upward-thrust branches, must be lovely bushes in the spring and summer.

But Rafiel didn't pay much attention to the details, because as he parked his SUV and got out, he got a strong whiff of shifter smell. And the smell only increased as he opened the garden gate and walked up to the porch.

On the porch, a woman stood crying by a pretentious reproduction Victorian mailbox. And she smelled unmistakably of shifter.

Kyrie thought he looked cold. Cold and lonely, with his arms wrapped around himself, standing in the snowstorm. She would have thought he would have come inside, into the warmth. She would have thought he would have come to where they were. And then she thought perhaps he was stopping himself from shifting, and that was all.

But when he turned around to face her, his features bore none of the strange distortions that presaged shifts. His eyes were their normal shape, as was his nose, and his face wasn't even slightly elongated as it seemed to get when he was about to change into a dragon. His teeth, bared, as they chattered against each other, retained their normal human bluntness. But he was pale, and his eyes were veiled—as though they were covered with the nictitating eyelids he grew in dragon form.

He seemed to be glaring at her. "What?" he asked, and his voice was edged with anger, and shimmered with sharp barbs. The signs to stay away were clear, but Kyrie couldn't leave him here, alone and furious.

"I . . . is there anything I can do to . . . help?" Kyrie asked.

"Oh, don't worry," he flung. "I'm not going to shift."

"I didn't think you were going to," she said, trying to keep her voice low and even, because she knew—she knew damn well—that in this mood Tom was like a small child, easily annoyed, easily angered by things he thought she had said, even when she couldn't be further from thinking it. "I just wanted to know why you were out here, alone and . . . and why you look so angry?"

"Why? Why I look so angry?" he asked. "What do you mean I look so angry? I'm being claimed. I'm being owned. By a creature so old we can't even guess at his motives. By a crime boss, Kyrie! And he . . . he uses people as instruments. He used Conan as a spy camera. And he probably can reach into Conan's mind all the time."

"I know. I realize how it feels, but . . ."

"But you sit there," Tom said. "And you talk to that creature, that . . . that dire wolf, even as he's going on about how he doesn't know what the Great Sky Dragon wants with me. He's talking about how ephemerals and shifters are different, and how our only loyalty is to shifters, and you are there, listening to him!"

"What did you expect me to do?" she asked. "Did you expect me to attack him? In the diner? Besides, he was giving us information we needed."

"Information!" His tone made it sound like the word should be a swear word. "Information! How do you know there is a word of truth in what he said?"

"Does it matter? Clearly there's *some* truth. I mean, I know it's tainted, that it's from his point of view. But, is it to some extent still true? Does it still have some contact with reality? Is it . . . is it going to work for us or against us?"

He was running his fingers through his hair, pulling it out of the bind that kept it in place at the back, scattering around wildly—making it look like a particularly energetic cat had been playing with his hair. "So is it?"

"I don't know," Kyrie said. She again managed to bring her voice down, to control her volume of speech. She knew he wasn't angry at her as such, truly she knew it, no matter how angry he might sound or how much it might seem to her like he was furious at her or perhaps—ridiculously—jealous of Dire. No, she mustn't sound like that. She must be calm and collected so that he would perhaps calm down. "But I know there is nothing we can do."

"Nothing we can do?" he said. "What do you mean nothing we can do? There has to be something we can do—there has to be a way to be free of all of this, hasn't there?" His eyes were wild, almost unfocused.

When Tom had first been hired by The George's erstwhile owner, he'd been addicted to drugs. Heroin, mostly, from what she understood of his stories. The drugs had been a misguided attempt to self-treat the shifting, to prevent himself from changing into a dragon whenever his emotions got control of him. Now, if Kyrie didn't know better, she'd think he was using again. There was a wildness to him, barely restrained and very much full of anger and something else, something seemingly uncontrollable. His blue eyes blazed with it as he said, "Why should I belong to someone? Belong as in be owned? Like a possession? A . . . thing? And only because I was born the way I am? Don't you understand, Kyrie, don't you see how wrong it is?"

Kyrie knew how wrong it was. She also understood, with startling clarity, at a glance, how different her background and Tom's were. He'd been left alone, to more or less raise himself. He might have been as unwanted as she was, as ignored, as disposable to those who were responsible for his existence. But unlike hers, his unsupervised childhood and barely supervised teenage years had been free of the control of strangers. His father might not have known or cared enough to control Tom and to make him follow rules, or even laws. But at least he'd not appointed revolving strangers to have power over Tom's life and determine what he could or couldn't do or say or wear to school.

A ward of the state since she was a few hours old, Kyrie had been passed from one controlling authority to another—foster families, social workers and the sometimes ironically named children advocates, all had passed her from person to person and there was nothing she could do except obey. She tried to convey this to Tom. "You think you're alone in this?" she said. "You think that it's because you're a shifter that strangers have a say over you? I was abandoned by my parents when I was just hours old," she said. "And from then on, I belonged to the state. Which in truth meant that I belonged to whomever the state appointed to look after a group of children. Strangers all, but they could determine everything, including what shots I got, and to what school I went. They could move me around to another foster family, uproot me from the neighborhood, leave me at the mercy of strangers."

He opened his mouth, but didn't answer. Instead, his mouth stayed open, then he closed it, with a snap. He put out a hand, and seemed like he would touch her face with his fingertips, only he let his hand fall before he could do it. "But that doesn't make it better, Kyrie," he finally said, his voice softer, but still seeming to simmer with outrage. "That doesn't make it any better. Yes, your upbringing was horrible, but that is supposed to be over. We're supposed to be our own people, now. We're supposed to be starting over. There shouldn't be anyone who can do this to us." His hand made a gesture in midair, which she supposed symbolized the control that the ancient shifters might have over them. "There shouldn't be anyone who can mess with our minds, our lives, what we are, this way."

Kyrie shrugged. "I didn't say my upbringing was horrible." And then caught herself saying it and thought how strange it was, because by various definitions, it had, indeed, been horrible. "I said that it w—" She shrugged. "It wasn't right. But then neither was yours. Just in very different ways. What I said is that I know this game. There is no point, when people think they own you, in just beating against it like . . . like a trapped bird ripping itself to shreds on the wire of the cage. When people think they own you, the only way you can get away with being yourself, the only way you can keep them off balance enough that they don't actually control you, is to play them one against the other. I think," she rubbed her forehead, as she thought of it. "I think we should do that. I think we should play the Ancient Ones against the dragons, the dragons against the Ancient Ones. I think we should go with the ones who demand least from us and—"

But Tom was shaking his head, making his black, curly hair fly about, like the ends of a whip. "No," he said. "No. We can't. We won't. Any concession we make to these people is like trading away a bit of ourselves and of who we are. Kyrie! Can't you see that they're evil? Can't you see them for what they are?"

"I can see they are very powerful," she said, hearing her voice toneless, and keeping it toneless, because otherwise she too would start yelling and next thing you knew, there would be people gathering to watch their argument. The only reason they hadn't gathered already, as far as she could see, was that it was snowing so hard, and they were in the back parking lot, while most people in The George were gathered up front, near the front entrance. "I can see they have mental and other powers that we lack. I can see too, that having lived so long, they have . . . they can call on contacts, on experience, on people they know. We can't do anything against that, either. So the only chance we have of defeating them, or even of holding them at arms' length, is to play them one against the other."

He shook his head. "There has to be another way. There has to." His hands were curling in fists. He looked at her, again unfocused. His face was contracted, as if in a spasm of pain. "I can't . . ." He shook his head. "They're not good, Kyrie. As people or as shifters. They're not good. We can't let them dictate to us. Ever."

"I'm not saying we should let them dictate to us." And now impatience crept into her voice. "I'm saying that we should use one to combat the other."

"No." He pressed his lips together, in narrow-lipped disapproval. "No."

"Then what are we to do?"

He faced her for a moment. His hands went at his hair again, pulling it back, but in fact snagging it in great handfuls, so that it hung in fantastical disarray around his face, making him look like an extra in a commercial picturing a society with no combs. "I'll figure out something," he said.

And with that the infuriating man started walking away. Kyrie ran after him, slipped on the ice and ended up having to clutch his shoulder to stay upright.

As he turned to look back at her, she said, "You can't go out there like that. Not in a T-shirt. Not . . . like that."

"Yes. Yes, I can," he said. His voice was absolutely flat, now, all emotion gone. "Yes I can. I need to cool off, Kyrie. Don't worry. I'll be back and I'll think of something."

She wanted to scream and shake him till his teeth fell out. It wasn't that she didn't love him. She was as conscious of loving him as she was that he was one of the more infuriating creatures alive—and possibly more infuriating than most dead ones too. Tom had a way of making her want to scream and stomp her foot. Sometimes, she almost understood his father who—trying to justify himself to her at one point—had told her that Tom had brought his disowning on himself, not by changing into a dragon, but because changing into a dragon was the last in a long line of disappointments and infuriating resistance to all normal behavior. His father hadn't disowned Tom because he was a dragon, but because he knew how out of control the human part of Tom was, and that, in a dragon, was terrifying.

But then she realized what Tom was saying. He needed to cool off. He needed to control himself. Which was the other side of the coin, that Tom's father had never seen or never been willing to see. Tom had an almost fanatical need for self-control. The things he'd done that seemed most out of control had more often than not been done to try to get control of himself. It might not be the best survival strategy in the world, but it was his, and who was Kyrie to try and change it? And what good would it do her to try?

Anything else she might tell him—put a coat on, take care of yourself, remember cars slide on ice and could kill you, remember you too might slip on ice—all of it would sound like she was trying to be his mother, and she didn't think maternal authority would go over any better than paternal.

She stepped back and away from him. She shook her head. She turned and walked towards the diner. At the door, she was almost run down by a wild-eyed Conan headed the other way—but she was done with trying to talk sense into dragons for the night, and she wasn't about to even try with this one. She might as well teach table manners to Not Dinner.

Instead, she went into the diner to meet with a sullen Keith protesting that he had to go, that truly he'd never meant to work today.

"Right, right," Kyrie said. "I'll call Anthony in." She wished Tom would give some thought to mundane considerations like the diner and who was cooking for the night, but that would probably be too much to ask for when he was convinced he could find a way for them to win, singlehanded, against the ancient shifters.

She snorted.

She wished him luck.

Rafiel walked up to stand beside the woman, who was so absorbed reading something printed on cheap, yellowish paper, that she didn't notice even when he stood right behind her, reading over her shoulder.

The pamphlet was the same he'd seen on a couple of phone poles around the diner. Pseudo Marxist exhortation for the rise of the masses by something that called itself the Rodent Liberation Front. He cleared his throat, causing the woman to jump and turn around.

She was much shorter than he was—all of maybe five-two—and had what was probably a whole lot of mousy-brown hair, which had been enhanced by a wash or a dye or something to have brilliant gold streaks. For something that elaborately dyed, it had not been styled at all, just caught back into a braid that was coming apart at the edges. It made her look curiously inoffensive and childlike. The look was completed by a dark brown overcoat, the neck surrounded with fluffy brown fake fur. She wore white socks and Mary Janes. The visitors' book at the aquarium identified her as a fifth-grade science teacher at Stainless Elementary, just around the corner.

She couldn't have been much larger than her students. And how exactly could she hide the fact that she was a shifter from them?

That was the strongest question on his mind, as she smelled, undeniably, unmistakably, like a shifter. How could she hide it? And why was she crying?

He cleared his throat, and she looked up to see that he was

looking at her, looming over her in fact. She let out a squeaky scream and looked up at him in complete alarm. Meanwhile, Rafiel went through and discarded many ways to start the conversation. He thought of asking her if she changed, or if she sometimes felt positively like an animal, or . . . a hundred other, quick-flashing and just as quickly discarded ideas.

The problem with all of them was that he couldn't really say any of them to a stranger. Not even to a stranger who, by smell alone, identified herself as one of his kind. He couldn't tell her he was one of her kind, either. It was one thing to question her, and another, quite different one, to let her hold his security in her hands. Particularly as she looked at him out of brown, tear-rimmed eyes.

"Officer Rafiel Trall, ma'am," he said, instead, as politely correct as he could be. "From the Goldport Police Department."

She squeaked again and put her hand in front of her face. Unfortunately this was the hand holding the Rodent Liberation Front pamphlet, and as it trembled in front of her face, it did nothing to make it easier for Rafiel not to mention that she smelled of shifter. But, objectively, he didn't need to reveal to her that he knew. Not even vaguely. What he needed to do was somehow determine when she'd been in the aquarium and what she'd done. If she'd been there with a large group of children, it was highly unlikely she'd either taken the time to dump an unsuspecting adult male into the tank or to steal the keys of the aquarium so she could come back and do it later. And he could check on her movements during the visit by talking to whoever had been there with her. If these things hadn't changed since his school days, every field trip, even every visit to the park, was facilitated not only by the teacher in charge, but by two or three aides and by a number of mothers who, apparently, lacked enough chaos in their lives and must, therefore, pursue it in these groups.

"I'm sorry if this is not a good time," he told the terrified eyes shimmering with tears. "But this is a very routine enquiry. You signed the book at the aquarium on the thirteenth?"

She blinked, as if this were not what she expected at all, and slowly lowered her hand. It was her turn to clear her throat, because, if he guessed right, she couldn't have spoken otherwise. "Yes, yes," she said. "I took my science class to the aquarium. We're studying environmental biology and the pollution of water courses, and how that affects endangered species of fish." Her voice was pipingly small, but he suspected that's how she normally talked.

"How many children would there be in the class?" Rafiel asked, fascinated by her recital of facts seeming calm enough, even as her eyes looked terrified.

She cleared her throat again. "Oh . . . there were two classes together, actually. I . . . I have them at different periods, you know. So it was forty children. Well, at least not exactly children, they're fifth graders, and they get very upset if we call them children, as they should, since they are, after all, almost teens."

"I see," he said. And he did in fact see that this woman probably lived in fear of her students, most of whom would be her height or probably taller than her. She would do anything rather than upset them or offend them. He wondered how effective that was, as a teaching discipline. He consulted his notebook for her name, which was . . . he squinted at it. Marina Gigio. "So, how many other adults were there to help supervise the . . . er . . . teens, Ms. Gigio?"

"Ms. Braeburn," she said. "And Ms. Hickey. They're teacher aides. And then there were five mothers, but I'd have to look at my paperwork to tell you their names. They vary, you know, with each field trip."

"I see," Rafiel said again. He did. That made eight adults to forty kids, leaving it on average to each adult to look after five of the kids. Only he doubted very much it worked that way. For one, the mother volunteers, from what he remembered from his own childhood, were far more interested in their own children's safety and behavior than in any other of the kids'. That was probably worse now, since political correctness and a certain paranoia amid parents would have taken its toll. No sane mother would dare scold or even caution another's child. At the end of that lay lawsuits or worse.

So, in fact, five of the adults would be looking after five or at the most—supposing there were a few siblings between the two classes— seven or eight kids. The rest would be left to the teachers and teacher's aides. And the rest, being fifth graders, would be a definite handful. At that age—Rafiel had cousins—they were still capable of most of the idiocy associated with very small children, but to it they had added the creative mischief of teenagers, from stupid pranks to holding hands or kissing when someone wasn't looking. And the world being what it was these days, holding hands or kissing could also lead to lawsuits.

The woman would have had her hands full. Rafiel nodded to her. "Did you see anything suspicious? Anything that . . . well . . . do you remember the shark area, and the point where you can climb stairs to a sort of platform and look down at the shark area?"

She nodded. "I've . . . I've read about it in the paper. Their finding remains there. Thinking that I let all the young people hang on the railing and look down, and they were all playing, you know—nothing vicious—but shoving each other and saying 'tonight you sleep with the fishes' . . . I couldn't have imagined how unstable it was. If I'd known, I'd never have let them up on it. When I think of what might have happened." She shuddered, or rather trembled, a trembling flutter that made Rafiel think of something he couldn't quite name.

"Well, I understand no one knew it was that unstable," he said. He didn't want to tell her that the area was perfectly stable, but that the safety cover of the tank had been removed. As far as he knew—and he would admit he hadn't looked at the paper much beyond the cryptozoological report on the front page—the newspaper was still reporting both findings of bodies at the aquarium as accidents or at the very worst mysterious deaths. "So you didn't see anyone else there? I mean, besides the group you took in?"

She shook her head. "No. Just the childr—young people. You know how it is when a school group goes to this type of place. The other visitors tend to get out of the way."

"Oh, yes," he said.

"Very considerate of most people, really," she said. "Giving the children a chance to learn."

"Yes," he said, firmly, not wishing to encourage her delusions or provoke a flow of stranger explanations. Instead, he said, "I was just wondering . . . if you saw anything else suspicious?"

"No," she said, with unusual firmness. She darted a look—he'd swear it—at the pamphlet she'd received in the mail, then looked up again. "Definitely not."

If she wasn't lying, then Rafiel would present his shifter form to the nearest vet for neutering. He frowned. He didn't want to do it, but something welled up in him—the meaning of her last name, the look of her flutter, and something else . . . a feeling.

He cast about for something he could claim ambiguously had been a guess at what she might have seen, should it fail to hit its mark. "Mouse, right?" he said at last.

She shriek-squeaked, and her hand darted for the door handle.

But Rafiel's hand was there first, holding onto the door handle, speaking in his best soothing, smooth voice, "It's all right, Ms. Gigio. It's all right. This is not about you. I just wanted to tell you I knew, and that it's all right."

But she turned, backing against the door, her back protected by it, and bared little teeth at him. "How do you know? How did you know?"

He didn't answer. He wasn't going to bare his throat that explicitly to her. He wasn't going to tell her in so many words. But he allowed his eyebrows to rise in an expression that was unmistakably *guess.*

"Oh," she said. She dropped the letter and covered her mouth with her hand. "Oh." And then, with something sparking at the back of her eyes. "Are there many of us, then? Around?"

He shrugged. "I know a few. I don't think there're many, no." He had no idea, of course, of how many Ancient Ones there might be. "Less than one percent of the population. Perhaps much less."

"Oh," she said again. "All . . . all the same thing?"

It took him a moment to realize what she was saying, then he shook his head slowly. "Not at all. In fact, I don't know of any two of the same mammals." The closest being himself and Kyrie, for all the good it did them. And Alice had been like him. "There's . . . there seems to be a gamut of shapes, from the most common to the extinct or even mythological."

"Oh," she said again, and let out air, as though deflating, though fortunately she didn't decrease in size as she did it. "I got this letter in the mail. I thought . . ."

"I know," Rafiel said. "I've seen those around the college. I thought they were a student prank."

"I did too," she said. "See them. I saw them outside The George this morning. I often go there for the pesto omelet."

And for the pheromones, Rafiel thought, but didn't say anything. Let her think that her actions were rational and consciously controlled. They needed all the illusions they could hold onto.

"But I thought it was a student prank too," she said.

"It might still be," Rafiel said, though he didn't for a minute believe it. "You know your last name means mouse in Italian. And it's possible."

"Yes, it is," she said, brightening up. It looked like a sudden weight had gone off her. "I mean, it's actually probable. How else would they know? Or . . . Or . . ." She seemed to run out of objections to the idea someone else might know. Rafiel thought this was also an exceptionally bad time to let her know that some shifters could smell out other shifters.

Instead, he just inclined his head, and said, "Will you tell me, then, what you saw at the aquarium? I realize it must have been something you didn't want to talk about to just anyone, perhaps something shapeshifter related?"

She looked up and managed to give the impression she was making complex calculations at the back of her mind. "Well . . ." she said. "Well . . ." And shrugged. "It's just something that could be shifters. I didn't want you to think I was crazy, that is, before I knew . . . you know . . . that . . . that you'd understand."

"I understand," he said. "What did you see?"

"It was in the aquarium area, when it changes over to the restaurant area, you know? It's always really hard to control the ki—young people there, because they always want to stay and eat at the restaurant, no matter how many times you tell them it's an expensive, sit-down place and they wouldn't really be pleased if a bunch of young people—who tend to be rowdier than grown-ups—took over their tables, and, you know . . ." She seemed to realize she was running on and finished lamely, "all that. So I was very busy talking to all of them, and Ms. Braeburn was actually standing by the entrance to the restaurant, herding them past, as it were, to make sure they didn't try to duck inside, and then I saw . . ."

She shook her head. "You know that area has all the huge tanks with the weird stuff? Squids and octopuses, and that huge crab tank, where there's a lens on the bottom, and you can crawl under the bottom and look up?"

He nodded. He hadn't paid that much attention to that area, but he vaguely remembered everything she mentioned.

"Oh, this is going to sound like I'm crazy," she said, and put her hands on either side of her face, as if to keep herself from blushing. It didn't work. A blush showed on her cheeks, on either side of her fingers. It made her, weirdly, very attractive, and Rafiel had to remind himself that when cats played with mice, the result was normally not pleasant.

"I swear, just as we managed to get the kids out of the area, a little naked man came out from under that area—you know, the area where you can crawl to look up and see the crabs and things, as if you were inside the aquarium. He looked Asian—I'd think Japanese. Or at least he looked like the Japanese in movies. And he looked very old. His hair was all white and he was almost bent in double. And . . . well, he was naked, so I looked more attentively." She seemed to realize how that might sound and gasped slightly, before saying, all in a rush, "I mean, I mean, because I'm familiar . . . because I know when you shift suddenly you often find yourself, you know, naked. So I looked, because he didn't look like a streaker or a flasher or any of that kind of person, so I thought, I thought . . . how odd, and maybe he was a shifter. Only it wasn't a real thought, I mean, with words or anything, just an impulse to look more closely at him and see, you know . . . what was wrong."

Rafiel refused to tread in the minefield of innuendo that surrounded that statement. Instead, he said, "And then?"

"Oh, that's the craziest part of all, and I've spent a lot of time wondering if I'd gone around the bend, you know? But this is the thing . . . he winked at me, when he saw me looking. Just winked with all the calm in the world. And then he . . . climbed the tank. He wasn't very big. Shorter than I. And you know the tanks are open at the top, right? So he climbed the tank and he . . . dropped into it. And then . . . I couldn't see him anymore."

"Do you mean he disappeared?"

She shook her head. "No, I don't think so. It's just as he splashed in, there was all this turmoil and then . . . there were just crabs and anemones there. Nothing out of the ordinary." She looked apologetic. "I hadn't counted the inhabitants of the tank before he dropped in."

"No one would have asked you to," he said, reassuringly.

"I confess," she said. "When I first heard of the bones and the arm found in the tank, I thought it might be a shark shifter, and that he hadn't changed in time . . . ?"

Rafiel hadn't thought of that, and that was a horrible idea, though it would certainly explain the moved-aside cover. And it wasn't like it was completely crazy. After all, sharks ate each other, too. And the remains being as sparse as they were, and having been in the water, how could he be sure the victims weren't shifters? But three shark shifters? All meeting the same fate? Unlikely.

"Thank you for your help, Ms. Gigio," he said. And then, because he felt he owed her something, he added, "I don't expect you'll have any more trouble with those pamphlets, but if you do, give me a call." He handed her one of his business cards. "I'll do what I can."

"Oh, thank you," she said, holding the card close to her chest. "That's so kind of you."

He didn't know what to answer to that, so he merely said, "Good evening, ma'am." And started towards the stairs. At which point, curiosity overtook him. There was something he had never fully understood about shifting. Oh, sure, Tom and Kyrie could go on and on about genes and about crossover from other species—borrowed genes or something like that—and about all this sort of pseudoscientific stuff, but what Rafiel wanted to know was what happened to the law of conservation of mass and energy when one shifted.

After all, Tom was easily five times his normal size when he shifted. Oh, sure, Tom was a muscular guy, but if you took his mass and distributed it across the bulk of the dragon, the dragon would be lighter than a cloud. Rafiel himself knew he was considerably heavier as a lion than as a man, though the lion was also much larger.

How would those differences in size play themselves over creatures that were much further from human at either end of the scale? What would a mouse shifter look like? Or a crab shifter, for that matter? He kept thinking of the report of the squirrel the size of a German shepherd. That would make finding shifters at the aquarium far easier.

"So . . . how big are you?" he asked. "When you shift?"

She blinked, and blushed, as if he'd asked her a very intimate question. "About . . ." she said. "Oh, normal size, you know? For a mouse."

And then, as if she'd broached the inadmissible, she opened her door and darted inside, leaving Rafiel rooted to the spot, thinking, *Cat and mouse. Bad idea.*

Tom was all too conscious of having been stubborn, and strange, and that he'd probably annoyed Kyrie—or at least deserved to annoy her. He felt guilty about walking away from their discussion, but he didn't know what else he could tell her, and he was very much afraid he would change into a dragon, right there in the parking lot.

He wrapped his arms around himself, shoving his hands under his arms to keep them warm, as he walked. He relished the sound of his boots against the snow. One of the good things about them was that they had such great traction. He also relished the fact that his hands and arms felt so cold they seemed to burn. Snow was settling all over him. One of the homeless who walked along Fairfax summer and winter was huddled in the recessed doorway of the realtors down the street.

He gave Tom an odd look from under disheveled bangs. "Whoa there, pal," he said. "You won't last long like that. They give coats for free down at St. Agnes. Got me this one." He patted his huge, multipocketed safari jacket. "Really warm."

Tom nodded, but walked on, without even slowing down. Wouldn't last long? How long could he last? How long did things like him live? And what happened to them when they went beyond the limits of normal human life? What did it do to you to live long enough to see all the normal people around you die? And their children, their grandchildren, everyone you could care for? Would it mean that you would come to think of them as ephemerals? As things? Creatures who didn't matter?

If that was true, then Tom didn't want to be a shifter. He didn't want to live to lose touch with everyone he knew—to see Keith's grandchildren get old and grey, and Anthony's great grandchildren die out. To lose all meaningful contact with people.

He stomped his feet, trying to find an outlet for his anger. He didn't want to be owned, he didn't want to owe anything to the Great Sky Dragon. Much less did he want to owe anything to the dire wolf, who had already proven that he had no respect for anyone, not even other, younger shifters—not even older shifters, if Old Joe was any indication.

And Old Joe was something else, working at Tom's mind. Where was he? Where could he have gone? It would be like Old Joe—Tom nurtured no illusions about his charity case—to have disappeared completely at the first sign of a threat. It would be like him . . . but it wouldn't be like him to go more than twenty-four hours without turning into an alligator and coming back to raid the diner dumpster. Particularly in this sort of cold weather when his shifter metabolism would be demanding protein.

Tom backtracked to where the homeless man sat. "Hey," he said.

The man looked back up at him. "Ah, you decided to come back for the coat? But I can't give you the coat, or I'll freeze, see." His speech was more articulate than Tom was used to from the people who would stay in doorways even when the weather turned bitterly cold. The main reason to not go to one of the free shelters was, normally, that they demanded sobriety and this person could not swear to it. "Go to St. Agnes. They will look after you."

"No, no," Tom said, his teeth chattering. "What I want to know is, have you heard of someone called Old Joe?"

"What? The gator?" the man said blinking.

It was Tom's turn to blink and then, in a sudden rush to seem innocent, "Gator?"

"Oh, he says he turns into a gator," he said. "We call him Gator, see?"

"Er . . . have you seen him?"

"Not since yesterday, I think." He shook his head. "He said he was heading out to the aquarium. Don't make no sense to me. The aquarium is closed."

"Er . . . yes, thank you." Tom said, as he started walking the other way again.

"St. Agnes," the homeless man screamed after him. "They'll fix you."

Tom nodded. He walked very fast away from the newly-gentrified area of Fairfax, the area where, since his arrival a year ago, the place had become clean, and all the street lamps worked, and where the businesses were bookstores and movie rental stores, restaurants and clothes stores.

As he walked, the stores changed slowly to "antique" shops, thrift shops, used bookshops, used CD shops, and then another two blocks down, it was down to new age stores, churches advertising free hot meals, and then a bit further on, to where the buildings on either side of the street were warehouses, most of them empty and shuttered against intruders.

Here, in the silence of the surroundings, Tom became aware of a strange sound—like an echo behind him. Feet crunching on snow, almost in perfect rhythm with his. He turned around. Sure enough, following him, at about a half-block distance, was Conan. Keeping him protected, Tom thought. Keeping an eye on him, more the like. A little, sentient spy camera, watching his every move.

"Go away," he yelled, turning around. "I don't need you."

Conan stopped. He looked up. He too had his arms wrapped

around himself, only one of his arms was rather shorter than the other, and it made him look even more pitiful. "But . . ." he said. "But . . ." And that was it. His lip trembled.

Tom had spent the last few months taking in every sad sack who stopped by the diner. But this was too much, to expect him to take on a sad sack who also happened to be not just a spy but an instrument used by the Great Sky Dragon. "Don't try it, Conan. You heard. You are a spy device for the old bastard. I don't want him around."

Conan opened his hands. "You don't understand," he said. "I don't have a choice. I was told to follow you, to not let anything happen to you."

"Did you know?" Tom asked. "Before you heard it from the . . ." He came closer, so he could talk to Conan. "From the dire wolf?"

Conan shook his head. He looked miserable. He must have rushed out, because not only hadn't he bothered to put his jacket on, he was still wearing his George apron. "No. He said I was to protect you. I remember being very confused about how I was to do that, considering that, you know . . . you were stronger than I . . . but he said . . ." He shrugged. "I'd just dragged myself back, you know, to . . . well, to the restaurant on the outskirts of town, where . . ."

Tom nodded. Where the point of contact with the triad was. He got that much.

"I expected him to kill me," Conan said. "He punishes failure horribly. I've seen him kill other people for failing."

"But you went back, anyway?" Tom asked. He couldn't understand it. "In your place, I'd have been putting as many miles between me and as many triads as possible as fast as possible."

Conan shook his head. "It's not that easy. First, they are everywhere, truly. When you least expect it, in some small town, some out of way place, you'll meet one of them. And then there's . . . when you first join? I knew they put a tracker in you. I didn't know he could . . . you know . . . see through my eyes or anything. But I knew he could tell where I was. And if I didn't come back, he would send someone for me. And then he would make it really unpleasant."

More unpleasant than death? Tom thought, but was afraid to ask. "So you went back."

"After months, I went back," Conan hung his head.

"I was wondering . . . I mean . . ." He shook his head. "I was almost dead but I came back in a few days, but you . . ."

Conan's eyes were huge. "I was caught in the burning building," he said. "Everyone else died. I must have managed to drag myself out before my brain . . ." He shook his head. "I don't even remember the first month."

"Oh."

"The arm . . ." he shrugged, "is the least of it. I understand bone is hard to grow. They told me . . . in another three months or so it should be normal."

"Oh," Tom said again, and thought that if Conan imagined this made him feel more charitable towards the Great Sky Dragon, he was a fool. All right, Tom might have been guilty of ripping out his arm and burning him, but it had been in self-defense. While the Great Sky Dragon was the one who had sent him after Tom.

"When he sent us out first, he had told us to kill you. Find the Pearl of Heaven, kill the thief. And then all of a sudden, when I came back, he wanted you alive. He wanted you protected." He shrugged. "I don't understand any of it, but I knew it was my chance to . . . to be accepted again. I didn't know he could see through my eyes until today. I thought I had to call him. I called him when you flew away." He sounded miserable. "When you went back to your house because of the dire wolf . . ."

Tom didn't understand it either, but of one thing he was sure. "I want you to go back, now, Conan, all right?"

Conan blinked at him, in complete confusion. "But I have to . . ."

"I want you to go back to the diner, and don't worry about me. Nothing is going to happen to me. Look, it's like this—if you stay here, I'm going to change and flame you. You can't flame me, because you're supposed to protect me, not kill me. If I flame you," Tom kept his voice steady, though he was, in fact, very sure he could never flame the hapless and helpless Conan, "you won't be able to follow me, anyway—and at best you'll have to come back as you did."

"No!"

"The Great Sky Dragon can't blame you for going back."

Conan opened his mouth to protest.

"No, look, I'm not going to get in any type of trouble. I just want to walk around for a while, until I calm down. Nothing will happen to me. I promise. And I won't let you come with me, anyway."

Conan opened his mouth again. "Don't you understand?" he asked, his voice vibrating and taut with despair. "If you want to flame me, do it. But I can't go back. Himself doesn't tolerate failure and I'm not very valuable to him. Not like you."

In Tom's mind an odd idea formed. If he was valuable to the Great Sky Dragon, then there was only one thing he could use to threaten the creature. "If you don't go back," he said, "I will kill myself. I'll throw myself from an underpass or fling myself under an eighteen-wheeler. I think if I destroy the brain, I won't come back. And I'd rather be dead than owned."

Conan started and looked up at Tom, as if trying to gauge how serious the threat was.

Tom looked back with desperate resolution. He *would* rather kill himself. Particularly if he was going to live millennia. A human lifetime of obeying someone was bad enough. An eternity would be hell on Earth. And then when he'd found out that the Great Sky Dragon could use his people—literally—as instruments . . . That was the worst of all. Tom could not face that. He let his revulsion show on his face, too.

Conan looked panicked, but nodded. He held his hands open on either side of his body, palms towards Tom, in instinctive appeasement. "All right," he said. "I'll go. I'll go."

And he turned around and started down the street. Tom hesitated. Did this mean the Great Sky Dragon was going to leave Tom alone? Or that he had someone else watching Tom?

Tom shrugged. It didn't matter. He continued down Fairfax, now solidly in the office neighborhood, all closed, of course, in the storm. Hands in his pockets, he walked on, under the falling snow. He was shivering, but that didn't matter.

What he wanted to know—what he very much needed to find out—is how he could rid himself from all the creatures who wanted to claim ownership of him, and make his life his own once more. He, who had never obeyed father nor mother, nanny or teacher, would not now turn his life over to more than half mad, dangerous old beings who played under no moral rules he could understand.

From deep within his jeans pocket, his phone rang.

Tom stepped off the road onto a space on the grounds of the aquarium, on the other side of the parking lot. In summer this was a pleasant-enough space with a little bridge over a carefully directed, and probably entirely artificial, small stream, trees, flowers, benches. Right then it was a winter wonderland, with icicles dripping off the trees and slippery ice underfoot.

Tom fished in his jeans pocket, thinking it was Kyrie, and answered the phone, his half-frozen fingers fumbling with the buttons.

"Tom?"

"Dad?"

"Oh, good. I have been delayed at the airport again. Something about flights to Denver being cancelled. Look, I really need you to go there, and to wait in the loft for the cable guy."

"Dad!" Tom turned around, to look at the frozen river. He had a feeling he'd heard something move or slither down there. It couldn't be water. That would be frozen. So what could it be?

"No. You see, I wouldn't ask if it were just because I want to watch TV, but in the beginning, at least, I'm going to be working from home, and I need the cable connection for the internet."

"Dad, I can't get to Denver," Tom said, drily, keeping his teeth from knocking together by an effort of will.

"Why not? How long would it take you to fly there? It's only a three-hour drive away. Flying couldn't be more than twenty minutes."

"Flying in the current blizzard would probably take about three hours," Tom said. He felt suddenly very tired. "And besides . . . look, I just can't."

"You know, I don't ask you to do this stuff every day," Edward Ormson said, in an aggrieved tone, from the other end of the connection. "It's just that this is really important to me, and I thought . . . Well, I thought our relationship was better these days."

Their relationship was better these days. Tom was very conscious that no matter what bad parents his parents might have been, he had been a truly horrible son, himself. And he owed his father for The George. "If I could at all, I would, Dad. It's just that I'm in the middle of a big mess just now."

"A mess? What type of a mess? Anything legal?"

His father was a corporate lawyer, and clearly, just now, a hammer in search of a nail.

"No," Tom said. "Look, it's just . . . not something I feel comfortable discussing on the phone."

"Did you eat someone?"

Tom dropped the phone. It went tumbling down over the brick parapet of the bridge and hit the river below with a hard thud. Under the bridge, there was that sound as if something had moved or slithered. It was so faint, that Tom couldn't be sure it had happened or if his half-frozen ears were giving him back impossible phantom sounds.

Rafiel got in his truck thinking that while the woman was a shifter, and seemed apparently harmless, yet he couldn't get involved with her. For one, the moment she found out he was a lion shifter . . . He shook his head. Cat and dragon might be one thing—and he still wasn't sure how that would play out in the end—but cat and mouse would be insane. It would require that he lose his marbles completely.

He got his cell phone from his pocket and dialed McKnight's cell phone. "Hey, Dick," he said, using McKnight's diminutive in an attempt to forestall more protests.

The answer from the other side of the phone had almost as much of a squeak as that of Ms. Gigio's, "Yes?"

"So . . . have you done the platform?" he asked.

"Yeah, yeah. We . . . I brought a team over." He spoke with such haste, such obviously tumbling guilt, that it was obvious to Rafiel that he had found something.

"What did you find?"

"We . . . uh . . . I found . . . that is . . . Michelle and I found a couple of used condoms, tied up, in the planters. We will have them processed and . . . and get back to you with the results."

"Thanks, McKnight. Do," Rafiel said, keeping the amusement, but not the forcefulness out of his voice.

He hesitated for a moment, starting the car away from Ms. Gigio's home. Where would he go now? He was dying to know what was happening with those condoms. Well . . . at least Lei had told the truth about that. Maybe.

Getting the phone again, he said, "Dick, can you give me the address of all of the aquarium's male employees? Female, too, while you're at it."

McKnight could. Or at least he could after much hemming and hawing and getting hold of the aquarium records from someone. He cleared his throat, nervously, and in a reedy voice gave Rafiel three male names—John Wagner, Carl Hoster and Jeremy Fry—and three female names—Suzanne Albert, Lillian Moore, Katlyn Jones—and addresses, all within a mile of the aquarium in the area where old Victorians had been converted into apartments, amid a lot of other, mostly cinder-block apartments, of fifties vintage. It mostly housed college students. And they were all close enough to the diner too.

Rafiel was feeling uneasy enough about Tom and Kyrie and whatever their little spat might have devolved into. Some part of him told him that, interested party or not, suspicious or not, he should have stayed around and refereed their argument. They were both younger than him, and both of them had far less experience of relationships.

Not that I can tell them a lot about relationships, Rafiel thought. *After all, I am the master of the love them and leave them.*

"Rafiel?"

He'd forgotten he'd left the cell phone on, and now looked at it in puzzlement, thereby putting his brakes on a little too late for the red light ahead. He hit a patch of ice as he braked and slid through the intersection to the glorious accompaniment of the horns of cars which swerved to avoid him. *Good thing I'm a policeman,* he thought as he took a deep breath, made sure he wasn't about to shift—his nails looked the same size, and there was nothing golden or furry about his hands—and said, "Yeah, McKnight?"

"Are you going to go talk to these people?" McKnight asked.

"That's the idea," Rafiel said.

"In this weather?"

"Well, all the more chance to find them at home, right?" Rafiel said, and hung up before McKnight would actively and loudly worry about his life or his safety or something.

Then he pressed one of his preset dials, and rang up The George.

Kyrie started worrying about Tom almost as soon as he left the parking lot. It wasn't that she was angry at him—or not exactly. A part of her understood that he couldn't bear to be controlled by someone else, much less someone who legally and morally should have no power over him.

Another part of her wanted to tell him to grow up already and that adults knew they couldn't have life all their own way, that they couldn't forever hold at bay the unpleasant parts of reality and those they would rather not deal with. But that part of her, she told herself, was firmly under control. Yes, she was sure that Tom was overreacting. But at the same time he was just as sure that she was underreacting, enduring the interference of the dire wolf in her affairs with excessive placidity and total lack of protest.

Which, she thought, was not really true. She could very easily—and happily, for that matter—allow herself to scream and rant. For all the good it would do.

But she would not allow herself to scream and rant at Tom. Because that would do no good. She was sure he'd gone off to cool off and that he too was trying to hold his temper in check. And she couldn't fault him. She preferred he did that than he shifted and took it out on all those nearby.

Keith was looking intently at her. "Is Anthony coming in?"

"In a few minutes," Kyrie said, keeping her voice calm. In her mind, she was imagining Tom walking blindly into the storm. She wished he had taken his jacket.

"I can't stay, Kyrie. I have to get home," Keith said. "I have no idea what happened to Summer. She must think I'm crazy. I bring her here for a coffee, and the next thing you know, I'm cooking."

"Yeah," Kyrie said. "Anthony is on his way." He'd sounded frankly relieved to be called in. Kyrie wondered what exactly his wife had been doing to make him so happy to hear from her. But Anthony solved it himself as he came in. "It's crazy just sitting in the house, watching reruns of *Friends*," he said. "I mean, it's a studio, and it's just snowing outside. And then Cecily is worried about . . . you know . . . the storm and whether the roof is going to cave in. Like . . . we're on the third floor down from the top of the building. If the roof caves in on us, we're in a world of trouble." He looked sheepish for a moment, as he divested himself of his jacket and put on his apron and the hat he wore while he was cooking—which was, granted, not as stylish as Tom's bandana, but served the same purpose of keeping hair out of the food. "She's not . . . I mean, I don't want you to think she's crazy or something. It's just she's not used to going through these blizzards. I guess for people who didn't grow up in Colorado it must look much worse than it is."

"Yeah, it does," Kyrie said. And still, in her mind, she saw Tom walking through the storm. How could he survive it? Could he survive it? She heard Dire saying that most of the young shifters died through their own stupidity and she gritted her teeth and pretended that everything was fine, and got orders, and put them on the carousel of spikes on the counter, for Anthony.

More people came in. Probably people who weren't all that familiar with Colorado, Kyrie thought, and who found it easier to weather the storm in here than alone in whatever tiny apartments they lived in. She kept a smile on her face, and worked as efficiently as she knew how, while Anthony turned out the meals in record time.

She didn't know how long it had been, when she heard the back door open. She set down the tray and the carafe of coffee on the counter, and ran down the hallway. "Tom," she started, with some idea of finishing the sentence with "Tom, I was so worried."

But instead of Tom, it was Conan, coming in. He was a vague shade between blue and lavender. His teeth beat a mad rhythm. His hair was so covered in snow that he might as well have been wearing a powdered wig.

"Where is Tom?" Kyrie asked.

Conan looked up at her, in mute misery. That look made thoughts run through her mind, thoughts she didn't like at all. There had been a fight and the Great Sky Dragon had killed Tom. After all, she remembered, the creature held it his right to discipline those he deemed to belong to him. Or else . . . or else, Tom had been run over. Or simply collapsed and frozen by the side of the road. "What. Happened. To. Tom?" she asked, her voice slow and controlled, even as she told herself that she would not shift. She would never shift. Not in the diner. Shifting wouldn't help anything. Conan already looked halfway between frozen and terrified.

He shook his head. "He is fine," he said, though the words weren't really easy to understand through his chattering teeth. "He's . . . he was fine when I left him."

And then, nerveless, as though his legs had turned to rubber under him and his body wasn't all that much more solid, Conan sank to his behind just inside the door of the diner. "He made me leave," he said. "He told me to leave. He made me leave. What if something happens to him?"

"Tom made you leave?"

A headshake. "No. Himself. He told me to leave. Tom said . . . he said he'd kill himself if I stayed with him, and the Grea—Himself said he meant it."

"Nothing will happen to Tom," Kyrie said. And bit her lip thinking that unfortunately she was growing as weary of the interference of elder shifters as Tom himself was. "It's all right. Come on." She helped him get up—or rather more or less pulled him up, by his arms, by main strength. "Come on. I'll get you coffee or something. You're frozen."

"He's out there, like that," Conan said. "In a T-shirt. What if something happens to him?"

"Tom is a big boy," Kyrie said. "He'll take care of himself. He used to live on the streets. It's not like he's a child whom we must look after."

She was telling herself that more than she was telling it to Conan. And she was so convincing that she almost believed it. At least for the next two hours, she managed to keep herself from freaking out thinking of Tom out there alone and what might happen to him.

It wasn't like the city was safe. There were the Ancient Ones, and whatever was throwing people to the sharks, and the Rodent Liberation Front and the triad. In fact, it was an interesting time to be a shifter in Goldport.

She was very close to losing all self-control, shifting, and loping about in the storm, trying to smell Tom out, when the phone rang.

"Hello," she said. "The George."

"Kyrie. It's Rafiel. Is Tom okay?"

And then, before she could control it, before she could remember that Tom was an adult and should be treated as such, all her anxiety came pouring out of her, "I hope so. But, Rafiel, he walked west on Fairfax two and a half hours ago and he hasn't come back."

"Uh. Does he have his phone with him?"

"Yes. Well . . . maybe. He should have it. But he isn't answering." An hour ago, in a moment of weakness, she'd tried to call three or four times. And another half a dozen times since.

"I see. You two fight?"

"No. Not really. He is just . . . he's mad at the . . . you know . . ."

"Yeah. I imagine." There was a pause, as if Rafiel were trying to think through things. "West on Fairfax?"

"Yeah."

"I see. I tell you what, I'll drive down the road a while and see if I can find him. What was he wearing?"

"What he was wearing when you last saw him. Jeans and a black T-shirt." She felt she needed to defend him against stupidity, even though Rafiel hadn't even paused in a significant manner. "He said he needed to cool off."

"Oh, yes. And I'm sure he has," Rafiel said. "Don't worry, okay? I'll see if I can find him."

Rafiel tried to call a couple of times. No answer. Stubborn dragon, he told himself about his friend, with something between annoyance and admiration. That Tom wasn't answering Kyrie might or might not make sense. She didn't seem to think they had argued, but Rafiel's experience of women—his mother, aunts and girl cousins included—told him that just because a woman thought that, it didn't mean the man she had emphatically not argued with thought the same.

He drove slowly down Fairfax seeing no movement, let alone movement by someone in jeans and a black T-shirt. Tom had black hair. He should have stood out like a sore thumb.

Unless, of course, he's passed out by the side of the road and covered in a mound of snow, in which case he is pretty much white. Rafiel felt a tightening in his stomach at the thought. How long could a dragon survive hypothermia? In either form? Oh, okay, so they were hard to kill, but was freezing one of the ways they could be killed? He didn't know. And it wasn't as if he was going to go in search of Dante Dire to ask him.

Dante Dire presented the other problem. Because Kyrie hadn't said anything about looking for two people, one following the other, he presumed that Conan hadn't gone with Tom. That meant Tom was out there without his human security cam. What if the bad guys had found him first? While Rafiel had got the idea that Dante Dire was cringingly afraid of the Great Sky Dragon, he didn't get the feeling that he was even vaguely impaired by moral considerations or feelings that he should not kill. Particularly—he suspected—no feelings that he should not kill dragons.

As stupid as it was that Dante Dire, sent to investigate the death of shifters, would end up killing shifters to get them out of his way, Rafiel suspected that this was a *nobody picks on my little brother but me* matter. After all, the Great Sky Dragon, supposed protector of all dragons, had killed at least one of their members in Goldport. The police had processed the body and Rafiel was sure he had been bitten in two in the parking lot of the Chinese restaurant. And the Great Sky Dragon had damn well near killed Tom, too, for all his new interest in protecting him.

Rafiel had now gone all the way to the west end of Fairfax. He turned around and started driving the other way, slowly. A movement from a doorway called his attention. It looked khaki, not black, but considering everything, perhaps with the snow it just looked that way.

Hopeful, he pulled up to the curb, stopped the car, jiggled a little in his seat, just to make sure at least one of his wheels wasn't on solid ice, parked and set the parking brake. "Hey there," he called to the indistinct, blurred form in the doorway.

The form stirred. Almost immediately, Rafiel realized it couldn't be Tom. This was someone older with white hair, probably taller and bulkier than Tom, though that was hard to tell, as he was huddled in the doorway with one of those Mylar space blankets over most of his body save for his shoulders and head. The flash of khaki was from the shoulders, covered in some sort of jacket. He looked at Rafiel from bleary eyes half hidden under unkempt bangs.

"Uh . . ." Rafiel said, jiggling his keys in his pocket. "Do you want a ride to a shelter?"

The eyes widened. "No shelter," he said, with something very akin to fear. He shook his head and rustled the corner of his shiny silver coverings. "I got my blanket."

"Oh. All right," Rafiel said. The man didn't seem drunk, but he seemed as averse to going into a shelter as, say, Tom or Kyrie or himself would have been. Rafiel sniffed the air, smelling nothing, but he wasn't sure he would have smelled anything as cold as it was. He would swear his ability to smell had frozen with his nose. Perhaps, he thought, he should come back and smell the man later. And, as the inanity of the thought struck, he snorted. Yeah, because he really needed to find another charity case for Tom. Old Joe wasn't enough. "Hey," he said, on impulse. "Did you see a guy go by here? About yea tall, wearing jeans and a black T-shirt? Black hair about shoulder long or a little longer?" How was it possible that he was suddenly so unsure of Tom's hair length? He almost sighed in exasperation at himself. Yes, Kyrie was far more interesting to look at, but he should have noticed his best male friend's hair length.

"I told him he needed a jacket," the old transient man said and nodded.

"Uh. You did? Good call."

"Yeah, he was going that way," the man said, pointing west. "If you are looking for him, going that way"—he pointed east, the direction Rafiel was now headed—"won't help."

"Right, but see, I went miles on Fairfax and I didn't—"

"He was looking for Old Joe," the derelict said. "Him that thinks he can be a gator? I told him last I heard Old Joe was headed for the aquarium. I don't know what he meant to do at the aquarium, though."

The aquarium, yeah, that would be like Tom. Let cryptozoology zanies take over the local paper. Let them get pictures of creatures that shouldn't possibly exist fighting it out in the parking lot of the aquarium. Tom, who shifted into one of the creatures, would immediately feel honor bound to go the aquarium. Why didn't I think of it before? "Thanks," he told the old man. "I'll . . . get you a coffee or something."

The man smiled, revealing very brown teeth. "Why, that would be very nice of you."

Back in the car, Rafiel turned around. *The aquarium. What are the odds?*

But it was a few minutes' drive there, at the most, and it wasn't as though he didn't have excuses he could give for being on the grounds. He turned onto Ocean Street and started driving slowly around the parking lot. And caught a flash of a black T-shirt—or mostly black, as it seemed mottled in white—as the person wearing it stepped off the garden path and disappeared from view.

Yeah, Tom, Rafiel thought, with a mix of concern and annoyance. *Because who else would think that late in the evening, in the middle of a snowstorm, is a good time to go explore the garden of the aquarium?*

Still, he wasn't at all sure and couldn't do more than hope that it was indeed Tom, as he parked on the street and jumped out. He ran across the garden, ice and—presumably—frozen grass crackling under his feet. "Tom," he yelled. "Tom."

And then he hit a patch of ice, and his feet went out from under him.

Tom heard Rafiel's voice. He'd walked down the slope towards the river, and he'd looked every place possible his phone might have hit the ice. But it was dark, he didn't have a flashlight and—as far as he could tell—his phone would now be covered by snow, and a lump amid the other lumps resting on the riverbed. While it might be possible to distinguish it from rocks and twigs by its shape, every minute that passed was making it more indistinct, and Tom had no idea how long he'd been looking. He didn't wear a watch—something Kyrie told him was silly. Normally he could rely on the clock on the wall of The George.

And now, between being cold and the snow falling all around muffling sound, he didn't know if five minutes had gone by, or an hour. Or more. Sometimes, the phone rang, but even that didn't make it any easier to find, because it seemed that, just as he had isolated an area the sound might be coming from, the ringing stopped again.

All of this was worsened by the fact that he had to look for the phone from the bank. He didn't think the river was frozen enough to support him. And while the "river" was probably no more than two feet deep, at most, Tom didn't want to get his feet and legs wet. He was cold enough.

On the other hand, he also didn't want to lose his phone. Not to mention that by now his father probably thought that he had eaten someone—instead of just having been startled while his fingers were half frozen. He didn't think, even if his father thought so, that he would feel obligated to call the police and report, but you never knew. For most of his life, Edward Ormson had been a fairly amoral—if not immoral—corporate lawyer. He'd encountered ethics and a sense of responsibility late in life. Like any midlife crisis, it could cause some very strange effects. He might suddenly feel an irresistible obligation to report imaginary crimes.

That's it, Tom thought. *I'll go back to The George and call him from there.* He climbed up from the bank of the river to the path, at least six feet above. Like all such canals, artificial or not, in Colorado, the bed for the little river was deep enough to accommodate a ten-times swollen volume in sudden flash floods.

Though, like the legendary Colorado blizzards, it was something he hadn't experienced for himself, he'd heard of summers when sudden snowstorms up in the mountains sent water thundering down the canyons below, to cause untold damage. So the design of every waterworks in Colorado accounted for those.

He struggled all the way to the road level, and looked towards Fairfax. And then thought that it had taken him probably a good hour to walk here, and that added to the point where he had effectively hung up on his father meant that Edward was probably concocting scarier and scarier stories to tell himself. Right.

Sighing, he started down to the riverbed again. He'd look just one more time. Then there was Rafiel's voice from the garden up there.

Definitely Rafiel's. And followed by a thud that indicated the idiot had just taken a header in the snow.

Tom cursed softly under his breath, and started climbing back up the steep bank. He wanted his phone. Badly. But considering the sounds he'd heard from under the bridge, he wasn't absolutely convinced there wasn't something or someone hiding there. Not so long ago, there had been a case in Denver of homeless men being found beheaded. Tom didn't remember—since at the time he didn't live in Colorado and all he had seen of the affair was the TV news that happened to be playing at a soup kitchen—whether the case had ever been resolved, or if there was still someone in Colorado, perhaps in the smaller towns now, whose hobby it was to kill males foolish enough to be out and unsheltered—and unobserved—in this sort of weather. So it probably wouldn't hurt, before he went down towards the river and made himself invisible to anyone driving by, for him to have backup.

Having made it all the way to the path beside the river, Tom looked in the direction the thud had come from. Rafiel had gotten up, and was dusting off his knees.

"Are you okay?" Tom said.

"I'm fine," Rafiel said, and glared at him. "You?"

"I'm great," Tom said. "I just dropped my phone. Down on the river." He paused a second. "Right after my father asked me if I'd eaten someone."

"Oh," Rafiel said. He looked uneasy. Had his parents ever asked him if he'd eaten someone? No. Never mind that. Probably not. Though Tom had yet to meet Rafiel's mom, Rafiel had brought his dad over for lunch at The George a couple of times.

An older, sturdier version of Rafiel, his hair white and giving less the impression of a leonine mane than his son's wild hair, Mr. Trall had impressed Tom as eminently sane. And eminently sane parents didn't leap to the conclusion their sons went around eating people, not even when the sons happened to have another, more carnivorous form. Which didn't help Tom at all, because his father wasn't sane.

Rafiel was fishing in the pocket of his jacket. "Here, why don't you call him on my phone?"

"Oh," Tom said, surprised the idea hadn't occurred to him, though considering how much ice he felt on top of his head, his brain was probably frozen solid. And not being a silicon-based life-form, this didn't help his thought processes at all. He took the phone and started dialing his father's number, all under what he couldn't help feeling was Rafiel's stern scrutiny.

"Hello? Dad?" Tom said, as the phone was answered on the other side.

"Tom. Oh. Good. I was . . . er . . . I've been worried."

Tom tried to grit his teeth, which was pretty hard, as they insisted on chattering together. "No, Dad, I didn't eat anyone."

"Oh." Pause. "Well, I didn't think you had. I was just . . . er . . . worried."

Please, don't let him have gone to the police, Tom thought, as he watched Rafiel turn on his heel and head back towards the truck. Tom had a vague moment of panic at the thought that Rafiel was just going to drive back. Well, at least he'd left him with the phone. But the slog back to The George seemed suddenly like too much of an effort to make. Tom was very cold and very tired, and maybe he should just lie down here and—

"So what sort of trouble are you in?" Edward Ormson asked, over the phone. "I notice you're using someone else's phone. Isn't that your policeman friend? Tom! You've been arrested."

Damn, damn, damn, damn, damn! His youthful antics had included several arrests, for vandalism, for joyriding, for possession. His father had bailed him out countless times. But did this justify—five years later—his father assuming he'd been arrested, just because he was using a policeman's phone? *Well, okay, yeah, it probably kind of does,* he thought.

"I'll get someone to come post bail as soon as—"

"I wasn't arrested, Dad. It's . . . hard to explain over the phone. Do you remember the pearl?" He raised his eyebrows and had trouble concentrating on the flow of conversation, as Rafiel was making his way back, a bundle of fabric swinging from one hand.

"You didn't steal it again?"

"No, I didn't steal anything. Ow." The last sound was because

Rafiel was roughly and very matter of factly putting a hooded sweat shirt over Tom's head and dressing him in it without so much as by your leave. It involved pulling Tom's hands through the sleeves, as if he'd been a child or a mental patient. "Ow, all right. I can dress myself, Rafiel."

"What?" Edward asked.

"Nothing. Rafiel has decided I'm not properly attired for the weather and is making me put on a hoodie." He glared at Rafiel.

"Seems sensible to me, if what I'm seeing on the weather channel is any indication," Edward said. "So, you were saying about this pearl."

"Not the pearl. The . . . owner of the pearl. He seems to think I belong to him. Because of who I am, you know?"

"Because you're my son and I worked for him?"

Sheesh. His dad could be surprisingly dense. "No, Dad. No. Because I am . . . you know, like him and his relatives."

"Oh. What is he doing? We could file a—"

"Father." Despite his annoyance Tom almost laughed. At least his father was trying to help. Which was, all things considered, not bad. "I am sure he wouldn't be the least intimidated by a legal order of some sort. He eats lawyers for breakfast. Probably literally."

Rafiel pulled the hood up over Tom's head. Tom said into the phone, "Look, I have to go. I'll call you from The George when I get there."

Right now the diner, with its warmth and warm coffee and food seemed to Tom like a vision of lost paradise. He hung up and gave Rafiel the phone. And then he noticed that Rafiel had a flashlight in his hand. One of the larger ones of the type people said the police often used as a weapon in a pinch. Tom stepped back. But Rafiel said, "Come on. Let's go look for your phone one last time."

"Kyrie will be worried," Tom said.

"Just a minute. We'll look for your phone and if we don't see it, with the flashlight, then we go back. And, you know, Kyrie is probably not that worried. She knows I'm looking for you."

Tom bit his tongue to avoid saying that of course that would calm down anyone's anxiety, because who could ever doubt that once

Rafiel was on the case everything would turn out for the best? But considering that Rafiel had found him, and gone out of his way to try to help him, his sarcasm would be misplaced. "All right," he said.

Seeing Tom subdued always frightened Rafiel a little. He'd been through law enforcement courses. He knew Tom's type.

Tom was the kind of person who usually had to be dragged away from whatever incident had just happened, still kicking and screaming and throwing a fit. The sort of person who could never get a traffic ticket without adding resisting arrest to the charges. The sort of person, in fact, who wasn't subdued unless he were very sick or very scared. Since Tom didn't look either, Rafiel had to assume freezing did something to shifter dragons.

Reptiles. Cold blood. Can't they die if they get cold enough? He didn't want to think about it, and besides, he'd given Tom a hoodie. Granted, it was Rafiel's size, and therefore a bit long on Tom, but that was good as it would go over Tom's hands.

Rafiel started towards the river, and then started, slowly, down the slope. His knee still hurt from banging it on the path when he had fallen and he had no intention of taking another header.

"Here," Tom said, stepping up beside him and offering him a hand. "My boots are sturdier than yours."

Rafiel took Tom's hand for support, half afraid that the very cold-feeling fingers would snap off under the grasp of his hand. He was sure—more than sure—that a normal person would have hypothermia from this adventure. But it always came back to . . . they weren't normal, were they?

They made it all the way to the bottom, where the frozen river glistened two steps from them. Unfortunately, it only glistened in the spots not covered up by snow. The rest was an amorphous, lumpy mess. He turned his flashlight on, and pointed it at the river and at that moment, Tom's phone rang. This helped Rafiel pinpoint the roughly rectangular snow-covered lump. "There," he said, nailing the shape with the beam of his flashlight. "Right there. Can you get it?"

Tom looked out speculatively. "I don't know if the ice will hold up. But if the ice breaks under me and I wet my feet, it's okay, because you'll give me a ride back to the diner, right?"

"Right," Rafiel said. Had the idiot thought that Rafiel was going to just come out, then leave him to freeze out here? "If parts of your body start breaking off from the cold I'm fairly sure Kyrie would kill me," he said, and grinned sheepishly at his friend. "So, yeah, I'll give you a ride back, you idiot."

Tom nodded and edged cautiously on top of the frozen river, with the sort of duck-footed waddle of someone trying to neither slip nor skate on the surface. In the middle of the river, he picked up the phone, then, as he was straightening, dropped it again.

"Would you stop that?" Rafiel asked impatiently. "The idea is to get back into the car and back to The George. Not to stand here and play find the phone."

But Tom shook his head, and bent, and picked up the phone again. He walked back close enough that he could whisper and Rafiel would hear him. "There's something in the tunnel under the little bridge, Rafiel. I saw a tail disappear that way."

A tail. Great. Rafiel was going to assume that, no matter how much Rafiel might want it to be otherwise, Tom didn't mean he had seen the friendly, furry, potentially wagging tail of a kitten or puppy. "Uh . . . a tail?"

"Reptilian. Dragging."

Rafiel frowned in the direction of the bridge and the shadows under it. It seemed to him, as he concentrated, that he did hear something very like a rustle from under there. But . . . a tail? "Perhaps the Great Sky Dragon sent one of your cousins to look after you."

"They're not my cousins."

"Whatever," Rafiel said, feeling an absurd pleasure, as if he'd scored a point. "They think they are."

"I'm hardly responsible for people's delusions."

How could someone like Tom, who didn't so much get in trouble as carry it into the lives of everyone around him, sound so much like a New England dowager?

"Yeah, but anyway, maybe he sent one of his underlings to look in on you?"

Tom shook his head. "Well, he did. Conan. But I sent him back his merry way. Or not merry." Tom frowned. "Besides," he whispered, "the tail looked like an alligator's."

"An alli—" Rafiel resisted an urge to smack his own forehead, and, shortly thereafter, an urge to smack Tom—hard—with the flashlight. "You mean Old Joe? The homeless guy said he told you he was at the aquarium."

"Yeah," Tom said. "I figure he's hiding out here, in alligator form."

"Is that why you're whispering? Look, what do you want with Old Joe, anyway? So he's hiding here, as an alligator. Perhaps we should leave him alone?"

Tom shook his head, which was par for the course. Of course he didn't think they should leave Old Joe alone, because that would be the life-preserving, not-getting-into-worse-trouble solution.

"Okay," Rafiel said. "So what do you want to do?"

"I figure he knows something," Tom whispered back. "And I want to find out what it is."

"Uh . . . what he knows is probably the best places to sleep when a storm threatens, and, Tom, you aren't even that with it. You ought to be indoors." And watched. By a nursemaid. Or a psychiatrist.

Tom shook his head again. Snow and ice flew from his dark hair. He frowned at Rafiel. He'd become alarmingly pale in the cold, so that he looked like he was wearing white pancake make-up, from which his lips—a vague shade of blue—the tip of his nose—a lovely violet—his dark eyebrows and his blue eyes emerged looking vaguely unnatural in all their chromatic glory. "Look, he knows something. And it's something that might help us. He knows about the Ancient Ones."

"Okay, even supposing he knows," Rafiel said impatiently, "what do you propose to do about this? And why are we whispering? If he didn't hear the cell phone ring, and doesn't know we're here, then he's way too addled to help us."

"That's not it," Tom said. "I don't want him to know we're about to go after him."

"We are? Into a sewer tunnel? After an alligator?"

"I don't think it's a sewer," Tom said, looking into the shadows under the bridge. "At least, I don't think the city would have an open sewer through a recreation area. I mean, I'm well aware that they're all crazy, but all the same, there's a difference between crazy and loony."

Not from where I'm standing, buddy. Aloud, Rafiel said, "Look at it this way—that connects to a drainage pipe somewhere. And that drainage pipe is connected, somewhere, to the Goldport sewers. You have heard of people flushing baby crocodiles, right?"

Tom made a sound of profound exasperation. "Yes, in New York City. Some science fiction writer or another wrote a very unpleasant story about it. But it's an urban legend, you know. No pet stores have sold crocodiles, that I remember. So it mustn't be legal anymore."

"Doesn't matter," Rafiel said, pragmatically. "It was legal back in the fifties. And crocodiles live forever."

"And migrate from New York City to Goldport, Colorado?" Tom shook his head. "Rafiel! Next thing you know, you're going to tell me we'll find Denver's lizard man from Cheeseman Park under there. Come on. Just come here, shine your flashlight under there. I promise I won't make you actually go under there and look amid all the dangerous animals."

He gave Rafiel one of his more irritating smiles.

"Oh, all right," Rafiel said, grudgingly.

For all that Tom had cajoled Rafiel into shining his light under the bridge, he was somewhat scared of what it might uncover. What if

Rafiel was correct, and it would show a bunch of dragons under there, all of them spying on Tom?

Choking back a laugh at the absurd image, Tom told himself he was getting worse than his father. Any moment now, he'd start asking himself if he'd eaten people.

Rafiel slip-skated to stand beside Tom, closer to the center of the river, and shone his flashlight searchingly into the space beneath the little arched bridge.

It was cozier under there than Tom expected—or at least, there was none of the trash he'd come to expect in that sort of place. He'd slept in that sort of place, sometimes, and it seemed never to be empty of a few rusting cans, a couple of unidentifiable, shredded cardboard boxes and perhaps the rotting body of a road-kill racoon. But under this bridge, it looked pretty clean. A couple of branches and some leaves, and other than that, just the clean shine of ice.

"Fine," Tom said. "I guess there isn't—"

But at that moment he heard the clack-clack-clack of alligator teeth that seemed to be Old Joe's way of laughing. It was faint and muffled, but definitely there. Tom grabbed Rafiel's wrist and aimed the flashlight at the place the sound had come from. There in the dark, Old Joe was squeezed under the place where the bridge came down to meet the bank and where it was, therefore, almost impossible to see.

Tom heard himself make a sound that was much like that of a steam train stopping. "Come out," he said, peremptorily. "Come out now."

He didn't know what he expected. Old Joe had obeyed him in the past, but in the past he'd caught Old Joe raiding The George's dumpster, and therefore he was, technically, trespassing on Tom's property. This time, Tom half-expected him to turn tail and run very fast, which, Tom understood, could be very fast indeed for an alligator.

Old Joe must have thought it too. For a moment there was a rebellious light in the tiny eyes, in the reflection of the flashlight. Rafiel must have thought of worse things, because he tried to pull the flashlight away from Tom and started to say, "Enough. You know—"

But Tom said, in his best voice of command, "Don't you dare.

Don't you even think about it. I thought you were dead. I've been worried sick for days. Now, you'll come out here, shift, and explain yourself."

Old Joe slithered forward, swinging his tail from side to side. Rafiel must have been still pretty unsure about what the creature meant to do, because he took a step backwards. But Tom stood his ground and Old Joe gave him a sheepish look, as if sorry that he had tried to scare him, or perhaps simply sorry that he hadn't managed to scare him.

He shifted, right there on the snow, and stayed sitting down on his butt on the ice, his hands around his knees. Rafiel made a sound and said, "I have clothes. In my car."

Old Joe gave him an indulgent, almost amused look, the sort of look grown-ups give cute little children. "No need," he said. "I will shift again, after you're gone." He looked up at Tom. "And now, what do you want? Why did you think I was dead?"

"Because of the dire wolf," Tom said. "You said he had talked to you and you clearly knew him, so I thought . . ." He felt as though he'd lost some of his capacity to command and his righteous indignation too, now that Old Joe was treating him as if he had been silly and alarmist.

Old Joe shrugged. "Yes. Dire is a bad person," he said. "He and his council of ancients, always dictating the way in which people are supposed to live, the way in which shifter people are supposed to be people, and whom we should respect and whom we shouldn't." He shook his head. "He's a very bad person." He looked up at Tom, intently. "You stay away from him."

"I have every intention of staying away from him," Tom said, hearing his own voice sound sullen, like an annoyed little boy's.

"You stay away from her, too."

"Her?" Tom said, with some strange notion that Rafiel had paid Old Joe to warn him against Kyrie.

"The girl that came to the aquarium, in the car," Old Joe said. "Just a little while ago."

Rafiel cleared his throat. "I know he spends more on his hair product than most third world nations produce in one year, but that wasn't a girl. It was my subordinate, McKnight. Though he might have had a girl with him," he said, vaguely remembering something about Michelle, one of the part-timers.

"No. Not the police people!" Old Joe looked aggrieved, like they were both very dense. "The other woman. She came by, after the police left, with a guy. She left without the guy."

"You mean . . ." Rafiel took a step towards the aquarium, but Tom held his wrist. He couldn't say anything. He wasn't about to cast aspersions on what Old Joe was saying right in front of Old Joe, but he held Rafiel's wrist and said, "Wait."

Then to Old Joe, he said, "And you haven't seen Dire again? He hasn't talked to you again? Tried to find out things about us?"

That embarrassed look that he suspected meant Old Joe was lying, flitted across the alligator's face again. "Well," he said. "He came and he did ask me some questions. Like, what had happened at the castle, and all, but he . . ." He shrugged. "I didn't tell him anything that could hurt you. I swear I didn't. And then I ran away so I didn't have to tell him anything else." He looked at Tom, a look much like a glare from under his fringe of hair. "That's all I know. Can I go now?" And without waiting for permission, he shifted, and ran—in alligator form—back under the bridge, in a clacking of teeth, much like a fugitive snicker.

"We've got to go to the aquarium," Rafiel said.

Which meant, Tom thought, that he wasn't thinking at all. How was he going to get in? And if he did, how was he going to justify going into the aquarium to look for a body just now? Tom was fairly sure his friend hadn't thought this through.

"Wait. Let's go to your car and discuss this first," he told Rafiel.

"But—"

"Wait."

In the car, Rafiel turned on the gas to start warming up the motor, so they could have heat soon.

"Rafiel, you can't go in there," Tom said. "You just can't."

"What do you mean, I can't?" Rafiel said. He reached for his phone, ready to call McKnight and ask him to come and process the scene.

"I meant, you can't." Tom looked very grave and slightly sad, which was very odd. If Rafiel didn't know him better, if Rafiel weren't sure this was one dragon who didn't go about pushing people into aquariums . . .

"Why not?" he asked belligerently, while behind his rational mind, there ran thoughts he wouldn't even acknowledge, much less express, such as that dragons were aquatic creatures and that, as aquatic creatures, they might have some craving or other relating to water and pushing people in it. "You know it's my duty. I'm a policeman. If there's a body in there—"

"*If*," Tom said. "But beyond that, Rafiel, how are you going to tell them you heard about it? Who are you going to say informed you? And how are you going to say you got in?"

Rafiel tapped his fingers on the seat beside him. "But . . . time is of the essence," he said. "If there is a corpse, the more complete it is, the better the picture we will get. I mean, with the other ones, we don't even know if they were already dead when they were dumped in. And if we're dealing with shifters . . ."

"Yes. Of course. Perhaps an anonymous phone call? From one of the phone booths remaining, at a convenience store not on Fairfax?" Tom said. "One of the ones in the less busy areas? You can park at the back, or even farther away than that, and I can call and tell the police that there is a corpse in the aquarium. But it has to be to the central station. And I can't be identified."

"Yeah," Rafiel said, thinking. "So long as you don't stay on the line. They'll try to keep you on the line, so that they can get to you. You must not do that. Say your piece and run, and we'll get out of there fast." As he spoke, he thought of the convenience store to go to, on Fer de Lance Street. Between the local pioneer museum and a high school, the place was guaranteed to be deserted today.

He started off, headed that way, by the shortest route possible. "Well, at least what Old Joe says," Rafiel said, "sort of narrows it down to a female employee of the aquarium. I had a list of names of male employees to interview, but now . . ."

"No," Tom said, seriously. His features were set in such a way that they seemed to be carved, and a muscle played on the side of his face, giving the impression that he was about to have a nervous breakdown or something. "No, don't be so sure. What you're not thinking about, Rafiel, is that . . . well . . . Old Joe is not the best of witnesses, you know? He often . . ." He shrugged.

"He often what? Drinks? Does drugs?"

Tom shook his head, emphatically. "No. Nothing like that. At least, not that I know, and I think I'd have been able to tell. No. But he sometimes seems to be . . . not quite anchored to reality, if you know what I mean?"

Rafiel quirked an eyebrow. Sometimes he wondered how anchored to reality they all were. Considering what they were, and what they could do, it would be a wonder if they didn't sometimes feel unmoored and adrift. "Okay," he said.

He pulled up behind the store, on Fer de Lance. Actually behind and on the other side of the street, so that no one associated him with the phone call. There wasn't anyone around, in any case. The high school was closed, as was the pioneer museum. The rest of the block had the sort of empty feel that areas of town had that aren't flourishing. Like the last houses that had stood there had just been bulldozed, and they hadn't come up with anything else to replace them. The vacant lots didn't even have trees or proper plants. Just a sort of scrubby grass, now completely covered by snow.

"What are you doing?" he said, realizing Tom was throwing himself over the front seat and towards the back.

Tom, now fully in the back seat, gave him a grin. "Getting out on the driver's side," he said. "It's towards the school, and that's firmly closed, so no one will see me."

He had the hood firmly pulled over his head, and started to open the door, then stopped. "Do you have a quarter? Because I can't use a credit card on this. It would be way too obvious."

Rafiel grabbed a quarter from the drink holder, where he normally kept parking-meter fodder. He flipped it at Tom, who grabbed it out of the air. Good to know he was getting the feeling in his hands back.

He watched Tom get out of the car, very quickly, cross the high school campus semidiagonally, so that any witness would say he came out of the school. Sometimes—he thought, as he watched Tom cross the street and run, hell-bent for leather, towards the convenience store, so fast that he wasn't any more than a brief dark blur amid the snow—it was easy to believe the things Tom told him about his teenage years. Casual juvenile delinquence would impart that sort of knowledge. How to trick the police, 101.

In less time than seemed possible, for what he needed to do, Tom was back, coming into the car through the back door and saying, "Drive, drive, drive."

Rafiel drove. "Who answered?"

"I think just the receptionist or dispatcher, or whatever. She told me she would transfer me to someone else, but I hung up." He grinned at Rafiel, a feral grin, and leaned forward on the seat. "I grabbed the phone with my sleeve. And I wiped the coin before putting it in."

Rafiel sighed. "Probably overkill," he said. "We are not exactly the most advanced scientific police in the world." He took a bunch of turns, very fast, not so much seeking to be physically far away from the convenience store, as seeking to be in a place no one would associate with the convenience store. In no time at all, it seemed, he was driving through an upscale neighborhood of the type that used to be a suburb in the days when the main form of commuting was the trolley car. Eight blocks or so, in a direct shot from downtown Goldport, this neighborhood was all shaded, set-back, two- and three-floor houses, which managed to look much like Christmas cards under the snow. "As long as they don't catch you in the act of putting the coin in, or dialing them up, that's pretty much it. Oh, if it's anyone but McKnight, they'll exert due diligence, too, by going to the clerk and asking if they saw someone call."

"Unlikely," Tom said. "I was at the back of the store the whole time. Unless he can see through brick walls . . ."

"Yes," Rafiel said, and then, because the way that Tom was

leaning forward over the seats was starting to give him visions of suddenly hitting a tree and ending up with Tom splattered all over his dashboard, "You know, we have laws about seat belts, in this state. As a policeman—"

Tom didn't answer. He just leaned back and buckled the seat belt. Then he made a sudden startled sound. "Kyrie," he said. "I haven't called Kyrie."

Kyrie was bargaining with fate. She was working, steadily, as if nothing had happened, but behind her smile, her ready quips at the customers, she was bargaining with fate.

She had started from the point of view that if Tom were to walk in, right then, she would only tell him how worried she'd been. She wouldn't make a big deal at all out of it. But since then, as the minutes passed and she heard neither from him nor from Rafiel, she'd started bargaining.

Okay, okay, if Tom walks in right now, she told herself, *I'll just smile and tell him how glad I am that he's alive.* Aware that she'd actually paused to listen for the sound of the back door opening up, she let out a hiss of frustration at herself. It wasn't sane, and it wasn't rational, but the thing was that she'd been expecting Tom to come in in response to her silent concession. She sighed at her own stupidity, and looked at the wall. Okay, he'd been gone more than two hours. What if he was frozen by the side of the road?

She could call Rafiel. She should call Rafiel. But what if Rafiel hadn't found him, yet? Or worse, what if Rafiel had found him? And he wasn't alive? In that case, the longer she took to find out about it, the better, right?

No. No. She was being stupid. It was unlikely he'd be dead, and if he was ill or severely hypothermic, of course she wanted to know. Needed to know. She set down the latest batch of orders and nudged

Conan, who was getting much better at tending tables, but who, despite lots of coffee, looked like death warmed over.

"Take over my tables for a little while, okay?" she asked.

He nodded. His gaze turned to her, said what he could not say in full voice. And it was something that Kyrie simply didn't want to hear. *What if he's dead? What if I left him and then the Ancient Ones killed him?*

Kyrie shook her head at him, slightly, denying her own misgivings as well as his. And then she stepped behind the counter and reached for the phone on the wall, trying to figure out how she could ask Rafiel questions without either giving away the shifter thing, or alarming Anthony, who was looking at her curiously. She was sure he had decided that she and Tom had had a spat. He was giving her that look of concern and gentle enquiry friends give you when they don't want to stick themselves in the middle of your marital disputes.

She took a deep breath. She could just ask Rafiel how it was going.

The phone rang, so suddenly and loudly that it made her jump. She fumbled for it, almost dropped it, managed to get it to her ear and say, "Hello?"

"Is that how you answer the phone for a business?" Tom's gently teasing voice was such a relief to hear that Kyrie felt her knees go weak, and tears sting behind her eyes.

"Idiot," she said.

"Um . . . that's also not the approved . . ." Tom said. She could see him grin as he spoke. And then, as though realizing he could only push his luck so far, he said, "Look, everything is okay. Sorry to take so long to call back, but we found Old Joe—"

"Old Joe?" Nothing could be further from her mind than the transient alligator shifter. She saw Anthony give her an odd look. Clearly that had also not figured in his speculation.

"Yeah. I'll explain when I get back. Look, it might be easier . . . if you can leave Anthony and Conan in charge and join us in the room at the bed-and-breakfast?" He chuckled softly. "I'd like to add girls to the repertoire of odd visitors I shower with."

"Idiot," she said again, very softly.

"Yes, I am. Conan made it back okay, right?"

"Yeah. Conan is fine. He's getting better at waiting tables, too."
Again, Kyrie was conscious of Anthony's baffled look at her. She did
her best to brazen it out, as she asked, "So you met Rafiel?" At least
she assumed so, unless he had now taken to using the royal we.

"Yeah. He'll be coming back with me. We're going by a doughnut
place first, though, apparently."

"What?"

"I don't know," Tom said. Kyrie could hear another voice in the
background, that she had to assume was Rafiel talking. "He says they
have a tracker in his car, and if he doesn't go by a doughnut place at
least once a week they kick him out of the force."

"Ha ha," Kyrie said.

"Yeah, I told him it was lame, too, but at least he's making an
effort at making fun of himself. A few more years and he should be
human. Hey. Stop hitting me. Police brutality. So, do you think you
can make it to the room? In about fifteen minutes?"

"I'll manage," Kyrie said.

"All right. And, listen . . . I'm an idiot. Sorry if I worried you."

She tried to deny that he worried her at all, but her mouth refused
to form quite that big a lie. "It's okay," she said, instead, because she
had bargained with fate, and she'd promised not to kill him, not to
maim him even slightly, and finally that she wasn't even going to yell
at him. "It's okay."

Tom thought the place must have been a Dunkin' Doughnuts in a
previous life, but it had now become—according to the sign hastily
painted on a facade in which the Dunkin' Doughnuts name was still
readable from the too-white shadow of the letters that used to cover
it—GOOD MORNING DOUGHNUTS.

The whole place had the sort of look of someone in limited
circumstances and hiding out under a false name to avoid

embarrassing the family. On the door, a hand-lettered sign read cash only please, which gave the impression that the people running it were planning to escape to South America at any moment, taking their ill-gotten gains with them.

But inside, it was surprisingly cozy, with aged but well-scrubbed formica tables, around which gathered bevies of retirees and housewives. This was clearly a gathering spot for a working-class neighborhood.

Behind the counter, a Chinese family made Tom tense, before he scolded himself that race had nothing to do with it. Yes, most dragon shifters might be Asian. But he clearly wasn't. And the dire wolf was just as bad as the Great Sky Dragon's triad. Perhaps worse, as at least it could be claimed that the Great Sky Dragon tried to protect all dragon shifters—while the dire wolf seemed to have very few loyalties but to himself. Tom wondered if Dire was representative of the Ancient Ones at all. Perhaps he'd just chosen to claim the role. There was no telling.

Rafiel was clearly known here. He ordered a dozen doughnuts, rapidly choosing the flavors, and grinning at Tom's bewildered expression. "I told you. We're required to visit these places. At least once a week."

Tom shook his head, smiling a little.

"Do you want coffee?" Rafiel asked. And when Tom nodded yes, he proceeded to order three. "I owe one to a guy in a doorway on Fairfax. He told me where to find you."

"The guy in a khaki jacket?" Tom asked.

"Yeah. He didn't seem to want to go to a shelter at any cost, and he had one of those Mylar blankets." Rafiel shrugged. "I wondered . . ." But never said what he wondered as he handed the bills over to the lady behind the counter.

Later in the truck, Tom said, "I wondered too. But he didn't smell of shifter."

"I know," Rafiel said. "Though to be honest, as cold as I was, I don't think I could smell anything."

"That's possible," Tom said. He bit his lip. "But I think I or you would have smelled something . . . even just a hint."

Rafiel nodded. He put a hand into the doughnut box, nudging it open in a way that bespoke long practice. He wedged a doughnut in his mouth, as he shifted into gear with his free hand. Then, with the doughnut still in his mouth, he backed out of the parking lot of the doughnut shop and onto the road.

"Why a dozen doughnuts?" Tom asked. "Seriously. Don't tell me they'd kick you out of the force. Why a dozen doughnuts?"

Rafiel took a bite of his doughnut, dipped into the box again for a napkin and wedged the napkin-wrapped doughnut into the cup holder on the dashboard, all while driving with one hand, in a way that Tom had to admit, given the snow and what looked to him no more visibility than about a palm beyond the windshield, seemed a bit cavalier.

"Energy," he said. "I think I'm going to have a long night of it. I don't think I can go and interview the male employees now, of course. But if Old Joe was right, and if there really was a body at the aquarium, I should get a call any minute now. And that usually means a few hours securing the scene, sweeping for evidence and all that. It's not a five-minute job."

"Right," Tom said.

"But first," Rafiel said, in all seriousness, "we must take the coffee to Khaki Guy, whom we'll do our best to sniff out, if he is a shifter. And then we must meet Kyrie. There's a meeting I'm not looking forward to."

"Why?" Tom said, surprised.

"Because I didn't call her as soon as I found you." He grinned wider and added, with every appearance of enjoying the thought, "She's going to rip my balls off and beat me with them."

Kyrie was glad they arrived at the room almost exactly fifteen minutes later. She had just the time to pick up Not Dinner, who, being a cat, and faced with a surfeit of stuffed furniture and other comfortable sleeping surfaces, had chosen to fall asleep in the bathtub. But he'd woken up when she first came into the bathroom, and scrabbled up her petting arm, until she held him under her chin and petted him, while he purred ecstatically.

She'd managed to get to the bed, with him trying to climb into her shirt, under the neckline, and install himself on her left shoulder, when she heard the key in the lock, and then Tom came in.

He still looked like nothing on earth, with his hair floating around him, in a wild dark cloud. He was wearing a hoodie she'd never seen on him, and which must be Rafiel's, since it was dark grey and said "Policemen Do It More Forcefully" across the chest. He was also carrying a doughnut and a cup of coffee. And he stood, just inside the door, grinning sheepishly at her, while Rafiel came in, behind him, and closed the door.

The weird thing, she thought, was that Rafiel looked scared, while Tom didn't. Tom looked more embarrassed, as if he'd done something horribly stupid. Which, of course, in a way, he had.

"Sorry," he said. "I still can't understand how you could take it so calmly." A blush climbed his cheeks. "But I guess you're more grown-up than I am. You've always been."

And she, who only a couple hours before was thinking exactly the same, shook her head. "No. I don't think it's a matter of being more or less grown-up. Truly. I think we're just . . . very different people." And then, for fear he'd interpret this as breaking up with him when, in fact, over the last hour or so she'd come to the conclusion she *couldn't* live without him, even if she tried, she added, "And that's okay. I mean, we're supposed to be. It would be very weird to fall in love with yourself, wouldn't it?"

Tom looked slyly at Rafiel and for just a moment, Kyrie thought he was going to say that Rafiel managed it fine. But instead, he shrugged a little, and that, Kyrie thought might in fact be a function of growing up. He'd learned not to bait the policeman.

"So . . . you said you needed to talk to me? Tell me . . . something?"

Tom nodded. "At least right now," he said, "I don't need to shower." And smiled. "I keep thinking I'm going to catch one of those horrible diseases you catch from washing too much. A fungus or something, because I destroyed the normal balance of the skin."

He walked to the vanity, and grabbed his hairbrush and started vigorously brushing his hair back, tying it neatly again, in his normal ponytail. While he did so, he talked. He told her of walking out—of thinking about a lot of things, though he wouldn't specify what those things were—of hearing that Old Joe might be at the aquarium and of wandering there. Then he told her about the phone, and how his father had thought he'd eaten someone.

Kyrie had to clench her hands into fists at this point, and make an effort not to speak out loud. Because she who never had parents, at least had an idea of what parents were supposed to be. And what they weren't. And she was fairly sure they weren't supposed to be like Edward Ormson. Oh, surely, his son was a strange creature. An enigma that they couldn't quite solve. But he should know Tom enough to know he wouldn't—couldn't—murder anyone. Much less eat him or her. Yes, she knew that Tom claimed to always be afraid of that also. Which was silly. Perhaps she knew him better than he knew himself, but she was quite aware that he would never do anything like that.

Thinking this she met his eyes in the mirror and they smiled at each other. He stepped back, slowly, to sit by her side on the bed, and hold her hand. "I shouldn't have gone away," he said. "Yes, I needed to cool off. But I needed to be with you as well. As is, I made you worry needlessly. Is . . . is Conan all right?"

"Very worried about you," Kyrie said. "He kept thinking the Ancient Ones might get you, and then the Great Sky Dragon might come for him."

Tom smiled, this time ruefully, and squeezed her hand a little. "I figured it was something like that."

"Okay, my story now," Rafiel said. He had sat backwards on the vanity chair, facing them, his arms around its middle, his chin resting atop of it. Despite his obvious grown-up proportions, the width of his shoulders, the glint of a five o'clock shadow in a tawny color that matched his leonine mane, he looked much like a truant boy. He told them, clearly, and doing the expressions and the voices of both himself and his interlocutors about his three interviews with aquarium visitors. "The thing," he said, "is that she told me there was another shifter, in the aquarium. She thought he was one of the spider crabs." He sighed. "So maybe that was the other shifter we smelled." He explained about his earlier interview with Ms. Gigio.

"Do you think she's the woman that Old Joe was warning you about?" Kyrie asked. "I mean . . ."

"I don't even know if Old Joe hallucinated the whole thing," Tom said. "Until there is proof to the contrary, I'd like to withhold opinion as to whom he was talking about."

Kyrie nodded. Rafiel looked up and shrugged a little. "She doesn't smell like a shifter. If she's only a crazy person who is pushing people into the shark tank . . . then she's not my problem."

"Rafiel!" Kyrie said, before she realized that she was going to say it, a note of indignation in her voice. "I can't believe you'd say that. What do you mean she's not your problem? You sound like . . . Dire . . . with all his talk about how ephemerals don't matter, how only shifters do."

Rafiel shook his head, even if a slight amount of color appeared over his high cheekbones. "You misunderstand me," he said. "That's not what I meant at all. Only that it won't require anything special from me—just police work, which I would do for any other case. It's not my problem as a shifter; I don't have to skulk and lie and find a way to make it all come out right. Only . . . only make sure that we find the culprit and she has a proper trial. Or he, if it's not Lei, but it's still not a shifter. It's the shifter angle that has me worried. Right now, the more I hear and the more I probe into this, the more I get worried that there is a shifter angle—it could be anyone, from Dante Dire, to this unknown spider crab shifter to . . ." He shook his head. "I don't think it could be Ms. Gigio. But it could definitely be the Rodent Liberation Front, whoever they are. Any rodent shifters crazy enough to try Marxist theory must be ready for everything."

"And crazy enough for anything," Tom said ruefully.

At that moment, Rafiel's phone rang. He picked it up and

answered. From their side, the conversation bordered on cryptic. Rafiel said, "Yeah, yeah, yeah. Right. I'll be there." And hung up, and got up to go.

"They found a corpse?" Tom asked, his body as taut as a bowstring, his tension seemingly communicating itself to Kyrie via the hand he held.

Rafiel nodded. "Yes. He's . . . He was almost not eaten at all—they'd . . . the sharks had just started on him, and they fished him out. Well . . . I don't know about not eaten at all." He looked a bit green and swallowed, as if the images his words evoked were getting to him, as well. "But he still has a face and lungs. And . . . well . . . they figure that they will be able to identify him, and look for signs that he was pushed into the tank while still alive. Or not."

Kyrie nodded.

"Glad I got the doughnuts," Rafiel told Tom. "It's going to be a long night. I'll call you guys or come by when I'm off."

And, with Kyrie holding tightly onto Notty, to prevent the orange fuzzball making a dash for the door, Kyrie and Tom stood up, to say goodbye to Rafiel, as he opened the door to leave.

And stopped, staring at the newspaper outside the door. It was one of the many peculiarities of the *Weekly Inquirer* that it was usually delivered late on the night of the day it was dated, sometime between eleven and midnight. Probably because it had started as a weekly paper, and there was less emphasis on the news being up to the minute, than on it being wittily or interestingly reported.

Only this time, none of them looked to see whether the news was properly reported. Instead, the three of them stared aghast at the headline, in screaming red, marching across the top of the front page: *Local Diner Haunted by Dragons.* Beneath it was a picture far clearer than any that zoological papers and magazines had ever boasted. It showed Tom and Conan both flying in dragon form. Tom was somewhat more distant—and therefore a little more blurred—but Conan was in the full glare of a very good electronic camera that had captured every scale and every fold of his skin in all its glory, as well as his mouth, open, the fangs parted, as if to roar.

"Wha—" Kyrie said in shock.

Rafiel swore under his breath. And then Notty took off, running down the carpeted hall. And Tom took off after it.

Tom caught the cat just short of the stairs. It required throwing himself headlong, his hand extended as if for the great baseball catch. What he caught was a tiny handful of spitting fury that he held very firmly, while bringing it up to his chest and standing up. He registered, distantly, that he'd just hit his knee hard, and that the wood beneath the carpet had far less give than he expected.

Holding Not Dinner, he limped back to the bedroom. Rafiel was still standing, holding the paper. "I have to go," he said, in a little, squeaky voice.

"But how . . ." Kyrie said.

Rafiel blushed. "I should have told you."

"What should you have told us?" Tom asked. "You saw someone take that picture?"

"Well . . . not quite that . . . But that Summer girl that Keith brought in? Right after you and Conan took off—" He turned to Kyrie. "This was when they were trying to rescue you, you know. Anyway, right after they took off, Keith's girlfriend was right there, at the back door, and I thought it was very weird. She said she'd got lost looking for the bathroom, but you know, it's not like it's all that hard to find, or like it's not properly marked, and right there . . ." He frowned. "I remember at the time thinking that something was wrong, and even more so when she disappeared right after. But then Dante Dire came in, and it just made me forget all that stuff."

"Yeah," Kyrie said. "I think he has that effect."

And Tom had to admit he did. "I'm sure," he said, feeling like his voice was constricted, "that it is all a matter of priorities. I mean, the dire wolf could kill us. What is the worst this woman could do? Make me move on?" He shrugged, attempting to look completely unaffected by this. "How bad would that be? I've moved so much, from town to town, and . . . all over." But he didn't want to move, and his heart was breaking over even the possibility of doing so. He didn't want to go anywhere. Let alone that he had Kyrie and a home, even if it was just a rented house, and apparently, now, a kitten.

He didn't want to leave the diner behind. It was the first time in his life that he felt invested in a place. He owned The George—half of it. It was his. He had shaped it already and would shape it more, make it something uniquely his, his own diner.

"I don't think it will come to that," Rafiel said. He stepped inside the door and flung the paper towards the bed. "At most, we'll say it's a good Photoshop job. I mean, Tom, who is going to believe in dragons? Seriously? If they'd caught me or Kyrie, it might be worse . . ." He shrugged. "Let's just take care that this doesn't happen again, okay?"

But how to make sure it didn't happen again was something completely different, Kyrie thought, as they got back into the diner, and Tom got the report from Anthony on what was prepared and what not. He tried to send Anthony home because it was best if Anthony went back and slept and came back in the morning, to relieve them when they would definitely need to rest, supposing there would be any rest that day.

They had barely got into the swing of their shift when Tom's phone rang, and he pulled it from his pocket. "It's Rafiel again," he said. And then, asking a puzzled Anthony to cover for them another five minutes, he pulled Kyrie with him into the storage area and put Rafiel on speaker.

"Hi," Rafiel said, between munching that indicated he was doing justice to the doughnuts he'd bought. "Look, I just came out to the car, with the excuse that I needed a doughnut."

"News on the body?" Kyrie asked.

"Well . . . yeah, kind of. But . . . the thing is . . ." He cleared his throat. "I got a phone call, from our medical examiner who was examining the . . . er . . . prophylactics they found in the planters."

Kyrie rolled her eyes. "You can say condoms, Rafiel. I know the word." An impish grin. "I've heard it a time or two."

A sound very much like a raspberry from the other end of the phone. "The medical examiner called it prophylactics. Of course, he also called the stuff inside genetic material, which he says exactly matches that of the first two vics."

"What, both of them?" Tom asked, sounding absolutely shocked.

"Well . . . no, one each. And no, there is no indication . . . I mean . . . the condoms were definitely used for . . . er . . . heterosexual sex. I mean . . . there were vaginal . . . secretions . . ." He paused in what seemed to Tom like an excess of embarrassment, like he had suddenly choked on it and couldn't go on. Tom grinned and waited, and eventually, after a noisy throat clearing, Rafiel came back on. "So it would seem that the male employees are not in fact a problem . . . though I can tell you, one of them, who apparently lives nearby and who dropped by to see if we needed him to show us or tell us anything, is definitely a shifter. His name is John Wagner. College student. Nice guy. Body builder. Works here part-time. I don't know what his shifted form is, but he . . . well . . . I'm fairly sure he doesn't have vaginal secretions."

"Unless his shifted form is as a woman," Tom said, wryly.

"Uh . . . I don't think so. You know, the other thing, the other part of the exam . . . of the . . ."

"Condoms," Kyrie said.

"Yeah. The other part of it is that it showed . . . well . . . The medical examiner thought this was from salve or cream, possibly a traditional medicinal one and that it should be easy to trace because of the exotic ingredient, but I'm not so sure. You see, there were . . . other cells on the sample. On the outside . . . They appear to be . . . Sharkskin cells. The examiner also thinks, possibly, because that was the shark tank, it might be someone who handles the sharks on a regular basis, although I don't even want to think what he imagines the handlers do with the sharks to get the cells in that particular region of their bodies."

Kyrie shrugged. "I bet you he thinks it's poor hygiene. And it might be."

"Oh, yes," Rafiel said. "It might be. On the other hand . . ."

"On the other hand, it could be something completely different," Kyrie said.

"Like someone who turns into a shark and back," Tom said. Because there was the very definite feel that the shift was never as complete as it seemed in either direction. More than once, Tom had shaken out his boots to find dragon scales inside them, even though he'd never worn them while a dragon and usually stepped well away from them before he shifted. And sometimes, when he washed his hair in the shower, one or two green and gold scales fell out.

"Yeah," Rafiel said. "That's what I'm very much afraid it is."

"In which case," Tom said, listening to Rafiel munch, "it's not so much a matter of maliciously pushing her—we'll assume her, since Old Joe said so—victims into the tank. It's more like your buying your doughnuts. A little snack to see her through the night."

The munching stopped. "Ew. Not like my doughnuts."

"Well, of course not," Tom hastened to say. "Unless you eat cannibal doughnuts." And then seized with sudden inspiration, "You know, Kyrie, we could do those next year for Halloween. Fill them with raspberry, or something, and put names on them . . . you know, like Joe or Mike, and call them cannibal doughnuts."

"Sure, we could," Kyrie said. "If our objective were to totally gross out and drive away our clientele. Besides, we can't do doughnuts properly. Not without a dedicated fryer."

"Maybe there will be enough money by the fall to buy another fryer," Tom said.

"Uh," Rafiel interrupted, "before you guys start arguing domestic arrangements, the other thing is, that I tried to find Old Joe, because, you know, since he was right about the last corpse—by the way, the name was Joseph Buckley; he was a software salesman—I thought he might be able to give me details and pinpoint who the woman might be he was talking about. But I can't find him anywhere."

Tom sighed. "He's very, very good at hiding. I think he's been doing it for centuries. If he's right about having been alive since before horses . . ."

"Yeah. Probably. Anyway . . . I can't figure out where he's gone, so if you hear something let me know."

And then he hung up, leaving them in the storage room, staring at each other.

"I wonder if John Wagner is a member of the Rodent Liberation Front," Tom said, biting the corner of his lip, in the way he did when he was thinking of something unpleasant. "I think he's one of our regulars. I remember the description, and also processing credit card bills for John Wagner."

Kyrie nodded. "Yeah, he is. He usually comes in for breakfast on Wednesday. And he's very fond of sweet bread, you know, Hawaiian bread. He always asks for a toast of that. Something about growing up in Hawaii."

"Interesting."

"Why interesting?" Kyrie asked.

"Because . . . if I remember correctly—and mind you, this is me remembering some cheap book or other that I read at some shelter for runaway teens, years ago—but if I remember correctly, Hawaii is the only place that has legends of shark shifters." He frowned. "Well, the Japanese might too. But Japanese shifter legends are very difficult to understand. I mean . . . they're not Western in structure. So even though I was very interested in all stories about shapeshifters, I don't think I remember any Japanese ones."

Kyrie nodded, but she felt her forehead wrinkle. "You know . . ." she said. "I . . . I don't know. I can't understand why I never smelled John Wagner. I mean, I serve him every week. You'd think I'd have sniffed him out."

Tom frowned. "Rafiel and I were talking about that, because of sniffing out Khaki Guy, you know. Both of us tried and neither of us could get a scent, but really . . . it's so cold, and then, the thing is . . . I've been homeless, but I washed. At least once a day. He clearly doesn't. There were smells, you know, of food and stuff, which I'm sure he's dropped on his clothes. And there was a smell of tobacco, too, and it was really hard to make out his smell amid all those, much less in the cold. So we don't know if he's a shifter, or just paranoid about shelters and closed-in situations. Which lots of people are, for reasons that have nothing to do with being shifters."

"Obviously," Kyrie said. "But John Wagner washes. I'm sure of it. He usually looks squeaky clean."

"Yes, but then when does he come in? Early early morning, right, before six a.m.? Before we quit. And I bet you he works days. So at six a.m. or before that, he's freshly washed, and probably has deodorant and aftershave on. Mix that with the smells of the diner—from fries to eggs and bacon—and you'd need to be looking for the smell of shifter to identify him. Or any other shifter."

"Yeah," Kyrie said. She nodded. "Well, I'm going to be looking for it, from now on. In just about everyone. Rodent Liberation Front and Ancient Ones and triads!" she said in a tone of great exasperation.

"Oh, my," Tom said, and smiled apologetically.

The aquarium was probably noisier than when it was open to the public, Rafiel thought, as he stood back, watching the frantic activity around him. People were snapping shots of the tank area and McKnight, with remarkable efficiency, probably born of the fact that Rafiel was frowning vaguely in his direction, was directing three people—three of Goldport's part-time officers, more used to breaking up drunken brawls among students than to doing crime scene processing—in combing through everything around there, including the planters by the side of shark tank.

And Rafiel, having quietly gotten away from the thick of things, had managed to sidle up to John Wagner, who was leaning against the far wall, under the plaque that explained the sharks' habits—unpleasant—and habitats—more extensive than Rafiel was comfortable thinking about.

He was a young guy, light-haired. Probably in his twenties, and he looked like he devoted serious time to body building. His file, as well as the brief conversation that Rafiel had had with him, indicated that Wagner was in college. Rafiel wondered what he majored in. Perhaps physical education or sports medicine?

Rafiel leaned beside him, casually. He noted that the man gave him a brief, amused, sidelong glance, and he returned a friendly smile. "So," he said, trying desperately to sound as if he was just making casual conversation, "you work out?"

The amused glance took him in again, and a lip curled ironically on the side. "A bit," the young man said. "Now and then."

And then Rafiel decided to go for broke, with the type of question that, should his interlocutor refuse to understand it or to respond, could be passed off as a joke of some sort—and which would certainly sound like a joke to anyone overhearing it. "In human form?" He had figured that Wagner's was the shifter-smell all around the shark area.

If he expected Wagner to be discomposed, he missed his mark. The smile only became a little broader, and he said, "Sure. The other one isn't really conducive to it. Unless I wanted to work on my ear muscles. And then there's all the drool."

"What?" Rafiel asked, unable to help himself. He cast a quick glance at the other people in the room, who were all surrounding something and taking pictures of it.

Wagner cackled, in unbecoming satisfaction. He muttered something under his breath that sounded disturbingly like "dumb ass," then added, "If you can smell me, what makes you think I can't smell you?"

"Oh," Rafiel said, now totally out of his depth. "Oh." He turned around to look at Wagner fully. The young man was grinning at him.

"Do you . . . do you know many of your . . . of our kind?" Rafiel asked. He'd never before interviewed anyone fully aware of what he himself was.

Wagner shrugged. "A couple. A friend back home, and then one more in college."

"Oh. What . . . are they?"

"Uh?"

"What forms do they take?" Rafiel said, his eye still on his subordinates and colleagues to make sure no one approached to hear this very strange conversation.

"Oh. My friend, Keith Kawamoto, back home was a bear. Which was very weird in Hawaii. Oh, sure, we had lots of fun roaming the beach late at night in our shifted forms. And he used to hang out in the Aiea Loop Trail. Weird-ass reports to everyone who would listen—and a lot of people who wouldn't—by the tourists. But who is going to believe tourists talking about a bear and a dog walking along the beach at low tide? Or a bear just hanging out? There was some enquiry once, to see if a circus that was passing through had lost a trained bear, but that was about it."

"And then here?"

Shrug. "There's a guy in the dorms who turns into a unicorn. Weird-ass thing to turn into, and of course no one believes it even if they see him. Sometimes we get reports of a white horse hanging about, is about it. It's assumed to be a prank." He shrugged. "After I smelled him out, we became pretty good friends. I keep telling him he's a unicorn so he can go in search of virgins, but he doesn't look like he'll ever have the courage, if you know what I mean." He waggled his eyebrows. "Engineering student and a bit of a dumb ass, but a nice guy."

His matter-of-fact approach to the situation and the way he seemed to have co-opted Rafiel as a buddy, whether Rafiel wanted to be one or not, were disconcerting enough that it took Rafiel a moment to collect himself. "So . . . you don't . . . I mean . . . I've had reports from . . . from another shifter . . . of a spider-crab shifter here in the aquarium. So I take it that's not true. I mean . . ."

"What? Because I didn't include him in my count? Nah, I didn't count him because I don't really know him. I know of him, but I don't know him. I think everyone in the aquarium—well, everyone who works here after-hours—has seen him. Weird-ass old Japanese guy, you know, all wrinkly and stuff. He looks like the Japanese guys in those reports they used to do where they found some old World War II soldier, who had been defending the same island in the Pacific for fifty years, ready to expel anyone who tried to land, only no one ever did."

"Uh . . ." Rafiel said. "So, you've talked to him?"

Wagner shook his head. "Nah. He doesn't talk to anyone. I don't even know if he speaks English, or if he was brought here in crab form." He shrugged. "I know he's been here for about ten years. It must be weird, you know, to have a form where if you shift you have to be near or in water. I don't know what I'd do if that were my problem. I mean, you can't always control when you shift."

Rafiel nodded. He couldn't imagine it either.

"So no one has talked to him?"

"Not that I know. Of course, the other people don't know he's a shifter. Anyone who is not expecting it, and who sees a little old man climb the side of an aquarium and plop inside, and disappear, thinks they're just seeing things, you know. So they talk about him as a ghost. If you go on-line, this aquarium is in Colorado's list of most haunted places. Just because of the old Japanese man. And they've made up all sorts of weird-ass shit about him. You know, that he was eaten by sharks here or some shit like that." He shrugged. "But as far as I know he's never talked to anyone. He just sits there and watches."

"I see," Rafiel said, wondering whether he was being lied to, and if so why. *Professional disinformation,* he thought. *You always wonder if they're lying to you. And if they are, why.* "So . . . did you smell him? The crab shifter? Is that why you know he's not a ghost?"

John Wagner looked startled. "You can't smell them. Not the water ones. Keith Kawamoto says he knows a dolphin one, and he said that, too. They don't smell like the rest of us. Why should they? Their signals will go over water, not air—"

"But—" Rafiel said. "How do you—"

"I've seen him shift. Watched him. I know what that looks like. Don't you?"

"Yeah . . . but . . . he doesn't smell? Of shifter?"

John Wagner shook his head. "And that's what worries me, you know? There could be others, in here." He gestured broadly at the tanks all around. "We'd never know. So . . . how could I find them if I can't smell them?"

"And do you have any idea?" Rafiel asked.

"Oh, sure," Wagner said. "You know, how when you shift you're always dying for a protein snack?"

Rafiel thought of Tom stuffing down pepperoni and cold cuts once, in a convenience store in the middle of Arizona. He thought of himself, dropping into the diner for bacon and eggs in the middle of the night, after a shift. He thought of sharks . . . "You mean?" he said, his voice sounding thick and queasy to his own ears. "You mean the sharks?"

John Wagner nodded. "Oh, yes," he said. "The sharks. And you know . . ." He shrugged. "Ah, hell. You grow up with legends about this stuff, you know? In Hawaii it's the beautiful girl who goes swimming with you at night and becomes a shark." He frowned slightly. "One of my college profs said it was a gynophobic fantasy like the vagina dentata. Dumb ass."

Rafiel, not sure he got the point, cleared his throat. "A girl," he said, "who turns into a shark. A girl from Hawaii? Like Lei Lani?"

Wagner shrugged. "Eh. Don't quote me on that. I have nothing against Lei. She's okay by me. Pretty easy on the eye too. Besides, I'm not too sure she's from Hawaii."

"What do you mean you're not too sure? I thought she was interning here, from the aquarium there or something?"

"Heard something like that too. 'Course, I didn't look at her resume or anything, you know. But . . ."

"But?"

"But I, well . . . At the end of the day I told her, you know, *Eh tita, pau hana?*"

"You told her tit what?" Rafiel asked, flabbergasted.

"Exactly. And she said just that. And she thought I was getting fresh or something . . ." He frowned. "And no Hawaiian girl would. That phrase is . . . eh . . . *So, strong sister, quitting time? Tita* is . . . a strong woman. When a Hawaiian *tita* comes after you, you run. Very strong personality. But she didn't get that at all. And anyone from

Hawaii would *know*." He paused. "And she didn't know *tako* is a octopus. And . . ." He shook his head. "She's just not right."

Kyrie saw him hanging around, outside the door. Dire. He was wearing a dark suit, and he was smoking, outside, pacing between the door and the side of the enclosure, where the diner had been expanded over what, in pictures from the thirties, had once been a covered porch.

She wondered if he was pacing out there because he, thanks to the latest Colorado laws, couldn't smoke inside. Or if he was pacing out there because he didn't want to come in.

She followed his movements with her gaze—watching the dark silhouette, the trail of red cigarette end. He looked nervous in his pacing, she thought as she wiped down a just-vacated table. Or perhaps he looked like a predator about to pounce. She'd gone to the zoo once, when she was about five, with the family she was staying with at the time. She remembered they had the tigers in altogether too-flimsy-looking enclosures. And she remembered a particularly large tiger pacing like that, while staring at her, as if she were next on his list of minimum daily requirement. Fifty pounds of skinny little girl. That was what Dante Dire's movement reminded her of, and she could feel his gaze almost burn through the window at her.

She looked over, as she took the tray back. Tom was cooking, his back turned. She was fairly sure he hadn't seen Dire. If he had, he'd say something.

And there was tension in each of Tom's muscles, in each of his movements. She wondered what he was thinking about. The murders? The newspaper article? The problems with Dante Dire? Or the semi-eternal, nearly all-powerful dragon who claimed ownership and full control of Tom, simply because Tom had been born with the ability to shift into a dragon.

She watched Tom flip a burger, and then he turned around to look at her. He raised an eyebrow, enquiringly. "Yes?"

"Nothing," she said, blushing a little, and disguising it by setting down the tray and ducking behind the counter to set the carafe back in its place so it could refill. "Nothing. I was just thinking that . . . as bad as things are, I don't want to lose this. I don't want to let this go. This is . . . what . . . us . . . our place. The George. It's . . ." She looked at him and was met with what looked like incomprehension, and blushed again. "It's the only home I've ever had," she said.

He looked blank a moment longer, and she realized, suddenly, that it wasn't incomprehension. It was Tom controlling his expressions and his emotions. Perhaps he thought she'd seen his naked emotions too often? Perhaps he thought she had come to his rescue once too often? Perhaps . . .

Or perhaps this was beyond thought and feeling. Perhaps it was just what men did. They didn't melt into tears at every turn. They didn't want women to feel they had to hold their hands and protect them. Kyrie saw it with sudden, distinct clarity. Oh, perhaps, in this age of the sensitive male, it was an ideal honored most often in the breach, but Kyrie could see it. From the earliest times of mankind, men had protected women, right? Women had been weaker, or at least more vulnerable while pregnant. It was a physical thing. For women, security and reproductive success had depended on having someone big and strong to protect them. But that meant that women often had to hold the someone big and strong together emotionally. And it meant that the someone big and strong didn't want to appear emotional to a prospective mate.

Tom swallowed. He managed to look perfectly impassive, but unbent a little as he said, "I know. I know. Me too. I don't want to lose this. But I keep thinking, and I don't know what to do. I can't . . . Kyrie, I can't ask the Great . . . I can't ask the creature to protect us. And I don't care if that's what he thought he was doing when he sent Conan to us. If we accept . . . if we ask his help . . . I'll never be able to call my own soul my own." He frowned and spoke, urgently, in what was little more than a whisper. "It would be the same as admitting I belong to him. If I'm his to protect, I'm his to order around."

"Yeah," Kyrie said. "Yeah. We'll think of something." She was thinking of something. She was thinking that if anything was going to be done about Dire, she would have to do it, and that she wasn't going to be able to tell Tom about it.

Oh, she could get angry about it. She could talk about stupid male pride. But what would it accomplish? She could see that he couldn't ask for help in this, not without bartering his—for lack of a better word—soul in the bargain. She wasn't even sure it was a male thing, but she was sure the male thing complicated it. Tom had to feel that he could defend home and woman. That much was obvious. He could not trade down on it.

"I'm going to take a break," she said. "For a moment. Conan has the tables and there's not that much."

"Okay," Tom said, and turned back towards the stove. Which, by itself, was a mark of his being worried, concerned, not thinking straight. Because, normally, he would have glanced back to make sure that Conan did have the tables and that the work wasn't overwhelming him. Kyrie didn't think it was. Maybe when Conan was starting, but this was his third night. His third night. Seemed like a month, at least.

She went by Conan on the way out, asked him to cover her tables. At the very least, she thought, she had to go out there and get rid of Dire before Tom saw him. Tom was tense enough already and not much could be gained from making him even more nervous.

She slipped out the front door, and only as the cold air outside hit her, did she think that Dire could kill her, out here, and perhaps make sure no one could see. But then again, she thought, that was one of those things she couldn't control, wasn't it? If he was going to kill her and mind-control people not to see her—as he would have to on a public street which, even in this snow day, had traffic, albeit foot traffic—then he could do it in the diner too. Or in her house. Or at the bed-and-breakfast. There was no safe place.

And if there was no safe place, there was no reason to be especially afraid of any place. She took a deep breath and looked up. Straight into Dire's eyes.

He smiled at her, a slow, welcome smile, and took a drag of his cigarette. "Hello, Kitten," he said, very softly, as though he were an older man, flirting with a younger girl in a cheesy movie from the seventies.

Kyrie felt a finger of unease crawl, coldly, up her spine. But he only smiled at her, a broader smile at what must have been her momentary, pinched look.

"You shouldn't be here," she said. "I mean, outside here. It will make our customers nervous to see someone roaming around outside, I mean . . ." She faltered. She couldn't explain why it would make the customers nervous. There was something, of course, to his step, to his look, that indicated he was on the prowl, that he was dangerous. But would normal people know that? Or did she see it, because she feared it?

"I'm not going to eat your customers, Kitten," he said, amused. He glanced at the diner then across the street, at the other, closed buildings. Down the block and across the street, white Christmas lights swung forlornly from the front of the hastily closed used bookstore. They normally turned them off when they left for the day, but they'd forgotten.

For some reason, those swaying lights were one of the saddest images Kyrie had ever seen. Dire lingered on them, then looked back at her. "To quote Bette Davis," he said, and smiled a little. "What a dump." He threw his cigarette on the ground and stepped on it. "What's a girl like you doing in a joint like this?"

She tightened her lips, mentally willing Tom not to look outside. She maneuvered, slightly, so that they were in the blind spot between the door to The George and the side enclosure. "In case you haven't noticed," she said, "I own the dump. Or at least half of it."

"Ah, yes, the diner named after the dragon slayer. Your boytoy has a weird sense of humor, doesn't he?" He looked at Kyrie. "Was he bragging that he kills other shifters? Was he actually proud of this?"

Kyrie thought of the painting of St. George and the dragon that Tom had hung over the back corner booth on the day they'd taken possession of The George. She remembered his words, "Because we have to be both the beast and the slayer."

She knew what Dire's opinions on this would be, and she'd be damned if she was going to give Tom up to some sort of insane punishment. She shrugged. "He has an odd sense of humor," she said.

"Ah. I see. Loyal." Dire said, and frowned slightly. "But I have a problem, you see? I was given a mission. As I told you and your friends, I'm sort of like a policeman, except the law I operate by is only the law of our own people. We don't"—he looked around with distaste—"recognize ephemeral law. But our law is nonetheless enforceable for applying only to us, and I'm the one sent to enforce it." He grinned, suddenly. "In other words, Kitten, I must find someone who is guilty. And I must deliver him to them. I was thinking your boyfriend might serve. But Daddy Dragon would get upset, and he can be a total bastard when he's pissed. So it would be better if it were that nice policeman."

"The—" Kyrie felt anger rise in her, and tried to keep it down. Getting furious at someone much more powerful than her wouldn't solve anything and it certainly wouldn't help anything. "What do you mean deliver him to them?"

"As the guilty one, you know?" Dire said, clearly unaware of the storm of emotions she was feeling. "I must find the guilty party, but they are not here, and they'll never know if it's the real guilty party, if you know what I mean. I could tell them it was." He shrugged. "So, your boyfriend or the policeman?"

"What?" she asked. And then the anger grabbed her. She glared at the ancient—and amoral—creature. "I don't think so. Not Tom. You wouldn't dare. Not Rafiel. Not even Conan. No. None of them is guilty. Not one. No."

"Well," he said, completely unconcerned by the rising tone of her voice. "It would be easier if it's not the dragons. Though if I told the Ancient Ones that it's the dragon boy, your boyfriend, they couldn't do anything, anyway, and . . ." He shrugged. "He might have to run away, true, because some of our members are less than sane and might want to strike anyway. But I would never. There's the daddy dragon. There's a treaty of sorts between our kinds. And I'm not stupid."

He shook his head. "No, I'm not stupid at all. I'm fine with telling them it was him, but he'd have to run, and if they came here and got you by accident . . . well . . . that would be a waste, wouldn't it?"

His gaze traveled lazily up and down her figure. "Wouldn't it? So, how about this? We work together. We pick a likely guilty party. Or a fall guy. It's all the same to me. I've asked enough, and I've gone to the site, and what I think happened is that these shifters were killing other shifters to serve their purposes." He shrugged. "This happens, right? It's one of the ways in which our kind can be very stupid. And why not everyone lives to be a full adult shifter. But then . . . then you came on the scene. And you played heroes. Okay. You're allowed to be heroes, I suppose. And they *were* preying on shifters. But then you killed a lot of innocent young ones. I'm not sure how it happened. Self-defense, or perhaps accidentally. I'm not going to ask. I'm just going to tell you that death on that order of magnitude requires a culprit, and I'll have to find one."

"Not here you don't have to find one," Kyrie said, sternly. She felt very angry. In fact she felt as though she could throw lightning bolts out of her eyes, she was so mad. "We already have the Great Sky Dragon to deal with. We have some reporter taking pictures of our shifted forms. We have the Rodent Liberation—"

"What?" Dante asked, his eyes very intent.

"Rodent Liberation Front. They—"

"No. The reporter part."

"Oh." Kyrie shrugged. "Front page of the *Weekly Inquirer* this morning."

He glared at her. "You let a reporter photograph you *shifting*?"

"No," she said. "We didn't let . . . she came to the diner, she—" Kyrie stopped short of saying that Keith had brought her. She didn't even know why, but her tongue just stopped short of it, as though a red light had gone on in her mind. "We found she'd taken pictures of Tom shifted. And Conan too." She paused and tried to bite her tongue, but it wouldn't stay still. "They were going to my rescue when you . . . were threatening me."

Dante Dire glared at her. He threw his head back. "I can't believe," he said, "that you thought you needed their help. I can't believe they are so foolish as to allow themselves to be photographed.

And I can't believe that dragons—dragons!—would shift where they could be seen. This is all a big muddle, and I will end up having to sort it out."

Kyrie, who felt weirdly grateful he had at least moved on from demanding that she choose a sacrificial victim for him to turn in to the Ancient Ones, started telling him not only didn't he have to sort it out, but this had nothing to do with him. "I don't think you—"

"Kyrie?" Tom had opened the door of the diner and stood looking at her and Dire. He nodded to Dire, as if he were a casual acquaintance and not an ancient horror who could destroy them all. "I wonder if you could come back from break," he said.

"Yes. Yes, of course," Kyrie said, walking away from Dire and practically scurrying towards the open door. "Of course."

She followed Tom in, and half expected to hear Dire come in behind them, but instead she heard something like a soft chuckle behind her. She didn't turn. She didn't look.

She followed Tom all the way past the areas of the counter that customers sat at. All the way to the cooking area, at the other end.

He smiled a little at her, as he turned to put a few burgers on the grill.

"Look, I didn't want to talk to him, but I thought—"

"That you didn't trust him out there, lurking, scaring our customers," Tom said. He smiled over his shoulder. "I got that. I was worried too."

"Yeah. He . . . was saying more of the same. That he needed to . . . to throw someone to the Ancient Ones."

"Or to the wolves," Tom said.

"Metaphorically," Kyrie said. "Look, it's just . . ."

"I know. I just went to rescue you. I wasn't sure you would get rid of him otherwise."

"Thank you," she said. And wondered if Tom had seen the dire wolf before she had, if he'd made plans . . . This wasn't the time to ask him. "Maybe you should go and get some sleep. I could get Anthony in early. And that would get you here for . . . for a little while longer than I am . . . You know . . . so we . . . so the diner is not without us."

The look he gave her over his shoulder was worried, this time. "Perhaps that would be better, yes," he said.

And she knew that he had understood what she couldn't explain. That she felt responsible for the customers in the diner. That a lot more of them than John Wagner and the mouse-teacher might be shifters. And that Dire might very well decide on one of them as a scapegoat. And she couldn't live with it.

Rafiel parked behind the diner, and pulled out his cell phone. "Yeah, McKnight?" as soon as McKnight answered.

"Yeah?" McKnight answered, cautiously.

"Two things. Look up any records for John Wagner and also . . . I don't know how you can do this, but . . ." He reasoned quickly that, of course, Dante Dire might have used another name. But he couldn't fly, so he presumably had to use some means of transport—airplanes. Even if private. And he would rent places. And while he could use another name, it was Rafiel's guess that most people didn't change all that often. Most shifters, either. They got comfy with a name and kept it, he guessed. "Check up on Dante Dire," he said. "Particularly anything having to do with Hawaii, and also when he might have come to town. Any place in Colorado he might have been."

"Dante . . . ?"

"Dante Dire," Rafiel spelled it.

"Who . . . ?"

"Just someone who's been around a lot, and I wonder . . ." He had a moment of fear. What if McKnight stumbled on something that—He stopped. That what? Tipped him to the fact that there were shapeshifters? Not likely. Rafiel suspected that for the average person it would take having their noses rubbed in it. In fact, they would have tumbled on to what was happening long ago if it weren't so. "He's just suspicious," he said. "Nothing definite, so don't break any laws, but check up on him, okay?"

There was a sound from the other side that might have been assent, and Rafiel said, "Right. I'll call back." And hung up. He cut his ignition and got out of the truck. Halfway through stepping down, he saw something through the snow.

He would never be able to swear to what it was. A dog, a bear, something rounding the building, or just—perhaps—a shadow. But he thought Dire, and having thought it, he followed the suspicious shadow around the building to the front.

And stopped, because in front of the building, leaning against the lamppost was the blond girl from the newspaper. There was something odd about her, but he couldn't put his finger on it, and he said, "I beg your pardon, you—"

And then it hit him. His human nose, not as sharp as his lion nose, was nonetheless acute enough to catch the smell of blood—the smell of death. Closer, closer, he saw that the girl was pale, dead—her eyes staring unseeing straight ahead. But she'd been propped up against the lamppost, and her clothes had been put back on. And she couldn't have been dead very long, because there was a steady drip-drip-drip of blood down the front of her clothes, from beneath her ski jacket.

For a moment he stood horrified, but his mind was working, behind it all. Dire. He was sure Dire was involved. Oh, he couldn't have done it now. No way that could have happened. But he had to be involved—somehow.

In his mind it all added up. Dante had killed the girl earlier, then . . . Then led him here. Like a gigantic joke. A joke perpetrated by an unfeeling, uncaring, ancient creature.

Like the shark murders—it would be just Dire's idea of a joke, to set it up, somehow, so that he could push into the tank guys who had been dallying with one of the female employees. The first time they'd seen him was around the aquarium. Perhaps he had a way in all along. Why shouldn't he? Rafiel had managed to get keys easily enough. And it would amuse some *thing* like Dire to create the impression of a shark shifter and see how they reacted.

With numbed fingers, Rafiel had—somehow—retrieved his phone from inside his jacket. He hit the redial button, staring at the corpse of the blond girl. "McKnight. Send the meat wagon and . . . and come along. There's been a . . . death. In front of The George. And get someone to check the visitor book at the aquarium. Find out if Dante Dire was there . . . anytime in the last month."

Tom woke up with the phone ringing, and a panicked Notty digging needle-sharp claws into his underarm, where he'd been nestling.

"Ow," he said, grabbing the furry body blindly in his right hand, then looking for the phone on the bedside table with his left. One of the good things of this split sleeping schedule was that he got the bed when Kyrie wasn't here. And her pillow still smelled like her, too.

"Yeah," he said, turning on the phone, and fully expecting it to be Kyrie telling him about some emergency at the diner. Before he heard any sound from the other side of the phone, he'd already covered the possibles in his mind. She might have run out of paper napkins. Or it could be the beef. Did he order more beef? Perhaps it was the dishwasher flaking again. They needed to buy a new one soon. "Yeah?"

"Oh, damn," Rafiel's voice. "Damn, damn, damn."

Tom sat up, setting Notty down beside him on the bed. "What?" His relations with Rafiel had been less than cordial at one point, but even back then, Rafiel had never called him for the purpose of cursing at him.

"Tom?" Rafiel said, as if surprised to hear him.

"You called me."

There was a silence on the other side, a silence during which Rafiel seemed to be taking several deep breaths. "Oh, shit, Tom, we're in so much trouble."

"What happened?" Tom said, jumping out of the bed and looking around for his clothes. He'd showered before going to bed, so he could probably skip it this time. Truth be told he had a shower problem—he enjoyed so much being able to shower when he pleased that he had a lot of showers even when not shifting back and forth. Unfortunately they did not have support groups for the hygiene-dependent. "Rafiel, what happened?" he repeated when no answer came.

"We found . . . a corpse," Rafiel's voice was distant, like he was holding the phone away from his mouth, or perhaps speaking in a tiny voice. "Just outside the diner. I'm calling you while McKnight is talking to Kyrie."

"Outside the diner!" Tom said. "In the parking lot again?"

"No, corner of Pride and Fairfax. By the lamppost. She was . . . propped up. Leaning against the post . . ."

"She?" Tom's mind went immediately to the woman whom Rafiel had found, the woman who was a mouse shifter.

"The . . . Summer Avenir. The reporter for the paper? The one that Keith talked to or brought in?"

"The one that published dragon pictures?"

"Yeah, we're going to have to talk to Conan. And the . . . whoever the triad members are in this area."

"She was killed by a dragon?" Tom asked.

"Well, she was killed by something with really big teeth," Rafiel said, in the tone of a man who has come to his rope's end and still has quite a bit to climb. "And then she was propped up. This is putting a damper on our normal story of attacks by wild animals, you know? It's clear"—he took a deep breath—"very clear it was one of us." He lowered his voice. "I can smell shifter all over the scene, still. I thought I'd seen Dire before, but . . . I don't know."

Tom moaned and dropped onto the bed, to put his socks on. His feet and in fact all his wounds from the encounter with the dire wolf were completely healed and the very faint scars would soon vanish. "We must make sure he stops."

"Who?" Rafiel said.

"Dire."

"Uh . . . yeah. I'd say that's a given. The question is how."

"I don't know," Tom said.

"You could"—Rafiel cleared his throat—"talk to the Great Sky Dragon."

Tom stopped, his hand on his sock, his mouth on the verge of uttering an absolute no. Instead, he took a deep breath. "You must see we can't, Rafiel. You must see we *can't*."

"Why not? If they are rival organizations, both ancient, why can't you talk to the Great Sky Dragon and make him deal with Dire? I mean, I know that Dire said he had a non-aggression pact with the triad, but it doesn't seem to me as if that pact is much good. How could it be? Otherwise he wouldn't have gone through all that trouble to make sure the triad knew he didn't intend to kill you."

Tom heard himself make a sound that was half annoyance and half anger. "I still can't ask for their help, Rafiel. If we ask for the help of a criminal organization, how can we, in the future, hold ourselves able to stop them? If we ask for the help of an organization that deals in drugs, that kills, that basically seems to view other humans—what did Dire call them?—ephemerals, as mere cattle to be milked, then how can we hope to stand for justice among our kind? Or anywhere?"

There was a long silence. Tom had the impression that Rafiel was running several arguments through his own head and discarding them just as fast as he thought them up. Finally he made a sound somewhere between a huff and a sigh. "Tom, we can't be so pure as the driven snow. I understand what you're saying. And standing for justice is very well—don't get me wrong. I'm as fond of graphic novels as Keith is. And justice and truth and all that, but Tom . . . I'm afraid he's going to kill one of us. I don't even know, you know . . . if he might not have set up the aquarium murders. He's . . . cunning, and he has an . . . odd sense of humor. Look at how he conned Kyrie into going to the house. At any point he could turn and decide to hold one of us—or all of us—responsible for those deaths and just kill us." Pause. "You know, it's quite likely it was him who killed this woman, without so much as a thought."

"Well, she did publish pictures of dragons in the newspaper," Tom said.

"But it could have been Photoshop. I mean, even if she had caught you mid-shifting, do you think that it couldn't be Photoshop? No one will take it seriously. Look at all the pictures of the alien that the tabloids keep following up on and publish. Do you believe he exists?"

"No," Tom said. "And no, I don't think anyone paid undue attention to the pictures. But they are pictures of our kind and . . . well . . . Dire is very old. At least assuming it was him. Though, frankly, the Great Sky Dragon is very old too, and I don't think any of his younger subordinates would have dared point out to him that times have changed."

"No," Rafiel said. "I'm sure they wouldn't. So . . . they killed this young woman. Without a thought. Because she was . . . an ephemeral."

"No, because she was an ephemeral they thought was threatening shifters." Tom found his mind going down the dangerous path that he knew these people's minds must take every time. He said matter of factly, "Think of it from their perspective, how it must have been throughout history. The discovery of a shifter would lead to a hunt for others. Death was always the end. Of course they would kill anyone that was a remote threat."

"Of course? You sound as if you approve."

"No. Understanding is not approving. There is a qualitative difference." He felt suddenly very tired. "You know, when I was on the streets, they had all these programs where you were supposed to mingle with the other runaways and empathize and understand them. Sometimes that's what you had to do for a meal. And the counselors always seemed to think that if you understood someone, you'd like them . . . and you know? It's not true. Sometimes the more you talk to a teenage habitual liar and drug pusher, the less you like them. But . . . but I do understand how they got to be the way they are. And at the same time . . ." He took a deep breath. "I understand how we could go that way. From the best of motives. Protecting ourselves and our friends. I understand how we could start deciding that . . . killing the occasional ephemeral meant nothing. Or even that we should kill a few every now and then, out of the blue, to keep the other ones in fear. I understand them, Rafiel. And it scares me. That's another reason not to ask for the Great Sky Dragon's help. That, and I'd like to continue being able to call my soul my own."

Rafiel huffed again and when he answered he was peevish. "Very well," he said, in a tone that implied it wasn't very well at all. "But I hope you know what to do, because this can't go on. With the deaths at the aquarium—and by the way, the latest one, Joe Buckley, had water in his lungs, so it wasn't a body disposal, it was murder by shark—and now some mysterious animal going around town killing people, not to mention what my colleagues are convinced is some madman who just propped up the body afterwards . . ." This time the sound was just a sigh. "I don't know how to cover up all of this, Tom. I just don't. And I'm an officer of the law. The killings must stop. And I think there's more than an even chance that it's all Dire. I'm . . . following up on it, but I really think there's a good chance he came to town before, you know, when they felt the deaths, and he set all this up. And we must stop him."

"I understand," Tom said and he did, and in this case he could even empathize. "I'll think of something. Look, I'll come down and help you talk to Conan, okay?"

After Rafiel hung up, Tom started tying his boots, a task made more complex by the fact that Notty was trying to help. "I'd better think of something, eh, Notty?" he said, as he petted the little round kitten head. "Or we are in deep, deep trouble."

Notty looked up at him with guileless intensely blue eyes that seemed to say he had every confidence in Tom's ability to make it all right. Tom wished he did too.

Every shifter could be a target, Kyrie thought. And even as she was thinking this, she had to put up with being interviewed by a young man with sparse red-blond hair and the slightly bulging blue eyes that always give the impression their possessor is desperately looking for a fairytale to believe in. He, somehow, seemed absolutely convinced that Kyrie must have a wild animal stashed somewhere, and must have deployed it to kill this woman journalist.

If only you knew, Kyrie thought, but just looked placidly at the man. "No," she said, in a firm voice, while she kept an eye on Conan who was dealing with the tables. She stood with her back to the counter. On the other side of it, Anthony was cooking orders. He'd been interviewed, but his interview had been very brief, since he hadn't left the stove since he'd come in at about four in the morning. And no, he hadn't seen any dead woman against the lamppost, though, frankly, if she'd been propped up and looked natural, he might not have noticed. After all, he'd been running in, and he'd been working what very much amounted to double shifts because of the weather and their being shorthanded. And now he had to go back to the stove before it went up in flames; did Officer McKnight mind?

Officer McKnight could not persist against Anthony's push to get back to work, and therefore he was now absolutely determined to make life difficult for Kyrie. Kyrie looked up and resisted an urge to smile. She wondered if she was supposed to cry into the table-wiping rag she was holding and confess that yes, she'd done it all.

She decided against it on principle. The man looked like he'd had his sense of humor surgically removed at birth and he might very well take her at her word. Instead, aloud, she said, with increasing firmness, "No, I was not mad at her for publishing the dragon pictures. Why should I be?"

"Well . . ." McKnight said, and looked at her with those bulging eyes, making her think he was going to dart an improbably long tongue out and catch a fly or something. "The thing is Ms. . . . . Smith, you and your . . . partner, Mr. Ormson own this diner half and half, right."

"Right," Kyrie said, wishing if he was going to pronounce Smith that way he would add "if that is indeed your real name."

"And this woman published pictures of dragons in the paper and said she'd seen them at the back door of your diner. Now . . . wouldn't you think people might be afraid to come here? That it might ruin your business?"

"What?" Kyrie asked, completely puzzled. "Are you truly asking me if I think that people are afraid of *dragons*? Are you afraid of dragons, Officer?"

"Well . . . that's neither here nor there, is it? I mean, I know that dragons are imaginary and I . . ." He shrugged. "But this is not about what I believe. Don't you think that people out there on the street might think that there are really dragons and that they might get attacked, if they come here?"

Kyrie shook her head. "No. In fact, considering all the recent movies and stories with good dragons, I think that if they were to believe dragons existed—and frankly I don't think even a lot of our college student clientele believes any such thing—they would be thrilled. If anything, that picture in the paper might bring us droves of customers." She realized as she said it that this was true, though certainly that was not how she and the others had first thought of it.

McKnight clearly hadn't thought of it that way either. He said, "But—" and then repeated "But, but," like it was the sound his brain gave off while sputtering and trying to start. "But you have to understand," he finally said. "Not everyone might have felt that way. And what if they were scared and stopped coming here. Wouldn't you have hated that reporter? Wouldn't you have thought of doing . . . something to her?"

"Something?" Kyrie said. She frowned. "What exactly are you suggesting? That I roamed the streets looking for a wild animal, whom I then convinced to chomp on this journalist, when she was conveniently just outside our door?" She glared. "Because a death by wild animal attack will, of course, hurt our business far *less* than rumors of dragons."

"Well, no, but you might . . . you might not have thought of that, as you were, you know . . ."

"Looking for a wild animal to kill her? Tell me, was it a mountain lion or a bear? And how did I keep it from killing me? My extrasensory powers?"

McKnight looked confused. Or rather, he looked more confused than normal. "But . . . but . . . if you had . . ."

"And what if I had grown wings and flown?" she asked. *Which I can't do. Though my boyfriend can.* "Do I have to answer hypothetical questions on that too?" She glared at him. "Given an ability to find wild animals disposed to kill inconvenient journalists at the drop of a hat, and supposing I had the superpowers to prevent them killing me, I still wouldn't have killed the journalist."

"Oh? Why not?"

"Because she was a person. A human being. And she'd done me no noticeable harm. Do you often kill people because they're annoying or sensationalist, Officer?"

"Me? Well, no, of course . . ." He seemed to finally realize he wasn't going to win this argument no matter how hard he tried. "Right," he said. "Right. Thank you, Ms. Smith. I will . . . I will go and ask your customers if they've seen anything."

Yes. Do, why don't you? Because that won't affect business at all, she thought irritably, as she ducked behind the counter, and found Anthony's gaze trained on her, half amusement, half awe.

"What?" she said.

"I think you have a bit of policeman caught between your teeth," he said.

"What?"

"Metaphorically speaking. I think that's what Tom calls biting off someone's head and beating them to death with it."

"Well," Kyrie said, deflated, as she got the carafe from the coffee maker and put the latest round of prepared orders on a tray to take out. Conan had been half handling all the orders, but she was fairly sure the breakfast crowd would prefer their eggs before they got all cold and rubbery. "He's dim."

"Yeah. I wonder why Rafiel didn't ask us the questions himself."

"Dunno. Dealing with some administrative stuff, I guess," Kyrie said, and started towards the tables, carrying the tray. She smiled and joked with her regulars. But her mind wasn't in it.

No, her mind was carefully processing the input of her nose. How many shifters were there in the diner? They knew for a fact that the diner had been soaked—some years ago—in pheromones designed to attract shifters. It had called her all the way from the bus station, in response to something—she wasn't sure what. For all she knew it had called her all the way from Cleveland where her last job had been. How many more people did it call? And what were their forms?

She didn't think they were implicated in the death of the journalist, Summer Avenir. She didn't think so, but you never knew. After all, the Ancient Ones weren't the only ones who could lose their heads when faced with something like pictures of shifters on the front page of their local paper and just outside their favorite diner. While Kyrie and Tom had no wish to associate wild animal attacks with their diner, some customer who just wanted to stop a threat might have more direct views of how to do so.

She saw Tom and Rafiel come in through the back door, poor Tom looking very pale and cranky, which made perfect sense, since he'd slept all of two and a half or three hours at most.

At the moment she saw them, she was standing by the front door and away from most of the occupied tables. She stood her ground, ostensibly waiting for them to go by her, so she could move freely.

But as they came close enough, she asked Rafiel in a whisper, "The teeth that killed the woman . . . They weren't alligator teeth, were they?"

Rafiel had a headache. No, it wasn't a headache as such because headaches were natural occurrences that came and went without much provocation. *This* headache was like a living thing, compounded half of pain, half of fear and mostly of anger. It sat on his brain, seeming to squeeze all rationality out of it.

He wanted to be mad at Tom for refusing to even consider calling the Great Sky Dragon and the triad to their aid. What was he doing?

Did he think they could play heroes all by themselves? Who were they against this ancient shifter group that permeated all nations and was a law unto itself. If the group decided whom to kill and whom to let live, to whom could they speak out against it? How could they when they were part of it too?

To some extent Dire was right when he told Rafiel and Kyrie that in the ancient times there had been many deaths, that in those days shifters were viewed as dangerous, as things to be eliminated.

But then again, weren't they dangerous? So many of them seemed to have a lust for killing and a total disregard for those outside their group.

Rafiel stood in the brightly lit parking lot and squinted against the light, and watched Tom walk from the inn, around the thawing slabs of ice in the parking lot. The sun was out, things were melting. Probably only to freeze again this night, but for now, ice was in retreat.

Rafiel squinted at Tom and thought to himself that if shifters were known, and if they were known for what they were, those creatures that Dire called ephemerals would be more than justified in exterminating them all, root and branch, the guilty with the innocent. But then . . . but then he and Tom and Kyrie were innocent.

And if we want to remain so, we'd best find a way to control those among our kind who aren't—those who are a danger to the society we live in. From there it followed that Tom had been right. They could not call on the Great Sky Dragon. They couldn't call on any of the old, corrupt organizations that looked down on the society amid which they lived and from which they derived the benefits of civilization. *No. It must be us. Me and you and me against the ancient shifter world. And Keith too, if he's willing.*

The ridiculous thought of the four of them facing down the Ancient Ones, much less the Ancient Ones, the triad and whatever was killing people at the aquarium—if it wasn't Dire or the crab shifter—made his head throb all the worse. The Rodent Liberation Front might be more their speed.

Tom, who always looked like heck when he was tired, now looked tired and grumpy and ill-awakened, with shadows under his eyes, and the sort of expression that suggested he was about to face a firing squad by the early dawn light.

He stomped across the parking lot towards Rafiel and greeted him with a grunt. They walked across the parking lot together, presumably, Rafiel thought, to talk to Conan. What Tom expected to get from Conan, if not the help of Conan's patron, was beyond him.

And then, as they got into the diner, and went close by Kyrie, he found his arm grabbed and Kyrie asked, "The teeth that killed the woman . . . They weren't alligator teeth, were they?"

Tom snorted behind Rafiel and said, with certainty. "It wasn't Old Joe."

But Kyrie was looking at Rafiel with those bright eyes of hers, that inquisitive all-attentive gaze she so rarely turned towards him. "Was it, Rafiel?"

He shook his head slowly. "Not so far as the examiner on the scene thought. He said bear or dog"—he shrugged—"only much, much bigger teeth. I could imagine, by a stretch of the imagination, its being a dragon, but not an alligator, no."

While he talked to Kyrie, Tom had gone behind both of them and into the glassed-in annex, where Conan was cleaning a table. Tom cheerfully helped him put the menus and condiment bottles back. Then he grabbed the wrist on Conan's good arm. Rafiel had no idea what he said to the man. Tom spoke in too low a voice to be heard. But Rafiel saw Conan pale, and then Tom shook his head and said something else, and Conan looked at him half in fear, but seemed calmer and nodded.

Rafiel wished he could hear it, but doubtless, through this headache, he wouldn't make any sense of it, in any case. Aloud he told Kyrie, "Looks like you'll have to take over all the waitressing. I think we're talking to Conan." He watched Tom take Conan to the table nearest the window—the one where the two sets of glassed-in walls met, and fortuitously the corner nearest the lamppost around which the dead woman had been wrapped.

"I won't sit people near there," Kyrie said, and turned to meet a couple who had just entered. Which left Rafiel with nothing to do but go talk to Conan.

Conan was sitting across from Tom, and as Rafiel approached, Tom got up. Before Rafiel was fully settled, Tom came back with three cups of coffee, a bowl full of the little packaged creamers, and a container of sugars. Conan hesitated and looked almost guilty taking the coffee. Or perhaps he just looked guilty. He looked guilty most of the time, a sort of cringing general-purpose guilt that made Rafiel's headache worse.

Tom looked at Rafiel as though expecting him to start the questioning, and Rafiel sighed. "The dead woman, out there?" he said.

"Yes. You asked me earlier," Conan said. "I didn't see anything."

"Really?" Rafiel asked, with withering sarcasm. "Were you waiting on people in this annex, then? Was there no one seated here?"

"Oh. Well, of course people were seated here. But . . . but it's dark out there. I didn't see anything." And then, as if with sudden inspiration. "Kyrie attended to people here too, and don't you think she would have spoken up if she'd seen something?"

Tom jerked forward, and Rafiel, fairly sure that he was going to come to Kyrie's defense, perhaps in a violent way, put a hand forward to stop him. "I'm sure she would have," he said. "I also know that these . . . creatures, whatever they might have been, from whichever side, have defenses that we can't begin to fathom. I'm fairly sure that Dire doesn't actually teleport, for instance. And if he can fake a phone call and make Kyrie actually hear my voice as if it came from her cell phone . . ." He shrugged. "It's possible they made themselves invisible.

"But you, Conan, aren't just one of us, one of the young shifters, are you?"

This brought him a wide-eyed glance from Conan, not an admission of guilt, not even, Rafiel thought, with an inward groan, an admission that Rafiel had somehow penetrated a deception. No. All that fish-eyed glare was pure shock, combined almost for sure with a calculation on Rafiel's mental health or lack thereof. "Of course I'm one of you," he said, in outraged protest. "What else would I be? I am twenty-three years old, and I was born in Tennessee. Knoxville. Mom and Dad own the Good Fortune Restaurant there. I was president of the Latin club in high school. Check it out. I'm in the yearbook."

"That's not what I meant," Rafiel said. *Though I worded it vaguely enough to catch something else, should it be there.* "What I mean is that the Great Sky Dragon sent you here to protect Tom. He has a link to your mind. Surely he wouldn't be fooled by whatever mind tricks Dire might be using. Surely, he would see whatever was happening. Did you not see anything? Sense his alarm in some way?" *Mind tricks. What if he convinces the victims of shark to just jump IN to the aquarium? Surely he can do it. Damn. How can one check that? Prove that? He probably doesn't even need to be there. Look what he did with Kyrie's phone.*

Conan shook his head. He looked miserable and on the edge of sniffling like a lost child. "I never . . . I didn't see anything. But . . . but before, when he spoke through me? I didn't see anything either. I wasn't . . . aware that he was doing anything."

Rafiel took a deep breath and drank a sip of hot, black coffee to fortify himself. "And could you have done it, Conan?"

This time he got the wide eyes and a look of almost panic. First Conan shook his head, then he opened his mouth. He looked like he was about to scream or run, but he did neither. Instead, he put his head in his good hand, and Rafiel fully expected him to show a tear-streaked face when he looked up. It wasn't. His face was perfectly dry, though his eyes looked reddened.

"Look, do you think I haven't asked myself this?" he asked. And, as though driven out of his voice by stress, the pseudo-Asian accent was gone, replaced by just the faintest hint of a Southern twang. "Ever since she was discovered I've asked myself this. He spoke through my mind. Could he also . . . do other things through my mind? I don't know. I don't know." He shook his head. "I don't know if he could have had me change and attack the girl. I think not, because if he could have, then when we were hunting Tom"—he looked at Tom— "why would he not do the same? Why would he leave us to our own devices?" He shrugged. "On the other hand, I think, why would he not have put a listening thing in our heads then as he did now, so he could advise us when we ran into trouble?" He shrugged again. "I don't know. I just don't know."

"Perhaps he didn't think it was worth it for just me," Tom said. "After all, I was just a young shifter, right? While here he knows he's up against the executioner sent by the Ancient Ones, right? So it would be more important. And he would send you, of course."

Conan started to shake his head, then shrugged again. "You might have been only a young one, but he was . . . By the end of it, we were all in full hunt for you. Though to be honest . . ." he looked pensive, "he only ever sent the young ones of us, never the old, experienced ones. Why, I don't know, just as I don't know why he wants you protected now." He looked suddenly embarrassed. "Only I'm kind of glad he does, because you're a nice guy and I don't want to be ordered to attack you."

"Would you, if he ordered you?" Tom asked.

Conan looked at Tom. And Rafiel felt as though he was seeing several thoughts flicker through Conan's mind. *No.* And then *yes* and then . . . Conan shrugged. "I'd like to think I wouldn't," he said, opening his hands on the tabletop, as if to show the absence of weapons. "But the thing is, if he ordered me, and I didn't obey, then I would be left . . ." He sighed. "With the absolute certainty of my own death. I belong to him. He's in my mind. Still, the prospect of waking up with myself, day after day, year after year, after killing someone who has become a friend . . ." He made a face. "Death might be preferable. On the other hand"—disarming smile—"I think I've proven I'm a coward and very attached to life. So . . . I don't know. The Great Sky Dragon would tell me to tell you that no, of course I wouldn't kill you, but I'm telling you the truth."

He seemed inordinately proud of it, and Rafiel who could feel the same gears turn in Tom's head that were turning in his—*what does he mean he doesn't know*, and *this is not a free man*—said, "It's always good to tell the truth. So, you don't know if you killed this woman or not?"

"I don't think I did," Conan said. "The thing was, see, we were fairly busy all night. Yes, there was a lull around four, but it wasn't a lull *in* the restaurant. It was just that no more people were arriving, not that the ones that were already here were leaving. A bunch of people came in and sat from three to five or so, just . . . here. Ordering more stuff, you know? So Kyrie and I were both very busy, all that time. I think Kyrie would have noticed if I'd left my tables unattended for any of that time. She would have asked me. You know she keeps an eye on me all the time. And I asked her . . . I asked her right after I heard. Just a quick question. And she said I'd been here all the time, helping with the tables."

"So it's improbable it was you," Rafiel said. "I presume that you don't have a way to cast the same sort of mind-invisibility thing that Dire does?"

"Not that I've ever heard of. And I've never heard of any of the senior dragons doing it . . . not even Himself. He usually appears in perfectly normal, reasonable ways."

"Except flying, yes," Rafiel said. "So you know of no reason why the Great Sky Dragon would want this woman dead? Wouldn't seeing dragons, one of them you, on the cover of the *Weekly Inquirer* unnerve him or enrage him?"

Conan shook his head. "I'm sure it wouldn't," he said.

"Why?" Rafiel asked.

"Because if it had I would have heard from him, or from one of the other ones, in the town, you know? Someone would have come to me and told me . . ." He seemed to run out of words or perhaps of imagination as to what they'd tell him.

"That you'd been a very naughty dragon?" Tom asked, seeming suddenly amused.

Conan nodded once. "That. I'm sure they would have. And he didn't. Which means he wasn't mad about the picture. Wasn't mad about showing myself. He is not . . ." A sudden lopsided smile. "I know it's playing into a stereotype a little, and perhaps it is wrong, but you know we Asians are supposed to be good with technology? Well . . . Himself is. He really is. He's very, very good with it. And he would have thought what I thought. That the dragons could be a Photoshop job, and that no one living in the world today would think they were real, unless they were shifters or already knew shifters themselves."

"But then . . . that leaves . . . Wait. What if she had gone after those you call senior dragons? I assume there are some of those here in town?"

Conan nodded once. "The Three Luck Dragon Restaurant where we . . ."

"Where I almost got killed?" Tom asked.

Conan's eyes opened wide. "You did? Was it there? I heard about it through the organization after I . . . came back. But I didn't know it had been done there, right at the center of our operations." Then to Rafiel: "That's where we met in the parking lot."

"And I assume the owner is one of you," Rafiel asked, and seeing the expression on Conan's face, hastened to add, "You don't have to answer that."

"She might have gone there," Conan said. "Yes. And harassed someone. But the thing is . . ." He shrugged again, an expressive, eloquent shrug that was almost a word in itself, a word that combined lack of knowledge with ability to acquire any. "The thing is that I don't think Himself would do it this way. For some reason he wants you protected." He gave Tom a look. "To be honest, it might be simply because you impressed him. Or Kyrie did. And because he is afraid that the Ancient Ones will take you out without his protection. I don't know. You don't ask that sort of question. But, anyway, if he wants to protect you, the last thing, the very last thing he would do was to come here, to leave the dead woman this close to your diner, and therefore call attention to you, right? He'd never do that. He's not stupid."

Rafiel didn't think the Great Sky Dragon was stupid at all. And even through his headache, he had to concede Conan's logic. He didn't see the Great Sky Dragon leaving a corpse that close to Tom, not if he wanted to protect him, at any rate.

His headache was worse. "Damn," he said. "That means it was probably Dire."

Conan nodded, sagely.

"Which means we need to figure out a way to deal with him."

"Deal with him?" Conan said. "You can't. Not alone. That's why Himself sent me, so that . . ."

Rafiel looked at Tom. Tom shook his head at him, but said nothing.

"Right," Rafiel said. "I think I'll take my headache and go see if I can come up with any new ideas."

Tom smiled at him, suddenly. "Where are you going to take your headache?"

"I don't know," Rafiel said. He had a savage need to be mad at someone and to be rude to someone, and he didn't want to do it here, and he didn't want to be mad at Tom. "I don't know. Maybe I'll drive in circles for a while till I think of somewhere to go."

The quizzical half-amused look he got back didn't really help his mood or sense of humor any. Nor did hearing Tom tell Conan—clearly, in answer to a question he didn't hear, "No, I don't want you to help. I don't want the Great Sky Dragon involved in this. It's between me and my *friends*. If the Great Sky Dragon gets involved I'll make sure to die. And then all his work and meddling will be for nothing."

Kyrie was worried and she didn't like to be worried. Or rather, she tried to minimize the time she spent being worried, tried to minimize the time she devoted to feeling stress. She much preferred, by far, to work on solutions than to turn over in her mind things that couldn't be helped.

But she was sure that it had been Dire who'd killed that poor woman. She remembered her own words to him—in haste and rage, and mostly wanting to get rid of him—about the reporter and the paper. Oh, she should have known better than to say that sort of thing to a psychopath, but she didn't feel guilty. Not exactly.

She had simply not been brought up with the idea that whatever she might say to someone might cause that person to go off and take it into his head to kill someone else. Though she'd grown up in foster homes, and some of her foster siblings had been less than stable, she'd never met with that level of volatility. Now she had. And she'd take it under advisement in the future. It had perhaps been stupid of her to speak of the poor girl. But Kyrie hadn't intended her death, and nothing could be served by castigating herself over crimes she hadn't meant to commit.

And yet, she felt a nettle of guilt and a nettle of worry, as she went about, waiting on tables. She would swear she smelled at least two shifters, perhaps more, though it was hard to tell through the smell of bacon and eggs and fresh-grilled pancakes.

However, when she stopped by the Poet—who had come in unusually late, and was clearly staying for breakfast—she could smell him—she was sure of it—the sharp tang of shifter around him.

She stopped long enough to refill his cup, and she could feel the smell rising from him, and then she noticed something else. What he had written on his notebook, in tiny, obsessively-neat block print, was "A modest proposal for a rodent revolution."

Rodents, Kyrie thought, moving away as he looked at her, and before he could realize she'd read over his shoulder. A Rodent Liberation Front. She wondered how real that was. It had seemed to—pardoning the pun—ferret out that school teacher rodent. Perhaps it had spies?

She shivered at the idea of an army of rodents spying on people. It reminded her of the movie *Ratatouille,* which she'd thought Tom would like, because, even though it was an animation for children, it was about a rat learning to be a chef. And since Tom had started culinary classes and was invested, heart and soul, in cooking the best he could for The George, Kyrie had thought this would be the perfect movie. Only the scene of the rats, flowing like a furry tide to take over the restaurant and do everything in it at night, had made Tom jump up and say, "Turn it off." Kyrie herself had felt pretty uncomfortable, too, though perhaps not as much as Tom, who'd said that all he could think was of a similar tide of rats taking over The George. The juxtaposition in his mind of rats and cooking surfaces just seemed to drive him crazy.

And yet . . . wouldn't such a furry tide of rats—such a group of shifters—have power? Shouldn't she be able to get help from them? She knew Tom didn't want to ask for help from the Great Sky Dragon. She understood it, even. But this was a diner customer.

The thought lasted all the walk back behind the counter, to replace the spent carafe and take up the filled one. Tom was behind the counter also taking over from Anthony and listening to Anthony's instructions on what was cooking and at what stage.

"I'll be back by six, right?" Anthony said. "Is that early enough for you? Because, you know, these double shifts are killing me, though Cecily says we could use the money because she wants a large screen TV. Where she plans to put the large screen TV in our apartment, I don't know, though doubtless I'll find out."

"You'll find out she wants to move to a bigger one," Tom said, in an amused tone, and Kyrie was surprised and admiring at once, that he could keep this calm and joke with Anthony like that, with everything that was hanging over their heads.

Anthony shrugged. "Ain't that the truth. But she's worth it. She's a great cook. Her steak is almost as good as yours. And I'm sorry, Tom, you're a good-looking man, but Cecily is much prettier."

Tom chuckled at that, and Anthony, putting his jacket on, ducked out of the counter and off towards the hallway. And Kyrie turned to Tom and said, "What about the RLF?"

Tom blinked at her. "Beg your pardon?"

"What about the Rodent Liberation Front?" Kyrie said. "What if we asked their help?"

"You're joking, right?"

"Well, they are a group of shifters, and they seem to be . . ." She looked up to see Tom's lips tremble. "Well, all right, the idea of an army of rats is somewhat creepy."

"Creepy isn't the half of it, and what I fear is not an army of rats," Tom said, "it is an army of rats, mice, gerbils, squirrels and guinea pigs."

"But . . . surely they could . . . do things?"

"Like what, nibble people to death?" Tom asked. Then shrugging, "Oh, I grant you they could probably be very useful in spying and that sort of thing, but . . ." He shook his head. "I don't know, Kyrie. All these organizations seem to come with their own, for lack of a better word, agenda: their own assumptions about who's in and who's out. I'd prefer to just be human."

Kyrie had to giggle at that. "Ah. Well. So would I, but we're not."

Tom shook his head. He frowned. "No. But perhaps we must be? I mean, I'm not going to deny, I can't deny, that I'm also something else, but we live in a society of humans and our parents . . . well . . . at least mine," he had the grace to blush, as if just remembering that she had no clue who or what her parents were, "are human. We owe humanity something . . . Even if we owe our kind something too." He looked annoyed, as though he'd just noticed that his tongue had got him hopelessly tangled. "Look, if I saw someone go after a . . . a mouse shifter, simply for being a mouse shifter and because the difference scared them, of course I would defend him or her. We owe each other that. But . . ."

"But if you found a mouse shifter nibbling on human babies at night and counting it as not mattering because he thought himself superior and more human than them . . . You'd eat the bastard?" Kyrie asked.

Tom flashed a smile. "Kill. Despite my dad's imagination, I do try very hard not to be a cannibal."

Kyrie chuckled. She could no more imagine Tom being a cannibal than she could imagine him being a mass murderer. Shifter or not, she knew her boyfriend held himself to a very stern standard. And would not, could not deviate. Not and remain himself. Which meant he couldn't ask for help. And that she would have to be the guarantor to the Great Sky Dragon that Tom wouldn't kill himself. She thought she could do that, if she had asked for help—and not him. If it were her debt.

A couple came in, and Kyrie went to seat them at a table by the window and take their order. The problem, when it came right down to it, was that Kyrie was also not absolutely sure that Tom could kill Dire even presuming he found a way to defeat his mind powers, no matter how much he thought Dire was dangerous to humans. She knew Tom. She thought Tom's own scruples would stop him. He would only kill when cornered. He would kill to protect his friends. But, given Dire's abilities, when Tom found himself cornered it might be too late.

Dire might not kill Tom. Kyrie wasn't sure how the truce of the Ancient Ones with the dragons would hold given an attack on a dragon. But she knew that he would hurt Tom. And wreak havoc on the rest of them.

And she saw no way out of it, she thought, as she set the two orders for French toast on the counter. They had to get rid of Dire, but Tom wouldn't let her ask for the help of anyone who might defeat the creature.

Rafiel didn't drive in circles. He drove through streets where people were making their cautious way to work—some of them for the first time in three days. It was slow going, and very broken progress, as he had to stop often to avoid ramming into the car in front of him, or else slow down for groups of schoolchildren slipping, sliding and giggling across an ice-patch on the crosswalk.

He stopped by a friendly doughnut shop—not his normal one—and grabbed two crullers and a tall cup of coffee, before retreating to the car parked in front of the shop, sparing just one grateful thought to his shifter metabolism that—thank heavens—allowed him to eat as much as he pleased of what he pleased.

The shop was in a neighborhood of small, remodeled townhouses and apartments. It had either been there since the middle of the twentieth century or someone had gone through a whole lot of trouble to make sure it looked as though it had. Though it had no tables, the interior had that green-formica and chrome look of the Fifties, and the sign over the shop blinked in pink and green neon good doughnuts. Which they were, or at least the crullers were—soft and moist. And the coffee was just as it should be, black as a murderer's soul, hot as hell and strong enough to peel paint—or stomach lining.

Rafiel's phone rang. He saw McKnight's cell number and took the phone to his ear with a "Yeah?"

"That guy you had me check on?"

"Dante Dire?"

"Yeah, I left a couple of the part-timers dealing with the data stuff. They didn't want to see the body."

"Yeah." *Smart part-timers.*

"Well, we didn't find signs that he was in the aquarium, but . . . well, his movements are kind of hard to check. He's all over. But he . . . well, he's been in Colorado for a couple of months. Also . . ."

"Also?"

"He made a killing in the stock market. Several times. He's either an amazing gambler, or he is crooked as hell."

Or he can read minds, Rafiel thought and shivered. "Thanks, McKnight."

Rafiel drank and ate in his car and considered his options.

He was about five blocks away from the aquarium. In the bewildering way towns in the west had of turning from residential to commercial and back again, this neighborhood became all offices as soon as you crossed under the expressway to the west. And then the aquarium was right there. He should go back to the aquarium. Oh, it was only one of the cases on his plate right now, but it was—arguably—the one he could actually do something about.

Whatever Tom and Kyrie had to say, he couldn't figure out how he could do anything about the dire wolf. And he certainly couldn't do anything about Conan and the Great Sky Dragon. He felt sorry for Conan, poor bastard, but that was about it. He didn't know where, if at all, the alligator fit in all this, and he'd be damned if he understood, even mildly, what was going on with a shifter crab. But whatever was going on at the aquarium he had to solve. There had to be a female involved, which seemed to rule out the old Japanese shifter. Unless, of course, the Japanese shifter disapproved of immoral behavior in his aquarium. Who knew? Morals had changed a lot, hadn't they, even in the last couple decades, let alone from whatever old era this shifter came from? And then there was always Dire. Dire's casual disregard for life. And even if they didn't find a trail showing he'd been in town, he might have been. And he might have mind-controlled those victims into jumping in the tank. To . . . make their life difficult? Keep them on their toes while he investigated their other alleged misdeeds?

His motives were almost impossible to fathom, except that it was pretty sure they weren't good. He seemed to take relish in casual emotional torture.

Or it could be a female at the aquarium.

He became aware that someone was knocking enthusiastically on the passenger side window, and looked away from pink and green neon to see Lei Lani's face surrounded by fluffy grey fake fur on a red ski jacket hood. She tapped the window again, and smiled.

Hello, suspect number . . . well, many.

He reached for the control on his door handle with a sugary hand and lowered the window. She smiled at him. "Officer Trall," she said. "I just came in for a coffee, and I saw you parked here. Nothing wrong in the doughnut shop, is there?"

He shook his head. "No. Just having breakfast. I'm afraid I was up all night and was starting to flag. But I am about to head back to the aquarium, to look at a few things."

"Oh, good. May I go to the aquarium now? I won't come near the crime scene. I know you guys have it all taped up and everything. I just want to go to the office and pick up some reports on shark health that I've been looking at which are urgent." Suddenly, her happy expression dimmed. "Well . . . if we don't end up having to kill half of them because we need to recover parts of people, and have the others shipped to parts unknown. I mean, who's going to come and look at our sharks, if they know they've eaten people?"

Rafiel shrugged. A tingle ran up and down his neck. His dad, now retired from the Goldport force had first told him about these *feelings*. The sense that *something* was wrong.

There was something to Lei Lani, to her talk, that made him suspect she knew something.

He doubted she could be *the* shark shifter, if there was one, because how did she convince her victims to go swimming in there? She didn't look strong enough to *push* men over. Unless she got them to lean over the tank somehow.

But she knew something, and she was trying to get him not to notice.

"Lots of people will come, probably," he said. "People do." He reassured her. "Why do you think they like sharks? Because they're fascinating marine creatures? No. Because they eat people. And this is their best chance at seeing them confined and safe, you know . . ."

She looked at him a moment, with huge, incredulous eyes, then blinked. "Perhaps. I guess being a shark expert, I have a soft spot for them. I don't think of them as . . . man-eaters."

And right there, Rafiel decided he needed to talk to Ms. Lani. Everyone thought of sharks as predators! And being, as they were, on semi-informal terms right now, it would probably be easier. But he'd like to reconcile what he'd heard from John Wagner about her with her comment that the male employees often had sex by the shark tank, and that, again, with the fact that the condoms found had vaginal secretions.

"Why don't you hop in?" he said. "If you're going to the aquarium, I might as well give you a ride." And because he had no intention of letting her go near the aquarium alone.

"Oh, thank you," she said, suddenly acting shy. "I could walk, you know? It's only a few blocks." She gestured vaguely across the way. "I live just over there. Normally I walk."

"Judging from the pedestrians I saw on the way here," Rafiel said, "there's quite a bit of ice on the sidewalks. I might as well give you a ride."

She got in, gingerly, and put her coffee cup on the dashboard as she sat down and buckled herself in, before picking the cup up again. "Thank you, really."

Rafiel backed out of the parking space and into the flow of traffic, while his passenger remained absolutely quiet. It wasn't till they were a block away that she said, still in that oddly shy tone, "So, I suppose I shouldn't ask you if you have made any progress? You said you don't discuss your investigations."

He answered with a shrug. "Well," he said, "we have made some progress. As you told us, there were some condoms discarded in the planters by the water." He watched carefully for her reactions, while seeming to ignore her.

"Oh?" she said, and raised an eyebrow. "I told you, I heard the guys at the aquarium talk, and that John Wagner? He's the worst. He has this . . . imaginary friend or whatever that he calls 'the drool'—you know, like it's a part of him, or a mobile, sentient weapon. If people displease him, he'll say 'fear the drool, I am basset,' and everyone laughs and all, and you know, he talks about how he used to own a basset and how much they drooled. But . . . it feels creepy somehow. And he keeps saying things like 'I'd never say anything impolite. Now the drool, he's a brazen bastard.' Like . . . like he's schizophrenic or something."

Rafiel was so horrified by the vision the words conjured, of the ebullient John Wagner turning into—of all things—a basset hound, that he could barely trust himself to speak. While silence lengthened, he caught himself thinking, *But . . . he can't be a shifter basset, can he? I mean I can imagine dog shifters, but would they be a particular breed?*

His limited knowledge of dog fancy told him that the current breeds favored as pets in the U.S. must all be of fairly recent creation. Recent, at least in evolutionary terms. And surely, surely, being relatively recent they couldn't have gotten enmeshed with human genes, could they? It seemed to him all the shifters he'd seen so far changed shapes into species and breeds that had been very long on the Earth. Some longer than humans. But then again, they had no idea how the shifting mechanism worked. Was it truly genetic? Or was there some other mechanism at work? Rafiel was hesitant to say it was magic, but then, wasn't magic just a name for a process no one understood yet? And after all, as far as they knew, dragons had never even existed.

"I'm sorry," Lei said, sounding distant, and somehow worried. "I didn't mean to cast aspersions on John. I mean, he's a nice guy and all. A little . . . extroverted, you'd call it, and he makes some jokes that could border on sexual harassment, but I'm sure he means well."

Oh, I wouldn't be sure of any such thing, Rafiel thought. Much as he'd liked the guy—and he realized with surprise that he had liked the guy, which was odd, considering that John Wagner appeared to consider him a dumb ass—he was quite sure it was part of Wagner's fundamental approach to the world to put the cat among the pigeons as much as humanly possible.

Which was why Rafiel was loath to think of what he'd said about Lei as meaning anything at all. For all he knew, Lei had simply made that sort of prissy comment about John Wagner being sexist, and

John had it in for her. Oh, not consciously. He didn't seem like the sort of guy who—fully aware of what he was doing—would be either vengeful or petty. But he might very well view casting doubt on her credentials and sending the police to look into her background as just a bit of fun and mischief. "No," he said, speaking to Lei. "That isn't it, you know. I didn't think you were particularly paranoid about John Wagner. I met him while we were processing the scene. He said he dropped by to see if we needed any help." Which, of course, was also the typical behavior of mass murderers, as Rafiel well knew. "He seems like a nice guy. Ebullient. But . . . but he didn't threaten me with the drool."

He was rewarded with a ladylike giggle and a small headshake. "I'm sure he only does that to his friends or people he works with and knows. I'm wondering if it was him . . . I mean, by the pool."

"No," Rafiel said decisively. "It couldn't be any of the men at the aquarium."

"Why not?" she asked. "I mean, did you—?"

"DNA test them? No. The semen in the condoms belonged to the last two victims, so you see, it couldn't be—"

"But, Officer!" she said and seemed within a breath of pointing out to him that they, after all, lived in the twenty-first century.

"No," he said, cutting her off. "You see, the outside of the condom had vaginal secretions." Now she looked surprised, staring at him. "And something else. Our analyst says that the outside of the condom also had minute fragments of sharkskin."

"Shark?" she asked, now looking truly surprised. "How do they know it's shark and not some other fish? I mean, I know there are preparations"—she blushed—"people use, to facilitate sex or heighten pleasure or . . ."

"No," Rafiel said. *Curiouser and curiouser. What does she know that requires this much enthusiasm to hide?* "This was shark. There is something in sharkskin called denticles. Our examiner says that they were on the outside of this condom. And please, don't ask me how. I wouldn't begin to be able to explain it." Which was true, he thought. *Not because I can't begin to explain, but because I wouldn't. If these shark particles are like the bits of hair and fluff I find on my bed after*

*a shifted night, or the scales that Tom is forever shaking out of his stuff,
then it would indicate that the shark itself is a shifter. Herself,
presumably, given the vaginal secretions. But how would a small
woman get her victim in before she shifted?*

"Uh," Lei said. She unzipped her ski jacket to reveal that
underneath she wore a semitransparent white blouse. Not
semitransparent in a way that would necessarily look racy or
provocative, but just as though a nice business blouse had been made
out of too thin a material and therefore allowed a vague translucence
to let forth the golden hues of her skin, the whiter tones of her bra,
and a pinkish spot in the middle, between her breasts which was
probably one of those rosettes with which bra manufacturers adorned
bras, for reasons Rafiel—who usually concerned himself far more
with the removal of their product than its purchase—couldn't
understand. He glanced sideways and into her black eyes, as she said,
"I think it is possible, isn't it, that they could have . . ." She shifted
uncomfortably in the seat. "You know . . . put stuff on the condom to
throw people off?"

Rafiel shrugged. He wasn't going to laugh the hypothesis off.
Mostly because once you got shifters involved in a crime scene, the
improbable was not only, often enough, possible, but it was,
strangely, often the most likely solution. After all, if you started with
the impossibility of someone changing shapes into an animal, then
wouldn't it follow that every other impossibility would be true? *My
disbelief was suspended from the neck until dead,* he thought. But still,
he spoke as if he were a normal policeman, and as if he didn't very
well know that all this involved shifters. "If that were the case," he
said, "wouldn't it have made much more sense to have tossed the
condoms away, out of the vicinity of the aquarium? And which of
the . . . stuff, do you suggest they put on the condom? The vaginal
secretions or the sharkskin?"

She seemed surprised, and squirmed some more, as he pulled
into a parking spot at the aquarium—which was still closed to visitors
and whose parking lot therefore remained empty. "I . . . I guess both?"
she said, at last, hesitantly.

"Um . . . okay. I could grant you both, at least if there were no woman involved . . ." He neglected to say that unless it was manual sex there would have been other traces. "Throwing in vaginal secretions might change our perception of the crime. But why the sharkskin? They can't have meant to throw suspicion on a shark. Unless," he said, as an idea occurred to him, "some woman at the aquarium is a craftswoman specializing in sword and knife handles made of sharkskin. They do those, don't they? I don't remember what they call it . . . Oh, yes, I do. Shagreen, isn't it?"

She shook her head. "I don't know," she said. "There are so many ways in which humans exploit the beautiful creatures." And then, as though catching sight of his shocked expression, she added, "Well, they are, you know, truly. Though my professor at college said that the natural historian always identifies with their subjects. Or at least, there is no other way to account for otherwise rational beings suddenly becoming misty-eyed over monitor lizards."

It might be true. "So, you went to college in Hawaii?" Or perhaps her lover was a were shark and she fed him . . . who knew? Perhaps all that stuff about John Wagner was because they were accomplices?

"University of Hawaii," she said. "Easiest thing, you know . . . I mean . . . it was my native state."

"You were born there?"

She laughed lightly. "Born and raised. I don't know when my first ancestors came to the isle. But since I'm a bit of a mix, I guess they all came at various times, over the course of history."

"Well . . ." he said, wondering if he too would get tagged with sexual harassment. "It's a very pleasant mix." There was something wrong here, something off to Lei's approaching him like this. What game *was* she playing? In these circumstances Rafiel often found it useful to give someone enough rope.

She seemed startled and blushed. "Thank you."

"Go and deal with your paperwork, or whatever you're going to do," Rafiel said. "I have to look at some things here on the grounds." The "some things" mostly applied to Old Joe. But he didn't want to tell her that. He doubted he could get much of rational value out of Old Joe. If anyone could do that, it would be Tom, and Tom was, alas, not around just now. But Rafiel was hoping to get ... something. "I'll come and see if you're ready afterwards."

He was sure Lei was up to something too. It would be easier to play along till he found what it was. He could check on old Joe, then drop in on Lei, suddenly. Perhaps he would catch her kissing a shark or something. He repressed a chuckle at the idea.

First, he hoped Old Joe could give him some inkling of whether Dire was likely to be afraid of anyone. And second, some idea of whether Old Joe knew the crab shifter at the aquarium. For neither of those conversations did he wish to have the curvaceous Lei around, particularly since Old Joe was probably going to be in his shifted form.

He knew his colleagues on the force had locked and sealed the shark chamber the night before after it became obvious that they were in fact dealing with murder. She wouldn't have the key to that, surely. McKnight was supposed to come in with the employees later on and supervise them while they fed the sharks and the other fish, so that no fish in those rooms would starve. But he didn't see anything wrong with letting Lei go and do whatever paperwork she needed to do. At least not if he could drop in on her unannounced.

He watched her go towards the aquarium and only as he saw her go in, did it occur to him that she'd never told him she had a key. Did she have a key? Surely interns wouldn't. Or did someone come to open the restaurant or aquarium at a designated time? Well, he'd find out. If she couldn't get in, she couldn't do much.

Getting out of the car, he ambled down to the stream. But it was flowing now, the water gurgling amid the remaining ice floes. Rafiel thought he saw what might have been a pair of alligator eyes and the snout of an alligator peeking from beneath the water, but he couldn't really tell.

"Come on," he said, speaking to the still air and wondering if he'd gone nuts. Surely anyone who heard him would think he had. "Come on, now, Old Joe? I need to talk to you. Tom's safety might be at stake."

Was that swishing sound an alligator's tail churning the stream? Or was it just the normal gurgling of the water augmented by his hopes?

He waited. But no snout broke the water, no alligator came towards him. No, it would not be this simple, Rafiel thought. No one was about to hand him the solution. He'd have to figure it out himself.

Kyrie waited till there was a lull early in the afternoon, when the diner was almost empty. Tom busied himself with those things he did when his cooking expertise was not needed—scrubbing the cooking surfaces, marinating meat, bringing out frozen dough and setting bread to rise. The bread was one of the few things Tom didn't make himself, from scratch. The woman, Laura, who had applied here some days ago, had offered baking skills, which, of course, would be a great help. Kyrie hoped she would show up for an interview as soon as the weather permitted it. For one, with the addition of Conan and the seeming disappearance of the unreliable waitress Beth, she was now the only woman on staff. For another, she wasn't sure how much longer Keith would want to continue working for them.

He had only ever been a part-time employee, because of his studies, but since he'd discovered Summer had taken pictures of Tom and Conan, he hadn't been back at all. Kyrie didn't know if he was upset with them, or if it had just finally been borne upon him how difficult and dangerous their position was. Probably both. She would have left them and herself far behind, by now, if she could. At least . . . she couldn't leave Tom. Any more than she could walk away from herself. But she would have left their shifter condition far behind.

As she walked towards the annex, she found herself daydreaming of a life in which neither she nor Tom were shifters. How peaceful the days would be and how devoid of unusual events.

Of course, she knew in her heart of hearts that the daydream was great foolishness. Because, if Tom hadn't been a shifter, he'd be living somewhere in New York City. Or perhaps he would have been sent to those Ivy League colleges where the wildest behavior is excused if the family pays enough. At any rate, he would never have crossed paths with her.

And besides, things were the way they were, so she must do what she must do. She felt a twinge of fear at the idea of exactly what she must do. Tom would disapprove. In fact, Tom would be very, very upset. If he ever found out. She didn't want to keep secrets from him. But sometimes people had to be kept in the dark for their own good. And in this case, Tom had to be kept in the dark for the continued ability to call his soul his own.

She approached Conan as he finished wiping a table, and spoke in an undertone, her ears listening for any sounds of approaching footsteps, which might be Tom coming to check on them. "Conan, do you have a way to contact the representatives of the dragon triad, here in town?"

She'd obviously been so careful that Conan himself had not heard her approach. He dropped the tray he'd been holding, and bent to retrieve it, his gaze fixed on her, his eyes big as saucers.

Seeing him open his mouth, and very much fearing how much noise he might make, she put her finger in front of her lips. He nodded and it seemed to her he looked a little pale, but when he straightened up, he whispered back, "Well, you know that Himself can take over my mind and . . . and listen in, but . . ."

"I don't mean like that," she said. "I mean, do you have a phone number to call or something? I presume that I could still approach them outside the Three Luck Dragon?" she asked.

"Inside," he said. "The owner. Yes."

"Then would you call whatever number you need to call and tell them I come in peace, but I want to talk to their leader?"

Conan gave her a long and analyzing stare, before giving her a very curt nod. "When?"

"After Tom goes back to the bed-and-breakfast to sleep," she said, "which I figure will be around six, because that's when Anthony will come in again."

"Oh," Conan said and then, "you haven't slept at all yourself."

Kyrie shrugged. "No. I can go twenty-four hours without sleeping. It just makes me more susceptible to shifting, but . . ."

He nodded. "I assume you . . . have a plan? And that you want our—the dragons' help with it?"

"Yes. Well . . . I want their help. I don't have a plan yet, but I'm sure one will emerge. Only, I must find out if they can help me, and then I must do what I can . . . I mean . . . I'm sure we can't fight this fight alone. And Tom won't ask for help." She saw him nod. "And Tom must never know of this."

Conan shrugged. "He won't learn it from me," he said. "Of course, the other dragons have their own . . . approach to honesty and promises."

"Meaning you can't promise me anything?" Kyrie asked, with alarm but not really surprised. She'd already once met the Great Sky Dragon's idea of morality. She wasn't sure he cared even for shifters that weren't his own kind.

After Anthony had come in, and Tom had gone back to the bed-and-breakfast to sleep, she went outside and—with trembling fingers—dialed the number Conan had given her. A heavily accented woman's voice answered, "Three Luck Dragon! How may I help you?"

Momentarily mute, Kyrie wondered if there was a polite way to say, May I speak to the boss dragon? Instead, she cleared her throat and said, "May I speak to the proprietor?"

The woman rattled something off, very fast, that appeared to be some Cantonese dialect, and Kyrie said, "Conan Lung told me to call. He said that the owner of the restaurant would speak to me."

There was a long silence, followed by the sound of cutlery and a rattle of plates and a voice saying something in an Asian language. Kyrie took a deep breath. Her thumb moved towards the disconnect button on the phone.

"Hello," a male voice said. It was a resonant voice, with almost no trace of an accent.

Caught off guard, Kyrie cleared her throat, nervously and said "Am I speaking to the owner of Three Luck Dragon?"

"Speaking," the voice said.

"Oh. Oh. Good. I wanted to talk about . . . about the owner of the diner . . . The George."

For a terribly long moment, while the speaker on the other side was silent, she thought he was going to ask "Who?"

But instead, when he spoke, he said, "The young dragon? The one whom Himself . . ."

"Yes." Kyrie hastened, not wanting to know if the man was about to say "the one whom Himself almost killed" or "the one whom Himself is protecting." That she didn't know which one the man was about to say betrayed her ambivalence about this being and about the step she was taking.

Was she doing the right thing? Or was she about to betray Tom's trust in her for nothing?

"I assume," the man said from the other side, his voice even more impersonal, colder, as though he were a receptionist talking to a stranger about some abstract transaction. "I assume that you do not wish to speak of this over the phone?"

Kyrie did not wish. No matter that Anthony was busy at the grill. No matter that she could go outside and attempt to talk from there. What she had to say was bound to make more than a few clients or passersby get curious. And then there was the fact that Summer might have friends or relatives coming around to see her place of death. There was already a clutter of flowers around the base of the pole, and one pink teddy bear clutching a heart. Summer's friends were bound to be journalists. Considering the paper was obsessed with cryptozoology, how would they react to hearing Kyrie talk of dragons. "It would be better if I may speak in person," she said. She remembered the parking lot, and the Great Sky Dragon in it. And all the other dragons around. Had this man—dragon—been there too? There was a great deal she'd rather do than see one of these dragons again. All else aside, they were a criminal organization and one populated by shifters, who could destroy her and Tom several times over. But she didn't have any choice. She'd run out of all choices.

"Come to the restaurant," the man said. "I'll be here. Ask for Mr. Lung."

Mr. Lung? Was he related to Conan?

⌐– –⌐ 🐈 ⌐– –⌐

Rafiel opened the door to the aquarium. It had been unlocked. The smell of fish and bleach—combined—hit his nostrils as well as damp air that seemed hot compared to the frosty air outside. He stepped into the shadows, lengthened since all the lights in the aquarium were off. He almost called out to Lei, except he remembered the offices were far enough around the corner that he was sure she couldn't hear him. He walked past the sealed door to the shark room, up a short flight of service stairs, now the only way to get past the shark room, to where the light of the floor-to-ceiling windows made the room with the anemones and crabs much brighter than the one belowstairs. He walked past the aquariums, looking curiously at the spider crab one. He wished he could tell that one of the giant, long-legged crabs— some of them looking as weathered and beaten as though they'd escaped from the mother of all clarified butter dishes—was a shifter. They all had moss growing on them. He squinted, reasoning that a shifter crab would have less moss, wouldn't it? Surely the moss sloughed off when the crabs shifted to human then back? Surely . . . But all of them seemed to have an even covering of the green stuff, and Rafiel started wondering if John Wagner had hallucinated it all. Perhaps for his own amusement. The man seemed to have a very odd sense of humor.

Normally he could have cut through the shark room to the office area, but now he had to make it across the silent restaurant, and then down another set of stairs, to the back.

As he got to the bottom floor, he saw light shining out of the office and called out, "Ms. Lani?"

She stuck her head out of the office, for just a moment. "I'll be ready in just a moment, Officer Trall."

"Oh. All right," he said. *Now what are you up to?*

"You may come in." Her voice sounded vaguely amused.

He ambled out of the hallway and into the cramped offices he had visited and searched before. On the wall, on a pegboard were the keys he had stolen and gotten copied, as well as several other sets of keys, which he assumed were to either other areas of the aquarium—areas he'd found no need to explore—or to the utility parts of the aquarium. At least he assumed that electrical circuits and such would be locked behind panels and couldn't be accessed by just anyone.

Other than that, the office consisted of a very long, narrow room, which might have, in some previous incarnation, been a hallway. It had no windows, and only two rows of desks, six on each side against the walls. While Lei Lani rummaged through the desk nearest the door, Rafiel walked up and down the rows of desks, to the small fridge set against the narrow far wall, and the coffee maker on top of the fridge. The coffee maker had coffee in it, and, inside, some blue mold over a residue sludge that might very well be sentient in itself, or perhaps even a shifter.

Rafiel eyed it dubiously. He was well aware, no matter how much he pretended not to be, that Tom and Kyrie thought there was something wrong with him, since he still lived with his parents, and he was the first to admit that perhaps he had leaned on parental protection too long. Until he'd met Kyrie and Tom, he had never seen other shifters manage for themselves, without normal people to cover up for them. But whatever his staying with his parents might betray about his character, it did not betray a lingering, overlong adolescence. To the contrary. Rafiel kept his area of the house neat, and had even acquired the reputation of a neat freak at the police station. If this coffee machine, or anything like it, were in the station, he'd be taking it out, rinsing it, washing it, then giving all his subordinates a lecture on keeping foodstuffs around as they molded. With a rueful smile, he thought that McKnight and the others must think he was a pure bundle of joy.

To distract himself from the machine, he turned his attention to the desks, once more. Above them were corkboards, with the usual family pictures and the like, showing that most people who worked here were pretty ordinary. One of the corkboards was ornamented with groups of young men standing around drinking beer and an inordinate number of pictures of a simpering blond in different bikinis. Rafiel presumed it was a young man's desk and, in fact, looking at the various groups in the pictures on the wall, quickly narrowed down the user of the desk to a tall, disheveled blond who looked like a football player. He was the youth who appeared in every picture and Rafiel had a vague memory of seeing him among the other employees the police had cursorily interviewed. Judging from the attention given to beer and girls amid the man's favorite memories, it wasn't hard to imagine him bringing girlfriends to the shark area to impress them. But then, the pictures were all of the same girl, and she didn't look like she'd be that much into sharp-toothed creatures.

Next to that desk was another one, whose remarkably neat and empty corkboard showed only two pictures. One had a soulful-eyed, sad-looking basset. The other, which was clearly a bought postcard, showed a donkey about to cross a busy highway and said, in yellow letters across the top "dumb ass." Rafiel thought the desk might as well be labeled as John Wagner's, and resisted a momentary impulse to look through the drawers. He truly had no reason to suspect John Wagner of anything, no matter how much he had—and he undoubtedly had—upset Lei. At least, judging from her comments on him. But then, Rafiel thought, those two would rub the other one the wrong way, wouldn't they? Lei Lani with her careful image, her nice clothes and manners, and John Wagner who seemed to believe his job was to repeatedly poke the universe in the eye.

He moved on to the next desk, and perked up because it was so obviously a woman's. Or perhaps he was letting his assumptions show, but he truly could not imagine any man, no matter his sexual orientation, adorning a desk with a collection of pretty kitten mugs, and owning a notepad in pink ornamented with butterflies. Besides, the collection of smiling kids in various stages of tooth loss and toothiness on the corkboard seemed to clinch the matter. They were all the same kids, he guessed, at different stages of growth. Or at least, the entire horde were redheaded and blue-eyed and had disturbingly vacuous expressions. "I guess she has what? Eight children?" he asked, more to distract himself from the contemplation of such a thing than to talk.

"What?" Lei said, the rustling of papers momentarily stopped.

"I said your . . . colleague seems to have eight children?"

She looked across and smiled. "Suzanne isn't married," she said, and, as though realizing that really didn't mean much in context, added, "She doesn't have any children. Those are her nephews and nieces."

"Oh," Rafiel said, embarrassed. He stepped across the other way, to look at the desk next to Lei's, which had pictures of what appeared to be bodybuilders on the corkboard, a note saying "Call me" and the number, and a collection of pink notebooks on the desk. He had just resolutely decided he wasn't going to say anything, much less ask it, when he noticed that Lei was staring intently at him, and blushing slightly.

He raised his eyebrows at her. It wasn't as if he could ask her why she was staring at him, of course, but raising eyebrows was surely allowed. She sighed and colored deeper, and looked down at her hands, which were resting on a pile of papers, from which protruded a couple of plastic baggies.

"Look," she said, "I was . . . curious . . . you know . . . after what you told me about what you found on the outside of the . . . of the preservatives."

"Yes?"

"Well . . . I looked in Lillian's desk . . . and . . . well . . ." She reached over and slid open the drawer in the middle of the desk.

Rafiel looked down at a welter of pencils and pens, a forlorn nest of paper clips, a confusion of rubber bands. Lei seemed to lose patience with him. She reached down and picked up a tube of something and put it on top of the desk.

Rafiel looked closer. "Petroleum jelly?" he said.

"Well . . ." Lei said. "You know, it's used for . . . you know . . . sex . . ."

"Yes, I know," Rafiel said. And, he imagined, for a dozen other things. He had a vague idea that it was also used for some sorts of closures that must resist water, like, say, wetsuits, which he knew were used when divers went in to clean the tanks.

"But that's not what . . . what made me . . . I mean . . . why I think I should tell you," Lei said. "It's this." She showed him some grey adherences to the slightly greasy outside of the tube. "I thought . . . it might be sharkskin." And then, looking up at his face, she looked like she was trying very hard not to give a sigh of exasperation. "We use petroleum jelly around the . . . you know . . . around the aquariums, on seals and valves and such, and I thought, she might have got sharkskin on it. We collect the skin for samples and such, you know, and that she . . . you know . . . then used it for . . . for other things."

Rafiel shrugged. He took the tube and reached for the end of one of the baggies under Lei's pile of papers. It came out from under the papers, scattering grey flakes as it was pulled away. It was full of what looked like white and grey dandruff.

"Oh," Lei said. And then. "Not that." She pulled the baggie away and put it on her desk. "Those are some samples I meant to send to the lab, for sharkskin diseases. Of course, now I don't know if our sharks . . ." She shrugged and looked pained.

"I need a plastic baggie, if I'm going to send this to analysis," Rafiel said. "And I must put a label on it, then seal it. And you must be willing to say I didn't tamper with it." Though of course, that didn't mean Lei Lani hadn't tampered with it, Rafiel thought but didn't say. Her finding this in the desk seemed very odd, and oddly convenient.

She primly got him a plastic baggie from her own desk, where she had a pile of them folded together. "We use them for samples," she said, as she handed him one.

"Curiously," he said, "we do too." Sealing the bag, he wrote on it with a marker from the desk drawer, saying what he had found and where. This would never hold up in a court of law, of course. There were so many ways in which it might have been tampered with. But at this point Rafiel was not operating on the assumption the matter would ever come to a court of law. Instead, he thought, this would end up in the court of Rafiel and it was for himself that he must collect evidence. And he wondered how stupid Ms. Lani thought he was.

Kyrie parked in front of the restaurant and got out of her car, shivering at the sight of the facade, at its cheery sign saying THREE LUCK DRAGON above another sign that proclaimed FOR YOUR HEALTH, WE DON'T USE MSG IN OUR COOKING.

Kyrie pulled her coat tighter around herself. She had very bad memories of this parking lot. Without meaning to, she looked toward the sky, afraid of a flapping of large wings, the sudden appearance of the Great Sky Dragon in all his golden and green glory. But the skies were empty and a sound somewhere between throat-clearing and a cough made her turn to look.

In the slightly open door of the restaurant, stood a middle-aged Asian gentleman, with impeccably cut salt-and-pepper hair and a big white apron. She took a deep breath. Three steps brought her close to him, and she had a moment of surprise, at noticing that he was wearing a shirt and tie under his apron.

"Ms. Smith?" he said, extending his hand.

She hesitated only fractionally before she shook it. It felt slightly cool to the touch. Not abnormally so. It was the same way Tom's skin usually felt, as if he'd been holding a glass with a cold drink all the time. Maybe it was something about the metabolism of dragon shifters, though Kyrie would bet the dragons were not actually cold-blooded.

The man held the door open to her. "Please come in."

He led her past the counter, manned by a small lady who was watching TV and doing accounts at the same time, then past the dining room where only three people sat at tables, and into a door that led into busy, noisy kitchen. Before she had more than a moment to recoil from the sound of pans banged together, the clash of plates, the way people yelled at each other across the room, she felt Mr.

Lung's cool hand on her elbow, and saw him pointing at yet another, narrower door.

She went through it to find herself in a very small room. There was only one table, long and narrow, covered in an immaculate white tablecloth. Three chairs, one on either of the longer sides of the table, and one at the end. At one corner of the table, the tablecloth had been pulled back, to reveal a cutting-board surface. That area was covered in cabbage and there was a cleaver amid it. On the other side sat a pile of papers that looked like account books, but which Kyrie could not presume to decipher, given they were written in Chinese ideograms.

Mr. Lung smiled and waved her to one of the chairs on the long side of the table, then sat himself on the facing one and took up the cleaver. "I hope you don't mind," he said, "if I work while we talk? I find it helps me concentrate. Also, we are a family operation. I don't cook, but I help with the preparation for the cooking. And then I take off the apron and serve at tables." Judging from his smile, one would think this was a pleasant social chat.

"You . . . know my name . . ." Kyrie said.

"Of course," he said, equably. "We met before. I mean, I've seen you. And I knew who you were. I was not . . . in my human form."

Kyrie thought of the assembly of dragons, of the Great Sky Dragon and of Tom—as she then thought—getting killed. She felt as if her throat would close.

Mr. Lung seemed to notice her discomfort. He set the cleaver down again, amid the chopped cabbage, gently, as if he were afraid the blade might scare her. "I know what it must have seemed like to you," he said. He joined his hands and rested them on the edge of the table, but kept his spotless shirt sleeves away from the cabbage. "But even then, I knew . . ." He shrugged. "He doesn't tell us much. He doesn't need to. He's like . . . the father of the family, and the father doesn't owe explanations to anyone, does he?" He smiled suddenly. "Well, now your attitudes here are different, but where I grew up the father could do as he pleased and didn't need to tell wife or children anything." For a moment it seemed to Kyrie as though he glanced across endless distances at a time she couldn't even imagine. "But we don't question him, and I haven't. I do have my suspicions, but I'm not so foolish as to share them, and besides, I might be quite wrong. But I can tell you he didn't mean to seriously punish the young dragon. If he had . . ." Mr. Lung shrugged.

He picked up the cleaver again, and resumed chopping cabbage. "If he had, you wouldn't be worried for the young dragon now, because he would be dead. Himself can be quite ruthless when he chooses. I don't think he has it in him to mind what other people feel or think." He shrugged again. "But he treated the young dragon very gently, particularly for someone who had just led him on a chase and defied him the way—what is his name? Mr. Ormson?—had."

Kyrie heard herself sniffle skeptically. "He had given people orders to kill him before."

Mr. Lung narrowed his eyes at her. "This is where I can't give you more detailed explanations, Ms. Smith. Partly, because they are only my conjectures. But I think . . . I think Himself found out something about Mr. Ormson when he met him in the flesh. And that's when he decided he could not kill him."

"Found out what?"

Mr. Lung shrugged. "I can't tell you that. All I can say is that the dragon triad looks after its own."

"But he's not . . . an Asian dragon."

"Sometimes the differences are smaller than you think," Mr. Lung said. "And not everything is as black and white as it appears. For now . . ." He chopped cabbage with a will. "Let's establish that it matters to Himself—in fact, it's important to him—that nothing should happen to the young dragon. So, anything I can do to help you with this . . ."

"He'll never join you, you know?" Kyrie felt forced to warn. "He just can't. He would . . . he will never give anyone that sort of authority over him."

Mr. Lung nodded. "I talked to his father," he said, as if he were admitting to a distasteful encounter. "I know all about Mr. Ormson's hatred of authority. All I can say is that he's very young."

Kyrie opened her mouth and almost said it wasn't the authority, it was the feeling of belonging absolutely to someone, and the fact that the triad was, after all, a criminal organization. But she realized in time that nothing could be gained from antagonizing the people she needed to help her, and almost smiled. It would be such a Tom thing to do, after all. Perhaps Tom was contagious. Instead, she closed her mouth. And when she opened it again, it was to say, "There's a dire wolf shifter in town."

"Ah, the executioner. We've . . . heard." The nimble fingers plied the cleaver impossibly fast, chopping exact, neat strips of cabbage. "We have . . . a pact with the Ancient Ones."

"I know. I don't know if Dante Dire intends to violate it," she said. And watched his eyebrows go up, as the cleaver stopped.

"What do you mean 'violate it'?" For just a moment, Mr. Lung's urbane mask seemed to slip. He set his mouth into what would have been a grin, except that it displayed far more of his small, sharp teeth than any natural grin could display. "He wouldn't dare."

Kyrie could swear she saw an extra pair of nictitating eyelids close, then open from the side, but she knew it couldn't be true. She looked away from him, hastily. "I don't know," she said. "I know the following: he's a sadist. He's not as much in control of himself as he thinks he is. He seems to have decided he likes me, or at least is not willing to hurt me, for now. And he's looking for a scapegoat for the deaths that brought him here."

"He should be more concerned," the dragon said, "with the other deaths. The ones that originally got you involved."

"Yes," Kyrie said. "But he doesn't seem concerned with searching out the true culprits or investigating anything. He wants to protect himself, and get out of here with his . . . reputation undiminished." Mentally she added to herself that at least she hoped he wanted to get out of there. The idea that he had a thing for her and that he might stick around to make himself agreeable to her was driving her insane. In the long list of suitors she'd rejected, Dante Dire was something she'd never met. Something she didn't need.

She started telling the dragon about her encounters with Dire and more, about what she sensed and feared from the creature. When she was done, Mr. Lung swept the cabbage into a mound, and looked at her over it. "So, you fear he might inadvertently kill the young dragon? While baiting him?" He looked skeptical. "We are not that frail, Ms. Smith. Nor that easy to kill."

"No," she said. "That is not what I fear at all. What I fear . . ." She shook her head. "You know Tom, such as he is." She smiled a little. "Hatred of authority and all, he insists on looking after those he thinks he's obliged to protect. To . . . to keep them from harm. As such, he's . . . well . . . he doesn't want me hurt. And he doesn't want Rafiel hurt, nor Keith, nor anyone in the diner. That girl reporter getting killed just outside the diner scared him. He thinks it's up to him to save us all. And I'm very afraid he's about to do something stupid."

Mr. Lung was quiet a long time. When he spoke, it was in measured tones. "I would say he will do something stupid. That sense that he must do something he's completely unprepared to do . . . I've seen it before. He will get hurt."

"Yes," Kyrie said, feeling a great wave of relief at being understood. "That's what I thought. He will get hurt."

"No," Mr. Lung said, with great decision, his face setting suddenly in sharp lines and angles. "No. Himself would not want him hurt. I will do what it takes. What is your plan?"

"Right," Rafiel said over the phone as he drove away from the doughnut shop where he had dropped off Lei Lani. "And I want you to check the backgrounds of the aquarium employees," and to McKnight's protests answered, "No, nothing special, okay? Just basically their resume. But check with the places where they're supposed to have studied and all."

"You . . . suspect one of them is an impostor?" McKnight asked.

"I don't know what I suspect," Rafiel said. "I just want to check it out."

"Oh," McKnight said. "Now?"

"Now would be good," Rafiel said, as sternly as he could. "Call me as soon as you have anything."

He hung up before McKnight could formulate an answer, and set a course towards the laboratory to drop off the petroleum jelly. He was fairly sure the petroleum jelly would have sharkskin in it. He was also fairly sure that the skin had come from the scrapings in that baggie Lei had on her desk. It had taken all of Rafiel's self-control—plus some—to avoid giving away how obvious all this was. Except that he could feel a theory assembling, like an itch at the back of his brain. If he had to bet, he would bet that Lei Lani was the shark shifter. And he would bet she took her dates to the aquarium and then . . . made a snack out of them.

The problem was, even if it proved that she hadn't gone to the University of Hawaii, even if it could be proven that she wasn't who she said she was . . . how could he be sure she was a shark shifter? And even if he were sure she was a shark shifter, how could he be sure that she was committing these heinous crimes? Or that she was committing them on purpose? Or that she knew what she was doing?

In a normal crime, you knew. And if you didn't know—if you weren't absolutely sure that the criminal knew right from wrong, or that he was in full possession of his faculties, you had the courts. Rafiel's job was supposed to be to provide a case to the courts. Not constituting himself judge, jury and executioner. That would make him no better than Dire.

No . . . he needed to go and talk to someone. He looked at the clock on the dashboard. Middle of the day. Normally both Kyrie and Tom would be at home and awake. He wasn't sure how the strange schedule was affecting things. He also knew they wouldn't be home. Rafiel had left their key with his father, who said his uncle would have the bathroom repaired in the next two or three days. But for now, Kyrie and Tom would be at the bed-and-breakfast. Or at least one of them would be. Almost for sure.

Rafiel parked in the back of The George. A quick look inside revealed Anthony at the grill, which meant Tom at least was off. The tables seemed to be attended to by Conan and Keith. That meant . . . maybe both Tom and Kyrie were off.

Turning away from The George, Rafiel crossed the parking lot, went up the broad stone steps flanked by sickly-looking stone lions—or perhaps dogs—and up to the front door of the bed-and-breakfast. The sign on the door said do come in, and Rafiel did. In response to a light tinkle from the bell affixed to the back of the front door, the kindly-looking, middle-aged proprietress came from the back of the house, wearing a frilly apron and smelling vaguely of vanilla.

"Hi," Rafiel said. "I'm here to see my friends, Mr. Ormson and Ms. Smith?" *And don't I sound like I have a truly interesting social life, the way I keep visiting Tom and Kyrie in their room.* He felt himself blush but smiled at the woman.

"Oh, sure. Just a moment," she said, heading to the antique mahogany desk in the middle of the room. "I'll just give them a ring to make sure they are decent and want to see you." Her smile somehow managed to soften the implication that he was an interloper or trying to disturb their privacy under false pretenses. She pressed some buttons, put the phone to her ear. "Mind you, I think only Mr. Ormson is in. Ms. Smith—" She stopped abruptly and her voice changed to the mad cheerfulness that people reserve for barely awakened males and slightly dangerous dogs, "Oh, hi, Mr. Ormson! Your friend, Mr.—" a pleading look at Rafiel.

"Trall."

"Mr. Trall is here. He would like to see you. Is it okay if I send him up?"

A series of rasps answered her and she said, "All righty, then. I'll send him up." And then, in her normal voice, to Rafiel. "He says to go on up. You know where the room is, I presume?"

"Oh, yes. I've been there before," Rafiel said. *Not that it would surprise anyone at the station to hear this. They would think that, at one stroke—so to put it—both my aloofness to my dates and my odd changes of clothes midday are explained.* The idea amused him, but it still made him blush, which he was fairly sure made him look very guilty.

He more or less ran up the stairs, all the way to the top floor, where he knocked lightly on Tom's door. There was the sound of steps approaching the door, and then a disheveled, unshaven Tom, in his underwear—and had Kyrie bought him jockey shorts with little dragons on them? Either that or Tom's sense of humor was worse than Rafiel had anticipated—holding a flailing kitten in one hand, opened the door.

"Hi," Rafiel said, walking in. "Sorry to disturb you. I can see I woke you."

"'Sokay," Tom mumbled, followed by something that might have been "Never mind." He closed the door and set the orange furball gently on the floor. "'Scuse me a moment?"

Rafiel nodded and Tom ducked into the bathroom and closed the door. Rafiel heard flushing and the shower running, then splashing of water. In what seemed like less than three minutes—spent mostly in pulling Not Dinner off Rafiel's pants, which he seemed to believe were the climbing part of a jungle gym—Tom opened the door again and emerged, wrapped in a white robe, with his hair in a towel.

"Nice turban," Rafiel said.

Tom glowered in response. He had shaving things out on the marble-topped vanity. A spray-on shaving cream can, and one of those razors that seemed to come with an ever-increasing number of blades. Even so, it all looked very Tom-like and unnecessarily difficult to Rafiel who, knowing Tom, was only surprised he didn't shave with a straight razor and use a brush to apply lather to his face. "I use an electric razor," he blurted out.

Tom, in the process of swathing his face in shaving cream, so that he looked like a turbaned Santa Claus, gave Rafiel a questioning look, then shrugged. "You're light-haired," he said, speaking in a weirdly stilted manner, almost not moving his lips—probably to avoid getting shaving cream in his mouth. He rinsed his hands. "To get my beard properly shaved, I need to grind the electric razor into my skin, and then I end up with burns. Besides," he shrugged, "when I started shaving, I was homeless. They have hand razors in those little kits shelters give away as charity. Electric razors not so much."

The idea that Tom had been homeless for years seemed insane, Rafiel thought, as Tom shaved a strip of cream off his face, rinsed the razor and looked at him. He had unearthly blue eyes, very intense in color. They looked like nothing so much as the blue on the type of pioneer enamelware often sold at touristy shops. It was disturbing to find himself under scrutiny by those sharp, bright eyes.

"Talk," Tom said.

"Hey, I'm supposed to say that," Rafiel said. "I'm the policeman."

He sat down on the one loveseat from which he had an unimpeded view of the bathroom. Tom, who had shaved another strip of cream and beard, shrugged. "If you didn't have something to talk about you wouldn't be here waking me."

"Well," Rafiel said. "I do need to talk to someone and you and Kyrie"—he shrugged—"are practically the only friends I have. At least the only friends I have that I'm not related to. And that I can . . . you know . . . be frank with."

"Right."

"But it's not like I know anything. It's more like I need to figure things out." Not Dinner, having ascended the heights of Rafiel's lap, was climbing under Rafiel's shirt. "What's he—?"

"Notty does that," Tom said, in a resigned tone. "Crawl under your clothes, I mean. He's a baby. Cold."

"I suppose," Rafiel said, though frankly, if he was going to have a feline getting in his clothes, he'd much rather—by far—it were Kyrie. "All right. Well, these are my suspicions." He proceeded to lay out the case against Lei Lani, such as he could make it out. Her half-truths, her exaggerations. As he was talking, the phone rang.

"Boss?" McKnight's voice.

"Yes?"

"That woman, Lei Lani?"

"Yes?"

"She doesn't seem to have graduated from the University of Hawaii. The aquarium there never heard of her, either."

"I see," Rafiel said. "Do a full records search, would you?" he said and hung up before McKnight could protest. He related the knowledge to Tom, who raised his eyebrows.

"But the fact she didn't attend the University of Hawaii," Tom said, as the blade went swish-swish across his face, rinse-rinse under the faucet, and then swish against his face again, "doesn't mean that she is a shark shifter."

"No," Rafiel said. "And that's what's making me uncomfortable. Look . . . I wish I could smell her out, but I can't. John Wagner says that aquatic shifters have pheromones you can only detect in water, which makes sense, of course, except that it makes it really hard to figure out who they are."

"Yeah," Tom said, rinsing the razor and setting it aside and then rinsing his face and drying it. He removed the towel from his hair, and started brushing the hair out vigorously. "The thing is—"

"The thing is that she might just have been taking boyfriends there, and when her boyfriends were found dead in the aquarium, she panicked and decided to put the guilt on someone else. It's entirely possible," he said, "that someone else is a shifter—shark or otherwise, and responsible for getting the victims in the tank once Ms. Lani is done with them. For all I know, the Japanese spider crab shifter—if there really is one—shoves people in the tank because he disapproves of fornication in the aquarium."

"Wouldn't the Japanese spider crab have done that before?" Tom said. "I mean, from what you said, he's been at the aquarium for years, right?"

"But we don't know that Ms. Lani or someone like her has been having fun at the aquarium for that long," Rafiel said. "This could be a response to something perceived as a new wave of immorality."

"I guess," Tom said nodding. "Which, of course, leaves us up a creek without a paddle, because we can't prove that Lei Lani is a shifter. And even if we could, how could we prove that she's the one getting them in the shark tank?" He crossed the room to where his tote bag was open on the floor, and retrieved underwear, jeans and a red T-shirt, then retreated with them all to the bathroom, closing the door till the barest crack remained open to allow the sound through. "I mean, the victims are dead. They can't exactly tell us what went on."

"The problem," Rafiel said, as Notty climbed the rest of the way inside his shirt and installed himself on his shoulder, under his shirt, his little orange fuzzy head protruding from Rafiel's collar and making a sound reminiscent of a badly tuned diesel engine, "is that if shifters weren't a secret, and I could tell my medical examiner what to look for, I'm sure they could find traces of whatever happened, maybe enough to tell us if we're looking for a crab shifter, a shark shifter or none of the above."

"Unless your medical examiner is a shifter himself," Tom said, emerging from the bathroom, and tying his hair back. "I wouldn't recommend it. If you're lucky, he'll recommend a psychiatric evaluation. If you're not, he might believe you."

Rafiel sighed. "I know. But we still have to figure out something."

"Yes," Tom said. "Yes, we do." He turned around to face Rafiel and smiled a little. "Nice second head, by the way."

Rafiel petted Notty's head protruding from his shirt. "Yeah, I think it will make me a veritable chick magnet."

"Not advisable. Notty would eat the chicks."

"Probably. But you know two heads . . ."

"Think better than one. Yes. Which reminds me . . . Could you . . . I mean, you have the keys to the aquarium, right? I mean, that's how you took Kyrie there before?"

Rafiel nodded.

"Well, then I think I might have an idea. We'll need to go by my house but I think there's something we can do."

Kyrie's head was whirling. Mr. Lung had believed her, when she said that Tom would not kill himself, provided it wasn't his independence that had been compromised. And he'd told her to let Conan Lung—whom he assured her was no relation, except in the way that all dragon shifters were supposed to be descended from the very first dragon—in on whatever the plan was. He promised that so long as Conan was with them, or where he could see them if they got in trouble, help would be instantaneous. So now, the question was—how to trap Dire?

And did she want to entrap him? Did she truly want to kill him? Despite everything that she'd told the owner of the Three Luck Dragon, she felt squeamish at the thought. After all, he hadn't tried to kill her. If that was what he wanted to do, he would have done it long ago. He'd pursued her, and tried to scare her and hurt her, but he had not actually sought to kill her.

Should she kill someone who wasn't trying to kill her? To say that he was a sadist—which, of course, he was—and was trying to terrorize her and hurt her just didn't seem enough reason to kill him. As she drove into the parking lot of The George and noted Rafiel's car parked where he normally parked when he was visiting, she sighed. It stretched the definition of self-defense to kill someone merely because they were psychopaths.

Oh, she was quite sure that Dire had killed plenty of people in his time. Well . . . she was almost sure he had killed Summer, the journalist. But horrible as that crime was, it was almost sure that he had done it to protect them. To keep them secret. Yes, of course it could be argued that by keeping their secret, he kept his own. But he could just as easily have killed them, and he hadn't. She opened the door of the car and got out onto the cool parking lot almost deserted in the after-lunch lull.

"Hello, Kitten Girl," a familiar voice said.

She spun around to see Dante Dire—in human aspect, wearing a well-tailored black suit, standing just steps from her. Her stomach knotted. Her heart sped up. She tasted bile at the back of her throat. He could read thoughts. Had he been reading her thoughts the last few minutes?

If so, he seemed in a strangely good mood. "I want you to know I've solved all our problems," he said, grinning at her. "I want you to know you don't have to worry anymore."

Our problems? What can he mean?

He laughed at what was, doubtlessly, her very confused expression. "Ah, I see you don't know. Well . . . it's like this. You know I came here to decide on who had killed a great deal of young ones, right? I was to do preliminary investigations, and then tell the council what I had found and wait for their decision. They'd probably send three or four more to verify my conclusions, and you know . . ." He put his hand in his pocket and made a sound of jingling, probably with change. "The truth is if they probed the problem, they would find that it was of course you and your friends . . . If it were just your friends, I wouldn't mind denouncing them. I don't know why the daddy dragon has an interest in Dragon Boy, but I'm sure—Dragon Boy not being one of his own nestlings, see?—that if push came to shove, he would let Dragon Boy go. And I could fulfill my mission and go back to my normal life."

As he spoke he approached her, and somehow his voice became lower and more seductive. "And let me tell you, my normal life is the sort of life anyone would dream of. I have my own private plane. I have bank accounts in every country. I've lived long enough to allow me to accumulate more money than I know what to do with. When I arrive somewhere, even if I arrive naked," he flashed her a smile, "I can always be properly attired and in a brand-new car within an hour."

He came very close, until his face was almost touching hers, and his voice descended till it was just a purr. "You can share that life with me, Kitten Girl. I can show you the world and everything beyond. Come on. You were made for better things than this dinky little diner."

Kyrie knew that he was doing something to her mind, even as he spoke, in that low seductive voice. She could feel her mind not so much changing as being changed for her. All of a sudden, as if she were looking through Dante Dire's eyes, the diner did look small and dinky—almost decayed, in fact, though they'd remodeled it extensively when they'd taken over three months ago.

Why do I want to do this? Is this really what I want to do with my life, serve hash and soup to students and people who are making barely more than minimum wage? Is this really how I want to spend every day? All of a sudden the place where she had at last felt she belonged seemed tacky—a squat of concrete, a glare of neon. And Tom, who was like the other half of her heart, seemed like a boring young man with curiously foreshortened ambition. All he wanted to do was take cooking classes and spend his life incrementally improving food and service at The George until it was the best diner in Colorado. In his free time, he did accounts or researched recipes. The most exciting thing they'd done in the last three months was take a weekend off and go to Denver to visit the *Titanic* exhibit at the Natural History Museum. Truth be told, Tom was a very boring man. And her life with him would be a very boring life.

In her mind's eye the years with Tom stretched endlessly, never too flush with money and forever living on the outside of all fashionable or even exotic entertainment. Nothing would ever happen, nothing ever break the routine.

"That's it," Dire said, softly, his face so close she could feel his warm breath on her skin. "That's exactly it. He'll kill you with boredom, Kitten Girl. He'll be the death of you.

"Or . . . you could come with me," he said. Through her mind there flashed, in succession, images of her in various designer clothes, images of her on a Mediterranean beach. Images of her eating in fine restaurants and taking airplanes. By Dire's side. And in her mind, for whatever reason, she was madly in love with Dire.

Kyrie didn't love Dire. In fact, she couldn't imagine being in love with any psychopath. She shook her head. "You're in my mind," she said, speaking through her clenched teeth, against the waves of love and attraction washing through her brain. "And you weren't invited."

He chuckled softly, in amusement. She raised her knee and hit him between the legs. Hard. The images vanished from her head. Before he could recover, before he could shift, before he could climb into her mind again, she ran, like mad, into the diner. She knew it wouldn't afford her much protection—or at least she thought it wouldn't—but she didn't care. She wanted away from that cold, dark mind.

She ran into the diner through the back door, and ran down the hallway into the diner itself. Anthony, who was peeling potatoes, turned around to give her a very puzzled look.

"I'm sorry," Kyrie said, ducking behind the counter. "I thought you'd need me. That I was away too long."

"No, you're fine. As you see, we don't have that many tables occupied."

"Yeah, I see," Kyrie said, as she put the apron on.

"Oh, Keith came in," Anthony said. "He says he can use the cash."

"Oh good," Kyrie said.

Anthony chopped the potatoes into sticks. "Well, with him here, rush hour wasn't really a problem. And Conan is getting better, despite that arm."

"Yeah. He's fairly smart," Kyrie said. Anthony said something about Conan singing really well, too, but Kyrie wasn't thinking of that. She was thinking of Dire, out in the parking lot. She didn't want to kill him. Not if she could help it. But she wasn't sure she could.

In Rafiel's car, Tom called Kyrie on the cell phone. Or rather he called The George, but it was she who answered, as he expected.

"Hi, Kyrie," he said.

She seemed faintly surprised and oddly suspicious. "Who is this?"

Had he slept such irregular hours that he still had sleep-voice? He didn't think so, but he cleared his throat all the same and said, "Me," with, he realized afterwards, the kind of confidence only a boyfriend would have in being recognized from such a syllable.

It seemed to work. Or at least she said, "Oh. I didn't expect you to be awake." She took a deep breath. "You know, *he* has impersonated Rafiel before . . ."

Tom took a look at Rafiel who was driving while tapping his fingers on the steering wheel in rhythm with some very strange song about never growing old. "Yeah. But only over the phone."

"We are talking over the phone!" Kyrie said, as if he'd taken leave of his senses.

"Oh . . . you mean . . ." Tom took a deep breath. "Well, I'm not going to ask you to go anywhere or anything, just wanted to know if Anthony is okay staying till six or so? Because it will be till then before I come back."

"All right," Kyrie said. "A long shift but . . . he's been pulling those."

It seemed very strange to Tom that she didn't ask him why or where he was going, or even what he was intending to do. It wasn't that Kyrie was overly inquisitive or determined to have him live in her pocket. It wasn't even that she demanded to know where he was at all times. But when he called to tell her he was going to be late for something, she asked why. Normal human curiosity. He thought of what Kyrie had said about Dire. "He has impersonated Rafiel before." But surely Dire wouldn't say that about himself if he was impersonating Kyrie. Besides, Tom remembered the description Kyrie had given of how Rafiel sounded over the phone—all breath, no voice . . . Kyrie didn't sound that way. And, on yet the other paw, Kyrie sounded exactly like she did when she was harassed and shorthanded.

"I'm sorry if I am putting you in a bind," he said. He'd discovered nine-tenths of a good relationship was preemptive apologizing even if you didn't know—sometimes he would say particularly if you didn't know—what you had done wrong. He'd found that his social skills, blunted by looking out only for himself for much too long, sometimes missed fine points of the effects his actions might have on Kyrie.

"You're not," Kyrie said. "I'll manage. Anthony was planning on staying at least that long, and Keith has come in. We're okay."

"Oh. I'm just . . . I'm with Rafiel. I'm helping him run an errand."

"All right. Call if you're going to be later than six. Or I'll worry."

"Right," Tom said, and hung up.

Rafiel, pulling into the parking lot of the aquarium, gave Tom a quizzical glance. Perhaps it was just Tom's expression—there was more amusement than there should have been. "She upset about you staying out late?"

Tom did his best to glare at Rafiel. He was fairly sure this was wasted effort. All his efforts to glare at the policeman before—glare him into silence; glare him into being sensible—had met with chuckles. This time was no exception. Tom shook his head. "If you're going to tell me 'better me than you,' even I am not stupid enough to buy that."

"Uh . . . no, dude. I'd rather it were me, but I didn't know she kept the shackles quite that tight."

"She doesn't." Tom frowned. He tried to think of how to explain what had disturbed him about the call. While he thought, Rafiel drove around the aquarium to the back, the overflow parking lot. They were all empty, but Tom imagined that the front parking lot, visible from Ocean and Congregation, was not the best choice for stealthy work. And they must be stealthy. Or at least not stupidly obvious. "It's . . ." He tried to figure out how to explain it. "It's more that she didn't seem her normal self."

"Oh?" Rafiel said, and for once there was no smirk behind his expression. "Do you think something is wrong?"

"It's quite possible," Tom said. "But she's at the diner, so . . ."

"So she's either safe, or there's nothing you can do to make her so."

"Yeah," Tom said. He didn't like it, but it was the truth. "If it's something that can happen in front of a whole bunch of people, my being there won't stop it."

They got out of the car and Rafiel led them to a side door, where, after trying a variety of keys, he found one that clicked the door open. Rafiel was carrying the cardboard box they'd gotten from Tom and Kyrie's house. It contained a surveillance system that Tom had been meaning to install around the diner.

"I must need to get my head examined," Rafiel said, as they stepped into the warmer, dark interior of the aquarium. "This is so many levels of illegal."

"Stealthy," Tom said. "Many levels of stealthy. We must make it stealthy. I mean . . . we can't solve this in the open. I mean, if you wanted to, what could you tell your assistant, what's his name? McQueen?"

"McKnight." Rafiel said with an odd sort of groan.

"What are you going to tell McKnight? That you smelled something funny while you were a lion? They'd have you committed. So . . . we have to do things . . . in creative ways."

"Right," Rafiel said. He gave the impression of speaking through clenched teeth. "Creative. Right."

Rafiel took them past banks of gurgling aquariums filled with fish. "Who feeds the fishies?" Tom asked. "Or do they eat each other or something?" He squinted at the label on the nearest tank, which said piranhas. The sound track of some nature program he must have watched, and forgotten, in childhood, ran through his head. Something about piranhas skeletonizing a cow in a matter of minutes. Tom had never been able to understand what a cow would be doing in the water, and he very much hoped that no one at the aquarium dropped a mooing heifer into the tank.

Rafiel waved a hand dismissively. "People can come in and feed them," he said. "That's not an issue. We only sealed the room with the sharks, but I understand it's open and McKnight comes in, when needed for personnel to clean the tank and feed the sharks, then he seals the room again." He looked over his shoulder. "At least that's the plan. I don't think it's happened yet."

He stopped outside a sealed door, and took out something very much like an exacto knife, with which he pulled—deftly—the police seal off the door and the handle. "I'm going to hell," he said under his breath.

"Well," Tom said. "If you're a believer, you know, it's a good question whether our kind has normal souls or if—"

"Tom, that isn't helpful."

"Well, I'm not a believer, myself, but it's a fascinating idea. Are we judged by the divinity of humans, or by some . . . you know, animal god?"

Rafiel pulled the door open. "Not right now it isn't a fascinating idea. I'm facing the problem of living with my guilt about breaking police regulations. I don't even want to *think* of anything else."

They were in the big dim room that Tom had heard described several times, but never seen till now. Walls and ceilings had been sculpted to look like the inside of a cave, stalactites and stalagmites delineating paths. Though, Tom thought, it was expecting rather too much of suspension of disbelief to think that the stalagmites had formed benches by natural processes. And the speckled-cement stairs with their metal railings, leading up to an observation platform— probably nine by nine feet wide—also with metal railings and planters with curiously plastic-looking flowers, just about killed that natural structure feel.

Rafiel went up to the platform and looked around nervously. He looked as if he expected doom to fall at any moment. Like . . . he thought his superiors would be psychically warned or something. And Tom, who'd been a juvenile delinquent and delighted in breaking rules long before he'd known he was a shifter, could only smile at him.

"It's not funny," Rafiel said. "I could be fired if anyone finds out about this." He clutched the grey box of surveillance equipment against his chest, as though it were a shield of righteousness. "Good lord, I could be *arrested*."

Tom didn't realize he was about to cackle till the sound bubbled out of his lips despite his best efforts. "Sorry, sorry," he said, to Rafiel's glare. "It's just I was thinking . . . we could be killed. We could be discovered as shifters—and ultimately killed—and you're worrying about being arrested. I mean . . . if they came for you, what's to stop you taking off in lion form?"

"What? Other than losing my identity, my family, everything I've worked for?"

Tom sobered up. He too could leave. At any moment, he could just go. It was easy. Take to the wing, and forget Kyrie and The George, and Keith and Rafiel and Anthony and Notty. No. What good was it to save yourself by losing everything that was important to you?

"Exactly," Rafiel said, softly, having read Tom's expressions without need for words. He shrugged. "But your point is taken too. In the maze of dangers we face, risking being arrested is not so very bad. And then I doubt we will be arrested, or even found out. At least with a bit of luck." He looked above himself, then around at the walls of the fake cave. "But we forgot something, Tom. Neither of us is an electrician. How are we going to put these up?" He waved the package containing two cameras and a mess of electrical stuff.

Tom grinned. "Well . . . you know . . ."

"Oh, don't tell me you used to wire cameras in people's houses while you were homeless. There are things I don't want to know."

This time Tom's gurgle of laughter poured out, without his ability to control it. "No. But when we had The George remodeled, the electrician didn't have an assistant. Nice man, but . . . you know, semi-retired. Did it cheap. One of Anthony's acquaintances."

"And?"

"Well, he needed help. Holding this, twisting that. Third hand kind of stuff. And I didn't have anything better to do. I was recovering from . . . near death. And he liked to talk . . . Seventies, you know, and no one wants to listen to him most of the time."

"So he taught you electrical stuff?"

"A bit. Jackleg stuff," Tom said. He brought out the little set of tools he'd slipped into the pocket of his jacket earlier, and grinned as Rafiel looked surprised. Just now and then he liked to upstage Mr. Unflappable Trall and be better prepared. He looked up and pointed to a light. "I think we'll tap that light," he said. "It's close enough to the stalactite and the plastic plants, that we can sort of run the wire behind and no one will know."

Rafiel looked at the light in turn. "Any idea how you'll reach it?"

"Oh, sure," Tom said. "I stand on the railing."

"Uh . . . I see. And if you fall?"

"I won't," Tom said.

"Really?"

"No. Because you're going to hold my ankles."

Rafiel looked up at Tom, who'd propped himself up, with a foot on either of the intersecting metal railings. He looked doubtfully down at the railings, which he wasn't even sure should be able to support that weight, then up again at Tom, who was fiddling with the light cover, and doing something underneath. After a while, Tom trailed a wire down, and pulled it, so it followed, kind of behind one of the cement stalactites that dropped down from the ceiling and around the edge of the railing.

"How much wire do you have?" Rafiel said.

"Enough," Tom said. "Right. I'm going to jump down now."

"Not while I'm holding you," Rafiel said, and stepped back.

Tom's feet wobbled on the railing, he started tilting forward. Rafiel reached up. Grabbed his wrist. Pulled. Something at the back of his mind said it was better for them to fall on the platform than on the tank. They toppled to the floor. Rafiel hit his elbow and his head, and gathered himself up. "Are you all right?" he asked Tom who had fallen in a heap, and was pale and shivering.

"Yeah," he said. "Yeah. Only . . ." He shook his head and scrambled to his knees and, on his knees, across the platform, to the planter, the box was tilted up against. Fishing in the box, he brought out the camera, which was about the diameter of a dime, and about as thick. He stuck it to one of the planters, well hidden in the foliage, the wire behind it. Then, as he seemed to make sure that the camera lens was unobstructed, he said, "When I was little, we had goldfish. At least, I wanted a pet, but you know, we lived in a condo. No place for pets, really, so my dad got me a bowl with goldfish. He also started calling them Schröedinger fish, because—well, I wasn't very interested and it wasn't in my room—it was in this passage between my room and the walk-in closet, and I didn't always remember to feed them. So Dad said every time we checked on them, it was not sure if they were alive or dead till we actually saw them. I remember this one time I forgot to feed them for like"—he narrowed his eyes with thought—"five days? When I came back to feed them, they all congregated in one spot, you know, clearly waiting for food.

"The sharks looked like that," he said and, for the first time, looked up to meet Rafiel's gaze. "Just like that. As if they were pet fish, used to being fed by people, you know?"

Rafiel sighed. "I'd say they are. I just wish we knew by whom."

"Well . . ." Tom said, and gestured towards the camera. "That will tell us, right?"

"Yeah," Rafiel said. "If they come in, of course. I mean, what with . . . you know . . ." He shrugged. "The room is sealed. Or will be again, once we leave. If it's a casual thing, if she just brings her boyfriends in, and someone . . . like the crab shifter, doesn't like it . . ."

"But if it's not," Tom said, "then we'll get it. The camera is motion-activated and it connects to my laptop, which is at the bed-and-breakfast. It will sound an alarm . . ." He gave an impish smile. "At least as soon as I install the program."

"Right," Rafiel said, but the idea didn't please him. There had to be another way around it, some other way to make things work. He didn't like the idea of just sitting down and waiting for some poor sap to be thrown in the shark tank. Not the least of which, because the poor sap would then be doomed. "So, why did you think you needed a surveillance system for The George?"

Tom stood up and dusted off the knees of his pants, as if this would fix the dust all over his clothes from having fallen headlong onto the observation platform. "I thought, you know, with the stuff that was happening at the back before . . . murder and all . . ." He shrugged. "I thought if a bunch of shifters were coming to the place, called by pheromones, we'd do as well to have early warning and proof if any of them had . . . control issues."

Rafiel, raising his eyebrows, reasoned that his friend trusted other shifters about as much as he did. They climbed down the stairs. Rafiel opened the door to the shark room, waited till Tom went by, then sealed the door again, initialing it once more, and putting in the date and time on the destroyed seal. "I'm going to hell." This time Tom didn't seem disposed to argue.

They walked quietly side by side along the deserted hallways, past the concrete trunk filled with plaster coins and Rafiel wondered if even very small children were fooled by it. He didn't remember ever being small enough to fall for that kind of fakery.

And then he wondered what they were going to do with the camera. While it had seemed like a good idea to set the camera in place, he now wondered how sane it was. Tom had been all enthusiastic about it, but it was probably just his happiness at getting to wire something. "Hey," he said, softly. "The other camera? Where do you intend to put it?"

Tom looked surprised. "Nowhere, really, I don't—"

He shut up abruptly, and Rafiel realized he had heard a sound, just before Tom stopped talking. Something like a soft footstep to their right. They were at the top of the stairs that led down to the aquarium with crabs and to the restaurant. For a second, he thought that it would be the crab shifter, emerging from his aquarium. Perhaps they could interrogate him.

But the person who came walking out of the shadows was Dante Dire—lank hair falling over his dark eyes, and his dark eyes sparkling with fury. "What are you doing here?" he asked.

Rafiel drew himself up and tried to hide the quiver of fear that ran through him on seeing the creature. Because he was not a fool, he remembered—all too well—that this creature could reach into his mind and change his thoughts; the idea paralyzed him. He could have endured any form or amount of physical torture, but the idea that someone—something—could change what he thought and how he felt . . . that he could not stand. "It would be better to ask what you are doing here," he said, keeping his voice steady. He was aware of Tom's having done something—he didn't know what. But Tom had been behind him as they walked, still in the shadows, Rafiel presumed, and now when Tom stepped forward there was nothing in his hands. He'd put the camera box down somewhere. And immediately Rafiel made himself stop thinking about the camera, and think only that they were there to gather evidence against the murderer who'd been throwing people into the shark tank. He put that thought in front, as it were, and hid all the rest—even his fear—behind it.

Dire's face hardened. "You have no business," he said, "trying to entrap innocent shifters."

"Innocent," Tom said, calling attention away from Rafiel—and presumably his thoughts. Rafiel felt as though something had been pressing against his thoughts, and the pressure now lifted, leaving him free to think clearly for a change. "Why do you think we're trying to entrap any shifters, innocent or otherwise?"

Dante Dire straightened up and stared, right over Rafiel's shoulder, at Tom. "Ah! You think I'm stupid and don't read the paper? I do. And the paper says there have been murders in this place.

And then, and then, I see you here, skulking, looking for clues. His mind," he pointed at Rafiel, "makes it clear enough he's looking for clues against someone he thinks is a shifter." He crossed his arms on his chest. "It's you or me, pretty Kitten Boy. We're going to have this out now. The way I told it to the girl, I need to kill someone who can plausibly be accused of having killed the young shifters. You will do as well as any."

Rafiel felt as though his heart had skipped in his chest. He felt fear surging through his veins, demanding loudly that he shift. "I have to investigate," he said. "I have to. It's my job."

"Bah. A job paid for ephemerals. A job in which you obey ephemerals. A job"—he spat out the word as if it were poison—"where you demean your nature for money. Money is easy, Kitten Boy, when you live almost forever. As you'd already have figured out, if you were made of stronger stuff. But you're not, and now you'll die for it." He glared at Rafiel. "Are you going to shift, or do I kill you as you are?"

And not all the forces in the hell he claimed awaited him could have kept Rafiel from shifting.

Tom felt as if he'd frozen in place. He'd thrown the box with the remaining camera behind some plastic bushes at the edge. He hoped he'd managed it before Dire saw it. He must have managed it, because Dire hadn't said anything about the box, just challenged their right to be there and announced that he was planning to kill Rafiel.

Stunned at the idea, Tom started to speak, but nothing came out of his mouth. It seemed to him that this was a duel. At least Dire had challenged Rafiel to a duel, challenged him to shift. If the intent were only to kill Rafiel, why not kill him as a human, without bothering with the lion form?

Except, of course, that Dire was a sadist. And the lion would, of course, provide him with a better fight, he thought, as lion and dire wolf stood facing each other, in this incongruous setting—tanks bubbled on either side, fish swam looking incuriously onto the scene. And Tom retreated until his back was against the concrete wall, while his brain worked feverishly.

His first thought—that Dire was doing this to gratify his sadistic impulses—was confirmed when, instead of going for the jugular, the huge prehistoric beast jumped at Rafiel and grabbed him by the scruff, much as a mother cat grabbing a baby. Only, it then lifted him off the ground and shook him, and threw him, sending him sprawling against one of the tanks.

For a moment, Tom, heart thumping at his throat, thought that Rafiel was already dead—that the dire wolf had broken his neck with that shake and toss. He heard something like a hiss come out of his mouth, and he realized what was about to happen. As he pulled off his shirt and dropped his pants—barely ahead of the process already twisting his limbs and covering his skin in green scales—he thought that he didn't want to fight the dire wolf. As ill-matched as Rafiel was against Dire, Tom was no better. He remembered the fight in the parking lot. He remembered that the dire wolf had almost killed him then. Why should now be any different?

But Rafiel was the closest thing he had to a best friend. If Tom stood by and watched the dire wolf finish Rafiel off in order to blame him for the deaths of hundreds of newborn shifters, just a few months ago, Tom would never be able to live with himself. Nor—he thought, ruefully, as his body contorted, in painful acrobatics, bending and twisting in a way it wasn't meant to, and as wings extruded from his back—would Kyrie want to live with him.

Dire was concentrating on Rafiel and hadn't seemed to notice Tom's shift, yet. Dire had swung the lion again, this time against the piranha tank. Tom flung himself into the fight, blindly. In the tight confines of the aquarium building, flying was no advantage, but he flung himself, aided by his wings, at the dire wolf and bit deep into what he could grab, which happened to be an ear, while letting out an ear-splitting hiss-roar that translated all his anger and frustration at this unreasonable ancient creature.

The dire wolf looked shocked—he turned a bloodied muzzle towards Tom, his eyes opened to their utmost in complete surprise. And Tom, instinct-driven, slashed his paw across the face, claws raking the eyes. Blood spurted. The dire wolf screamed. And the part of Tom that remained very much human was aware that this was a momentary advantage. The creature would recover. Eventually it would regrow its eyes. Until then, it might very well be able to look through their eyes. He couldn't allow it time to recover.

Leaping across the room, he grabbed Rafiel by the scruff even as Rafiel, dizzy and battle-mad, tried to grab at him. But grabbing the scruff seemed to paralyze him, and Tom—fairly sure that in normal circumstances he'd have a hard time lifting Rafiel and trying to hold as gently as possible so he didn't wound Rafiel more—ran down the stairs with his friend held between his teeth.

Down the stairs and at a run through the aquarium—was that a Japanese man hiding in the shadows? and had he winked at Tom?—and turning sharply left, down a narrow corridor between tanks and . . .

Tom hit the exterior door with his full body weight. As he hit, he thought Dire might have locked it, but the door was already opening, letting them out into the cold air, where Tom dropped Rafiel and concentrated on changing. The dragon argued that Rafiel would make a really good protein snack, but Tom forced his limbs to shift, decontort. Before he could fully form words, he said, "Now, Rafiel, shift." The words came out half roar, half hiss, with only the barest vocalization behind them. And then Tom's eyes cleared and he realized Rafiel was already human, trying to walk to the car on a leg that bent the wrong way.

"Your keys?" Tom said.

Rafiel looked at him, his eyes full of pain, but reached for a bracelet at his wrist—metal but of the sort of links that stretched, so that it stayed with him through his shifts. He pulled the key and handed it to Tom, who opened the car, climbed in, and flung the passenger door open, just in time for Rafiel to climb in. He saw Dire's car parked next to them.

"Drive, drive, drive," Rafiel said. And Tom was driving, as fast as he knew how, down the still-half-iced streets, breathing deeply, telling himself that residual panic didn't justify shifting, that he would not—could not—shift. He tasted Rafiel's blood in his mouth, from the wounds the dire wolf had made at the back of Rafiel's neck, and it didn't help him keep control. Not at all.

It was a while—and Tom had no clue where he was, having driven more or less blindly—before Rafiel said, softly, "Thank you."

"What?" Tom asked, hearing his own voice ill-humored and combative. "Why?"

"Well . . . you . . . saved my life."

"As opposed to just letting you die? What do you think I am?"

"Brave. I know that creature scares the living daylights out of me. I don't know if I'd be able to make myself intervene in a fight between him and you."

"Don't worry about it," Tom said, hoping his dismissive tone would stop the conversation. He'd never learned to take compliments, and he wasn't ready for gratitude for doing what he had to do—what was clearly required of him as a human being. He just wanted to get back to the bed-and-breakfast and have a shower and—

"Damn," he said.

"What?"

"I left my boots in the aquarium."

Rafiel laughed. It was weak laughter. Not so much amusement, as a reflex of relief. He remembered Tom, once, running naked down the street, save for his all-prized jacket and his boots.

"It's not funny," Tom said.

"Yes, it is. You have an unnatural attachment to those boots."

"They're mine, and I like them," Tom said. Still driving like a maniac, he turned to glower at Rafiel. "I haven't had many things in my life that I could hold onto, you know? Things that were mine, I mean."

"Yes, but why in the name of all that's holy would the things you want to hold onto be items of apparel when you are a shifter?" Rafiel asked, smiling.

Tom shrugged. "It was all I had before settling down. All I had were the clothes on my back."

"Right. Well, it's unlikely the creature knows how attached you are to your boots, so you'll probably be safe," he said. "Meaning he won't piss in them. And if he does, I'll buy you new boots."

"Thank you. I like the ones I have."

"Unnatural," Rafiel said. "But I'm not going back to get them. Not even for you, my friend."

"Ah, look, the dire wolf will probably be gone and besides we can't leave them behind. Someone will go to the aquarium. Someone will know we broke in."

Rafiel looked at him, disbelieving. "You have to be joking."

"No, I'm not. It's my boots, and they'll figure out they're mine, and next thing you know, they'll be talking about my pushing people into the shark tank or something."

Rafiel groaned, seeing what he meant. "Oh okay, fine. But if the car is still there, I'm not going in. I'm just not. And I suspect we left blood all over the floor and isn't that enough to show I was there? What do the boots matter? I'll just have to try to divert any investigation that—"

"Rafiel, you were shifted. They'll find lion's blood." He gave Rafiel a sideways look. "On the other hand, unless I'm wrong, you also left your cell phone and your clothes and your official identification there. So you'll have to have a really good story to explain having been in there . . ."

"I could tell them I lost them this morning, when I was there with Lei."

"What? And your clothes? Shredded as if you'd burst out of them?"

Rafiel groaned and heard himself swearing softly. "Fine, we'll go back. I'm trying to figure out how the day could get any worse."

Which was a stupid thing to say, he realized, as he heard the siren behind him, and saw the flashing lights in the rear view mirror. "Don't worry," he told Tom, as Tom smashed his foot on the gas. "I'm a policeman."

"What, naked, in the car, with another man, in public? How much authority will you have, Officer Trall?"

"They . . . uh." Naked in public was the problem. They'd bring him up on an indecency charge so fast. He looked back. "We could get dressed."

"Fast enough? Before he comes up to the window?"

It might have been possible if they were being followed by a police car. The cop would have had to park way behind them, and then approach them carefully. But Rafiel could see that there was a motorcycle cop in hot pursuit. "We can't outrun it. He probably already has my license plate and—"

"Right," Tom said. "There's only one thing to do. But afterwards, you have to get me a burger. No. A dozen of them."

"Sure thing," Rafiel said, not absolutely sure what Tom meant to do and not caring either. "I have money under the seat, with the clothes. We don't even have to wait till we get my wallet." At this point, anything Tom could do to get them out of this fix was worth it.

"Right." Tom said. "But you have to drive. Can you drive?"

"Sure. I'll use my left foot."

Tom pulled over and stopped. Something to the way he clenched the wheel, the way his nails seemed to elongate slowly, the way his bone structure appeared to change, made Rafiel want to scream, *Don't shift in my car.* But when Tom was already this much on edge, all the scream would do was cause him to shift immediately. He bit his tongue and held his breath.

Tom rolled down the window, then grasped the handle. His voice all hissy and slurpy, as if his dental structure had already shifted, he said, "The moment I get out, drive. Just drive straight. I'll catch up."

"Tom . . . don't—" He was going to tell him not to eat the man, but didn't have time.

There was a voice from the open window. "Sir, you were doing . . . What—"

Tom opened the door and leapt out, while shifting—so that the effect was rather like a kernel of corn popping—bursting and exploding into a massive, much larger form, as it escaped the confines of its skin.

There was a strangled scream from the policeman, and Rafiel switched seats and closed the door and drove straight ahead. He was on Fairfax, he realized. The world's longest, straight thoroughfare. It was listed in the *Guinness Book of World Records* as such. He hoped it was long enough to allow Rafiel to still be on it whenever Tom caught up.

"Don't eat him," Rafiel yelled and rolled up the window, as he drove. He didn't know if Tom had heard him.

Perhaps ten blocks ahead, as Rafiel entered a definitely seedy area of abandoned warehouses and graffitied overpasses, he saw a shadow fall over the car. A shadow such as if a really large dragon body had flown overhead. And then, in front of a warehouse, Tom stood, extending his thumb in the universal gesture of the hitchhiker.

Rafiel stopped and unlocked the door. As Tom got in, he looked for signs of blood around his mouth or something. Trying to keep it light, he said, "You know, hitchhiking naked is a felony. And we don't even go into what eating a policeman might be. The force disapproves of it."

Tom stopped, in the middle of buckling his seatbelt. "I didn't eat him," he said. "He started screaming for mercy as soon as I was fully out of the car. I just flew away after that. I figure there's no way he's going to tell anyone what happened, and your license plate will never be mentioned."

"You sure?" Rafiel said.

"I'm sure. If I'd eaten him, you wouldn't look so tasty right about now."

Rafiel wasn't absolutely sure whether Tom was joking, but then again, he also wasn't willing to tempt fate. "Clothes are under the seat. We should put something on before we go to a drive-through," he said.

"And afterwards?" Tom said.

"Afterwards," Rafiel said, "we go get your damn boots."

When they got to the aquarium, Lei Lani was just ahead of them, opening the door on the restaurant side. Rafiel tried to remember whether they might have left it unlocked—whether they might—perhaps—have left via that entrance. He couldn't remember. Clearly, being concussed and dangling from a berserker dragon's jaws did something to the memory. But it didn't matter, he thought. After all, Dire might have left the door open, too.

She was in the process of opening the door as they came up behind her—wearing tracksuits and looking rather disheveled and, in Rafiel's case, limping, but seeming much more respectable than they'd been before. Tom, who had inhaled five burgers in the ten blocks here, even had a little color and seemed reasonably human. At least, Rafiel hoped so, because if he had looked tasty to Tom, then Lei must look positively tender.

Still, she turned and looked at them, seeming puzzled. "Oh, Officer Trall . . ." she said. "I . . . didn't expect to see you. I realized there was another report that I left behind."

Or perhaps another colleague to try to implicate. Or, Rafiel thought, not quite sure why, but catching something shifty about her eyes, a look of discomfort. *Or perhaps you've decided it's too late to cover things up, and so are going to leave without a forwarding address.*

He was fairly sure this last wasn't true. Not unless McKnight had been so clumsy in his prodding that she now knew, or suspected, that the police had found the lies about her background. *McKnight? Incompetent? What are the odds?* he thought, sarcastically, and barely suppressed a groan. A look at Tom revealed an expression so full of distress and a gaze desperately attempting to make several speeches, that Rafiel almost groaned again.

He wished he could mind-talk to Tom and inform him that, yes, yes, he had realized they needed to retrieve their things before Lei Lani found them. Meanwhile he would have to hope she didn't notice they were wearing identical stretch-shoes.

She didn't seem to. When he said, "I forgot my wallet," she merely gave him a wry look and said, "You seem to do that a lot."

Rafiel shrugged. "I drop it," he said. "I need bigger pockets or a briefcase or something. But then, if I had a briefcase, I'd probably leave it behind."

She smiled and didn't comment on that, and turned right, to go to the office. Rafiel turned the other way, towards the piranha room, his heart accelerating. The dire wolf would be there, right there, ready to jump out at him.

But the room was quiet and empty, except for the gurgling of the tanks and the sound the piranhas made swimming back and forth. Tom's clothes and boots were where he had left them, by the tank. Rafiel's were quite shredded, so he transferred his wallet and ID and cell phone from the shreds, then bundled them up.

He looked up to see Tom standing, holding his own clothes and the box for the cameras. "Here," he told Tom, thrusting his bloodied, shredded clothes at him. "Take this to the car, okay?"

He got raised eyebrows in response.

"I'm going to go ask Lei Lani for a date," Rafiel said.

"What?" Tom's voice came out louder than the half whisper in which they'd been speaking, like a small outburst of sudden indignation. "Excuse me?"

"Shhh." Rafiel said, gesturing down with his hand. "It's not what you think," he said, in a whisper.

"Isn't it? This is a heck of a time to work on your social life, Rafiel," Tom said, but he lowered his voice to a whisper as well.

"It's not my social life," Rafiel said. "It's . . . you know how . . ."

He concentrated on listening for the slightest sound. His hearing was more acute than normal human, but he heard nothing. Not close enough for Lei Lani to hear. And yet, he didn't feel comfortable. He sighed. "Come to the car."

Tom shrugged and followed him to the car. Rafiel threw his shredded clothes in the back. Tom sat on the passenger side and started changing. Rafiel, his gaze sweeping the parking lot to make sure they were quite alone, explained. "I've been worried," he said. "About the camera and how all this was going to work."

Tom frowned at him. "Duh. Whoever it is brings a date there, and then the computer sounds the alarm, and then—duh—we catch her. Or him."

"No," Rafiel said, very patiently. He loved Tom like the brother he'd never had. Truly, he did. But elaborate plans were not the man's main strength. His greatest act of heroism had been on the spur of the moment. Most of what Tom did seemed to be on the spur of the moment. "Yeah, we will have footage of whatever happens. It's even possible we'll know who it is, and what they're doing. If they're shifters, we could go and kill them in cold blood, and stop the deaths. Of course, then we'll have Dire on our tails, but that's something else again. But . . . Tom, the poor sap who is brought here will die. There is no way we can get to him in time."

"Oh," Tom said. "Unless we're expecting it?"

"How can we be expecting it, if it's a stranger?" he said. "By the time the camera beeps, they'll already be in the aquarium. There is nothing we can do. Except collect the remains."

Tom frowned. "Damn. I hadn't thought that through. I don't think it's going to be that easy to sit there, waiting, you know, while . . . some poor sap . . . Damn, Rafiel, I don't even think I can do it. I mean, I know he'd probably die anyway, whether this is part of our trap or not. But I don't want to be . . . I'd feel like an accomplice."

"No, it wouldn't work," Rafiel said. "Which is why I'm going in there and ask Lei Lani for a date."

Tom frowned at him. "Because you think she's the murderer?"

Rafiel shrugged. "Not exactly. But I think there is a good chance she might be. I think it's quite possible she's a shark shifter. Which might or might not mean anything. I've also found she's never attended the University of Hawaii, at least not under this name." He shrugged. "All of it might have other, innocent explanations, and if this were a normal investigation, where I could share my suspicions with my colleagues, it wouldn't be the time for a desperate gamble. But it isn't a casual investigation—it's a life-and-death one. And . . . other people will die. Plus, Dire seems to have settled on me as the sacrificial victim for him to execute."

"Dire will just be furious," Tom said, "if we go after Lani and she's a shifter."

"I think Dire is furious now. There is one thing I know we can't do, Tom, and that's face Dire, the triads and the aquarium murderer all at the same time. For the last week I've walked on eggshells, afraid one or the other of those are about to give us away. I can't go on like that. Let's start taking the enemies down one at a time. The aquarium murderer, at least until further notice, is not more powerful than us, so let's take that one on first. Then we'll figure out some way to get Dire. And then the triads . . ." He shrugged. "Perhaps they'll just go away."

"Fat chance," Tom said.

Rafiel shrugged again. "One at a time. So, I'm going in and asking Ms. Lani out."

"But . . . like that?" Tom asked. "You are all bruised, have two big gashes on the back of your neck, and you probably broke your ankle."

Rafiel shrugged. "So, I tell her I got in a fight in the course of duty. You know there is little that a woman loves better than a hero."

Tom stared at him for a long time, then sighed and shook his head. "The worst part, Mr. Hero, is that you'll probably pull it off."

Rafiel gave him a feline grin. "Of course I will."

Kyrie looked from one to the other of the men, her mouth half open, as though all the words had escaped her and weren't coming back. Rafiel looked like he'd been put into an industrial threshing machine. His forehead was scratched, his arm showed blood through the shirt. He was walking as if he had—at the very least—a seriously bruised ankle.

Tom looked hungry. In fact, despite the fact that he'd announced to her, up front, that he'd already eaten, and even though his story made it clear he'd had something like ten hamburgers, he looked starved, and sniffed the air as if trying to inhale calories through sniffing in stray particles of cooking meat.

And yet, both of them looked as happy, as full of themselves as boys who had pulled off a really good prank. It had to be one of those male things, because she couldn't begin to imagine what was going through their minds. "And you went back?" she said. "For the boots and the ID?"

"And the clothes," Rafiel said, enthusiastically. "My clothes. Well, the shreds of them."

"I see," Kyrie said.

"It wasn't a big deal," Tom said, as his head swiveled to follow a gyro platter carried by Keith. "Dire wasn't there when we went back."

Yes, of course, that made it all right, Kyrie thought, as she sighed and despaired of explaining to these overgrown boys that, after all, Dante Dire had the power of messing with their minds. He might have made it seem that there was no one there. He might have jumped them from a dark corner. He might still be waiting to—She couldn't say any of it, certainly not in the diner, although the three of them were occupying the corner booth, under the picture of the dragon slayer, and there were no other occupied booths in this part of the diner.

Keith stopped by and dropped a plate entirely filled with gyro shavings and souvlaki in front of Tom, who looked up at him, surprised, "How did you know?"

Keith shrugged. "Meat-seeking behavior," he said. "I've come to know it." He looked from Rafiel to Tom. "What have you two been doing with yourselves?" he asked. And then paused, and bent over towards the table, his hands on the formica. "It isn't about Summer

Avenir, right? I mean . . . is there some big fight going on that you guys haven't told me about?"

Kyrie sighed and shifted further into the booth. "Come. You can hear about it."

But Keith shook his head, and looked around at the tables. "Nah. Conan went to take a nap, he said, and that would leave the tables unattended."

Kyrie frowned. This sudden reluctance to run away with the shifter circus was not like Keith at all. A look at the young man showed her dark circles around his eyes and a general impression of being less than healthy. "Huh," she said.

"It's nothing, okay?" Keith said. He shrugged. "It's just that, you know, you guys always said that being a shifter was no picnic, that there was stuff . . . but you know, for me, it was all about fighting and . . . well, it was like being a superhero."

"Yeah, so you told us," Tom said.

"Only, then . . . Summer turned out to be the granddaughter of the newspaper owner, and to have been after cryptozoology stuff, and she endangered you and got herself killed . . . and now I know it's not . . ."—he looked at them, intently—"I assume it wasn't one of you. I wouldn't have come back if I thought it had been one of you."

"No," Kyrie said, shocked. "No. It's . . . one of the people we're fighting."

"People!" Keith said. "Somehow, no, I don't think it's people."

Kyrie felt shocked as if she'd been punched. "What about us?"

Keith sighed. "I want to say of course you're people . . ." he said. "I want to say it . . . but . . ." He looked away. "It would help if Tom didn't look like he could happily take a chunk out of a passing diner."

Tom, finger-deep in gyro meat, looked up. "Hey!"

"No . . . I know you're not like that," Keith said. "And of course you can trust me, and all. But . . . these . . . creatures, like the ones we fought against before . . . It's not like a computer game, and it's not like a comic, and it's not like being superheroes."

"We never said . . ."

"I know you didn't. But I'm an idiot, okay . . . and I thought . . ." He shrugged. "I thought a whole lot of stupid things. But it's not fun anymore. It's serious. And the things you guys fight, they're really serious too. I take it the . . . creature you're fighting is the one who was in here the other day talking about how I was just a transitive or something and—"

"Ephemeral," Tom said. "Because you live less than we do, and he—"

"Yeah. I got the gist. Anyway . . . I take it that's the big bad, and I wish you luck and all, but I want no part of it. I . . ." He took a deep breath. "I might as well tell you that I've applied for a scholarship to do the last two years of college abroad, in Italy. I was accepted. I'll be leaving at the end of the month. That's my two-weeks' notice."

They all looked at him, stunned. Oh, Kyrie understood what he was saying. In fact, they'd been the first to tell him that it wasn't fun, it wasn't like being a superhero, it wasn't anything of the kind. But Keith had been, in a way, the one normal human admitted to their fraternity, the one they could trust.

The one, Kyrie thought, *who reassures us that we're still human.*

"Sure," Tom said, sounding deflated. "Sure. I just . . . tell me the exact date and I'll make sure you have your check a couple of days in advance so that you can cash it before you fly, okay?"

Keith looked startled. Had he forgotten that Tom tried to take care of people no matter what? "Okay," he said, as he walked away.

And he couldn't be that mad at them, Kyrie thought, at least not consciously, because having seen Rafiel eye Tom's food jealously, he brought him a plate of meat as well, and silverware for both of them. "Anthony thinks you have a tapeworm," he said, walking away. "Both of you."

"You know," Rafiel said, "Dante Dire would say we need to kill Keith, to ensure our own safety."

Kyrie shook her head, feeling vaguely impatient. Dire could say whatever he wanted. Keith could say whatever he wanted for that matter. She could understand Dire's point about how hard it was to consider as people and as equals, people who didn't consider you human. But she was sure of something and that was that Dire was far more dangerous to Keith than Keith ever could be to any of them. The other thing was that Kyrie was fairly sure people were just . . .

people. It was just that shifters had so many more means of causing harm than people who didn't at the drop of a hat grow claws and fangs. "You still didn't tell me," she said with a trace of impatience, "what you were doing at the aquarium today?"

"Oh," Tom shrugged and looked sheepish, managing to look much like a kid caught with his hand in the cookie jar. "We were installing a camera."

"Installing a what?"

"A camera. In that platform area where, clearly, there's been screwing going on."

"Why?" Kyrie asked. The idea was unfathomable. "So you guys could have your very own private porn channel? Isn't it kind of gruesome? I mean considering . . ."

"No," Tom said. "It's for an alarm. I've already installed the software in my laptop. You and I are going to keep watch on it. By turns. It beeps, you see . . . when someone moves in front of the camera and activates it."

"We're going to keep watch on it by turns?" Kyrie asked. "And what exactly do we do about The George, Tom? You still need to cook, and without Keith, or with Keith on reduced hours, I still need to wait tables. What do we do about that?"

The minute she said it, Tom's face fell, and she felt as though she were the most horrible woman alive. "Look, I can see where it's important, but . . ."

Rafiel cleared his throat. "You're right, Kyrie," he said. "That's why I have a plan. We couldn't just wait, see?"

Tom nodded. "So, Rafiel came up with something. Rafiel says, and he's right that we'd start with the weakest enemy and move on towards the strongest, because, you know, we can't fight all of them at the same time."

"No," Kyrie said. "But I don't think this will help us fight at all."

"No, it will," Rafiel said. "I think that the Lani chick likes me. Oh, I don't mean she's in love with me or anything," he answered Tom's knowing smile. "That's not it at all. But the thing is, she has sort of come on to me and hinted since she first met me. If she's the aquarium killer, and if she is a shark shifter, perhaps I look tasty."

"Officer Mignon," Tom mumbled.

"Something like that. But in any case"—Rafiel shrugged—"she has tried to, you know, hint that she would be okay going out more than once. And in fact, you know, she came up to my car outside the doughnut shop, when I didn't even know she knew my car . . . so . . . I think, particularly if she's guilty and is worried about it—but even if she isn't guilty and her boyfriends just keep taking headers into the shark tank through no fault of her own . . ." He stopped and looked lost.

Kyrie said, "No." Tom made some indeterminate sound.

"No, really," Rafiel said. "I've gone on dates with women before. Truly. Some people don't seem to think I'm that horrible."

"I didn't mean that," Kyrie said. "It's more, I'd prefer you don't run that risk."

Rafiel looked towards Tom who was eating, oblivious to them. So he assumed Tom wasn't jealous. Which was good, because he didn't think Kyrie meant it in any other way than as a caring friend. "How much more of a risk is doing nothing?" Rafiel asked. "I almost died today, and I wasn't doing anything I thought was dangerous, except maybe to my moral health."

"Well, you were trying to solve the aquarium murders," Kyrie said. "And if anything, this is more likely to bring Dire on you, since he said that you should not investigate these murders."

"Yeah," Rafiel admitted. "But you see . . . that only makes it obligatory that I do something. How am I going to live with myself, knowing that I stopped an investigation because someone who doesn't consider humans as such told me to stop? How can I go on? And besides, Kyrie—"

"And besides, Kyrie," Tom said. "Even if we don't do anything at all, Dire will end up killing us. Or at least, he will kill one of us so he can blame all of the deaths on that one person and skip off back to his affairs, his reputation as executioner untarnished. He doesn't care who he blames. After what I did to him," Tom's voice became rueful as he said this, "it's very probable that the pact with the dragons won't even hold him back anymore."

"So we'll do something about the aquarium murders," Rafiel said. "And then we'll figure out some way to get Dire. Because we have to. It's him or us."

"And through all of this," Tom said, "we'll try to keep Conan safe. Frankly, we shouldn't even let him know what we intend to do. Conan shouldn't cross the street by himself, much less get involved in intrigue and conspiracy."

"So," Rafiel said, "I asked Lei Lani out tonight. And she said yes."

The expression of complete surprise on Kyrie's face was totally worth it.

Kyrie bit her tongue hard. Listening to Rafiel's plan, she realized that it made the perfect trap for Dire. She couldn't imagine how the two men kept imagining they would be allowed to deal with each of the threats in turn—without more than one of them imposing themselves upon their notice at the same time.

It was clear, to her, at least. Dire had been watching them. Dire had been watching the aquarium. Dire knew they wanted to catch and punish the aquarium killer. They were not going to be allowed to do it without interference. It would never happen.

And they couldn't simply go after Dire in cold blood, anyway. If they went after Dire in any way that couldn't be construed as self-defense, and if they went to the triads for help, the only thing that would happen would be that the Ancient Ones would accuse the dragons of murder, and a war would break out. Mr. Lung had warned Kyrie against that.

So the best thing was to get Dire to come after them. Which the aquarium trap seemed like the perfect setup for.

But that meant that Kyrie had to arrange the night shift, somehow, so Conan could be free, without Tom knowing. First, she thought, she would go to the bed-and-breakfast and talk to Conan. And then, if he could perhaps pretend to be sick . . . then Kyrie would have an excuse to ask Keith to work.

"If you guys get in the car," Rafiel said, "and wait in it, perhaps a block from the aquarium, then you can get me in time. Not that I should need help. I mean . . . I've fought other shifters before, but . . . I'd prefer to have backup."

"Of course," Tom said. "But not in our car. In the supply van."

Kyrie saw Rafiel give Tom a surprised look and Tom sighed, long-suffering. "You can see into the car. But the old supply van, the one without the George logo, we can sit in the back—well, we can sit in the back once I throw in a couple of cushions—and no one will see us. Or even know we're there. Just an anonymous van parked by the side of the road."

Kyrie knocked at the door to Conan's room, which was in the bottom floor, just off the entrance. There was a sound of shuffling, from inside, and then Conan's voice, "Yes?"

"It's Kyrie," she whispered. She'd left Tom taking care of her tables, with the excuse that she had to go take a shower to wake up, since she hadn't slept in . . . much too long.

Conan opened the door, and looked at her, somewhat surprised. "Kyrie?"

"I need to talk to you. May I come in?"

"Yeah, sure." He threw the door open into a room that was about a quarter the size of theirs—just a little bigger than the destroyed bathroom at home. It had a daybed against one wall, a small dresser and a desk opposite. At the end of it the door opened into a tiny bathroom, where she could just see the glass door of a stand-up shower, with what looked like a pair of underwear drying draped over it.

Without meaning to, she looked down. Conan was wearing pants—or rather shorts and a baggy white T-shirt. "Is anything wrong?" he asked her.

"Yes and no," she said. She closed the door, then leaned against the desk while he slumped on his bed, and looked at her. And she explained. She explained everything. What had happened, what the plan was.

"But, Kyrie, I can't," he said. He put his hands on his head, grabbing a handful of his straight black hair on either side. "I can't do that. He told me he'd kill himself, and the Great Sky Dragon said he meant it."

"He would kill himself," Kyrie said. "If he had to be . . . beholden to the Great Sky Dragon, yes. But don't you see in this case he doesn't have to? Even if he finds out I asked for help, I'll be the one he's mad at, you see. I'll be the one who is indebted to the triads. He's not."

Conan looked at her, blinking, and it took her a moment to realize he was fighting back tears. "I'm not sure he's not right, Kyrie," he said, pitifully. "If I had any choice, now—which I don't—I'd choose not to belong to the Great Sky Dragon, too." And seeing Kyrie flinch, he must have realized what she'd thought, because he smiled. "I don't know if he's still listening to me, no. He might be. Or he might have turned off when Tom told him he wouldn't allow me to follow him around." A small frown. "I don't think so, though, or Mr. Lung would have told you that you needed to do something else to get his attention, than just have me around. He didn't, so I guess . . . Himself is watching. And he now knows I'd prefer not to belong to him, which is fine. I would. If he didn't know that before . . ." Conan shrugged. "I don't think he cares. I'm not *important* like Tom and I never had a choice."

Kyrie sighed. In her mind only one thing mattered right now. She didn't want to appear callous towards Conan. She even liked Conan in a way, though he was definitely one of the strays that Tom was so prone to picking up. But she didn't have time or patience, just now, to discuss his philosophy of life. "Does this mean you won't help?" she asked.

"No," Conan said. "It doesn't. I'll help, of course. It's not like I have a choice, you know. I have to help. Or die. And I'm not ready to die."

"I was going to suggest you take my car, because—"

Conan shook his head. He looked very sad. "If I know how my people work, I expect there will be a car brought to me in the next hour, a car that Tom won't identify. And just tell Tom I have a cough and decided not to work because I might be contagious. The only thing I want to know . . ." He paused.

"Yes?"

"Is what they intend to use me as, other than possibly bait. It's not that I mind. It can't be much worse than all the other things I've had to do. I just wish I had more of an inkling of what will happen than 'Conan will watch, and then we'll intervene.'" He looked very tired. "Doesn't matter. I'm sure better minds than mine will handle it."

Kyrie was caught between a desire to bitch-slap him and a desire to free him from his vassalage.

Kyrie hoped that Dante Dire had the place under surveillance of some sort. She had to—simply had to—arrange for him to follow them that night. She wasn't quite sure how to do it, except, of course, by managing to pretend that the last thing she wanted was for him to follow them.

There was a good chance she wouldn't need to do anything to get him to follow them. She suspected he had gone after Tom and Rafiel after seeing them leave the bed-and-breakfast. If that was the case, any of them going near the aquarium was likely to cause Dire to follow. She just wished she could be sure. She also wished she could be sure that Tom hadn't blinded him for a few weeks. Because if Tom had, then it was going to be very hard to entrap him.

While Tom was busy at the grill and Keith was keeping up with the tables, in the brief post-dinner lull, and before Anthony came in to spell Tom, she took the time to go outside, into the parking lot, looking for Dire's car.

Instead, she found Dire himself, standing outside the back door, smoking. His dark eyes, she noted, looked fine.

He grinned at her, as if he knew what she was looking at. In the next few words, he proved he did. "Well, Kitten," he said, "you and your boyfriend are very rude." He shrugged. "Not that I resent it from you. I like my women with a bit of spirit."

"I am not your woman," Kyrie said.

He grinned again, flashing white between taut lips. "Oh yes," he said. "I know that. But you know, shifters' lives are long and all that might yet change. Your boyfriend is too dumb to know what's good for him, so he's not likely to make old bones."

"I think my boyfriend is perfectly fine," she said, snappishly. And meaning the snap, too, because Dire annoyed her—besides putting a chill up her spine—and because she thought he would expect her to react this way.

Dire shrugged. He took a pull on his cigarette, making the tip glow bright. "I'm sure you do. You're both very young. Young as ephemerals. But he doesn't understand that, when needed, one must sacrifice a friend . . . or two." His gaze on her was speculative, and she felt as though she were being considered as a "sacrifice."

"And have you sacrificed many *friends*?" she asked, wrapping her arms around herself.

If she expected him to flinch or look guilty, she would have been sorely disappointed. He threw his head back and laughed. "One or two . . . dozen. But I'm still here, aren't I?"

"Yes," Kyrie said, and judging the time to be right, added, "In fact, I wish you weren't here so much. What are you doing here, all the time? Are you following us?" Mentally, she projected the feeling/idea that tonight of all nights she didn't want him around.

She watched his eyes quicken, but nothing more in his gaze gave away that he'd caught on to something. His voice was quite disinterested and amused as he said, "I find you entertaining."

Tom felt awkward and stupid. Which, he supposed, in many ways he was. At least when the many ways involved human interaction. He felt very strange taking time off and getting into the supply van with Kyrie. Kyrie drove till they were outside the aquarium, about the time that Rafiel would be starting his date. It was unlikely, of course, that Lei Lani would be dragging Rafiel to the aquarium at the beginning of the date—even if Rafiel was right in his suspicions. Even if she intended to drag him there later.

But they didn't want to be too far away to intervene if she did take him there. The time was quite likely to be too short, then. And the idea was not to have Rafiel get himself killed. For one, even if they got the woman immediately afterwards, the police tended to get religious when one of them got killed. They would leave no stone unturned. And when it came to murders committed by shifters, Tom would very much like to let mossy stones lie. And for another . . . Tom liked the lion bastard. Life wouldn't be nearly as much fun without a friend in the police, he thought. Why, they might not get pulled into whichever murder was going on, on the vaguest suspicion that a shifter might be involved.

So, they'd taken the laptop—still quiescent—and driven to a block from the aquarium, where they'd parked on a darkened side street. The van smelled of old cabbage and—strangely, since Tom didn't remember carrying any in it—stale crackers. It had only two seats, since the back was normally filled with crates and boxes of supplies for the diner. In summer and fall, he and Kyrie had taken the van to the farmers' market early every morning, when Anthony came in to relieve them. They'd got better deals, and better produce too. Though Tom had probably gone overboard on the apricots, which was why they had about a hundred jars of jam in the cold room at The George. Which would come in really handy the minute he learned to make homemade bread.

But because he and Kyrie rarely got to go out alone, because he didn't want them to sit in the front seats and be obvious, and because he was a fool, he'd made sure the van was clean and he'd brought a blanket to spread on the metallic floor that had long since lost its carpet, if it had ever had one.

He'd also brought two very large throw pillows from their room.

It was only when Kyrie had looked at the blanket and the pillows, and turned an inquisitive glance towards him, that he realized how it might look. "What?" he said. "What? I thought it would be more comfortable than the bare floor and all, while we wait."

She had smiled just a little, an odd, Mona Lisa smile. "I'm sure it will be," she had said all soft and breezily.

And now they were parked on a side street, less than a block from the aquarium. It was a narrow street and at this point pretty much deserted, with what looked like an empty—with broken windows—house on one side, and a park on the other. They left the front seats and went to the back, where they sat primly on the pillows across from each other, and they put the laptop up, its back against the front seats. The laptop had been a gift from Tom's father and, until now, he'd never used it for anything more exciting than doing the accounting for The George.

But the laptop wasn't being exciting either. A blank screen with a field of stars streaming past—his screen saver—stared back at them.

Tom looked at it, then looked at Kyrie. The laptop was supposed to beep if it caught anything, and just now, Tom was disposed to let the laptop do its thing and not give it undue attention. Because, after all, if you couldn't trust your laptop, what could you trust?

Instead he looked over at Kyrie. He was dating the only woman in the world who could look like a goddess in worn jeans and a utilitarian brown sweat shirt. The brown brought out the olive tones in her skin, and went seamlessly with the layer-dyed hair which was her only concession to vanity. Well, she had one other, but he wasn't sure whether that was due to vanity or to her belief that this was her good-luck charm, much like his boots were his—but she was wearing her red feather earring, dangling from her ear, jewel-bright against her dark hair. It seemed to highlight her dark-red lips, which were jewellike enough even without the benefit of lipstick.

He longed to trace with his hands the outline of her breasts under the sweat shirt. His lips ached for her lips. It had been . . . a week, maybe more, since he had so much as hugged her. And he wondered if she now thought he was a perfect idiot, since he'd shifted in the bathroom. He wondered if he'd ruined her respect for him, and if now it would be only a matter of time before she told him they couldn't go on like this.

"I'm an idiot," he said. And as she turned to look at him, he went on, honestly. "If I had half a lick of sense, when I knew I'd be spending at least an hour and probably more in a van with the most beautiful woman in the world, I'd have had the good sense to bring champagne and chocolates, or something."

"We couldn't have champagne," she said. "We can't afford to be tipsy."

"Apple cider then," he said. "Something to make you feel as special as just being near you makes me feel."

For a moment he thought he'd upset her. Her mouth opened in an "Oh." and her eyes widened, as though surprised. And then, unaccountably, she was in his arms, her body warm against his. He frantically searched for her lips and found them, kissing her desperately, as if he could only draw breath through her mouth. "Kyrie," he said. "Oh, Kyrie."

Halfway through dinner, Rafiel found himself hoping that Lei Lani wasn't the murderer, whether or not she was a shifter. And he wanted her to be a shifter. He really did. Because then she would understand him—and he could maybe even marry her.

He didn't know what it was exactly, and he'd have been hard pressed to say, but he felt happy in her presence. Very happy. Almost on the edge of drunk.

Tuscany Bay, the fashionable restaurant to which he'd decided to take her, despite the nonsensical name, turned out to be a very decent Italian place, with dancing and a jazz band that played softly melodic sounds. And being around Lei seemed to erase Rafiel's pains, so that, after a dinner of grilled salmon, he could stand on his bruised ankle, and lead her in a heartfelt—and possibly slightly obscene— slow dance.

They danced one song, two, and Rafiel was conscious that most people in the place were staring at them, and he was sure—absolutely sure—that everyone of them was envying him. Lei was wearing a simple—almost severe—black and white dress, and the cutest little fedora tilted sideways on her head. Beneath it, her hair was loose, brushed till glossy and dark as sin.

After the second song, she said, "I think we should go out. You know, for a walk."

And he was fine with that. He'd have gone anywhere with her. At the door, when they picked up their coats from the coat check, the coat check lady whispered to Lei, "Don't let him drive," and Rafiel could not understand why. Did she think he was drunk? How could he be? He had drunk iced tea all evening.

But it didn't matter. As they walked outside, the cold air did feel invigorating. Lei put her arm in his. Above the skies had cleared and a million stars seemed to sparkle in the deep black velvet of the night.

He was a little surprised when they got to the aquarium and she opened the door. There was something about the aquarium. Something he was supposed to remember. But he had no idea what. And he was sure it couldn't be very important. After all, he was lucky. He had Lei Lani, right there.

Tom had just said, "Oh, I'm such an idiot," against the soft depths of Kyrie's tapestry-dyed hair, when the alarm sounded. For a moment, for just a moment, he thought it was ringing inside his head. Reminding him there was a reason he didn't usually allow himself to lose control, that he might at any moment lose control of himself and shift, which would work about as well in the van as it had in the bathroom.

He tried to tell the alarm to stuff it, but it continued to ring, quite oblivious to his opinions, and it dawned on Tom that it was the sound from the laptop at about the same time that Kyrie pulled away and said, "Damn, the laptop."

"Yeah," Tom said. "Yeah." It wasn't the most coherent response in the world, but it was the one he had, and he was going to stick to it.

Kyrie touched the button that made the screen saver stop scrolling by and brought the transmission from the camera to them in vivid, bold color. Tom remembered, irrelevantly, his father going on about how he'd picked that laptop because of the wonderful movie screen. All the same it took him a moment to figure out what he was looking at.

"Oh, good lord," Kyrie said. "Is he crazy or stupid?"

And then Tom realized he was looking at Rafiel and Lei Lani, without clothes, in what used to euphemistically be called a moment of passion. He jumped to the front seat and out. He had gone five steps before he realized that Kyrie hadn't been as fast. And it took him only two seconds to see a dire wolf round on him, from outside. It was growling in a low tone, and of course there were no words in its growl. But Tom would swear it was saying "Payback time, Dragon Boy."

Kyrie removed her earring, and then her clothes and leapt from the van even as she shifted. As a panther, she interposed herself between Dire and Tom. She growled, a fierce, loud growl that meant that he wouldn't be allowed to touch Tom, and she willed Tom to go past her. Willed it with all her mind.

There was Dire, standing in front of them, blocking the access to the aquarium. How long before Lei Lani took it into her head to drown Rafiel? They'd been naked and . . . um . . . Tom had no idea how long it was supposed to last. Movies had given him a range of times from a couple of minutes to hours, and he had no idea which one was closer to the truth.

But he knew, or at least he suspected that when the fun and games were done, it would be the final swim for Rafiel, a swim from which he would not return.

He could tell from the way Kyrie—in panther form, her fur velvet-dark—interposed herself between him and Dire, that she meant for him to go past. But how could he go past when Kyrie's life was at risk? He remembered what Dire could do. And he wasn't willing to see him treat Kyrie as he'd treated Rafiel.

Oh, Dire might want Kyrie, or at least he might think so. But did he want her more than he wanted to fulfill his *duty* and return, once more victorious, to his cosmopolitan lifestyle? And Kyrie would make as good a sacrifice to Dire's lifestyle as Rafiel.

Tom realized his body had made the decision for him because while he thought, he had stripped bare and untied his boots. He now stepped out of his boots, and spoke, in his slurpy almost-dragon voice, "Attack me, you prehistoric horror. Or can you only defeat girls?"

And then he shifted.

Damn the man, Kyrie thought, a passenger in the back of the panther's mind, even as Dire lunged at her and tossed her aside, while he rounded on Tom.

Kyrie landed heavily on a scruffy front lawn, and tried to get up. And couldn't. At first she thought she must be paralyzed, and then she realized Tom wasn't moving either. After issuing his challenge and leaping, he'd landed heavily, as if he couldn't control his paws, and now was half lying on the street, while Dire circled around him, growling, with every appearance of enjoyment.

He was going to kill Tom, she realized. He was in their minds. He was controlling them. And he was going to kill Tom. And then probably kill her.

Don't be silly, Kitten Girl, his voice said in her mind, with a suggestion of indecent laughter. *That would be a waste.*

She wanted to get up. She tried with all her mind and heart to get up. But she couldn't. She couldn't move.

And then, from above, came the flap of wings.

Tom heard the flap of wings. His eyes—about the only part of him not paralyzed—turned upward in time to see huge wings, descending. He wanted to protest, to say no. He hadn't asked for help. Even there, at death's door, he hadn't asked for help.

Let Dire kill him, but at least he would die free, and not owe his life to a criminal dragon.

Laughter filled his mind, and then a voice he remembered all too well. *Commendable*, it said. *Or perhaps crazy. Never mind. Go now. You are free. Go take care of your friend.*

And suddenly Tom could move, and he could see Kyrie move too. She was leaping towards the aquarium ahead of him. So she'd heard the golden bastard in her mind as well. And the golden bastard was interposing himself between Tom and Kyrie and Dire. The dire wolf screamed a sound of pure fury and Tom, who hadn't wanted the Great Sky Dragon's help, nonetheless hoped the Great Sky Dragon was doing to Dire what he did to them, and rifling through his mind, and using it. He hoped so, as he lurched, as fast as he could towards the aquarium.

Kyrie hit the aquarium door first, full lope, and rebounded back, shocked. Locked. The door was locked. The cat in whose mind Kyrie was couldn't understand it, even as Kyrie forced it to try to turn the knob. Until she felt a dragon claw rest, gently, on her shoulder, moving her aside.

The cat felt threatened and wanted to fight, but Kyrie was in control and she forced the body to step aside. And felt it recoil in terror and put belly to the ground and growl softly, as the dragon faced the door and opened his massive jaws, and let loose a stream of white-hot flame.

The door cracked. The outer lining of metal melted and ran. The inside layer of wood charred. The door fell inward, and Kyrie forced the great cat to leap in, over the smoldering door, and down a hallway, to where a door stood open with a seal ripped in two, and Kyrie lunged up the hallway, and loped up the stairs to the platform, in time to see . . . Rafiel, in human form, leaning over the railing and getting a push, and falling, falling headlong into the shark tank.

He made a sound of panic as he fell, and his shape blurred and changed. It was the lion that hit the water with a loud splash. The cover of the tank, removed, stood to the side.

A woman laughed, and turned to Kyrie. "I see. Why don't you join your boyfriend?"

Tom wanted to scream "No," but what came out of the dragon's mouth was a long, incoherent growl, as he rushed in, past Kyrie and almost past the woman on the platform.

The thought in his mind was that he must go and rescue Rafiel. He must. But he had a moment to think that if the woman stayed where she was, she might find a way to push Kyrie in. And he couldn't allow that, so he did what seemed all too logical to the dragon, and grabbed at the woman, pulling her in with him, as he plunged in after Rafiel.

The sharks hadn't started on Rafiel, who was trying to swim, his lion body quite adept at swimming, but not so much at reaching up to the edge of the tank lid and climbing out. He growled softly, whenever he tried and failed. And he looked—the human in Tom's dragon mind thought—very much like a drowned cat.

He thought all this as he plunged in, hitting the water with a great splash and going down-down-down, drawing a deep breath scented with what seemed like intoxicating perfume, and realizing he was breathing under water.

He came up beneath Rafiel, lifting him, pushing him up with his own body, till the lion's paws touched the edge of the opening, and then the dragon gave the lion a little shove, pushing him out.

And he felt a shark—skin rough as sandpaper—touch his back paw. Something from a nature program about sharks turning, or circling or something before biting crossed the dragon's mind, and the dragon did what came instinctively. It snapped downward and it bit at the shark. Hard. The shark flopped. Blood poured out. Other sharks rushed in.

Feeding frenzy, Tom's human mind thought and pushed, with all its might, at the dragon's body, impelling it, mind over matter, to the opening, its wings unfurling, half jumping, half flying out of the tank.

On the way he picked up the lion, who had been cowering on the edge of the tank where the covering rested, and lifted him all the way to the platform.

And before he could shift and talk or look around for Kyrie, he heard an unholy growl.

Dante Dire, Kyrie thought. And—through the panther's mind, confused, blurred—went the thought that he'd escaped the Great Sky Dragon. Somehow. She would hate to imagine how.

And then she was plunging after him, madly. She felt him bite her, attack her, too ravening to care who she was, too maddened with rage to care whether he could just mind-control her instead.

From the shadows a dragon emerged. No. Two dragons. One of them red and with a foreshortened arm. And a very wet lion. They all fell on Dire, and Kyrie couldn't honestly say who was attacking what, except that Dire seemed to be everywhere at once, his teeth biting and his claws scraping, but never enough to get hold of them.

And then he seemed to regain control. Suddenly, the horrible smell she remembered from her kitchen when he'd attacked her there, surrounded them. And into their minds poured Dire's voice, *If you are done now, I can kill you.*

But at the same moment, two other voices sounded. "I don't think so," said a tremulous voice and, looking over, Kyrie was surprised to see Old Joe standing, for once, very straight. Next to him was an old Japanese gentleman, looking faintly amused.

You! Dire said. *You. You're weak. You can never face me.*

"We're not weak," the Japanese gentleman said. His accent was, clearly, the real thing, but not that incomprehensible. "We are free. We would have nothing to do with your council and your rules. We told you before it was wrong to separate yourself from humanity."

"We told you it would come to no good," Old Joe said, his voice clearer and more firm than it had ever been, at least that Kyrie had heard it.

"No good, uh?" Dire had shifted. He was human, looking at them with scornfully curled lip. "I am the executioner. Even the Daddy Dragon couldn't face me. He cares too much for his whelp to use his form too long. He was afraid I would hurt the body he was borrowing." He grinned. "And I won. Because I don't care for anything but myself. Come," he said, and shifted, in a single, fluid movement. *Come now, we'll see who is stronger.*

It all happened too fast. There were suddenly an alligator and a giant spider crab. And they shifted, and the crab was stabbing at the dire wolf, while the alligator seemed to be everywhere at once, biting and slicing. The dire wolf's teeth closed on hard carapace and armored back. The alligator's teeth clack-clacked in what sounded like laughter.

There was a howl, a growl of pent-up fury, and suddenly the dire wolf was not there.

"He will come back," Tom said softly. And Kyrie realized he had shifted, and so had she, and they were both naked, hugging on the top step of the platform.

Before she could answer, a dripping-wet Rafiel walked around the shark tank, below them, and halfway up the stairs. "I'll be damned if I can explain all the trace on the scene now," he said, ruefully. "They're going to find scales, and blood of at least three different animals. But," he said, "I don't think that the murders will go on." He looked incredibly tired and somehow defeated, even as he announced good news. "She . . . shifted as she died. They will find human remains in the tank this time. Female."

Tom, pulling Kyrie against him, shuddered. And Kyrie said, "Why did you let things get that advanced?"

"I don't know. It could be some form of pheromones," he said. "Or else, she put something in my drink." He looked up, his golden eyes very sad. "I know that it was all delusion. I know she just wanted a snack. But for a moment, it was like being a kid again, back when I was in love with Alice." He shrugged and sat on the bottom step of the platform, and leaned against the railing. "I guess time never winds backwards."

And Kyrie who remembered something from the fight, looked to the other side of the steps, where Conan sat, looking just as dejected as Rafiel. "Conan," she said, "what was it Dire said, about the Great Sky Dragon borrowing your form?"

Conan shook. He looked up at her, seeming drained and pale. "He . . . he didn't . . . I mean, he can't be everywhere at once, but just like he can listen through his underlings . . . he can make us take his form. With all of his powers. Only if he does it for long, we die."

Kyrie blinked at him. "He made you take his form?"

"Just . . . just for a moment. Then he realized I couldn't stand it . . ."

"And he realized he cared for you?" Tom said, skeptically.

Conan shook his head. "No. He realized he cared for *you*. And he thought . . ." He sighed. "He thought you wouldn't forgive him if he killed me. Even when . . . even if it was to kill Dire. So he . . . let me go. He told me . . . in my mind, that I was now yours. That I'm to do what you tell me."

Tom coughed. "Mine?" Something like a choked laughter

escaped him. "No offense, Conan, you're a nice guy. But the only person I ever wanted to be mine was Kyrie, and it wasn't in that sense. If he gave you to me, I give you to yourself. You're yours."

"I was afraid of that," Conan said, dolefully.

"Afraid," Kyrie said.

Conan shrugged. "Yes. I don't know how . . . not to belong to someone. I've taken orders from someone since before I was an adult. I'm not used to being my own person."

"Try it," she said, not without sympathy. "You can get used to it. And you still belong to us. Just as a friend, not a . . . possession."

"Truly?" he asked. "And I can . . . still work at The George?"

Kyrie felt Tom tremble with silent laughter. "If you want to. But I thought you were going to sing for your supper."

Conan blushed. "Maybe someday. But for now, I'm just glad to have a job."

"And on that, gentlemen and lady," Tom said, "I'm starving, and I think we should go to The George for some food. Because, you know it and I know it, that the old bastard is going to come back and try to kill us and right now another shift might kill *me*."

"Maybe he won't try to kill us," Old Joe said. He was standing alone. The crab shifter was nowhere to be seen. "Maybe he's afraid now?"

"I very much doubt it," Tom said, drily. But he added, "And Joe? Thank you. You saved our lives, I think."

Old Joe shrugged, but blushed and said, "You do what you have to."

"Yeah," Tom said. "At any rate, let's go eat something. What about your friend? Does he want to come?"

"Who? He? No. He never does. He doesn't feel very comfortable as a human, anymore. All he wants is his aquarium and to watch life go by."

Two weeks later, Tom woke up from sleep in his back porch, at his and Kyrie's house, looking up at the ceiling some past occupier had painted a deep pink. The bathroom had been repaired. The house was silent. Kyrie's breathing wasn't audible from her bedroom, and neither was what he was sure must be Notty's quite industrial-sized purr.

He wasn't sure what had wakened him, but Dire was on his mind. He hadn't seen Dire or heard from him for two weeks, and he wanted Old Joe to be right. He wanted it to be that Dire had gone away forever.

And just as he thought this he heard the voice in his mind. *Hey, Dragon Boy, come and be killed!* With the words came a flash—the view of Dire, in his animal form, waiting, down the street from Tom, in a little park, where pine trees covered in snow stood silent guard over a gazebo and stone boulders. In summer, the park was frequented by everyone in the neighborhood. But in winter no one ever went there, and the little lake in the middle was iced over— though not enough for anyone to skate on it.

It was the perfect place, Tom thought, for a duel. A shifter duel. But he was thousands of years younger than Dire. And he knew he couldn't fight the mind powers.

Or did he? There was something Dire had said, about how the Great Sky Dragon himself had been defeated because he cared too much for his subordinate. Perhaps he was right. Perhaps the way to fight with the mind, the way the Ancient Ones did, came from not caring.

Yes. It does, Dante Dire said in his mind. *It comes from us having seen the generations unfold and caring for nothing. You love life, that's your weakness. While we love only death, even our own, if it comes to that.*

And something in Tom's mind beat against the words. Denied them. He didn't care if they were true. He would not accept them. That was no way to live.

He got up, undressed silently. On his way out the door, he opened Kyrie's door a crack—enough to see her sleeping, under the moonlight, on her side, her face supported on her arm. Notty was nestled in her hair, purring. They looked peaceful. Domestic.

And Tom went out, into the cold dark night.

On his front porch, after closing the door carefully behind himself, he shifted.

He flew into the park. Dante waited for him, shifted, in the deepest dark, near where the trees clustered, just by the lakeside.

So good of you to come and die, he said. And Tom could feel him casting cold binds of domination and power over his mind. Nets of cold control.

But Tom held on to what he knew was true. To what he loved. The image of Kyrie and Notty, sleeping in the moonlight. The George, shining like a neon jewel through the snow. Anthony at the grill. Conan tending tables. The images burned within him like warm fires. Like home fires, calling to his heart.

Mine, mine, mine, he said, and while he caught Dire trying to hold on to these images, to threaten them, to tell Tom they were weaknesses, he couldn't hold them.

Tom's love for his family, his friends, his diner, shone through, warming his soul, and Dire's cold thoughts slipped off. He had only hatred and barrenness to offer. And those were never very strong weapons.

After that, it was easy. The dragon, after all, could fly. The dire wolf couldn't. He looked almost small, in the dark, amid the trees and the snow.

The vicious teeth tried to rend Tom's wing, as Tom approached, but Tom flipped over, suddenly, and bit the dire wolf's neck. Hard.

Tom grabbed it by the neck and shook it, as Dire started to shift, under his jaws—guessing Tom would have more trouble killing a human than an animal. A pitiful human fist hit the dragon's scales. A forlorn human scream echoed. Again and again, Dire tried to cast his cold uncaring spell upon Tom's mind—Tom pressed harder.

He tasted blood, and recoiled from it, but forced his jaws to close. The taste made him gag, but he persisted. Bone crunched. Dire's head and body fell, two separate parts.

It was truth that Dire loved death and pain—or causing them. But Tom loved life. And while Tom lived he would keep those he loved safe. Which meant Dire must die.

Afterwards, Tom took the head, and the body, and swam with them, deep into the cold, dark lake—after breaking the ice covering on it. He found that there were caves, on either side of the lake, leading quite deep under the city, perhaps to what had once been mines and were now flooded. He put the head and the body in separate tunnels, and blocked the entrance with large stones. He didn't want either ever found.

And then, half frozen, he swam back, and walked home.

After a shower, after rinsing his mouth with mouthwash, again and again, and again, Tom put his robe on and went to the kitchen, where he put paid to two packages of sandwich ham while the dozen eggs they had just bought boiled enough to not be repulsive.

When the craving for protein abated, still feeling chilled, Tom opened the door to Kyrie's room and called, softly, "Kyrie?"

She opened her eyes, and Notty's head shot up. "Yes?"

"Do you mind if I sleep here? Just sleep? I mean . . . I just . . . want to be with you."

Kyrie sat up in bed. "What's wrong?"

"Nothing. I'm just . . . I'm very cold."

"Are you coming down with something?"

"I don't think so. I'm just . . . I just need company."

She shifted to one side of the double bed, taking Notty with her, leaving him space. Tom climbed in, and curled up on the mattress, looking at Kyrie and Notty, who was now parading back and forth between the two of them and purring, the contented purr of a cat with two body servants.

"Kyrie," Tom said, wanting to talk, wanting to explain this feeling that wasn't regret or guilt, but had shades of both. He'd taken a life. He'd killed someone who'd lived thousands of years. He'd had to do it. None of them would be safe till he was dead. So why was it that this thing he'd done made him feel so cut off from the rest of humanity?

He moved fractionally towards Kyrie. "Listen," he said.

Notty jumped up, back arched and hissed towards Tom. His pose was so possessive of Kyrie that Tom laughed aloud. "Yes, yes, your girl cat, Notty. I'll behave."

He petted the ruffled kitten till Kyrie said, softly, "What is it?"

He looked at her. Her eyes were half closed. He smiled. The talk would wait. Tonight was not the night to try to explain what he'd done or how he felt. He wanted more than anything to hold Kyrie, to love her. But tonight was not the night for that, either.

Let the night close itself upon its horror. Let wonders unfold another time. "Nothing," he said quietly.

He petted Notty till he passed from wakefulness into a dream where he was holding Kyrie in the midst of a field of snow. And it was very warm.

When they got into The George, in the evening, they found Conan and Anthony sitting at the back booth, in front of what looked like a veritable mound of bread. Sitting across from them was a young woman with brown hair, hazel eyes and a blade of a nose. She looked towards them and extended a hand and spoke, in a pleasant contralto, "Hi. I'm Laura Miller. You must think I'm the most unreliable person alive, but I simply couldn't come in before. I had to take care of some family matters . . . But I'm here now, and I'm free to interview for the job, if you still want to consider me. And I brought some samples of my baking with me."

"Consider her," Anthony said. He picked a roll from the confusion of bread. "She makes this Italian bread . . . My mom would weep, I tell you."

Tom, grinning, turned towards her. "Well, as you can see, I have to consider you. And we were taking care of family matters, too. I have no idea how to interview you, just now, my mind is still in a whirl. So . . . is there anything you want to tell me?"

The woman blinked at him, then looked toward Kyrie, then, perhaps having decided that if they were crazy they weren't, at least, unpleasant, rattled off quickly, "I can do gourmet cooking, but really, I don't like it as much as a variety of good plain cooking. I truly do need to bake, though. Cookies, biscuits, breads, muffins, scones, pies, fancy pastries, whatever. I like making breads and pies and biscuits and muffins most of all, though. Cornbread's fun to make, both Northern and Southern. So's gingerbread. With or without rum sauce. Fresh pitas are like a miracle, puffing themselves up like little balloons. Stews and soups and prep cooking are satisfying, too. But not as good as baking. But I can get the bucket of scrams ready for morning rush, and get the onions and peppers for morning and lunch rush, and chop the salad, and mix up the tsatsiki.

"I can do a lot of prep cooking. I can do quantity cooking. I can run an industrial dishwasher. But I really love baking. Just don't ask me to do gourmet dinners where everything needs to be perfectly plated. My idea of decorative plating is to put the juice with the cherries and onions over the pork loin rather than beside it. And maybe to have carrots and green beans by the pork loin instead of potatoes and corn. But fancy plating with everything all pointing in perfect directions and swirled sauces? It all tastes the same in the mouth, anyway. And unless it's someone's birthday, I don't frost cakes fancy. Just tasty. I like to do one-offs, but that's why I don't like fancy frosting every day. Special should be special. And pies are either lattice, pierced, open, or have a couple of shapes out with tart cutters. If The George wants Martha Stewart, you can hire her. But I do use my grandma's pie crust recipe. And she won blue ribbons." She stopped, giving the impression that she'd run out of breath.

And Kyrie looked at Tom and found him looking at her. And she wondered how the woman would do with shifters and madness, but, hell, Anthony seemed to do well enough even while being totally clueless. And frankly, the list of breads was enough to make her want to drool.

She winked at Tom. He winked back and they said at the same time, "You're hired."

Just at that moment, she thought she smelled a vague shifter's scent beneath the smell of all the baking. Was their new employee a shifter?

But Tom was saying, "We'll discuss terms, okay? But we're flexible, since one of the really important qualities I wanted was someone who could bake." He'd somehow got hold of a little curlicue of a roll sprinkled with what looked like cheese, and was eating it, merrily. "And you certainly can do that."

Laura smiled, and at that moment the bell behind the front door tinkled. Edward Ormson, whom Kyrie always thought looked like an older and better-dressed version of Tom, came in. He was pulling a flight bag, and looked up at the group of them with a quizzical smile. "Oh, good," he said, to no one in particular. He looked at Tom, "I assume everything is well and you still haven't eaten anyone?"

Did Laura's eyes widen just a little? Kyrie couldn't tell, and Tom was laughing. "No, Dad. I haven't. And yeah, everything is fine."

"First day they opened the passes, so first day I could get here. I will go and check in at the hotel later, but I thought I'd come and see how you were doing, and make sure everything was okay."

Tom felt . . . oddly amused and tender. His father had driven here, as soon as the snow stopped for two days and the mountain passes opened, to make sure everything was okay. He could have called. He could have asked someone else to check on them. But no. Edward Ormson, who hated making himself uncomfortable, had driven a mountain road that would still have patches of ice and which was probably crowded with long-delayed travelers, to come here and check on his son.

They'd all come a long way.

But Tom still had no idea whatsoever how to express his affection for his father. So he did the only thing he knew how to do. He stepped behind the counter, and took off his jacket, putting it on the shelf under there. Then he put on his apron and his bandana, and said, "Okay, Dad. I'll make you dinner before you go to your hotel. What would you like?"

His dad grinned. "Noah's boy."

"We don't eat people," Tom said. "I thought we'd established that."

"No, no. See, you have all the diner slang in the menu, so I went and studied it, on-line. 'Noah's boy' is ham. You know. Ham. In the Bible."

Kyrie giggled, and Tom gave her an indulgent smile. "Um . . . I don't think we have that in the menu, but sure. I'll make it. One Noah's boy, coming up. And then I'll discuss your pay and hours, Laura."

A look over his shoulder showed him that Laura was made of uncommonly resilient stuff. She was smiling a little and had sat down at the booth.

The front door tinkled, to let in the dinner rush hour, and Kyrie put her apron on, ready to go attend to the tables.

The Poet came in and sat at his table, with his notebook. Tom wondered if the Poet truly was a member of the Rodent Liberation Front, and, if so, if he was the squirrel that shifted to the size of a German shepherd and smoked cigarettes. Anything was possible, he guessed. But he hoped the Rodent Liberation Front would be still now for a while, and let them have at least a little peace.

Kyrie was still behind the counter. Before going back out, she touched his shoulder with her warm hand. It wasn't even a public display of affection. But it was enough.

And The George's neon signs shone softly, while a fresh snowfall started—big, fluffy flakes, blanketing Goldport in quietness and cold.